CROSSING LINES SERIES

A. D. JUSTICE

A.D. Justice

Lines are for crossing.
Rules are for breaking.

FINE LINE
A CROSSING LINES NOVEL

USA Today Bestselling Author
A.D. JUSTICE

PROLOGUE

A Terrible Idea
Nick

"For the record, this is a terrible idea."

My director, Calvin Montgomery, locks his angry eyes on me while speaking to the handler who will be assigned to me—if Calvin approves the operation, that is.

"Sir, Special Agent Nick Tucker has repeatedly proved what a valuable asset he is in the field. He's one of our best. He has outscored most of his peers in both field and psychological profile tests—even those who have previous undercover experience. We can't deny the man has the skills we need on this assignment. He deserves this chance."

"Yes, I can read the reports as well as you can, Jack. But Nick doesn't have any true undercover experience—not even on short-term cases, and the others do. Maybe they didn't score as well on the psych tests because they're already accustomed to living among the criminal element and acting as one of them. Did that ever occur to you? We both know how hard this life is even for a few months, but the case you're asking me to put Nick on is potentially a multiyear mission."

Calvin turns his penetrating gaze to me, constantly assessing my every reaction, looking for a weakness and a reason to deny my involvement. I've been in hectic firefights before and kept my cool, though. My time in the military, working for Steele Security, and providing private security for billionaire Dominic Powers before joining the DEA prepared me for most every perilous situation they can throw at me. Drawing on my inner strength, I keep my expression passive, my breathing regular, and my instinct to remind him he's driven a desk for too many years to remember what working in the field is actually like under wraps.

"You'll be cut off from everyone you know, Nick. You'll essentially divorce your entire life—for years. Your friends, your family, wife, girlfriend, boyfriend. *Everyone.* You hear me? And that's the easy part of the job. Even contact with Jack will be sparse, especially due to the group you'll infiltrate, so you'll be making decisions on the fly. Any outside affiliation will be scrutinized—and these guys won't ask questions first. They'll shoot you in the head and replace you with the next guy in line. I'm not convinced you truly understand what you'll have to do to be one of them."

"I can assure you, I do understand."

"Is that right? This UC op has been issued special permission to break the very laws you've sworn to uphold. Your psych profile shows a strong sense of duty and a penchant for following the rules to the letter. So, you'd be fine if they order you to force some young kid to sell drugs on the street corner and bring you every penny of the money he made? Then rough him up if he doesn't bring you enough?"

The visual that pops into my brain before I can stop it makes my heart rate increase instantly, the artery in my neck jerking and giving away my reaction.

"Or maybe it's not a him. Maybe it's a her. You'd willingly force a young woman into prostitution, selling her to any Joe Blow off the street, who'll do whatever the fuck he wants to do to her? You can make them believe you don't care about her at all, just how much money she brings in for getting her John's rocks off? What if that means her customer gets to beat the shit out of her just because he has mommy issues? I mean, as long as he doesn't kill her and she can perform for her next trick, what the fuck does it matter, right?"

My stomach churns with disgust, and the room around me turns red with my rage. But I tamp down those feelings inside my chest until they form a mangled ball full of drive and determination to see this through to the end.

"I'll do whatever the fuck I have to do to stop these bastards. The longer we sit here repeatedly arguing the same points and imagining hypothetical situations, the more time they have to commit those very crimes. Sir."

"I'm sure I don't have to remind you we're after the major charges to shut them down for good. Small-time hoods are a dime a dozen. We want the source—their suppliers. Local reports say this group is using a prescription drug that hasn't even cleared the FDA yet. It's highly effective and lethal in the wrong hands. That's in addition to the influx of opioids and other controlled substances from their Mexican drug cartel affiliation. We can't blow the entire operation because you feel the need to feed your savior complex over every sob story you hear. Most of those women asked for it anyway—they probably even enjoy it."

"I'm well aware of what we're after and how to do my job." Inside, I'm seething; outside, I display a calm demeanor.

He's testing me, that much I know. His last comment was to gauge my knee-jerk reaction because that's exactly how this gang thinks. If Calvin approves my request for undercover work, the group I'll join will say and do a lot worse to me than my director has ever even thought about. If I can't handle my boss yanking my chain inside the comfort of his office in our secure, air-conditioned building, I have no business being an undercover agent where anything and everything can go wrong.

Will go wrong.

Something always does.

To stay alive, I have to think fast on my feet, improvise, and give an award-winning performance.

No time like the present to start earning a few of those golden statuettes.

"Sir, I can handle anything they throw at me. I've been in intense situations in my career, starting in the Army, through private details, and in my time with the DEA. I'm ready to take my career to the next level, and I need undercover experience to do that. This wasn't Jack's idea—I requested to be assigned to this case."

The muscles around Calvin's eyes contract, crinkling the skin until only small slits remain. He draws a slow circle around his mouth with his thumb and forefinger before resting his chin on his hand. With my gaze locked on to his, I wait for him to make his decision. The first one to blink will be Calvin, because I am all in.

"All right, Special Agent Tucker, you've convinced me to give you a chance. On one condition."

"What condition is that?"

"If at any time you suspect your cover is blown, or your gut warns you that something is off and they've turned on you, get out of there. To hell with the case and the charges. Call Jack, get to the safe house, do whatever it takes to extract yourself from the situation."

"I appreciate your concern, sir, but it won't come to that. I'll see this through till the end."

"All right. We'll get your name, background, and criminal

history established. Congratulations, Nick. You have the distinct honor of pledging to one of the most notorious motorcycle gangs in the world. The Devil's Dominion rules their LA territory with an iron fist. I only hope they don't turn that fist on you."

"Thank you, sir. I won't let you down."

~

Six Months Later

"ARE YOU SURE YOU'RE READY TO APPROACH THEM, NICK? NO need to rush things." Jack paces in his kitchen while I sit at the table and finish my coffee.

Jack Collins fits the bill for a retired biker. He is a handler, but he's curated his entire life around the motorcycle club lifestyle to avoid arousing any suspicions. He hasn't pledged to any outfit, but he is known by enough bikers that no one questions his presence, and no one crosses him. He has the don't-fuck-with-me air down pat.

His long black and gray hair is pulled back in a low ponytail. His sun-weathered skin bears the ravages of years on the open road—the deep-set wrinkles, the sunspots, the year-round dark tan. His brown eyes are keen, assessing a man and his intentions with a quick glance. The skin on his hands matches his face, but his grip is as strong as a man half his age. The long span of his career gives him advantages others could only hope to attain one day.

"It's time, Jack. You're my handler, you know I'm ready, and you know that shit is escalating out there. My hair has grown out, along with my beard. All my ink is finished—nothing overly distinguishable but still believable. My criminal background is airtight, and my stints in San Quentin and Pelican Bay legitimize my badass felon status."

"You can't use words like *legitimize* around these guys, Nick." Jack scrubs his hand down his face.

"I can talk real dumb too, Jack. Like I ain't got no schooling or nothing."

"Make fun of this all you want, Nick. But I'm telling you, these guys have a grittiness about them, a certain way they talk, a language all their own. It's a combination of the motorcycle gang lingo and prison slang."

"Trust me, I got this. I've mastered how they speak, the motorcycle gang terms, and the prison slang. I've memorized my background and rehearsed how I became a badass ex-convict, looking to join the baddest MC club around. One point that is pure genius on your part is showing I was part of a Tijuana-based gang before I was sent to prison. Thanks for that."

"Anything I can do to keep you from having to murder someone as part of your initiation. Because that's what they usually require—and could still order you to do it. But we'll cross that bridge when we have to. If you can patch in, you won't have to do the lowly probie bullshit. That'll at least give you a leg up in earning their trust and working your way up the chain faster than most.

"If you have to improvise and add anything to your history, don't forget to tell me immediately. We can build your experience around whatever you need, but it could take a little time to get it on paper. And don't say gang. You know how one-percenters feel about that word."

"Striking the word gang from my vocabulary now. And I'll try to keep the improvisation to a minimum, but I'm sure it'll come up. My documented history is solid, but that doesn't account for the things I never got caught doing. If you happen to have any former gang members in your back pocket, that would be useful too."

"I'll see what I can do. You never know, this old dog may still have a few tricks you don't know about."

One thing about Jack Collins, he always has another trick up his sleeve no one else knows about. How he stayed one step ahead of the agents under his charge when he went weeks without hearing from them is a mystery in our world. He takes his job home with him every night, and the safety of his agents is his first priority. I know I am in good hands.

"Thanks for the coffee. I'm heading back to my dinky little apartment to get into character. They're having a party at their clubhouse tomorrow night, so I'll use that opportunity to make my presence known."

"Good luck, kid. Don't die."

"That's the nicest thing you've ever said to me, Jack." I smile over my shoulder as I leave his bachelor pad and climb onto my bike.

My new life waits for me, in the gritty, dirty underbelly of the criminal world. Getting the approval for this level of under-cover work is a boost to my ego and a rush to my senses. The heightened danger, constantly surveilling my surroundings, and testing my ability to decipher friend from foe within a matter of seconds will take my career to the next level.

I feel as if I've found my purpose in life. Finally.

∽

Major Mistakes
Savannah

THE WOMAN STARING AT ME LOOKS FAMILIAR, BUT I DON'T KNOW her. Not anymore anyway. Her red hair is longer than when she was younger. Her deep green eyes hold so many secrets, ones she'll never tell. She's also much thinner than she used to be—a telltale sign of stress and depression settling in over the long haul. The sad fact is, I used to know her very well. But now she's only the outer shell of the vibrant, bubbly personality I remember from just a couple of years ago. The light in her eyes is dim now, barely perceptible even when I'm searching for it.

"When did this happen, exactly? How did I become *this* woman?" I stare into the hollow green eyes reflected in the mirror, talking to myself. Again.

A loud bang on my apartment door abruptly ends my one-sided conversation. My heart drops, and a groan escapes from my throat. Dread covers me like a lead blanket. There's only one person that can be…the one person I really don't want to see, much less spend the evening around. But I don't have a choice. I'm trapped, like a frightened, timid animal in a cage.

After removing the door chain and unlocking the multiple bolts I had installed, the door swings open before I can even grab the knob.

"Why the fuck do you have the door locked like that? Who are you hiding in here?" Butch pushes past me, moving from one room to the next through my apartment as he searches for the invisible man.

"There's no one here except me. Just like last time. And the time before that. You know I always keep all the door locks in place when I'm here alone."

It's a phobia I have—an intense fear that drives me to check the locks several times before going to bed every night. He knows this about me, because he's complained about it every time he's stayed at my apartment. Thankfully, that hasn't happened in a very long time.

He stomps toward me in his heavy leather boots, the ones he wears every day because they best protect his feet and ankles while he's riding his motorcycle. It's strange how what I initially thought was intriguing, dangerous, and sexy about him when we met are the very traits that make me want to run away and start a new life somewhere else today.

I just haven't figured out how to get away from him yet.

"Pack all your shit. We're leaving."

"What?" I whirl around on my heel and stare at him, completely dumbfounded.

"We're moving. Prez is sending me and a couple of other guys to DC to induct a smaller club into ours. We have to try them out, see if they're worthy enough to wear the Devil's Dominion colors. This is my chance to show him I'm officer material and get on the voting ballot to move up in the club. I've been waiting years for this day."

The only thought in my mind is that my opportunity to get away from him is finally here. The day I've been waiting to come for far too long. There's no way I can move from LA to DC—they're at completely opposite ends of the country. Literally from one coast to the other. My entire life is here in LA, including my job and the few friends I had before I started seeing Butch.

Maybe my friends will take me back when I get rid of him.

"That's great news for you, Butch. I'm glad the president finally sees your potential in the club, and I hope they make you an officer soon. But I can't just up and move across country with you. My job is here—my entire career I've worked years to establish. I also have a lease on this apartment I can't just break."

I'm listing every logical reason I can think of, no matter how lame it will inevitably sound to him. He doesn't care about excuses—he only cares about results. More specifically, he only cares about the results he wants to see.

"Wouldn't that just fucking thrill you? Wouldn't you just love for me to go across the fucking country for the next six months and leave you here alone so you can fuck every swinging dick that crosses your path? Of course you're going with me, you stupid bitch. Who the fuck do you think is gonna drive the truck behind us and haul our shit across the country? All our stuff won't fit on our fucking bikes, you moron. Now, pack your shit like I said."

With his final command, he shoves me and slams my head into the wall, catching the edge of the doorframe with the full blunt force of the impact. Even with my eyes closed, I can feel the room spinning. Nausea settles into my gut and the bile churns, threatening to work its way up my throat. The pain in my skull makes me whimper. His only reply is a disgusted huff.

"Now, rent the fucking moving truck, pack your shit, and let's go to DC before I'm too old to ride my damn bike anymore."

After I hear the door open, he hurls one last threat at me. "If you even think of trying to get out of this, I'll kill every single person you love. All your fucking friends from the hospital. Your mom. Your sister. Try me, bitch. I dare you."

He stomps out, the chains on his boots and belt clinking with every step, growing fainter until I hear the engine of his bike roar to life. Funny, or not funny, how it reminds me so much of his own terrible roar. After he rides away, I open my eyes and gingerly move off the wall where he left me.

The door to my apartment is standing wide open.

He knows my paralyzing fear of leaving the door unlocked. Irrational or not, it's still there.

I want to rush to lock every bolt, but the first step in that direction reminds me of my head injury. The disorientation, nausea, and I are not new friends. With slow movements, I lift my hand to feel the goose egg forming behind my ear. I'm not even surprised to find blood on my fingers when I lower my arm again.

My walk to the door is slow as I calculate each step and how much farther I have to go. My chest is heaving from the building anxiety. When the door is finally locked—every bolt is secured and every chain is in place, my pounding heart slows enough so I can breathe normally again.

After I put a cold compress on the back of my head, I slide onto the couch and carefully lie back on the throw pillows. I waste a few minutes daydreaming about never leaving my apartment again, never unlocking the door again, while waiting for the throbbing in my head to subside. As often as I dream about this, I should've already found the master plan for leaving Butch in my dust.

Since nothing else I've tried so far has worked, I pick up my laptop and rent the moving van as the asshole commanded. A one-way trip to Washington, DC coming up, sans the excitement a cross-country trip should elicit. The only way I can describe how I feel about what I just did is I'm positive I've just signed my own death certificate.

In fact, the longer I'm around Butch, the more I realize that outcome is inevitable—it's only a matter of time. The odds there will come a day when it's him or me increase with our every encounter. I let my eyes drift up to the ceiling, staring at nothing in particular while thinking about my situation. My job as an emergency room nurse is stressful and adrenaline-filled, but it pales in comparison to a single interaction with Butch. In an ironic twist, I would be required by law to report potential domestic abuse if one of my patients presented with the same signs I bear.

He wasn't always like this. When I first met him, the tall, muscular, brooding man was much sexier. His brown hair was longer than other men I'd dated before, but it gave him an edgier appearance. Eyes so brown they're almost black sparkled with playfulness and teasing. But it was all a charade—he was pretending to be someone he wasn't. And he was so good at it for so long—long enough to ensure I fell for him. Long enough to ensure I was caught in his trap. When I look at him now, all I see is the ugliness inside. Any desire that once burned for him has long been doused.

Thankfully, those nights with him have dwindled to an occasional visit—and only when he needs me to do something for him. He disappeared for a couple of weeks one time, and I thought he'd found someone else to prey upon. Selfishly, I hoped he had—but then I immediately felt bad for wishing him on anyone else. Unfortunately, one day, he simply walked back into my apartment as if he'd been here all along. No explanation. No questions.

His visits have been sporadic since that day. Usually when he's drunk and looking for somewhere to crash after a night out with his friends. He passes out in my bed, and I sleep on the couch, unable to stand being in the same room with him any longer than absolutely necessary. His insane jealousy makes no sense to me whatsoever. We are not a couple and haven't been for a very long time, yet he calls me every name in the book when he accuses me of seeing other men.

Not that I'm the least bit interested in even trying to date. I still can't get rid of the last mistake I made.

Now he shows up and demands I move across the country with him. I'm having a hard time wrapping my head around this one. It's not like either of us wants to be with the other. That much is clear. But I believe he'll make good on his threat to kill everyone I love. In fact, I have no doubt he will.

One problem at a time, though. Before we even reach the East Coast, I have to survive the actual 3,000-mile trip with him and his buddies. That should be fun—waiting for them to pass out on the bed from the abundance of drugs and alcohol so I can grab the extra linens and sleep on the nasty floor. But I prefer the floor over touching any of them. Maybe I'll sleep in the truck…with the doors locked…under the guise of protecting our belongings.

A few hours later when I walk into the hospital for the night shift, my heart is heavy, and all my feelings show on my face. My coworker takes one look at me, and her face falls.

"What has Butch done now?" Stella puts her hands on her

hips and draws in a deep breath. She already knows she won't like the answer.

After explaining the series of events and the commandment Butch issued, I watch her face for the disappointment I know will come. On one hand, I completely understand it, and I was even the same way…before I became the abused and battered victim. Life is now divided into two sections: BB and AB. Before Butch and After Butch.

Before Butch, I said no man would ever lay a hand on me and live to tell about it.

No man would ever abuse me in any way—physically, mentally, or verbally. I would leave him in a heartbeat.

No man would replace my job, my dreams, or my friends—the sacred relationships I'd always held so dear.

After Butch, I withdrew from my friends.

My dreams took a back seat.

Self-esteem was what others had, but not me.

I miss the Before Butch version of myself. But now I feel as if I'm in too deep and can't claw my way out. One thing I've realized after looking back over the past eighteen months is none of this happened suddenly. He chipped away at the very core of me little by little, bit by bit, day by day. Until the very spark that made me *me* disappeared. And I allowed him to do it.

It's my fault.

If I'd been stronger, smarter, faster…maybe I would've seen the warning signs for what they really were.

Huge signs that flashed "Bridge Out Ahead."

But his apologies were so sincere at first. So heartfelt. He was remorseful and promised those bad things would never happen again.

He'd drunk too much. He always liked to fight when he drank. Such a man's man.

He was under too much stress. Work was a constant sore

spot. His coworkers or his boss never liked him. They always made up a reason to get rid of him.

Of course, that was before I found out the truth about him. Before I understood what being in a one-percenter motorcycle club really meant. When I made the mistake of calling his club a gang during a heated argument, I saw stars after he backhanded me for disrespecting his brothers.

That was the day the apologies stopped and the real threats began. Old ladies didn't leave bona fide club members. Ever. It wasn't the woman's decision whether to stay or go. She just did what she was told and lived with what she got. He warned me to be glad I wasn't a sheep—one of the women they pass around to each other indiscriminately, using at will for any hedonistic pleasure they wanted to indulge in at the moment.

Ignoring the pleas and concern in Stella's eyes, I continue updating her on my plans. "I'm turning in my two-week notice tonight. That date was the earliest I could get a moving truck big enough for my stuff plus theirs anyway. I'm so glad it has a towing hitch for my car too."

I leave Stella, disappointed expression and all, to start my rounds and focus on the emergency cases. I wish I could stop time so my shift would never end. But working in busy emergency rooms always makes the time go by faster than the slower pace, comparatively, on the medical-surgical floors. Before I know it, the sun rises and a new day dawns, and I have to face the unpleasantness of packing all my belongings.

Two weeks will pass in the blink of an eye.

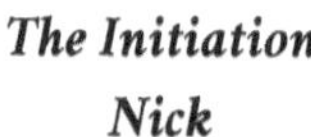

The Initiation
Nick

"YOU READY FOR TONIGHT?" JACK'S SERIOUS EXPRESSION GIVES

away his thoughts. Unusual for him after the years of handling undercover officers.

"I'm as ready as I'll ever be." I slide my arm into my cut and complete the persona of Renegade.

Turns out, the idea to convince them I was part of a Tijuana-based club was a stroke of genius on Jack's part. The Devils' ties to the Mexican cartel are already in place, but with my joining them, the full backing of the cartel is implied, giving them more muscle than they already have. An ATF agent has been working a few members of that gang over the last several years, so inter-agency cooperation kicked in, and my alibi was instantly airtight. With my background in prison and ties to the Mexican cartel-sanctioned motorcycle club firmly in place, I approached the Devils with an offer they couldn't refuse.

The Devils' already long reach just increased with no effort on their part. At least as far as their reputation with rival clubs is concerned. Keeping those other clubs at arm's length while the Devils conduct business is vital to maintaining their dominance in the territory. When the club president realized the possibilities I could bring, the dollar signs in his eyes were so bright, they rivaled the neon signs of the Vegas strip.

Headbanger, also known as Bobby Blalock, is the club president. He has a rap sheet longer than my leg, along with countless other crimes he's never been charged with committing. Or ordering. His officers and many other members are all too eager to carry out plans on his behalf. They're brothers in colors, but they're also all vying for the attention of one man. The one who can make or break them in the club.

Tonight is initiation for a few new prospects who are on their way to becoming full patch members. The ceremony to patch in is a big deal to these guys—it seals their identity and their place in the family.

I've been riding with the Devils for the past two weeks. Hanging out with them in the clubhouse provides a completely unique perspective on the inner workings of a notorious outlaw gang. Some of the guys have done hard time, and it's a miracle most aren't still in prison. I've had to bite my tongue way too many times already—something my director knew about me before he approved the assignment.

My moral compass always points due north. Always.

Their skewed sense of right and wrong doesn't mesh well with me. In fact, we're like oil and water at the very core. The only peace I have is when we're on the open road, the wind whipping around me, and the road rushing by under my wheels. The sense of freedom on a motorcycle is the sole only thing I have in common with these guys. It's the only time we're even remotely on the same page.

The long ride to the initiation grounds in the hot, arid desert of Southern California gives me time to get myself back into character. Jack stressed over and over how I have to be part of the group to avoid suspicion. Because of the high stakes, I've been given special clearance to break the laws I've sworn to uphold. But there are oaths I've taken, and I have no intention of reneging on them.

There are lines I refuse to cross.

There are rules I refuse to break—even for the greater good and the thrill of closing the case.

But I have to act like there are no lines I won't cross. To be convincing, I have to put Nick Tucker away and be Renegade to the bone. In my mind, I have to think of Renegade as a completely different person. It's the only way I can pull this off.

He's an ex-con, fresh out of a maximum-security prison, and that has to be my persona. As a convicted felon on parole, I can't legally cross the border to ride with my old club because the pigs will nab Renegade immediately. I can't exactly drive my motorcycle through the underground tunnels to cross the border. Of course, as Renegade, I have the contacts, so I could find an illegal way, like a fake passport or hidden in a caravan. But I'd take that risk only for a golden opportunity, a sure thing.

Renegade has talked a good game in his two weeks with the Devils. Tonight, Prez will present me with the final piece of my colors—the top rocker panel for my cut—because I scored the largest shipment of meth and negotiated the best deal for the club he's ever seen. Compliments of my DEA and ATF friends.

When I finally roll up to their private hideaway in the desert, my Renegade character is in full swing. After grabbing a couple of beers from the cooler, I stroll over to where the officers are hanging out with a few of the lifers—the men who have been part of the club for so long, they aren't required to attend all church meetings and outings anymore, but they're every bit a part of the club as any other member. They can come and go as they please, though most stay more than they leave. This is the only life they know.

"Good of you to bring me a beer, Renegade." Axle reaches for one of the longneck bottles I'm carrying, so I hand it over without a fuss. He's one of the most respected lifers in the group. His experience combined with his naturally level head makes for a powerful ally in a group of trigger-happy thugs. Despite Axle's advanced age and lack of officer status, no man in this group wants to tangle with him.

"You know I always got your back, Ax."

"Back atcha, kid." He takes a long pull from the bottle but keeps his eyes locked on mine. "Heard about that big score you got for us. I'm impressed—and I don't impress easily. Good job."

"Appreciate it, man. Just glad I could help out."

"Well, well, look who's coming our way. The new prospects are here, and they brought their offerings to the Devils with them." Nutcrusher, the club vice president, stands and rubs his hands together, eager to get down to business.

When I glance over my shoulder at the approaching

prospects, my stomach drops to my knees and my empty hand curls into a tight fist.

Their "offerings" are new sheep, women being shoved into the midst of the already rowdy scene. The three prospects are each forcing a woman to walk in front of them. The women alternate from stumbling ahead a few steps to digging their heels in to try to stop, only to be shoved from behind and start the process all over again. Their eyes are wide and full of fear. Their faces are tear-stained and their hair is disheveled—and not from the ride here since they arrived in the club van.

I'm positive these three women have already been used as offerings before the new patches ever brought them to meet the brothers. Before I consciously realize I'm moving, my feet develop a mind of their own and take a step forward. Then I feel a hand on my shoulder, holding me back.

"What you see tonight will test your mettle, boy. You've never been around anything like this, I can already tell. But I guarantee, if you blow your cover now, you'll never see anything at all, ever again."

Shocked by his words, I whip my head around and meet Axle's knowing gaze.

"Use it, kid. Use everything you have to see and do as a member to take them down. As shitty as it sounds, you can't save these women and do what you came here to do at the same time. Keep your eyes on the end goal, son, and make them pay for their crimes when it's all said and done."

"What are you talking about, Axle?" He knows. We both know he knows. But I'll be damned if I'll blow my own cover.

"I'm CIA, Nick Tucker from the DEA family. I've been on this case for a long time, waiting for my foreign target to make his move so I can take him down. I told you, I got your back."

"The CIA can't operate on US soil, Ax. Everyone knows that."

His grin resembles one connected to an inside joke.

Everyone else is clueless, and one person holds all the aces in his hand. "Sure we don't. I'm on loan to whichever agency wants to take the credit for the bust when it goes down. If you're still here when it happens, maybe that'll be the DEA."

Before I can reply, the shrill shriek of a woman's scream combined with ripping fabric fills the air, making my guts churn with disgust. Any man who would lay a hand on a woman in anger or abuse is no man at all. He's a pussy who knows he couldn't stand toe-to-toe with a real man.

The crowd that gathers around the three women—to watch, to encourage, or to participate—are the worst of the underworld. Preying on the defenseless and taking advantage of those who are hanging on by a thread as it is.

"Come with me, Renegade. This is as good as this scene gets. It's all downhill from here, and I don't think you can stop yourself from intervening yet." Axle guides me away from the ruckus.

I can still hear their pleas to stop. Their screams that echo through the desert air. Their cries for someone to please help them...to make it stop.

But I do nothing.

What kind of man does that make me?

"When they finish with the girls, they'll take them back to the clubhouse, and the club doctor will patch them up. They'll use them as sheep, or they'll cycle them into the prostitution ring and run them on the streets. They're not easy on them, but they don't permanently damage them either. Headbanger has a strict rule on that part since it affects his cash flow."

"Axle, your explanation doesn't help me one fucking bit. Do you even hear yourself? Of course they're permanently damaged now. Maybe not in the way you meant, but they still are." He nods in understanding, and he knows he can't say much more to justify what we've witnessed. "Where did they get those girls? Did they kidnap them?"

"No. They pick up hitchhikers or strays. Bring them into the family. Give them food, a place to sleep, and the protection of a notorious motorcycle club. But they expect the girls to earn their keep one way or another. This may be the first time you've ever seen this, but it won't be the last. It won't even be the worst thing you've seen by the time your undercover operation ends."

The silence between us only seems to amplify the mixture of screams and catcalls behind us.

"Talk to me, Axle. Tell me about life in the CIA. Were you in the service? Anything, man. Talk about the fucking weather. I don't care."

"This gets easier, kid. You'll learn to compartmentalize shit like this. Picture those assholes in prison orange, enduring the same fate they're subjecting those girls to right now at the hands of a big, angry brute in their cell, where they have nowhere else to run. Then make that your end goal and sole mission in life. Find what gets you through the rough spots one day at a time. Your assignment will be over before you know it. Then you can put all this bullshit behind you."

I don't see that happening.

CHAPTER 1

Savannah—Two Years Later

"We're moving you out of that apartment today. I've been waiting for this day forever. No more excuses about waiting until your lease is up." Karen slings her backpack over her shoulder and jingles her car keys in her hand. "Let's go do this."

"What if he's still there?"

"That's why my husband and his friends are meeting us. We need their muscles to carry your furniture, and the fact that they're all cops doesn't hurt either." Karen smiles broadly, knowing Butch wouldn't dare start something with them around. "You know, you're welcome to stay with Spencer and me anytime you want. For example, if you wake up in the middle of the night scared and don't want to be alone anymore. Or if you just want to have a slumber party full of alcohol and junk food. Just show up at my house and make yourself at home."

"That sounds like so much fun. I don't know how to thank you for this, Karen." The shame of my situation is almost unbearable. All the time I've wasted, being afraid of Butch and what he'd do if I said or did the wrong thing when he was around. Not living my life to the fullest, enjoying every minute of every day. Not doing all the things I've wanted to do when I wanted to do them. Not spending time with my family so I could keep them as far away from that bastard as possible.

Being controlled and dominated by a cruel man.

"You can thank me by staying away from him for good. By calling the police if he comes anywhere near you again. By asking for help if he finds a way to back you into a corner again. I will get you out—one way or another. You are not alone in this, and you are not to blame." Karen grabs my arms to emphasize her words, and I consciously avoid wincing in pain from the pressure on my bruised skin. She doesn't know the bruises are there; I've hid them well.

Guess old habits do die hard.

"You have my word. Once I'm rid of him, it will be once and for all. There will be no going back or letting him in again for any reason. I've honestly wanted this for a long time, but I never could make it work. I think this time will definitely be different. For the first time in a long time, I have hope for a better life."

"It's all yours, babe. All yours for the taking. Once we get you moved, we'll work on finding you a real man. I'm sure Spencer has at least one single, handsome friend we can set you up with."

"Oh, no. No, no, no. I'm not interested in anything remotely resembling a man in my life. I'll just borrow your husband and his friends for heavy-lifting duties and scaring away bad guys. That's as close to having another man as I want to get."

"Woman-to-woman…friend-to-friend…I have to be brutally honest with you, Savannah."

"Go ahead. I know you. You'll explode if you don't get it out."

"It's not you I'm worried about as much as it's your poor, neglected, prune-shriveled va-jay-jay. I mean, it's seriously been three years since you took it out for a sit and spin? No squats in the cucumber patch? No gland-to-gland combat? We're both mandatory reporters, and you are definitely way past neglecting the old bearded clam. I think I need to turn you in to the nearest hot policeman."

Before meeting Karen, I'd almost forgotten how good it felt to simply laugh with a friend. To say whatever crazy thought came to my mind without fear of ridicule or reprisal. To have someone on my side, in my corner, standing by me no matter where the chips may fall. Stella was the last person I was semi-close to, but my friendship with Stella was nothing like the one I now have with Karen. We tease each other relentlessly, and I always tell her she elbowed her way into my heart, never taking no for an answer.

And saved my life in the process.

Now she's adding fun, love, and laughter too. Maybe the old me will emerge like a butterfly coming out of a cocoon.

We arrive at my apartment complex and find Spencer is already here waiting for us with his own small army. He pulls Karen into his arms, a warm, sweet smile on his face as he looks at her and kisses her hello. He's not at all shy or embarrassed by public displays of affection—or showing how completely and utterly in love he is.

Watching the two of them embrace, I'd swear the depth of their love for each other is their source of strength.

Butch insisted love was a weakness. A way other people could use you without explanation or a chance for retribution. He didn't believe anything that exposed your vulnerabilities could possibly make you stronger.

Butch was wrong.

I see it so clearly now, watching my friends. They give me something to aspire to reach in relationship goals—one day, possibly. The way I feel right now, I'd never trust a man enough to feel safe with him. To give him all of me and believe he'd do the same. Perhaps I'll find that man at some point in my life, but I plan to focus on myself first.

My goals.

My hopes.

My dreams.

I've put them on the back burner for a man who wasn't worth even a second of my time. Today is the first day of the new me.

"Hi, Savannah. Good to see you." Spencer turns his attention to me, keeping his arm wrapped around Karen's waist.

"Thank you for doing this, Spence. I don't know how to repay your kindness—and all your friends. I wish you'd let me pay you for your trouble." My gaze drifts to each of his friends standing by the moving truck—and I immediately regret it. Though they try to mask their thoughts, I see the judging stares and disgusted glances.

I can't exactly hide the black eye I'm sporting, though it has mostly faded to light green bruising.

They're asking why I've stayed so long.

They're questioning what I've done to deserve this.

They want to know why I'm so weak and spineless to let someone treat me this way.

I've experienced these reactions so many times from other people. Until they've walked a mile in my shoes, they'll never understand what it takes to be able to get out of a situation like this. Now that I've lived it, I can honestly say I didn't have a fucking clue what I was talking about when I used to pass those same judgments on other women.

"You're not paying us one single penny. We're happy to help." Spencer releases Karen and steps toward me. "Can I have your keys? Jake and I are going up to your apartment to make sure it's safe. Stay here with Terry, Jarod, and Trent until you hear from us. Then you and Karen can pack your things and we'll get you away from this asshole." Jake steps up next to Spencer and inclines his head at me as Spencer speaks.

"Sure. This one is the door key, this one is to the top bolt, and this one is the bottom bolt." I hand the keys over, feeling guilty for allowing complete strangers to stick their necks out for me. They're off duty, doing this as a favor to Spencer.

"I sure hope he's up there. And I hope he puts up a fight. At the very least, a little resistance. All I need is one good reason to take him down." Jake cracks his knuckles and sneers his lip. "I'm more than willing to pay him back on your behalf, Savannah."

Could I have been wrong? Could their expressions I took for judgment against me have been disgust with Butch instead? Have I read others wrong too?

"I appreciate the offer, Jake. But I don't want you to get in trouble because of me."

"You're looking at it all wrong, sweetheart. All he has to do is touch me wrong one time and he's assaulted a police officer. That's a serious offense, one he'd be hauled away in handcuffs over." Jake smiles, hopeful for the chance to arrest Butch and avenge me in one fell swoop.

One can hope he's in my apartment. Right?

Both fortunately and unfortunately, Butch wasn't in my apartment, and he never showed up while we were there, packing and moving all my belongings out, cleaning up afterward, and leaving the complex without a trace we'd ever been there. While I would've enjoyed seeing him hauled away in handcuffs by a few of DC's finest detectives, I'll take the stealthy approach we pulled off over a confrontation with him any day.

My new home is actually in a newer apartment, but the rent is affordable, and the neighborhood is on the trendier side. This area is nice and safe. I spotted a small coffee shop down the street. Cozy and quaint, it looks like the perfect place to work on my secret project. Something I've decided to do just for myself as much as for others.

"This place looks great!" Karen walks in like she lives here—after unlocking all my locks and bolts with the extra key I gave her—and I wouldn't have it any other way. "You must've been up all night, unpacking and decorating your new place."

"I couldn't sleep. I was too excited to close my eyes."

She drops her purse on the couch, places her hand on her hip, and quirks one eyebrow up at me. "For the record, I'm letting you get away with that abbreviated answer because there is some truth to it. Don't think for one second you'll get away with that shit in the future, though."

"Fine. I was also checking the door and window locks every five minutes and thirty-six seconds. And my ears were oddly in tune with every loud engine that drove past, regardless of the hour."

"I knew I should've spent the night with you last night, even though you insisted you'd be fine. It's really too bad Butch didn't show up yesterday. I would've enjoyed seeing the guys take care of him. But that also means he has no idea where you are now. There are over six million people in the DC metro area. You could live in Virginia or Maryland now for all he knows."

"But he knows where I work. He could follow me home from the hospital." With that thought, I can't help but glance nervously around my small condo, even knowing he isn't inside it. It's a reflex, as if mentioning his name will actually conjure the man out of thin air. "And it's not like you can just move in with me, so enough of the guilt trip for not spending the night."

"Let's devise a plan in case he does show up at the hospital or spots you on the road on the way home." Karen gives me her undivided attention. "Watch your surroundings at all times. We'll alert human resources and arrange for a security guard to escort you to your car every morning. If you think anyone is following you, don't go home. Drive straight to the police station and call me on the way. I'll get Spencer and the guys on the case immediately. Stay in public sight, and never yell for help. Always yell 'Fire.' That draws more people faster than screaming for help does."

"You are definitely married to a cop."

"I need to ask Spencer about self-defense classes. I'll go with you. We can do it on our days off." The wheels in Karen's head are spinning, making plans and mental to-do lists. All to ensure my safety and security.

My best friend is the best person.

"Have a seat. I'll get us a couple of sodas from the fridge, and we'll just bask in the newness of my new little home." True to her nature, she refuses the seat and checks out my decorating skills instead.

"You have great taste, Savannah. I don't know why you chose the noble but overworked profession of nursing over interior design. You could star in your own remodeling TV show by now." Karen pops the top on the Coke can and sips as she strolls to the master bedroom. "I love how you arranged this. You need to come over to my house and help me figure out how to rearrange and redecorate."

"You want to change your bedroom?"

"Oh no, not just the bedroom. My house. I want you to redo my whole house."

"That's more than just a weekend project, Karen."

"Yeah, I know. I'm good with however long it takes. Gives me time to parade Spencer's friends around and see which one you mesh with best."

"Sit. Stop with the matchmaking. Talk to me about more important topics."

We settle on the couch, facing the floor-to-ceiling windows that let in all the natural light I could ever want, and stare at the landscape of Meridian Hill Park only a block away. A light dusting of snow covers the bare trees, shrubs, and grassy areas. The temperatures haven't dropped enough for the snow to stick to the pavement yet, and the cold wind hasn't stopped anyone from enjoying the park.

"You know I only want you to be happy and loved, right? The way Spence loves me and puts me first in everything he does. I want that happy home life for you too." Karen's unusually serious tone makes my breath catch. I swing my eyes up to read her expression. Should've known I'd only find kindness and compassion there.

"I do know that, Karen. Sometimes when I watch you and Spence together, I'm overwhelmed by how much I wish I had what you two have. It's not envy—it's a goal I've set for myself. But whether the man for me is one of Spencer's friends or not doesn't make a difference right now.

"I've lost myself over the last three years. Butch was a different man when I first met him, though I should've recognized the warning signs and red flags for what they really were. The blinders I wore were my fault, and I accept the blame for that. But when the switch flipped and the abuse started, it wasn't just physical injuries. The mental damage he caused nearly destroyed me. Before I even consider looking at another man, I have to be okay with looking at myself in the mirror again.

"There's a fine line between love and hate. I need to find my way back across that line."

"You know I don't judge you for staying with him as long as you did. The threats, the violence, and being in the constant state of fight-or-flight takes a terrible toll on your overall well-being. But I am so thankful you're away from him now, and I'm so proud of you for finding the courage and strength to do it. Just to be clear, though. I will have you committed on a seventy-two-hour psychiatric hold if you let him back in now. You have all the support you need from me, Spence, and a host of DC's finest."

"That seventy-two-hour hold kind of sounds appealing. A little vacation. I could use a long weekend away. Can you arrange for that evaluation to be done in the Bahamas?"

"Your sarcastic humor is what first told me we'd be best friends. You know you're not going off to a Caribbean island for a mental-health check and leaving me here to work your shifts. We go mental together, or we don't go at all."

"Good to know your priorities are in order."

"Did you expect anything less of me?" A sly smile spreads across her face.

"No. In fact, I would've been very disappointed in you if you had replied any other way."

"You know me too well. There's no mystery left in our relationship…no hidden gems for you to uncover."

"I haven't met all of your personalities yet. I'm sure you have plenty of mysteries left for me to figure out."

Days bled into weeks with no sign or word from Butch. Over that time, I began to find purpose in my work again. Meaning in my life. A new direction to take and a way to use what I've been through for good. The exciting prospects of new projects, secret plans, and shifts at the hospital consumed my time. I fell into bed every day completely exhausted and thoroughly content for the first time in years.

"Have a good day. I'm off for the next four days, and I am not coming in for anyone or anything." I've already briefed the incoming day nurse on the status of each patient and completed all my charting from the night shift. All that's left is to clock out and stroll through the doors.

The snow flurries swirl in the wind outside and the skies are a gloomy shade of gray, but nothing can dampen my mood today. My neighborhood has a quaint little coffee shop at the end of the block. The scents and the scenery are calling my name. My laptop, a table with a view, and a piping hot cup of coffee are all I need to work on my life-defining purpose—a new business venture to help other women in my predicament. I'm writing a book for women in abusive relationships, and I need time and inspiration to add another chapter to the hardest story I've ever told.

My own.

No time like the present.

CHAPTER 2

Nick

"This shit is for the birds. What the fuck am I even doing here?"

The wind coming off the water of the canal is colder than I remember when I step out of my brownstone in old Georgetown. I haven't been back in DC for so long, I've forgotten how cold it can get. Lucky me. Just when I arrive back in town, the weatherman predicts we'll have the coldest winter on record. Although, we haven't even officially reached the first day of winter yet, leaving me little optimism for the remainder of the season. Guess I got a little too comfortable in the Southern California sun. With the collar of my leather bomber jacket flipped up as a shield against the wind, I shove my hands in my pockets and keep walking toward a small coffee shop in the Adams Morgan neighborhood of DC. I found it by accident one day while wandering around aimlessly, and I've made the two-mile walk there every morning since. Holiday lights, decorations, and Christmas trees line my path, adding to the festive vibe of the neighborhood.

The best thing about this quaint little shop is it's not a chain. There are no hipster kids taking up all the seats, trying to appear cool or studious. This place just serves great coffee with equally delicious food, and everyone leaves me the fuck alone. I've come here every day for the last two weeks, ordered the same drink, and walked the couple of miles back to my brownstone in Georgetown.

Routine. Order. Peace.

I order my usual coffee and move to the end of the counter to wait for my name to be called. The bell over the door chimes so frequently with customers coming and going, I've almost tuned it out. But the energy in the café changes instantly, becoming stifling from the nervous electricity arcs crackling in the air. The tingling sensation zings up my spine before I even turn my head to look at who just walked in the shop.

"Get your fucking ass up and get out of here right now!"

The shop is filled with people this morning. They're talking, laughing, or furiously typing on their phones. But they all stop at the same time. I know, because the only noise in the room now is coming from the mouth-breathing bottom-feeder causing a scene. I drop my head forward because I know—I fucking *know*—no one else will step in and stop him. They'll watch. They'll say what a dick he is under their breath. One may be brave enough to threaten to call the police, but that won't faze a motherfucker like him.

I know his type all too well. He'll get off on showing them just how fucking evil he can be. The person who will take the brunt of his pathetic display of power will be the defenseless woman sitting in the coffee shop. No doubt she thought she'd be safe in such a busy public place. But this dickhead is banking on being the only tough guy in a room full of nonfat soy latte drinkers. Not a flask of whiskey in sight.

"I said get the fuck up!"

The unmistakable sound of scraping against the wood floor

followed by a chair toppling over suggests he's jerked her out of the seat.

Still, no one moves.

"Let go! You're hurting me!" Her shrill shrieks fill the coffee shop, and I close my eyes, willing the scene to go away.

But it doesn't, and she's terrified. Still, no one says a word or tries to intervene in any way.

"You don't know what *hurt* is yet. But you will after this fucking stunt."

"Stop! I have to get my laptop and my purse."

"You spend too much time on that fucking thing anyway. You must be talking to some other guy. You're such a slut. I should stomp that fucking thing into a million pieces so you can't whore around anymore."

No one steps forward to stop him or his ridiculous tirade.

She cries out in pain, and I can't take it any longer. I turn around and stride toward him, determination set in my stance and murderous rage written on my face. As if on cue, every person between him and me takes two steps back, giving me plenty of room to move. "Get your fucking hands off her before I break them off your arms and shove them so far up your ass, you'll be able to wave at people from the back of your fucking throat."

The expression on his face is priceless. He's a big guy, but then I am too. The difference is, I'm a hell of a lot meaner than he has ever thought about being. I've committed acts of violence that would make him piss in his pants like a little baby. Breaking him with one punch will be the easiest task on my to-do list for the day.

"Who the fuck are you?" His sneer and intense stare-down are meant to intimidate me.

I'd laugh in his face if I weren't so pissed off over his treatment of this beautiful, terrified lady.

"I'm the man who's going to fuck you up one side and down

the other if you don't take your hands off her right now. I won't say it again."

I know the instant he decides to call my bluff. He's gotten away with this too many times. He's been given too many idle threats by guys who didn't have the ass to back up their words. He thinks he'll get away with it again with me because his fingers on his left hand tighten on her arm and he jerks her harder toward his chest as he nonchalantly drops his right hand. She loses her balance and falls into him, causing him to manhandle her even more until she regains her footing.

His right arm juts toward me, but I see his pathetic punch coming from a mile away. That's when I take him. A quick, swift jab to his nose makes his head snap backward. The pop of the bone breaking echoes through the room, and he stumbles backward before crumpling to the ground. His hand is still firmly wrapped around her bicep, though, so I rush forward to break his hold and keep her from falling to the floor with him. Once I free her of his grip, I instinctively wrap my arm around her waist, pulling her into me, and move her farther away from him.

The small shop erupts in claps and cheers as the dickhead lies bleeding on the floor, but she buries her face in my chest to hide. Shame, embarrassment, guilt—I've seen all the emotions written in her posture and her reaction too many times to count. And every single time, it enrages me because the abused woman thinks it's her fault instead of the man who can't fucking control himself. If I never see this unwarranted shame on an innocent woman's face again, it'll be too soon.

But I'm not ready for what else I see when this lady in particular finally peers up at me.

Through the tears shining in her deep green eyes and the black streaks of wet mascara on her face, she looks up at me with admiration. Adoration. Her champion. A hero.

"Are you okay? Did he hurt you?" Somehow, I manage to ask

her the most basic questions about her well-being, but she has rattled me to my core without uttering a single word.

I'm no hero. I can't even say I'm a good man anymore.

"I'm okay. Thank you for what you did, stepping in like that. I can't tell you how much I appreciate it."

I wipe the mascara away with the pad of my thumb. Dickhead has embarrassed her enough for today. She doesn't need raccoon eyes to add insult to injury.

As the dickhead tries to stand, two police officers step into the café. He wipes the blood from his face when he's finally on his feet then startles from the red smear on his hand. His angry gaze flies up to me and amps up tenfold when his eyes trail my arm around her midsection. An ugly snarl covers his face, and I pull her tighter into me out of sheer spite. My eyebrow quirks up, and a smirk covers my face.

It's a blatant dare. He knows it. I know it. I don't fucking care. He can bring his A game, and he'll still get his ass beaten down.

"What's going on here?" One of the officers takes control of the situation. His authoritative tone defuses the angry spark in dickhead's eyes.

"That guy just punched me and broke my nose." He points to me, and the officers' gazes follow his finger.

"Is that true?"

"Absolutely."

Several patrons start chiming in at once.

"That man was abusing that woman."

"He got punched in the nose because he was hurting her."

"That's not all that happened, Officer. That man saved her."

"Okay, okay. Everyone calm down until we get to the bottom of this. We need to see some ID." One officer takes the name and information of the other guy. "Butch McMahan. Is the address on your license still correct?"

"Yes, sir."

Oh, *now* he's polite and respectful.

The other officer approaches me cautiously. "You got some ID?"

"Sure, Officer." I smile and pull my own badge out from under my jacket. "Special Agent Nick Tucker, DEA."

All the color drains from Butch's face. My smirk morphs into the first real smile I've had in a long time.

"Special Agent Tucker, can you tell me what happened here?"

"Absolutely." I give him the play-by-play of the events leading up to the altercation that rendered Bitch temporarily dazed and incapacitated on the floor. Every time I say "Bitch," he corrects me with "Butch," but I keep going. It's the little things that make me feel better. Like calling Butch "Bitch." By the time I finish relaying the events, both cops have to actively work to avoid laughing out loud.

I don't even try to hide my mirth. Bitch deserves it.

Then one of the officers checks the license of the woman still clinging to me. "Savannah Fields. Is this address still correct?"

"No. That's my old address. I moved a couple of months ago but haven't had my license updated."

"What's your new address, then?" The cop waits with his pen pressed against the paper, looking up when she doesn't answer.

"I don't want to give it out." Her eyes jerk toward Butch then back to the officer's. I immediately understand the situation.

"Let's step outside so she can give you her information in private, Officer."

"Absolutely. Better yet, I have another idea. Frank, can you take Mr. McMahan outside and finish getting his information, away from Miss Fields?"

"My pleasure. Step outside, sir. We're not finished yet." The other officer opens the door and motions with his head for Butch to step through.

When the door is closed and Savannah is assured he can't

hear her, she rattles off her new address to the officer, and it's immediately committed to my memory.

"I don't want to press charges, Officer. It'll only provoke him more than he already is."

"Are you sure about that, Miss Fields? This is a clear-cut case of simple assault and battery. You have plenty of credible witnesses who are more than happy to testify to that fact, if needed."

I watch her face as she weighs the pros and cons, and I know the very second she's made up her mind. "No, I just want him to leave me alone and put all this behind me once and for all."

The problem is, I've been around men like Butch for the past two years. He won't leave her alone. He won't let this slight against him go unanswered. His pride has been wounded whether he leaves here in the back of the patrol car or not. And he will want revenge for that insult. But her mind is made up, and she urges the officer to wrap this up so everyone can get back to their business.

With the paperwork done, Bitch and the other office rejoin us in the warmth of the coffee shop.

"I want him arrested." Bitch thrusts his finger at me as he approaches, and I'm sorely tempted to break it. "He assaulted me. Broke my nose. Look at me."

"Go ahead and press charges. Savannah and I will both press charges against you too, and we'll see who walks out of the precinct and who spends the night." My blatant dare is meant to incite him again. He doesn't take much goading to push him over the edge, and I'm in the mood to have another go at him.

The cop finishes writing on his form and turns to Bitch. "Here's the deal. You can either leave now and stay away from her for good, and I mean *forever*, Mr. McMahan. Or, we can arrest you right now for assault and battery. You can try to press charges against Special Agent Tucker, but I guarantee his director will have already talked to the chief of police before we even get to the station."

Butch hesitates for just a moment, weighing his options, before he concedes. "I'll leave. I never want to see her again anyway."

The cop turns to Savannah. "Go file a restraining order against him. If he breaks it, we'll haul him in."

"Like a piece of paper can save her if I wanted to get to her."

"Did you just threaten her in front of me? Because I'll arrest you right here and now if you want to play this stupid game." The cop grabs his cuffs and advances on Bitch.

"No, no, I'm not threatening her. If you're finished with me, I'll go now."

"That would be best. Stay away from her. Don't call her. Don't look for her. If you see her out somewhere, turn and walk the other way. You get me?"

He nods then storms out the door. A collective sigh echoes through the shop when the door closes behind him. When I look down at Savannah, I'm surprised to find her still attached to me even after Butch is gone. The two cops leave soon after Savannah promises to pursue the restraining order so they can arrest his ass when he approaches her again. They know he will —they've seen the signs too many times, too.

"You okay?" I wait for her to tip her face up to me, and those emerald-green eyes hypnotize me instantly.

She nods. "I think I'm okay now. Thank you for not leaving me to deal with this mess alone."

"My pleasure, Savannah. Let me grab a hot coffee then I'll walk you home to make sure you get there safely. Can I get you anything?"

"I think I'm already jittery enough. I don't need more caffeine to add to it." She laughs nervously and glances away. "I'll just grab my things then I'll be ready to go."

With my coffee in hand and Savannah's laptop bag slung

over my shoulder, she and I set off on foot. The chilly air hits us the second we step out of the café. "Good thing your place is only at the end of the block. You'd freeze to death if you had to walk much farther."

She nods and looks down, a sure sign of the low self-esteem. "I know, but I'm too fat, so I need the exercise. Butch used to complain about my weight frequently."

I place my hand on her arm, careful not to alarm her, and halt her steps. "That's not what I said at all. You're gorgeous, built, and sexy as hell. I don't give a shit what that fucking moron said—you're perfect exactly the way you are right now. From what I've seen and felt, you have all the right curves in all the right places."

Her face burns bright red and her eyes drop to the ground, but a smile spreads across her face. "Thank you, Nick. That's very sweet of you to say."

With a chuckle, I shake my head. "I've never been accused of being *sweet* before." We continue our short walk to her apartment building. "Do you mind if I come up for a minute? Before you get the wrong idea, I only want to make sure he's not waiting for you up there before I leave you alone."

"Um, sure. I guess that's a good idea, considering he just showed up in my neighborhood today, and I have no idea how he found out where I live now."

"You're still in scrubs, so I'm guessing you work nights. Any chance he could've followed you home from work?"

"Maybe. But I was very careful, watching all around me and everything. I didn't even drive to work today. I took the Metro and walked to the coffee shop."

I can tell she's very uneasy about being alone with me in the elevator, but I know this guy isn't going to give up as easily as he said. So I take advantage of the time to learn more about the clusterfuck that just happened. "I take it Butch McMahan is your ex-boyfriend?"

"Unfortunately. It's actually a long, ugly story, but we haven't been more than acquaintances for about three years. Though, he obviously thinks that means he owns me and gets to boss me around. I know the cop was adamant about the restraining order, but it won't do any good to get one. It may even make the situation worse because Butch would take it as a dare. I don't want his temper to escalate."

I'm leaning against the elevator wall as we slowly climb to the fifth floor, watching her every move and expression, when a sobering fact hits me.

The threat of danger to Savannah is far from being over. Undercover work sharpened my gut instincts. My intuition kept me alive at times I could just as easily have died, but I heeded the warnings even when I questioned the logic behind doing so. I learned quickly not to ignore them, and right now, they're screaming at the top of their lungs at me.

Can I simply walk away knowing that?

CHAPTER 3

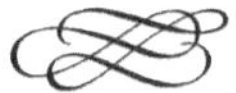

Savannah

This enormous man moving through my apartment like he owns it is reassuring and intimidating at the same time. And sexy. Very, very sexy. That's something I shouldn't even be thinking about right now. I've sworn off men completely until I get my own shit together. I don't need another complication in my life right now. I mean, I haven't even fully gotten rid of Butch yet, despite my best attempts. I wouldn't feel right about starting something with another man with that kind of loser baggage still clinging to me.

But there's something innately calming and reassuring about Nick. He didn't even flinch over the extra time it took to open all my dead bolts and door locks—and lock them back again once we were inside. Now, I can't help but follow him around like a lost puppy and watch his every move, explaining my reasoning for decorating or furniture arrangement. He has no idea how much I appreciate his good-natured replies to my rambling. He's definitely lethal to the female population in those jeans that cling to his legs perfectly, outlining the

43

muscular tree trunks underneath the denim fabric. And I find myself jealous of the thermal Henley stretching across his broad shoulders, thick chest, and muscular arms, clinging to his fine physique like a tattoo.

Speaking of a tattoo, I see hints of extensive ink across his chest now and then when he moves in just the right way. The tips of an elaborate design peek out from under his shirt, and I'm dying to ask him if I can see it. When we walked into my apartment, he took off his jacket and draped it over his arm, no expectations for me to pick it up off the floor wherever he decided to drop it. Unlike someone else I know but wish I didn't.

"You don't have an alarm system?" His tone is nonchalant, absent any judgment or condemnation. But I have a feeling it's anything but benign from the way he thoroughly checks and rechecks my doors and windows, as if I don't check them a hundred times a day without his help.

"No. I'm only renting and have no intentions of buying this place, so I didn't see the point in investing the money."

He nods his head, but his demeanor clearly says he doesn't agree with me. "Maybe you'll change your mind after the incident today."

When I'm silent for too long, he turns and pierces me with his amber-colored eyes that make me think of a shot of whiskey —smooth and warm, but with an extra kick that comes from out of nowhere. But something deeper in them speaks to me. I feel an instant connection to him, past the acts of kindness he's shown me.

"Maybe."

I can't tell him I don't have the extra money for a security monitoring system right now. I've already put myself in an embarrassing situation, and I'm working hard to get out of it. The investments in my future endeavors coupled with the usual moving expenses hit my savings account harder than I originally estimated, so I'll need time to save up enough money to cover more than the necessities. Living in DC is not cheap, and I'm well aware I could move to another town and get away from Butch. I could pick any small town or big city in the world, but I refuse to run and hide from a place I've grown to call home. Maybe that makes me stupid. Or stubborn. Or both. But I refuse to leave behind the best friends I've ever known just because of a poor excuse for a man.

There's definitely much more to Nick Tucker than the rough exterior and the savior attitude I've seen so far. The way he carries himself screams confidence and capability—but he also gives off enough signals to let everyone know to keep a wide berth. When he speaks, his message is short and to the point. Even on the walk to my apartment, the limited conversation we had was all about me. He seemed hesitant to share anything about himself—personal or otherwise.

Yet, he cares. Even about a stranger embroiled in the drama of domestic abuse, probable frequent flyer at the local police station, and general wimp of a woman, for all he knows. First impressions are as hard to overcome as false beliefs about women who don't flee from domestic violence.

"I have some friends in the security business. To the public, they've closed up shop and redirected their efforts elsewhere. To those of us who know them, they still provide the best security services anyone would ever need, all while keeping it under the radar. They're good friends of mine, so I'd trust them with my life, and I don't say that about anyone else. If you'll let me, I'd like to call them to install a security system for you."

"But you don't know me. Why would you do that?" No man would call in a favor like that for someone he didn't know. He only knows my name because I had to give it to the police officer. We literally just met a few minutes ago. What does he expect in return?

His eyes drop to the floor, and a dark shadow passes over his expression. There's so much regret deep inside this man. Pain seeps out of his very essence, troubling him so much, even a stranger can see it. "You don't deserve how he treated you. You're entitled to feel safe in your own home." He shrugs his muscular shoulders, still not meeting my gaze head on. "If I can help take some of that away, I want to try."

"I appreciate the offer, but I can't let you do that. It's very kind of you to be so concerned about me, though. You have a good heart, Nick." I'm not flirting—I'm being as sincere as possible. Maybe I missed a few huge warning signs with the other guy, but my eyes are wide open now.

"I don't think your friend would agree with that assessment of me, but I'll admit to having a strong sense of right and wrong. My protective instincts have always been fairly keen, too. Sorry if I crossed the line with my offer. Sometimes I do get a little overzealous...but that's only because of what I've seen in my line of work."

When he speaks this time, those amber eyes lock on to mine and hold me captive. I almost feel bad about turning down his offer to help. It seems so important to him.

"Your friends in security, did you use to work with them?" I'm genuinely curious about Nick, but maybe I'll learn more about him by asking about his friends rather than about him directly.

"Yeah. We were all Army buddies first. Reaper started his own security company when he left the service. I worked for him for a while before I took a private security job with the software mogul Dominic Powers. Now I'm with the DEA. Reaper had his security business for several years before all the guys settled down with families, but they couldn't stand being out of the thick of things for long. Now they take high-powered but low-visibility cases."

"You mean they handle undercover work, don't you?"

"Something like that." Is that a small smile? Finally, some type of reaction from him. Amused by my amusement.

"I've always been fascinated by that type of work. I never could do it myself, but I love watching documentaries about other people who do it. It's intriguing."

That amused look is gone, replaced by a haunted expression I can't even begin to guess about.

He pulls a card out of his wallet and writes something on the back. "Here's my contact info, and my personal cell is on there. If you change your mind or if he shows up here, call me. My address is on the back if you ever need a nearby place to escape to. I'm only a couple of miles from here—in Georgetown. Don't hesitate to call or drop by if you need help."

With that, he slides his jacket over his muscular arms and back. "Lock up behind me. Stay safe, Savannah."

"Thank you again for everything. Are you sure you don't want me to drive you home? It's getting pretty cold out there."

"No, I like to walk. Thanks anyway. Enjoy the rest of your day." Before the door closes behind him, he graces me with a full-face smile.

Straight white teeth against naturally tanned skin. Short hair that looks black on sight, but closer inspection reveals the dark brown mixture. Well-groomed beard that adds to his rugged and handsome appearance. But that real smile makes me weak in the knees.

After he's gone, I realize he never asked for my number. That really shouldn't disappoint me as much as it does. I shouldn't care whether he wants to call me or not. I certainly shouldn't wonder if he has a girlfriend, or recount that I didn't see a ring on his finger.

And I definitely shouldn't tell Karen about him.

For the next few hours, I keep myself busy writing and plotting my next couple of chapters, motivated even more by the events of the morning. The distinctive rumble of a motorcycle engine slowly moving by catches my attention. My heart races, my hands shake, and my palms sweat. Sliding along the wall to the window, I peek through the crack between the curtains and the wall without giving away my location. My breath hitches in my chest, and I stand motionless while staring down at Butch. He's stopped in front of my building, casing the scene. My only consolation is he doesn't know which apartment is mine. The tenant names aren't listed on the door buzzer for safety concerns—exactly like this situation. Still, if someone opens the door and holds it for him, he would find me all too soon.

He raises his hand, his forefinger pointed outward and his thumb extended upward, forming a mock gun. Then he slowly moves his hand across the building, pretending to shoot when he reaches each window. Though he doesn't know which one I'm in, the threat is obvious. And real—because he has no idea I'm watching, but he's taking the time to see it through regardless.

I can't breathe.

I'm never going to get away from him. He doesn't even care about me, much less love me. So why can't he just leave me alone?

His arm drops limply to his side, and his spine straightens. A large figure steps out of the shadows, slowly approaching Butch's bike. A hood covers the second man's head and his hands are in his jacket pockets, but I'd recognize that strut anywhere.

Nick is out there with Butch.

So many thoughts rush through my mind, I can barely keep up with them. Was the entire scene at the coffee shop a ruse to get me to trust Nick? Is he in league with Butch and the motor-cycle gang? I can't chance moving to slide the window open, but then, I wouldn't be able to hear them from the fifth floor anyway.

Butch makes a show of turning the ignition key off and

putting the kickstand down. He stands and climbs off his bike. An anxiety attack is imminent. There's no way I can fight off these two muscular brutes if they turn on me. I slide my cell out of my pocket and prepare to dial 9-1-1. If they walk toward the building, I'm running and dialing at the same time.

Butch faces Nick, his arms hanging loosely at his sides, but his fists are ready. That stance is all too familiar. Butch is about to sucker-punch Nick. Maybe they're not friends, after all. My imagination is all over the place, along with my paranoia and anxiety. Butch takes a swing, but Nick easily ducks before delivering a powerful blow to Butch's stomach, one fist after the other.

Butch doubles over in pain and drops to his knees in the middle of the road, coughing and spitting on the ground. Nick takes that opportunity to snatch something out of Butch's vest pocket then spikes it on the asphalt in front of Butch. Then I realize what it is—or was. Butch's cell phone. Nick stomps on what's left of it with the heel of his boot, further demolishing it and grinding it into dust.

Nick doesn't walk away before adding insult to injury. He smiles and gives Butch an imaginary tip of his hat. Then Nick strolls off without a care in the world while Butch tries to catch his breath and stand up straight again. He holds his side as he straddles his motorcycle then glances down at the broken pieces of his phone before putting his bike into gear and riding away.

First, I'm dying to call Nick and ask him what the hell just happened. Then I realize he never left my neighborhood when he left my apartment. He knew Butch would show up, and he waited out in the cold wind and snow for hours.

Second, there's no way in hell I can keep any of this from Karen and Spencer. She will flip her shit on me for not calling her immediately, and I'm sure Spencer will want to meet Nick. Either way, I'll be in an embarrassing predicament—Karen with her matchmaking plans and Spencer with his law enforcement brotherhood bond pushing me on a man I just met.

Lastly, watching Nick dishing out what I've taken from Butch was way too hot. I wish I'd videoed it on my phone so I could replay it a million and one times. From what I've seen of him so far, Nick Tucker is the perfect man. Did I mention he's also a fine specimen to examine?

If I wait much longer, I run the risk of facing a thoroughly pissed-off best friend, so I fish my phone from my pocket again. Funny, I don't even remember putting it back in there. When she answers, she's her usual chipper self. Until I recount the coffee shop scene. I only get as far as Butch dragging me out of my seat before she becomes unhinged.

"What the hell, Savannah? Why are you just now calling me? Spence! Spence! Where is your gun? I'm going to neuter Butch and spare the world from any chance of him reproducing any satanic spawn in his image."

"What?" I can hear the confusion in Spencer's tone, and it makes me laugh.

"Hold on, Karen. Let me finish the whole story first. You'll enjoy it."

"There's more? Let me put you on speaker so Spence can hear too. He may have better ideas of how to rid Butch of his cock and balls. Maybe some dry ice. Think that would freeze them off, babe?"

"Please don't talk about dry-icing anyone's cock and balls. It causes me physical pain. Savannah, please tell us your story so we can change the subject. Quickly."

An image of Spencer protectively covering his junk with his hand flashes in my mind, and I choke back a laugh. Then I recount everything—from start to finish—for both of them. When I reach the end of the story, I'm met with complete silence on the other end of the line.

"Karen? Spence? Did I lose you?"

"No. We're here. Just in shock." Spencer answers first, which is odd, but the hesitancy in his voice is even more so.

"What? Do you know Nick?"

"You haven't been watching the news lately, have you?"

"No. Why? I've been asleep during the day or on my way to work most evenings."

"Nick Tucker is the agent who was involved in that shootout with the Devil's Dominion motorcycle gang in LA a few months ago. He'd been undercover with them for two years, and his cover was blown after he saved those kidnapped actresses."

"So, he's one of the good guys, then?" I knew it.

"Well, technically, yes. But Savannah, he was one of them for two years. I'm sure there were things he had to do to prove his allegiance. That's a long time to be in with one of those gangs and not be like them. He had to fit in. If they'd ever questioned his loyalty to them, they would've just killed him. He may be a federal agent, but he may not be completely harmless either. Just be careful, okay?"

And just like that, my walls go back up again.

CHAPTER 4

Nick

My morning coffee run takes me by Savannah's building. Curiosity gets the better of me, so I have to look up at her condo, but I don't catch any movement as I walk by. Within a few minutes, my favorite coffee shop is in sight, and my craving intensifies. When I step inside, those emerald-green eyes lift to meet mine, and a smile lights up her face.

What was I thinking about craving again?

"Good morning, Savannah. How's your day going?"

"Good morning. So far, so good. You?"

"About the same." I walk to the counter and order my usual, feeling her eyes boring into my back the entire time. After I waste a few minutes making small talk with the barista, I quickly turn before Savannah can avert her eyes.

Busted.

Staring straight at me. Checking me out. From the angle of her gaze, she was looking at my ass. From the way she's chewing on her bottom lip, I'd say she liked it. Without asking or waiting for an invitation, I take a seat at her table, sipping my coffee and ignoring her surprised reaction.

"What are you working on so early this morning?" I incline my head toward her laptop.

"Um, I'm…um, writing a book." Her cheeks flush, and she lowers her gaze to the table, as if she's waiting for me to ridicule her for such an absurd idea. That, however, is the furthest thing from my mind.

"What's it about?" I lean in, giving her my full attention.

"I want to help other women who are in abusive relationships, so it's about what I've experienced and what I wish I'd done differently." She searches my eyes and waits for the other shoe to drop.

"I'm impressed. That's incredibly thoughtful and insightful of you. When you become famous and hit the talk-show circuit, I'll be able to say, 'I knew her when.' You'll be my claim to fame." The truth is, I mean every word of it.

Gratitude shimmers in her eyes before she swallows hard, regaining control over her composure. "Thank you for saying that, Nick. I don't expect that will happen at all, but I appreciate the vote of confidence."

"Of course. I won't keep you from working any longer, then. Have a good one." Just as I push back from the table, a picture of me flashes up on the TV mounted over the barista bar.

"Looks like you have your own claim to fame." Her eyes remain glued to the screen as the images change.

The first one is of me in character, decked out as a member of the Devil's Dominion motorcycle club with my long, scruffy hair and scraggly beard, wearing my cut with the club colors boldly displayed on my back. The next image looks more like I do today, with my short, military-style haircut, neatly trimmed beard, and sporting a DEA jacket. The trial for the members running drugs, guns, prostitution rings, and kidnapping schemes is underway. The more attention it garners, the more my face is flashed on every TV screen across the nation.

My cover was blown shortly after the gang takedown. One of the surviving members made sure to sing like a fucking canary to anyone who'd listen—after I saved his pathetic life. An overly eager journalist was all too willing to accommodate his anonymity in exchange for my name—all to get the scoop on everyone else. When the journalist ran with the story and my pictures, he annihilated any chance I have to go undercover again—ever. There's no outlaw organization in North America that won't recognize me on the spot by the time this trial is over—whether it's a motorcycle gang or an organized crime syndicate. They'd never believe I'd turned rogue either. My blood bleeds DEA and following the law to the letter, and that's the tune every reporter sings about me now.

Calvin, my director, already warned me that this do-gooder character they've made me out to be could all be fueled by the gang's lawyers...to discredit me and relish my epic fall from grace when my gang crimes are revealed. Pointing out all my flaws after making me out to be the best agent since James Bond will be part of their defense. My fall from grace will help create an ounce of doubt in the jurors' minds toward the gang members—or at least some hesitation to throw the entire book at them. My sins will be broadcast from every satellite and antennae across the nation, all in the name of discrediting me and getting those low-life thugs off the hook.

This is another reason Calvin didn't think I was ready for undercover work. The aftermath can be fucking brutal.

"I wish they'd quit running that load of bullshit. They're only trying to sensationalize the trial and get the public more engaged." I shake my head, disgusted with how slowly the wheels of justice turn sometimes, and start toward the door. "That's my cue to exit stage left. Good luck with your book."

"Hey, Nick?" The tentative tone in her voice grabs my attention.

"Yeah?"

"Do you miss it?" Her eyes roam over my face while she waits for me to answer, searching for any clue of my real feelings.

"Miss what, exactly?" I'm not sure what to make of her question or why she's so concerned about it.

"Undercover work, I guess." She shrugs unconvincingly. "Being part of the motorcycle club."

"Miss being part of those fucked-up losers? No, I don't miss that at all. Undercover work…wasn't exactly what I thought it would be. I don't appreciate that my option to participate in undercover operations has been taken from me now, but I'm still considering my options for the future. Riding a desk isn't my cup of tea."

She bites on the end of her pen, a subconscious behavior showing she's nervous about what she has to say next. "There's something else I should tell you. Um, Butch stopped in front of my building yesterday. I don't think he saw me, but I saw him."

That memory brings a smile to my face. "Yeah, I figured he would. I waited around for him to show his fugly mug. An idiot thug like him couldn't resist, not even realizing all he accomplished was showing his entire hand."

"What do you mean?"

"I knew he was tracking you somehow. He found you here in the coffee shop after you said you moved without telling him where you went, didn't he? When he rolled up at your building, I approached him, made a few not so vague threats to his person, and took his phone from him."

"His phone? Why would you take his phone? What does that have to do with anything?" Her eyebrows draw down, her head tilts to the side, and her lips part slightly. On top of being too fucking beautiful to look at, she's so damn cute when she scrunches up her face.

"He had an app on it so he could trace you. It was still open when I snatched his phone from his cut. It was a burner phone. With a guy like him, I made an educated guess he doesn't have your number memorized. Still, I suggest changing your phone number and your email address in case he's actually smarter than he looks."

"You mean I went to all the trouble of packing and moving in secret, to a new location he knew nothing about, only to have him track me with an app on his phone? Oh my gosh, Nick. I feel so stupid. I should've anticipated something like that, but the thought honestly never crossed my mind. I can't believe you stayed out in the cold for so long, waiting for him to show just so you could make him leave me alone. Saying thank you—again—seems so inadequate. The news anchor had it completely correct when he said you're an undercover hero."

"I'm no hero, Savannah. Not at all. But I've witnessed first-hand how some sorry excuse for a man treats women. If I can help keep one of them away from you, I'll do whatever needs to be done."

"He's one of them, you know."

My head snaps back toward her fast enough to give me whiplash. "He's one of who?"

"The Devil's Dominion motorcycle club. The club president sent him out here a little over two years ago to oversee bringing a smaller gang into their circle. Things didn't go too smoothly with that assignment, though. He never told me anything, of course. But his voice is naturally loud, so I overheard everything he said about it when he came around me. He wouldn't go back out to LA because he'd failed at the assignment he was given, and he knew he'd never be promoted to an officer after that."

"He was a Devil, and he doesn't know who I am?" I can't

fucking believe what I'm hearing. "And he just ditched his colors and ran?"

"Butch never watched TV—not even the news—so it doesn't surprise me he didn't recognize you. He hasn't owned a TV since he put his foot through one before we left LA because something someone said pissed him off. I kept mine off when he was around so he wouldn't break it. As far as his colors, I was never involved in that side of his life, so I don't know much about how it works. The other group didn't like the raw deal they were getting, and there were more of them than there were Devils here, so they ran Butch and a couple of his buddies off. It was after that when he quit wearing his vest with their patches. Is that what you mean?"

"Yeah, a cut is the vest, and the colors are the patches—the top and bottom rocker panels and the middle patch. Under the club bylaws, he's supposed to wear his colors every time he's on his bike. He must've tucked his tail and run when the other club refused him. Rather than make believers of them himself, or even call in the reinforcements to help him, he just dropped his colors and hid instead. He's even more of a coward than I thought. What do you know? I've given Bitch way too much credit."

She snickers at my choice nickname for him. "He may not be too bright, but don't underestimate him, Nick. He's as cruel and malicious as they come."

"I'm sure he is. But there's always someone bigger, badder, and meaner just around the corner. Let me know if he comes sniffing around, looking to cause trouble for you again. I'll make good on those threats I made."

Not that I think she will, but the offer stands. I can't stand guard outside her place day and night, but I'll gladly jump on my bike, whisk around the stalled traffic, and make a quick dash of the two miles separating us to face off with that dickhead again. All this pent-up energy and frustration have to vent somewhere.

For some reason, I'm still standing here, staring into those emerald-green eyes and those flaming strands of auburn-colored hair that are pulled back in some kind of beautiful, intricate braid. I'm sure I look like a fucking idiot. What I'm thinking about her is the last thing I need right now. My life is complicated enough as it is. After two raps on the table with my knuckles, I make my exit. "That book won't write itself, Savannah. I'll leave you to it."

OVER THE NEXT TWO WEEKS, SAVANNAH IS IN MY FAVORITE coffee shop every morning in her nursing scrubs, sitting in the same seat, with her fingers furiously flying across the keyboard. My routine is also the same—walk in, say hello, grab my usual order, and take a seat with her while she types away on her laptop. After the first couple of days, I noticed she rarely ate, still stuck on that stupid fucking notion that she's too fat. So I started ordering breakfast to go with my coffee. She isn't fat. She is *fine*. And watching her enjoy the variety of menu items I deliver to her every day gives me an unusual satisfaction.

These visits with Savannah are not dates. I'm just getting to know the beautiful redhead with emerald-green eyes better every day. There's a difference. Besides, I'm enjoying just spending time with her. The aroma of coffee mixed with cinnamon buns and every other imaginable pastry is the icing on the piece of delicious red velvet cake sitting across from me. Plus, she's smart and funny. For the first time in a long time, I enjoy talking to someone about everyday mundane topics instead of the logistics of an undercover operation.

"So, tell me, what made you leave your private employer and join the DEA?" She watches me over the rim of her mug, blowing on the piping hot java before touching it to her mouth. I can't help but watch every movement of her lips and tongue until they disappear behind the bottom of her cup.

"The owner of the company, Dominic Powers, got married. He and his wife Sofia had a baby. Dominic hired someone else to run the company while he sat back and made the money. His home has state-of-the-art security with monitoring stations and impenetrable fences. My unique services were no longer required, not at the level I was used to providing anyway. After serving in the Army, I still had a strong conviction of serving my country, so the DEA became my new home."

"And the undercover work? Weren't you scared? I mean, if they'd found out you were a federal agent, they would've killed you on the spot." She looks at me with awe, waiting for my reply.

"They would have—and actually tried to there at the end. They almost succeeded in killing a buddy of mine from the CIA. He joined late in the investigation for a different reason, but he ended up blowing his cover to save a girl he was in love with. Almost blew my entire case, but so far, it hasn't completely unraveled. Once the trials are over, I'll be able to breathe freely again."

"I can't tell you how impressed I am with everything you've done. You've been all over the world. Done all kinds of work. Met all kinds of people. You've faced real-life situations that would make me pee the bed if I only dreamed about them. Besides work, what do you like to do?"

"I've been undercover for the past two years, until recently. I don't do anything besides work. Except go to the gym, if that counts as a hobby. I use weights to work off stress and keep in peak physical condition. Never know when you'll need that extra bit of ass to back up your threats."

She smiles and her eyes sparkle. Like emeralds. "You, threaten someone? Surely not. I can't even imagine that. You're just a big teddy bear." She puts her hand on my arm as she speaks. An innocent act to emphasize her tease, but the mere contact of her soft skin ignites every nerve in my body.

Fuck. It's been way too long since I've enjoyed the scents and sounds of a willing and beautiful woman underneath me. And I shouldn't be thinking any of the thoughts about a certain auburn-haired woman that are running through my mind. Or seeing any of the visions surrounding her that are parading through my mind's eye at the moment. "Yeah. You just keep thinking that, darlin'."

"You're still my hero, Nick. My undercover hero. Don't you ever forget it."

"No, you won't let me forget that moniker for shit." We laugh together, comfortable with the playful joking between us. "Speaking of the gym, I should get going."

"Will I see you tomorrow? Same time, same place?" There's a hopeful tone to her voice that wasn't there yesterday or the day before when she asked me the same question.

"Never know what tomorrow holds, darlin'." My standard response doesn't have quite as much conviction as it's held every other time I've used it either. Maybe we're both looking forward to seeing each other tomorrow.

Maybe a little too much. I leave with a wink and a quick wave before I say something I'll regret later. I'm not looking for romance. She's not looking for a good time. We're definitely not a match made in heaven.

Thinking of working off pent-up frustration leaves me with two options. One, start going through my little black book and seeing which friend-with-benefits still feels friendly after I've been away more than two years. Or two, go to the gym and hit the weights until I lose control of all voluntary muscle movement and regret my decision in the morning.

The gym it is.

After a quick jog back to my brownstone, I change into my

dark gray sweat pants, throw on a tank top, and slide my thick hoodie over my head. After stuffing a change of clothes in my old gym bag, I'm out the door and on my way to wear myself out. Bypassing all the boutique gyms in the area, I head toward a man's-man gym—no machines, only heavy weights that take two hands to lift. No yoga classes. No Zen rooms. No safe spaces. Just free weights, free water, and freedom to work out undisturbed. Down the steps and into the basement I go, to my favorite unknown gym, The Dungeon.

Many other agents work out here from every agency identified by initials. We share a mutual understanding of how a labor-intensive workout helps more than any mandated therapy session could. Punishing ourselves while simultaneously making our bodies harder and stronger is the ultimate win-win scenario. Likely the only one of those we'll ever have in our line of work.

Hours pass as I lift weights until I've pushed my muscles beyond fatigue and into exhaustion. It hurts so good, though. My arms are made of cooked spaghetti now, and I can barely push the bar back up on the holder on my last rep. After putting my weights back on the racks, I hit the treadmill for a long stretch of my legs and my lungs. This is when I completely clear my mind, only listening to the way my feet fall on the conveyor belt and focusing on keeping my breathing consistent. The rest of the world doesn't exist for this hour. It's mine and mine alone.

It's when I'm in the shower with the scalding hot water soothing my exhausted muscles that my thoughts are overrun once again. The news coverage is still running. The nickname the anchor gave me is used every day on every station now. The way Savannah looked at me when she called me an undercover hero was the same way she looked at me when I tossed Bitch around like a little bitch doll for manhandling her.

That expression will change when the smear campaign begins.

The higher they rise, the further they fall.

And currently, they're trying to launch me and my super-hero alter ego they've created into the fucking stratosphere.

Back in my brownstone, I grab a gallon of water from the refrigerator and stand in the open door, guzzling it down to quench my thirst and cool my engines. Out of nowhere, someone starts pounding on my door and frantically screaming my name. On my way to the commotion, I drop the jug of water on the table and grab my gun instead. When I jerk the door open, I find a battered and bloodied Savannah.

Her once expertly styled hair now hangs in tatters—parts of it frizzy but still in place, and other large chunks hang loose. Two large sections next to her scalp are matted and still wet with blood. One eye is nearly swollen shut, and both her lips are busted and bleeding. Her cheeks show scrapes and abrasions, while bruises in the shapes of long fingers are already forming in angry red tendrils on her neck. Some of these injuries very recently occurred because not enough time has passed for the coagulation process to begin, but others are at least a couple of hours older.

That son of a bitch.

"Nick."

Her voice breaks when she says my name, then her knees buckle under her weight. I easily scoop her up with one arm and carry her inside my home. All the adrenaline and rage flowing through my veins must flush the lactic acid from my muscles because I am primed and ready to give Bitch the beat-down of his life.

CHAPTER 5

Savannah

The sensation of strength and warmth envelops me, and I feel protected and sheltered for the first time in far too many years. Every inch of my body hurts, but Nick's muscular arms cradle me with such care, I feel as well cared for as a newborn baby. His scent is soothing too—sandalwood mixed with hints of the aroma of coffee, reminding me of the first time he saved me. Those scents are forever ingrained in my psyche and associated with Nick.

Safe. Secure. Protected. Cherished.

He places me on the soft cushions of his couch and covers with me a blanket. "Just relax, darlin'. You're safe. I'm here with you, and I guarantee he won't get through me to reach you."

With one hand on my shoulder, giving me all the reassurance and sharing his strength, he uses the other to call the police. A fleeting thought to protest getting them involved pops into my mind, but I quickly dismiss it. Butch has had way too many chances, and this time, he's gone way too far. Nick gives the police his address and a rundown of my injuries, then he pauses—the first sign of hesitancy I detect.

"Savannah, do you need to go to the hospital? Did he...did he rape you?" He's seething just below the surface, barely able to contain his anger. But it's all directed at Butch, that much I already know.

"No, he didn't. He wasn't interested in that kind of power. Tell them to send Detective Spencer Donovan. He's my best friend's husband."

Nick finishes the conversation with the dispatcher and releases a long, heavy sigh after he hangs up. "They got a hold of Detective Donovan. He will be here in a few minutes, darlin'. We'll get Butch, and he'll pay for every mark he put on you. Just rest until your friend gets here."

Sure enough, only a few minutes pass before someone knocks on the door, identifying himself as a DC detective. Nick partially opens the door and checks his identification before inviting him inside, even though I'm right here and can hear Spencer's voice loud and clear. After giving Spencer all my pertinent information and assuring both men, again, I don't want to go to the hospital, I begin telling them what happened today.

"I'd been out for the early part of the day, running errands and shopping. When I got back to my apartment, my arms were full of bags and I was distracted, so I didn't notice if anything was out of the ordinary. But looking back, I realize now a couple of my dead bolts were too easy to turn. I remember opening the door and kicking it closed behind me, knowing I still had to secure all the locks before I put up my groceries. Before I even had time to set the bags down in the kitchen, Butch hit me from behind and sent me flying across the table. So he was already inside before I arrived home."

From there, I continue describing the attack in chronological order to the best of my spotty memory, retracing my steps, backing up, and adding to the details as flashes return to me. The punches to my face and head, the kicks to my abdomen and back, the objects hurtling through the air at me from so many directions. The indiscriminate screaming and yelling mixed with items crashing and breaking all around me. Chunks of time are missing from when I went in and out of consciousness, only to awaken to Butch's manic tirade again.

"I don't know how long the entire attack lasted—but it wasn't over with quickly. When I woke the final time, he was gone, and I didn't wait around to see if he was coming back."

"Did he give you any indication of what set him off?" I know Spencer has to ask that; it's part of his job. But there is no finding reason in an extremely unreasonable man.

"He kept saying he wasn't going to let me out of a sweet deal so easily. That it'd be over his dead body. But I have no idea what he meant. We haven't been romantically involved in years. I've made it perfectly clear multiple times I want nothing more to do with him. I even moved and didn't tell him where I was going. He was crazed, but I have no idea why."

After more questions and Nick sharing the details of the altercations he's had with Butch, I'm once again urged to go get a piece of paper that says he can't come within 500 yards of me. Because criminals always follow the law, and abusers are always remorseful enough to simply stop abusing others.

That piece of paper won't help me, no matter what laws are behind it.

If they can't get to Butch to arrest him for the assault I've endured, how will they find him to arrest him for breaking a restraining order?

Spencer promises a warrant will be issued for his arrest. If they find him, they'll take him in and hold him—until he makes bail. And I'll hold my breath and wait for that to happen. He's like a cockroach—scurrying into the dark places to hide from any light. Only coming out when something he wants is there, unsuspecting and unprotected.

Nick takes several pictures of my injuries with both an instant camera and with his phone. He understands as well as I do that this situation is far from over. But what can they do until Butch is found and put behind bars?

"Do you want me to escort you back to your apartment? I need to talk to your neighbors and document the state of your place." Spencer slides his pen into his shirt pocket, signaling we're finished here and he's ready to go.

But I'm not ready to go back there at all. The thought of it nearly sends me into a full-fledged panic attack. Without realizing I'm doing it, I shake my head.

"No, she's not going back there for a while. She's in no shape to be alone, and she doesn't have a security system. Yet. Butch could walk back in there at any time, if he even left the building at all. Look at her injuries—there's no telling how long he held her there against her will. He has stalked and harassed and abused her enough." Nick partially steps between Spencer and me, shielding me with his body even if he doesn't realize he's doing it.

"Nick, do you want to join me when I check out her apartment?" Spencer is hesitant to leave me here alone with Nick, especially after our last conversation about him.

"Here—just take my keys and let yourself in. If he's there, you can arrest him or shoot him." I pick up my small bag off the floor and hand over my keys. "I don't care if you have to go through all my things."

Spencer is obviously unsure about leaving me in Nick's care but takes the keys anyway. "I'll bring them back to you as soon as I'm finished with my reports. Call my cell if you need me before then. Will you be here? With Nick?"

"She will." Nick answers before I can and lays his hand on my shoulder, but I nod at Spencer and give him a small smile, silently telling him not to worry.

"I'm safe here, Spencer. Nick is a DEA agent. He knows how to handle Butch if he's stupid enough to come around here." Nick gently squeezes my shoulder in response.

I glance up at him, gratitude glimmering in my eyes and blurring my vision. He looks down at me, concern mixed with the inherent air of authority etched in his masculine features, then his face softens. A shadow passes over his eyes, like a rain cloud blotting out the sun on a bright day. Then he walks to the door to see Spencer out.

So many questions are answered in that one telltale sign, a rare glimpse into the man who reveals so little of himself to others. Nick lives with as many regrets as I do. They may not be anywhere near the same types of disappointments, but they still create the life-altering sense of shame that is nearly impossible to live under. I know from personal experience how the weight of past mistakes suffocates and binds until almost all hope is lost. The doubts nag and remind of all the bad decisions made in the past, badgering the mind and troubling the soul. Too many wishes to count have been wasted on seeking a way to turn back time and undo the years of unnecessary guilt.

A realization hits me from out of nowhere, sucker-punching me in the gut and stealing all my breath. That painfully deep pool of sorrow and self-loathing I just glimpsed in Nick's eyes... is the exact same hollow gaze I see when I look in the mirror.

"Savannah, you know Karen will be livid when I talk to her." Spence turns in the doorway, craning his neck around Nick to see me. "You may want to warn Nick about her, too."

"When you tell her what happened, please tell her every minute detail so I don't have to repeat any of it. Then tell her I love her...and remind her how much she loves me."

Spencer chuckles and shakes his head. "I'll be back soon, Savannah. Stay inside. Rest. We'll get him."

"Thank you, Spencer. And I love you too."

"Feeling's mutual, Savannah."

Nick closes the door after watching Spencer walk away, I presume to see what kind of car he drives so Nick will recognize it on sight next time. Unable to hold my head up any longer, I stretch out on the couch and try to find a comfortable position, one that doesn't put too much pressure on all my aches and pains and abrasions and contusions. When the door closes, I hear Nick lock the knob. Then the dead bolt. A second later, metal slides across metal, mixed the distinct sound of a chain clinking. Stupid, hot tears fill my closed eyes from the simplest gesture no one else even would've noticed.

Nick secured all the locks on his door. For me. From the short time he's been around me, he knows exactly what I need to feel safe and secure. Even though a logical part of my brain knows those locks can't protect me—obviously, as evidenced by my current state—it's an irrational need I can't do without. But those locks ease the storm that rages inside me, the one that grows more out of control when all I can fixate on is their unlocked status.

My self-doubt creeps in, and I don't want him to think I'm emotionally unstable, despite the fact that I am, actually, emotionally distraught...overwrought...frazzled...jittery. I hold my breath in an attempt to squelch the flood of sensations inside before the dam breaks, and I start blubbering out of control.

Then I feel the slightest touch on my face, so feathery and light, I question if I actually felt it. When I feel it a second time, I slowly open my eyes and find Nick sitting on the coffee table next to me, cleaning my wounds with a cotton swab. His focused expression shows his attention to detail, but the extra care he takes to avoid inflicting more pain while doctoring my injuries pushes me over the edge. Once the tears start, there's no stopping them. Like water escaping over a full spillway, rivers flow uncontrollably from my eyes.

Nick lifts his eyes to mine, startled at first—probably thinking he hurt me in some way—then realization settles into his features. He nods wordlessly in understanding. We move in tandem, each sensing what the other will do beforehand. His arms extend as I sit upright on the couch. He pulls me into his arms as I move into his lap. He cradles me like a baby, holding me close to his chest as he moves to the couch. I bury my head in the crook of his neck just before the sobs rack my body. He rocks me, whispering words of comfort as I rest my aching cheek against his chest, soaking his shirt with the torrent still pouring from my eyes.

Time passes—minutes into hours—while he comforts me. And I soak up every second of it, selfishly taking every ounce of security and reassurance he gives me. When I'm finally calm enough—and dehydrated enough—to stop the waterworks, I remain motionless in his arms and use my unique vantage point to examine him much closer than usual.

His chest is solid as a rock, yet remarkably easy to cuddle against.

His arms are thick and muscular, but gentle and comforting.

His voice is deep and masculine, full of intimidation for those who cross him. But lying here in his care, that same voice encouraged me to let it all out because I was safe with him. That voice soothed my frayed nerves and calmed my racing heart when the panic set in and the anxiety threatened to pull me under.

He's my undercover hero, even if he can't see it because of the blinders he wears when he looks at himself. But that's okay, because one day soon, he'll see himself exactly how I see him, through my eyes. I'll make sure of it. He tries to hide his soft heart and his protective nature behind a gruff exterior and threatening air. But now that I've seen the man inside, I wonder how I ever could've missed him.

"Thank you." I intentionally keep my voice soft, afraid I'll break the trance we're both in and he'll jump up, ready to leave me behind. "I'm sorry I brought all this to your doorstep. Literally."

"You're welcome. But you haven't done anything to be sorry about. I hate that this happened to you, but I'm glad you came to me. At least I know you're safe from him while you're here with me. He said he'd let you go over his dead body? I'm not seeing a downside to that proposition."

I can't help but notice how he kept his lips close to my head when he spoke. How low and sensual his voice sounded, like a velvety-soft caress over my skin. How his thumb lightly strokes my lower back, slowly back and forth, as if he's my attentive lover.

Maybe this is the most inappropriate time to entertain such flights of fancy. But Nick isn't the one who hurt me. He isn't the one who left me for dead. He isn't the one who has threatened me day in and day out over the last few years.

Nick is the one who saved me...not only from Butch, but from myself. If I look hard enough, maybe I can see myself with him in the future.

CHAPTER 6

Nick

The beautiful redhead in my arms reminds me of so many women who paraded in and out of the club headquarters in LA. The majority of those women wanted to be there—on some level anyway. They endured abuse and were passed around freely among the brothers, like a water canteen for a group of men stranded in the desert too long. They weren't allowed to complain. They couldn't say no to any demand. And they didn't have a choice of which man had his turn next. Had they had any alternative other than living on the street in a cardboard box, I'm sure they would've jumped at it instead. But the relative safety of being inside a notorious outlaw biker gang hangout was better than what most of them already had faced on the outside.

My imagination is incapable of seeing Savannah in a place like that, though. Her entire disposition is the complete opposite of every sheep or old lady I met in my two-plus years undercover. She's the epitome of my dream woman, but she's definitely here in the flesh. Her plump, round ass fits perfectly in my lap. Her waist is small enough for my arms to wrap around at least a couple of times. Her long, red hair is thick and smells of vanilla and violet, especially so close to my face that I can't avoid it. Even with the now clotted injuries to her scalp, the scrapes, bruises, and puffy contusions on her face, she's the most beautiful woman I've ever seen. Or held.

But this can never be. The thought I'm having of holding her forever is really just wishful thinking, never to come to fruition. I have to admit, it's a really great dream, though.

She apologized for bringing her problems to me, as if I'd want her to go anywhere else at this point. Helping her is not a hardship for me. Doing what's right is every bit as much a part of me as my fingerprints are. This is what identifies and makes me who I am, what distinguishes me from everyone else out there. In some small way, maybe I also wonder if helping her will absolve me of some of my other sins...the laws I broke while undercover...the women I didn't protect because my cover came first. The ones I allowed to suffer so I wouldn't be killed for being a DEA agent.

"I don't want to impose on your generosity, Nick. You've been too good to me as it is. When Spencer gets back from checking everything out, I can go back to my apartment."

She can't see my smile from the way she's cradled in my arms, so I don't try to hide it at all. There's no conviction in her voice. If she actually wanted to stay in her place alone, she would've insisted. She would've stated she was going back, not left it up to me to decide for her. She doesn't want to impose, but she doesn't get that she's not an imposition to me. At all. Time to make a believer out of her.

"You're not going back to your apartment tonight. Or tomorrow. You can go back after you've healed and after we've had a top-of-the-line security system installed. For the record, I'm fairly blunt about what I think and what I want. If you ever impose, I'll tell you straight up. If I tell you I want you to come to me if you need help, that's exactly what I mean. And when I say you're staying here with me, where I know for a fact that you're safe, your pretty little ass isn't going anywhere. Got it?"

I can feel her smile against my chest at the same time her tense muscles relax again, her body melting against mine. "Got it, Nick. Thank you again. Thank you, thank you, thank you."

"While you're here, I expect you to make yourself at home. If there's something you want in the kitchen, it's yours. If there's something you want to watch on TV, you're welcome to the remote. If you need anything from the store, just tell me. We're thick as thieves, you and I."

"Then you have to give me some way to earn my keep around here." She raises her head from my chest to look at me. I hope to hell she can't read minds, because that offer is way too fucking tempting to turn down. "I'm a great cook. Let me feed you while I'm here."

Not exactly the same thing I thought she was offering, and I like my original thought better. Still, a home-cooked meal is not something I'll easily turn down.

"Deal, with a couple of exceptions. Don't even think about doing anything tonight. Probably not tomorrow either. You've been through hell. And if you don't feel up to cooking any other day you're here, then don't. No expectations. No tit for tat. You are a guest who's making herself at home here. Feeling at home means if you don't want to cook, we order takeout. Plain and simple."

"I can work with those stipulations." She smiles—or tries to. The bruises on her cheeks and the busted lips make it difficult for her to accomplish a full smile.

Seeing her injuries ignites the fury in me all over again. If I could get my hands on Butch, Savannah would never worry about him hurting her again. Fucker ghosted two weeks ago—not a sighting, not a word, nothing. Then all of a sudden, he's lying in wait for her inside her apartment. For all he knew, she could've died from her injuries after he left her unconscious on the floor. After spending a couple of hours every day with her over the last two weeks, I've gotten to know her fairly well. What makes her tick. Things she likes and doesn't like. Dreams and aspirations she has for her life.

She's not a casualty of a case I'm working while undercover.

A knock at the door pulls me from my murderous thoughts. Visions of Butch strung up by his balls, screaming in pain in a shrill, high-pitched voice retreat to the back of my mind. I'm sure it's Spencer at the door, coming back to deliver Savannah's keys. At the moment, I'm considering leaving Detective Donovan outside the door just so I don't have to move Savannah off my lap. We're both very comfortable in our current positions, and I felt her breath catch before she released it in a disappointed sigh. She thinks she's sly, this fiery little minx in my arms, but I can tell she wants more than friendship from me.

I'm not sure I'm capable of giving more.

I'm also not sure she's truly ready to want more.

Still, neither of us offers to move to answer the door. She's also considering her options, and that makes me want to grin much more than it fucking should.

"I should probably get that. I'm sure it's your detective friend stopping back by. He was already worried about leaving you here with me. We shouldn't cause him more concern by pretending we don't hear him at the door." My lips are against her hair as I speak, brushing along the shell of her ear. She leans closer into me. My arms tighten around her. My brain knows it should make me get up, but my fucking body is revolting against letting her go.

A louder and longer bang on the door signals Spencer's increasing frustration. "Savannah, are you in there?"

"Why don't you go take a hot shower? Use the one in my bedroom—it has a walk-in shower with a seat. Use the seat. I don't want to go in there and find you passed out on the floor. There are clean towels on the heated rack. Yell if you need anything at all."

"God, yes, that sounds like heaven. I think I will take you up on that." She looks up at me again. "I can't thank you enough. For everything."

"No reason to thank me, darlin'. It's my pleasure."

After I help her stand and make sure she's steady on her feet, I go to the door and let Spencer in. Savannah is already in my bathroom, adjusting the hot water for the shower when he walks into my living room. I can always spot a career cop—their eyes scan everything in the room, unabashedly looking at every single item in their surroundings, taking in the scene and processing it on the spot, whether it's considered rude by normal standards or not.

"Savannah okay?" His eyes assess me now, and I already know what he thinks of me. It's clear as fucking day.

"She will be. She had somewhat of a breakdown after you left, but I think she got most of it out."

"I packed a few of her things I thought she may want. I've had to do similar for Karen before when she got stuck working double shifts at the hospital because of the weather and stuff. Where is she anyway?" He hands me a small duffle bag with a few articles of clothes and toiletries then glances over my shoulder, toward the hallway.

"She just now went to take a shower."

Spencer nods, maintaining eye contact, and puts his hands on his hips. "At the risk of sounding cliché, this is the part where I warn you about not hurting her. She's a good person, and she doesn't deserve to be treated the way she has been."

"No one deserves that." My voice is flat, and my statement is blunt for a reason. While I wholeheartedly agree Savannah doesn't deserve this, I adamantly believe no one else does either.

"Of course not, but I'm not here for everyone else. I'm here for her. I don't know what your intentions are, but I know you were undercover with the same gang Butch is in. Since I don't believe in coincidences, I'm more than uncomfortable with your budding relationship with my wife's best friend. So maybe you can explain how you just happened to get mixed up with a woman who was mixed up with a gang member from the very gang you just spent two years riding with."

"Detective Donovan, I'm a trained DEA Special Agent. Now, maybe you don't understand the grueling nature of our training or what it takes to become a Special Agent, but I can assure you that not a fucking one of those low-life fuckers were friends of mine. I put my life on the line every fucking day just to take them down. I didn't risk everything I've worked my entire career to build, spend two years of my life gathering intel and putting up with their bullshit, just to choke when they're finally going to trial for their many, many crimes."

He has the decency to show his embarrassment over his idiotic blunder. "You're right. I'm sorry, man. Savannah has just been through enough hell, and I'd never forgive myself if she went through even more because I didn't ask the tough questions."

"Don't sweat it. She needs friends like that. I'm glad she has you."

He fishes her keys out of his pocket and extends his hand to me. I take them and put them on the coffee table in plain sight. "Thanks. Find anything interesting in her apartment?"

"Yeah, but you're not going to like it."

"Let's hear it." I stiffen my spine and school my features. Undercover expressionless mode activated.

"He left a note there—for you. I had to turn the actual note in for evidence, but here's what it said."

He holds out his phone, so I take it and study the picture of the note Bitch left me at Savannah's apartment.

. . .

You Fucking Undercover Pig—

How are my sloppy seconds? You think you can take her from me before I've released her? You know the rules—none of the bitches leave the club before a Devil says she can. I'll be back to collect my property...and you'll show the world what a piece of shit you are.

Signed,

Suck My Dick

"What a charming letter. He really missed his calling. I'm thinking he could get a high-level gig writing greeting cards." I hand Spencer's phone back to him, unconcerned with Butch's insignificant threat against me. But his continued threats against Savannah do concern me because he's already shown he will carry those out without hesitation.

"Has Savannah said anything else about Butch's comment regarding not letting his sweet deal go?"

"No, she hasn't talked about it at all, actually. The trauma of everything he did hit her at once. I've literally sat here for hours and held her while she cried it all out, reassuring her that she's safe and I'll keep her that way. She hasn't mentioned anything else about his ranting and raving."

"I don't know what he meant." A siren's voice replies from the hallway behind me.

When I turn to look at her, I realize exactly how true my initial thought is. She's freshly showered, with wet hair hanging in long, natural curls. She has a towel wrapped around her neck, partially covering her shoulders. But that's not exactly what's captured my attention and refuses to let me look away. One thing I didn't consider when I suggested a shower is what she'd wear afterward. Seeing her in one of my T-shirts and a pair of my boxer briefs is fucking hotter than I ever could've imagined. And I can imagine a lot.

Bruised and battered or not, Savannah Fields is stunningly

beautiful. So much so, she takes my breath away just looking at her.

"Okay, just checking. I'll keep digging for additional information. I've issued a BOLO for him. If any of our guys sees him, he'll go away for a long time. I brought your keys back, and I have a message from Karen. She will be calling you later so you'd better answer on the first ring, and she's subject to stop by here at any time of the day or night to check on you."

Savannah smiles, the appreciation for her friend warming her from the inside out. She glows with love for Karen—the one friend I've heard all about during our daily meetings over coffee. "Tell her I'll call her tomorrow morning when I wake up. I've had a very long and painful day. I'm taking some ibuprofen and going to bed soon. Now that I've had a hot shower, I'll pass right out."

"Not until you've eaten first. Then I'll tuck you in and let you sleep till noon tomorrow if you want." I raise one eyebrow in mock challenge.

Her familiar laugh is music to my ears. "Fine. Let me rephrase. I'm eating first, then going to bed."

Satisfied Savannah is indeed as well as she can be under the circumstances, Spencer leaves before I head to the kitchen and start cooking. Chicken alfredo is my specialty, and pasta cures anything that ails. After she finishes a plate of food, complete with garlic bread and a glass of wine, her eyes start closing on their own.

Scooping her into my arms, I carry her to the guest bedroom and tuck her into the bed. She's out as soon as her head hits the pillow and the blankets cover her body. I watch her for a moment, sleeping peacefully after such a terrifying day, and make her a solemn vow.

"For you, I will try my damnedest to be the undercover hero you deserve."

After making sure the front door is locked, cleaning up the

kitchen, and scrolling through the channels, searching for anything that will take my mind off the horrors Savannah endured today, I finally give up and head to bed. After a quick hot shower to rinse off, I climb into my bed and stare at the ceiling until sleep finally overtakes me.

An hour later, I wake to the sensation of the hairs on the back of my neck standing on end. Someone is in my room, moving toward me. I curl my hands into fists, ready to tear into whoever was stupid enough to pull this stunt. I watch the dark figure move to the foot of my bed, then bump into it. A hand reaches out and feels the way around to the opposite side of the bed—a small, dainty hand. When she reaches the head of the bed, she gently pulls back the covers and gingerly slides into bed beside me. Then she moves over until she's pressed up against me, her head finding a comfortable spot on my chest and her arm draping across my abdomen.

Within seconds, her breathing slows to an even, easy pace as she rests peacefully with my arm wrapped around her.

My breathing, however, is anything but slow and easy.

CHAPTER 7

Savannah

When I open my eyes after the best sleep I've had in years, I realize there's a very hard body under my cheek. My eyes roam the length of that fine, chiseled body until they locate my arm. My hand is splayed out on his stomach, precariously low and definitely inappropriately placed for someone I've only known a couple of weeks. A man who hasn't shown the slightest interest in kissing me, much less being molested by me in my sleep first thing in the morning.

The problem is, now that I've realized where my hand is resting, any sudden movement will be overtly obvious. And embarrassing. This requires delicate and deliberate extrication. Preferably before he even wakes and realizes the full magnitude of my blunder.

If I pretend to stretch, maybe?

No. I can tell without moving more than it takes to breathe that my whole body is sore—much more so than when I went to bed last night. Engaging all my muscles at once for a good, full-body stretch would be excruciating.

The longer I lie here, arguing with myself, the longer my hand rests in a dangerous location.

Then there's the whole topic of "'What are you doing in my bed?' for $500, Alex." Not that I think Nick would mind since I had awful nightmares despite being tired to the bone. Snuggling next to him kept the monster away all night. I wouldn't have slept a wink without him after the first dream woke me.

I'm just going to make sure he's still asleep, then gently lift my hand from his…nether regions. As easily and slowly as I can, I lift my head to look at his gorgeous sleeping face.

And find whiskey-colored amber eyes looking directly at me. Wide awake and wide open, with amusement and something else shining brightly in those golden flecks. That something else is need and desire. Oh God, definitely desire, if the involuntary rising of my hand is any indication.

"Good morning, darlin'. Sleep well?"

"Best sleep of my life. You?"

"Can't complain. At all. Slept really, really well."

"Guess you're wondering how I got in here." I smile sweetly—on purpose.

"Not at all. I watched you sneak in and crawl into bed with me."

"Oh. Really? I had a bad dream."

"I figured. It's fine—I don't mind that you came in here with me. If that's what you wanted, all you had to do was say so."

I feel like there's an intentional double meaning to his offer.

Hand still rising…still rising…

Followed by awkward silence and actively searching for somewhere to set my gaze upon. Anywhere but at my hand.

Do not look at the hand.

This isn't uncomfortable at all.

"How do you feel today?"

The sudden loss of complete silence in the room startles me, making me jump. Even though it sends pain throughout my entire body, the jolt to my system does accomplish removing my hand from his dick. At least I don't have to make up an excuse to stop touching him now.

"Umm, really sore. Really, really sore, to be honest. It even hurts to breathe normally."

"I'm going to take this moment to point out the obvious." He pauses and I hold my breath, afraid of what he'll say next. "You're an ER nurse. You know better than anyone if you should go get checked out. My non-medical expert opinion is you should've let me take you to the hospital last night. But since you didn't, I'm offering to take you now. Breathing normally shouldn't cause you pain."

"Here's a little secret you may not know, Nick. Nurses are terrible patients. We hate being on the receiving end of medical care. It is better to give care than to receive care, in our expert opinion. Last night, I wasn't mentally prepared to go to the hospital. I mean, I work there, and I don't want my coworkers seeing me like this."

"Savannah, I completely understand what you're saying." His voice is tender, understanding. That doesn't mean I don't hear the "but" that's coming next. "But guys who abuse women are counting on you to hide what they do. No evidence, no crime. By hiding out and suffering through the injuries on your own, you're actually shielding him."

"You're right, Nick. On one hand, you're exactly right. On the other, the people I work with every day will think of me as being weak. They'll ask why I've tolerated his behavior, they'll question what I've done to deserve it. They'll look at me differently every day for the rest of the time I work there."

He sits up and turns his upper body to face me. "Your friends will want to help you. They may be hurt that you didn't turn to them for help, but they will stand by your side and defend you. The backbiters who aren't your friends can go fuck themselves. If you're really that concerned about what others will think of you, don't tell them about anything except this time. He's a crazy ex, so they can keep an eye out for him. They will not blame you for this, darlin'."

"All right." His point is valid, and if Karen were in my situation, I'd tell her the same thing. Taking my own advice isn't an easy pill to swallow, though.

He drags his hand down his face, releasing a long sigh between clenched teeth. "I'm sorry, Savannah. I don't mean to push you into something you don't want to do. Tell me what to do, from an emergency room nurse perspective. If a woman showed up, presenting with your same symptoms, would she need medical attention?"

"You play dirty, Nick." There's only a hint of a smile on his lips, but it fully reaches his eyes. He knows he's won. "If she were my patient, I'd recommend she at least have X-rays of her ribs to make sure there was no danger of a broken rib puncturing a lung."

He nods, probably expecting as much. I have a sneaking suspicion he's at least had field medical training. Not as extensive as my training, of course, but enough to patch up a friend and get them off the battlefield when necessary. That's what he's trying to do with me—patch up his friend after I've limped off the battlefield, worse for wear.

"Do you think that patient will let me take her to have her ribs checked out now?" He cocks his head to the side before allowing that stunning smile to overtake his gorgeous face.

"Maybe...after she eats breakfast, since they won't let her have anything once she gets there."

"You've just given me a great idea. I think I have a bright future in hostage negotiations since undercover work is out of the question now. Breakfast is coming up in twenty, so you have time to get dressed while I'm cooking."

"Just so we're clear, I won't forget how you twisted my arm. I will use your tactics against you one day, and you won't have a leg to stand on. You'll have to give in to my every whim."

"One day?" He chuckles and stands, looking like a real-life Adonis in snug-fitting black boxer briefs…and nothing else. Chiseled chest. Trim waist. That sexy V low on his abdomen. Muscular legs. He is absolutely the full package. "Pretty sure we passed the 'one day' mark a while back."

He walks off toward the kitchen, while I stay in his bed to watch him leave. Holy hell. He looks just as good from the back as he does from the front. These thoughts shouldn't be running through my mind, and I feel guilty for even entertaining the notion there could be anything between us. All this baggage that still haunts me isn't fair to bring into any new relationship. Although, I do have to admit, Nick handles Butch and all his bullshit better than anyone I know, myself included. The truth is, I don't think I deserve Nick or anything he's doing for me out of the kindness of his heart.

But the more time I spend with him, the harder I find it to think of not having him in my life.

When I hear him taking pans out of the cupboard, I reluctantly move to get out of bed. Fighting for every inch, I finally reach the side of the bed and clench my jaw before attempting to stand. I've managed to roll over onto my stomach, thinking incorrectly that would make it easier to slide off the bed, and every inch of my body is on fire from the short distance I just covered.

"Can I help?" Nick asks from the doorway.

In my defense, I'm not normally a constant crybaby. But I've cried more in front of him than anyone else in my life. Tears of frustration and pain sting my eyes because I know I can't even get out of bed without his help. Had I not stayed with him last night, I would be in a world of trouble today.

"Okay." I manage to mumble a reply without completely breaking.

He grabs a top sheet from the closet and folds it in half a couple of times. From the opposite side of the bed, he gently pushes as much of it underneath me as he can. "I'll help you roll over onto the sheet—slow and easy—but tell me if anything hurts too much. Okay?"

I nod, unable to speak because of the ball of emotion that's stuck in my throat.

With gentle hands and a reassuring tone, he helps me to roll over on my back, straightening the part of the sheet that was under me as I roll. He uses both sides of the sheet as support under my back to lift and move me to the edge of the bed. When I sit up and slide my legs off the bed, that's also with Nick's support. Once I'm sitting erect and the tips of my toes are touching the floor, he's kneeling down on one knee in front of me, watching my reactions with eagle-eye precision.

"Talk to me, Savannah. Are you in a lot of pain? Did I hurt you?"

I shake my head. "You didn't hurt me at all. I was just thinking I'm actually in a lot worse shape than I originally thought. If you hadn't been here last night...if I hadn't stayed here..."

"Don't think like that. I'm here, and you're here with me. We'll do this together. You need time to heal, and you need help while you heal. I won't leave you alone. You can stay here as long as you need to. When you're ready to go back to your place, I'll make sure you feel safe doing it. I won't abandon you." He reaches up and cups my cheek in his big hand, his natural body heat warming me inside and out.

Like a frightened puppy craving human attention, I lean into his hand and close my eyes, soaking up the connection I feel building between us every minute we're together. Whether a relationship builds fast or slow, the pace doesn't define its depth. This bond I feel with Nick didn't develop immediately. We didn't experience the whole "love at first sight" phenomenon, but my feelings are dangerously close to that. I can't say he feels the same, but I can say I pray that he does. Or will, eventually.

And that scares me.

Straightening my spine, I inhale carefully and open my eyes, finding his still closely watching me. "That was a good idea to use the draw sheet. You have more medical experience than you admit."

"You never know, I may have a few more tricks up my sleeve."

"Let's see if one of those tricks is helping me to stand. I hope once I get up, I'll be able to walk on my own. You never realize how much you use your abdominal muscles for every little move until you can't use them at all."

"Put your arms around my neck. When I stand, use me to help pull yourself up. I'll wrap my arms around your waist to hold you steady, but I don't want to put too much pressure on your sore areas."

I do as he says, and at the last second, his hands slide under my behind to help push me upright. Leaning back a little, I give him a playful side-eye glance. "Did you just cop a feel on an injured and defenseless woman?"

He grins, and mischief shines in his eyes. "No more than you did when you thought I was still asleep this morning." He waggles his eyebrows, both playfully and seductively, and I hide my face in his neck.

"Stop trying to make me laugh. It hurts!" I say, through both my laughter and pain. His deep chuckle rumbles in my ear in response.

"I took a chance that your ass wasn't hurt as badly as your ribs are. Hopefully that was a good guess."

"Yes, it was a great guess, and surprisingly helpful. Thank you, Nick. You're the best man I've ever met."

He goes completely still, making me worry I've crossed an

unknown line, but he doesn't release me. There's such a fine line between right and wrong sometimes. When I move my face from the hiding place against his neck, I pluck up the courage to meet him eye-to-eye. The expression on his face nearly shatters my heart into a million pieces.

It's pure, unadulterated, palpable gratitude.

He searches my eyes and face, not asking the question that's on the tip of his tongue. The one I see in his eyes, though he tries to hide it.

"I meant every word, Nick. You're brave and you're strong. You're thoughtful and considerate. You take care of me and show me how to take care of myself. You're easy to talk to but refuse to let anyone run over you. You're funny and sweet, but serious and mean when you have to be. I don't know one single man who would've done everything you've done for me—or even a fraction of it. You are, hands down, the best man I've ever known."

He opens his mouth to speak but stops himself before it's too late. He shakes his head while keeping his eyes locked on mine. "You never cease to amaze me. Thank you for saying that."

That look—the one he's giving me now—the one that tells me he desperately wants to believe me, steals what little breath I have in my lungs. He needs to believe me. But he's not quite there yet. That seals my heart's fate. It's not about "fixing him." He's perfect exactly the way he is now. My heart is now focused on helping him see the many wonderful qualities he possesses, the traits I've seen since day one. For me, this is more than the good friend mission I originally set out on. I know, beyond a shadow of a doubt, I've already fallen for him.

"The bag Spencer brought over for you is in the bathroom. But let's make sure you can walk alone before I go cook your breakfast."

After I take a few steps, I assure him I'll be okay alone in the bathroom and promise to yell for him if I need anything at all.

With the door closed behind me, I glare at the commode and silently contemplate how I'll manage the whole sitting maneuver alone, while knowing there's no way in hell I'm asking Nick to help me out with *that*.

Though it takes much more out of me than it should, I manage to use the vanity to help brace myself as I sit and stand again. Rifling through my bag, I find my brush and a few hair bands. Thank you, Spencer! With my hair pulled up in a high, messy bun, my teeth brushed, and my comfy yoga pants and long-sleeved T-shirt on, I feel somewhat human again.

Nick has a tasty breakfast waiting for me when I finally join him in the kitchen. Instead of eating at the table, he puts our plates on the bar so I can slide on and off the higher stool easier. It really is the little things that matter the most.

We take my car to the hospital so I can use my employee parking decal and retrieve my badge I left in the glove compartment when I drove to Nick's last night. Bypassing the triage desk, we walk in through the ambulance bay and straight into the secure area. It's a relatively slow day, so one of the doctors is behind the desk, catching up on his charting when I approach.

"Holy shit, Savannah! What happened to you?" His eyes immediately move to size up Nick, the brawny brute standing behind me.

"Can you check me out, Dr. Wattress? I think I may have a couple of cracked ribs, but I just want to be sure they don't move and cause more damage." I reach back and grab Nick's hand, wordlessly conveying he's here to help me.

"Of course. Let's get you into a room and see what's going on with your injuries." He chooses an open exam room and ushers Nick and me inside. He gives me a gown to change into and closes the curtain, giving me a little privacy. I slide the curtain back to let them know I'm ready. Technically, I'm supposed to remove my bra and panties too, but that's not happening. They were hard enough to get into the first time.

Nick immediately notices the bed is too low for me to comfortably sit down, so he moves to the far side and raises it until the height is just right for me. Every move I make, he's right there to help me.

"Who did this to you, Savannah?" Dr. Wattress asks when he begins checking my injuries.

I'm quiet for a heartbeat too long, so Nick answers for me. "Her ex who can't seem to take a hint. She moved to get away from him, and he found her again."

The doctor looks up at Nick, anger rolling off him in waves. "When you get a hold of him, don't bring him to my emergency room for treatment."

"Understood, Doc. If I get my hands on him, he's more likely to need a good mortician than a physician."

"Nick has been taking good care of me, even though I haven't made it too easy on him." I smile up at Nick, but that quickly changes when the doctor touches my ribs. "Ouch!"

"When did this happen?"

"Yesterday."

"And you're just now coming to see me?" Dr. Wattress shakes his head, clearly not pleased with my decision-making skills. "You definitely have a few broken ribs, I can tell you that without X-rays. There's really no danger of them moving or puncturing anything if you follow doctor's orders to the letter."

"She will." Nick's confident reply makes the doctor smile. "Just tell me what they are, and I'll make sure of it."

He goes through a list of dos and don'ts with Nick. Ice packs. Ibuprofen. Cough if I feel the urge, to help reduce the chance of pneumonia—just hold a pillow against my side to lessen the impact. Six weeks off work, taking extra care the first two weeks. Move around as much as I'm able, to help keep fluids moving freely. Come back immediately if I reinjure my ribs or have any shortness of breath.

All things I could've told Nick before we got here, but he

wouldn't have taken my word for it after our hostage-negotiation discussion.

The doctor writes a prescription for a stronger pain medication to use at night to help me sleep through the discomfort and tells me he'll submit the medical documentation for my required time off. Back in the car an hour later, Nick picks up my prescription for me before driving us back to his place with a triumphant smirk on his face.

"What are you so happy about?" I ask teasingly.

"One, I was right about a lot of things. Two, I really like that doctor. And three, you have to stay with me for the next two weeks so I can make sure you follow his orders to a T."

"He didn't say I had to stay with you for the next two weeks, Nick."

"Yes, he did. Would you like to go back and ask him?" He glances at me over his shoulder, hoping I'll accept his dare.

"No, because you two will just conspire against me."

"Like I said, you're staying with me for the next couple of weeks so I can make sure you behave. Doctor's orders."

Funny thing is, "behave" isn't the first word that comes to mind when I think about spending two weeks with Nick at his place.

It's not even in the top ten thoughts.

CHAPTER 8

Nick

With Savannah resting comfortably on my couch, I retreat to my bedroom with the intention of making a few calls. Butch's ability to access not only her building but her apartment is a huge red flag, one I can't quite put my finger on at the moment. I know for a fact that she has multiple locks on her door and uses every one of them. The sinking feeling in my gut tells me Butch went to great lengths to get to her—but not because he's distraught that she dumped him.

He's after something else entirely.

I casually stroll back into the living room where Savannah is watching the news and fighting to keep her eyes open. Taking a seat on the coffee table across from her, I pick up her keys Spencer left and hand them to her. She looks at me then down at her keys, confusion and apprehension clear in her expression.

"Are any keys missing from your key ring?" I intentionally keep my tone light and my demeanor calm. There's no need to cause her even more alarm if I'm simply being hypervigilant. As usual.

Her eyebrows draw down, and her eyes crinkle slightly in the corner, as much as she can with the swelling anyway, but she goes through each key on the ring as I asked. "No, they're all here. I don't keep the building's garage door key on here anymore since I've been taking the Metro to work lately. It's still in my car from when I drove over here yesterday."

"Where did you have it before that?"

"Hidden inside my apartment. Why?" She lays the keys down beside me and gives me her full attention, preparing for a long explanation.

"Just a hunch I'm working on."

She's silent for a minute, waiting for me to continue, but that only results in us staring at each other. "Nick, that's not enough. I need more than that."

"Does Butch keep anything in your car? Did he ever use it?"

"No, to both questions. He was always on his motorcycle, and he always insisted I drive my car instead of riding with him. Said it ruined his image to have someone riding bitch. That was fine with me—I didn't want to stay in the places he went any longer than I absolutely had to anyway. He went to the seediest parts of town he could find. There were always other gang members around with half-dressed women who I'm sure were strung out on drugs."

"But he insisted you go with him to those places? Did he make you hang around very long?" I'm getting a clearer picture, and I don't like it at all.

"No, not long at all. It was usually to change the bandages on his friend's wounds...or to look at whatever new rash someone had." A chill runs up her spine, and she shakes involuntarily in disgust. "After I'd played doctor and helped as much as I could, I got the hell out of there. Tell me what you're thinking. What has he done to my car? Did he put a tracker on it?"

"I don't think he has anything that high-tech. But I do think he's after something specific, more than getting his rocks off by beating up a woman."

Pulling my cell out of my pocket, I call Calvin at the agency and ask him to send a low-key forensics team to my townhouse. Savannah's eyes grow wide with fear.

"What are you doing? What's going on, Nick?"

"It's best to wait until they get here. Do you have Spencer's number in your phone?"

"Yes, I do." She pulls up his contact info, and we wait for him to pick up. "Hi, Spencer. Nick needs to talk to you."

She hands the phone to me, and I tell him about the team on the way to my apartment then ask if he can join us since he's involved in the assault and battery charges against Butch. He promises to be here within minutes. He obviously understands the urgency, and Savannah feels the increasing pressure from all the stress. In case my gut is correct, I can't tell her anything just yet and possibly taint the findings.

But I'll do whatever it takes to protect her.

"Just trust me. I would never do anything to hurt you, and I won't let anyone else hurt you either. I'm doing all of this to protect you."

"I trust you."

Though she has every reason never to trust another man in her life, she freely gives it to me. That realization is humbling. A knock on my door stops me from saying something neither of us is ready to hear. The feeling is there, on the edge of the proverbial cliff, but I'm not ready to take the leap off it just yet.

Tim, another Special Agent I've known for quite a while, is standing on the threshold. His team waits a few spaces down by the unmarked forensics van with the gear stowed inside, ready to get to work. We shake hands in a friendly reunion and a quick catch-up of what we've each been doing since we saw each other last. While we're chatting, Spencer pulls up and joins us. After I introduce them, I turn my request to Savannah's friend.

"Spencer, I need you to stay in here with Savannah and me while Tim does his job. We'll need a third-party witness to verify whatever Tim finds hasn't been tampered with by either Savannah or me. Every step of this is being done by the book to protect all of us in the long run."

"You got it. I'll go in and keep her company now." Spencer leaves Tim and me alone to finish our conversation in private.

"What do you need us to do, Nick?" Tim looks puzzled and intrigued, ready to dive into the job at hand.

"Cover every inch of Savannah's car. Don't leave anything unchecked. But try not to look like a DEA agent searching the car. Act like you're a mechanic or something—leave the hood open." I explain her prior relationship with Butch, his ties to the Devils, and the recent events. "I don't think he's found what he's looking for, and my gut tells me whatever it is will be found in her car."

"The Devils are about to go to trial, you're the main under-cover officer for the DEA, and you're involved with the ex-girl-friend of a club member? Have you lost your fucking mind, Nick?" Tim stares me down, looking at me as if he has no clue who I am.

"Did you hear a fucking word I just told you? I met her in a coffee shop—while he was manhandling her. You think I'd just stand by and let that shit happen, especially after everything I've seen? I told her she had a safe place to get away from him if she ever needed it. Well, step inside the door and take a look at her. She fucking needed it, man. He could've killed her." My voice gets louder with each passing second. My blood boils while rushing through my veins.

Tim curses under his breath and steps around me. He opens the door, walks inside, and comes back out with a bottle of water. "I see what you mean. Any chance she's in on this with him to help the Devils? To get any information or intel on you?"

"Zero chance." I place my hands on my hips and wait for him to drop the subject.

"Don't say I didn't warn you. When you tell Calvin the whole story, he'll ream you a new asshole, and you know it."

"Let me handle Calvin. You handle searching the car. I'm going inside now so I can't be accused of trying to hide any evidence you may find."

"If there's anything there, the Devils' lawyer may accuse you of planting it."

"Anyone who'd believe I'd plant something, especially on someone I consider a friend, is a moron."

"Yeah, well, the world is full of them, my friend. Any spin they can put on the story to make the good guys look bad is a good spin."

Maybe he's right—maybe I'm damned if I do and damned if I don't. But my conscience will be clear, and I'll be able to look at myself in the mirror without questioning which lines I'll cross today.

Savannah is sitting up on the couch with a pillow pressed to her side when I walk back into the brownstone, leaving Tim and his team to do their job. She has a blanket draped over her lap, and she's nervously biting her thumbnail. Something hitches in my chest—a twinge of life I haven't felt in a very long time. Years. I refused to let myself get close to anyone while I was undercover. There was no way I'd trust anyone in that world with my real identity and no way I'd start a relationship under false pretenses. Plus, when shit went down, she would've been the first target on their hit list.

Since I've been back in DC, I've had zero interest in anything except getting back to my normal self. Putting the past couple years behind me and letting go of all the guilt over what I didn't do about the crimes I witnessed. Trying to reconcile the man I thought I was before the assignment began with the man I had to be while undercover. When I condemned them for lying and dealing underhandedly, the mirror told me I was doing the same things they were. When I couldn't wait to bust them and send them away for life for the crimes they committed, my conscience reminded me about all the times I watched or participated in those very crimes.

Being around Savannah brings a breath of fresh air to my stale existence. One I didn't even know was missing until getting better acquainted with her. When I look at her injuries, I vacillate between wanting to dedicate my life to showing her how a real man should treat her and wanting to rip Butch's head from his body and shove it up his ass.

The struggle is real.

But when she looks at me like that—like I hung the fucking moon and stars—I can't help but think my former self is making a full comeback, pushing the corrupt man inside me out of the way. Maybe she's exactly what I need in my life. Someone to take care of, someone to help, someone who will listen when I share the details of my days—the good, the bad, the ups, the downs.

Someone to love.

Someone who can love me.

Not that she's ready for a relationship. She hasn't even been able to get rid of the last guy. I doubt she'd appreciate me adding more stress by trying to start something new. Bad timing and all.

"Nick?"

"Yeah?"

"Are...you okay?" Her eyes narrow as she cuts them sideways at me.

"Fine. Why?"

"Well, because you've just been standing there staring at me. Not saying anything at all."

"Have I?"

Staring at her isn't a hardship on me. Looking away from her is.

When I don't elaborate, she stands, pushing the pillow harder into her side as she moves. I start to protest, but she shakes her head. "The doctor said I need to move around frequently, remember?"

I nod, smiling while letting her have that one.

She walks to me, pain in every step, but that doesn't stop her. When she reaches me, she places her hand on my chest and peers up at me, her emerald-green eyes searching mine. "What's going on out there that has you so distracted?"

"There's a team of DEA forensic agents searching your car for drugs or other contraband."

Reading people and gauging reactions are skills I've spent years training and refining. Knowing when they're lying, when they're holding out, and when they're about to pull the gun they have hidden in their back waistband has saved my ass too many times to count. Studying Savannah's face and reaction to that news tells me everything I need to know. She doesn't have a clue why we'd look for anything in her car.

Sometimes I wish I could still be that naïve...that trusting of other people.

But not today. Today, I'm glad I'm listening to my instincts, so when I take Butch out of the equation, he's out for good with no possibility of ever hurting Savannah again. In any way.

"I don't understand. Why would you think I'd have drugs, Nick?" Pain flashes in her eyes. Hurt because I'd think so little of her.

"Savannah, I know better than that. I don't think you'd do that at all. But I do think Butch has hidden them in your car, and I think he was so pissed off over not being able to get into your building's garage to get them, he broke in to your apartment to look for the key. Then he attacked you when you walked in on him in the act."

After helping her back to the couch, I order delivery for all of us. My friends will be hungry when they've finished with her car, and I need to make sure she eats more than enough to keep a bird alive, too. By the time the food delivery is expected, Tim and team join us inside the living room, smiles from ear to ear covering their faces. The delivery guy shows up just behind them, so I throw a couple of bills in his direction and tell everyone to help themselves after I fix Savannah's plate.

"The good news is," Tim begins, "I can't tell you much about what we found. And that in itself should tell you enough about what we found."

"There's a calling card?" I hold my slice of pizza in midair, waiting for the confirmation I've been dying to hear.

"Definite calling card. Enough that I can guarantee Savannah can't be held responsible under the constructive possession laws." Tim beams, knowing the significance of his find.

"I'm sorry—I have no idea what that means." Savannah's eyes dart back and forth between Tim and me, waiting for a better explanation.

Tim takes pity on her. "What I'm saying is, I know without a shadow of a doubt you had no idea what was hidden in your car, so you can't be held responsible for possession."

"Did you leave everything exactly as you found it?" Not that I doubt his ability to do his job, but I'm leaving no stone unturned in this maneuver.

"I'm insulted you even thought it was necessary to ask me that, Tucker."

"Just making sure. Calm your tits, Tim. Now, Savannah, tell me every move you'd normally make in your car before you started taking the Metro to work. Where did you go? How long did you stay there? Where did you park? Don't leave out any detail, no matter how small you may think it is. Do you think you can do that?"

"Sure, I can do that. Then what happens?"

"Then we wait."

CHAPTER 9

Savannah

"What's a calling card?"

Now that we're alone, I feel more comfortable asking Nick all my questions that weren't answered earlier. Not that the other men would've minded, but they were so involved in the logistics and planning of every detail of the upcoming operations, I didn't want to delay their conversation by asking them to explain all their jargon to me.

Besides, now I have even more to talk about with Nick. More reasons to stay right beside him. More reasons to stare at his handsome face and finely built physique. The way he looks at me when we talk has changed. When we first met, I saw mostly pity in his eyes. That bothered me more than I would admit.

Now, I see admiration in those whiskey-colored eyes. I also see desire—and not only when I accidentally molest him in the bed. I caught him watching me several times when we were eating pizza earlier. When Tim tried a little too hard to get to know me, I was secretly thrilled Nick immediately shut him down. Not in a jealous, possessive way, but his reaction was enough to let me know he didn't appreciate the intrusion.

Maybe there's hope after all.

"A calling card is the signature way drug distributors package their shit for the street dealers to sell. The major players are arrogant, and they want everyone on the street to know who's running the show. Butch is in over his head, so I'm going to help him drown."

"I feel guilty getting you involved in all this, you know? I've caused you so much trouble in the so little time you've known me. You must think I'm one big walking disaster."

He surprises me by kneeling in front me, gently cupping my face in his big hands, and holding my gaze with his intense stare. "No, Savannah. In fact, I've never thought that, and you're not allowed to think that either. You don't have a clue how amazing you are, do you?"

This smoldering attraction I've been fighting just lit up in a fully involved five-alarm fire.

Without thinking, without overanalyzing, without asking for permission, I lean toward him and press my lips to his. Gently at first, in case he doesn't reciprocate, but he takes control after about a second. He slides his hands around my head, threading his fingers through my hair as they glide. I can tell he's being so easy with me, treating me like a porcelain doll. But I can't feel my injuries at the moment. I can only feel the sensation of every nerve ending firing at once and my body being set on fire, all from his tender touch and simple kiss.

When his tongue swipes across my lips, my resulting gasp gives him full access to claim my mouth. I lean back on the couch cushions and wrap my hands around his neck, pulling him with me so that he's partially lying on me. Though I'm sore and have bruises covering most of my body, the weight of his body on me feels like heaven. The warmth of his hands on my skin and the velvety smoothness of his tongue send chills over my body, fanning out like ripples in still water.

He breaks the kiss first, ever so slowly, and presses his forehead against mine while we both try to slow our racing hearts. I can feel his pulse jumping in his neck, and it makes me want to kiss him all over again. With a look, a touch, a gesture, Nick Tucker makes me feel beautiful, desired, and needed.

"That was the hottest fucking kiss." His words are a strained whisper, full of longing and a thirst for me. I know, because I feel it all the way to my soul.

"It definitely was. Now I need a cold shower before I combust."

He smiles, releases a small chuckle, and gently kisses my cheek. "Believe me when I say it kills me to stop this. But if you kiss me like that again, I'm afraid you'll have a lot more broken bones after I throw you over my shoulder, haul you into the bedroom, and bend you in more ways than a pretzel."

"Oh my God. Why do I get the feeling all the extra broken bones would be so worth it?"

"Savannah, you're really not helping, darlin'. The situation is hard enough as it is." He waggles his eyebrows at me, and the butterflies in my chest not only take flight but break out into an impromptu *Riverdance* production.

"Just so you know, I feel it too."

"I don't see how you couldn't feel it since it's lying on your leg right now."

We both break out laughing, and I immediately regret it. Grabbing my trusty pillow, I push it into my broken ribs for support and alternate between laughing and howling "ow" repeatedly.

"Okay, so we both needed that laugh. And maybe we should let the current broken bones heal before we break new ones. I'm not sure I'm up to it today, after all." I stroke his cheek, feeling the words but refusing to say them now. It's too soon. No one feels—*that*—this soon.

"It's nice, being able to joke with you. But know this about me, Savannah. There's only one part of you I'd ever break—and that's any desire you may have for another man. I'll make sure that's completely obliterated, to the point that even looking doesn't appeal to you."

"I believe you, Nick...because I'm already there."

"Darlin', I'm so glad to hear that." Then his smile falters, and a concerned expression takes its place. "But don't feel pressured to say that. You don't owe me anything in return for my help, and the last thing I want you to think is I expect any kind of payment."

"I'd never think that about you, Nick. And I hope you know I understand the difference between gratitude and what I actually feel for you."

"You have no idea how happy I am to know we're on the same page. You get some rest while I get some work done. I'm running the logistics on this operation, so I'm going to make sure the plan is airtight before we make the first move. Yell if you need anything at all."

"Can you bring my laptop out of my bag? I have a few things I want to look into myself."

"You got it."

While Nick is at the kitchen table, eyeball-deep in maps, routes, and plans, I boot up my laptop and start researching how to volunteer in various positions with our local women's shelter. After what I've been through and how much help I've been given because of nothing more than the kindness of strangers, volunteering to help others in similar situations is the least I can do.

When I find the website, I fill out all the forms and consent to a background check. I'm looking forward to putting a different spin on my circumstances and crossing that fine line between fear and courage. Even though putting myself in front of others and sharing my story scares me, I feel I need to step into the spotlight and make myself more vulnerable before I can fully be strong again. Trial by fire. Actions speak louder than words. Every cloud has a silver lining. All the inspirational sayings that are meant to encourage and inspire swirl in my head, but even without them, I know I'm making the right move.

Just as I open my document to continue working on my book, with a new chapter inspired by recent revelations, my phone rings, and I realize I neglected to call my best friend first thing this morning.

"Hello?" I know exactly who's calling, but I'm still trying to figure out a way to defuse the situation.

"Don't act like you don't know who this is or why I'm calling, Savannah Fields. How dare you let me find out from one of the day nurses that you showed up in the emergency room with broken ribs! If you weren't already injured, I'd be over there kicking your ass right now."

"That's actually the only part of me that doesn't hurt."

"Spence said Nick is taking good care of you." Her tone changes, letting me know she's not actually mad at me for anything. Worried about my well-being, but not mad. "I'm glad someone is. You know you could've stayed with us if you needed a place to hide."

"Staying here with Nick is actually working out to my benefit. He knows how Butch operates, and he's working on a plan to make sure Butch stays out of my life forever. When I first came here, it was because I was too terrified to go anywhere else, plus his brownstone was closer than your place. But I'm staying because he takes such good care of me, Karen. He keeps the nightmares at bay." I describe what happened last night and this morning—sneaking into his bed and waking up in a compromising position.

"After all that, he still had to help you out of bed?" Karen laughs heartily at my expense, but I don't mind. My pillow is tight against my ribs, so my occasional outbursts don't hurt as bad. "Well, if all that hasn't scared him away, nothing will, my friend. Sounds like you have a keeper there. Spencer has even given his seal of approval, and you know that doesn't come easily for him."

"We're both taking things really slowly. I've brought a lot of shitty baggage with me. It's a little hard to start something new on solid ground when it feels like quicksand will swallow you at any time."

"You know what your problem is, Savannah? You don't give yourself nearly enough credit. Butch is shit, but he's not your shitty baggage. You got away from him. What he continues to do is all on him—not you. Don't take the blame for any of his bullshit anymore. Make him own what he's done, and you own the brave things you've done."

"Thank you, Karen. You know I needed to hear that. I love you."

"I love you too. Now when do I get to meet Nick, hook him up to a lie detector, and play 150 Questions with cords that deliver electric shocks for every lie?"

"Stop making me laugh! It hurts!" She laughs in my ear. "You can meet him, if you behave. Besides, he doesn't lie. He's brutally honest, so I don't think you'll need to use the electricity on him."

"He sounds too good to be true. I'll be the judge of his honesty. But not tomorrow. You may not have considered this, but the third day after an injury is always the worst, so I'm afraid you'll feel worse tomorrow. So, can we get this on the books for the day after tomorrow? I'm off, Spence is off, and you're there. Perfect timing." I'm almost positive Karen has our entire evening already planned out in her head.

"That's good with me. Let me check with Nick to make sure

he's okay with it, though."

"Check with Nick about what?" Speak of the tall, handsome, irresistible devil, and he appears out of nowhere. He sits on the couch beside me, fingering the long curls of my ponytail while he waits for my answer.

"My best friend wants to meet you. She's bringing her own lie-detector machine, complete with an electric chair to shock you when you lie."

"I have no reason to lie, but she's welcome to use mine if she doesn't want to lug hers across town." One side of his mouth lifts in amusement as he winks at me. "The day after tomorrow is good with me. We can eat here if you're not ready to go out to a restaurant by then. But if you want to go out, it'll be our first official date. Your call, darlin'."

"Date, huh? You wouldn't be embarrassed to take me out like this? All busted up with black, purple, and green bruises everywhere?"

"Nope. Not at all. You're still just as beautiful to me."

"Oh my God, Savannah! If you don't marry him by tomorrow, I just might!" Karen yells into the phone loud enough for Nick to hear her.

"You're already taken, Karen," Nick yells back with a chuckle. Then he looks dead into my eyes and adds, "And so am I."

Karen's excited squeal nearly bursts my eardrum. At least she's breathing, because I can't right now.

He leans over and presses his soft, plump lips against mine. He trails his fingertips along my cheek, barely touching me but leaving his invisible brand on my skin. Marking me…as his.

Our eyes remain locked when he pulls back. A knowing smirk crosses his face while I fight to maintain my composure. When I'm finally able to speak again, I confirm our plans with Karen. "We're definitely going out to a nice restaurant. Nick and I are having that first date."

After we eat dinner together, I'm so tired I can barely keep my eyes open. Nick helps me up, and we walk toward the bedrooms together. He smiles down at me when we reach the hallway. "Where are you sleeping tonight?"

He knows the answer. He just wants to hear me say it.

"Smartass." I walk into his bedroom, his responding chuckle rumbling through his chest. I secretly love how relaxed and comfortable we are with each other. Now I can see—and feel—what was lacking in every other relationship I've ever attempted to have.

If I feel this strongly about him after only a couple of weeks of spending time with him, getting to know him inside and out, I can't imagine what a few more weeks will do. He helps me into bed then takes his spot beside me. He wraps his arm around me protectively when I lay my head in the crook of his shoulder. Warm, safe, and protected, I close my eyes and sleep soundly all night.

The next day is, unfortunately, as Karen predicted and I expected. Everywhere I wasn't sore yesterday hurts today. Everywhere I was sore yesterday is worse now. Nick looks down at me before we attempt to get out of bed. "Well, darlin', how do you feel today?"

"It hurts to blink. Can I just stay in bed all day?"

"Afraid not. The doctor said you need to keep moving throughout the day, remember? No pneumonia allowed. Besides, that would just make your muscles hurt longer. Come on, I'll help you out of bed. You can shower first. Maybe the hot water will help. Then we'll go by your apartment and get more of your things to bring back here. Plus, I want to look around for myself."

"You're sure we'll be safe if he shows up while we're there?"

"You and I will be perfectly safe. I can only wish he'd show up while I'm there. Please, God, let him show up."

CHAPTER 10

Nick

Showered, dressed, and fed, Savannah says she feels a little better than she did first thing this morning. We're on our way to her apartment now. How Butch got inside still bothers me. Time to bring up the touchy subject with her again.

"Darlin', I really don't like the idea of your apartment not having more security than it does. I'm in no hurry for you to leave my place, but when you do move back in to your condo, I'd like to know it's under the safest possible conditions."

"It sounds like you have a very complex system in mind. I spent my extra money on moving, buying a new laptop, and taking marketing classes for my book. Now I'm not able to work overtime for a month and a half, so it'll be a while before I can do anything extra like that." She looks out the window as she explains, not wanting to make eye contact with me.

"You never know when a great opportunity will just fall into your lap."

"What have you done, Nick?"

"Me? Nothing. Nothing at all."

We arrive at her building, and I feel the anxiety rolling off her and crashing into me before we even exit my truck. She looks up at the building and inhales a haggard breath. Though the sudden expansion of her lungs and ribs causes a jolt of pain to cut through her, the fear of going inside overrides it.

"Hey, look at me." I speak softly to get her attention without startling her.

Her gaze shifts to meet mine. All color has drained from her face. Her green eyes are huge, and her pupils are dilated. She looks at me, waiting for the strength and courage to leave the relative safety of my vehicle.

"He will not touch you—not one hair on that beautiful head of yours. If he's stupid enough to be here again, he'll leave in a body bag before I let him lay one finger on you. I've got you, darlin'. You have nothing to worry about."

"I worry about you, too, Nick. I worry that Butch will find some way to take you away from me."

"Not even a remote possibility, darlin'. Can we go up and get your clothes now? I'm really looking forward to our date tomorrow night. But if you'd rather go naked, we can do that. We'll be the talk of the town."

She rewards me with a small smile for that. "Okay, let's go up there and get it over with."

Before we reach the outer door, another resident is leaving and holds the door open for us. He's a younger guy, barely out of his teens, and obviously thinks he's being helpful. He doesn't have a clue how his politeness could cost someone their life.

Strike one.

Inside the elevator, she's practically glued to my side as we watch the floors tick by on the lighted panel. Taking a second to glance around, I notice there are no security cameras in the elevators, and there were none in the entryway.

Strike two.

I wrap my arm around her, and she molds her body against mine. I'm enjoying how she seems to fit against me like the missing piece of a jigsaw puzzle a little too much. When the elevator stops and we stroll down the hallway together, a sense of dread settles in my gut from out of the blue. This time, it's not over concern about her apartment not being safe enough—I'm facing the fact that she has her own place and will be leaving mine soon.

Years of being alone have suddenly caught up with me, and I don't want to be alone anymore.

She stops at her door and begins unlocking the dead bolts, and I take the time to inspect the door closely. There are light scratches around the locks and the bolts, other scratches in the paint where the door meets the frame, indicating someone worked to pick all the locks and gain entry into her condo. She just arrived home at the worst possible time.

Yet none of her neighbors heard anything, called the police, or came to her aid.

Strike three.

The door to her condo swings open, but she stands motionless at the threshold, staring inside at the mess left behind. From where we stand, I can see her overturned dining table and a few broken chairs surrounding it. Shattered glass from broken vases litters the floor. The groceries she'd bought are scattered throughout the room.

"I'm with you, babe. Right beside you every step of the way. Let's go inside."

She nods, but her actions are almost robotic. Dealing with the aftermath of the attack brings back too many terrible memories, but this must be done one way or another. For me, I wouldn't have it any other way than being right here with her to help her work through the pain and fear. When she slips her hand into mine, I realize she's putting her full trust in me yet again to protect her. I'll be her undercover hero, in whatever capacity she needs.

I step inside first, and she follows in my footsteps, staying close to me in case a monster steps out of the shadows. With my other hand, I unholster the gun on my hip and hold it at the ready. When she looks up at me, she appears to be a little more comforted than just a moment ago. She knows I meant what I said about Butch leaving in a body bag. If it comes down to him or her, there's really no choice to be made.

"We're going to check every possible hiding place in each room first to make sure we're completely alone. Then while you pack, I'll straighten up, so you don't have to look at this mess anymore. Are you ready?"

She nods again, this time more animatedly, letting me know she feels more secure. After I lock the door behind us, we move from room to room together, checking in every closet, behind every door, and under every piece of intact furniture. Butch was frantic in his search, hitting every room and leaving a path of chaos and destruction. Satisfied that we're alone and no one will get past me to hurt her, she releases her death grip on my hand and walks into her closet to begin picking out the additional items she'll need. I grab her suitcases from the top shelf and lay them out for her easy access. While she's busy with that, I set out to clean up and make her home feel as close to normal as possible.

When I've finished righting her furniture, picking up shattered debris, and sweeping up broken glass in the other rooms, I move back into to her bedroom. She's sitting at her vanity table, staring at her still-bruised face. The swelling is down considerably since she first showed up at my door, but it's nowhere near gone. Neither are the discolorations around her eye, on her cheeks, or on her neck. Those are the visible injuries. Under her shirt, the bruises on her ribs and back are worse, as I suspected they would be before they get better.

It's on the tip of my tongue to say, "What's on your mind, gorgeous?", but I know she'd assume I'm only attempting to distract her from her current thoughts. I'm not—all I see is her beauty shining through—but I hold my tongue anyway.

"Last room to clean up. Do you need any help packing your clothes and one million and one shoes?"

"One million and one? Does one of my feet not get a shoe?" She can't stop the small grin that breaks free despite her resistance. "I think I've packed everything I'll need. To be honest, I didn't leave much here—most everything I have is coming with me. Except my scrubs, of course, since I won't be working during the next couple of weeks."

"You can work all you want." I wait for her to give me the side-eye before continuing. "On your book. While sitting on my couch. Safe in my house."

"I should've known there was a catch." She shakes her head, but I don't miss the smile she attempts to hide. She secretly enjoys all the doting she's receiving. And maybe I'm enjoying giving it more than I've realized before now.

Over the next few minutes, I straighten up her bedroom to erase all traces of Butch's presence. Putting the mattress and box spring back on the bed frame and picking up the mess Butch left behind doesn't take long. When I've finished, I zip her suitcases closed and pull them with one hand.

"Shall we?" I offer my other arm to her, and she wraps her hand around it, pulling close to me again.

When we reach her living room, she stops and looks around. "This is amazing, Nick. I thought it would take hours to make a dent in the damage he did. It's almost back to normal, minus the broken furniture I'll have to replace now."

"We'll come back another day, and I'll take all the garbage out. I didn't want to leave you up here alone to get everything out of here today. At least you can walk through here without stepping on anything now." She squeezes my arm and leans her head against me.

"Thank you, Nick. What would I have done without you?" Her voice is a little watery, clogged with emotion, so I simply kiss her on the top of the head in response.

We leave the building without incident, and I help her climb into my vehicle for the short drive back to my place. Glancing over at her in the passenger seat of my truck, I can tell this short excursion has worn her out, probably more from the emotional aspect than anything. She leans her head against the back of the seat and fights sleep as I take my time, slowing at yellow lights and actually coming to a full stop at the stop signs.

When I pull into my driveway and kill the engine, I almost hate to wake her to get her inside. But the chilly weather starts to permeate the interior of the truck almost immediately, preventing me from sitting here and staring at her for too long.

"Are we already back home?" Her eyes are still closed, and her voice is heavy with sleep, but she knows where we are. *Home.* Funny. I've never thought of my brownstone as home until she said it.

"We're home, darlin'. Let's get you inside so you can finish that nap under your blanket."

After getting her settled on the couch, I grab her suitcases from the truck and put them in the bedroom. Then I take my spot at the kitchen table and review the plan to nab Butch for the umpteenth time. Now more than ever, I want him out of her life. For her safety, of course. But for more selfish reasons I've only just realized.

When she said she didn't know what she'd do without me, it struck a chord deep inside me. One that, now that she rang it, can't be unrung now. Will she still want me when he's no longer a threat? Will her feelings for me diminish when she's free to live her life again?

Or will she be ready to pursue something more serious... more permanent?

While she sleeps, I decide to make that phone call I've been putting off for far too long. I feel partially responsible for Butch even having the opportunity to get to her. Had I followed my gut and insisted on helping her, she wouldn't be all beaten up, sleeping on my couch right now. Then again, had I interfered when she didn't want my help, she might not have spoken to me afterward. Now, I think she'll understand both my motives and the dire need for the additional layer of security.

"Hey Reaper, it's Nick Tucker. Long time since we've talked, my friend."

"Nick Tucker, it has been way too long. What can I do you for?" Noah Steele, my former employer and longtime friend, is one of the best men I know. He's never too busy to help out a brother in need.

I explain Savannah's situation and ask for his expert help to safeguard her condo. He's particularly interested in hearing about Butch and his ties to the Devils. Noah and his team were there to help during a tight spot when I was undercover. Knowing what those fuckers were capable of, Noah jumps at the chance to help us out.

"Consider it done, Nick. I've got a couple of men in the area I'd trust with my life. If Silas is back in DC, I'll ask him to swing by and try to break in after they're done. If he can't get inside, no one can."

We talk for a while longer, chatting about the crazed news coverage over the notorious outlaw gang and all the nicknames the media outlets have given me, over and above their favorite— the Undercover Hero.

"Special Agent Adonis is my personal favorite." Noah laughs out loud at my expense.

"Yeah, yeah. Whatever, man."

"Brianna said to tell you she likes Undercover Stud Muffin,

and she thinks you should change your business cards to match it." Noah is still laughing, and I hear his wife's laughter join in on the roast in the background.

"Tell Brianna I said hello." I will never live this down for the rest of my life.

"Undercover Panty Charmer is Bull's favorite."

"Okay, that's enough running down all my nicknames. I'm sure each of you can add even more humiliating titles to the already long list, but I've really had enough of the whole press thing now."

I'm thinking I should've just gone to Home Depot and bought a home monitoring system to install on my own.

"My guys will be there by the first of next week. Is that soon enough?"

"That's great. She's staying here with me for a couple of weeks anyway. That'll give us time to try out the new system and let her get used to it before she goes back home."

There's that word again.

Home.

"Speaking of Silas, when will you know if he's in town?"

"I can try to get a hold of him right now if you need him."

"If you don't mind, that'd be great. I need an extra hand from someone I know I can trust for my side project with Butch. We're all hands on deck as it is, but I can't leave Savannah unprotected, and I'm sure as hell not letting her tag along. Thanks for your help, Reap."

"Anytime, my friend. I'll send Silas in your direction if he's back on US soil. If not, we'll figure something else out. I won't leave you hanging."

We disconnect and I step into the doorway, checking on Savannah. She's still sleeping soundly on the couch, wrapped up in the blanket, and I ask myself which moment it was that made me fall so hard for her.

CHAPTER 11

Savannah

Bad decision #856 of this week alone is insisting we go out on a real date instead of having dinner in my pajamas at Nick's house. And the personal flaw I can't seem to move past is my stubborn nature, and that's preventing me from telling Nick that clothes hurt my ribs even more than breathing does. But our first date is important to me. It feels like we need this milestone to say we have the beginnings of a real relationship, not just a fly-by-night passing.

I can hear the conversation with my mother now.

"So where did Nick take you on your first date?" Asked in the standard judgy-Mom tone.

"To his kitchen, where we had pizza and breadsticks while relaxing in our pajamas. Then we cuddled in his bed until I fell asleep with my cheek on his chest and his arm around me to keep the monsters in the dark from getting to me."

"That's not a date, Savannah. That's a booty call."

"No one says 'booty call' anymore, Mom. It's called 'Netflix and

chill,' and we didn't even watch Netflix. It was an awesome first date, though."

That's not exactly the most romantic version of how I've pictured our time together. Then again, being in near tears from the clothes squeezing me in the wrong places isn't exactly romantic either. Even though the temperature is far too cold for me to wear my soft cotton pullover dress, that's exactly what I've decided on. My thick wool overcoat should help shield me from the whipping winds, no longer than the minute or two we'll be outside. I'll just hurry as fast as I can in my current state to get from the truck to the door of the restaurant.

Changing clothes takes me an entire ten minutes because every time I move, it hurts more than the last. I'm so screwed.

When I finally sit down at the mirror to put on a little makeup, I realize I need a lot of makeup to hide the rainbow of colors my face is currently sporting. Dabbing carefully, I apply plenty of concealer and foundation, then I even out the tone with a dusting of loose powder. A little blush then some nice eyeshadow round it out.

And, ta-da…all my bruises are still visible. They're just very well accessorized with other colors now.

Finally dressed, complete with full makeup and my hair styled in a way other than a ponytail or messy bun, I realize there's absolutely no way I can walk in heels tonight. I grab my thigh-high boots from my available selection of shoes. They're low-heeled, so I don't have to worry about tripping over air and hurting myself even worse.

When I finally emerge from the bathroom, Nick whistles a long, low catcall as his eyes drink me in. I feel them skimming across my skin, like light touches from his fingertips all over my body. My insecurities melt away, and excited butterflies flutter in my belly, ready for the first date I've had in…years. That realization would actually make me sad, if not for the handsome and sexy man leaning against the doorframe, watching my every move with hungry eyes and waiting to whisk me away for the evening.

"You look absolutely gorgeous. I'll be the envy of every man in there tonight. Maybe I should just keep you at home instead, so I don't get into any fights when someone tries to steal you away from me." He leans over and kisses me softly, and I briefly consider taking him up on that offer.

"There's no man alive who could take me away from you, Nick. But we should get going before you talk me into the idea of just staying home. Karen is looking forward to meeting you after everything she's heard about you from Spence and me. If we're a no-show, she'll hunt us both down, and it won't be pretty when she finds us."

"Only if you're sure you feel up to it. You sleep with me at night, remember? I know you're nowhere near healed yet, no matter how much you pretend you're better off than you really are."

"You know, it's a little scary how you can see through me sometimes. You're right, I'll probably pay for it later tonight. And when I say I will, I mean you will, too. But..."

"But?" His eyes twinkle like stars in the dark sky. He knows I was about to admit to something that would embarrass me.

"But tonight is important to me. It's our first date. Even though we've spent a lot of time together, and even though I'm sort of even living with you, tonight kind of feels like our beginning."

He smiles, understanding shining in his eyes, but he slowly shakes his head. "No, darlin', tonight is not our beginning. Not for me anyway. We began the first day I laid eyes on you, when you captured me with those gorgeous green eyes. Then every morning when we met for coffee and you shared your hopes and dreams for the future with me. Our first official date may be tonight, but I've been yours for weeks now. Now that we've gotten much better acquainted, I know my feelings for you won't ever diminish."

"Nick." His name comes out on a whisper as I place my hand on his cheek. Tears well up in my eyes, and I fight the intense emotion rising inside me and prevent them from falling. "You have no idea how much that means to me coming from you. But there's something we should talk about before we go any further. You may change your mind about me."

"Darlin', I don't care about your past or anything you think must be the worst thing in the world. I can guarantee, whatever you have to share isn't as bad as some of the things I've had to do. I'm not even worried about what you want to tell me. But since it's important to you, I'll be glad to listen. Then we'll get back to our regularly scheduled lives."

"You make love feel so easy." I didn't mean to just blurt out the words, but I couldn't hold them in any longer. He makes me feel so much—so many feelings that are new and exciting. Hope blooms inside of me like a rare flower in a barren desert.

With lightning speed, he cups my face in his hands and covers my lips with his. With the sweetest, softest kiss, he sets my body ablaze and liquifies me where I stand. He pulls back, emotion swimming in the amber depths of his eyes. "I love you, Savannah. It may seem too soon to some. Others will think it's because of the situation we're in, but they're all wrong. It's you —the woman I've spent mornings, days, and nights with—who has captured my heart. I'm not some young kid who's never had a real relationship. I've made my share of mistakes. But this I can guarantee you, I will never want another after you. If you walk away from me tomorrow, or after fifty years of marriage, no one else will ever have my heart."

Thinking I'd get out of here this evening without messing up my makeup or my clothes was a silly wish. I'm blubbering like a baby, tears of complete joy that I wouldn't trade for all the smiles in the world if it meant I never heard those touching words of love from Nick Tucker. Those were meant for just my ears, never to be heard by another woman from his lips. I couldn't create a better man if I tried, even with a genie and a million wishes.

When we finally arrive at the restaurant, Nick pulls up to the front door and hops out of the truck. He comes around to my side and helps me slide out without too much jarring. "Wait inside where it's warm, darlin'. I'll park the truck and be right back."

My undercover hero.

Karen and Spencer are already inside when I walk in. They'd put our name on the list for a table and are waiting for Nick and me at the bar. Karen is sipping on a glass of water when I step up beside her and wrap my arm around her shoulders.

"I've missed my best friend. I thought for sure you'd show up at Nick's brownstone to see us."

Her head whips around in my direction, and she nearly jumps out of her seat. "Savannah! I've missed you too! Believe me, I was already headed out to the car with my keys in my hand when Spencer stopped me. He assured me you were in good hands before pressuring me to let Nick handle your care." Her eyes scan my face and neck, noting each and every contusion, abrasion, and swollen spot. The green, black, red, and purple marks of the bruises are impossible to hide, no matter how hard I tried. But even if I'd had stage makeup that can hide full-body tattoos, Karen would still be able to find them. She lowers her voice and continues. "Spence told me that asshole did a number on you this time, but he didn't accurately describe the severity. Dr. Wattress should've kept you inpatient."

"No, he shouldn't have either. I know it looks bad, but I am on the mend. I have the best caregiver. He even dropped me off at the door while he parks the truck and walks in the cold alone."

"There's your undercover lover now. There's no mistaking

his face—it's on the news every day." Karen smiles at Nick as he approaches. He walks directly to me, greets Spencer with one hand while the other wraps around me.

"You must be Karen." Nick accepts her extended hand. "Nick Tucker."

"It's nice to finally meet you. I've heard all about you. Thanks to the news, I guess everyone knows your every secret now. I was looking forward to grilling you with my prepared questions, all 150 of them." Karen breaks out into a full-face grin before she laughs, letting Nick know she's only teasing.

"Don't believe everything you hear on the news. Fake news is a real thing, Karen. They've reported shit about me that I've never even heard of, so it makes me wonder what else I've believed without knowing the full truth. Besides, if I were really a superhero in disguise, Savannah would've already told you." Nick looks down at me and winks.

The hostess calls our name, and we follow her to the table. Over the next couple of hours, the four of us enjoy our meals, the company, and the ambiance of the restaurant. Not that Nick's place isn't great, but sometimes a girl needs to get dolled up and go outside. Even though staying home with Nick was more than appealing, I'm so glad we forced ourselves to leave and head out with friends tonight. We laugh, though I try to keep mine to a light chuckle. We make silly toasts in jest of each other. And we celebrate a momentous occasion.

"I'd like to make a toast, and there's no one I'd rather share this with." Karen raises her glass, so the rest of us follow suit. "We just recently found out…Spencer and I are going to be parents. I'm pregnant!"

My resulting yelp really, really hurts—but I wouldn't take it back for the world. My best friend is going to have a baby, and I couldn't be more thrilled for her. She rushes around the table to hug me, knowing I move like a senior citizen at the moment.

With my arms around her neck, I squeeze her tightly and whisper my congratulations.

"I'm so happy for you, Karen. I love you. You'll be the best mom ever."

She wipes tears from the corner of her eyes and retakes her seat. "Thank you. It was definitely a surprise—we weren't trying at all. My grandma always said no child is an accident. A surprise, maybe. A blessing, always. But never a mistake."

"I was wondering why you weren't drinking wine. I thought it was in solidarity with me since I can't have any with my pain meds."

"That's exactly what it is, Savannah. I love you so much, I'd deprive myself of wine just because you can't have any."

"You're such a liar. You'd drink the whole bottle by yourself and leave me with none if you could."

After stuffing ourselves with the best Italian food DC offers and topping that off with the most decadent dessert on the menu, we say our goodnights and prepare to leave. Nick, being Nick, won't let me out of the restaurant until he's pulled the truck back to the front door to pick me up. Though I don't expect the special treatment, I do love the way he takes care of me. The special touches he adds that show he's put extra thought into the details.

He really is the best man.

Mom will be so impressed with him, she may even try to take him away from me and keep him all to herself.

That thought makes me chuckle to myself.

When the full-size truck rolls up to the curb, I hug Karen and Spencer good night, congratulate them again, and promise to make plans to just hang out—in comfortable clothes—again very soon. With that, Nick helps me into the truck and takes me home.

Home.

I keep using that word when I refer to wherever he is. It just feels so right.

Back inside his brownstone, he helped me change out of my dressy clothes and back into my oversize T-shirt and comfortable yoga pants. He slid his fingers along my skin, checking my wounds while sharing his love. Every place he found a bruise, he left hot kisses to help it heal faster. Where there were abrasions, he lovingly stroked my skin, telling me the places would heal without leaving a single scar as a reminder. I only wanted help to change because holding my arms over my head to take the dress off alone was too much to ask after a night of sitting upright, talking, and laughing. But he gave me so much more than I asked for—he realized what I needed and gave it all to me freely.

Though the doctor said to move around, all the excitement of the night zapped all my energy. We retreat to the couch to unwind from the festivities and chat about Karen's surprise news. With all seriousness, I turn to face him and take his hand in mine.

"Nick, you should know this about me. If it changes your mind about us, I will not think less of you. Just please be honest with me, that's all I ask."

"Always will be. You can tell me anything, darlin'."

"I've had female problems as far back as I can remember. Skipped periods, extremely painful cycles, so much irregularity since puberty. I've had some tests done in the past, and it doesn't appear I'll be able to conceive. My body just doesn't work like it's supposed to, so babies probably aren't a possibility for me. Ever."

I wait with bated breath for his response. What man would want a woman who can't have children?

"I'm still waiting for whatever it is that makes you think I wouldn't want to be with you anymore. Was that it?"

Thinking he's obviously teasing me, my eyes fly up to meet

his, and I'm already fighting back hot, stinging tears. But there's no jest in his expression. There's no falseness in his eyes. Once again, my undercover hero just reduced the entire mountain down to a molehill.

"Yes, that was it. No kids, Nick. We can't have a family. No little Nick Juniors running around the house. No one to carry on the family name and traditions."

"That's not what you just said. You have medical issues that prevent you from getting pregnant. That's fine. That doesn't mean we can't still have a full life and a large family if that's what we decide we want. All that matters to me is I spend every day with you. You are the best part of my life, Savannah. Anything extra is just the cherry on top."

I'm blubbering. Again. Crying like a baby. Tears of joy streak my perfectly applied makeup. Black mascara pools on my fingers with every swipe. I can only imagine how much of a mess I must look like right now. "I love you so much, Nick. I never thought I could love someone so much, especially not so fast. And I swear I won't spend the rest of my life crying like an idiot…but after everything I've been through, my emotions are a mess. I either shut down completely or cry uncontrollably. It's embarrassing."

"Never be embarrassed with me…and never feel as if you have to hide any emotion from me. Sad tears, happy tears, sappy tears. They're part of you, and I'll take all of you I can get." He leans over to kiss me, and I'm completely lost in this wonderful man beside me, until I hear my name being announced on the local evening news.

"In this shot, you can see Special Agent Nick Tucker out with his new leading lady. But we have serious questions about the nature of their relationship, and who Nick Tucker really is, behind the scenes. In this closeup picture, you can clearly see that Savannah Fields, Special Agent Tucker's new flame, has bruising all over her face and neck that is consistent with domestic abuse."

All I can do is gape at the television.

"And, with the new allegations surrounding Special Agent Tucker and the crimes he committed against women on behalf of the Devil's Dominion motorcycle club, we have to ask the hard questions. Did the undercover outlaw gang life change Nick Tucker, the pride of the DEA? Is he physically and mentally abusing Savannah Fields? Were his crimes while undercover absolutely necessary in order to complete his mission, or did they conveniently hide his true colors behind the safety of his badge? We have more from eyewitnesses at the restaurant tonight who claim they overheard Miss Fields referring to the source of her injuries as none other than Nick Tucker himself. More news, coming up next."

CHAPTER 12

Nick

For the next ten minutes and thirty-seven seconds, I stare dumbfounded at the TV, listening to the news anchor drone on and on. About me. About my sins. About my crimes. The long litany of offenses bringing back every haunting memory as she reads each one off the teleprompter, speaking as if she knows every intimate detail about me.

Hitchhiking females kidnapped off the street, brought into the fold, and forced into prostitution.

Involvement in skirmishes with rival gangs, resulting in injuries and deaths.

Women bought, sold, traded, or just plain given away within the club.

Sheep, those who didn't belong to any one biker, forced into street-level drug dealing on behalf of the club.

Rampant physical and sexual abuse against any woman without a "property of" patch...and even some with the patch, with her man's consent...from any and all members, at any time they choose, in any way they want.

Every tick of the second hand makes the bile in my stomach churn even more. Any thought I had of leaving those deeds under the rug, neatly hidden from the light of day, is completely obliterated now. My chance to confess to Savannah and try to help her understand the circumstances I faced while undercover was just annihilated by a partially fake news report. The report of the crimes committed by the Devils was true. My part in those crimes was not true. Not that I can completely absolve myself of all the violations I allowed to happen, but I'd still prefer she heard it from me first.

Time to face the music.

"Savannah." Her name leaves my lips before I dare to look at her, knowing the disappointment I'll see on her face will gut me. I feel enough like a failure as it is. My gaze swings over to hers just as she wraps her hand around mine and squeezes it.

"Nick, I can't believe they're comparing you to all those bikers and accusing you of doing this to me. You're nothing like those men. You'd never hurt me. I'm calling them to set the record straight. This is bullshit."

"Wait, darlin'. Hold up a minute. No, I'd never hurt you, but I didn't stop those guys from hurting all those other women. I'm just as guilty as they are—I watched them commit all kinds of unspeakable acts, and I did nothing. For two years, I was complicit in every crime they committed against those women. At first, I walked away from the scene so I wouldn't say anything. But I could only do that for so long before they started to question me."

"Nick—I know all of this. Don't you think I know you had to do things while undercover that you wouldn't normally do? I'm glad you did, no matter what it was at the time. Thanks to you, those violent men are off the streets. They're going to pay for their crimes. What you did was for the greater good—you were looking at the long game, no matter what it cost you in the short run. That takes more than guts and courage, Nick. That takes commitment and sacrifice.

"You're *nothing* like them, no matter what you had to do to seem like you were one of them. I know that, and I think deep down, you know too. You have to forgive yourself. I know that's easier said than done, but it's eating you alive and keeping you from being truly happy. You deserve as much happiness as anyone else. Even more. You gave up two years of your life to keep the rest of us safe from men like that. How many people would be willing to do that, much less put their life on the line every day of those two years? If the Devils didn't turn on you, a rival gang could have. Or a drug cartel. Or anyone else."

"Why does it sound like such a good idea coming from you?"

"Which part sounds good? What am I getting credit for?"

"Convincing me to forgive myself and let it go. That I deserve at least that much after all I gave up over the last couple of years. For the record, the biker life is not the life for me. I learned I enjoy hot showers, soap, and soft beds on the regular." At last, I can start to joke about serving hard time with a biker gang.

"I'm glad to hear that. So, can I call the news now and tell them they got the story all wrong? That it was actually one of the Devils who did this to me—not you?"

"Unfortunately, no. Somehow, I think they'd find an even bigger story in the fact that the ex-girlfriend of a former Devil is now living in my home and going out on dinner dates with me. The spin and sensationalism of that story would eclipse the false accusations that I beat you."

"Oh shit, Nick. I didn't even think of it that way. What if that does get out? Will you be in trouble? I mean, I can explain everything—how it all happened."

"No one will believe it was all a coincidence, darlin'. If they don't turn on me, they'll turn on you and accuse you of using me to get your boyfriend out of trouble. Or some other bullshit about us fighting over you and you getting caught in the cross-fire. There are so many possibilities of how that narrative could go."

We settle back on the couch, Savannah taking her time to find a comfortable spot snuggled next to me. The news is too depressing—and infuriating—so I change the channel and find something we will actually enjoy. Just when the chaos seems to die down and we can enjoy some alone time, my cell phone rings. This late at night, that's never a good sign. I grab it off the coffee table and stare at the name on the caller ID for a moment before deciding to get it over with now instead of later.

"Calvin. What can I do for you?"

He starts yelling immediately, loud enough for Savannah to hear every word he says, even with the phone pressed against my ear. He rants and raves about my very public relationship with her, already knowing who she is but not realizing we were letting the rest of the world in on our little secret just yet.

"Do you know how this looks, Tucker? You're dating the former girlfriend of a member of the very gang we're prosecuting. How fucking stupid are you? Don't tell me you couldn't keep your dick in your pants for a few months longer to give us time to send these assholes to prison! How can you not see this is a conflict of interest?"

"How can it be a conflict of interest when she was never part of the gang? Her ex-boyfriend has been here over the last couple of years, not even an active member of the Devils after his assignment fell through. And I didn't meet her until they'd already been arrested—under a multi-agency cooperative effort, by the way, and the charges had already been filed. This is standard spin-doctor bullshit, sir. My relationship with her doesn't change the crimes they committed. They tried to murder a federal agent, for fuck's sake!"

"You should know as well as anyone that perception is key when it comes to how the public will view this. And right now, what everyone will see is that our lead undercover agent is sleeping with the fucking enemy."

"What do you suggest we do, sir? Hold a press conference? Do a few interviews?"

"Did you fall and bust your fucking head? No. You don't publicly say or do anything else. Get her out of your house and lay low until this shitshow blows over."

He hangs up without waiting for a reply from me. Just as well, he wouldn't have liked what I had to say anyway. Savannah isn't going anywhere—at least not until the security system is in place and she's mentally and physically ready to go back to her apartment. Not a moment before. And definitely not because my director thinks he can direct my personal life. After I turn off my cell phone for the night, I wrap my arms around Savannah and resume watching the movie with her.

Like nothing happened.

Because nothing did. Nothing wrong anyway. Everything between us is right. Right as rain.

Before long, Savannah is sacked out in my arms, sleeping soundly after the excitement of our first date. I chuckle to myself over that term. Not because of how much it meant to her, but because of how backward our relationship is. We started living together before we ever had our first date. We were eyeballs-deep in love before we officially had dinner out together. And we were planning our future together before I met her best friend.

But why not?

Nothing else in my life has been traditional or had any semblance of normalcy. My time in the service was spent under constant fire, enemies around every corner waiting for the opportunity to wipe me from existence. When I worked for Steele Security, I was under similar circumstances, but on a much smaller scale. My private security time with Dominic Powers brought danger and near-death experiences. Now that

I'm older, it's nice to enjoy the simple pleasures in life and not wonder who's lurking in the dark, waiting to blow up my Humvee with an IED.

I'm finally at a place in my life where falling in love is a perk, not a burden.

Savannah stirs in my arms, and a light moan escapes her lips. I look down at her, expecting her to wake and ask me to take her to bed. Instead, she tightens her grip around my waist and adjusts her head to a more comfortable spot on my chest. Another first for me—sleeping with a woman without fucking all night then sending her packing in the morning. Relationships were never in my bag of tricks before I met her. One-night stands that turned into full-weekend romps between the sheets were. Occasional friends with benefits—only the ones who weren't looking for more—satisfied my itch.

But I threw that little black book in the trash. With her around, I know I won't need it again.

Fuck if I don't need a cold shower right now, with her warm body pressed against mine. The way she wraps herself around me when we sleep is a complete turn-on—even unintentionally. When she's healed and able, I have so many plans to ravage her perfect body, count how many times she screams my name in one night, and wipe her memory clean of any man she knew before me. She doesn't realize the depths of my feelings for her yet. But she will.

Soon.

"Darlin', I need to take you to bed." That's the fucking understatement of the year. I need to do a whole lot more than that, but for tonight, holding her in my arms will have to do.

"Mmm, do we have to move?"

"I'm afraid so. If I leave you lying here like this all night, you'll be even sorer in the morning. You need to stretch out, my love."

Her eyes flutter open, and she cranes her neck to look up at me. "My love?"

"That's right. You are, aren't you?"

Her beautiful smile lights up her sleepy eyes. "I am. And you're mine."

"No question about that, darlin'. I'm all yours." After working my way out of her grip, I help her up, and we walk hand in hand to the bedroom. She steps into the bathroom to wash her face, and I climb into bed, keeping the covers turned back until she's held closely in my arms again. When she finds her comfortable place again, I release a long, relaxing breath. Now I can sleep.

"Nick?"

"Yeah, babe?"

"I know you said you didn't care about my past and didn't need to know any of it, but there is something else I want to tell you. Something I think you need to know."

"Okay. Hit me."

"When I first met Butch, I didn't know what he was. He rode a motorcycle, but a lot of men ride them. They're not all criminals. But it didn't take too long to realize exactly what kind of man he was, and our relationship, if you can even call it that, deteriorated quickly. A few weeks ago, when I moved to get away from him, it wasn't because we'd just broken up and I had to find somewhere else to live. He and I haven't been... together...in more than three years. He showed up now and then when he ordered me to go somewhere with him. But we haven't been in an intimate relationship since long before I moved here from LA. You know how the gang treated women... so I didn't want you to think I was one of their sheep."

"Darlin', I never thought you were one of their women. But I have to tell you, I'm more than a little pleased to know it's been a long time since you were last with him. On the other hand, thinking about being the last man you'll ever be with will keep me up all night now. Visions of your beautiful body underneath mine, screaming out my name until the neighbors call the cops, and watching you fall asleep in the afterglow of your multiple orgasms will haunt me all fucking night."

"Thanks for that visual. Like I said, it's been more than three years since I've had sex. Now we'll both be awake all night with no way to cure what ails us. How much longer will it be until my ribs are healed again?"

"Considering it's only been a couple of days since they were injured, five weeks, five days, and three hours. I can figure out the exact number of minutes when all my blood returns to my veins. Since I'm a nice guy and a very giving lover, I'll put you out of your three-year misery first. Lie back, darlin'. I'm going to take care of you right now. There's just one thing I need you to take care of for me, though."

"What's that?" Her words come out breathy, the excitement building inside her as I fold back the covers and slide down her body.

"You have to count how many times you scream my name for me. I'll be a little preoccupied down here and may miss one. If you lose count, I'll have to start all over again."

"Oh...my..." Then my tongue goes to work. "*Nick!*"

"Mm-hmm...that's what I want to hear. That was one. Keep going, darlin'. The night is still young. You're so fucking sweet."

CHAPTER 13

Savannah

Our first date changed our relationship in so many ways. When Nick met my best friend and they actually got along, I knew he was a special man. When his boss basically ordered him to stop seeing me, or at least being seen in public with me, and he refused, I knew he meant it when he said he loved me. But when he said he was adamant about erasing any other man from my memory, I thought it was mostly macho talk.

Until he proved it to me. Over and over. All night long. Until I begged him to stop because I couldn't take anymore. He was more than pleased with himself, and I was more than pleased with his performance. I did feel guilty because I didn't get a chance to perform for him, but when I moved to try, he wouldn't let me.

"Not until you're well, darlin'. I'm a big boy. It won't kill me to wait a few more weeks until I know it won't hurt you. Trust me, the *forty-six times* you screamed my name was more than enough satisfaction for me."

I actually did keep count. Not because he ordered me to—although I momentarily contemplated "accidentally" losing count so he would have to start over—but because I was genuinely curious too. Turns out, forty-six was technically past my limit, but he wanted to see if we could make it to fifty. My body couldn't take it...and neither could his neighbors, because they started banging on the wall and yelling for us to shut the hell up.

We fell asleep, completely exhausted, after an uncontrollable laughing spell.

In the days since then, we've grown so much closer. We talk about everything—no topic is off-limits—he wants to know my thoughts, he wants to hear what I think, and he wants to share everything with me. What a novel idea—a relationship is a partnership is a relationship. I love this connection we have, where even the silence is comfortable and the atmosphere is nurturing.

These are the thoughts that I cling to as we drive to my apartment to meet his security friends. They're going to install new protective measures, including meeting with the superintendent about making the main entry and the enclosed garage more secure. Nick says they're very persuasive men, and when the super sees the extent of my injuries after a lunatic broke in and managed to get up to the fifth floor undetected, he thinks the building's board of directors will invest in additional measures.

That's all well and good, but in the back of my mind, I know it means I'll be moving back in to my condo soon. Alone. Without Nick. Sleeping single in my queen-size bed. No hard body that scares the monsters away and keeps me warm all night to cuddle against. I'm well aware that I'm too old to react like such a juvenile over the situation. I'm also well aware that staying at Nick's brownstone was only a temporary solution to help me until I'm healed enough to be on my own again.

That doesn't make leaving him any easier.

He must sense my apprehension as we near the building, because he squeezes my hand before bringing it to his lips. "Don't worry, darlin'. I'm here with you, and I'm not going anywhere. They will fix the breaches—to my satisfaction—one way or another. You won't fight this battle alone."

That's not the battle I'm concerned about fighting alone, but I hold my tongue. One step at a time. It's not as if he's kicking me out of his apartment and his life. Two weeks is more like a vacation, not a marriage. Apparently, I just become attached way too easily, and I'm definitely attached to Nick.

"For fuck's sake, did you see that?" I shield my face with my hand, wishing I had a wide-brimmed hat to hide under.

"Yeah, they've been watching us for a while. It's aggravating, isn't it?"

Another aspect of his job hits home with his reply. His sixth sense is much more honed and refined than mine. I only noticed the person snapping pictures of us as we passed because the sun reflected off the chrome on the car and caught my eye. But Nick knew we were being followed and photographed well before I realized it. We'll be fodder for the local news again. I never thought I'd say this, but I'm starting to miss all the political mudslinging between the opposing parties that kept them busy before Nick and I became household names.

"Your director will be thrilled to see all these pictures on the news tonight."

"Babe, I'm not worried about it, so you shouldn't be either."

"I feel responsible. If I'd gone to Karen's house instead of yours, none of this would be happening."

"There was a reason you came to me, Savannah. We're meant to be together. I never believed in fate and finding that one person I'm supposed to be with until I met you. Now I can see everything that happened, happened for a reason. If that means my director gets pissed and yells at me again, I can guarantee it won't be the last time. He'll get mad about something else after this blows over. That's his job—staying on his agents' asses to keep all of us in line."

"You're pretty laid-back for a Special Agent. I thought you were all type A personalities."

"Oh, I am definitely type A. I've just learned how to control it when needed, and how to release it when I need to let all hell break loose on someone."

We arrive at my building, and he pulls into one of the surface-level parking spots in front of the building. He gets out of the truck and walks around to my side. I sit still, not because I expect him to treat me like a porcelain doll, but because the memories of this place are so vivid, I can still taste the blood in my mouth. That old anxiety I thought I'd left behind, with Nick's help, starts building in my chest and threatens to emerge as a strangled scream. I push it down, focusing on my breathing as I work to calm my racing heart.

Then I feel Nick's hand slide around my waist, keeping his grip loose but letting me know he's there. I didn't even realize he'd opened my door yet. "Darlin', tell me if you can't do this. I'll take you away from here right now, and I'll handle this myself. At first, I thought it would help if you heard the changes we're demanding, but now I'm not so sure anymore."

Somewhere in my logical mind, I hear his words and process them. He'll take me away for now, but the changes will still be implemented. The security will still be put into place. I'll still move back into my condo alone. Whether it's today, tomorrow, or next week, I will have to face the fact that I'll be here alone again at some point.

Maybe I should've realized this sooner, but the weight of my thoughts changes my view of everything. I've allowed Butch to rob me of my independence, of my freedom, of my right to live in my home without fear of him. If I don't woman up, go in there with Nick, and make my own demands heard, I'm essentially allowing Butch to win. He wins at ruining my life, making me completely dependent on someone else for my sense of security, and taking away what I've worked for my entire life.

"No, I'm ready. Let's do this. I'm glad you're here with me, but they're going to listen to what I have to say, too."

Nick smiles, genuinely and warmly, before kissing me softly. "That's my girl. I knew that feisty fighter in you would regroup and show up sooner or later."

"She's here now, and she's ready to kick ass."

When we reach the main door, a large, imposing figure steps into view just inside. Nick feels my hesitation in my faltering steps. "That's Silas Steele, Noah's brother. He's one of the good guys. Noah said he'd call Silas to see if he was in town to help us out with Operation Bitch."

"Was he undercover with you?"

"No, but he helped resolve the case in his own way. He's an officer with the CIA, so he's very skilled at interrogation techniques and extracting needed information from people. Since my case involved international arms dealers, the DEA was able to pull in Silas to help through interagency cooperation. The fact that he's the brother of one of the best friends I've ever had didn't hurt either."

"If you like him, then I'll like him. Butch should take off running in the opposite direction if he sees you two men walking toward him."

Nick chuckles darkly beside me, the low timbre of his laugh rumbling through his chest over the mental images of Butch tucking tail and running. "Nah, we don't want him to do that. We want him to stand and fight so we can end this once and for all."

Nick opens the door for me, and I step into the lobby of my building. Silas smiles at me, instantly changing his appearance from daunting and intimidating to warm and friendly.

"You must be Savannah. My brother Noah told me all about you. Seems you've captured the heart of our elusive Special

Agent Friskme. Millions of women claim to have drugs hidden somewhere on their person, so he'll frisk them until he finds the contraband."

"Not you too, Silas." Nick shakes his head. "Noah, Brianna, and Bull already gave me enough shit over the pet names I've been given."

"Dude, the comments on social media posts about you are gold. Pure gold. I've laughed my ass off. You should've known better than to let your cover get blown by one of those shit-heads. You'll find no sympathy here."

"Yeah, you just remember you said that, Silas Steele. What goes around, comes around, my friend."

Silas laughs, shrugging off Nick's warning like it's nothing. "Noah's men are already upstairs. You can fill me in on the plan to lure this Butch character in so we can trap him and kill him."

"Silas. Really? You sound like Shadow. Is that how the CIA trains you? Just kill everyone who gets in your way?"

"Yep."

Silas's reply makes me laugh, even though I doubt he's kidding. When we exit the elevator on the fifth floor, two men are standing outside my door. Since neither Nick nor Silas flinches, I assume these are the two men we're here to meet. Silas reaches them first and extends his hand toward the one nearest us.

"Roman, how are you?" He claps one hand on Roman's shoulder, while shaking hands with the other.

"Good. I didn't know you were back in the States. When did you get home?" Roman replies to Silas, giving me a moment to silently assess him. He's not as thick as Nick, but he's tall and muscular, nonetheless. His hair is a lighter brown, and he has that playboy vibe some men just naturally exude. But his eyes are kind, showing the good guy underneath.

"You know I never let anyone know my travel plans ahead of

time. My whole family sics Liz on me when I do." Laughter fills the hallway, all at Silas's expense.

Nick turns to me to explain. "Liz is a friend of Noah's wife, and she has taken quite a liking to Silas. Even though she's old enough to be his mother."

"She wants to be a super spy with me and regularly makes my life hell when she's around. No one tell her how much I secretly love her, though." Silas grins then turns to the second man. "Brad, it's been a long time, brother. Are you here with all the latest technology gadgets for Savannah's condo?"

"Hey, Silas. You know I am. When I'm done, she'll be better protected than Beyoncé and Fort Knox combined."

"I like Brad," I chime in. "Brad is my new best friend."

"Savannah, I hope you don't mind, but we've already broken in to your condo several times, trying out new ideas and testing our equipment. We also took out all the broken furniture and the garbage for you. Everything is as good as new in there now." Roman holds out a set of keys toward me, and I immediately notice how few there are on the ring.

"Don't worry. We added a biometric lock that only opens for you and a digital lock that triggers a complete security shutdown if the wrong numbers are attempted too many times. We have cameras in the hallway and elevators now, and everything is monitored from a central, secure location with facial recognition technology. You also have a new secure door and a panic alarm inside."

"You and I are going to be BFFs too." The men laugh, amused by my commentary.

Brad asks for my hand and places it on a scanner in a large metal case. After he scans my entire hand into the system, we try out the biometric locks. I'm like a kid in a candy store with all the new gadgets and upgraded security. Locking my door will be much more fun with these new toys than my old, no-tech dead bolts.

"Have you already had words with the super?" Nick asks, looking between Roman and Brad.

"We did. When we were able to get into the lobby without any trouble at all, we paid him a visit. He was more than a little taken aback when we walked into his 'secure office' with no forewarning. Then I explained what happened to Savannah, and I may have insinuated I'd be back to visit him if anything else happened to her. After that, he was very receptive to our suggestions and upgrades. He even assured us he'll take care of getting funding approved through the board of directors. Seems the owners are sensitive to being sued over breach of contract after they lost their last lawsuit." Roman's smile is downright devious, but if that's what it takes to create a cone of protection around my building, I'm all for it.

"So, are you moving back in to your condo tonight, Savannah?" Silas asks, genuinely interested and not just fishing for information.

"No, she's not." Nick replies for me, and I cut my eyes up at him, raising my eyebrows in silent question. "What? It hasn't even been two weeks yet, and your doctor has you out of work for six weeks. You're still under my direct care and supervision right now."

"Man, you'd be better off just admitting you don't want her to leave than trying to pull the old 'doctor's orders' routine." Silas laughs and playfully punches Nick's arm. "Admit it, you are wrapped around her little finger, my friend."

"I have no reason to deny it. She knows it. I know it. You know it. Every news outlet in DC knows it, even though they accuse me of beating her up. Still, it's only been about a week since she was hurt initially, and I'm not taking any chances with her being reinjured."

"Fine, Undercover Lover—which is my personal favorite nickname, by the way—have it your way. Everyone go inside so I can find the holes in your security system. Savannah won't get to use it any time soon, but the next tenant will be thrilled with all the upgrades."

Silas urges the four of us inside so he can get to work on breaking in, cracking the codes, and just playing the bad guy in general. Every time Silas finds a way in, Brad and Roman tweak whatever failed, until the very last try. When Silas pops up behind me from out of nowhere, I simultaneously scream and jump, then grab my side as I try to catch my breath.

"Where the hell did you come from?" When I'm finally able to speak, I search my surroundings for a hidden door.

"I broke in to the condo next door and crawled through the heating duct right into your condo. This building has huge ducts." Silas smiles broadly, proud of his ingenuity.

"Adding motion sensors to the heating ducts now," Brad replies, unimpressed.

"At least now I know this place will be locked up tight." Nick steps behind me and wraps his arms around me. "That doesn't change the fact that you're not leaving my home or my bed yet."

I rest my arms on top of his, squeezing in response. "You don't have to tell me twice. You've spoiled me. I can't sleep without you now."

"Good to know my evil plan is working."

"You know I'll eventually have to come back here, right? I mean, as attached as I am to you already, you'll want your space back."

"Let's just take it one day at a time. We're in no hurry. Besides, even if you decided to stay here tonight, that doesn't mean I can't stay with you. Or that we won't see each other again. It just means half of my bed will be really cold and lonely without you in it."

Becoming attached to Nick is easy.

Falling in love with him was inevitable.

Feeling at peace with our relationship, regardless of what we face, is pure bliss.

Silas, Roman, and Brad finish demonstrating every feature of the new system they installed in my condo. Roman showed me how the cameras monitor every floor and elevator via an app on his phone. The lobby doors will be replaced with stylish yet ultra-secure doors that only the residents will be able to open.

Then they leave with promises to let us know when the doors are installed. Nick, of course, refuses to let me stay in my condo without him until those doors are in place.

Then again, he did offer to help me christen every room and leave good and long-lasting memories in place of the old ones once I'm completely healed. That's one more offer from him I simply can't refuse.

CHAPTER 14

Nick

"Can you just get back to the fucking topic at hand? I swear to God, I will shoot you myself if you change the subject again." I sit back, cross my arms over my body, and glare at Silas.

Fucker just laughs at me as if I'm a fucking comedian.

"Man, you are in an extra pissy mood since Savannah left you. News flash, brother—she just went back to her own condo. The one that's only two miles from your brownstone. You could run if you wanted and be there faster than driving in DC traffic. You two haven't known each other long enough to live together permanently yet. It's not like she broke up with you and went running back to Butch." Silas smirks at me, like he gives the best relationship advice in the world.

"What do you know? You're a fucking spy. You lie for a living. When's the last time you had a serious girlfriend?"

"Seventh grade. Worst four days of my life. I thought we'd never break up."

"That's it. I'm shooting you and putting us both out of our

misery." I glare at him, giving him my worst—or best—intimidation stare. Bad thing is, he knows me too fucking well, so it only makes him laugh harder. "Can we get back to finalizing the plan to take out Butch once and for all?"

"Yeah, yeah, okay. Spoilsport. I was thinking, maybe we should invite Liz for this op. Butch wouldn't stand a chance against her."

He's really testing my nerves today. "We're not letting Liz in on our plan. No fucking way. She stays with Noah and Brianna and their kids, wherever they are. And that's not here, in harm's way, with a convicted felon, one-percenter, biker gang criminal who has no qualms about hurting women. You must miss Liz. You keep bringing her up."

"Just trying to lighten the tension in this room, brother. You're a different man without Savannah here to level out your moods."

Funny thing, I never realized that very fact until the words left his mouth. Before Savannah, I was angry all the time and hated the world, hated what I'd become. Then she brought light and love and fresh air into my life and made me a better man without conscious effort. She made me *want* to be the best man I possibly could be—for her. Since she went back to her condo and I don't have her with me all the time, I've regressed to that moody, unapproachable bastard.

Time to snap out of that shit.

"You're right—I'm being ridiculous. My bad, man. Knowing he's still out there, regardless of how well protected she is, makes me nuts. The thought of not getting to her in time haunts me."

"Her condo has the best security in the world. It's better protected than the White House."

"But she's not always in her condo, is she?"

"I know she hasn't gone back to work yet. What's she been

up to?" I'd swear Silas is stalling for some reason, but talking about Savannah does make me feel better.

"She started volunteering at the family crisis center to help other domestic abuse victims. She loves it. She's manning the phones right now, talking to women who are looking for a way to get out of a bad situation. She spends a few hours a day there. No physical work, but she leaves both completely drained and full of excitement."

"That's great. She's making a difference for others and helping herself at the same time. Have you decided when you're going back to work?"

"I haven't decided what I'm going to do yet. I can't go back to undercover work since everyone knows my face now. And with Savannah in my life, I wouldn't want to do that anyway. It definitely doesn't suck that I have more than two years' worth of my salary saved and all my accrued time off just waiting for me to burn through it. My director ordered me to take off the mandatory eight-week decompression time after the long-term operation ended, so I'm just waiting for some huge epiphany to fall out of the sky and smack me on the head."

"I'll keep that in mind."

Someone knocks on my door, and I lift my gaze to Silas's. "Are you expecting someone, Silas?"

"Just Roman and Brad. They said they'd be glad to lend their expertise on this job."

After I let Roman and Brad in, the four of us sit at the table and review every aspect of the plan, consider every possible failure, and identify potential contingencies. When we're satisfied that we've covered all the bases we can possibly think of, I pass out a round of cold longneck beers, and we settle in front of the TV.

"You really should sit this one out, Nick." Roman takes a swig of his beer. "You're technically still on administrative leave, the trial is heating up, and you probably need to stay with

Savannah in case anything goes wrong with getting Butch. She wouldn't feel safe with anyone else. Plus, she'd be worried about you the whole time."

"As much as I hate to admit it, I know you're right. I can't jeopardize the trial with an unsanctioned undercover operation. And I damn sure can't risk Savannah running out on one of you to try to help me. She's likely to pull some shit like that, too." I chuckle, thinking about how she has nightmares without me beside her in bed, but she doesn't give herself enough credit. She wouldn't hesitate to face that very monster head on if she thought she could help me.

"So we're good to go for tomorrow night?" Silas asks.

"We are absolutely ready. Butch doesn't know Savannah is off work, so she'll drive her car to the hospital tomorrow night. She'll go in one door where Nick will be waiting for her, and they'll exit through another door so Butch won't see her leave. Her car will stay parked there, and we'll watch it all night if needed. The van Brad will record and monitor everything from is already in play, so it won't seem out of place.

"Butch's head will be on the chopping block soon if he doesn't move that heroin, and he knows it. That's why he went crazy trying to get to it. The Mexican cartel that the Devils were in bed with isn't a forgiving bunch." Roman finishes off his beer and grabs another from the refrigerator. "I almost want to hold on to the packages and let them deal with him."

"Tell me about it. If we ever found his body, it'd be in pieces strewn to the four corners of the world. I don't know which would be better—knowing he's dead, or seeing him behind bars." At this point, I'm thinking six feet under would be best so the fucker can't come back at all.

We finish by agreeing on the time each man will be at his assigned position, then I head to pick up Savannah from the shelter. Men aren't usually allowed to know or visit the secret location, but since I'm a federal agent, I have automatic clearance. Still, I wait in the truck for her to emerge from the building so no one is anxious about my presence. She'll be finished with her shift soon, and I can't wait to hear about her day. Her excitement over helping others has grown after every time she's volunteered. Watching her blossom and become more confident in her abilities are added benefits for me. She smiles and laughs more. No topic is left off the table, and she shares her entire day with me. Her passion for the difference she's making makes me miss my own.

Before long, she steps out of the front door, sporting the brightest smile when she spots me parked close to the road. The single-story building is mostly tan with light, mint-green accents, nothing spectacular that would draw the eye when passing by on a daily basis. There's no obvious sign advertising the services, and that's the entire point. It's unassuming and boring, not creating unnecessary attention to the people seeking solace inside. A high fence encloses the lot behind the building, with English ivy covering the slats and obstructing the view of the yard. From Savannah's description, I know there's a playground and space for outdoor activities for the kids and mothers to enjoy without prying eyes.

Behind her, the center's director emerges from the building, walking at a brisk pace toward my truck. She's a big woman, much taller than Savannah with large bone structure and muscular build. She keeps her blond hair short, letting her natural curls maintain her hairstyle for her. She motions for me to roll down my window before she even reaches the truck.

"Good afternoon, Miss Linda. How are you?"

"You know you're not allowed to be here."

Well, hello to you too.

"Actually, I am allowed to be here, and we've already covered this." I flash my badge, showing I'm a federal agent and officer of the law, and follow it up with an intentional smirk.

"Maybe you should just find somewhere else to park and

wait for Savannah, or she could drive herself. It's not as if she needs a babysitter or hand-holding. Your sitting out here in your truck day after day may cause others to park here. We don't want anyone loitering around the building where women and children are hiding from estranged spouses."

"I'm not loitering, Linda. And my truck doesn't draw attention any more than your car parked right over there does. As far as Savannah driving herself, she's not my prisoner by any means, if that's what you're insinuating. She's a grown woman who can make up her own mind, go where she wants to go, and do whatever she wants to do. For reasons I'm not at liberty to discuss with you, I'm giving her a ride back and forth for the time being."

Linda purses her lips, clearly not happy with not having the last word in our battle of wills. If she thinks for one second she's entitled to boss me around, she has another think coming. She turns and walks away, her shoes smacking the ground with annoyance with every step. Savannah and I cut our eyes at each other before busting out in laughter.

"Hello, darlin'. How was your day?"

"It was good until the last few minutes. I made a new friend today. Hopefully you'll be able to meet her soon. She's really sweet."

After helping Savannah into the truck, I slide back behind the wheel and start to drive. "That'd be great. So, she's a resident there?"

"Yes. Her name is Miranda Petrovio, and she's hiding from an abusive ex. She said they were never married, but that didn't stop him from trying to own her. He's apparently a really bad man, even worse than Butch. She's still too scared to say much about him, even to me, and she's extra careful around windows. Makes me wonder if I'm not being careful enough. I mean, I know I live on the fifth floor, but I don't have blackout curtains and thick fabric shades. When I leave any building, I look around to see if he's waiting there, but I do go out and live my life."

"You never know what Miranda has been through or how he's brainwashed her. It'll take time to deprogram her mind from the abuse. You know I want you to be careful, but not to the point where you're a shut-in. That's no kind of life for anyone."

"Remember last night when you mentioned taking me to the shooting range and teaching me a few things?"

"Sure do."

"Maybe we can take her with us one time. I thought maybe it would be good for her to get out with people who will look after her and teach her self-defense at the same time."

"Maybe. Let's see if she'll even meet me first." And from there, I can make a judgment call on whether it'd be a good idea. Reading people is part of my job, and I'd definitely want a good read on her before I put a gun in the hands of a total stranger, especially around Savannah. "Tomorrow night, do you want to stay at your place or mine?"

"What's special about tomorrow night?"

"We're moving forward with the plan to nab Butch. It's time to get him off the streets and off your back."

"Let's stay at my place, then, and put the extra security measures to work. We can even hit the panic button and seal all the windows and the bedroom door. No one in or out until I unlock it."

"Darlin', I'm fine with staying there if it makes you feel safer. But we'll have to do without the panic-room setting. Besides, I was hoping you'd let me have another go at him."

She laughs, though there's little humor in it. "Oh, I know you'd love that. But I'd probably be a nervous wreck."

"You know, your lack of faith in my skills is a little insulting. I've manhandled him twice now without a single scratch on me. What makes you think he could take me in a fight?"

"It's not that, Nick. He doesn't hold a candle to you in any way. But he also wouldn't hesitate to kill you if he had the chance. He has no conscience and has no issue with fighting dirty. He didn't see you coming the other times, but if this goes south tomorrow night, he'll be the one coming for you. And coming for blood in any way he can get it. So it's more that I know how evil he really is, and I don't want to risk losing you."

"I know exactly what kind of man he is, and he doesn't scare me, babe. But for your peace of mind, we'll stay at your place. Anywhere I'm with you is fine with me."

I finish telling her the details of our sting operation and the part she'll play. The *only* part she'll play—drive her car to the hospital with Spencer tailing her, watching her every move. Then she'll walk inside, where I'll be waiting to escort her right back outside and whisk her away to safety with me.

"Are you saying I'll be your prisoner?" she asks teasingly, throwing my words to Linda back at me.

"Nope. We're going to your condo. I'll be yours."

"Oh, I really like the sound of that."

"We're going to my place right now because it's closer. There are some sounds I really like to hear you make, too. Very loud sounds that piss off the neighbors."

"Have I mentioned 'Undercover Lover' is now my favorite?"

My lead foot presses harder on the gas, speeding through the streets and swerving around cars moving too slowly. I can't wait to get her home.

CHAPTER 15

Savannah

*D*riving to the hospital again after what seems like a long time away feels surreal. Before the last couple of weeks with Nick, the Metro was my primary means of transportation. Now that I know what's hiding in my car, I sort of wish I were back on the subway train instead. But this is the plan to arrest Butch once and for all. Spencer lags several cars behind me, leaving enough space to avoid being spotted.

My eyes keep darting to my rearview mirror all on their own, watching for a big, burly man on a motorcycle to come roaring up beside me.

So far, so good.

When I reach the hospital, I park in my usual spot and take my time gathering my coat and bag before exiting the car. I'm trying my hardest to do everything as ordinarily as possible in case I'm being watched. It's a strange feeling, wondering if someone is right behind me, waiting to harm me. Or worse. Then I feel him before I see him. I feel his eyes on me and his strength flowing toward me.

Nick is hiding just inside the hospital doors, waiting for me to join him, watching me with his eagle eyes as I make my way across the parking lot. He's barely visible to me, but I know it's him, and that gives me courage to keep moving. He gave me tips before we left his place to help me act and react normally, rather than trying to focus on being normal. I'm not sure his tips sank in, though, because I feel very obvious. Then I see him smile at me and nod his head, and I feel better about...walking normally.

I've mastered walking. Go me.

I bite my lip to keep from laughing out loud at myself.

Once I'm inside the hospital and away from the glass doors, Nick folds his arms around me, pulling me into the familiar warmth of his chest, and I melt into him. The sandalwood scent of his cologne envelops me as much as his embrace does, reminding me of the day we met in the coffee shop. Even though only a couple of months have passed since that day, the changes I've embraced have made me a different person. I'm not a former soldier like Nick, ready to take on an entire motorcycle gang with my bare hands. But I'm not the trampled-down delicate flower I once was either.

Volunteering in the crisis center has opened my eyes to a lot of facts I never considered before. When those women feel beaten down or foolish for putting up with the shit they tolerated for years, I point out how strong they were for leaving when they thought they had nowhere else to go. When they are ashamed for allowing their kids to see the environment they endured, I remind them of how they fled with the clothes on their backs and nothing else, just so their children would have a better life one day.

Those women helped me realize how the changes I implemented in my own life have made me a stronger person. The mirror they put in front of my face doesn't show the hollow-eyed, scared woman I used to see. Not that I want to run into

Butch in a dark alley or anything stupid like that. But his threats and taunts won't keep me under his thumb ever again.

"You've been working long enough tonight. How about I take you home now?" Nick leans down and kisses me, making me forget everything else in the process.

"Excellent idea. It has been a long night, and my feet are tired from being on them for so long." I smile up at him, playing along and loving our comfort level with each other.

"By all means, allow me to sweep you off your feet then, my love."

"Trust me, you already have, Nick."

Once I'm securely tucked into his truck, he drives back to my condo where the extreme security system awaits. Maybe the extra measures are overkill with a highly trained DEA agent locked inside with me, but I haven't quite reached the point where I'm comfortable with completely throwing caution to the wind yet.

Thankfully, Nick knows how to pick his battles, and this isn't one of them.

Nick puts his cell phone in the dash holder and sends the phone call through the truck's speakers. "Everyone on the line?"

Silas, Roman, Spencer, and Brad all respond to let Nick know the conferencing worked.

"Talk to me, Spence. Did she have a tail on her?"

"No sign of Butch on his motorcycle, but I did identify a car following her from her building to the hospital."

"There's a woman inside the car, no sign of anyone else with her. She's circling the parking lot for the third time now since Savannah walked inside," Brad adds.

"What make and model car is she driving?"

"It's a black Honda CR-V. Older model, around 2001. She's parking now. Let's see if she gets out."

The silence on the line kills me as we all hold our collective breaths, waiting to see what move the mystery woman will make.

"She's wearing a cut with a Devil's Dominion rocker panel and 'Property of' patch. She's not very bright, wearing such easily identifiable clothing while picking up enough heroin to send her to jail for life for intent to distribute." I can just see Roman shaking his head as he speaks. "She's circling the car, trying a little too hard to be nonchalant. She has no idea what she's doing."

"And yet, she's doing it for Butch anyway. He doesn't care if she gets sent to prison for life or some rival drug dealer offs her in the parking lot. As long as he gets his stash and saves his own neck, no one else matters." Nick's fingers curl around the steering wheel, his knuckles turning white from the tight grip he has on it. "I've seen it too many times over the last couple of years. That P.O. patch means nothing when it comes down to choosing between the woman and the money. It's always the money for them."

Staring at Nick, I realize how true his words are and how he's the complete opposite. No amount of money would buy his allegiance or replace who he loves. He would give up everything else in his life for the sake of love and honor.

"She's going for it. She's on the ground, working her way under the wheel well to find the package. Once she has it, she'll take it back to Butch, and we'll have his exact location no matter what hole he slithers into. They won't find the tracker for a while." Brad's proud of his contributions, and I have to agree I'm infinitely appreciative of his work.

"And now she's on the move with it. Silas, you got her?" Roman asks.

"Absolutely. Stay on your toes, men. The game is afoot."

I'm thankful to have the package of heroin out of my car, but now I have so many questions. Without a doubt, the answers will haunt me. I reach up and hit the mute button on his phone.

"Nick, she knew exactly where to look, didn't she?"

"Sounds like it, darlin'."

"So, this isn't the first time he's hidden drugs somewhere in my car and let me transport them for him." I don't even have to phrase it as a question. The truth has already sucker-punched me in the gut.

"No, babe. In my experience, you were transporting drugs for him every time he made you go somewhere with him or told you to meet him out. There's a reason why you always had to drive your car and never ride on his bike. Every biker's old lady I knew while undercover rode with their man and proudly wore the 'Property of' patch on their back." He glances over at me, gauging my reaction.

"All these years, I've worked my ass off to save people's lives…and he used me to move drugs that will kill them. Had I been caught with them, I would've lost everything—my nursing license, my job, my apartment, my car, my freedom—and I wouldn't have had a clue until it was too late."

Nick nods, understanding my inner turmoil all too well, but also knowing words won't really comfort me right now.

"Nick?"

"Yeah, babe?"

"Can I shoot him when we catch him? It would save us a lot of trouble in the long run and save the taxpayers a lot of money on the trial."

"As much as I want to give you everything you want, you know I can't agree to that, darlin'."

"I know… I probably wouldn't be able to pull the trigger either. But it felt good to say it anyway."

Nick laughs and nods. "I'm sure it did. Almost as good as it felt hearing you say it, I bet."

"She's heading south, getting on the interstate." Silas's voice breaks the silence in the cab, bringing my thoughts back to the task in front of us. "Twenty dollars says she heads to Washington Highlands. He probably found a vacant rowhouse to assert squatter's rights in."

"Or he's taken over her house and lets her do all the work for him. What a man." Roman sounds as if he'd like to shoot Butch himself. He'll have to get in line.

We arrive at my building, and Nick takes the call off speaker until we reach my door. Once inside, he hits the speaker button again and puts the phone on the counter. Silas is still following her, changing lanes and taking exits only to get right back on the interstate. He's singing along with the radio as he drives and occasionally interrupts the song, giving a full description of his every move. The comic relief is just that—relief, in this very stressful situation.

"Everyone owes me twenty dollars when I get back. We're exiting the interstate and heading straight to Atlantic Street, Southeast. I called it."

Everyone hurls insults at Silas, telling him he's full of shit if he thinks he's getting any money from anyone. I can't help but laugh at the brotherhood and camaraderie these men have. Silas parks a couple of blocks away from where the Honda CR-V stops at a rowhouse, also called by Silas. The woman looks around nervously before darting inside with the package tucked under her arm.

We disconnect when Silas says he'll call back when there's something to report. After a couple of hours, the phone rings, and I nearly jump out of my seat.

"Talk to me, man," Nick says when he answers the phone.

"Our boy Butch is here. Do you want me to snuff him out now so we can call it a night?"

"What the hell is it with you CIA guys? When I worked with Shadow, he wanted to kill everyone too."

"It's just cleaner that way, Nick. No offense to anyone."

I'm still not really sure if Silas is kidding or not when he says things like this. If I had to guess, I'd say he's serious. Deadly serious.

"We need to arrest him, Silas."

"Yeah, well, that may be your agency's stance, but it's not mine. I don't have the authority to arrest him. But I do have other skills that will come in very handy should you change your mind. He's here with a group of his biker buddies, all piled up in a small, run-down rowhouse. From the records search, looks like the woman owns it and they all just moved in on her. So what's the plan now that you won't let me just take them all out at once and be done with it?"

"Leave it. When he starts cutting that heroin, he'll come find us. I want to nail him to the wall on more than just an intent to distribute charge. I want to make sure he never steps foot outside of a prison again."

"And which charge do you think would do that?"

"The premeditated attempted murder of a federal agent, for starters."

CHAPTER 16

Savannah

ick's words send shivers down my spine, and I'm pretty sure my heart just stopped beating. "What did you do?"

"Technically, I didn't do it. Tim did. But the gist is, Tim took the real heroin and replaced it with a look-alike substance. Once Butch realizes it's fake, and it won't take him long, he'll know it was me, and he'll come for his real heroin. He's on the line for a lot of money, and he's looking to make a lot more considering how much they hid in your car. He'll cut other substances into it and make the stash at least three times bigger."

"How about that? You do have a devious side. I never would've thought it, Nick. Learn something new every day." Silas chuckles on the line, but I don't find anything funny about the situation.

"Thanks for your help, Silas. Stay close—I'm sure you'll hear from me again soon."

"You got it, brother. I won't be far away. Call anytime."

Nick pockets his phone while keeping his intense gaze on me. "You have that worried expression on your face again."

"Maybe I'm just not used to what you do for a living. I know you've been in much more danger than this before. Doesn't mean I have to like it."

"Can't say I'd react any differently if our roles were reversed. Don't even give it another thought. I'll be fine, and several very good men have my back."

Nick's phone chimes with an incoming text, so he glances at the screen. "Roman just parked your car in the garage. I'll go meet him to get your keys back."

"For the record, I know you're only doing that so you can change the subject when you get back."

"Ah hell, I was hoping it'd take you longer than a few weeks to figure out my tricks."

"Yeah. No."

He walks out into the hallway laughing, leaving me standing here alone with a gigantic smile on my face.

I love that man.

He's back just as quickly as he left, and I realize that I didn't rush to lock the door behind him. For the first time in years, it slipped my mind.

"Your car is safely parked back in the garage under the building. Now, we wait."

The next few days pass by without incident. Although Nick was surprised Butch hadn't made a move yet, he also wasn't alarmed. Then Nick received a call neither of us expected, and most of the bravado I'd built up immediately evaporated.

"I'm afraid I have some potentially upsetting news, darlin'."

I stop what I'm doing and give him my full attention. "What is it?"

"My director called and said it's time for me to come back to work. They think it sends a better message if I'm on the job when the trial kicks off next week. I'd hoped to extend my time off until Butch is out of the way, but unless he makes a move this weekend, that's not going to happen."

"Well, we knew that was a possibility. You can't take off forever. Although, it would be nice to be independently wealthy and never have to work again, wouldn't it?"

"Let's keep playing the lottery. Maybe we'll win and retire to our own private island one day."

We settle on the couch, cuddling and watching TV, when the news shows pictures of Nick and me again. Their love affair with him is long over, and they spout his crimes while he was undercover every chance they get. The gang members Nick knew are next up on the screen, claiming entrapment and accusing Nick of ordering them to commit the crimes they're accused of, as if he were the president of the club instead of Bobby Blalock.

"It's pretty obvious why Calvin wants me back now. My absence makes me look guilty." He sounds so gloomy, like he lost his best friend.

"Hey." I turn to face him. "There's nothing we can't get through together. You've been my rock since day one, before I even realized it. You saved me when I wasn't able to save myself. Now let me be your rock. When you feel like everything is at its worst, think about how much I love you. That's one thing you'll never question or doubt."

Gravity draws me to him with the force of colliding stars, the same stars that burst behind my eyelids when his lips press against mine. With a single stroke of his tongue across mine, I'm pulled under his splendid spell, never to be released again. An immediate urgency consumes us as the excitement low in my belly grows. Butterflies flutter in my chest, threatening to bubble up out of my throat at any second.

Summoning my inner strength, the last of my reserves, I break our kiss to look deeply into Nick's eyes, conveying my message without saying a word. At first, there's a slight hint of confusion in his expression, but it quickly changes to understanding. And anticipation.

"You're sure?"

"Positive."

"I don't want to hurt you, darlin'. I know your broken ribs are still painful."

"Then make love to me slow and easy, Nick. But when you take me, know that you take all of me. All my love. All my heart. Don't break it."

"That is one thing you'll never have to worry about, darlin'. I'd never break your heart."

Moving down the hall on cloud nine, my feet never touching the floor, I'm back in his embrace the second we step into my bedroom. Sensual kisses on my neck heighten my eagerness. Smoldering licks of his tongue increase my impatience. Then our souls connect, and the final missing link is fused inside us, a bond we created that will never be broken.

The sweat drips off his brow as he holds my gaze, and I let him see all of me. All my insecurities. My inner questions. With every move and every breath and every expression, I show him how much I love him and need him and want him. When the dams break and my heart is laid bare to him, I see in his eyes the same love that has consumed me. As I call out his name and every muscle in his body tenses, the only thought I have in my mind is that this incredible man loves me as much as I love him.

He'll be here tomorrow...the same as he is tonight. He'll stand beside me, no matter what troubles and trials the future brings. He'll be my best friend and my lover and my world. But more than that, I'll be his too. Equals in love. Partners in life. Soul mates forever. As we descend from the highest high, spiraling toward the bottom below, I don't fear the fall. Nick will be there to catch me because he's falling with me.

"Did I hurt you, darlin'?" He strokes one cheek with his thumb and leaves sweet kisses on the other.

"No, babe, you didn't hurt me at all. I've never felt as amazing as I do right now."

"I love you, Savannah."

"I love you too, my undercover lover."

He chuckles in the dark, then silence overtakes us, and we fall asleep in each other's arms. Completely happy. Completely in love. Completely complete.

Now that the soreness in my body is improving day by day, I have so much more energy, and I'm ready to dive back into life headfirst. Nick and I spend the weekend together, strolling the electric streets of the Adams Morgan neighborhood of DC. One of the rooftop bars draws our attention Saturday evening, so we climb the stairs, and the hostess seats us under an outdoor heater. Between the heat radiating from above us and the way we're completely bundled up in parkas and hats, we're able to enjoy the sights and scenes of this popular area. Add the free-flowing alcohol, and I'm feeling no cold and no pain after a couple of drinks.

Music plays through the outdoor speakers, loud enough to enjoy but not enough to distract our conversation. Nick and I spend hours, talking, drinking, and munching on appetizers—simply sharing our entire life stories. Funny childhood stories. Embarrassing teenage tales. He tells me about some of his cases he worked before going undercover. I share stories of some of my more interesting emergency room patients. For the hours we spend on the rooftop just talking and laughing, I completely forget about anything else.

Nick pays our tab and we leave the bar, walking home since it's not far and plenty of people are still milling around. Restaurants and trendy bars are abundant in this neighborhood—and it's always been relatively safe. Still, I'm hugged up to Nick as we walk, my arm around his waist and my body pressed against him while his arm wraps around me. Without warning, he stops walking and pushes me until my back is against a tree. The bare limbs jut out above us, covered with tiny white lights like stars twinkling in the night skies.

His lips gently caress the sensitive skin of my neck, from my ear to my collarbone and back again. Then he moves to the other side and repeats his ministrations. Even in this cold air, my body is heating to the boiling point. I can see my breath hanging in the air like small puffs of smoke escaping from my overheating core. This is pure heaven and hell…and I wouldn't change it for anything in the world.

When he moves back up to my ear and whispers to me, the cold instantly seeps into my every pore, and pure terror replaces all other sensations.

"We're being followed, darlin'. I'm not sure who it is yet, but I don't think it's Butch. Stay close to me. If I tell you to run, get inside a restaurant or a bar and call the police. Do you understand?"

I nod robotically. "Yes."

"That's my girl. Let's just walk casually. They've been watching us for a while and haven't tried to approach us. That tells me they're tailing us to find out where I live, probably tied to the case somehow. But I'm not taking any chances with your safety to find out who they are."

We start walking again for a few steps before a taxi passes us. Nick flags it down, and we dash into the back seat, heading in the opposite direction of the men following us. When we drive by, Nick gets a good look at their faces, shock and annoyance clear in their expressions.

"Where to?" the cabbie asks.

Nick gives my address, and we ride the rest of the way in silence. Nick, in quiet retrospection. Me, in complete terror. Who would be following us if not Butch?

Late night activities led to sleeping in Sunday morning. After brunch, we spend the rest of the day lounging in my condo, purposely doing nothing more than spending time together. We venture out of bed once or twice, making refueling runs to the refrigerator or the door for delivery. Nick takes his time worshiping my body and making me feel cherished. My ribs only hurt now when touched, but he's still extra careful to avoid doing anything that would cause me pain. But he makes sure he does anything and everything needed for my pleasure. My body is spent, and a smile is permanently affixed to my face now. Not that I'm complaining. Late Sunday night, Nick leaves for his apartment, knowing he has to be at work early in the morning.

My condo is too quiet without him here, but I'll survive. I always do somehow. Sleep finally overtakes me, and I wake to the chiming of my alarm clock. I'm volunteering early at the crisis center this week. Most of my time is spent on the phones, helping convince battered women to flee to safety. But since I've been on the mend, I've spent more time restocking the residents' rooms with soap, shampoo, and towels. While it may sound as if I'm little more than a maid, the benefits I reap from it are so much more valuable to me.

Miranda is quickly becoming a friend I desperately want to help. In the short time since I met her, she has opened up to me more than anyone else at the center. She hasn't shared much about her life before, but I do know she was treated more like property than a person. Her ex was a cruel man who enjoyed demeaning her in front of others. Because of the humiliation he subjected her to, she finds it difficult to look others in the eye.

But she's opening up to me, and it's a beautiful thing.

When I walk into the center, Linda is reprimanding one of the staff members for allowing her boyfriend to drop her off at work. The younger girl, Patty, counters, saying she wouldn't be able to show up for work at all without a ride, but Linda isn't having it. I understand both of their points all too well. Working in the emergency room, I have no choice but to show up for work, even during inclement weather, whether I have reliable transportation or not.

"If you need a ride tomorrow, call me. I don't mind swinging by to get you or coming in earlier." I smile at Patty as I walk around them.

"Thank you, Savannah. If you're sure you don't mind, I may have to do that."

"I don't mind at all."

I start making my rounds—as a nurse, I can't think of it any other way, it seems—and refill the used goods in each resident's room. When I reach Miranda's room, she's chewing on her thumbnail and pacing the floor. Her eyes are cast down, staring at the floor as she walks back and forth, and she hasn't noticed my presence in her room yet.

"Miranda, are you okay? What's wrong?"

"One of my friends was killed. I just found out." She stops in her tracks and looks up at me, her eyes haunted. "I will kill myself before I let him take me back to hell."

CHAPTER 17

Savannah

"Miranda, don't say that. I'm so sorry about your friend, and I wish I could help take away that pain. But you're safe here. He doesn't know where you are. Even if he somehow finds you, I won't let him take you anywhere."

She drops her hand from her mouth and rushes to me, throwing her arms around my neck and squeezing. Her voice quivers almost as much as her body shakes. "Thank you for saying that, Savannah. You're the only friend I have left in the world now."

"Even if that's true, you still have me." I write down my cell phone number and my address for her, telling her to call anytime she needs me. "And if you ever need to run from here, run to me. You know, Nick did the same for me. He gave me his address after he witnessed Butch harassing me, and I had to use it. I showed up at his place out of the blue, beat-up and bringing trouble with me. Not once has he ever made me feel like a burden to him. And you're not one to me either."

She wipes tears from her eyes as she turns away from me. "I

think he murdered my friend to try to find out where I am. I couldn't put you in that kind of danger."

"If that's true, then you need to call me before anyone else if you feel you're in danger. Nick just upgraded my apartment with state-of-the-art security. He wouldn't be able to get in to hurt either of us, trust me. If I found out he hurt you when I could've helped, that would kill me, Miranda."

She nods, even though she's not fully ready to commit yet. "Okay, you win. Thank you again, Savannah."

Right now, she doesn't want to appear ungrateful, so she agrees. But if push comes to shove, at least she knows where she can escape to safety. If she'll only swallow her pride and let me help.

"Do you want to talk about your friend? Is there anything I can do to help?"

"Believe me, you're already helping. I appreciate you more than you know. I really need time to process everything, though. I found out about it just before you got here, so my head really isn't on straight right now."

"I completely understand. If you need to talk later, you know how to reach me." I hug her before continuing on to the next room, but she stays on my mind the rest of the day. Unable to attend a friend's funeral out of fear her ex will find her, on top of suspecting that same man murdered a close friend in a desperate attempt to find her.

That has to be pure torture. I couldn't imagine being kept away from Karen and Spencer. Miranda has to feel utterly and totally alone in the world right now. I know all too well people have multiple facets to their personalities, but she has been nothing but sweet to me since the day I met her. My heart breaks for her.

As I make my way toward the front of the large building, pushing my now-empty supply cart, sounds of terrified screaming and angry shouting slow my steps. Something terrible is happening, and all the women and children are panicking.

"I said shut the fuck up!" Gunshots ring out, echoing throughout the building and bouncing off the walls.

My feet come to a complete stop, and my lungs freeze in my chest. I feel every shot in my soul, because I know that voice. And I know he won't hesitate to kill every person in this building, woman or child, as long as he gets what he wants.

And what he wants is me.

"Savannah, what's going on?" Miranda steals up beside me, making me nearly jump out of my skin.

"My ex is here. He followed me somehow." I think for a second, trying to figure out what to do. I hand Miranda my unlocked cell phone. "Call Nick Tucker. Tell him Butch is here and what's going on. I'm going outside to draw Butch away from everyone. As soon as he steps out the door, pull the emergency alarm and lock down the facility."

"Savannah, you can't do that! He'll kill you!" The fear on Miranda's face mirrors my own, but I can't put an entire building full of women and children at risk when they've already given up everything they had for a modicum of safety.

"I'm so scared I can't think straight, Miranda. But I do know one thing. I can't live with the death of innocent people on my conscience. The other people here shouldn't have to suffer because of me. Please call Nick, right now. Tell him I said to hurry...and that I love him."

With brisk steps, I move to the emergency exit and push the bar, setting off the alarm. At this point, I'm betting we need all the help we can get, as fast as we can get it. The alarm will alert the monitoring company, who will call to verify there's an actual emergency. When no one from the center answers, they'll dispatch our local fire department and police units as a precaution. While the response time won't be terrible, it's also not immediate, but it's all I have at the moment.

Moving around the side of the building, I make my way to the very front parking lot. The building is close enough to the road to draw more attention from passersby. Anything that could possibly help. When I reach the end of the line, I stand frozen in my spot, shaking from head to toe. My hands are cold, my mouth is dry, and I'm second-guessing my decision with every second that ticks by.

Then I realize the building is eerily quiet.

The alarm is off.

There's no screaming coming from inside.

Dear God. What has he done?

"Butch! I'm out here! Come out here and face me like a man!" I scream at him as loud as I can. The force exerted against my ribs sends shock waves of pain through my body, threatening to bring me to my knees, but I push the swells of nausea aside. I can't focus on that right now.

He steps to the front door, smiling at me with an evil grin that sends cold chills up and down my spine. "Well, I'm here, you fucking bitch. What are you going to do now?"

Before I can answer, he jerks a child from behind him and presses the barrel of the gun to the young boy's head.

"Nice fucking try by pulling the alarm, you whore. You must be even stupider than I thought you were. One call from the alarm company and I killed that shit on the spot. If any of those stupid whores inside suddenly tries to get smart, little Jamal here will pay the price. So, let me tell you the same thing—get your stupid fat ass inside right now, or I'll shoot him in the fucking head right in front of you."

I didn't account for this scenario at all. In my mind, he left everyone else alone and just came after me. After all, that's what he wants, right?

"Now!" His screamed command jolts me from my inner turmoil, making my feet move toward him independently of all conscious thought.

When I get close enough to him, he pushes Jamal back inside then grabs my arm, jerking me as hard as he can. I scream out in pain, but that only serves to satisfy him even more. He shoves me through the doorway and locks it behind us. Everyone who was unfortunate enough to be in the center is hunkered down in the entertainment room, lined against the wall three deep. Tears stream down every person's face—women and children alike. All the terror they've endured in their lives is conjured in one person.

Butch.

And I brought him here.

"You have me. Let them go."

"Don't you dare try to tell me what to fucking do, bitch. No one is leaving. I'll shoot them all, one by one, right in front of you if you pull that shit again." He walks over to a mother of three and points the gun at her head. "Should I show you right now?"

"No! No. I believe you. I believe you!" I put my hands up in the universal gesture for stop, as if the subliminal message will do any good with him.

"I don't think you do." He swings his arm around, leveling it at Linda, and pulls the trigger. She crumples to the floor, her eyes wide open and fixed in a death stare. The room spins around me as terror-filled screams reverberate off the walls, each one hitting me like a thousand sharp knives.

Butch walks to me, unaffected by his heinous deed, and roughly grabs my face. "Call that undercover pig you've been fucking and tell him to bring me my shit right now. My real shit. If he shows up here with that fucking talcum powder bull-shit, everyone in here will eat a fucking bullet for dinner." He releases me with a snap of his wrist, making my head jerk violently.

"I-I don't have m-my cell phone on me to call him. I n-need a phone." My reply is stammered; I can barely get the words out.

I don't want to draw attention to Miranda by telling him I already asked her to call Nick for me. That may be just the excuse he needs to kill her too.

He looks at me with contempt and skepticism. "Who doesn't have their fucking cell phone in their pocket these days?"

I run my hands over my pockets, showing him they're empty. "I'm serious. I don't have it with me."

"Here, Savannah. You can use mine." Miranda stands and extends her hand to me, returning my cell without giving away our prior plan.

My hands shake uncontrollably, but somehow, I manage to dial the phone.

"Put it on speaker, you two-bit whore. I want to hear every word."

"She doesn't need the speaker. You can hear me just fine from right here." Nick steps into the room with his gun drawn and his sights set squarely on Butch's chest. His eyes drop to Linda's lifeless body lying on the floor, and I know his hatred for Butch has surpassed his previous contempt.

I end the call and slip my cell back into Miranda's hand before giving her a slight push toward her place in the crowd of people crouched on the floor. Out of sight, out of mind is my hope. There's little chance I'll come out of this unscathed. Knowing Butch's savagery, I shudder to think what he'll do just to inflict pain on me. My biggest fear at the moment is he'll use Nick for that very purpose.

But seeing Nick in action, completely at ease in his element, makes me think we may all have a chance to walk away.

"Well, well, well, if it isn't the undercover pig himself. You got balls showing up here like this. Alone. Thinking you can just waltz in here and take over because you wear a fucking badge. We all know you're just as bad as any so-called criminal you arrest. You were one of us—that means you did every dirty little deed we did. And now you're a fucking rat pig, so that makes you even worse."

"I know exactly who and what I am, Bitch. I'm a DEA Special Agent. I was undercover to stop a bunch of badass wannabes who didn't have the guts or brains to make it on his own. You're a pathetic loser and you know it. When you leave here today, it'll be in either handcuffs or a body bag. When I leave, it'll be in my nice vehicle, going back to my nice home, and lying in bed next to my fine girlfriend. Now drop your fucking gun before I put a hole in your chest big enough to drive my truck through."

Butch smirks and my blood runs cold.

"You put your gun down…or I'll blow her fucking head off right here, right now. Do you want to see her brains? I bet they're as pretty as she is." Another Devil steps out from behind the open door, giving up his hiding place behind me. The cold metal of his gun digs into my temple while his rough hand squeezes my neck. "Maybe I'll fuck her first and let you watch. Hard decision."

Tears well up in my eyes. Hope is fleeting, and I can feel every ounce of it draining from my body. I trust Nick, but two against one, using me as leverage, is a no-win scenario. A sudden, loud crash behind me makes me jump. A split second later, I'm on the floor in the middle of flailing arms and legs. When I finally work free of the tangled limbs, I'm beyond relieved to see Silas has the other Devil in a full-body lock, sporting a wide grin on his face.

"Are you okay, Savannah?" Silas asks. All I can do is nod. I think I'm okay. "Good. Be with you in just a second. Let me help this troubled young man go to sleep."

Glancing over at Nick, I see he's engaged in a brawl with Butch, taking out his frustrations on him one punch at a time. Butch staggers backward and Nick follows, delivering one punishing blow after the other. As I watch Nick in action, the thought crosses my mind that he could easily knock Butch out with a single punch, but he's enjoying beating the shit out of him too much to do that. When Butch falls flat on his ass, Nick stands over him and reads him his rights.

Nick reaches to grab his handcuffs, but they're on the ground a few feet away after falling out during their brawl. One of the ladies huddled nearby crawls toward them and pushes them across the tile floor. When Nick reaches to grab them, Butch capitalizes on Nick's off-balance position to push free and run. Nick jumps to his feet, fast on Butch's tail. In the blink of an eye, I take off running after Nick.

"Savannah, no!" I hear Miranda scream as I run, but the words don't register. I know Butch. He'll kill Nick first, then he'll come back and kill the rest of us.

When I burst through the front door of the building, Nick and Butch are squared off against each other again. Nick has his gun drawn, cars are stopped on the side of the road, and the onlookers all have their phones trained on the men. Instead of calling for help, they're videoing the showdown happening in the parking lot.

"You're just in time, little whore." Butch's gaze swings from me to Nick just before he draws a gun from the side of his motorcycle. "Say goodbye to your double-crossing pig. I hope he fucked your brains out last night...because it'll be his last time."

CHAPTER 18

Nick

An ugly sneer crosses his face then he pulls the trigger.

The painful scream that follows turns my blood to ice and stills my heart. He never intended to shoot me—Savannah was always his target.

And that bullet found its mark.

The thumping rumble of a motorcycle leaving the scene registers in the back of my mind as I rush to her side, holstering my gun and withdrawing my cell to call an ambulance. Blood is already pooling on the ground underneath her. Dark blood, almost black, covers her abdomen. In a matter of seconds, she goes from loud, shrill screams of pain to low, quiet whimpers.

She's already lost a lot of blood.

I rip her shirt open and wipe away the blood covering her skin, trying to find the wound so I can apply pressure and slow the loss. When I finally locate the hole, she's even quieter than just seconds before.

"No, Savannah! No! You hold on. Do you hear me? Don't

you dare fucking give up on me now!" I jerk my shirt off my back and use it to put pressure on the wound.

The plethora of sirens from police, EMS, and Fire/Rescue vehicles coming from behind me bring little relief with them. The entry hole is low in her abdomen...lower, in her pelvic region. The internal damage a bullet does in that region is catastrophic. I've been in this line of work long enough to know that without a confirmation from a doctor. The ride to the hospital will be the longest ride of our lives.

Multiple sets of tires screech to a halt, and a host of men and women descend on us from every side, hauling every piece of medical equipment they have. I'm pushed out of the way to make room for all the emergency procedures they need to perform to try to save her life. I pray it's enough to keep her going until they can get her into the operating room.

The paramedic calls out her stats before issuing medical directives to the others, letting them know what he's doing and what he expects them to do. I hear terms like bilateral IVs with fluid bolus, run them wide open, and hypotensive. I know enough to understand none of that equals good news about her condition.

"This will be a load and go. Get those bilateral lines in right now. Let's move fast, ladies and gents." The paramedic in charge points to two EMTs then down to Savannah's hands.

"What's her name?" The paramedic swings his gaze to me, and it's then that I realize I've dropped to my knees at her head.

"Savannah Fields." I'm running on autopilot. I have no idea how I even answered him with a coherent response. If asked, I couldn't even tell him my own name at this very moment.

"Hey dear, can you tell me your name?" His voice is loud, nearly shouting at her, and he rubs her shoulder to get her attention.

When she moans in response, my heart nearly leaps out of my chest. "Savannah."

"Savannah, do you know what today is?"

She answers correctly while the flurry of activity continues around her.

"Do you remember what happened to you?" The paramedic continues to ask questions, but I think he's checking her mental status more than anything. He's already performed a rapid medical assessment on the rest of her body.

"Shot." Her voice is weak, but I thank God it's there at all. Her sweet voice is music to my ears.

He looks up at me again. "Do you have any idea what caliber bullet hit her?"

"Yeah, he had a 9mm." The paramedic nods before signaling the rest of the team to wrap it up.

"We're taking you to the hospital now, dear. You'll feel a lot of hands moving you onto the gurney then we'll load you into the back of the ambulance. I'll be back there with you the whole time." The paramedic asks which hospital she prefers, so I give him the name of the one where she works and assure her that I'll be right behind the ambulance until I'm by her side again.

Only minutes after arriving, the ambulance takes off, running lights and sirens at breakneck speed out of the area. The fire and rescue crews are still on the scene, picking up discarded medical supplies and plastic wrappings. The police canvass the scene, writing up reports of the shooting and gathering information from eyewitnesses. A young rookie cop calls out to me to stop when I jog toward my truck.

"Hold up. We need to talk to you about what happened here." The young buck puffs out his chest and gives me his practiced stern expression.

"Ask all you want—at the fucking hospital, you moron. I'm not standing here one more second with you while she's fighting for her life."

He yells at me again when I turn to leave, but I ignore his commands. I hear a familiar voice tell him to let me go. When I glance over my shoulder as I slide into my truck, I see Spencer taking charge of the scene. He nods at me, knowing there's no stopping me, and he wouldn't try to anyway. I grab an extra shirt from my gym bag in the back seat and quickly pull it over my head before throwing the truck into gear.

Red lights and stop signs are all one big blur on my way to the emergency room. My lead foot lets me catch up with the ambulance before they even pull it into the emergency bay. By the time they're unloading her, I've already parked and run to the double doors to walk in with them. There's no way anyone can make me stay in the waiting room and leave her back here alone. My badge comes in handy when my presence is questioned—it gets me out of speaking at all. They just nod and keep working. As long as I'm not a psycho civilian, I'm allowed to wait here, out of their way.

Watch and wait.

The emergency room doctor orders X-rays and imaging immediately, telling the staff to clear the way for Savannah —"stat." Then he instructs another nurse to page the specialist in female pelvic medicine and reconstructive surgery for an immediate and urgent consult. Two nurses wheel Savannah by me on the way to radiology. Her skin is pale, and her breathing is slow. Tubes are attached to each arm, and an oxygen mask covers her nose and mouth. Bags of IV solution hang above her head as do bags of blood. Wires snake out from the blanket covering her, and my eyes follow them to the heart monitor. I'm not a doctor, but I know a fast heartbeat and a low blood pressure are not good signs in an emergency situation. But as long as that heart monitor records a beating heart, my heart will keep beating too.

The logical part of me knows she's only been away for mere minutes, but it feels like an eternity. I pace back and forth in front of her room in the emergency department, straining my ears to catch any word of her condition. She's lost so much blood. They have to get her into surgery immediately and fix her.

Don't they?

"Nick!" A frantic voice yells my name from behind me. I whirl around to find Karen rushing toward me. "What have they said?"

"I don't know anything yet." I relay the bits and pieces I've picked up while stalking outside the door. The color drains from her face.

"You're sure they said to page the reconstructive surgeon?"

"Yeah. That's not a title I'd know without hearing it first. Why? What does that mean?"

"That's Dr. Jeff Smith. He's a brilliant surgeon, but he's only called in on the very worst cases. The ones other doctors don't want to attempt because of the complexity and bad odds. He will definitely help her, but it means the bullet did extensive damage, Nick."

Karen and I talk for a few more minutes while we wait together. This is where Karen works too, so she has access to every bit of information we could possibly need, but she opts to wait and hear it from the doctor with me. She's a good friend, because if I had her access, I'd be on that computer reading every single word.

"Karen, are you here with Savannah?" A tall man wearing a white lab coat approaches us. He's not much older than me, but one glance at the name embroidered over his chest pocket tells me this is the genius surgeon who holds the love of my life's life in his hands. Dr. Jeff Smith.

"Yes, Dr. Jeff. This is Nick, Savannah's...fiancé. You can tell us both—I'll vouch for him."

"Come with me. She'll need your support."

We follow Dr. Smith through several twists and turns in the hallways until we reach doors with bright red no-entry signs and large white AUTHORIZED ADMITTANCE ONLY lettering across them. Behind those secure doors, several people in surgical scrubs are preparing Savannah as quickly as they can.

We reach her bedside, and I place my hand on her arm. Her eyelashes flutter a few times before she opens her eyes to look up at me. I can see and feel her relief, the reassurance she feels from simply knowing I'm here with her.

"Savannah, I've been called in because of the severity of your pelvic trauma. The impact of the bullet has injured your uterus and is causing a lot of bleeding. The damage to your uterus is severe and irreparable. I am uncertain as to the damage to your ovaries. In order to save your life, I have to perform an emergency hysterectomy to remove the uterus. After this surgery, you will never be able to become pregnant. Do you understand what I've just explained to you?"

His tone of voice is kind, but his message is direct. As a federal agent, I understand the need for bluntness. It leaves no room for misunderstanding or confusion. As a man who only wants to protect the woman he loves, the finality of the doctor's words strikes like a knife to my gut.

I wish that bullet had hit me instead.

I should've shot him instead of waiting for him to comply with my commands. He was unarmed and fleeing at first. My training kicked in—I couldn't use lethal force against an unarmed man. Had I merely pulled the trigger, Savannah wouldn't be in this position now and Butch would be dead. I'd gladly pay any price to go back and change my decision now. The strict rules I've followed have now cost me more than I could've ever imagined.

This is all my fault.

Tears stream out of Savannah's eyes like free-flowing waterfalls. Her bottom lip quivers uncontrollably until she pulls it between her teeth to try to stop it. She closes her eyes, but that does nothing to stem the tide of tears falling. She nods her head and weakly whispers her consent to surgery. "I understand, Dr. Jeff."

"We're taking you into the OR immediately. I'll give you a minute or two with your friends, but that's all we can spare." He turns his gaze to me. "The OR nurse will call the surgical waiting room to give you periodic updates during the procedure. Try to make yourself as comfortable as possible. We all have a long night ahead of us."

He claps me on the shoulder as he leaves, a sign of understanding just how devastating this news and this predicament is for all of us. I lean over the side of the bed, being careful not to jar her too much, but I want to be as close to her as I can get.

"Darlin', I'll be right here waiting for you when you get out of surgery. No matter how long it takes or how long I have to wait to see you again. And I'll be by your side, taking care of you every minute of every day afterward. I'm so sorry I didn't get to you in time. I'm so sorry, baby."

She squeezes my arm—not hard, but it's there. I don't know how she has the strength or energy to move at all, but she doesn't respond verbally.

"I love you, Savannah. I loved you yesterday. I love you today. And I'll love you tomorrow. Nothing can ever change that. I only love you more every day."

Her tears increase again, but she remains quiet. I know what's running through her mind. Her self-esteem has been battered and beaten for years. This blow is too much for her to take. All at the hands of that fucker Butch. When I'm finished with him, he will regret not turning that gun on me instead of her. He has no idea what he just unlocked deep inside of me. No one does. Not yet anyway.

"We have to go now. You can wait just outside those doors in the surgical waiting room. We'll call the phone in there to give you status updates." The OR nurse unlocks the wheels of the bed and takes Savannah away.

Karen wraps her hand around my arm and tugs me toward the direction we came in. "We'll be here for a while, Nick. Let's go find some coffee and the waiting room. She's in good hands. Trust me."

Karen's emergency room training must be running on all cylinders, but my training just flew out the fucking window. I can't think straight for shit. My brain basically just shuts down, allowing Karen to lead me through the hospital corridors until we're seated in a room full of uncomfortable chairs with bad hospital coffee in hand. I don't even remember getting here.

Some undercover hero I turned out to be.

"Nick?"

"Yeah."

"Did you hear a word I just said?"

"No. Sorry."

"I said, she's going to be fine. She has lost a lot of blood, but they got her here fast. She has the best of the best surgeons. She's strong, and she was conscious when we just saw her. All very good signs."

"You're right. They're absolutely good signs that she'll pull through. But she never should've been in this predicament in the first place. She wouldn't have been hurt if it hadn't been for me."

"That's not true at all. She's tried getting away from Butch for years. He has hurt her in so many ways. This is all on him. Not you, Nick."

"I'll lose her after this. She won't see me anymore once she's released from the hospital."

"Why do you say that?"

I think she knows why, from the expression on her face. But in case I don't know everything about Savannah, she wants to reserve the right to reassure me.

"Because one night when we talked about our future, Savannah told me she wanted to have fertility testing done first.

She had doubts about her ability to become pregnant and said she wasn't sure she would marry me if that were the case, because she felt like she would be taking an important part of my future away from me. Well, now we know the answer to that question for sure, don't we?"

"You told her it doesn't matter to you, didn't you?"

"Of course, I did. And I meant it. All I need is her for the rest of my life. Everything else is optional."

"Give her some time, Nick. What happened tonight is already a lot to take in, and now she knows she can't have kids in addition to almost being killed. On top of that, she thinks she's letting you down, because that's just her personality. Let her come to terms with the trauma first, then she'll come to terms with you and your acceptance of her—just the way she is. One step at a time and it'll all be okay. Eventually."

"I'm not so sure. She wouldn't even look at me back there once she knew the severity of her injuries. Under normal circumstances, she would've turned to me for comfort. Before Dr. Jeff gave her the news, I felt how much she needed me. After, she wouldn't look at me at all. She's already pulling away from me."

Hours pass with frequent updates from the OR staff.

She's doing well.

Everything is going as planned.

She's tolerating the surgery well. Nothing unexpected.

The surgery is over. They're just finishing up. The doctor will come to the waiting room to talk to you when he's done in here.

She's being moved to recovery. They'll monitor her back there for about an hour. Dr. Smith is on his way to you now.

My nerves are shot, waiting for Dr. Smith to walk into this waiting room. They've already assured us she did fine in surgery. But the specifics about the damage that 9mm bullet caused are what I'm dreading now.

The surgeon finally comes in and pulls up a chair across

from us. The expression he wears is serious—all business—but maybe he has to separate his work from his life like I do. Compartmentalize to survive and stay sane.

"Savannah is in recovery now. The surgery took longer than I planned because the internal damage was extensive. I had held out hope to save her uterus going in, but that was not even remotely possible. To stop the bleeding, I had to remove it and close several nicks in her uterine artery. She'll have to stay in the hospital for a while. We'll need to monitor her closely for bleeding and any signs of infection.

"She'll be moved to ICU for close observation over the next several days, but I've left instructions for them to let you two see her for a minute or two. Don't expect more than that, though. The ICU nurses have a lot on their hands and not a lot of extra time. Also, don't expect her to be able to stay awake. She has a pain pump and we've already given her quite a lot of pain medicine, but I know just seeing her will make you feel better. Any questions?"

"Does she know for certain you had to do a hysterectomy?" I hold my breath and wait for the reply I know is coming.

"She knows. She may not remember all the details when she first wakes up, though."

Savannah

The intense stinging slices through me before I even open my eyes. I'm not sure where I am, why I'm here, or what happened to me at the moment. The searing pain makes it hard to concentrate on clearing my foggy brain. When I try to move, my limbs feel extra heavy, almost like dead weights are attached to me.

The faint beeping of the heart monitor and hiss of the oxygen cannula are unmistakable clues, sounds I'm used to hearing on a daily basis. Fighting against the lead weights on my eyelids, I finally pry them open and glace around. The dim room with curtain partitions between the rows of beds and soft lights overhead is all too familiar. I'm in the recovery room at the hospital.

I've had surgery. Major surgery, if my pain level is any indication. All at once, the events come rushing back to me like scenes playing on a movie projector. Butch. Nick. Linda. The family crisis center. The gun hidden in his motorcycle. The crude remarks. The cruel smirk. The blast from the muzzle.

Then complete darkness consumed me as Nick screamed for me to hold on.

Dr. Jeff telling me I'll never have children of my own.

Even though I knew that was a possibility before, now it's a certainty beyond the realm of medical intervention. My thoughts are jumbled in a haze of anesthesia and pain medicine, but my heart understands perfectly. Nick's words of reassurance swirl in my head, but that was when the situation was mostly hypothetical—and potentially fixable.

I'm past that point now. Theory has become reality. Tears leak from the corners of my eyes, and I let them flow, falling unchecked to the pillow beneath my head.

"There she is. You sure gave me a scare, Savannah." One of my nurse friends slides up to my side and grasps my hand. Her voice is low and reassuring, but she can't mask the tint of sadness in it. "You're in recovery now, sweetie. You came through the surgery with flying colors. Just rest now. We'll move you out of here in an hour or so."

The click of my pain pump administering the next dose means I'll be out again in about fifteen seconds or so. The pain in my body and the pain in my soul will disappear into the black abyss, where even dreams can't reach me. My thoughts revert back to Nick just before I slip into a deep sleep, squeezing my heart with a pain that's every bit as real as any other part of me. I wish he were here with me.

When I wake next, I'm being moved into my bed in the intensive care unit. While I shouldn't be surprised since I'm a gunshot wound survivor, I'm still alarmed by the level of care and attention Dr. Jeff obviously thinks I need. Glancing around the room, I see more nurses I know very well since the ER and ICU share nurses in dire situations. Then I see those whiskey-colored amber eyes locked on me. He's with Karen and one of the nurses appears to be briefing them on my condition, but his attention is homed in on me.

"Excuse me." I read his lips as he steps around the nurse and makes a beeline for me. He's immediately beside me, his long legs making quick work of the distance. He grips the side rails of the bed so hard, I wonder if he'll leave imprints. "Hi, darlin'. How do you feel? Do you need anything?"

I shake my head from side to side, thinking about how sad he seems. The pain radiating from his eyes is palpable. He blames himself for Butch's actions. Opening my hand, I signal for him to take it in his. First, I look down at our entwined fingers, thinking about how much I love him, before meeting his penetrating gaze again. My throat is still raw from being intubated, but I manage to speak to him in a whisper. "This isn't your fault, Nick. None of it. I don't blame you, so you can't blame yourself either."

A pained smile makes a brief showing before retreating behind his mask of steel. "Savannah, I wish he'd shot me. I thought he was gunning for me—I completely read him wrong, and look what my fuckup caused. This is my job, it's what I'm trained to do, and I failed. I failed you. That is all on me."

I shake my head again. "Then this is my fault for ever getting involved with him in the first place."

"No, babe, you are the victim here. You're the survivor. But you're not responsible for him."

This time, I nod. "Neither are you, Nick."

He stammers for a few seconds, wanting to argue with me but knowing he'd only be arguing with his own point if he does. Then he smiles—really smiles—at me, and my heart does flips in my chest. The heart monitor picks up on the effect he has on me, making his eyes jerk to the screen. When he looks back down at me, he squeezes my hand and leans over the rail to kiss my cheek. "They won't let me stay long because you need your rest. But I wanted you to know I'm here. I'm not going anywhere. I love you."

"Go home, Nick. You won't be able to see me for several more hours. There's no need for you to live in the hospital."

"She's right." Karen speaks up from the foot of my bed. "Listen to the ER nurse, she knows what she's talking about. The fact that she's talking at all tells me she'll be okay."

My only response is a small smile. I don't think I'll ever be okay again. But I don't say that out loud.

"Hey, get that thought out of your head right now," Nick's soothing voice chastises me. "You're alive and soon will be well. That's all that matters to me."

Emotion nearly chokes me, squeezing my throat and threatening to overcome me. Tears well up in my eyes without warning and without mercy.

"You know, don't you, sweetie?" Karen asks.

I nod, my chin and bottom lip quivering too much to risk trying to speak.

"I'm so sorry this happened to you, Savannah. We talked to Dr. Jeff before your surgery and afterward. There was no other way he could save your life. Believe me, Nick and I would both much rather have you just as you are than risk losing you completely.

"All this tragedy is too much to deal with right now, but when you've healed, you'll see things more clearly. Listen to me, babbling on, trying to console you and really sucking at it. I'll be my usual blunt self now, so listen up. Even though it feels like it right now, I promise you this isn't the end of the world. This isn't the end of your life. So, wallow in your grief for now, get it all out while you're in here. When you're discharged, Savannah's new outlook on life starts immediately. Got it?"

I love my best friend.

"Got it. Now, get out. My drugs are kicking in."

"That's my girl. Love you, doll. I'll be back to check on you later today."

Nick leans over, places a lingering kiss on my forehead, and cups my cheek. "I love you, darlin'. Nothing will ever change how I feel about you. Just remember that. I'll be back this evening during visitor hours."

Time passes but means nothing in here. I don't know if it's daylight or dark out, but the pain management drugs are working wonders, so that's all that matters. Well, that, and I've come to a decision during my more lucid moments. It's not a huge revelation or anything, just a facet I hadn't considered until I had so much time on my hands.

I'm letting Nick go.

I believe him when he says my inability to have children won't affect his love for me. He's too good of a man to let that sway his feelings. But he will blame himself for Butch shooting me for the rest of our lives. Every time he looks at me, he'll see what he deems as his failure to protect me. When Karen's belly starts protruding, he'll be consumed with guilt over not being able to give me the same. Guilt, because he thinks he neglected to do his job, even though reading Butch's mind was never in his job description.

I've argued all the points in my mind, wavering between breaking up and breaking down, but the dilemma always ends with the same solution. Now to tell him I don't want to see him anymore, so he doesn't spend another moment of his life waiting for me. This is not a conversation I'm looking forward to having, and I'm sure he'll blame the medications as he refuses to accept my decision. Eventually, he'll understand this is what's best for both of us.

Maybe, eventually, I'll convince myself of that too.

When he shows up for the evening visitation, I know with one glance he's had no rest. He looks worse than I do...or at least than I think I look. Having no mirror in this room is both a curse and a blessing.

He picks up my hand and kisses the back of it before holding it to his cheek and closing his eyes, reveling in our connection.

The stubble of his beard prickles my skin, reminding me of the intimate times we've shared. My fingers develop a mind of their own, turning to stroke his skin and lightly scratch his beard. My heart is already breaking inside my chest, just thinking about telling him goodbye.

"Nick." My voice cracks on his name, and his eyes fly open. "Sit down. There's something I need to say."

"No. No fucking way. You're not doing this to me, Savannah. I love you, and you're not pushing me away from you now. I'm not the type of man who tucks tail and runs at the first sign of trouble. This is important to you, and I respect that, but it's only a bump in the road to me. Nothing we can't work out and move past. I'm not running or walking away from you. Ever."

"Nick, I need you to listen. It's hard for me to talk."

"Good. Then shut your mouth and let me just be here with you. I'll do all the talking, and you can just rest your jaws. I've already told you, whether or not you can have a baby doesn't matter to me. You matter to me, and no one else will ever take your place in my heart. Now, if you want me to live the rest of my life alone, without anyone to love because you took my heart with you when you left me, that's up to you."

"You know, my mother tried to guilt-trip me my entire life. Really doesn't work on me now that I'm grown. Please listen to me."

"Go ahead and say it. My answer won't change, but I'll listen to you anyway."

"I need you to leave and never come back, Nick. I love everything about you. You're truly the best man I know. Because of that, you shouldn't have to spend the rest of your life feeling guilty for something that wasn't your fault. Every time you look at me, or see a baby, or anything related to children, that's exactly where your mind will go. Then I'll see that disturbed expression and know it's because of me. We'll never fully be happy together with this between us. I love you too much not to want to see you happy. This is how we're both hardwired, so there's no blame."

He stares hard at me, his brain working overtime to process everything I've said and play it out in his mind. "Darlin', please don't do this. I love you."

He can't deny the truth of the matter. Every ounce of pain, regret, and acknowledgment shows in his features. The despondent look in his eyes. The gloomy expression on his face. The downward turn of his mouth.

"I know you do… I love you too. And it's because of that love that I have no choice *but* to do this. You have to go, Nick, and don't come back. Move on with your life knowing that I want you to be happy and I want the very best for you. More than anything, that's my hope for you." My heart disintegrates inside me when I untangle my hand from his.

He straightens his spine and pulls the mask back over his face. "Savannah Fields, I refuse to let you push me away or cut me out of your life because you have some crazy idea that I could ever be happy without you. You are my happiness. Without you, there's no reason for me to even try. I'm going to go now because you need to rest and recuperate, but I'm leaving you with these words to mull over."

I raise my eyebrows in question, unable to formulate and verbalize the question in my mind to ask what he means.

"There's nothing we can't get through together. You've been my rock since day one, before I even realized it. You saved me when I wasn't able to save myself. Now, let me be your rock. When you feel like everything is at its worst, think about how much I love you. That's one thing you'll never question or doubt."

My words…used against me in the worst way possible—because I believe he means it. I watch him walk away, shoulders hunched and sadness permeating every part of his being. Knowing I caused him more pain than anyone else ever has kills me. Where is that pain medicine when I need it because I'm sure this broken heart will kill me before anything else can.

OVER A WEEK LATER, I'VE BEEN MOVED OUT OF THE ICU AND into the step-down unit. While my care isn't as critical, they still keep a very close watch on me. The change in my demeanor has been a sore subject lately. True to his word, Nick has stayed away, but only because that's what I asked him to do. He'd never force himself on me, though I know he still asks about me multiple times a day because Karen's phone pings constantly while she's here.

Karen knows I'm miserable without him, but she's giving me time to figure that out on my own. The problem is I don't need time to know how much I miss him. That's not the problem. I've never questioned my feelings for him. Only our ability to slay the monster in our closet.

"You look better now that you're able to sit up a little more." Karen washes my hair in the plastic bin made specifically for bedridden patients. A real shower would feel like pure heaven right now.

"I really can't tell you how badly being unable to take care of myself sucks."

"Well, I must admit, you're making a much better patient than I would. You've already been in the hospital ten days without losing your mind."

"It's only been ten days? I was sure it was more like thirty."

She chuckles. "I'm sure it feels like it. But Dr. Jeff said you're healing faster than he thought you would. A couple more weeks in here and you'll probably be ready to go home."

A couple more weeks without Nick. Then a few more. Maybe in a few years, I'll stop counting the days since I last saw him.

Karen called my mom and sister to tell them what happened to me the first night during my surgery. The two of them were here every day during the first week—before I sent them home because there's not much they can do to help while I'm still in the hospital. Every time they knocked on my door, it made me hope it was Nick coming to see me, to convince me I was wrong, and he can be happy with me. Karen hears my gasp with the current knocking, but her only response is to arch an eyebrow at me.

"Come in," I call out.

When Miranda steps into my hospital room, I'm shocked beyond words. She never leaves the crisis center for her own safety. Even after Butch terrorized every woman and child in the place, I was told Miranda still refused to step outside the doors.

"Miranda, I'm surprised to see you. But I'm so glad you're here." I introduce Karen and Miranda, briefly explaining how I know each woman.

"I'm sorry I didn't come to see you sooner. Believe me, it's not because I didn't want to check on you. After everything that happened, I was even more afraid to leave my room than usual. Then I realized, you're the only friend I have. There's no excuse for me to let you down after all you've done for me. I also brought your cell phone. It's been going off several times a day, and it was selfish of me not to bring it to you. Other people care about you, and I'm sure they're looking for answers."

Karen finishes washing my hair, so I tell Miranda to have a seat while she dries and styles it in a messy bun. Miranda hands my phone to me, and I scroll through the messages while Karen performs her magic.

Every single message is from Nick.

I love you.

I miss you.

You're wrong, you know. Every time I look at you, all I see is happiness for the rest of my life.

You're so beautiful—even when you drool in your sleep.

Darlin', you are my life. Don't you see that?

Longer texts tell me about his days at work and his nights sitting out in the hallway, guarding my door. Butch is still at large despite a city-wide manhunt, but Nick assures me he will get his man. He tells me not to worry because he has everything under control. The messages are a daily journal of his life since I've been stuck in this hospital room, keeping me updated on everything he's doing as if we're still speaking. As if everything is completely normal.

Those butterflies take up in my chest again, making my heart flutter like crazy. When I glance up at Karen, I see a knowing smirk on her face.

Nick

Savannah just read all my texts from the last ten days. I know because the read receipt finally showed up on my phone. The three little dots dancing on my text message screen give me hope she's realized this whole breaking up with me bullshit won't work. I'm not going anywhere. If she didn't love me anymore, that would be different. I'd leave her alone to live her life. But she does love me, and we both know it. She's throwing away the best thing either of us has ever known, all for a complete misconception she's convinced herself is reality.

I won't let her toss me aside that easily. I won't let her toss *us* aside that easily. We've proved time and again we're perfect for each other. She'll have to work a little harder at convincing me she doesn't want to be in my life anymore. Karen told me Savannah didn't have her phone with her but encouraged me to keep sending my daily messages anyway, keeping her informed of every mundane detail of my day, reminding her of our deep connection that time apart can't diminish. The impact of reading one after the other all at once would be immense. I hope she's right, because I'm legit dying without talking to her every day.

It's so good to read about your days. The highlight of mine was a shampoo and hairstyle by Karen.

I stare at the message far too long, trying to read between the lines instead of just talking to her while she's in a talkative mood.

Me: *I volunteer as tribute to give you a sponge bath. You don't even have to get out of bed.*

Savannah: *Very kind of you to offer. Can you guarantee hot water and silky-smooth skin? Because you'll have to shave my legs to make good on that promise.*

Me: *Darlin', for you, I'll promise silky-smooth everything.*

Savannah: *You're not in here yet.*

She doesn't have to tell me twice. I'm running down the hospital corridor before I've even finished reading the message. When I burst through the door, Karen is putting away her hairbrushes and shampoo, Miranda is kicked back in the visitor's chair, and Savannah is in her bed with a beautiful smile on her face.

"Miranda, let's go grab some coffee and give them some privacy." Karen winks at me as she and Miranda leave the room.

"Karen told me you've been here every morning, every lunch break, and every night. Nick, you know that's not healthy. You have to go home and rest." Savannah looks every bit as beautiful as she did the first day I met her.

"You don't have to worry about me. I get enough rest. I come here every day in case you need me. Or in case you decide you want me again."

"Nick." She breathes my name. "I've never not wanted you."

"Then what are you doing, Savannah? We're meant to be together. No matter what, we'll work through any issues together. We're stronger together than we could ever be apart. And being apart is killing me."

"And the other thing? The whole never forgiving yourself for what you can't control?"

"I've given that a lot of thought over the last ten days. Honestly, I can see why you'd think I'd react that way. Everything you've known about me has been duty, honor, and keeping my word. And that's exactly why you should believe me when I say, I could never look at you and feel hurt, disappointed, or as if anything is lacking in my life. Would kids be nice? Sure. But winning the lottery and buying that private island just for the two of us would too. As long as we're together, I don't need anything or anyone else to make me happy. Do I want to give you the world? You bet your fine ass, I do. But I want to give you all my love first and foremost. Without your love, nothing else matters."

Tears fall from her eyes onto her cheeks, but this time, they're tears of joy instead of pain. They're tears of relief instead of burden. They're tears of love instead of goodbye. She holds out her arms, and I rush into them, holding her close to me without jarring her still-recovering body too much. She squeezes me as hard as she can, burying her face in my chest and releasing all the pent-up tension she's held on to alone.

When she calms down, she gingerly moves over in the bed, giving me room to settle in beside her.

"If you're going to sleep at the hospital, the least you can do is sleep with me. You know I sleep better with you by my side."

"That's the best offer I've had in eleven whole days."

"One day longer than we've been apart, huh?"

We both chuckle and settle back into our relationship as if nothing happened. Because it really didn't. She had a moment of doubt and needed to let it play out naturally. When her theory lost steam, she knew there was no other option but for us to be together.

"Thank you for not giving up on me. I was in a really dark and heavily medicated place that day. Karen had a long talk with me today while doing my hair and helped me see the error of my ways."

"Hmm. I guess I owe Karen the best damn baby shower ever thrown, then. We're talking parade-sized balloons, tons of confetti, and a full jazz band. Whatever she wants."

"She wants us to be happy, and she convinced me of how miserable I've been without you and how stupid my decision was. Mostly, she helped me to realize I pushed you away before you had a chance to push me away, and that wasn't fair to either of us since neither of us actually wants that."

"She's a very smart woman. I'm glad you listened to her. This isn't something I'm proud of, per se, but my next option was to kidnap you and keep you chained to my bed until you relented. Although, I still say that plan has merit."

"See, this is part of why I love you. You make me laugh even when it hurts."

After I give her a very thorough bed bath, her dinner arrives and I help feed her, despite her protests she can manage that task on her own. I know she can—but it feels good to be here with her again. And I know I'll have to leave her in a few minutes for a previous engagement.

"I'll be back later tonight. There's something I have to go take care of right now. Is that offer to sleep with you still good?"

"That's a standing offer, Nick. You're welcome in my bed anytime."

With a thorough kiss goodbye, and a thousand-pound weight lifted from my chest, I reluctantly leave her side. There's only one person who could pry me away from her, and I have a bullet with his name on it. Butch slithered out of his hiding place long enough to be spotted, so now I'm holding my own venomous snake roundup.

There are a few lights on inside the dilapidated house in Washington Highlands when I drive by, but I keep going until I'm a couple of blocks away. The sun has already set, and the dark of night is quickly falling, giving me inherent cover when moving between the houses. Some are vacant, long ago abandoned and never claimed by new residents. The working streetlights are spotty at best. Most have been shot out or shattered by rocks. The cold has driven most people inside, huddled around open fires to try to keep warm.

Tonight, the cold doesn't bother me. The ice in my veins has numbed me to the chill in the air.

I held Savannah in my arms as she lay dying in that parking lot. More of her blood soaked into the asphalt than ran in her veins. Time was not on her side, and had we not been so close to a hospital, she would've died in the ambulance on the way. Part of me did die that day when I thought I'd lose her. The pallor of her skin matched the coolness when I held her, begging her not to leave me. In that moment, I realized I can cross that fine line between right and wrong. For her, I will cross every line, break every rule, and annihilate every man who tries to take her from me.

Tonight, one man still poses a direct threat, and he'll pay for his crimes. All of them. Tonight, I'm the judge, jury, and executioner all rolled into one. If his friends get in the way, it'll be their own fault when they're little more than collateral damage. Moving through the shadows toward the back door of the rundown shack, I listen to every sound and watch every shadow. He will not escape my wrath one more day.

The lack of shades or curtains on the back window gives me a perfect line of sight into the house. Five men, two women, and Butch are camped out in the main room. Worn-out mattresses are scattered across the floor, and beer cans litter the walkways. A metal barrel sits in the middle of the room with an open fire still burning inside. A shed at the rear property line catches my eye, no doubt where they hid their motorcycles to avoid being spotted in this neighborhood.

A quick look in the shed reveals all six motorcycles are

stuffed inside. The red plastic gasoline can gives me an idea of how to evacuate the house in one fell swoop. Once the gas can is empty and the motorcycles are drenched, I strike a match I pilfered from the shed and toss it into the middle of the room. The fumes catch up in a roaring blaze instantly, so I retreat to the side of the house to enjoy the show. One thing a motorhead loves is his ride, and these guys have no other possessions to their names. When they hit the back steps, they'll be frantic to reach their bikes.

Loud, agitated shouts carry on the night air as the occupants of the house empty into the backyard. At first, they try to bat the flames away to get through the door to their bikes. Then, one of the geniuses decides to grab the water hose instead. While they're busy fighting with the frozen-solid hose and with each other, I steal into the house and kick the barrel over, the fire and hot coals spreading across the floor and bedding. The old wooden house is basically one big pile of kindling, ready to disintegrate into ashes with a single spark. I exit out the front door, leaving it standing wide open to ensure the fire has plenty of fresh oxygen and whipping winds to feed it.

"What the fuck is going on?" one of the men shouts when he looks over his shoulder and finds his hideout nearly fully ablaze.

The fire in the shed heats the motorcycles' gas tanks to the tipping point, causing one after the other to explode. Pieces of metal and rubber and unidentifiable parts land haphazardly in the yard. I smile, pleased with the devastation they feel, but I'm done with the tit for tat games. This ends tonight, and it ends on my terms.

Stepping out of the shadows with my gun drawn, suppressor in place and arm extended, I realize what Shadow and Silas have tried to tell me over the years is true. While CIA officers work under much different rules than the rest of us, sometimes their methods are necessary. Sometimes their course of action is the best way in the long run. When Savannah no longer has to look over her shoulder, waiting for some low-life asshole to take his revenge, every move I've made tonight will be worth it.

The shock of seeing me registers on Butch's face first before morphing into anger. Then he realizes I have no intentions of arresting him. I have no plans of taking him anywhere. This is it for him. The murderous rage written on my face tells him more than words ever could. He opens his mouth to spew his vitriol at me, and I pull the trigger, hitting him square in the chest.

He falls to the ground with raucous screams, grabbing his wound and writhing in pain. I take a step closer and fire again, hitting him in the head and silencing him forever. The other five men decide to rush me at once, thinking they can overtake me before I pick them off one by one. But they're wrong. Dead wrong.

The two women huddle together, crying loudly and begging for their lives.

"Go. If you say a word to anyone, I'll hunt you down, and no one will ever find your bodies."

They run off into the night. Where, I don't know, nor do I care. By the time they sober up from all the drugs I just burned up inside the house, they probably won't even remember where they were.

"I'm impressed." Silas steps out of the shadows, catching me off guard.

"Fuck, man. I could've shot you just now!"

"No, you couldn't. You didn't even know I was standing here watching your entire show. Sloppy, Nick. That kind of shit will get you killed. But if you're looking for a new job once the trial is over, I may know an agency that's hiring someone with your skills and brass cojones."

"I'm definitely interested. Let's talk more—somewhere away from here before we're both caught at the scene of the crime."

Silas lifts his cell to his ear and smiles. "I need a cleanup and containment crew immediately." He gives the address of our current location and a description of the two women I just let flee from the scene. My eyebrows draw down, and I tilt my head to the side, silently questioning his motives. Surely, he didn't just order an agency-sanctioned hit on those two women.

"What? We leave no witnesses, Nick. Ever. Better get used to change, buddy." He claps me on the shoulder, understanding the conflict I'm fighting inside me. "Those women were running to more bikers a few blocks over. You know better than anyone, the sheep are loyal to their masters. These men are dead, and that house will be nothing but rubble in a matter of minutes. They're already looking for new guys to replace the dead ones because they have no one else. Go back to the hospital, lie down next to Savannah, then tell me if you'd change one single thing about tonight. If not, you know you're ready, and I'll help you out. If your conscience still bothers you because you didn't make the world a safer place exactly by the book, maybe you should stay with the DEA."

His words circle in my thoughts on the drive back to the hospital. Everything has always been black and white for me. There were no shades of gray in between. There were no alternate lines in the sand. It was this or that. Period. Now, there's an entire rainbow of colors separating the line between right and wrong. That fine line just became a great divide, and I'm not sure how to jump across it.

I leave Silas to direct the cleanup crew and head back to where I'm needed most. When I step into the hospital room and find Savannah sleeping soundly with the first happy expression on her face since all this bullshit started, I feel a sense of peace envelop me like never before. That's when I know that Silas was right, and there's no going back for me now. Once the trial is over, I'll tender my resignation to the DEA and join him at the CIA. Though it means more international travel and visiting dangerous places, I won't be recognized in those circles.

Changing my appearance will mean more than unkempt hair and a scraggly beard to hide my face.

She stirs when I slide into bed beside her, her eyes flittering open to make sure it's actually me. Her eyes close again automatically, but she's smiling, safe and secure in my embrace. We have a long road ahead of us, months until she's fully recovered and back to her usual self. But those months will be filled with love and laughter and the discovery of a whole new world, one we've never known before.

One I only want to experience and explore with her. With my head back against the pillow and my love at my side, I slip into the most peaceful sleep I've had in the last couple of weeks. The events of the night are not even an afterthought now—because she's safe and because she's mine.

"I'm glad you came back, Nick. I was afraid you'd get busy and wouldn't make it back tonight. You have no idea how much I've missed you."

"Darlin', I think I have a pretty good idea, if it's anywhere close to how much I've missed you. I thought I was going to lose you forever in that parking lot. Holding you while telling you to keep fighting will always be the worst memory I have. But holding you while telling you how much I love you will always be my favorite. Never leave me again, Savannah. I'm a strong man, but losing you is one thing I can't handle."

"You don't have to worry about that, Nick. You'll never get rid of me now. I'm afraid you're stuck with me for life." Her voice is sleepy, and her words are meant partly in jest, but I'm completely serious.

"Savannah?"

"Hmm?"

"Marry me," I whisper against her head.

"Okay," she whispers back.

CHAPTER 21

Savannah—Three Months Later

"*P*ut that box down! Are you crazy?" Nick grabs the box from my hands and gives me an irritated look. It doesn't work, but he gets an A for effort.

"Nick, I'm completely healed now, and this is a box of scarves. It doesn't even weigh as much as my purse does."

"Please go pack up your kitchen items so I can move you out of this condo before you change your mind." He leans over and kisses me for the hundredth time. Maybe I'll keep picking up light boxes until he becomes more distracted.

"I can read your mind. Go pack your shit, right now."

Anyone listening would take that as a threat, but I know my sweetheart of a man, and that simply shows how much he wants me to move in with him. Permanently. I'm as giddy about this move as he is; we've just been waiting for the right time after my stint in the hospital. Now that I'm completely—and finally—healed from all my injuries, I can't wait to start my new life with the man of my dreams.

In our new home—a real house in the suburbs, where there's

plenty of bright sunshine, cherry trees in bloom, and spacious yards with beautiful green grass. We chose Arlington, Virginia as our new spot to put down roots. It's just outside the craziness of DC, but it still is every bit as vibrant and upbeat as Adams Morgan.

Nick sold his brownstone almost as soon as he put it on the market. He, Roman, and Silas talked to my superintendent about letting me out of my lease early. With all the security upgrades they made to my place, the building management isn't losing any money by letting me out of my lease early. Plus, the super is really afraid of these three hulking men, especially when they all crowd into his office at once, so he didn't put up much of a fight.

As I'm in the kitchen throwing pots and pans into a moving box, doing as I'm told, my cell phone rings. One glance at the screen and a smile crosses my face. "Hey, Miranda. How are you?"

"Hi, Savannah. I'm fine, thank you. I need to ask you for a favor, and I feel like a terrible friend for even asking."

"What do you need, hon?"

"I was wondering if you could come by the center to talk with me? I have an idea I want to run by you, but it's not the kind of thing we can talk about over the phone. It's about a way I really think I can help you, after everything you've done for me. But I know this is probably the last place you want to see right now, so I feel terrible even asking. Believe me, I wouldn't if this wasn't important."

She's right; I haven't returned to the shelter since the ambulance carried me away that awful day, and I haven't wanted to even one time. The sights and sounds of that day are never far from my mind. As happy as Nick makes me, the nightmares threaten to return every night. There's one nightmare that will never return, that much I'm sure of. Though I don't know the details of what happened, and I'm probably better off that way,

Nick assured me I never have to worry about running into Butch again.

That's all I need to know.

I'm learning techniques to keep the monsters at bay on my own because I can't always rely on Nick to save the day. Or night. Whatever. Finding my own strength and standing on my own two feet are important to me, even if it takes time to overcome the demons when I close my eyes.

But Miranda's voice is so hopeful, while simultaneously being cautious. She doesn't want to get her hopes up in case I decline her request. But at the same time, whatever it is she wants to discuss is important to her.

"Do you mind if Nick comes with me?"

"No, I don't mind at all. Actually, that would be perfect. Please? I'm sorry to ask—I know it's really very selfish of me, considering I have such a hard time leaving here, so I should understand why you'd have a hard time coming back."

"No, it's fine. I understand why you're concerned about leaving. You don't know where your ex is or where you could run into him. We're packing right now, but we can come later this evening. Is that okay?"

"Perfect. Thank you so much."

We chat for a few more minutes until Nick stands in the kitchen doorway, staring at me like I've grown an extra head, then Miranda and I disconnect. I smile up at him from my spot on the floor, and he simply shakes his head at me. "Do you plan on finishing this room anytime today?"

"It's on my to-do list."

"You're definitely feeling better. Getting all sassy and feisty. I love it."

"Good, because you're only going to get more and more of it."

"I'll take it all, darlin'. Every bit you have to offer."

"Hey, I have some potentially upsetting plans for us this evening."

"Okay. What's up?"

I relay the call with Miranda and her request for us to come talk with her. A dark shadow passes over his face, the memory of that day nearly three months ago still fresh in his mind too. "She wouldn't ask for no reason, Nick. Whatever she has to say, she really wants to talk to us about it. I'm okay with going back there as long as you're with me. Are you okay with it?"

"As long as you're by my side at all times, yes."

"I'll go too. You two may need backup," Silas says as he passes by with another taped box.

"Perfect. We're both safe since Silas has our back. So, we're good to go, right?" I stand and wrap my arms around Nick's waist, push up on my toes, and press a long kiss to his lips.

"You know, this kind of distraction works on me a little too well. How can I say no to you when you ask me like that?" His arms encircle my waist, and his mouth covers mine. The panty-melting kiss he lays on me is hot enough to make me spontaneously combust.

And he thinks I hold the magic power over him. No way that's an accurate assumption.

"We're never going to get Savannah moved out of here if you two keep taking kissing breaks." Silas walks back by again, heading to grab another box.

"Okay, now I feel guilty. Let's get back to work. Our friends are doing all the hard labor." With one last kiss, I start taking my plates down from the cabinets and wrapping them in paper.

Before I know it, we've finished packing and carrying all my boxes down to the moving truck. Well, I watched Nick, Silas, and Roman carry the boxes down, but telling them where to put them in the back of the truck was a full-time job in itself.

Roman offers to drive the truck to our new home so we don't

have to make an extra trip back into DC to visit Miranda at the shelter. We found a great deal on a three-bedroom home in a nice neighborhood. It's close enough to drive back into the city for work, but far enough away that we don't miss the craziness of the congested traffic at other times. There's a mother-in-law apartment over the detached garage that would be perfect as an office.

When I was first able to sit up after surgery, Karen brought my laptop to the hospital so I could continue working on my book. Since I've been off on medical leave, I've finished writing my story and found a talented editor to help make me sound halfway decent. I'm excited to see what the future holds when I release this self-help book. If just one woman saves herself and walks away from an abusive relationship after reading my story, it'll have been worth the time and effort.

After two more weeks, I'll finally be headed back to my job as a nurse, too. I've traded the night shift for days, though. Karen also moved to the day shift since it's easier on her both while she's pregnant and after the baby is born. I'm thrilled we'll still work together, and the added bonus is I'll be home with Nick every night.

"So, Undercover Lover, are you glad the trial bullshit is over?" Silas asks from the back seat.

"Absolutely. Having my entire life splashed across every news outlet on TV and the internet got old really fast. Thank God for Axle, huh? He showed up with all that video footage of Bobby Blalock ordering hits and shit, and all of a sudden, the lawyers were clamoring for deals. Hey, that reminds me, how'd you get my picture scrubbed from everywhere so fast?" Nick glances at Silas in the rearview mirror.

"Ah, you know, the delete key works wonders. You should try it sometime." Silas hedges, refusing to give us a straight answer.

"I will, as soon as you get me in at The Farm."

"You'll hear from them anytime now. Actually, you and

Roman both will. I've proposed a three-man team of CIA officers for special operations, working in conjunction with the NSA. Good news is we'll be stateside most of the time. An occasional trip here or there, but no long stints or moving to foreign field offices in our future. They're reviewing your files and background information now, but they'll contact you soon."

"Sounds like a great opportunity. Let's get started."

Nick's enthusiasm is contagious—and magnificent to hear. He's changed so much from the man I first met. He's still the best man I know, but now he's also the happiest. The changes we've made in our lives and in each other's is nothing short of fate. He's my soul mate, regardless of what obstacles have been thrown in front of us.

We walk into the center hand in hand, with Silas covering our backs for good measure. Terrifying memories try to halt my forward motion, but Nick's hand on my lower back reminds me of how far we've come in a short time. There's no going backward now, and no letting old ghosts ruin the good thing we've found.

Miranda meets us just inside the door, throws her arms around my neck, and bounces up and down. She's virtually giddy with excitement and eagerness, though I don't have a clue why yet.

"Miranda, this is Silas Steele. Silas, this is my friend, Miranda Petrovio."

"Hello, Silas." Miranda extends her hand to Silas. When I look up at him, he has an odd expression on his face as he studies Miranda.

"Hi, Miranda. Have we met before? You look very familiar."

"Um, no, I don't think so. But I hear that a lot. I always say I have a very common face. Maybe you just remember me from that awful day. I was here in the middle of everything." She laughs nervously and turns her head away, extending her hand to an empty table in the common room. "Let's have a seat."

"I'll wait over here by the door, just to be on the safe side. Yell if you need me. Nice to meet you, Miranda." Silas walks backward, keeping his eyes trained on us.

Odd.

"It's nice to meet you too, Silas." Miranda takes the seat with her back to Silas, which I notice immediately.

As paranoid as she usually is, she would never sit with her back to the door anytime I volunteered here. In fact, she was adamant about having her back to the wall so she could keep her eyes on the door at all times. My initial thought is she's uncomfortable with Silas's probing stare, and I quickly dismiss my uncertainty as paranoia from coming back here. Besides, Silas can be rather unnerving at times to anyone who doesn't know him. I chalk it up to the CIA officer ingrained in him.

Miranda leans forward, a wide smile covering her face, and grasps my hands in hers. "Thank you so much for coming. Hear me out before you say anything, please, because I know how crazy this is going to sound. But you've been such a good friend to me when I had no one, and if there's something I can do to help you, then I want to do it. You've helped me, talked to me, and trusted me to help you. I've literally had no one else for so long, but you've made me feel like part of your life. There's a way I can help you both with something you want more than anything. I want to offer to do this, because I know you'd never ask it of me."

"What are you talking about? Tell me!" I'm getting excited just listening to her enthusiasm.

"When you were in the hospital, I saw how deeply depressed you were over not being able to have a baby. But I realized it's more than that—it's who you are. You love, you take care of others, you give your whole heart, and it's a beautiful thing. I want to help give that opportunity back to you, Savannah. I'd love to carry your baby for you so you two lovebirds can be parents. You don't deserve what that monster did to you. You shouldn't have to pay for his sins for the rest of your life."

She stops talking, but I can't find my voice or even a coherent thought to attempt to muddle through. I stare at her in disbelief, positive I've misunderstood her intentions. Nick seems to be under the same mute spell because he's sitting beside me, motionless and slack-jawed.

"Let me try to explain further. I'd be a gestational carrier only—not a surrogate mother. Your egg will be fertilized by Nick then implanted into me, so the baby will be one hundred percent yours and Nick's. I would literally only be an incubator for your embryo until the delivery, but this way, you can still have your own baby. Do you understand what I'm suggesting?"

I'm shocked beyond words. How do I respond to an offer like this? How can I say yes, but then again, how can I say no to a baby that would be wholly Nick's and mine?

"Miranda, we—"

"Yes. The answer is yes, we would love that." Nick cuts me off before I can reject such a generous offer. My head jerks toward him, and any question I have in my mind clears when I look at his handsome face. "This is what you want, darlin'. This is why I almost lost you—because you were afraid of what I'd constantly think about not having children of our own. That's not what I think about at all, though, babe. But I know how important this is to you, and she's offering the opportunity of a lifetime. I think we should take it and enjoy every minute of the journey."

"Listen to him, Savannah. He understands. This is the best way I know how to thank you for all your kindness. I want to do this for you. You're the only friend I have left in the world."

With pure joy bubbling up inside my chest, I fly out of my seat and around the table to hug Miranda. Once I wrap my arms around her, I can't force myself to let her go. This amazing gift she's offering gives me more hope than I've had in this area of my life in years, even if nothing goes right in the process. I've never felt whole, thinking I was unable to conceive all those years, even though my logical side chided my emotional side for even entertaining that notion.

"I have one condition," I state when I finally release her. "Nick, do you mind if she moves in to the apartment above the garage while she's pregnant? I want to have her as close as possible during the pregnancy. Just in case she needs help or protection or ice cream."

"That's a great idea, darlin'. We would be right there to help you, Miranda. We'll help take care of you and protect you, but you'd still have your own private space. More so than here. And I'd feel better knowing Savannah would have a friend there when I'm away for work. Plus, your ex would have no idea to look for you in Arlington. I think we'd all feel better with you living close by. What do you say, Miranda?"

"Oh my gosh—I can't believe you'd want me to live there with you. If you're sure I won't be in the way, then yes, I'd love to. After the baby's born, I'll find a job and get my own place, I promise. I won't overstay my welcome."

"We'll worry about that when the time comes." Miranda and I giggle together like two adolescent school girls making plans for a sleepover party.

I'm overwhelmed with hope because of the mere possibility she's offering us. After all these years, after the deep depression and dark hole I found myself in after my hysterectomy, I can see a light at the end of the tunnel. And it feels a lot like a dream coming true.

CHAPTER 22

Nick

I've never known Silas to be so transparent before. The way he watches Miranda is uncharacteristically obvious for him and goes against everything in his training. He observes and handles people for a living, yet he's giving away the home field advantage when it comes to his interest in Miranda and who she is.

When he asked if they'd ever met, I almost choked on the very air I'd inhaled. This is a man who doesn't forget a face and is a master of disguise. He knows damn well if he has met her before. My guess is he'd know the date, time of day, and circumstances surrounding the meeting without a hitch. And it's much more than seeing her face when he was my backup when we faced down Butch and his demon buddy. His tone was certain, and he was testing her honesty.

But then he backed off. And I mean he backed all the way to the door, like a sentinel standing guard. If she were a threat to us, he wouldn't have budged, and he would've called her on it immediately. Still, there's a story to be told there, and my gut tells me we'll be hot on that case soon enough. Makes me wonder if she's why he volunteered to join us for the meeting at the center.

That's one reason why I jumped at the opportunity she so readily offered before Savannah could turn her down. If her offer is bona fide, I'm all for giving Savannah a baby right now. Tomorrow, if I could. If her offer is a ruse, I'm all for exposing her treachery as soon as possible. Either way, Savannah's suggestion of having Miranda move in to the apartment over our garage was perfectly timed and expertly played, even though she doesn't realize it.

Keep friends close and enemies closer mentality.

One thing I know for sure, Savannah is overjoyed with the idea. Miranda had better not be playing on my girl's emotions, only to use her for some bullshit scheme. Her disappointment would be unbearable. My anger would be unmanageable. My plan is to take it one day at a time and watch Miranda like a hawk in the event I need to step in and knock heads around.

On the ride home, Savannah can't stop talking about Miranda's generosity and how incredible she is to give us such a wonderful gift. Her faith in humanity is beautiful and balances my constant suspicion of everyone in the world. We're complete opposite ends of the spectrum, but the way we complement each other just works for us. In this case, her excitement seeps into me, making me hope for the best despite my wariness.

The Special Agent in me says to prepare for the worst-case scenario, though.

Savannah researches gestational surrogacy and in vitro insemination protocols on her phone and relays the information she finds. The procedures. The time frames. The number of eggs they implant at one time. The odds of having multiple babies if more than one embryo is implanted. The odds of the fertilized eggs not taking. Through all of her chatter, Silas is silent in the back seat, never weighing in one way or another.

"What's on your mind, Silas?" I get straight to the point. I'd rather have all our cards on the table.

"A trip I have to take that just popped up. I'll probably be out on a flight first thing in the morning, but I'll be back before you're even settled into your first training class at The Farm, though."

"Where are you headed?" I raise my eyes up to the rearview mirror, meeting Silas's stoic gaze, while knowing his reply will probably create more questions than answers for me.

"Moscow."

Fuck me running. That is the last place I would've expected him to say. This just became much more complicated than I originally thought.

The sinking feeling in my gut warns me this will not end well.

"You'll let me know if plans change?" Savannah is still busy on her phone, not paying much attention to us, but Silas understands my question perfectly.

"Absolutely. As soon as I know for sure, you'll be the first to know."

Roman is already at the house with the moving truck and has carried in all the boxes, saving us a lot of time. The three of us start moving the furniture into place while Savannah begins unpacking the boxes and identifying where she'll hang the wall decorations. By the time we finish unloading the truck and getting everything in place, it's late and we're all more than ready to crash.

While Savannah is busy in another room, I catch Silas alone. "Just before Savannah was shot, we started walking home one evening from a rooftop bar in Adams Morgan. Two guys were tailing us, a little too obvious to be one of ours. At the time, I thought maybe it had something to do with the case and the trial, but now I'm not so sure. What do you think?"

"What did they look like?"

"Extremely average—from their features to their build. Nothing remarkable about them. Except their very angry expressions when we jumped into a passing cab and sped off in the opposite direction."

Silas nods, his expression giving nothing away, as usual. "I don't think they had anything to do with the case or the trial. But I'll find out more as soon as I can. If they posed a threat to you, you wouldn't still be here three months later. You haven't seen them again since then?"

"No, and I haven't seen a new tail replace them either."

"Good. They were probably reprimanded for being spotted and losing you, so the teams have been pulled back to give you some space. I'll find out more as soon as possible. Keep doing everything you'd normally do until I get back...then we'll talk."

After seeing Roman and Silas off with a promise of an elaborate dinner out somewhere with unlimited alcohol to repay them for all their help, Savannah and I climb into our shared bed in our new house. She lies on her side, and I move close behind her, sliding my arm over her waist and pulling our bodies together. A small moan escapes from her lips, fully content in my arms. I get it—this is the best feeling in the world. Well, it runs a close second or third anyway. There are other feelings I can think of that are much better...in fact, at the moment, I can't seem to think of anything else but how damn good it feels to be buried inside her.

"Mmm, did you bring your gun to bed with you, or are you just happy to see me?"

"Both. I definitely brought my gun to bed with me. Let me show you how I use it."

Sinking into her body, I lose myself in the warmth that envelops me. The noises she makes fill the room, rising on a crescendo until the exquisite tones of her desires prompt me to seek the next and the next. Everything about her is intoxicating. The way my name sounds falling from her lips. How she grips my shoulders and claws my back when the pressure inside builds. The way she shudders and shakes under my touch. Her heavy breaths from all the attention I lavish on her from head to toe. The feel of her muscles contracting and relaxing around me before her body falls limp, exhausted from our endeavors but with an expression of complete satisfaction on her beautiful face.

We lie in the soft glow of the moonlight streaming through the blinds, our bodies still entwined and each breathing heavily. Our house is now a home and holds every ounce of love we possess. What's funny is this was never the life I wanted. When I was a younger man, the adventure I sought was in faraway places and dangerous situations. The thrill of the chase and the excitement of living the escapades most people only read about was my idea of a perfect life. Single. No attachments to tie me down.

That version of life is as far away from what I want now as east is from west. Without Savannah, without what we have, I'd have no life at all. No reason to go on. As cliché as that sounds, it's the fucking honest truth. Finding her, getting to know her, and falling in love with her changed me from the inside out. I don't have to question if I'm a good man anymore. One look in her eyes is all the proof I need. She sees straight into my soul and what she finds is good enough for her. I never want to be only "good enough," though, so I keep reaching, keep striving to deserve the adoration she so easily gives me.

"You saved me, Savannah." My confession is barely a whisper in the darkness, but it's out there now.

"I think you have that backward, babe. How did I save you?"

"When I moved back to DC, I was a completely lost soul. My compass was broken, and I just wandered aimlessly between my brownstone and the coffee shop. Even though I was a good actor and I was good at keeping people at arm's length, I was nowhere near being happy. You brought all the light, love, and happiness into my life. I didn't even know this level of bliss was real. If I'm living in a fantasy world, don't ever burst my bubble. I like it here."

"I love living in this bubble with you. But it's not a fantasy, this is our life, and it only gets better from here. You've rescued me physically, you've literally saved my life—you've convinced me that heroes do exist. More than that, you've shown me that true love is real, regardless of how messy life gets or how hard it is. I know you'll never desert me, you'll never hurt me, and you'll never break my heart...because you're the best man I've ever known, Nick."

We fall asleep wrapped in each other's arms and secure in our love. Whatever happens next, happens. But we'll get through it together...good or bad.

Over the next few days, Savannah and I work to finish unpacking every box, setting up every room, and hanging every picture. When I say we, I mean me, of course, since I insist on doing all the heavy lifting. She supervises. It works. When we reach the apartment over the garage, she drags me to the furniture store and chooses a few new pieces to make it as homey as possible for Miranda. We venture over to the nursery furniture, and I watch as she fingers every item, from the crib to the rocker-glider chair to the changing table. She keeps saying if it's meant to be, it will be, but she can't hide how much she wants it to be.

"Have you thought about setting a date for our wedding yet? It may be caveman-ish of me, but I really want to see Savannah Fields changed to Savannah Tucker. Soon. How about tomorrow? Is tomorrow too soon?" I intentionally change the subject before her thoughts go too far down the baby-making path.

Her nervous laugh causes a flash of alarm to run through me. "I actually thought I dreamed you proposed to me. It was a wonderful dream."

"It definitely was not a dream. You already said yes, so you can't take it back now."

"Zero chance of that happening, my love. What about a long weekend trip to Vegas, a drive-thru wedding in a rented car, and a honeymoon where we never leave the hotel room? They have room service. We can be back before you start with the CIA Monday morning."

"Can you be more perfect for me? I'm making the reservations tonight. Nonrefundable tickets." I lean down and kiss her, but I'm not kidding about making travel plans.

"Fine with me. I'll go pack our clothes. Let's leave tomorrow when I get off work—Thursday to Sunday is a perfect short getaway."

AFTER A LONG WEEKEND OF DRIVE-THRU NUPTIALS, CHAMPAGNE and strawberries delivered to our suite, and nonstop love-making on every surface in our expansive room, we're flying back to DC as Mr. and Mrs. for the first time in my life, and the only time this will happen. Six months ago, if someone had told me that getting married would've made me the happiest man on the planet, I would've shot them in the head and put them out of their misery. Now, I'd buy them a beer and convince them to join the newlywed cult if they hadn't already.

When we pull into the garage back at our home, we sit in silence inside the truck, holding hands and staring at our wedding bands. The diamond will come, we'll pick it out together, but the forever bands on our ring fingers hold the most meaning to me. "Mrs. Tucker, are you ready to be carried across the threshold and start the rest of our lives together in our own home?"

"Absolutely, Mr. Tucker. I love you...so much."

After getting her out of the truck, I carry her across the

threshold and straight up to our bedroom. We have a few hours left before I have to report to The Farm for training. Thanks to my previous experience, I don't have to live there like some of the recruits do. I'll be home most every night and weekends, but some of the spy boot camp sessions will require more of my time than others. With our combined work schedules, we're flexible enough to work around the time apart.

Speaking of flexible, the gorgeous redhead beckoning me with her big emerald-green eyes is very bendy and flexible, and I'm one lucky son of a bitch to have landed her. She straddles my waist, lowering herself on me until she's fully seated, taking all of me. She begins to move, throwing her head back in ecstasy and releasing the sexiest fucking moans I've ever heard. Like a jigsaw puzzle that's been completed at last, being joined as one with the only woman I've ever honestly loved feels as if the missing piece of the puzzle inside me found its mate.

My soul mate.

Before I drift off to sleep, exhausted from the long day and nighttime acrobatics, my phone chimes with a text. I pick it up and glance at the screen, releasing a sigh of relief over the message from Silas.

Okay to move forward with your plans, but there's much more to the story than we thought. I'll fill you in when I get home. See you tomorrow.

Savannah

The past few months have been nonstop running from one place to another for both Nick and me. After our whirlwind weekend in Vegas, Nick started his new job, and the grueling training schedule has kept him super busy. Miranda didn't have many possessions at the shelter, so she and I were able to move everything without help. She was thrilled to have more than a single room at a crowded shelter. The privacy and proximity afforded by her new home brought her to tears—happy tears. Karen has been over several times, looking as if she is ready to pop at any time, but she's as invested in Miranda as I am. I've enjoyed having another friend nearby as much as Miranda has enjoyed getting to know Karen.

Nick comes home most every night, but sometimes it's very late and he's completely exhausted. However, his schedule hasn't stopped him from making time to help ensure the entire in vitro fertilization process flowed smoothly. The first few appointments were for Miranda and me—medication to synchronize our ovulation cycles to prime my body for the extraction. Medication for her so her body can prepare to accept the embryo. Then the trigger shot for me—the last step before they collect my eggs.

Nick and I talked at length about how many embryos we'd want implanted, then sat down together to share our decision with Miranda. Since she'd be the one impacted the most, we wanted to make sure she was on board with us and understood what she faced. I shouldn't have been worried about her reaction, but I couldn't just assume she'd be fine with whatever we decided to do with her body.

Turns out, she was fine with whatever we wanted to do with her body.

We assured her that two implanted embryos were enough for us. If they both take, we'd get two for the price of one, considering we may never have the opportunity for such an amazing gestational surrogate again. If only one embryo implanted, we'd be equally as thrilled and consider ourselves blessed to have a baby at all.

After all the buildup—watching the calendar, going to doctor appointments, getting shots, taking medication, having the egg retrieval performed, and fertilizing the eggs in a laboratory then having them transferred to her uterus—we were finally ready for the big day. It was time for the pregnancy test. I was so nervous and excited, I couldn't eat or sleep all weekend, waiting for the end of the fourteen days to pass. The wait was more than excruciating—it was downright cruel and unusual punishment. The entire process was mentally grueling.

And it all came down to one little test and a positive or negative sign.

While Miranda took the test into the bathroom with her, I slipped into Nick's lap, wrapped my arm around his neck, and laid my head on his shoulder. He smelled so good, the combination of sandalwood and coffee reminding me of the first day we met. Believe it or not, that memory calmed my racing heart. I remembered how I felt, looking up into his eyes when he knocked Butch on his ass. Nick was my hero that day, and he's still my hero today. He was my rock that day, and he's still my rock today. No matter what Miranda's pee showed, we would still have each other, and that was all that mattered.

A few minutes later, Miranda emerged from the bathroom with the stick in her hand. Her eyes were downcast and her feet moved slowly toward me. The doctor warned us several times that the embryos might not attach the first time. That's why they take plenty of eggs and freeze the embryos that are not implanted right away. If she was willing, I reasoned we could always try it again after another cycle of medication and clinic visits.

She handed the positive pregnancy test stick to me and grinned from ear to ear. "Congratulations, Savannah. We're pregnant!"

At first, I was completely speechless. I had prepared to be let down after the first try, knowing many people have to try more than once before an embryo attaches. But I sat there holding my breath and pinching myself, waiting to wake up from a wonderful dream. Nick squeezed me, wrapping both arms around me and burying his face against my neck. He kissed the delicate skin there, moving up to my jawline, across my cheek, and finally capturing my lips. His soft, lingering touch brought me out of my trance. He pulled his head back, looked into my eyes, and smiled warmly at me.

"We're having a baby, darlin'."

With screams and shouts loud enough to alert the entire neighborhood, I jumped up from Nick's lap and danced around in excitement. Then I grabbed Miranda and hugged her, so very thankful for this incredible gift she's given us.

That was six weeks ago. It's now June, the beginning of summer, and we're preparing for an ultrasound to confirm the embryo is developing and thriving. This has been another excruciating wait. Are we having one or two babies? Does it even matter? We're having a baby! Another concern I've pushed to the back of my mind is the frequency of miscarriages after IVF. But Miranda has been great about my overprotectiveness and checking on her multiple times a day, even between patients while I'm at work. She refers to me as her helicopter mom, but I think she secretly likes the attention.

"Miranda Petrovio family." The nurse stands in the doorway, holding it open with her hip when she calls us into the exam room.

Miranda is already in her paper gown and leaning back on the exam table. She looks relieved when we join her, and the full understanding of the enormous task she's agreed to hits me like a runaway train. She's completely alone without Nick and me. No family to help her. No one to turn to for advice or just to lend an ear and a shoulder. And now she's pregnant with a baby that's not hers, all to help someone she barely knew just a few short months ago.

Nick and I take seats beside her, and I reach over to grasp her hand. She squeezes mine in return, and I notice her visibly relax. The doctor steps into the room, and the sonogram technician readies her supplies. When they find what they're looking for, they turn the screen so all of us can see the images with them.

And there it is...

Or, I should say, there they are...

Two distinct embryonic sacs.

We're having twins.

I'm hyperventilating.

I don't think Miranda is breathing at all. Her eyes are bugging out of her head and her mouth is wide open, but I don't see her chest moving. I can't stop mine from heaving.

"Hell yeah!" Nick shouts from beside me, drawing everyone's attention and breaking the spell Miranda and I are both under.

Everyone in the room bursts out in laughter and huge smiles. At least we're breathing normally again. Congratulatory hugs are passed around freely. Miranda doesn't release me when we hug, though. Instead, she slides over a little to give me room to recline beside her. Then she looks at the technician.

"These are her babies. I'm just carrying them for her. Can you please show her again?"

"Of course. Congratulations, mamas. You should both be very proud." The technician slides the wand over Miranda's stomach again until she finds the two raspberry-sized babies. Two separate, tiny heartbeats. Two distinct pieces of Nick and me that I love instantly at first glance.

Yes, I do believe in love at first sight. Because I'm totally and completely in love with our babies right now.

"No wonder I've had so much morning sickness and been so tired lately. These two babies are already zapping my energy." Miranda laughs but keeps her eyes glued to the screen. "Savannah, I'm so happy for you. You're going to be the best mom ever."

We leave the clinic with the next appointment scheduled at the regular obstetrician's office. Miranda is doing well, and the babies seem to be thriving in her womb, so the IVF clinic's job is done. We climb into Nick's truck, and my phone starts to ring.

"Hey Karen, I should've known you'd call right about now." I love my best friend.

"Oh yeah? Is all the magic gone from our relationship? Am I that predictable?"

"Only when you want to know all the details about my baby mama." It's a running joke between us. I've told a few people at work that Miranda is pregnant with my baby and then laugh hysterically when they're unsure of how to reply.

"How is your baby doing?" Karen asks with a smile in her voice.

"My babies—plural—are doing good. Twins, Karen! We're so excited!"

"Oh, love, I'm so happy for you and Nick! That's the best news I've heard all day. Well, maybe the second-best news."

"You have other news? Tell me!"

"My water broke. Spence and I are on the way to the hospital to have this baby today!"

"Oh my God! Nick—you have to turn around and get to the hospital right now!" I realize after I scream at him that my words could be misconstrued. His horrified expression confirms my suspicion a little too late. "Sorry, Karen's in labor. We're having a baby today. Let's take Miranda home first so she can rest, then we'll go to the hospital."

"Thank you—I was going to say the nausea is a little much. I'd love to see her baby, but I'm afraid the hospital odors would completely do me in right now."

"You got it. Tell Karen we'll be there as soon as we can." Nick keeps a level head while I freak out enough for both of us. Excitement overload.

Hours later, I'm sitting beside my best friend, holding my goddaughter in my arms, and promising her I'll always be here to help take care of her. After we returned from our impromptu wedding in Vegas, Karen chastised me for not asking her to be my matron of honor but relented after I reminded her that she couldn't travel. She forgave me then asked me to be Kate's godmother. Naturally, I said yes. Holding this precious baby and showering her with love, I can't imagine how much stronger my love for my babies will be when I finally hold them in my arms.

"When you have yours, I'll be there with you, Savannah. I can't wait until that day."

"I can't either." My gaze lifts to meet Nick's, and I instantly feel his love flowing into me. "We're going to have a great family."

"You bet your sweet ass, we are." Nick winks then takes Kate from my arms.

If I could actually get pregnant, it would spontaneously occur from seeing Nick Tucker with a tiny baby girl in his arms.

TIME FLIES WHEN YOU'RE HAVING FUN, A BEST FRIEND WITH A newborn, a woman pregnant with your twin babies, and a husband in training day and night at The Farm or wherever else they decide to send him. Another holiday season has passed, and another new year has now begun, bringing promises of everything I've ever wanted. But time really doesn't care if you're ready for the upcoming changes or not. They happen regardless of the best-laid plans or whether it's under the ideal circumstances.

For us, those changes are a baby boy and a baby girl who will be delivered via a scheduled Cesarean section. Thankfully, both Miranda and the babies had an uneventful pregnancy, by medical terms. Every day was a magical event for me. The first time they moved. The first time they had the hiccups. The protruding feet and elbows just under her skin. All the major milestones that I was able to experience with her as if I experienced them myself.

When I step back inside the labor and delivery ward, I feel as if I just left here after Karen's little bundle of joy was born. That was more than half a year ago now, and this time, we're here for our own flesh and blood. A day I didn't think could happen just a short year ago, yet here I am, waiting for my twins. I'm scared and thrilled and scared some more and so damn happy, I can't keep it all inside.

Nick and I scrub in with the doctors to give Miranda all the support we can and watch the delivery of our babies. Nothing in the operating room will bother me—I've seen much worse in the emergency room. But my heart is pounding so hard, I feel light-headed. Two pediatricians are on standby to grab the twins and perform assessments the moment they emerge. They've appeared healthy all along, but the doctors' presence just makes sense under the circumstances.

Nick and I sit on either side of Miranda's head, and I slip my hand under the sterile cover to hold hers. She grips it tightly, scared and nervous about what's to come, but there's no turning back now. She turns her face toward me and whispers.

"I'm so glad you're here with me. I know there's nowhere else you'd be right now, but I'm so grateful for you, Savannah."

"I'm the grateful one, Miranda. You're giving me the greatest gifts I could ever ask for—and they're both fully Nick and me. I've never known anyone as selfless as you are. No one else would've done this for me." I lean over and kiss her forehead. She's become like a younger sister to me, especially in the time since she's been living over our garage.

Once the obstetrician begins, the entire birthing sequence seems to be over in the blink of an eye. Everyone proceeds in orchestrated movements, the entire team knowing their specific job to the point of perfection. Once the pediatricians have given the all clear for the twins, two nurses approach Nick and me, each offering us a swaddled baby. Pictures are snapped and too many tears to count are shed, but every single moment is perfectly perfect.

Once we're moved to a private room, Miranda sleeps while Nick and I enjoy quiet time with our babies, lying on the fold-out couch with Gavin and Kinsley Tucker snuggled between us. For the next eight weeks, I'll take care of Miranda along with the new loves of my life. It's the least I can do to repay her for this incredible life she's given Nick and me. Now I understand what it means to wear your heart on your sleeve, because my heart is now completely laid bare, embodied by these three perfect humans lying here with me.

In the last seven months, while Miranda rested and Nick worked countless hours, I spent my free time working on my book. Refining every word. Pouring my heart and soul into every chapter. Reliving the hell that I endured under that monster's thumb. Sharing the wholly embarrassing details of why I stayed, why I allowed the abuse, and why I didn't tell anyone. Writing that and baring my soul for the world to judge was cathartic for me, even if no one else appreciated my work. That book was for me; it signaled a major turning point in my life that I wouldn't change if I could. Everything that happened, regardless of how painful or humiliating it was at the time, brought me to where I am today. Made me the woman I am right now. Gave me the strength to stand when every cell inside me screamed to crumble into a million pieces.

When I hit publish, I rushed to the bathroom and vomited from sheer nerves.

Then I put the marketing tips I'd learned to use and started promoting my book. All 352 pages contained bits and pieces of me, and I was proud of what I'd accomplished. When I poured that energy into my campaigns, women from all walks of life snatched it up and sent it soaring up the charts. The success I realized from that one book will never outweigh the validation I received from the very women I expected to tear me apart.

Emails from all over poured in, thanking me for being brave enough to share my experiences. Many fled from the abusive relationships they'd been imprisoned in for years because they realized if I could do it, they could too. Two weeks before Gavin and Kinsley were scheduled to be born, I turned in my resignation from the ER department to write full time, working from home where my whole life exists.

My next book will be for women who can't have children of their own, and I'll share my amazing story with them. A story of hope and love and laughter and tears and amazing people along the way. Again, if I can help just one, it's worth all the blood, sweat, and tears I pour into it.

I never actually believed I'd have a happily ever after. I thought those were only meant for dreams and fairy tales, the stuff fictional books were made of. But now that I'm living a life that's better than anything I could've dreamed or hoped for, it's clear what was missing in those early days of bitter disappointment.

Nick Tucker was missing. My soul mate. My forever. There's a fine line between heaven and hell, and I know without a doubt I've crossed that line. From my torturous hell before Nick, and straight into my blissful heaven with him.

I simply couldn't ask for more than what I have right now.

I don't need locks on my heart and locks on my door anymore.

Silas—Moscow, Russia

"I'm surprised to see you. I didn't know you were coming." He narrows his eyes and stares at me suspiciously. He's a large man, formidable back in his heyday, but that was many years ago. Today, he'd sooner reach for his gun and blow a hole in my gut than spar with me. Can't say I blame him.

My Russian contact is leery of surprise visits, especially when I haven't been here in quite some time. That's what happens after living in a military-ruled country that still leans strongly to Communism and enjoys torturing citizens for information. Sure, to the rest of the world, they're now a republic. But that's just the face they wear and the front they show. Walk a mile on the wild side of Moscow then tell me that bullshit party line is real.

The KGB would haul Dmitri away right now if they thought it would gain them an inch. The cold war may have ended years ago, but there's a secret war still raging with no signs of slowing down. And they're playing for keeps, though most of the world has no idea what's going on behind the iron curtain. And that's exactly how they want it.

"If you'd known I was coming, it wouldn't have been a surprise." I purposely keep my hands visible. I mean him no harm. I'm here for answers only he can give.

"What do you want, Silas? I'm in no mood for fun and games. It's been a long day, and I'm ready to get out of here."

I walk farther into his office at the government's fortified complex in the heart of Moscow. There are cameras and voice recorders all over the building; I'm not stupid. But then, they knew I was here the second my plane touched down on the tarmac. My visit here is for unofficial business, but if it turns out to be even remotely what I suspect, the NSA and CIA will duke it out for investigating rights. Good thing I've already assembled a team of three highly skilled and able officers to handle just such an investigation.

Two of them will be starting their training next week with a significant advantage over their classmates because of their previous experience. Now they're learning the spy and asset component, the psychology behind turning a loyalist to a separatist, along with how to blend into a crowd, to become unrecognizable, to become invisible when needed. Very special skills when "sharpshooting assassin" is added to the curriculum vitae.

Glancing over his shoulder, I rest my gaze on the only personal item I've ever known Dmitri to display in his office. It's a picture of his twin daughters—beautiful girls with long black hair, eyes almost as black as coal, straight, thin noses, and perfectly bright complexions.

"I'm here as a friend, Dmitri. How about you and I go find the bottom of a Chernobyl-poisoned bottle of vodka and catch up?" Friends in our business are hard to come by. Dmitri knows this better than anyone, I'm sure of it.

"Your Russian has improved since the last time I saw you. Have you been practicing on someone?"

"No, my Russian has always been impeccable. You were just too drunk to notice when I was here the last time."

Dmitri laughs, the smile reaching his eyes and showing he's warming up to me at last. That's no small feat in the bitter cold of Moscow, even in early spring. "Okay, let's have a drink and regale each other with tales of the good old days."

We walk silently through the corridors until we're well outside the building. There's a time and place for everything, but his office inside the Moscow Kremlin complex is not the place for idle chitchat. And especially not for the questions I have for him. The beauty inside the walled compound—the five palaces, four cathedrals, and the Kremlin Towers with spires reaching to the sky—masks the true inner workings of the secret government operations. To the public eye, most of the government's work is handled at the Moscow White House, a few miles away. But to those of us in the trade, we know the Kremlin is where the clandestine operations begin and end.

We walk along the Moskva River, then cross the bridge to head to Gorky Park. Despite the cool evening temperature and the time it takes to reach our destination by foot, I'd rather walk the entire distance than chance getting into the wrong car. Besides, traffic in Moscow is terrible, and driving would probably take longer than walking. The time out in the cold air gives me time to think and breathe. Being back here isn't exactly easy for me, but with the high stakes involved, I don't have another choice.

The odds of someone from the KGB following us are high, and I'm not keen on being snatched into an unmarked van and whisked away for questioning. On paper, the KGB as it once was doesn't even exist anymore after it was disbanded and split into two units. But as the powerful regime leader declared, "There's no such thing as a former KGB man." That same leader has worked behind the scenes to reestablish his elite police force, full of henchmen, assassins, and ruthless torturers.

Dmitri and I are careful and take our time before deciding where to stop for a drink, leisurely strolling in the old section of the park until we find a pub tucked away on a side street. We choose a booth away from the other patrons, one that allows a view of the front door and anyone who may try to get too close. The music playing in the background is enough to drown out our conversation on any external listening devices their government has in their arsenal.

My toys are slightly more advanced and higher tech. If the tables were reversed and I were spying on them, I'd have their every word in my ear, clear as a bell. Thankfully, they haven't quite caught up with our advanced gadgets yet. However, their medieval torture methods to extract information are top of the line, and I prefer to avoid them at all costs.

Dmitri orders shots and beer for both of us before turning his keen and penetrating gaze on me. "Silas, why are you here?"

"Tell me, Dmitri. How are your daughters, Mira and Kira?"

He strikes a match, lighting his cigar and taking a few drags on it before hardening his eyes and staring me down amidst the smoke swirling between us. The blunt end of his cigar glows in an angry red shade, much like the coloring overtaking his face at the moment.

"I told you I'm in no mood to play games. Speak your mind or get the fuck out of my sight. I'm giving you this one warning because we've been friendly in the past, but don't mistake this pass for weakness. I will gut you like a fucking fish and dump your body in the river, never to be seen again."

The waitress sets our drinks down in front of us, then pauses to take our orders. Dmitri dismisses her with a simple wave of his hand. I wait until she's out of earshot to continue.

"Calm down, Dmitri. I'm here to help you and your daughters. But I need you to level with me about what's really going on. What has happened to them?"

"You're not only asking me to commit treason against my

country, you're asking me to put my family's lives in real danger. This I cannot do. Go home. Mind your own business. Forget you know me." He throws his shot back then chases it with the entire pint of beer before slamming the mug on the table.

Before he has an opportunity to slide out of the booth, I stand and toss enough rubles on the table to cover our drinks plus a hefty tip. He cuts his eyes up at me, distrust and murderous contempt shining in his eyes.

"You know, your daughters are very beautiful. I know you've always been very proud of them. Their picture is the only personal memento you have in your office. That's a very telling sign, one I'm sure your superiors also picked up on and used as leverage against you. But I assure you, I'm not the guilty party in this. It seems there's something awry in your own government. A blurred line is far too easy to cross—and that's exactly what they created when they used your children against you after all your years of faithful service."

I begin to walk away then stop and look back over my shoulder. "There are slight differences in your girls, even though they're identical twins. For one, Mira has a much softer expression in her eyes than Kira does. Mira's a considerably gentler soul, isn't she? Not quite as fierce and resilient as Kira."

Before I reach the plane for my return flight home, I predict Dmitri Petrov will desperately want a meeting to resume our conversation.

And I'll be waiting for him.

Outside the pub, I pull my heavy overcoat tightly around me, flipping my collar up and pulling my hat down lower on my head. The wind whips around me, and the setting sun makes the air even colder. Without Dmitri's help, I'll have to go off my own assumptions and start directly with the source. I'd hoped to have a little more intel in my back pocket first, but his lack of answers is telling enough.

"Silas, wait."

That didn't take as long as I thought it would.

I stop and turn sideways, casting a glance at Dmitri over my shoulder. The primary reason I'm here is to help make sure a friend doesn't get caught in the cross fire of whatever covert operation the Russians have underway. The fact that I've known Dmitri almost the entire time I've worked in the CIA is a distant second. Our friendship, loosely labeled, is one of convenience and mutual benefit. The moment I'm no longer of use to him, he'd throw me under the bus. As it turns out, we can both help each other this time.

"Suddenly feeling chatty, Dmitri?"

"Do you really think you can help?" The pleading in his eyes isn't fake, but that's about the only fact I'm certain of right now.

"Do you really think you have any other options? I have an idea of what's going on, and if I'm right, you're the one who's playing games—very dangerous games."

He nods, not so much in agreement with my jab that he's behind the duplicity, but that knowing and doing nothing about it makes him complicit.

"Come to my house tonight. You can stay in our guest bedroom, we'll talk, and I'll drive you back to the airport in the morning."

"When you say airport, you don't really mean Siberian prison camp, do you?"

"Not this time. Next time, maybe."

He calls his driver to come pick us up, and we wait inside the pub, throwing back shots of vodka and snacking on caviar, until he arrives. The black sedan idles alongside the curb, and we walk out together. A moment of hesitation hits me before I slide into Dmitri's car, but I'm banking on his love for his kids to overrule his love of Mother Russia.

Our conversation on the way to his house in the suburbs is benign—nothing the driver or any other prying ears can use against us. When we arrive, his wife Natalya waits for us in the doorway, wringing her hands. The telltale sign of excessive worry gives me comfort—that I'm not walking into a trap.

"Silas, hello, it's been a long time." Natalya greets me with a wary expression despite her warm words.

"Don't worry, Nat. I'm here to help if I can." I kiss both of her cheeks, trying to reassure her of my intentions. She visibly relaxes, dropping her hands to her sides before inviting me in.

"This house is clean. I do my own bug-proofing so Nat and I can have private conversations. We can talk freely here." Dmitri sits at the dining table and begins filling his plate. Nat grabs another plate for me, and I join them for a full meal.

"Dmitri, tell me what's going on. I know you know, so don't bullshit me. And don't leave anything out."

He lowers his fork and levels me with his keen glare. "Will you save both of my girls? No matter what you find?"

"You know I'll do my best, Dmitri. That's the only promise I can give you."

"They were taken to America…by the GRU."

So Russia's largest foreign intelligence agency is hard at work on US soil.

***

**Silas's story continues in *Blurred Line*.
Read Roman's story in *Hard Line*.**

Want more of Nick Tucker? Read ***Her Dom*** and ***Her Dom's Lesson***!

Want more of Nick, Silas, Roman, Reaper, Bull, Rebel, and Shadow? Find them and more the ***Steele Security series***: ***Wicked Games***, ***Wicked Ties***, ***Wicked Nights***, ***Wicked Intentions***, and ***Wicked Shadows!***

ACKNOWLEDGMENTS

Writing a book is no small feat. As for me, I put my heart and soul into the story, taking time away from family and friends to finish writing just one more chapter. When I finally reach those two little magical words, a weight is lifted from my shoulders and I'm able to breathe again. Until I start the next book.

My writing journey includes conferring with several people I trust and admire to give feedback and suggestions. There are also people who encourage and support me along the way, taking a chance on a new type of book or a storyline outside the norm. Those who aren't afraid to step outside the box and give "different" a chance. These are my people—my tribe—whether they realize it or not.

Acknowledgments are hard to write because I never want to leave anyone out or make anyone feel their place in my life isn't important. If you've ever read my books, you hold a special place in my heart. There are a few special people I want to recognize for helping make this book special to me.

First and foremost, I thank my Lord and Savior, Jesus Christ, for his unending love, mercy, and forgiveness of a sinner like me. Without Him, I am nothing. Yes, when I say I fall short, I realize I fall way short, but thankfully, there's no such thing as being too far from Him. He knows my heart.

Dr. Jeff in this story is a real person, doctor, and specialty surgeon. He provided the verbatim narrative he would've used for a patient in the situation described in this book. Many thanks to him for taking time to help ensure the scene was as close to reality as possible.

Vanessa, Dr. Jeff's wife, is a very good friend of mine, and she acted as the go-between for our conversation despite her own hectic schedule. As always, she was so gracious and willing to help in any way she could. Thank you for being such a good friend.

Nita Banks, thank you for all the questions you answered and insight you gave. We both know you love me...it's really past time for you to admit it.

Michelle Dare and T.K. Leigh, thank you for all your support —every single day. I'm so thankful for your friendship, your insights, and all your advice. You can never leave me...because I'd find you. Love you ladies with all my heart!

A.M. Hargrove, Liv Morris, Beth Hurley, and Tabitha Charisse, thank you for being my guinea pigs and reading this story before this book was made available to the masses. Your friendship and your feedback mean the world to me!

Lisa Hollett with Silently Correcting Your Grammar, my editor and my friend, thank you once again for working through this book with me, polishing it until it shines, and laughing with me along the way. Your witty banter makes editing (more) fun. Funner? The Funnest? Just kidding!

Wander Aguiar, the photographer for the covers in this series, is always wonderful to work with—although he does make choosing one photo very difficult.

And to my readers, whether you love, like, or hate this book, thank you for taking your time to read it. Thank you for your reviews, even if all you say is you liked it or not. Thank you for your support—you have no idea how much every little bit means to an author.

All my love to you,
Angel

Lines are for crossing.
Rules are for breaking.

BLURRED LINE

—A CROSSING LINES NOVEL—

USA Today Bestselling Author
A.D. JUSTICE

PROLOGUE

Silas—Moscow, Russia

"I'm surprised to see you. I didn't know you were coming." He narrows his eyes and stares at me suspiciously. He's a large man, formidable back in his heyday, but that was many years ago. Today, he'd sooner reach for his gun and blow a hole in my gut than spar with me. Can't say I blame him.

My Russian contact is leery of surprise visits, especially when I haven't been here in quite some time. That's what happens after living in a military-ruled country that still leans strongly to Communism and enjoys torturing citizens for information. Sure, to the rest of the world, they're now a republic. But that's just the face they wear and the front they show. Walk a mile on the wild side of Moscow then tell me that bullshit party line is real.

The KGB would haul Dmitri away right now if they thought it would gain them an inch. The cold war may have ended years ago, but there's a secret war still raging with no signs of slowing down. And they're playing for keeps, though most of the world has no idea what's going on behind the iron curtain. And that's exactly how they want it.

"If you'd known I was coming, it wouldn't have been a surprise." I purposely keep my hands visible. I mean him no harm. I'm here for answers only he can give.

"What do you want, Silas? I'm in no mood for fun and games. It's been a long day, and I'm ready to get out of here."

I walk farther into his office at the government's fortified complex in the heart of Moscow. There are cameras and voice recorders all over the building; I'm not stupid. But then, they knew I was here the second my plane touched down on the tarmac. My visit here is for unofficial business, but if it turns out to be even remotely what I suspect, the NSA and CIA will duke it out for investigating rights. Good thing I've already assembled a team of three highly skilled and able officers to handle just such an investigation.

Two of them will be starting their training next week with a significant advantage over their classmates because of their previous experience. Now they're learning the spy and asset component, the psychology behind turning a loyalist to a separatist, along with how to blend into a crowd, to become unrecognizable, to become invisible when needed. Very special skills when "sharpshooting assassin" is added to the curriculum vitae.

Glancing over his shoulder, I rest my gaze on the only personal item I've ever known Dmitri to display in his office. It's a picture of his twin daughters—beautiful girls with long black hair, eyes almost as black as coal, straight, thin noses, and perfectly bright complexions.

"I'm here as a friend, Dmitri. How about you and I go find the bottom of a Chernobyl-poisoned bottle of vodka and catch up?" Friends in our business are hard to come by. Dmitri knows this better than anyone, I'm sure of it.

"Your Russian has improved since the last time I saw you. Have you been practicing on someone?"

"No, my Russian has always been impeccable. You were just too drunk to notice when I was here the last time."

Dmitri laughs, the smile reaching his eyes and showing he's warming up to me at last. That's no small feat in the bitter cold of Moscow, even in early spring. "Okay, let's have a drink and regale each other with tales of the good old days."

We walk silently through the corridors until we're well outside the building. There's a time and place for everything, but his office inside the Moscow Kremlin complex is not the place for idle chitchat. And especially not for the questions I have for him. The beauty inside the walled compound—the five palaces, four cathedrals, and the Kremlin Towers with spires reaching to the sky—masks the true inner workings of the secret government operations. To the public eye, most of the government's work is handled at the Moscow White House, a few miles away. But to those of us in the trade, we know the Kremlin is where the clandestine operations begin and end.

We walk along the Moskva River, then cross the bridge to head to Gorky Park. Despite the cool evening temperature and the time it takes to reach our destination by foot, I'd rather walk the entire distance than chance getting into the wrong car. Besides, traffic in Moscow is terrible, and driving would probably take longer than walking. The time out in the cold air gives me time to think and breathe. Being back here isn't exactly easy for me, but with the high stakes involved, I don't have another choice.

The odds of someone from the KGB following us are high, and I'm not keen on being snatched into an unmarked van and whisked away for questioning. On paper, the KGB as it once was doesn't even exist anymore after it was disbanded and split into two units. But as the powerful regime leader declared, "There's no such thing as a former KGB man." That same leader has worked behind the scenes to reestablish his elite police force, full of henchmen, assassins, and ruthless torturers.

Dmitri and I are careful and take our time before deciding where to stop for a drink, leisurely strolling in the old section of the park until we find a pub tucked away on a side street. We choose a booth away from the other patrons, one that allows a view of the front door and anyone who may try to get too close. The music playing in the background is enough to drown out our conversation on any external listening devices their government has in their arsenal.

My toys are slightly more advanced and higher tech. If the tables were reversed and I were spying on them, I'd have their every word in my ear, clear as a bell. Thankfully, they haven't quite caught up with our advanced gadgets yet. However, their medieval torture methods to extract information are top of the line, and I prefer to avoid them at all costs.

Dmitri orders shots and beer for both of us before turning his keen and penetrating gaze on me. "Silas, why are you here?"

"Tell me, Dmitri. How are your daughters, Mira and Kira?"

He strikes a match, lighting his cigar and taking a few drags on it before hardening his eyes and staring me down amidst the smoke swirling between us. The blunt end of his cigar glows in an angry red shade, much like the coloring overtaking his face at the moment.

"I told you I'm in no mood to play games. Speak your mind or get the fuck out of my sight. I'm giving you this one warning because we've been friendly in the past, but don't mistake this pass for weakness. I will gut you like a fucking fish and dump your body in the river, never to be seen again."

The waitress sets our drinks down in front of us, then pauses to take our orders. Dmitri dismisses her with a simple wave of his hand. I wait until she's out of earshot to continue.

"Calm down, Dmitri. I'm here to help you and your daughters. But I need you to level with me about what's really going on. What has happened to them?"

"You're not only asking me to commit treason against my

country, you're asking me to put my family's lives in real danger. This I cannot do. Go home. Mind your own business. Forget you know me." He throws his shot back then chases it with the entire pint of beer before slamming the mug on the table.

Before he has an opportunity to slide out of the booth, I stand and toss enough rubles on the table to cover our drinks plus a hefty tip. He cuts his eyes up at me, distrust and murderous contempt shining in his eyes.

"You know, your daughters are very beautiful. I know you've always been very proud of them. Their picture is the only personal memento you have in your office. That's a very telling sign, one I'm sure your superiors also picked up on and used as leverage against you. But I assure you, I'm not the guilty party in this. It seems there's something awry in your own government. A blurred line is far too easy to cross—and that's exactly what they created when they used your children against you after all your years of faithful service."

I begin to walk away then stop and look back over my shoulder. "There are slight differences in your girls, even though they're identical twins. For one, Mira has a much softer expression in her eyes than Kira does. Mira's a considerably gentler soul, isn't she? Not quite as fierce and resilient as Kira."

Before I reach the plane for my return flight home, I predict Dmitri Petrov will desperately want a meeting to resume our conversation.

And I'll be waiting for him.

Outside the pub, I pull my heavy overcoat tightly around me, flipping my collar up and pulling my hat down lower on my head. The wind whips around me, and the setting sun makes the air even colder. Without Dmitri's help, I'll have to go off my own assumptions and start directly with the source. I'd hoped to have a little more intel in my back pocket first, but his lack of answers is telling enough.

"Silas, wait."

That didn't take as long as I thought it would.

I stop and turn sideways, casting a glance at Dmitri over my shoulder. The primary reason I'm here is to help make sure a friend doesn't get caught in the cross fire of whatever covert operation the Russians have underway. The fact that I've known Dmitri almost the entire time I've worked in the CIA is a distant second. Our friendship, loosely labeled, is one of convenience and mutual benefit. The moment I'm no longer of use to him, he'd throw me under the bus. As it turns out, we can both help each other this time.

"Suddenly feeling chatty, Dmitri?"

"Do you really think you can help?" The pleading in his eyes isn't fake, but that's about the only fact I'm certain of right now.

"Do you really think you have any other options? I have an idea of what's going on, and if I'm right, you're the one who's playing games—very dangerous games."

He nods, not so much in agreement with my jab that he's behind the duplicity, but that knowing and doing nothing about it makes him complicit.

"Come to my house tonight. You can stay in our guest bedroom, we'll talk, and I'll drive you back to the airport in the morning."

"When you say airport, you don't really mean Siberian prison camp, do you?"

"Not this time. Next time, maybe."

He calls his driver to come pick us up, and we wait inside the pub, throwing back shots of vodka and snacking on caviar, until he arrives. The black sedan idles alongside the curb, and we walk out together. A moment of hesitation hits me before I slide into Dmitri's car, but I'm banking on his love for his kids to overrule his love of Mother Russia.

Our conversation on the way to his house in the suburbs is benign—nothing the driver or any other prying ears can use against us. When we arrive, his wife Natalya waits for us in the doorway, wringing her hands. The telltale sign of excessive worry gives me comfort—that I'm not walking into a trap.

"Silas, hello, it's been a long time." Natalya greets me with a wary expression despite her warm words.

"Don't worry, Nat. I'm here to help if I can." I kiss both of her cheeks, trying to reassure her of my intentions. She visibly relaxes, dropping her hands to her sides before inviting me in.

"This house is clean. I do my own bug-proofing so Nat and I can have private conversations. We can talk freely here." Dmitri sits at the dining table and begins filling his plate. Nat grabs another plate for me, and I join them for a full meal.

"Dmitri, tell me what's going on. I know you know, so don't bullshit me. And don't leave anything out."

He lowers his fork and levels me with his keen glare. "Will you save both of my girls? No matter what you find?"

"You know I'll do my best, Dmitri. That's the only promise I can give you."

"They were taken to America…by the GRU."

So Russia's largest foreign intelligence agency is hard at work on US soil.

CHAPTER 1

Kira—Eighteen Months Later

Going through the motions day after day and pretending to give two shits about the man sitting across from me is exhausting. He's droning on endlessly about his golf game, as if his commentary on the sport is the most exciting topic ever. As if I care one bit about golf or his swing or how close to par he was during his last game. Close to par is still subpar, that much I know about him. It's winter, for crying out loud. No one golfs in the snow.

But it's my job to pretend I care. He must believe I'm hanging on his every word, dying to know his next magnificent revelation—like a new fucking golf glove he's trying out or something else equally as asinine. We're sitting in a bar that's only a couple of blocks from Capitol Hill, chatting over drinks and flirting as if we're really into each other. The sad thing is, he honestly thinks I want to go home with him tonight. He has no clue I'd rather stab myself in the eye than spend one second longer than I have to with him.

"David, you make it all sound so easy. But I've tried hitting that tiny little ball before, and it's so hard, especially when you have to chase it all over the course. What else do you do for fun?" I pick up my vodka and orange juice, intentionally holding the stirring straw provocatively between my lips. On cue, his eyes drop to my mouth, his lips part, and his breaths increase. He's so fucking predictable. Not that he has a snowball's chance in hell of getting anything from me tonight, but he doesn't need to know that yet.

"I'd love to show you all kinds of things we can do for fun. Your satisfaction is guaranteed."

And I guarantee there's no fucking way that will ever happen.

"Aren't you always working, though?" I stick out my bottom lip, pouting like a child while trying to get him back on topic.

This demure act is slowly killing me inside.

"Well, yes, that's true. My job is very, very important, and it requires a lot of my time. I'm on call twenty-four seven, in case the senator needs me to work on an urgent matter for him. You know, he gets all the glory while I do all the hard work behind the scenes. He only takes the information I give him and argues the points in our favor. I'm the backbone of his entire office. He'd completely fail at his job without me." David raises his glass and downs another shot of bourbon then signals the waitress for another.

That's right...keep drinking. The more you swallow, the looser your tongue becomes.

"That's so not fair. You should be sitting in the Senator's office instead of him. He'd be lucky to sit in your chair. Maybe you can show me his office one day soon. I bet he has a huge… desk." I run my fingernail along his forearm, driving home my insinuation.

He shrugs one shoulder and smirks, clearly trying to be nonchalant but failing miserably at it, as the waitress sets a new glass in front of him. "We can go tonight, if that's what you want. You know, I have keys to the office and can go in there whenever I want. What do you say, baby?"

Baby. Inwardly, I cringe every time he calls me that little pet name. It's not the term of endearment as much as it is the irritating man behind it.

"I say we have a couple more for the road, then go make exciting use of that huge desk." I pick up my glass and make a show of the lack of alcohol. "Can you get me a shot of vodka from the bar? The waitress is busy, and the bartender serves you faster than he does me."

"Of course, baby. I'll be right back. Ronnie, the bartender, knows me. I come in here a lot."

When he leaves our booth, I pull the small vial of tasteless, odorless liquid from between my breasts and empty it into his glass. It mixes with his bourbon instantly, undetectable to the human eye or tongue. The first real smile of the night crosses my face. Soon, I'll be rid of this loser and on to better marks.

He returns with two shots—the straight vodka I requested and another I recognize instantly. I literally force myself not to roll my eyes at his blatant attempt to be cute. My inner voice tells me to stab *him* in the eye, steal the keys, and get this over with as soon as possible.

"Here's your vodka." He sets the shot glass in front of me, and I smile appreciatively, as expected, before I toss it back. "Now for a little something sweeter. Here's your first screaming orgasm of the night, and here's to many more."

When he lifts his bourbon for a toast, I happily raise mine to clink our glasses together. "To many more, indeed."

Just not with you.

The contents of his glass disappear, sliding down his throat before a devious smile crawls across his face. My response is more relaxed, knowing by the time we reach the congressional offices, he'll start to feel the effects of the extra kick I slipped him.

With the tab paid, we leave the bar and walk hand in hand the two blocks back to the office building. By the time we reach the south side entry doors, David is already feeling the effects of all the alcohol he drank plus the extra sedative. We should have just enough time to make it through the security checkpoint and up to the eighth floor before he becomes too sloppy drunk to manage.

The open, airy interior of the Hart Building is much more modern than the older Senate offices. The halls teem with people at all hours of the day and night, especially when significant bills are on the cusp of passing and those involved want to stake their claims. This evening is no different, with staffers rushing back and forth between offices and conference rooms. Their attention is focused on their specific assignments, so they don't even bother glancing in our direction.

David throws his arm over my shoulders as we walk down the spacious hallway together, leaning his face close to mine as he whispers loudly. "You are so fucking beautiful. I can't wait to bend you over the desk, pull your long blond hair, and smack that perfect ass every time you scream my name."

"Let's hope the office is empty, then. What a sight the others would see if they're still working."

"The Senator hasn't been in the office all week. His daughter is getting married this weekend, so he's overseeing the huge tent going up in his backyard. The other staffers left before I did today, so his office is all ours."

The office doors are solid glass, allowing natural light from the central atrium to illuminate the external spaces. Walking past the aides' offices and desks in the outer area, we stop in front of a thick, wooden door that conveys the opulence and prestige of the position without the need for further explanation. He retrieves his keys from his pocket, unlocks the door, and lets me step inside first.

The senator's inner sanctum is two-stories high, and every

bit as lavish as I imagined it would be. The rich mahogany wainscoting wraps around the bottom half of the room, and the masculine, dark-green walls stretch up to the ceiling. Large works of art adorn the high walls, each one costing more money than I've made in my entire life. The hypocrisy is astounding—they don't serve the people here. They help themselves while riding on the backs of the people.

He moves behind me, wrapping his arms around my waist and burying his face in my neck. His body sways back and forth, unable to steady himself with the room spinning so fast around him. "Are you ready to have some real fun?"

"Absolutely."

His arms drop from my sides just before his knees give out, and his body crumples to the floor in a heap of drunkenness. I step over him and walk behind the big desk, the one that holds all the information I need to copy before I can leave here. The docking port for the senator's laptop is empty, but his desktop computer is still on. The encryption on his password is strong, but not enough to prevent my portable brute-force attack software from identifying the letters, numbers, and special characters in milliseconds.

After I make myself a system administrator, nothing stops me from copying the data I need to a flash drive. Rifling through his computer files gives me extra ammunition. He apparently believes his computer is safe from any prying eyes, if the very personal pictures and documents he has "hidden" under a folder entitled "Personal Folder" are any indication. Those, I conceal in a special folder on my flash drive. I may need them later.

After I've copied everything that could be used as leverage against him, along with the highly classified files on the server that I still need to comb through, I replace the folders with a spyware program renamed to match each one. No matter which icon a user clicks on, it'll open another door to the network that won't be detected for some time.

When I finish my job, I make sure everything in the office appears precisely as it was before I entered. The chair is back in place, and the monitor is turned off, nothing showing I was ever here. With the exception of the aide still passed out on the floor, of course. I'll never see him again since my cover is that I'm only a tourist here in DC and I'm heading back to San Diego soon. But if I ever have the displeasure of his company again, my reason for leaving him here to sleep it off is explained easily enough. And it'll be all his fault since he drank too much and left me alone in a strange place.

As I leave the office, I don't bother to close the heavy wooden door to the senator's private office behind me. If anyone walking by sees David and wants to help him, more power to them. But no one seems to notice anything when I step out into the main corridor. Everyone is anxious to get home after working extra-long hours on a Friday, well past the time average workers have already gone back to their families. I step into the thick of the passing group, easily absorbed by the masses as we make our way down to the lobby level and out the east side of the building. After I step out into the crisp, night air, I hail a taxi and ride away from the scene of the crime, leaving no trace of my real self.

When I reach the interior of my small home in Alexandria, Virginia, I reset the alarm, kick my high heels off, and pull the blond wig off my head. In the summer, the wig and the net holding my long black hair in place can get uncomfortably hot —close to the point of feeling as if a heat stroke is imminent if I'm not careful. But January in Washington, DC, is cold enough not to notice I'm wearing it for the most part. Before I even make it to my bedroom, my phone starts ringing, and I know who it is before looking at the screen.

"Hello?"

"Hello. This is Erika with HairBenders Salon. I'm calling to confirm your appointment on Wednesday morning at 9:15 at our Cameron Station Boulevard location."

"Thank you for the reminder, Erika. I will be there."

We disconnect, and I grab my laptop out of the safe. Before I hand this flash drive over at the designated drop Wednesday morning, I want to memorize everything that's on it. I'll also make my own copy. The information I nabbed could come in handy one day if I play my cards right. Every move I make must be calculated, weighed, and measured first. Every step I take must be plotted and coordinated. The dangers are too real, and the odds are stacked against me, but sometimes there's no choice but to roll the dice and hope for the best.

I'll have to face the consequences of getting caught red-handed with the classified information if my cover is somehow blown. Sometimes the risk is worth the gamble.

With the jump drive inserted into my laptop, I open the folders and mentally prepare myself to go through the highly classified data, document by document. My near-photographic memory is both a blessing and a curse, but right now I'm going with a blessing. It helps me connect the dots when I have to recall information from something I read ten documents ago, but my memories can't be admitted as evidence the same as physical documents can.

Some of the files contain information I already know. Nothing too exciting—the Americans are watching the Russians who are watching the Americans. The ones they know about anyway. My name still isn't on the list, so I'll survive another day. Time gets away from me the deeper I dive into the senator's files. My stomach growls, reminding me I haven't eaten anything since this morning.

My cheap-ass date only sprang for the alcohol because he thought he'd get lucky tonight, but the joke's on him. I stand

and stretch before walking to the refrigerator to stare inside until something I want to eat magically appears.

I'm still waiting…and staring.

After I quickly calculate the time it takes to cook something from scratch versus the time it takes to order delivery, my decision is made. Chinese food delivered hot to my door, it is. The shower calls my name, mainly stemming from my need to wash any remnants of that loser off my skin. But the truth is I've grown weary in my bones of this job and how much it demands of me every time I step out the door.

This is not the life I'd planned when I was a child. If there were any way I could wash it all away, watch it flow down the drain with the bathwater, I would take that shot in a second.

CHAPTER 2

Silas

Kira walks down the hall to the bathroom and leaves the door standing wide open behind her as she adjusts the water. Telltale sounds of her undressing before opening the shower door help me visualize her every move. Before leaving the safety of my hiding place in the shadows inside her home, I wait another few seconds, listening intently to verify she's actually inside the tub.

As a fellow spy, she would know the tricks of the trade already. Our number one offensive move is confusing the enemy by making him believe we're doing one thing when we're actually using misdirection to gain the upper hand. When I hear the water falling in waves, I know she's washing and rinsing her hair, letting the water pool in her long black hair before releasing it with one large splash. Now that I'm confident she didn't sense my presence inside the house with her, I move silently toward her laptop.

She's obviously not on her game tonight. No spy worth his—or her—salt leaves a computer unlocked, the flash drive plugged in, and the stolen documents still open on the desktop. With a few clicks, I erase all evidence of their existence from her computer and eject the flash drive. Just as I slip it into my pocket, the sound of water coming from the bathroom falls silent, then the shower door opens again. The noise of the hairdryer covers my exit from her house, just in time to avoid the teenager delivering her food.

From my vantage point outside, I wait and watch the exchange. Usually, I'd be long gone from the scene, but not this time. Not with this case. Nothing about this situation fits the conventional mold, from the person I'm watching to the reasons why I'm doing it. Even Kira's actions don't match the typical spy patterns. She's all over the board—unpredictable and difficult to follow one minute, to downright sloppy and amateurish the next.

After she pays the delivery boy and closes the door, I watch with a smirk I couldn't contain even if I wanted to, which I don't. She hasn't yet realized both the drive and the data she saved are gone, but she will as soon as she sits down to eat and finish perusing the pilfered classified documents. This is where her predictable response will kick in—she'll run to the door, fling it open, and rush outside, straight into the cold January air, without protection or checking her surroundings first. All mistakes even rookies at The Farm don't make during their initial training.

She is an enigma wrapped in a contradiction.

Thankfully, she can't hear the chuckle that escapes from me when she reacts exactly as I suspected she would. The front door stands wide open while she rushes around the perimeter of her house in nothing but her bathrobe and slippers. When she makes it back around to the front, she stands on the porch, her eyes scanning up and down the street in front of her house. But she can't see me from where I'm watching at the moment.

In fact, she hasn't seen, heard, or felt me watching her at

any time in the past year and a half since I returned from Moscow. Standard GRU training should've refined her skills and honed her senses to be able to identify a tail with barely a second glance, even one carried out by a seasoned agent like myself. She can get an invitation into a senator's office, maneuver through secure areas, and steal information from a secure system, and yet, she has tunnel vision where her own safety is concerned. Like not covering the keypad when she enabled the alarm, giving me a full view of her four-digit code. The inconsistencies in her skills and deeds don't make sense to me.

Her shoulders droop noticeably when she releases a defeated sigh. She drops her head back, closes her eyes, and curls her hands into tight fists. If she could kick her own ass right now, she most definitely would. But there's more than anger in her body language. A pained expression crosses her features before being quickly replaced with almost paralyzing fear. She knows she fucked up and there's no way to explain it away, no way to reclaim the data now—from either her computer or from Senator Hunt's. When I wiped hers, I made sure it was wiped CIA clean.

Even I couldn't retrieve it now if I wanted to.

This surveillance is throwing me off my game. I've never been one to show my hand like this, and now she knows without a shadow of a doubt she's being watched. She knows someone was in her home. She knows the data she stole earlier tonight was taken right out from under her nose as soon as she let her guard down. If I'd revealed myself to anyone else in the trade, I'd be a dead man by morning. But with Kira, I'm betting on another angle.

The desperation she so easily displays—from the way she covers her face with her hands before running her fingers through her still damp hair to the way she keeps glancing up and down the street, as if the flash drive will mysteriously appear out of thin air—tells me I've hit the jackpot with reading this peculiar Russian spy.

She'll be reckless enough to try to get back into the senator's office. The same senator who just happens to be on The United Senate Select Committee on Intelligence.

When she turns and walks back into her house, I remain in place for a while longer. Now she knows her cover is blown so she'll be watching for movement, looking for any vehicle that seems out of place in her quiet little part of the neighborhood. I'm guessing that dinner she ordered isn't looking too appealing right now, with her stomach in knots and her nerves set on edge. She has plans to make to try to find a way back into the secure offices now, especially since she burned her bridge with the aide tonight.

An hour after the house is completely dark and still, I stroll over to the next street, slide behind the wheel of my car, and make my way back to my apartment. There's only one viable prospect for her now, and I have my own preparations to make to attend the black-tie political fundraising event, where the buy-in for a plate easily costs $1,000, but that's lowballing compared to the individual donations of $30,000 or more. This is the life in DC—someone is always fundraising for something, and someone else is always more than willing to donate to it for a favor in return.

I need to dust off my tuxedo and get an invitation to the party for myself. I have a hot date all lined up for tomorrow night—she just doesn't know it yet.

Back inside my apartment, I sit down with my secure CIA laptop to check out the contents of the flash drive. At first glance, it seems she copied everything she could find in hopes of finding anything of use. It'll take time to go through all the documents and identify any significant national security risks we're facing as a result of this breach. That research will have to wait until later, though, when I can give it to one of my side-kicks. It's already been a long day and night.

Stick a fork in me, I'm completely done.

WHEN I STEP INTO THE ATRIUM OF THE RONALD REAGAN Building on Saturday evening, my undercover training immediately kicks in. The room is as tall as it is long, with a rounded glass dome that adjoins the third-floor ceiling. Both upper floors are wide-open promenades, providing an excellent view of the grand room below. Flowing rolls of white gossamer fabric are draped all the way from the glass above to the floor below, gathered strategically to create the ambiance and rich tone of the gala. The music from the jazz band on the stage at the far end of the room carries on the room's acoustics, adding to the overall mood and vibe.

A waiter approaches with a tray full of champagne flutes, so I take one to sip on as I begin mingling with the crowd. Saying hello to complete strangers as I work my way through the party, acting as if I know them and I belong here, keeps suspicious eyes from staring too long. They return a polite greeting and quickly resume their conversations. Listening for tidbits of information as I pass by is second nature to me now. It comes as naturally as breathing. I'm just waiting for the right conversation to catch my ear.

When I slow and turn, taking a lingering perusal of the people at the party, my gaze locks on the sexiest woman in the entire room, standing regally at the top of the stairs, unaware of her beauty and allure. Kira's long black hair shimmers, catching the soft white twinkle of the lights and reflecting them like tiny bursts of starlight. In a sea of black cocktail dresses, she stands out even more in her pure-white, floor-length gown that leaves one shoulder bare and clings to her every curve, beckoning every man in the room to her beauty.

Then it hits me. That's precisely her intention—mesmerize and hypnotize the men with her exquisiteness, then knock them on their ass with a hidden syringe or a tiny vial of liquid sleeping medicine. The congresspeople, aides, and other staffers in the room have the access she desperately needs. Experience tells me she's meeting someone soon to turn over the information she stole—someone who expects nothing less than success. Whichever unwitting victim falls into her web will do, as long as she can use him to get back into the secure office and on the secure servers.

I have other plans for her, though.

She's descending from the top of the wide, runner-covered stairway, three stories up, so I have plenty of time to drink her in while formulating my approach. After dropping off my champagne glass on an empty table, I weave through the crowd with my sights set on her, watching her every move to coordinate my own to match. She reaches the bottom of the steps just as I reach the edge of the crowd and enjoy an unobstructed view of her.

She starts by assessing every individual to find the perfect mark—who's here, who's vulnerable, who's alone. She takes a step into the crowd but quickly realizes her task won't be quite as easy as she thought. Most people don't show up to these elaborate fundraising events alone, and for a good reason. They're here to rub elbows and tap shoulders to get their own politicians more funding. Every connection in this circuit only helps the cause in the end—the more lips flapping and hands extending for handouts, the better.

When she identifies her target, her facial expression changes, and she morphs into character. She's on the prowl now, stalking her prey as she moves past the elaborately decorated round tables and the throngs of people laughing and chatting each other up. Following her line of sight, I realize which victim she's chosen for tonight's performance, and I instantly recognize him.

She's in way over her head, but she doesn't have a clue.

Moving quickly and silently through the crowd, I slip around all the obstacles in my path until I'm directly in front of her. The tables line the walls, leaving enough room in the middle for a decently sized dance floor. Several couples are taking advantage of the slow, sultry jazz sounds carrying over the air. When she raises her arm to touch the man's shoulder, I grab her hand just before her fingers have a chance to graze his jacket.

With my other arm wrapped around her waist, I walk her backward a few steps, surprised expression and all, until we reach the dance floor. We begin swaying to the music, our feet moving naturally to the beat, our bodies in sync without conscious effort. As if we've danced together our entire lives. Her intoxicating perfume fills my nostrils, making me want to bury my face in her neck and inhale every bit of her essence. She keeps her dark eyes glued to mine. The shock is still registered in them, but it's now mixed with a little excitement and a little leeriness.

I'm curious to see which emotion wins in the end.

"Not that I don't appreciate the dance, but I have to ask. Do I know you?"

She doesn't know me—that's not her real question. That's merely a polite way of saying, "Who the fuck are you?"

"We've never met." That's not a lie. "But you were about to make a huge mistake, and I felt a strong need to save you from yourself."

"I was about to make a huge mistake? What do you mean?" Waves of suspicion churn in her eyes.

"The man you were about to flirt with? I know him, and he's not someone you want to double-cross. He's not an unsuspecting senator's aide who's too scared to report he was outwitted by a young lady he snuck into his boss's office. The man behind us has the means and the determination to hunt you down and kill you for much less."

Her confusion clears, giving way to clarity. The angry red tinge creeps up her skin, starting at her neck and disappearing into her hairline. I tighten my arm around her waist, holding her against me before she decides to scale my body like a beautiful little spider monkey and choke me out with her bare hands.

"You. Son. Of. A. Bitch!" She hisses the insult at me in an irate whisper, enunciating each word with marked aversion. If we were alone, this would be a very different scene. She's a bit of a wildcat when provoked. This may be an inappropriate time to tell her how fucking sexy she is when she's mad. "You're the one who broke into my house!"

"To be fair, you broke into my government first. Now, there are a lot of things I can sweep under the rug and pretend I didn't see, but that's not one of them. On top to that, you're a Russian spy, and our countries historically haven't been the best of friends. The only reason you're not in custody right now is because of your father. Try that shit again, though, and you're headed for Guantanamo Bay, where they'll hold you for interrogation for as long as they want. I'm not *that* tight with your dad."

"That's a ridiculous accusation. I'm not a spy. But it's very convenient for you to claim to know my father when I have no way to verify it. Especially since I don't even know your name. Maybe you're the Russian spy, trying to work me and turn me against my country. Maybe I should call for security right now."

"Now, Kira, don't try to bluff me. Dmitri is a friend, and he's beside himself with worry about you. I gave him my word I'd help you as much as possible, but I won't help you steal top-secret information from my country and hand it over to yours. I've done enough favors for you over the last eighteen months, tracking you down and keeping you out of prison, or worse— out of the real bad guys' hands. And my name is Silas."

She glances nervously around the room, her eyes jumping from one spot to another. I chuckle, mostly to myself, but I can't hide my amusement.

"What's so funny?"

"You're looking for an escape route. Do you really think I would've revealed my upper hand if it was my real ace in the hole?"

"There's nothing you could possibly have on me, Silas. You have nothing to hold over my head to threaten me with. My laptop is completely clean. Thanks to you."

"You may be surprised by the things I know. May surprise you even more when you realize you didn't even have a clue about the truth of the matter. But I do have a few questions—a few holes in the story you can help fill in. So why don't we call a truce—broker our own peace treaty right now—and help each other out?"

The music continues, we keep swaying, and the wheels keep turning in her mind. She has been trained to work assets, turn them to support her country, or give her the information she wants in exchange for something else. She hasn't been in this situation before—where she's the one being worked and giving up the information to the enemy. No time like the present to learn on the job.

"What do you know that I don't? You have to give me something to go on other than you know my dad's name."

"I know more than your dad's name. Your mom, Nat, knows me too. She even cooked for me the last time I visited their house—the one Dmitri sweeps for bugs himself so they can have private conversations. He also keeps a picture of you and Mira on his desk in his office at the Kremlin. It's the only personal item he has there—the only one he's ever been proud enough of to show others. I'm guessing he assumed his KGB days would keep his family safe, though he should've known his own government better than that.

Communists aren't known for their friendships or loyalty to anyone."

"Haven't you kept up with current political affairs? Russia hasn't been a communist country for a very long time."

"Ah, yes, of course. United Russia. Because the last election wasn't rigged at all, right? Come on, Kira. I've given you enough information to prove I know you and your family. I also know that you secretly like me, even though you don't want to admit it."

Now she laughs, a genuine one that reaches her eyes and lights up her face. "And why would you say that, Silas?"

"Because you're still dancing with me, without even noticing the music stopped a couple of minutes ago."

CHAPTER 3

Kira

Tall, dark, and handsome. Fit, muscular, and stealthy. Not prone to following the rules, making plans up as he goes, and approaching life-and-death decisions as a game to be won.

Definitely CIA.

FBI agents follow the rules to the letter, never veering off the beaten path. They're much more serious and don't negotiate with outsiders. Silas is an officer who can change to fit his environment. The chameleon who can never be caught. He was invisible last night, leaving no trace of being in my house, other than his deliberate acts of stealing my flash drive and wiping my computer clean. Now tonight, he's dressed in an Armani tuxedo, tailored to fit his massive frame in an all-too-appealing fashion. His easygoing disposition is no doubt meant to subdue and disorient his victims, never seeing the runaway train that hit them until he's long out of sight.

He's not wrong about one thing, though. Once he started talking and I got lost in his deep blue eyes, everyone else in the room faded to black. His air of authority is innate. It's in the way he moves, the way he speaks, and the way he commands respect with no effort at all. His dazzling features disarm me with barely any struggle. His thick arms enveloped me in a comforting cocoon, and his alluring cologne pulled me even further under his spell.

We were still dancing, our bodies aligned and swaying in time to our own song, and I didn't even realize the band had stopped playing. He infuriated me and scared me and concerned me, but he also made me feel protected. I've never felt simultaneously so powerless and powerful in my life, and that is the very sensation that finally brings me back to my senses. The flashing red "warning" sign in my mind reminds me that spies can't be trusted no matter how enticing their promises are. They're trained to lie, steal, cheat, and kill to get what they need.

I should know.

What he needs from me is yet to be seen, but admitting my subterfuge right off the bat isn't fucking happening, no matter how charming and dashing he is.

"I'm still dancing with you because I'm still entertaining this ridiculous theory you're working on that I'm a Russian spy. Do you even hear the slightest bit of a Russian accent in my voice?"

"No, I don't. You're very good at what you do. And your English is perfect. That's all part of your training. You'd be surprised how well I can speak Russian."

He leans down, and his lips brush the shell of my ear. The deep and sensual timbre of his murmur makes goosebumps fan out across my bare skin.

"You look beautiful tonight." He speaks in perfect Russian, giving away no hint of an American accent.

"That sounded very seductive in your gravelly whisper. If I spoke or understood Russian, I may have liked what you said, but we'll never know."

He laughs and rolls his eyes, clearly knowing I'm lying through my teeth. "Tell you what I'll do. If this doesn't prove it to you, nothing will."

We walk to the edge of the dance floor, and he pulls out a chair at one of the empty tables for me to sit. He releases my hand, slides into the chair beside me, and reaches into his pants pocket, retrieving his cell phone. After a few clicks, he presses the phone to his ear and begins speaking in Russian. "There's someone here you need to convince to let me help her. She's being very stubborn, seems to be a strong family trait."

Then he hands the phone to me.

"Hello?"

"Kira?" My mom's voice fills the line, relief and fear fighting for first place in her tone. "Is it really you? Please listen to Silas. He's our friend—he's only trying to help you."

I push the phone back into his hand as fast as I can, as if it's a ticking bomb about to explode. Everything about this situation runs counter to my training, to what's expected of me, to what's keeping me alive. Speaking to my family back in Russia is expressly forbidden. The traced phone calls would absolutely blow my cover and put my entire family in grave danger.

"Hey Nat, she's a little shy to talk right now. Probably afraid my phone calls can be tracked. I think hearing your voice did the trick, though. We'll talk again soon."

"You shouldn't have done that." I glare at him, ready to kill him with my bare hands and take my chances in this crowded room.

"Relax, Kira. My phone is secure, untraceable, and undetectable. No one except you and I know about that call. I had to show you I'm not bullshitting so you'd believe me. I'll help you get on a plane back to Moscow, but then my part in any of this is over. If you step foot on American soil again, you'll be detained immediately and indefinitely."

"Why would you help me like this at all? What do you owe my father?"

"Nothing. This isn't for him, exactly. He benefits from my interference, but I'm mainly looking out for a friend."

"I don't understand. How do I know your friend?"

"You don't. But your sister Mira does."

"Mira?" I'm so confused. Silas acts as if I should understand his explanations and reasoning without questioning him, but none of this makes sense to me in the least.

"She's a good person, and I don't want to see her end up in a supermax federal prison, or worse, because you refuse to comply with the laws of this country. Years of living in a sound-proof isolation cell would be worse than death for her. I'm only trying to spare her from trouble with immigration, interrogation, and prison time for as long as I can." His charming smile and easygoing personality instantly change, revealing the lethally serious man underneath.

"But..." I pause, trying to connect my thoughts and words coherently. "Mira's already in prison. Are you saying you can get into the prison where she's being held?"

He tilts his head to the side and the corners of his eyes contract. Then he lifts his eyebrows and immediately lowers them again, putting his own pieces of the puzzle together. "Someone told you Mira's in prison, huh? My guess is they're using that cover story to make sure you keep toeing the line."

I sit up straighter, instantly more interested in what Silas has to say. "Don't play games with me, Silas. Do you know her? Is she okay?"

"She's perfectly fine. She's safe, she's happy, and she's living with a very loving family."

His answers are intentionally vague regarding where she is, I understand that. He's doing his job, getting ready to put me on a plane back to Russia for stealing top-secret and other classified documents from a secure server in a controlled-access government building. But she's my twin—and I've felt like half of me has been missing without being able to talk to her. All this time, I've believed my handlers—and they lied to my face every fucking day about my sister. What else have they lied about? What else do I not know?

My throat starts to clog, burning with tears that I force back down and refuse to let fall from my eyes. So many emotions run through me at once—but the most prevalent feeling of them all is regret. Because if Silas has his way, I'll never see Mira again.

"Can we go somewhere a little quieter and more private so we can talk? I'd like to hear more about Mira."

"We can talk on the way to the airstrip. There's a private jet waiting to take you to Moscow tonight."

He stands and extends his hand to help me up. I robotically accept his offer while trying to formulate how I'll ditch him once we step outside the building. If I get into the car with him, my life as I know it will be finished. There's no way I'm going back to Moscow. Not ever. Not even to see my parents, as much as I miss them. He has a job to do—I respect that. But his succeeding at his job would mean certain death for me. Had he been captured in Russia under the same circumstances, no one would give him the second chance I'm hell-bent on taking for myself.

We move through the crowded room, and I try to keep my expression neutral. All I can think is I'm being marched out to face the firing squad. My every step is harder and harder to take until my feet feel as if they're weighted down by concrete shoes.

A large crowd of interns—judging by how young they appear to be—with huge smiles on their faces and nearly empty glasses in their hands, weaves between the tight spaces around the tables and chairs, heading for the dance floor. At least some people are having fun at this party. A few of the girls start dancing well before they've moved out of our way, obviously a little tipsy and ready to have a good time. One of them grabs my arms and urges me to dance with her.

The unwitting stranger pulls my hand loose from Silas's grip.

Then I realize I'm free—and I allow her to pull me farther away from him while her friends fill in the space between Silas and me. He starts to push his way through the crowd, walking toward me, but the young studs in hot pursuit of the pretty girls prevent him from getting closer. The easygoing man I first met is long gone, replaced by the serious officer underneath. His facial features turn to stone. His eyes are as sharp as an eagle's and as cold as a marble slab—and he's determined to have me in custody.

But this is my chance, the only one I will have in the foreseeable future since my cover is blown and my real identity is out. While the horde of young revelers enjoys the upbeat music coming from the band—jumping, dancing, and forming a human wall separating me from Silas—I make a run for the exit door at the back of the room. If the alarm sounds when I run through the door, so be it. Maybe it'll create more of a diversion and give me extra time to get away.

When I push the door, I'm relieved to find it's unlocked. No extra bells and whistles are going off, so I can only assume it's because the enormous space is packed with people for tonight's fundraising event. Whatever the reason isn't important now that I'm in the clear, so to speak. I can still almost feel his hot breath breathing down my neck. In my rush, I left my coat in the cloakroom, and the thin material of my evening gown doesn't offer much protection from the winter winds whipping between the buildings. Running in heels isn't exactly graceful, but the line of taxis dropping off passengers along the sidewalk provides a modicum of cover, making it seem as if I'm only hurrying to reach an open cab before it's gone again.

When I slide into the back seat and slam the door closed

behind me, I give the driver my address. "There's an extra $50 tip if you get me there in less than ten minutes."

"You got it, lady."

He guns the engine, and the tires squeal as he pulls away from the curb. I turn to look out the back window and realize how narrowly I escaped Silas's grasp. He was reaching for the door and just barely missed the handle when we sped away. He lowers his chin and narrows his eyes, watching intently with the expression of an assassin who just accepted a direct challenge. That's not what gives me chills, though. He hasn't moved from his spot on the sidewalk despite the distance the cabbie has already put between us.

How long has Silas been watching me?

What else does he know?

The only option I have now is to reach my house, change clothes, and throw an extra set of clothing into a bag in record time, then clear out of there before he shows up. My heart is running away in my chest, pounding so hard, my skin is visibly jumping with each beat under the thin fabric of my dress. I know I should be planning my next move—where I'll hide out now that I know the rest of the government agencies will be after me—but all I can think about is what Silas said while we were dancing.

Mira isn't behind bars. She isn't being held in a dark, cold cell somewhere, being tortured for information. She's happy and healthy and being taken care of by an American family.

But Silas is a spy, too. He's trained to tell lies for a living, to make others believe every word that falls from his lips. I have to consider his story about Mira could be a carefully constructed scheme to get information from me. Maybe they broke her and that's how he found me, intending to finish the job by finishing me.

My mother wouldn't be in on a scheme like that, though. She'd die before she'd help anyone hurt us. In this entire confusing and maddening situation, that's the only fact I can cling to and not second-guess.

She said Silas would help me.

However, she doesn't know what I've discovered. And with that damning information in my head, I can't leave. If only I could convince Silas to help me instead of just throwing me on a plane back to Moscow. But that would've been a highly unlikely "if," even before I ditched him at the gala.

True to his word, the cab driver ran every red light and stop sign between the Reagan Building and my house to get the promised extra tip for getting me home in record time. I discreetly slide the $100 bill out of my bra and hand it to him. "Keep the change."

"Hey, thanks, lady!"

His night is made. Mine is falling apart. Story of my life.

I rush to the front porch, retrieve the hidden spare key, and head straight for my bedroom closet. After I kick off my shoes and leave the beautiful gown in a crumpled pile on the floor, I pull an oversized black hoodie over my head, slide black leggings over my legs, and complete the blackness of my mood with matching socks and boots. Extra jeans, sweaters, undergarments, and sneakers are shoved into a duffle bag, along with a stack of hidden cash and new identification, before I rush to the living room to grab my laptop and phone.

Everything else I've accumulated will have to stay. There's no time for sentimental attachments to material things when I live my life on the run day after day. With my electronics safely stashed in my bag, I turn from the table and take two steps toward the front door...before two strong arms grab me from behind. One muscular leg wraps around mine, hooking my ankle and preventing me from fighting back. Wrapped in a blanket of thick muscle and hard body, I can't even move.

My front door swings open, and Silas steps inside the frame, taking up the entire space with his enormous size. He crosses his arms, lowers his chin toward his chest, and glares menacingly at me. One thing I've learned about the men in this business—they don't care if the enemy is male or female. The same treatment is doled out regardless of sex, strength, or circumstances. From the way Silas is burning holes through me with the anger in his eyes, I'm not looking forward to the next few minutes.

"Kira, that was an incredibly stupid move." Silas moves inside and closes the door behind him. "As I recall, I offered to help you leave this country without being captured and sent to Gitmo for being a Russian spy and stealing top-secret government documents."

He takes the duffle bag from my tight grip with no effort at all and makes a point of looking it over. Then he cuts his eyes back to mine, barely hiding the anger seething just underneath. "And yet, this packed getaway bag makes me believe you were planning to disappear and continue your attack on my country."

When I don't reply, he shifts his eyes from mine to the man behind me. After a barely perceptible nod from Silas, I feel the tight coil of muscles encircle my neck a split second before I slip into complete darkness.

CHAPTER 4

Kira

I begin to rouse to the gentle rocking of a moving vehicle. Instinct nudges me before realization sets in, and I sit straight up with a start. We're well outside the city now, and everything is pitch black. Silas is driving; I can make out his silhouette from the back seat. Two large men flank me, leaving me very little room to move between their hulking forms. In fact, I think my cheek rested on one man's shoulder before I woke.

"Which one of you choked me out?"

A dark chuckle rumbles through the chest of the man to my left. "That was me, but I didn't choke you. It's a special technique that just helps you go right to sleep with no fuss."

I don't know this dickhead from Adam, and I have no idea where they're taking me or what they're planning to do to me once we get there. Years of training kick in, and I react violently, regardless of the massive men sandwiching me in the middle of the back seat, regardless of the moving vehicle, and regardless of the dark streets with no discernible landmarks to tell me where I am.

When my elbow connects with his nose, the familiar pop of bone and cartilage giving way echoes through the vehicle. His eyes shut involuntarily, and his hands fly to cover his face on pure reflex. I lunge for the car door on the other side of him, ready to tuck and roll before disappearing into the night, far from these men. Just as my fingers wrap around the door handle, two strong arms grab me from behind and haul me across the seat into his lap.

"Calm the fuck down. We're not here to hurt you—unless you make us."

"The fuck you say. He just knocked me out, and you three loaded me into a vehicle against my will. Now we're in the middle of Bumfuck, Egypt, and you think I should just go along and trust you?"

"I think you just broke my fucking nose." The other man glares over at me while wiping the blood from his face. The man holding me suppresses a chuckle, while Silas's deep laugh rumbles through the car without apology.

"And? You're lucky that's all I broke. What would you do if you woke up in a car with three strangers? Who the hell are you guys anyway?" I try to get a look at his face, but the lack of light works against me. I'm sure that is part of why they're taking me somewhere into the countryside of Virginia, if I had to guess.

He's silent, but Silas speaks up from the front. "That's Roman. The man on the other side of you is Nick."

"Well, I would say it's nice to meet you, but considering the circumstances, it's not." All three men laugh even though I didn't actually mean it as a joke. "Where are you taking me?"

Nick moves me back to my seat in the middle then secures the seat belt around me, pulling it tight across my body until it locks me in place.

"We're going to a safe house to talk." Silas is being especially tight-lipped and more reserved than he was at the gala. I realize that's my fault. He's punishing me for running away from him, but he'd do the same if our roles were reversed.

"Is that CIA code for you're taking me out to a remote field to kill me and dispose of my body?" I did mean that as a joke to lighten the mood in the car, if possible, but there's no reaction for a few seconds.

"What makes you think we're CIA?" Maybe Silas doesn't have a sense of humor after all.

"Because you bend the rules to suit you. Other agencies with three initials don't do that—they follow the rules to the letter. CIA officers only follow rules that benefit them."

Nick smiles, and I see a slight nod of his head. He knows what I said is true. I'm not judging since I obviously make decisions on the fly, all depending on the circumstances and pressures I'm under.

The car begins to slow, then Silas makes a right turn onto a long, darkened driveway. The gravel crunches under the weight of the tires as we creep toward the house hidden among the trees. Their idea of a safe house is vastly different than the city apartments and homes the GRU has. This location is more like the places we use to question traitors—isolated, secure, and soundproof. This situation doesn't bode well for me.

When we park, Roman gets out and turns to take my arm. Rather than exiting on the opposite side, Nick moves across the seat toward me, keeping me securely between the two of them. There's no way I can outrun all three of these men anyway— even if I knew where I was and which way to run. Once we're all out of the car, Silas walks behind us as Nick and Roman walk beside me, each gripping my arms until we're inside the house and the door is locked behind us.

The entryway opens directly into a large living room to the left and dining room to the right. After seeing the modern floor plan and comfortable furnishings, I now realize this house is newer than I initially thought. The unpaved driveway conjured images of an older dwelling—one other people wouldn't often visit.

"Have a seat." Silas walks through the dining room into the kitchen, and I sit on the plush leather sofa. While he's in the other room, I take the opportunity to glance around the fully decorated home. If this is a place for torture, they don't leave any evidence of it behind. "Here. This will wet your whistle and help you talk all night if needed."

He extends his hand to offer a bottle of cold water, so I take it from him and twist the cap, noting that it hasn't been opened before now. No unknown additives to help loosen my tongue. With his other hand, he swings a chair around to sit directly in front of me, our knees touching from the close quarters. Nick and Roman remain standing, guarding the exits with their large frames. I cut my gaze between the two men before rolling my eyes at them.

"You two can sit down. I won't try to run as long as we're only talking. But I'm not getting on an airplane. The only way I'm going back is if you shoot me and send me back in a casket."

They ignore me and maintain their vigilant stance instead.

"What were you looking for in the senator's office?" Silas pulls my attention back to him.

He's such a handsome man, still in his tuxedo, but now without the bow tie. The top couple buttons of his crisp white shirt are undone, hinting at his finely tuned body underneath. He stands a full head and shoulders taller than me, with a fully muscled frame perfectly proportionate to his height. I've caught glimpses of the different facets of his personality. His suave and debonair side and his playful nature.

But right now, he's in all-business mode, impatiently waiting for me to explain my actions. This man is very different from the one I danced with just a short time ago. That man was warm and inviting, but the man sitting in front of me is cold and calculating. There is no line he wouldn't cross to neutralize a threat.

What he doesn't understand is how volatile the bomb I'm about to drop in his lap is. He doesn't realize that in order to defend the country he loves, he'll have to cross the line he never thought he'd have to face. He'll have to betray his country in order to save it.

My silence stretches a little too long, and his patience is wearing a bit too thin. He leans forward, puts his forearms on his knees, and pierces me with his deep blue eyes. I've noticed they change with his mood. When he's friendly and accommodating, they're a warm, inviting shade of blue. Malleable and friendly, they draw others in on the premise of trust, honor, and duty. When he goes into interrogation mode, like now, the warmth completely disappears, replaced by an iciness that chills me to the bone. I have no doubt this man is a trained killer and has no misgivings about using his unique skills.

"We're doing this the easy way at the moment, Kira. But this is the last time I will ask nicely. You think you've pegged CIA officers so well. So, believe me when I say this. If I don't get a complete and honest answer right now, you'll find out firsthand exactly what I'm capable of doing in order to protect and serve my country. I know what you are and why you're here. You've been here illegally, silently observing but not actively conspiring against us. Until tonight. Now that you've stepped up your game, I want to know why—what prompted the change in your behavior. And you will tell me everything."

I'd like to have the warm and flirty Silas back now. But he's long gone, and I'm afraid he won't be back anytime soon.

"My sister and I were brought here against our will twenty years ago. We were only ten years old when we were ripped from our mother's arms, Silas. You say you know her? Then you know she doesn't exactly wear her heart on her sleeve when it comes to showing her emotions. So imagine seeing her have a complete breakdown, right in front of you, while men you don't know, have never even seen before, drag you away from the only home you've ever had. All they would tell us was that we'd have a new family soon and to forget about our old one if we knew what was good for us.

"We grew up here in America, taking English lessons until we were fluent, and all traces of our Russian accents were gone. We went to school here, just like every other American teenager. But we had extra lessons after school—learning fighting skills, staying up-to-date on the latest technology advancements, and training how to get in and out of buildings undetected. We didn't know what we were being prepared to do throughout our teenage years, only that we had to keep everything a secret from everyone else. We were one person by day and a completely different person at night. Then we turned eighteen and were forced into this life—no questions of what we wanted to do with our lives, no options to go off to college somewhere, and no mention of our future. Nothing we've done since we were ten has been our choice. You have to believe me."

I'm fully aware all my blurted confession is entirely off topic, even though he already warned me about not answering his direct questions. But this is all information he needs to know, nevertheless. I need him to understand what occurred in the past, so the path we should take in the present and the future is crystal clear.

"That's a very touching story. I'm perplexed, though, because you told me everything except what I asked." With a menacing expression covering his face, he starts rolling up his sleeves, revealing his muscular forearms.

"I'm trying to tell you everything—so you'll get the big picture and understand what's happening. Just give me a chance to explain."

"By all means, continue." He waves his hand in front of him, but the skepticism in his voice is loud and clear.

"There are more people like Mira and me planted here, waiting to be activated. They've been here for years, working in every walk of life, rising to the top of corporate ladders, or just hosting new recruits in their homes. They're also in the government, from a secretary in the FBI to a staffer in a congressman's office…maybe even a senator himself. They're doing their jobs normally and living their daily lives until they hear from their mentor. Then they cross that line and become a spy again."

"Are you saying the senator whose office you broke into is a Russian asset?" His expression matches his voice, wholly skeptical and ready to toss me into a cell then forget I exist.

"I don't know what his exact capacity is, but I do know he's important to whatever the current project is. He has ties to the Academy and the GRU somehow. That's part of why I had to get into his computer—to find out what he's doing and why."

"The Academy?"

"The training center that runs all of our operations."

"How do they do that—get your orders to you? What's their process?"

"They send the encrypted orders to our handlers, but never directly to the operative, and no one here has all the information about any single op. The information is divided up between several players, only giving each person the information about their specific job. There's also always at least one layer of contact between everyone—the GRU and us, and between the activated operatives."

"How do you know the senator is involved?" Silas's expression doesn't change, but something in the air around us makes me think he's starting to believe me. The twenty-questions game is a one-way street, and I understand why, but we're wasting valuable time.

"Have you ever heard pieces of different conversations, picked up on various tidbits of information, then put them all together, and they made a perfectly clear picture?"

He nods without verbally confirming, but at least he's giving me that much.

"That's exactly what I've done. You probably expect me to point to one specific detail or give you one concrete shred of evidence to prove it. I can't do that without going through everything on that flash drive."

"Yeah, that's not happening. Do you think I'm gullible? Do you really think I'd just hand that over so you can memorize every top-secret detail in there and pass them on to your superiors? Try again. That's almost more of an insult than your stealing from my country. You really think I'm that stupid?"

"What? No, I don't think you're stupid at all. I don't want to give that information to my superiors—I wanted to use it to save my sister! I was going to change the documents before handing the flash drive off to them at our drop site Wednesday morning. They told me my sister was sitting in a prison cell at a black site because of me, Silas. They said she was being tortured and would eventually be killed—all because they thought she was me when she was caught. I've only continued working with them to get close to the senator. They said they'd find a way to get Mira out if I did this, even if it meant they had to do a prisoner exchange."

"They're open to an exchange, huh? Who do they claim to have to exchange?"

This conversation just took a very unexpected change in direction, and I'm not sure how to answer that question. If the name I give him is a high-value asset, he'll trade Mira and me in a heartbeat. If not, I've just inadvertently given up a valuable leverage opportunity. After a quick glance around the room, I confirm all eyes are on me, and if possible, they would burn holes through me with the intensity of their stares. They all want to hear the answer to that question—which tells me I need to sit on that information for as long as possible.

"Is my sister really okay?" My voice cracks at the end, but I push the emotions clogging my throat back down.

Remember your training.

I hear Olga Vladimirovna, my instructor at the Academy, in my head, relentlessly pushing me to train longer, fight harder, and show no weaknesses.

Silas doesn't move, doesn't flinch, doesn't even seem to breathe for far too long. Then he nods again. His shoulders lift as he inhales deeply then releases his breath in a resigned sigh. "Mira is fine. I wasn't lying when I said she's living with a family who loves her very much. She's working as the nanny for their children now. The three of us are the only ones who know about her past, and her former employer has no clue how to find her." He motions toward Nick and Roman as he speaks, but I can't look away from him. "And I plan to keep it that way."

"I want to see her. Please, just take me to her."

Silas shakes his head. "You can forget about that."

CHAPTER 5

Silas

"What do you think? Do you believe her?" Nick eyes me, carefully watching my every reaction. He has more skin in this game than anyone, so I understand his concern. Kira's sister lives in his house, helps care for his babies, and has become a best friend to his wife. An international incident would take both ladies down with one fail swoop.

"I don't know, man. On the one hand, I'd say she's telling the truth. On the other, I know she's a trained GRU operative—and they're not far removed from the KGB days. Same trainers. Same expectations. Same results." I shake my head, more irritated with myself than anything else. I'm too close to this case to make rational decisions. There's way too much at stake in this game. The blurred lines are not part and parcel of my usual method, and I don't like it.

Nick nods, understanding my confused state, and heads back into the living room to babysit our guest.

"The great Silas Steele can't decide if a Russian spy is lying to him or not? What the hell is going on here?" Roman glares at me as if I've lost my mind. Maybe I have. "What the fuck, man? You got the hots for her?"

"What? No, of course not. Fuck off."

"You fuck off. You're lying to me right now. You've been compromised—either fuck her out of your system or step aside and let us do our job. We don't have time to wait. We need to know what time and where her dead drop is so we can get eyes on it right now."

I know Roman is right about part of what he's saying, but my gut is conflicted for a reason. That doesn't mean his words don't thoroughly piss me off, though. I've listened to my instincts and stayed alive in much more dire circumstances than this. Not trusting my senses now would be a huge mistake—but that's about all I'm sure of at this point.

"Back off, Roman. You have no idea what you're talking about." I cut my glare to meet his and watch him instantly relax his rigid stance. "I know how to do my job—and that's exactly what I'm doing. If this senator is selling our secrets or in any way working with a foreign government under the table, we need to find out every detail so we can shut him down."

"You're right about that, of course. But it's not like you not to know if someone is lying to you or not. What gives?" He isn't letting this one go after all.

"I think it's because I know her sister so well. When I confronted Mira about her previous employer, she didn't even try to deny it. She admitted everything, answered every question, and gave me more information that any informant ever has in my career.

"Kira, on the other hand, started out being deceitful to me, running from me, trying to ditch me. Lying about one of our senators and claiming she only wants to save her sister would be a good stall tactic. But if she happens to be telling the truth, sending her back to Russia would be a huge mistake. I don't want to make any rash decisions about her fate I'll regret later."

"Well, they do look exactly alike. I can see where that could be confusing."

"They may look alike to you, but not to me. They're complete opposites. Kira is hard, cunning, and adventurous. Mira is soft, sweet, and prefers the sidelines. I could see the differences in them in a picture their father has of them when they're maybe eight years old. Their personality traits make them as different as night and day, even in their appearance."

"That may be—to you—but not to me. From where I stand, they're the spitting image of each other, which is probably why the GRU wanted them so badly. I hear your objection, buddy, but your vision isn't clear on this one. That girl in there has your head spinning, whether you want to acknowledge it or not. She's exactly your type. I'm betting none of your other liaisons with other CIA officers over the years hold a candle to her." Roman flashes a shit-eating grin, confident in his ability to profile me, and walks off before I can object.

I slide my cell out of my pocket and dial my deputy director to fill him in on what we're facing and advise him of my plans.

"Graves."

"Chuck, this is Silas. I need to apprise you of a situation."

Over the next few minutes, I give him the rundown of the night and the accusations Kira leveled against a sitting senator. As usual, he's quiet while listening to all the facts, then gets straight to the point with his directive.

"Get to the bottom of it, Steele. Find out if she's lying or telling the truth. Don't let her out of your sight for even one fucking second. If she needs to take a piss, you'd better be right beside her, handing her the fucking toilet paper. You have two weeks to prove or disprove her allegations before she's on a plane bound for Russia."

"Two weeks? Sir, this will amount to a full-scale investigation. Two weeks isn't much time to collect intel and make a definitive decision."

"It's all the time you're getting, Steele. She's a known, admitted Russian spy. On American soil. I'm doing you a favor by giving you two weeks at all. She should be on the tarmac, headed back to her Mother Russia right now. I suggest you keep her on a very short, tight leash, because if she fucks us, it's your ass that'll feel it."

"Understood, sir."

When I start to rejoin them in the living room, I hear Kira questioning Nick about her sister. I watch her for a few moments before she realizes I've stepped back into the room, studying her movements, the words she chooses, and the information she's trying to get out of him.

"Can't you just tell me where she is?" Kira's pleading has no effect on Nick.

"No." Nick's stoic expression nearly makes me laugh out loud. I haven't seen any signs that she's an assassin, but then again, I wouldn't put it past her.

"They told me she'd been caught and was being tortured at a black site because of me. She took an assignment I was supposed to run, and then she never came back. I've blamed myself and tried to find a way to get her out for the past year. I miss her so much. She's the only family member I've been able to hold on to all these years. They let us talk to Mom and Dad on the phone twice a year, but never more than that. Mira's the only real family I have."

Tears slide down her cheeks, but I have to question if they're crocodile tears—it's part of my training and part of my job. I just don't know her well enough yet to read her real emotions. She's kept them repressed longer than any normal person, and from such an early age, so she has impressive control over them. All the more reason why my guard is up, and I'm leery as hell of everything she says.

"Can I talk to her on the phone? Will you call her? Let me just hear from her that she's okay." The desperate pleading in her voice now is genuine. She's unsure if we've told her the truth about Mira.

"Nick, why don't you go pick Mira up and bring her here? Roman and I can entertain Kira for a while. Maybe you can bring Brad back with you too." Nick hesitates for only a second before reading my mind.

"Sure, I can do that. Call if you need anything else while I'm out. We'll be back here very soon." With that, Nick leaves us alone with a very apprehensive prisoner.

Roman locks the door and resets the house alarm once Nick is off the porch. The motion sensors around the house will alert us if anyone unexpected shows up. The doors and windows are set to remain locked unless the deactivate code is entered. The only way out is if she breaks a window or someone rams the door. From the frightened expression on her face, she knows all too well she's trapped.

When she lifts the bottle of water to her lips, I notice her hand shaking as she takes a drink. Is that from nerves or an extra dump of adrenaline as she readies herself for the flight-or-fight response? At this point, I'm going with nerves. She's made no move to get up from the couch. Her eyes aren't focused on anything in particular. She's merely staring off into space, lost in her own thoughts while she attempts to make sense of everything.

Her world as she knew it was thoroughly and completely upended. The truths she based her life and actions on turned out to be lies, all designed to use and manipulate her. The people she trusted revealed their true character. Now she's clinging to the one hope she has left in the world, and that's her sister—the only genuinely loyal person she has ever known.

"I will be very upfront with you, Kira, as long as you're honest with me. If at any time you lie to me or try to run from me again, you'll be forcibly removed from my country. Do we understand each other?"

"Absolutely."

"We've been given two weeks to get to the bottom of this allegation. If we don't have indisputable and irrefutable evidence by then, I've been ordered to put you on a plane bound for Moscow. This is normally a full-scale FBI investigation that could take months and teams of agents to complete. We have a team of three, plus a couple of Russian spies, to accomplish an impossible mission in record time."

"I'm up for it if you are." Her eyes meet mine, and I see the fire and determination ignite in them again.

"I reviewed all the documents on your flash drive. Nothing in there directly implicates Senator Hunt in any type of espionage ring, unless they're using very sophisticated ciphers." Roman folds his arms over his chest. The accusation in his tone is heard loud and clear.

"That's not my fault. I copied as many documents from his office computer as I could, hoping I had the ones that would be useful. Silas knows I didn't have time to delete or alter anything before he stole the flash drive from my house. If you'd let me review them with you, I may be able to put two and two together easier."

"I am not sharing classified documents with you for any reason. Now, if the damaging evidence isn't on his computer in his office, exactly where do you think we'll find it, then?" Roman is testing her, seeing if she'll take the bait.

"You don't really think the only place he works is in his office, do you? I'm sure he works on his laptop at home or on his phone whenever he travels. His docking station was empty, so he must've taken his laptop with him. He's one of the last men in the world to carry a briefcase with actual papers in it. I'm sure at least some are classified, top-secret documents."

"You didn't complete surveillance on him before you worked your way into his office and into his files, did you?" Roman pins her with a look of utter disgust.

"No, I took a calculated risk, betting that the information would be on his computer in his office, where he'd most likely access the Intelligence Committee files."

"Wow. We really are starting from scratch on this case, aren't we? How are we supposed to wrap it up within two weeks?" Roman looks at me for answers, but I don't have them yet.

"We'll work this the same way we work any other case. One blind leap of faith at a time. We'll start with the basics, weed through the garbage, and hope we come out smelling like roses in the end. There will be a lot of surveillance, little to no sleep, and being spread very thin since we won't have a lot of help." I shrug my shoulders, not knowing what else to say to make him feel better about our odds.

"What happens at the end of that time? What if we find incriminating evidence but not enough to prove his involvement?" Roman asks.

"You, Nick, and I will probably keep working the case until resolution, but it'll be without Kira's help."

"What about Mira? Will she be sent back with her sister?"

"I didn't tell the deputy director about Mira."

Roman's jaw drops, and he stares at me in utter disbelief. "Better watch out for those blurred lines, Silas. They'll trip you up every time."

"I hear you. But I think I crossed that line about a year and a half ago when I recognized Mira and didn't turn them both in immediately when I found Kira. Something about it just never felt like the right thing to do, though."

"For all of our sakes, I hope you're right."

Off the record, I hope I'm right, too.

CHAPTER 6

Kira

wo weeks?

That's all the time they're giving us to find hard evidence against a heavily involved politician? How is that even possible?

If that's true, we're wasting time sitting in this house, hashing out who trusts whom instead of just getting the job done. We need to move with what we already know and figure out the rest as we go. If I'm sent back to Moscow, I'll be executed within days. They'll interrogate me first for any information that could possibly help them, but they'll get rid of me, nonetheless. Mira will have to spend her life in the shadows, always looking over her shoulder out of fear someone will find her.

"Silas, we should go to his house in the DC area and check it out. Right now. We can slip inside, get his briefcase, and check the contents right there while we're in his office. He'll never know we were there. Maybe we'll get lucky and find the documents in his possession. It's entirely possible he keeps them at home instead of at the office. His aide said the senator's been out of the office all week because his daughter is getting married at his house this weekend. Maybe he took the evidence home with him."

"I've never found working by luck to be…lucky." Silas slowly cocks one eyebrow at me, as if my idea is the craziest suggestion he's ever heard. "We need to stake out his house, check his security system, note their schedules—along with their neighbors and any rent-a-cops. He could also live in a gated community. There's a lot more to this job than just a simple B&E. Plus, if the wedding is at his house, too many people will be going in and out for us to slip in undetected."

We don't have enough time for a full-scale stakeout approach. I start to voice my objection, but the motion sensor alarm catches my attention instead. The front door slowly opens, and Nick enters first. He stops in the doorway to glance around before fully stepping inside. Standing directly behind him is my sister, Mira. When she sees me, her bottom jaw drops, and her eyes remain wide and unblinking. Her hands fly to her face, covering her mouth as her eyes start to water. She shakes her head, disbelief clearly showing in her features.

When I stand, I extend my arms out to either side, and she rushes into my embrace without saying a word. We hold each other, not moving other than to squeeze each other tighter and tighter. Mira's sobs break free, tearing through her body and making her shake uncontrollably in my arms. I've never seen her react so intensely before, so I'm naturally concerned by her outburst. I slide my hands to her shoulders and push until she's an arm's length from me.

"Mira…talk to me. What is it? What happened to you?"

"Kira, I can't believe you're actually here. My last assignment went bad…very bad. When the explosives detonated in this old building, the structural integrity was worse than we'd anticipated. All that was left of the two-story structure was rubble.

That's when I realized I finally had a chance to get out. They'd think I was still inside until the debris was cleared, and by then, I'd be well hidden away.

"So, I ran straight to a women's shelter, where I knew men weren't allowed and they wouldn't find me. But I found ways to check the message system without being traced. I intercepted one of the messages they sent back to Moscow. They reported you were dead, Kira. They told Moscow I was missing in action, presumed a deserter, so they interrogated and executed you when you didn't tell them where to find me. All this time, I've believed you were dead because of me, and that I was all alone. I'm just so happy you're alive."

She throws her arms around my neck again, squeezing tighter this time, while softly chanting "thank you" over and over again. Since we were little kids, I've been the one to help Mira stand on her own two feet, show her she is more than capable, and encourage her to keep fighting. She was never cut out for the life we were forced into living, and I've always felt it was my responsibility to keep her alive. Over the last year I've been looking for her, I've questioned if she withered up and died, or fought and blossomed like the magnificent rebel I know she is deep inside.

"I'm fine, sissy. They never interrogated me. They never hurt me in any way. They asked me several questions about you, but that was nothing. That communication was sent to draw you out because they had no idea where you were. I'm just so thankful you didn't fall for their tricks. You found a good hiding place, because I've been looking for you for the past year and a half and didn't find a single trace of you."

"I'm not living in the shelter anymore. I met the most wonderful woman while I was there. Her name is Savannah and, when you meet her, you'll love her as much as I do. You'll see." Mira's smile lights up her face and reminds me again how much I've missed her. She has always been the bright sunshine that chases away the gloomy gray clouds in my mind.

"As much as I'd love to meet her, I'm not sure I'll get that chance, sis. Silas caught me stealing top-secret information from a senator's office, so I'm to be returned to Moscow in two weeks. We have until then to get the proof we need, or they'll shut down the investigation as a false accusation. There's a lot to do and not a lot of time left for socializing."

Mira's smile fades as her face drops, and it breaks my heart to see the amount of pain in her eyes. Realization of what will happen soon sets in, and she starts shaking her head. "No. Silas, no, you can't send her back now. You know what'll happen to her if you do. They'll execute her and dump her body in a land-fill without a second thought. You have to do something to stop this."

As he's a man who has lived his life in the shadows and under the cloak of anonymity, the uneasiness of being thrust into the spotlight is painfully obvious in his expression. On the one hand, he doesn't want to let Mira down by telling her the hard truth. On the other hand, I don't think he agrees with what his superior ordered him to do, so his heart isn't in it, but he knows he can't shirk his duties.

"This decision wasn't up to him, Mira. It wasn't his call to make. He tried to argue against it, but he has to follow orders or face the consequences. It's not fair of us to ask him to do anything other than what's right. I took those documents for a good reason, and I wasn't going to give the information over to the GRU, but what I did was illegal, regardless."

"What's right? How is giving you a one-way ticket to your own execution anywhere near right? If they send you back, they'll have to send me back too. There's no way I can live with myself knowing what's happening to you in Moscow while I'm here, living the comfortable life in Virginia."

"And I can't let you do that. You're not paying for my

mistakes." I kiss her cheek, knowing the only thing we have in common besides our appearance is our stubborn streak. Neither of us is good at backing down once we've made up our mind.

But there's no sense in arguing the point any further now. There's too much to do and not enough time to do it the way I'd prefer—and definitely not enough time to handle it the way Silas insists. I can only hope to change their minds once the solid proof is in my hands, and I fill in the blanks with the knowledge in my head. Maybe throw in an extra measure of information that I have hidden up my sleeve—in case of a rainy day...or a life-or-death emergency.

"She's telling the truth, Silas." A man I didn't notice before now speaks up, his head popping up from behind a thick metal case. He's tall with a lean build, but he's not scrawny. His muscles simply aren't as bulky as the other men in the room. He's unassuming yet attractive with his short brown hair and green eyes. He's definitely one of them, blending in, gathering intel, not drawing attention to himself. "And there's no way in hell I'll let you go back to Russia, Mira. You know that."

"Kira, this is Brad." Mira moves to stand beside him. She has an obvious affection for him if the shy smile and stolen glances are any indication. From the way he looks at her, I'd say the feeling is more than mutual. "Brad, this is my sister, Kira."

Brad takes her hand in his before walking over to me. He extends his other hand, and I accept it as we exchange greetings. "Have you known my sister long?"

"Savannah introduced us soon after they met, so about a year a half ago now."

"You're a friend of the mysterious Savannah, too? Seems everyone knows her except me."

"She's my wife," Nick says. He's visibly still leery of me—unwilling to share more than the most basic information. The very least of what he's absolutely required to share with me.

"Oh, okay. Well, hopefully I'll get to meet her one day. My sister seems very taken with her. So, Brad, who was telling the truth and about what?"

Silas nods, giving Brad permission to explain. "You, Kira. You were telling the truth about not planning to give the classified documents to the GRU. The results were a little fuzzy when you said the decision wasn't up to Silas, but emotions can alter the results of the scan. Or, it also could be that part of you blames him for the situation. Either way, you have a strong reaction to him. More focused questioning would tell me what the truth is."

"Or you could just ask me directly."

"The answer to that question isn't really germane to the investigation." So, Brad is obviously the tech guru of the group. Direct, unemotional responses when he's focused on the problem at hand.

"But it could give us insight into her state of mind overall. Maybe we should ask her." Silas smiles, making me question if he has an actual playful side after all.

"I don't blame you, Silas. What I did is not your responsibility. Do I wish you hadn't caught me? Of course. But it is what it is." I turn my attention back to Brad. "How did you know I was telling the truth?"

Before Brad can reply, Nick interjects. "We have access to advanced technology. That's all you need to know about it."

"Fair enough. So, what's the plan, then? What's the next move?" I look at Silas and find him staring at me intently.

"The next move…is to go back to your house, get whatever you need to get ready for a black-tie affair, and show up for the wedding being held in the senator's home tomorrow."

"How will we get in at this late date? RSVPs have to be sent weeks in advance for events like that."

"We've already got that covered. Don't worry."

"Won't his aide be there? He could still recognize me, even without the blond wig."

"No, he's too low on the totem pole to be invited to an important event like that. The senator's only daughter is getting married then leaving the country for six months. They only want the cream of the crop at the reception. There will be so many people moving in and out of the house and the huge event tent set up in his backyard, they won't notice a couple of guests lost in their enormous mansion."

"Are you asking me to be your date for a wedding, Silas?" I try to lighten the somber mood of the room with a little humor, but the heated look in his eyes makes my heart race instead.

"Absolutely. And you know what the standing rule for wedding dates is, right?"

Years of training taught me to suppress my feelings, not to get emotionally involved in any mission, and view sex on the job as a necessary means to an end. No man has ever affected me while I was working in character, using him to get what I needed. Come to think of it, even the few men I dated as myself never really knew me. They never actually affected me enough to elicit real feelings.

So how, after being captured in the act and subsequently questioned by this man, do I have butterflies fluttering in my chest from a single flirtatious question?

"What rule is that?" I finally find my voice.

"You can't wear white and upstage the bride. We'll have to find you another dress because you'd definitely steal the show in that white dress you were wearing earlier."

I've never felt so stupid before in all my life. I completely misread the meaning behind his question.

CHAPTER 7

Silas

Brad, Nick, and Roman have escorted the ladies back to Kira's place to pack her belongings since she won't be living there again anytime soon. Or ever. Looks like she'll live here with me for the next couple of weeks while we sort through the accusations to determine if she's stalling, lying, or telling the truth.

Even though Roman has already checked the documents and I trust him with my life, I decide to take a look at them myself while they're gone. He's a good man and a great soldier, but after years in this game, there may be hidden keys I'd notice that he wouldn't. I'm leaving no stone unturned in this operation. The first few are run-of-the-mill internal sharing of information, nothing exciting or eye-opening about the content.

Then one catches my eye, making my spy senses tingle all over. Even as part of the Intelligence Committee, the senator would have no need for this information. It was classified "eyes only" when the case was opened years ago, meaning only a specific set of people have clearance to see it. And I know for a fact that he wasn't one of them, because I was.

"Now why would you be interested in this?" I steeple my hands in front of my face and let all possible, even improbable, situations run through my mind. One thing I've learned from working with all types of people all over the world—never underestimate your opponent. Or your coworker.

When the front door opens, I hear Brad, Nick, Mira, and Kira all laughing—at Roman's expense, from the sounds of it. That makes me smile. He's excellent at his job…but not so much with personal relationships. Forcing him into close quarters with others who acknowledge their feelings is good exposure for him…and good entertainment for me.

Before anyone walks into my office, I shut down the application and close my laptop. The words on that page are ingrained in my memory, though, and none of the possibilities of why Senator Hunt pilfered that specific investigation are good.

I step into the living room and see why everyone is laughing at Roman. He has multiple duffle bags draped over his arms while trying to maneuver large suitcases through the front door. But Brad's, Nick's, Kira's, and Mira's arms are empty. Multiple straps slide off his shoulders, falling to his forearm and making him release the suitcases. He looks like a one-man vaudeville show, juggling multiple items that were never meant to be juggled.

"Did you lose a bet, Roman?" I can't help but laugh after I ask.

"He's actually in the process of losing said bet. He was bragging, as usual, saying he could carry everything she owned and then some without any help from us. So, we're letting him prove his worth. We're not convinced yet." Nick folds his arms across his chest, his smug expression intact, and continues watching Roman struggle alone.

"For fuck's sake, give us a bag, Roman, and let us help you." I grab one of the large suitcases from his grip and pull it inside the house before also taking the one in his other hand. Then I turn my attention to Kira. "Did you find anything to wear to the wedding tomorrow evening?"

"No, sorry. The only thing I have that's formal enough is the white dress I wore earlier, and we both know that won't work."

"That's not a problem. There are plenty of places nearby that'll have something appropriate for you to wear. We'll have time to go tomorrow since it's an evening wedding."

"Who gets married in January in the DC area anyway? It's too fucking cold. Why not wait until the cherry trees are in bloom and everything's beautiful again?" Kira shakes her head and takes a couple duffle bags from Roman.

"Senator Hunt's daughter is marrying a doctor who's volunteering with Doctors Without Borders. They wanted to get married before they leave the country for the next six months so their families can witness it." I had the same question and did a little research while they were away. The weather is too cold and snowy for a traditional wedding, but it seems Hunt's daughter is marrying a genuinely good man.

"Sounds like you need your invitations now." Brad boots up his unique laptop—the one specifically designed for him by the best of the best in the CIA technology center for all his high-tech needs.

With a few simple keystrokes, Brad updates the attendee list with the pictures for the aliases Kira and I will use to get into the exclusive event. I'm counting heavily on the mother and father of the bride to be too busy and overcome with emotion to notice us roaming around their home unsupervised. Good thing I can think of a distraction or two should we get caught coming out of one of the bedrooms. Being caught in the act of rifling through their drawers would be a little harder to explain, though.

"We've accomplished as much tonight as we possibly can, so

everyone should head home, get some rest, and be ready to go again first thing tomorrow. Kira needs a dress, we need comms, and I need an up-to-date blueprint of the house so I can get a feel for the layout and where he'd possibly hide valuables. We still have a lot to do and no extra time to do it in."

"I'll have the blueprint for you first thing in the morning, Silas. Check your email when you wake up." Brad places his hand on Mira's lower back, giving her a silent cue that she has to say goodbye now.

Mira wraps her arms around Kira's neck and holds on for half a minute or more. Tears stream down both of their faces, neither wanting to be the first to let go after being apart for so long and not knowing the other's fate.

"Mira, why don't you plan on going shopping with Kira tomorrow? It'll be a good outing for you two to spend more time together without actually making you a party to this operation."

"Thank you, Silas. I appreciate that."

As Nick, Brad, and Mira are leaving, I tell Roman to head home, too. We have a long day tomorrow, and Kira isn't going anywhere else tonight without me. With the house locked up and protected by the best alarm system available, we'll both be able to rest for the remainder of the night without any extra security shifts. Plus, now that she's assured her sister is close by, safe, and still accessible to her, she doesn't seem too keen on leaving anymore.

"It has been a long day and an equally long evening. I'll take your stuff to your room for you." I pick up her suitcases and gesture toward the hall. "Do you need anything else for now?"

"No, I brought everything I need from my place. Thank you, though. Are you going to bed too?"

We reach the guest bedroom, and I open the door for her then place her bags beside the bed. "No, I've lived on much less sleep than I'll get tonight for many years. I'll be fine. The bathroom is right through that door over there. Plenty of closet space for your clothes over here. You're not confined to this room. If you want anything from the kitchen, it's yours. No need to ask. If you want to hang out in the den and watch TV for a while, you're welcome to it. Make yourself at home."

"Thank you for this, Silas. Sincerely. I'm drained, so I think I'll just go to bed now. Like you said, we have a lot to do tomorrow, and we need to get an early start."

"Until tomorrow, then."

ROMAN AND NICK AGREED TO TAKE BOTH KIRA AND MIRA shopping while Brad and I finish working on the logistics of getting lost in the senator's mansion while scores of workers are milling about. To clarify, Roman didn't exactly agree—but he complied with direct orders, regardless. He had a few choice words to call me before he left on his mandated shopping mission, but spending time with the ladies will do him good. He thinks he's such a player, but I know where his head and heart are. Even if he's still clueless.

"Brad, I've been given permission to read you in on this case so I can share the details of this document with you. This was listed as 'eyes only,' and I was one of the few people allowed to know the details of the investigation. I remember the case vividly, because I was going back and forth to Moscow at the time, chasing ghosts that made me look like an incompetent fool. By the time I figured out one clue to their hideout location, they'd already moved somewhere else, and I had to start all over again. My failure on that case is something I've never forgotten, and what I saw still haunts me to this day.

"The thing is, not one single US official was ever identified as a potential target—no one even with any distant ties to the suspects. But we knew there had to be someone with connections helping them because they were always one step ahead of us, and that shit just doesn't happen. Senator Hunt was not part of the special committee appointed to review the details, and our director made a decision to intentionally keep it out of the Senate's reach."

"So how did Senator Hunt get it, then? It's not like Langley's server is on a cloud." Brad's question is rhetorical, knowing I don't have that answer yet.

While he reads the entire document, his question echoes in my mind. There's only one way that document got out of Langley…and none of the possible scenarios gives me any peace. When he looks up from the screen, he wears a perplexed expression.

"This information is very high level. What am I missing? What's in the fine print?"

For the next thirty minutes, I walk Brad through every detail of the case. How it began, where it took us, and why we were never able to bring it to full closure. Every officer has one case that haunts him, gives him nightmares, and makes him second-guess his place in the agency. This one has been the thorn in my side for years, knowing there had to be a piece of the puzzle missing but driving myself crazy trying to find it. Now that I've caught a glimpse of it, I have a sick feeling in the pit of my stomach and an acute desire to ignore the truth. Because there's no going back once I've crossed the line drawn in front of me.

"What are you going to do, Silas?" The concern in his eyes is evidence of the danger we're walking into. This doesn't affect only me—the lives of our entire team are now in jeopardy.

"I'm going to do my job, even though I know exactly what that means if I'm caught before I have irrefutable proof. Even that may not be enough to get me off the hook."

"What does that mean, Silas?"

"It means I think the senator is in some very shady shit, and in order to prove it, I'll have to read Kira in on the case, too. She may not know what this document means, but she may have some insight into Moscow's involvement from the past. If I can get information out of her, it may help us figure out why he has this document at all."

"But that's treason, Silas. You can't do that—there's no coming back from betraying your country, especially since you're a career CIA officer. Everything you've ever done to protect and serve will be dissected and questioned. Every mistake you've ever made, even if you've corrected it since then, and every judgment call you've made that falls outside the lines will be put on trial for the world to be your judge, jury, and executioner."

"Trust me, Brad. The CIA won't allow it to go that far. It'll be covered up, along with my body in the middle of the Sahara Desert where no evidence will ever be found. It'll be a miracle if I can pull this off, so I completely understand if you want to walk away now."

"I'm not going anywhere, man. You and your brother have never let me down, and I'm not about to turn my back on you now. I'll keep all eyes off you as long as I can."

"Thanks, Brad. I'm glad to have you on my side. I still have a shit-ton of other files to read through first, but this is the only one that has raised huge red flags so far. Let's see if there are more before I tell her anything about it."

The driveway alarm chimes, alerting me to an incoming vehicle. After a quick check of the monitors, I verify it's Nick and the gang returning from their shopping excursion. A pan of the camera rewards me with a closeup shot of Roman's face. His expression screams he's disgusted, disgruntled, and displeased, making me burst out laughing at his expense. I can almost feel his eyes burning straight through me when they land on the camera. Then he flips me off, holding up his middle finger all the way up the driveway.

The ladies are chatting up a storm when they walk into the

house. If I didn't already know them, I wouldn't have pegged them for Russian spies. They sound like the normal, average American woman. The dress, the shoes, the hair, the makeup—every detail every other woman I've ever known has focused on when dressing for a black-tie affair. Part of me wishes I'd never recognized Mira that day I met her in the women's shelter when she was hiding from her handlers under an alias. But her fake name wasn't too far off from her real name. She used the name Miranda Petrovia to hide in plain sight.

Kira is holding a long garment bag in one hand and a shoe box in the other. Her makeup has been professionally applied, and her black hair is expertly styled in a sweeping updo. She's beautiful with her long hair worn down and flowing across her shoulders, but I have to say this new style is doubly appealing, exposing the soft skin of her slender neck.

"Well, it's not white, but I can't guarantee she won't upstage the bride, Silas. This dress was made for her—no one can wear it like she does. Even I have to admit she looks sinfully sexy in it." Mira raises her eyebrows, driving her point home.

After hearing that, I know I'm probably in for a long night.

CHAPTER 8

Kira

Shopping and getting made up at the salon took longer than I had anticipated, so by the time I got back, Silas and I only had a couple of hours left before we had to leave for Senator Hunt's estate. Silas greeted us as he usually did, made small talk for a few minutes, then disappeared into his bedroom. And closed the door. At first, I assumed he was getting dressed in his tuxedo, so I retreated to my bedroom, and Mira helped me put on my dress and not mess up my hair or makeup in the process.

That was forty-five minutes ago, and Silas still hasn't emerged from behind his closed door.

"Stop worrying. You look beautiful, exactly like you fit in their world. No one will question your presence there." Mira grabs my shoulders and holds me in place, making me look her in the eye. "Let loose and have fun on your date with Silas tonight every chance you get."

"It's not a date, sis. We're actually working and just pretending to be on a date." I shake my head at her. I know she only wants me to be happy, to drop my walls of steel and let someone in besides her for once.

"Deny it all you want, but we're twins. I've known Silas for a while now. When he could've turned me in and sent me to an actual black site, he showed me mercy instead. I didn't know until recently, but he also followed you since the day he figured out who I was. He made sure you were safe and stayed out of trouble. Even when he caught you breaking into the secure servers, he fought to keep you on the case with him. He's a good man, and he's a good match for you. I'm making it my personal mission to make sure you two realize how perfect you are for each other."

Her enthusiasm would be contagious if I didn't already know I'll be forcibly removed from the country in less than two weeks now. "Mira, I'll be gone soon. We don't exactly have enough time to date, marry, and live happily ever after in that time. In fact, we couldn't even finish a round of antibiotics in that short time. I appreciate why you're trying to do this, but there's no sense in pursuing something that can never be."

The door to Silas's room opens, and he comes strolling out, wearing his tailor-made tuxedo and looking far too sexy for the female population to take. One look at me and he stops in his tracks. His jaw is slack, and his eyes are wide, slowly dragging up and down my body. My cheeks burn, and my heart races from the heat in his gaze.

The dress I picked out is the most gorgeous formal dress I've ever seen. The glamorous silver-beaded and sequined bodice has a sweetheart neckline, dipping in the middle to reveal just enough cleavage to be stunningly sexy. The long, sheer, off-shoulder sleeves are beaded, continuing the sparkling sheen of the top, while the skirt is pure peach satin, showing enough thigh to carry off the sultry vibe. The train begins from the material gathered at the waist, long and sheer in the back and is also covered in beads and sequins. The entire ensemble catches the light as I move and twinkles like stars in the dark skies.

"Kira, you look absolutely ravishing. I mean, I thought you were beautiful before, but now I can't tear my eyes away from you. Your sister is right—you could wear a burlap sack, and you'd still upstage the bride. There's no way to avoid it." Silas keeps staring at me, caressing my exposed skin with his gaze, touching me with the desire in his eyes, and heating me from the inside out.

He clears his throat, breaking the trance we're both under, and extends his hand toward me. "We should leave now, so we're not fashionably late."

I slip my hand into his, marveling at how mine seems to disappear in the size of his, yet there's no fear associated with it. Only security and safety. These hands would never harm me; that much I already know about Silas. "Let me grab my coat on the way out, and we'll be on our way."

"Wear the long coat—the thick wool one. That way, when you take it off in front of everyone, I'll hear all the gasps and moans when they get a look at you. Every man will be jealous of me as it is, but it'll be like unwrapping a present in front of an audience." Silas's smile covers his entire face. He nods enthusiastically, urging me to accept his request.

"Gasps and moans? You can't be serious."

"I am deadly serious. Gasps from the ladies, moans from the guys. It'll be beautiful. Trust me."

"Famous last words." I turn to head toward my bedroom to grab the coat but stop in my tracks. "Hang on. How do you know I have a long wool coat? I haven't worn it around you."

"I may have watched you a time or two in the last year or so." He shrugs, completely unashamed.

"Stalker." I shake my head and walk off, smiling to myself while listening to his laughter echo down the hall.

As asked, I grab my long coat on the way out and wrap it

around me. Actually, it works perfectly because it shields me from the biting winds, and it has plenty of hidden pockets in the inner lining to hide documents, pictures, flash drives, or anything else we need to smuggle out of the senator's home. Silas opens the car door for me, and I slide into the luxurious leather seat then watch him walk around the front with his confident gait and smooth swagger.

When we arrive at the senator's mansion inside a gated and private-security-patrolled community, just as Silas called it, the valet parks the vehicle while we walk up the steps to the enormous front door. On the ride over, we reviewed the plan and discussed what we'd do in case of an emergency. Now the game is afoot, and the strategy is in motion. My fingers are crossed, and my silent prayers are going up, hoping we find what we're looking for here.

Once inside, I understand why their daughter chose to get married here rather than in a church or at a destination wedding. The entrance is unlike any house I've ever seen. The large circular entryway alone is close to the size of a ballroom. The stairs curve around the right side of the room, leading up to an open second-floor landing. The arched openings and decorative black wrought-iron railing will provide a perfect view of the bride as she descends the steps toward her husband-to-be.

The reception tent has been erected in the backyard, just off the veranda directly behind where the wedding is being held. Once the guests start to move toward the reception, the temporary bottleneck will give Silas and me a chance to get lost in the shuffle of the crowd.

Staff dressed in full tuxedos, complete with top hats and tails, check the invitations before escorting us to our assigned seats. We're not high enough on the guest list to warrant a place in the front of the room, but that's better for us and our reason for being here. Sticking to the shadows and avoiding any spotlights are paramount to our success tonight. We sit patiently, quietly chatting with each other, while we wait for the main event to begin.

"You look familiar. Have we met?" A man stops beside Silas and eyes him suspiciously.

"No, Chuck, you don't know me at all. So, move on before you blow my cover and have to explain to the agency exactly how that happened." Silas speaks in a hushed voice, but his words are clear. What I can't figure out is how he did that without moving his lips.

"You look just like one of my employees. Spitting image of him, actually. Tall guy. Popular with the ladies. Working on a case that could end his career for good with one misstep. I'd hate to see that happen to him. He's been with me forever."

"If he's such a good guy, then maybe you should put a little trust in him and back him up when he needs it. I'm sure he'd appreciate your help. And your faith." Silas cuts his eyes up to Chuck, making the other man smile broadly.

"Maybe you're right. If he were here tonight—which he isn't —but if he were, I'd tell him to check out the senator's office on the second floor, behind the master bedroom. The senator is so proud of it that he took a few of us on a tour a while ago. You wouldn't believe the hidden wall safe or the secret drawer in his desk."

"I'm sure your employee would be very interested to hear all about that home office. It sounds like the perfect setup since I've wanted to remodel my home office for a while now. Do you think the senator would mind if my date and I took a peek at it after the ceremony?"

"His daughter has so many activities planned for her reception that I doubt the senator would ever know if you took a stroll upstairs. He's more focused on spending every minute he can with his daughter before she and her new husband fly off to Uzbekistan for six months. The father-daughter dance is high on his list, as is watching her cut the cake. I wouldn't linger, just in case, but I could've sworn I saw someone tampering with the security camera for that part of the house."

"What a shame. And this looks like such a nice neighborhood, too. We'll keep an eye out for any nefarious characters."

Chuck raises his eyes to meet mine after that comment, revealing his real impression of me. "See that you do. We wouldn't want them roaming loose in our country, would we?"

"You know, my boss has told me on many, many occasions that I'm the best judge of character he's ever met. He's even written commendations for me on my interviewing skills, saying I'm better than a polygraph test because no one has ever beaten me with a lie. With all those compliments over the years, you'd think he'd listen to me now and then. I could make him look so good to his superiors—if he'd just get out of my way and let me do my job."

Chuck's expression changes right before my eyes. "You're right. If you've worked for him that long and have received that many compliments, he shouldn't worry you're about to make the biggest mistake of your life. I guess if you're willing to gamble with your life, then he should let you play Russian roulette until the game is over…one way or another."

Silas inhales a long and deep breath, drawing his spine up completely straight and rigid until his lungs are fully expanded. Chuck takes the hint and walks off to his seat, leaving the conversation on that somber note. I watch Silas for a moment, taking in his handsome face, his wide shoulders, and his broad chest. I'm sure he does have a way with the ladies, and I'm sure he's had his way with plenty of them. He's easy to talk to, with a wicked sense of humor and quick, witty comebacks. But his intelligence is even more impressive. With one look, he can definitely gauge friend from foe, and he already has a plan in place to outwit his opponents before they even know they're in the game.

But right now, he's fighting against his temper. He usually

keeps it under firm control, never giving anyone the upper hand by making him react instead of act. Chuck seems to hold that power over him, though.

"You need to breathe. You've been holding that breath for a long time. If you pass out, I can't pick you up off the floor. You'll just have to lie down there and watch the wedding from an odd angle when you wake up."

He slowly turns his head to look at me, a deadpan expression on his face. But I see a small twitch in the corner of his mouth. He wants to smile, but he also wants to stay mad for a little longer.

"Silas, that man is your friend, whether he told you what you wanted to hear or not. He wouldn't have said those things if he weren't trying to help you get in and out without getting caught and if he didn't care about you successfully completing this mission. I have a feeling this isn't exactly sanctioned, so if you're caught, you go down alone. He can't shield you from the repercussions of your actions. He trusts you, or he wouldn't have said one word to you, especially knowing you're here undercover. It's me he doesn't trust—the Russian roulette comment wasn't exactly subtle—but you can't blame him for that. You don't trust me either."

He finally releases the breath he's held since Chuck walked away and nods, wordlessly telling me he knows I'm right.

He leans over toward me. Our faces are so close, we must appear as lovers to everyone else around us. His voice is soft when he whispers to me, mirth sparkling in his blue eyes as he stares into mine. "Would you really have left me on the floor?"

"You're damn right, I would have. Try it and find out, big boy."

He chuckles and slides his arm around me, pulling me into his side. "Remind me to make you pay for that comment in some subtle way later."

"I'll put it on the list."

~

AFTER THE CEREMONY IS OVER, WE INTENTIONALLY WAIT FOR THE other guests to file into the line for the reception so we can be in the very back. Just our luck, we can't sneak up the stairs because the staff stands on both sides, giving each guest a wedding favor bag and ushering us through the French doors at a brisk pace. The bridal party will be waiting for all the guests to settle in before making their toasts, after all.

Why I didn't realize the event tent would be every bit as luxurious and adorned as the house is beyond me. This family spared no expense for their little girl's wedding. From the hardwood floors, to the crystal chandeliers, to the fountain of flowing champagne, to the perfectly decorated tables, to the enormous wedding cake—every minute detail has been considered and executed flawlessly.

We find seats closest to the exit and suffer through the funny stories and the touching moments of the bride's and groom's lives. Finally, the DJ announces it's time to break in the brandnew dance floor, and Silas and I prepare to make our move. Only...now we look like living statues with the megawatt spotlight shining directly on us before it moves on to the next table.

"The bride has a special request of her treasured guests tonight. Before she takes the floor with her new husband in their first dance, she asks for all the couples in the room to step out onto the dance floor first. She wants to see love shine all around her on her wedding night. So, come on, friends and family. Make her dream a reality—take your partner by the hand, hold each other close, and let's get it on!"

Marvin Gaye's soulful voice fills the tent, and couples from every direction make their way to the dance floor. Waiters mingle between the tables, encouraging stragglers to comply. Silas stands, takes my hand, and pulls me from my seat to standing.

"You heard the man. Let's get it on." He winks and leads me to an open spot. Then he slides his arms around my waist, pulls my body tight against his, and we start to sway from side to side, keeping time with the music.

With my hands locked behind his neck, our bodies meld into one, flowing with the music and with the beat of our own hearts. His strong arms linked around my waist make me feel sheltered and protected. The spicy scent of his intoxicating cologne makes me feel heady and reckless. Maybe it is from years of living on the edge, from never having someone I cared about other than my sister, or the heavy toll my profession has taken on me, but at this moment in his arms, there is nothing else I want more.

No secret searches for hidden evidence.

No more danger, intrigue, or conspiracies.

No more spying or scheming.

Deep down, a quiet life with someone to love, and someone to love me in return, is all I've ever really wanted.

When the song finally ends, and the newlyweds take their place for their first dance as husband and wife, Silas and I casually walk out of the tent, up the stairs, and straight into the senator's home office. I watch with sheer admiration as he breaks into the hidden safe as though he were simply opening a cabinet door. The secret drawer wasn't so well hidden that Silas couldn't locate it, open it, and rifle through all the contents.

At the end of the evening, everything I'd hoped to find here eluded me. We leave empty-handed. I don't even have the heart to talk about it on the ride home.

"We'll keep looking, Kira. This isn't the end."

No? Then why do I feel like I just ran headlong into a brick wall on a dead-end street?

Silas

"You know it'll send up a huge red flag if I don't make that dead drop in the morning. My handler has already called to check in, and I confirmed I'd be there. That means I told her I accomplished my mission of getting into the senator's office." Kira slides into the seat beside me at the kitchen table.

In the last couple of evenings since we attended the wedding, Mira and Brad have been coming over to help. It seems the extra company and time spent together has made Kira more relaxed around me. The personality underneath her guarded persona is finally emerging, and even Nick is smiling and talking to her more now. Maybe Nick gleaned more insight into her character the night they went back to her old house to pack her clothes and toiletries.

For Kira to come to me with this request must mean she's starting to trust me.

Part of me wishes the feeling were mutual, because the more I'm around her, the more I like her. But Chuck's "Russian roulette" comment is stuck in my mind. My concern isn't only with Kira, but with who else she works with on the other side.

"And how do you suggest we manage that? They'll be on the lookout for anyone out of place. I'm sure they're trained to spot tails the same as I am, and there's no way in hell you're going alone."

When I lean back in my chair and look in her eyes, I plainly see the regret shining in them. While I feel for her predicament, and I honestly do, I won't make the mistake of giving her a chance to double-cross me. There's too much at stake, just as Chuck so eloquently alluded to in front of her. It was one thing when I personally escorted her to a wedding at the senator's house, but it's quite another to send her out to a dead drop site alone. She's not as adept at this spy business as I am. She's not as cunning and ruthless as she likes to think she is.

But that may be her MO while her every move is being watched.

"I can do it for her." Mira sits in the chair beside Kira and holds her hand.

"No fucking way!" Kira, Brad, Nick, Roman, and I all answer at the same time, with the exact same words.

"Tough room." Mira laughs off our reaction. She's used to us now after all the time she has spent around us while living with Nick's family.

"You've been out of the game for the last year and a half, love. If you put yourself back in it now, even to help your sister, you're risking your freedom. You never know if the drop site is being watched by another agency—or other Russian operatives." Brad could never be a spy—he not only wears his emotions on his sleeve, but his facial expressions give away his every thought.

"He's right, Mira. We won't risk your safety. Kira, why don't you and I head out to your drop site tonight and leave it ahead of the scheduled time? Nick can take your sister back home, where you know she's well cared for and very safe."

"All right. You and I will go late tonight, Silas. You can stand guard from behind cover in case anyone else is watching. If I get caught, at least you'll still be in the clear."

"Just be careful out there, sis." The two sisters look at each other, hesitant to leave the other's side again. "I want you to know I really am happy now, and you will be too very soon. Savannah is like a sister to me, and Nick is the big brother we never had. When this is over, and Silas finds a way to keep you off that airplane, they'll be your family too. That's just who they are."

Mira's eyes cut over to me as she hugs her sister goodbye. "Very subtle message, Mira. No one else caught on to that secret spy message you just sent me at all."

"Hey, this is like 'Spy vs. Spy,' in real life, isn't it?" Brad asks, his face beaming with pride over his corny joke.

"Yes, we're exactly like that." I can't help but laugh and be grateful for Brad's ability to defuse the tension of the situation with such a simple notion. Within seconds, even Nick, with his serious nature can't hold back, and now we're all laughing together.

After everyone leaves, Kira and I sit down at the table and hash out the plan for later tonight. "Where are you supposed to leave the flash drive?"

"Taped under a bench in the pavilion at Armistead Boothe Park on Cameron Station Boulevard."

"Okay, that's not too far from here. We can go late tonight and be back here in no time."

I pull up the map of the park and surrounding area online, so we can walk through our every step before arriving. Before walking into any potential trap, I want to know every possible entry and exit point, the best spot for observing the vicinity, and where we're most likely to encounter trouble.

"I think I'll go try to get some rest before we head out tonight. Do you need any other information from me before I do?" Kira pushes back from the table and stands with her hands clasped together, uncertainty emanating from her entire being.

"No, I think I'm good for now. Thanks."

"Silas?" She stops in the hall before she makes it through the doorway.

"Yeah?"

"I know none of this has been easy for you. I understand the predicament I've put you in—working with me, protecting my sister, and protecting your country. For what it's worth, I am sorry about that, but I do appreciate everything you're doing. You don't trust me, and I don't blame you. If I were in your shoes, I wouldn't trust me either. But you can believe I'd never do anything to hurt Mira, and going rogue now would only expose her. That's one thing I would never do—no matter what the consequences to me may be."

Part of me wants to believe she's being sincere. A small part of me may even put some stock in what she's saying. But the undercover officer inside warns me against it. He reminds me that self-preservation makes people do things they would never consider doing otherwise. Detestable acts that they later regret, but in that split second of decision, they value their own lives over everyone else's.

Including a dearly loved sister.

I've seen the aftermath of family members turning on other family members to save their own skin. It happens more than I'd prefer to think about, and that's precisely why I have to fight the urge to believe she wouldn't do anything to jeopardize Mira or this mission. No matter how much I'd enjoy the luxury of thinking she's actually on my side in this.

That's why I haven't broken my vow and told her about the discrepancies I found in the senator's files. It's why I review the rest of the flash drive contents when she is asleep at night, or for that solid hour locked inside my room while she was busy dressing for the wedding. And why I haven't explained to her all the reasons behind my reassuring her our investigation isn't over. She believes it is because we didn't find anything during our search of his home office—and she's mentally preparing herself to be forcibly removed from the country.

"Thank you for saying that. I appreciate it, Kira. But I really hope your loyalty to your sister is never put to the test."

We remain motionless, staring at each other for several heartbeats. The connection I've felt with her is real—it's like a tether holding me in place near her now. I've had more than a year to watch her from a distance, get to know her intimately without ever saying a word to her, and analyze her every expression, gesture, and mannerism. While I followed her, I memorized everything about her. Not quite at the stalker level, but thorough enough to be effective at my job. But sharing this space with her now, knowing everything I know about her, makes me question how much of my observation was for the job and how much was for me.

The hopeful expression she wore when she pledged her allegiance to me falls as she realizes my trust issues with her run deeper than a few words can bridge. She slowly nods, and a small, sad smile makes a brief appearance. "Our handlers tested our bond every single day since we were first torn from our mother's arms and thrust into this life. My loyalty to her has never faltered in twenty years, and I'm not about to break my longstanding record now. Good night, Silas."

"Good night, Kira."

After changing into my black cargo pants and sweatshirt, I return to the den and settle on the couch to comb through all the information I've gathered so far. One more time, as I always do. I'm deep in thought, trying to fit two puzzle pieces together that don't want to match when I hear the bedroom door open. I glance down at my watch and realize it's only been forty-five minutes since she left me to nap before our late-night rendezvous in the park.

"Couldn't sleep?"

"No. And there's no use in trying now."

She sits at the other end of the couch and turns her body to face me, bending one leg with her foot underneath her. She's wearing a pale pink tank top and matching shorts. Her long black hair is pulled to the side, hanging over one shoulder, and she's twirling a strand between her fingers. Seeing her like this, out of her natural element, makes her seem so vulnerable and lost. At the party when I first met her, she was working the scene and identifying her next mark. She was focused on the end goal and confident in her abilities.

In the days since that first meeting, I've fought against the recurring thoughts that she's not the villain I've painted her to be in my mind.

She knows how to get the job done, that's for sure, but the purpose that drives her to do it isn't anywhere in the same hemisphere as mine. My means and methods may cross lines at times, pushing the regulations and breaking a few rules now and then, but my objective never changes. Service to my country is first and foremost. Period.

Watching her silently fight her fears now, I see her in a different light. Even though we're different, I think I'm starting to unwrap that enigma and understand why she's so hard to read.

First and foremost, she's an actress.

Plain and simple.

In order to survive in this clandestine lifestyle from such an early age, the only way she could keep herself together and focus on one mission at a time, she had to pretend she knew what she was doing and what she wanted out of it. That's the only way she knows how to do this spy thing—it's all an imaginary world, and she's just a player acting out her role on an extremely treacherous stage.

"Care for some free professional advice?"

She stills and raises her gaze to meet mine. "Absolutely." That's a lie in the purest sense of the word, though I'm not convinced she even realizes she's lying. She's still acting, and that answer is the one she thinks she's supposed to give in this circumstance.

"One, if you actually want to be an undercover officer, your heart has to be in it. You have to fight for what you believe in, not what you've been told you believe in. Two, acting the part will only get you so far. You actually have to become the person you're pretending to be. You have to know her inside and out—how she would react in different situations, how she would handle problems, her entire personality profile—it all has to be ingrained in you. And three, your heart isn't in this, you don't know what you believe in, and you don't know who you are."

"Are you saying I'm not good at my job, Silas?" She arches one eyebrow, daring me to give the wrong answer to her loaded question.

"No, that's not what I'm saying. But I am saying this isn't the life you want, the career you chose, or what you feel is your true calling in life. And to those of us who live and breathe this work, it shows. You've dealt with everyday civilians up until now, haven't you? You haven't been on any counterintelligence missions, have you? Haven't dealt with any battle-hardened soldiers?"

"Yes, all of that is true. My assignments have revolved around getting information out of ordinary people. Executive assistants with loose tongues. Senate staffers with loose zippers. No one who has already been taught the trade, though."

"The man you singled out and almost approached at the fundraiser where we met? He would've read you like a children's book, and we never would've found your body when he was finished with you. Could you not sense that from his carriage and demeanor?"

"I sensed he had connections and could get me into the secure areas. He was right there with several other senators and high-level officials. That's exactly the type of person I needed to complete my job."

"No, love. He wasn't there with them. They were with him. There's a difference. When a man walks into a room and everyone flocks to his side, that man is the one with all the power. Not the followers. He was the center of attention—and they were all vying for five minutes with him. Not the other way around."

"Why are you telling me this? Are you trying to help me to be a better spy against America?" She folds her arms over her chest and tips her head to the side. She's clearly annoyed with me.

"Not at all." I can't help but chuckle. "I'm trying to save you. You're in deep water, way over your head, and you're very close to going under for good. Get out of this business and find something else to do with your life. I would hate to get the news that the wrong person figured out who you really are."

"Thanks for the pep talk. Maybe we should head out to the park now and get this over with before I have time to say the wrong thing to the wrong person and end up dead. It'll be incredibly obvious if I'm killed and you put the flash drive on the wrong bench in my absence."

The smile covering my face as she walks away is genuine. Her false bravado aside, that smartass retort just ratcheted up my respect for her. "Don't worry, love. I'll protect you."

Without a moment's hesitation, she holds up her middle finger, extending her arm as far toward me as it'll reach, just before she disappears into her bedroom. That makes me lean my head back on the couch and release a deep belly laugh. If nothing else, at least the time I have left with Kira will most definitely be entertaining.

~

WHEN WE REACH THE AREA IN ALEXANDRIA, I PULL INTO A SPACE in the Home Depot parking lot and turn off the truck. A few third shift employees are working, so my vehicle doesn't seem out of place. The park is a couple of blocks from the back side of the building, but we're not taking any chances of being spotted driving around and casing the vicinity.

"We're on foot from here. Stay close to me, Kira, and stay on your guard. We're going out on a limb doing this with no prior reconnaissance and no idea if your coworkers are out here watching, especially the night before a scheduled drop."

Outside the truck, we hold hands as we walk toward the park. We look like any other normal couple out for an extremely late-night stroll. The windows of most of the houses and apartments along the tree-lined street are dark, their inhabitants sound asleep. A small sedan pulls into one of the parallel parking spots, horribly missing the mark. Four young ladies tumble out of a car as we pass by, dressed to the nines after a night out and all walking on wobbly legs and spiky heels. I wrap my arm around Kira's shoulders and pull her face into mine as we pass them, giving the illusion that we're lovers and can't keep our lips off each other. Not that they'd recognize our faces through their beer goggles, but we can't be too careful. I've acted shit-faced drunk many times before when it gave me a marked advantage over my target.

Whistles and catcalls follow us as the girls cheer us on. "Girl-friend! Take that fine specimen of a man home and rock his world!"

"If you don't want him, send him back here! I'll take him!"

Kira rises to the challenge when she stops me, lifts up on her toes, and plants her lips on mine. Her hand glides along my cheek as her soft tongue slides against my lips. Before her actions even register on my shocked brain, my arms wrap around her waist, my lips part, and my tongue slides along hers. Just like that, the sparks I've heard about so many times but never experienced ignite all at once behind my eyes. In a split second, I take control of the kiss she initiated and deepen it. With intentional steps, I back her against a tree and lean into her.

She wraps her arms around my neck and runs her fingers through the hair at the nape of my neck. Her nails trail against my skin with the lightest of scrapes, but the sensation is enough to set my blood boiling. Her breasts push against me, and I feel the rapid rise and fall of her chest from her labored breathing. I brush my fingers along her neck then up to her chin, holding it lightly when I end the kiss and pull back only far enough to look directly into her eyes.

What I'd give to read her mind right now.

Alexandria just experienced a heat wave in the dead of winter.

"Fuck, that's so hot! Now I have to go watch porn and check the batteries in Bob." The girl's words are slurred, but it seems her vision is perfectly fine.

"Who the hell is Bob?" One of the other girls asks, laughing hysterically in her drunken state.

"My battery-operated boyfriend, Sheila. You should already know that—you have one too."

"Oh yeah. Fuck, we need a man to kiss us like that. I think my panties just melted right off me."

All four ladies completely lose their composure, leaning on each other while fighting the fits of laughter overtaking them. The harder they try to stop laughing, the worse it makes their situation. While they're too busy paying attention to each other,

Kira and I take the opportunity to disappear around the corner before they compose themselves.

We walk in silence around the perimeter of pavilion area of the park, sticking to the shadows and invisible spots, stopping and listening for any sounds that indicate we're not alone. After several passes around the immediate area and almost an hour of watching and waiting, I'm finally convinced enough that we're alone. I motion for Kira to make her way to the bench then I draw my pistol to cover her, keeping my vantage point in the dark.

She takes the small envelope with the flash drive that contains some real but irrelevant documents, along with some top-secret but doctored documents, and sits on the bench as if she belongs there at two in the morning. She slides forward, plants her hands on either side of her legs, and wraps her fingers around the edge of the bench. Then she stands and walks back toward the way we came in the park, not drawing attention to my location. Her hands are empty…and the package is securely attached to the underside of the bench.

I have to give her credit…that sleight-of-hand trick was expertly executed.

I'd say she's done that once or twice before tonight.

CHAPTER 10

Silas

After I jog around to meet her at the park entrance, we leave the area in the same manner we entered, as a couple completely captivated by each other. With my arm around her shoulders and hers under my coat, wrapped around my waist, we stroll through the empty neighborhood until we reach the truck. I open her door first and help her in, keeping up appearances in case we're under surveillance. She finally looks up at me again, and for just a second, she drops the act, and I get a glimpse of the real Kira Petrova.

The real Kira is beautiful, inside and out.

When our eyes meet for that one moment in time, I feel something more sincere with her than with any other woman I've ever known.

She's shy and unsure and brave and bold. She's trapped in a life she can't simply walk away from, and she's being used by two competing governments, yet she still puts her trust in me with nothing more than my word as a promise.

An overwhelming and undeniable urge to know her inside

and out overcomes me. A call I actively fight against to prevent another impromptu kiss that would be wholly inappropriate this time.

But damn if it wouldn't feel so right.

I stop myself from doing something stupid by closing her door and hurrying around to the driver side. When I'm settled behind the wheel, I start to put the truck in gear, but she stops me before I can drive away.

"Silas? Are you upset with me for kissing you? You haven't really spoken to me since then. That was just part of our cover —because of what those young ladies were saying. If I hadn't reacted that way, anyone watching would've questioned if we were really together."

"No, I'm not mad about that hot as fuck kiss at all. And I'm not still thinking about it until this very second. At all. But if you want to convince anyone else that we're together, all you have to do is say the word." With a wink and a smile, I let her know I'm only teasing her.

She laughs off my harmless flirting. "You'll be the first one to know if we need to convince anyone else that we're hopelessly in love."

Regardless of how passionate that kiss was or that fact that I've only actually known Kira for a few days now, this outing has made us more relaxed in each other's company. Not that I'm ready to give her the Silas Steele badge of trust yet, but I am impressed with how she took my advice about becoming her alias, and how fast she reacted on the fly when we were being taunted. If the circumstances were different, maybe we would make a good team.

THE NEXT MORNING, KIRA IS ALREADY UP AND DRESSED WHEN I stumble into the kitchen in my pajama pants. The aroma of freshly brewed coffee woke me from my deep slumber, but I didn't expect to find her wide awake so early after our late-night activities.

"What's on your mind, Kira?"

"I guess I am pretty obvious, huh?"

"Yep. Up early. On your third cup of coffee. Already showered and dressed. Gnawing your fingernails down to the quick. All very subtle giveaways." I take a long sip of the burning-hot lava from a mug and immediately feel the fog clearing from between my ears.

"How do you know I've had three cups of coffee?" She looks genuinely confused, and I decide to use it to my advantage.

"Didn't I tell you? One of my many abilities is reading minds. I know your every thought." I arch one eyebrow suggestively, and her face lights up like a Christmas tree.

Interesting.

"If you can read minds, you wouldn't have asked me what's on my mind." She crosses her arms over her body and waits for my real explanation.

I chuckle and nod toward the coffee pot. "Half the pot is missing already. You're the only one who could've chugged it this morning. So, let's have it. What's bothering you?"

"We've looked through everything this guy has, but we haven't found any evidence of his collusion. But I know he's somehow tied to this passing of classified information. I've heard his name—I wasn't supposed to hear it, but my handler didn't know I was in the safe house at the time. Something isn't adding up with his connection. I can't put my finger on what's off, and I'm running out of time."

"Tell me why this assignment is so important to you. Help me understand why you need to do this."

"When I was around twenty and just barely out of field training, the Academy sent over a lot of girls who would cycle in and out. I didn't think anything about it at first, other than they had completed the training they needed and were sent out on their assignments. I believed the lies they fed us. Then a couple of years later, I was working in the Miami area, getting insider information from an executive assistant in the FBI office there. I didn't realize how important the files she gave me over lunch were until later that night. By then, I was too late.

"The FBI agents had been watching a massage parlor down there. They suspected the owner of human trafficking. So, I opened the file and started looking through the pictures they'd taken. Some were regular customers, you know? Just going in for a regular massage. But there were several in a row of young girls going in, with notes that they didn't come back out. I stared at one face in particular and I couldn't believe what I saw. It was one of the girls who'd left field training early.

"When I confronted my handler at the time about it, I was severely reprimanded for even asking the question, but she finally relented and told me what they'd reassigned that young girl to do. She'd been abused all that time, moved from place to place to give new men a chance to do whatever they wanted to do to her. After that, I was moved out of Miami and sent here to work. They thought this was far enough away from their activities in Florida for me to forget what I'd seen and focus on my new assignment.

"So, imagine my surprise when all these years later, the same massage parlor name is brought up in a conversation between two handlers—mine and one other. Then they mentioned Senator Hunt's connection to it, and I knew they were still up to their old tricks. So, I did some digging of my own without telling anyone I was looking into him. He has another home in the Miami area, and when he's there, he frequents that very place."

"What's the name of it?" My blood turns to ice in my veins, so cold even my hot coffee can't thaw it because I already know exactly what she'll say. It's like a nightmare that keeps returning to haunt me, even though it's many years later.

"Pure Delight Spa."

The desire to ram my fist through the wall is overpowering, but I find the strength to refrain from somewhere deep inside. Knowing this mission isn't finished stays my hand, but knowing a prior mission remains incomplete stirs my blood.

"Tell me everything you know about it." My reaction is more intense than I intended to show, revealing my hand before I've had a chance to process everything.

"You know I'm more than willing to share everything I know, especially if it'll help put an end to the abuse of innocent people. But this feels a lot like a one-sided relationship, Silas. You need to share what you know, too. There may be details I can give you to fill in the full picture. But if I have no idea what you're working on or what you're looking for, we could be running in circles and chasing our tails."

She has a valid point—I'll give her that. But keeping secrets was drilled into me from the start of my career until now. There are very few people I trust implicitly, and I can count them all on one hand. The fact that she already knows about this particular establishment does make me somewhat more comfortable in sharing the rest of the information with her now.

"Several years ago, I was read in on a top-secret assignment regarding that very place. The intel wasn't widely known because the report had been restricted to our eyes only. Russian chatter had been intercepted and decoded by our Signals Intelligence division. The message referred to an international human trafficking ring, and one of the main locations was that very place in Miami." That is the abridged version of the story. The extremely redacted and abridged version.

"Why do I get the feeling you're holding out on me?" Kira rolls her eyes before cutting them sideways toward me.

"Okay, you want the entire story? Here goes. Another officer had a Russian asset he was working for this case. He got a lot of information from her about the next time they were bringing the new batch of girls into the spa—how, when, where, everything. For the entire two weeks before the sting, we took turns driving to the location, parking the car, and walking into a nearby establishment. We'd stay there all day to make it seem like we were working. Technically, we were, but if anyone was casing the neighborhood, our cars had to be easily recognizable as belonging there.

"The day finally came around, and we were more than ready to take down every single person. In the time we were waiting for them to arrive, we were researching their other locations and other illegal activities. They'd set up an extensive network of human trafficking…including a segment of very disturbing offers to sell underage children."

Just the memory of what I saw still haunts me to this day, forcing an involuntary shudder to tear through me.

"Silas, I'm so sorry. That must've been terrible."

"It definitely was. That was one of the worst cases I've ever worked in my entire career. Which made me even more determined to catch the man behind the scheme and take him down by any means necessary. He was so fucking bold. He thought he had everything locked up tight and no one could touch him. When he finally showed up, it was very late at night.

"He, um…" I push the feelings welling up in my chest back down. Now is not the time to dwell on them. "He pulled up in a moving truck, plenty of room in the back to conduct any business he wanted. Before he got the girls out of the back, he chose one to make an example of for the others. I heard her screams from inside that truck, but I was ordered to stand down. We didn't have intel on what else was inside that truck, and the danger to the public was too much to risk for one girl. Or so my deputy director said."

Several moments of silence pass while I mentally relive that dark scene.

"What happened next, Silas?" Kira's voice is soft and soothing. She knows what's next, but she's hoping she's wrong.

"We finally got a visual inside the truck, and I went completely off the rails. I didn't wait for the team to be ready to move. I didn't wait for my backup to reach his vantage point. I just jerked the door open and couldn't believe my eyes. She was already dead by the time we rushed the truck. Instinct and pure hate took over, and I ripped that man apart with my bare hands —just like he did to that poor girl.

"The discussion with the Russian ambassador was a little more civil than mine with the fucker in the back of that truck, but their government got the message, despite the lack of bluntness I preferred. She died because of me. I was there to stop the trafficking, but also to save those young girls. But I didn't do my job—I didn't stop that monster from hurting her, I didn't get her out of that truck in time, and I didn't save her life."

"That wasn't your fault, Silas. You followed orders, just like we've all had to do. That doesn't make you a bad person or any other negative depiction you have stored in your mind. You did what you had to do for your job." She puts her hand on my arm, offering solace and reassurance with the warmth of her touch.

"Yeah. For my job. And what would've happened if I hadn't followed orders? Face being written up for insubordination? Get a week's vacation without pay for disobeying my scene commander? It's not like they would've fired me or arrested me. Even if they did, saving her would've been worth it." I roughly drag my hand through my hair then over my face. The mental images flashing through my mind are enough to choke me out.

"You didn't know that the truck wasn't rigged to explode. You didn't know if you were walking into a trap that would've killed not only you but your entire team. There's no way to know if the outcome would've been any different."

"Just the chance of saving her would've been better than living with her death on my conscience all these years. They prepared her body, and I escorted her back home to Russia. That's when I met your father at the Kremlin. He was there to apprehend me and throw me into a Russian prison for killing their man—until he saw what all that fucker did to the poor girl. I remember the scene very clearly. He said she reminded him too much of his own daughters, and he was enormously shaken up by all of it. The state of her body, the thought of something like that happening to Mira or you, and knowing his government had a hand in it. But I never realized the Academy was helping by feeding girls to that maniac. I'm glad I killed him."

"Wait. I remember when that happened. That was about ten years ago, right? Our handlers tried to keep us from watching the local news. They said most everything reported about Russia was intentional misinformation to confuse and disarm us. But that specific incident rattled them worse than anything I'd ever seen before. That was you?"

"That was me."

Her brows furrow and she stares hard at nothing, focusing all her brain power on one spot on the table. I've seen that expression before—she's trying to access old memories. Some morsel of information is there on the cusp, waiting to be realized and put into context. Maybe something that didn't make sense at the time, but bringing it out in the open now will answer unresolved questions.

"What is it, Kira? You've remembered something, but you don't want to tell me."

"Silas, you killed Ivan Sokolov. He was one of Russia's most respected foreign relations ministers. What you just told me doesn't match the story released to the Russian media at all. My handler shared that release with me because there was so much buzz about it. She knew I'd hear about it one way or another, so she tried to get ahead of the American version. The Russian embassy claimed he was captured and tortured by the American government because he was falsely accused of spying when he was here on a goodwill mission."

"Typical propaganda to keep the citizens of our countries at odds with each other."

"But when Ivan died, his brother Viktor was alive and well, safely hidden inside Russia. They were partners in everything they did. You didn't see one's name in the Russian news without seeing the other—except when Ivan died. Viktor swore vengeance in a rare outburst to a journalist, but he quickly changed his tune soon after. My guess is the Kremlin silenced him and scrubbed the story."

"His brother? Our research never revealed he had a brother. No names, no mention of any surviving family members, nothing. How is that? What did he look like?"

"Viktor was quite a bit younger than Ivan—maybe a decade or so. I never saw Viktor's face in the news, only Ivan's. My guess is Ivan kept his brother's name hidden and out of reach of the foreign press for his protection. That way, no one could touch his little brother because no one knew who he was or what he looked like. Then when Ivan died, the Kremlin continued covering him for their own benefit. Someone who never existed is an invaluable resource to the GRU."

"Absolutely. And he'd be a ghost to us, nearly impossible to find."

"Nearly?"

"Nearly."

We have a lot of work to do.

Kira

"Senator Hunt's daughter left last night for her Caribbean honeymoon before heading to Uzbekistan for the next six months. Then Hunt announced he's taking a short vacation at his home away from home in Miami to relax and recuperate from the stress of overseeing the wedding in his home. He'll be there for the next three weeks, possibly longer." Silas beat me to the kitchen this morning. From his bright and chipper mood, I'd say he's already on his third cup of coffee. Seems to be a pattern in this house.

"Well, good morning to you too. I did sleep well. Thank you for asking. And yes, it does look like a beautiful day out there. We should go do something fun for a change. All we do is work, work, work. You know what Johnny says about all work and no play. It's really not a good thing." I grab a mug from the cupboard and fill it full of hot deliciousness to jump-start my brain and hopefully put me in as good a mood as Silas seems to be. "Who's your source anyway? His impromptu trip seems a little too convenient, doesn't it? Maybe he's onto us."

"My source is airtight, so don't you worry your pretty little head about that. And there's no way he's onto us. For future reference, I don't get made when I'm undercover unless I want to."

"Airtight, huh? So who is this magical, never wrong source of yours, and how do I get one?" I join him at the table, sipping my coffee and racking my brain for ideas of how to speed up this waiting game.

He holds up the local newspaper, showing the picture of Senator Hunt watching his daughter drive away in the posh stretch limousine after the wedding. The entire story is about how much time he and his wife have dedicated to the wedding, how stressful yet fun it's been for them both, and how they need a few days away to recharge their batteries before the next congressional session begins.

As if they did any of the actual wedding preparations themselves. They had servants to attend to every single detail for them. All they had to do was be home and dressed on time. They probably even had help with that.

I may be a little angry with that sham of a family right now with everything that's happening right under our noses.

After Silas shared his heartbreaking story last night and I relived the painful memories from my own past, just the idea of the bastard getting away with his depravity is enough to drive me into a murderous rage. My thoughts and feelings are obviously bleeding over into my disposition this morning.

"Really? Your secret weapon is the newspaper that everyone in a hundred-mile radius reads?" My tone remains deadpan, but I'm fighting a smile and a laugh with everything I have.

I'm trying to hold on to my anger to stay focused on the case. Every day with Silas is muddying the waters, making it harder and harder for me to keep him in his own little box inside my mind. His easygoing personality combined with his muscular build and sexy lips leave me with the most inappropriate thoughts about my jailer.

"Yes, this story tells me everything I need to know. He's not concerned about returning to the scene of the crime, so to speak, so he has no clue he's being watched. If we catch him in the spa while the illegal activity is occurring, we have probable cause to bring him in and question him, even if he is a sitting senator. So, how would you like to go to Miami with me?"

I'm sure I'm hearing things.

"What?"

"Let's go to Miami. My brother has a huge house there. We can crash at his place. Not sure if he's there or at their place in California, but he won't mind either way. If they're in Florida now, you'll love his wife, Brianna. She's the best. We'll be right there at the beach, enjoying the sun, sand, and surf in between taking down bad guys. You said yourself we need to have some fun."

"Silas, I only have a few more days left before your deputy director makes me leave the country. We don't have time to lounge around on the beach and play in the ocean." Has he lost his mind?

"Hmm. You're right, we don't have much of that two-week decree left, do we?" He scratches his chin, pretending to be deep in thought but failing miserably. The ruse only endears him to me even more. "I have the perfect solution. We'll go to Miami, let the clock run out on Graves's two-week investigation bullshit, do our job, and shut this fucker down once and for all. Because, Kira, I can't sleep one more night knowing I left a piece of shit like him on the street because I followed orders. I swore I'd never do that again, no matter what the cost, no matter what line I have to cross. This is more than worth it to me—it feels like a chance to make amends for what I failed to do before. Is that worth the consequences to you?"

"Absolutely. Give me ten minutes to pack, and I'll be ready to go. Are we driving? I'm guessing getting on a plane will be next to impossible for me. I'm sure my face has been distributed to all the airports within driving distance of here." I don't even need time to think about what's right or wrong. We both need this win to help wipe our slates clean again.

"Ordinarily, yes, flying would be a problem. But since my brother runs a very successful security firm, and sometimes has to escort clients on his company jet, I think we can squeeze you past security at the private airstrip just before we board his plane." There's a mischievous twinkle in his eye that is adorable.

"I'm going to pack right now. I've never been on a private jet before. And despite having worked in Miami years ago, I never actually got to go to the beach and get in the ocean." Before I can stop myself, I throw my arms around his neck and kiss his cheek. "Thank you so much for breaking the rules to try to stop him. Even if this doesn't work out the way we want, just the fact that we did everything in our power to stop it means the world to me."

"Since you were denied the complete joy of doing nothing but enjoying the scenery, that's the first stop on our agenda. We have to rectify that wrong as soon as possible. This dreary cold weather here is depressing, and I miss the electric vibe in Miami. You can thank me by packing your bikini and joining me on the beach to soak up some rays."

"Consider this as payment in full, then. I'm packing two bikinis right now."

The change in Silas's demeanor from last night until today is literally dark to daylight. But I'm not complaining or questioning his decision. I'm simply going with it. This case took a very personal turn for him, and I completely understand his need to right the wrongs of his past. Not that I think he did anything unethical—all soldiers are taught to follow orders to the letter. And that's what we've both been, regardless of titles or jobs. We're soldiers at our core. The one deep inside Silas is screaming for justice and absolution.

I'm praying he finds it on this trip because, win or lose, he may no longer have a job when we get back. And I certainly will no longer be allowed to stay on American soil to help him with anything. This is most definitely a now-or-never trip.

All those thoughts flow through my mind as I pack for our trip, stuffing a variety of clothing options into the suitcase since I have no idea what may be needed.

Black clothes? Check.

Dress clothes? Check.

Bikinis? Check.

Although, the only time I've ever even worn one was while working during a pool party, trying to get close to an FBI informant to find out what secrets he held. They've never even been wet, aside from the first wash. Maybe this time, I'll actually make it to the beach and into the ocean for the first time.

When my sister and I were taken away from our parents, the Academy said we were young enough to forget our blood families but old enough not to need coddling anymore. But they were so wrong. I never forgot my parents, not for one second, and the biannual calls home only made my homesickness worse. Even at that tender young age, I had learned to hide my true feelings and only react in the way they expected me to. So I pushed the enormous ball of emotions as far down inside me as I could.

Mira wasn't as agile with her reactions. She learned over time, but she still wore her feelings on her sleeve. From the time we were little kids until now, she's been a hopeless romantic. I've never told her, but I've always admired her for holding on to that piece of humanity. That hope to keep the spark alive inside her that one day she'd have a normal life and a normal family to love. Her beliefs ran counter to our training in every way.

We never were to fall in love.

We never were to care about anyone else.

We never were to put anything above completing the mission.

Any deviation from the rules was considered treason and punishable by watching our parents being shot by a firing squad.

For the first time in as far back as I can remember, I feel a sliver of hope for my future. I'm not naïve or delusional—I fully understand they intend to send me back to Moscow to face my failure. But I'm hopeful my contributions and information will help get my request for asylum approved. And that's a very different feeling for me—to hope, to dare to dream, to want something more for myself.

If I'm completely honest with myself, maybe I also want to explore the attraction between Silas and me to see where it leads us. The desire is mutual, and the temptation is strong. The chemistry between us is real and so tangible, the air crackles with electricity around us. There's no way I'm the only one who thinks it…feels it…wants it.

"Are you almost ready to go?" Silas startles me from my ruminating, making me jump out of shock. Something else I'm not used to—having someone sneak up on me.

"Almost." I stuff another pair of shoes into my suitcase and zip it up. "Now I am."

"What were you thinking about just now, before you realized I was standing here?" He's leaning against the doorjamb, assessing me with those X-ray vision eyes of his.

"If I tell you, it may not come true."

"If you tell me, maybe I can help make it come true."

I have a strong feeling we're not talking about the same thing right now. And just the thought of what he's possibly offering me is enough to make me salivate uncontrollably.

"Um, I was just, um, hoping we'd actually have a chance to

enjoy the beach and the ocean. Work always seems to get in the way of the things I'd prefer to do."

"Kira, I personally guarantee at least one day of lounging on the sand and playing in the waves. But just so you know, I don't buy that's what you were thinking for one second." He raises his eyebrows at me, waiting for me to argue or acknowledge his assumption.

But I'm not ready to share my innermost thoughts or feelings with him quite yet. Despite spending twenty-four hours a day with him for the last week or so and getting to know him better than I ever anticipated, I'm more afraid of revealing my feelings and making a complete fool out of myself than facing an army on my own.

"Shouldn't we be leaving now?" I grab my suitcase and start walking toward the door. But he doesn't move to let me pass.

He raises his hand to my face, barely tracing my cheek with his fingertips. I can feel the warmth in his eyes, heating my skin. From no more than a touch, my breath hitches, making my lungs work for every bit of oxygen they draw. "You never have to hide anything from me, Kira. One day, I hope you'll realize that."

He takes the suitcase from my hand and carries it out to his truck. With the house locked up and our plan to fly away to Miami set in stone, there's no looking back now. I'm so excited, I can barely make myself sit still in this seat. Even knowing the wrath we'll face when we finally return...or we're apprehended as fugitives in Florida. Either way.

When we board the private jet without a hitch, I'm literally giddy with excitement. Looking around the high-class cabin, I instantly feel out of my element. I've never experienced anything this luxurious before, and apart from the trip home, it's unlikely I ever will again. That makes this trip all that much more special, so I plan to soak up every second of it. The plush leather chair calls my name, so I take a seat and buckle up.

Silas sits beside me, wearing that same spicy cologne that makes me want to bury my nose in his neck and stay there for an inappropriate and uncomfortable amount of time.

"Penny for your thoughts."

When I lift my eyes up to his, I realize I've been staring at his neck like a vampire dying of thirst. This is not awkward at all.

"I was just wondering what kind of cologne you wear. You always smell so good."

"If it makes you feel any better, I've wondered that about you a lot."

"Yeah?"

"Oh yeah. When I'm around you. When I'm alone. When you're asleep. When you drink all the coffee and don't leave any for me. I wonder about it a lot."

We're not talking about cologne anymore. I'm certain of it.

"Sounds like we have more in common than we realized. Except for the drinking all the coffee part. Somehow you make sure to leave some for me when you're the first one up."

"I'm a nice guy like that. Ladies should always finish first."

"Good morning from the flight deck. We are preparing for takeoff. For your safety, please make sure your seat belts are fastened, and all luggage is stowed."

If the pilot hadn't interrupted at that exact moment, I would probably already be in Silas's lap right now, covering every inch of myself in his intoxicating scent.

"Noah's house is amazing. You'll love it. There's a pool in the backyard, the whole place is surrounded by a brick fence, state-of-the-art security system, and every amenity you could ever dream of. But when we get there, we're changing clothes, grabbing food and drinks to go, and heading straight for the beach. The rest of the day, we're not giving up our spot in the sand. We both need a relaxing day before we hit it hard tomorrow. Think you can handle that?"

"That sounds like heaven. I'm positive I can handle that. And if anything happens that causes me to say I've changed my mind, you can just handcuff me to the beach chair until my attitude improves."

"With a few tweaks, some minor alterations, that plan has incredible merit. I'll keep that request in mind for later."

What thoughts this man conjures with just a few words…

"So, how did you get drawn into this cloak-and-dagger world? Just from what I know about you, I'd say you could've been anything you wanted to be. Are you an adrenaline junkie? Pathological liar? Functioning schizophrenic?" I'm genuinely interested in what makes him tick. He takes a moment to consider his answer. I can almost see the wheels turning in his head, trying to decide if he should tell me the truth or not.

"You wouldn't know it if you met him today, but my father wasn't always the warm and fuzzy type. He was cold as ice and hard as stone when I was growing up. He expected me to return home immediately after college and follow in his footsteps in the corporate world of business. But I knew before I left for school that I wanted to travel the world and experience life to the fullest, not sit behind a desk inside a plush office all day.

"So, I chose political science as my major and became fluent in several foreign languages. It was really one step at a time. I never set out to become a CIA officer, but the clandestine lifestyle, the worldwide travel, and the constant adrenaline rush of working an asset in the most perilous location in the world were impossible to pass up. I started right out of college and have been doing this ever since. I can't imagine doing anything else now."

"How did your father take your career choice?"

"Dear old dad did not disappoint. He did exactly as I thought he would, confirming my profiling skills were already on point before I even started CIA training. He immediately disowned me and told me never to come home again. I still talked to my mom, brother, and sister when I wasn't deep undercover, but I didn't go back home for many years after that. Turns out, my brother also let Dad down when he joined the Army immediately after high school graduation, leaving my sister home alone with his tyrannical demands. Then Noah and I were both disowned—by our father and our sister, for leaving her."

"Wow. You said he's different now. How did it all get resolved?"

"There's nothing like an unexpected cancer diagnosis to put petty differences into perspective. He retired as CEO of a major insurance company, and they still live in the huge house I grew up in, completely remodeled now. The only difference is, now it's always full of the laughter and pitter-patter of grandbaby feet. I think the grandkids stay with them more than they do their parents."

"What are your siblings' names again?"

"Noah and Chaise. Noah is married to Brianna. Chaise is married to Bull."

"Bull?"

Silas laughs and nods. "Noah and his Delta Force brothers worked together after they left the service. They all still go by their old nicknames."

"Ah, that makes sense. So, what's Noah's nickname?"

"Reaper. The other two guys are Rebel and Shadow."

"Sounds like you have quite an interesting extended family. I'm a little jealous. I've always wanted a large family. You know my family and my history, so you also know that dream was always out of the question."

"At one time, it wasn't possible, that's true. But soon you'll have a chance to start over and make it happen. Don't give up on it if that's what you still want."

I know he means well, but my new start isn't exactly what he thinks it'll be. However, I don't want to dampen the good mood and the fun waiting for us when we land. "Maybe you're right."

The corners of his eyes crinkle, and he cocks one eyebrow

upward. "Kira, let's make a promise to each other right now. This promise can never be broken for any reason."

"What promise is that?"

"We'll be honest with each other, regardless of the cost or how painful the words are to say aloud. No matter what it's about. Just the cold, hard truth. Can you do that?"

"Sure, I can do that. Can you? What about the classified information you're not supposed to share?"

"If it's something I can't tell you, I'll just say that. I won't lie about it. Will that work?"

"That works."

"Good. Now, let's back up for a minute. There was zero conviction in your voice when you said I may be right. Why do you think you'll never have what you want?"

Regardless of how painful the truth is, right? Here goes nothing. "There's no 'maybe' to it, Silas. I'll never have a home, a husband, or any children. When my flight lands in Moscow, I'll be grabbed off the plane and taken to an interrogation site. Once they're satisfied that they've squeezed every last drop of information out of me, it'll be as if I never even existed. They'll destroy anything remotely related to me, including that picture my dad keeps on his desk. In fact, if you can get a message to him to hide it immediately, I'd appreciate it. Just that old picture would probably get Mom and Dad killed too."

He scrubs his hand over his face, leaving it covering his mouth as he considers my words. I stare out the window to avoid the temptation to try to read his mind through the intensity of his gaze.

"I know I don't have to ask this, but it's too important not to say anything. Mira will have to watch over her shoulder for the rest of her life. She and I worked missions together for years. They know she defected against them, even if she hasn't made it official yet. Even taking her act of treason against them off the table, they know it could be too detrimental to the Academy to leave her out on the lam once they have me in custody. Please help take care of her."

"Let's take this one day at a time. We have a long way to go before we have to cross that bridge. Mira's fine—she's in very capable hands. Today, my only focus is taking care of you. Bikini, beer, beach. Sand, surf, sun. If it doesn't involve one of those, it's not a priority for today. Deal?"

"Deal." I raise my eyes to meet his. "I can't wait to see you in a bikini."

His responding smile is immediate and reaches from ear to ear. "Play your cards right, and you just might."

The rest of the two-and-a-half-hour flight flew by in the blink of an eye. Silas and I spent every moment talking about everyday, normal topics. For a short time, we didn't live in a world entrenched in treachery, buried in lies, or corrupted by enemies. We were just a man and a woman, getting to know each other on a profoundly personal level. We dropped the façade of our cover personalities and let our real selves step out into the sunlight.

There may have even been some harmless flirting, a couple not-so-subtle sexual innuendos thrown around the cabin, and more than a few heated glances.

I've never been so anxious to be seen in a bikini in my entire life. We're wheels down and making a landing now, but my thoughts are already several steps ahead. Silas had an epiphany about rectifying the mistakes of his past. Mine is a little more selfish, but this is the only time I have left. No matter how short or long this Miami trip lasts, I'll live every minute to the fullest. If that means making a complete fool of myself by trying to initiate a short-term relationship with Silas while we're here, so be it.

At least I won't die without checking that item off my new Why Not list. If I don't have much time left, why not do what I want to do—right now? No time like the present.

CHAPTER 12

Silas

We step out of the jet directly into the warm Miami sun, even when it's the dead of winter everywhere else in the country. Kira stops for a moment and soaks it in, with her face tilting upward, her eyes closing of their own accord, and her lips curling into a beautiful smile. The serene expression on her face captivates me, halting my feet and seizing my breath. The slight breeze blows her long black hair away from her face and makes her shirt cling to her curves, leaving me to openly ogle her natural beauty. I'm using all my willpower to avoid pulling her into my arms and crushing my lips against hers before disappearing into the Caribbean with her for the foreseeable future.

"You'll get more sun with your bikini on, you know." I purposely brush my lips across the shell of her ear and murmur the words. A shiver runs through her that has nothing to do with the wind blowing around us.

"I just needed a moment to soak it all in. Now I'm ready." She smiles up at me, her face beaming with bliss.

We cruise away from the private airstrip with the top down on our rental car, heading to my brother's secure estate for some much-needed rest and relaxation. Kira's enthusiasm is contagious as she takes in the sights and sounds of the vibrant city, not having been here in many years. Today is about giving her what she needs, but the selfish part of me hopes she opts for avoiding the crowds in lieu of more private locales.

Now that I have her here alone, I'm not too interested in sharing her with anyone else.

When I pull into Noah's gated driveway, she pulls her sunglasses off her face and openly gapes at our surroundings. He's done exceptionally well for himself with his security business, and his enormous home set behind tall brick fences only reveals part of the picture. With the code keyed in, the gates swing open—and our day of being a South Beach tourist begins.

Kira starts to jump out of the car the second I put it into Park, but I grab her arm to halt her momentum. She whips her head around, looking at me as if I've lost my mind—her excitement is barely contained as it is. Keeping my face passive is nearly impossible.

"Remember my rule."

Her brows draw down, and confusion mars her beautiful face. "What rule is that?"

"You're only allowed to have fun today. Whatever you want to do is fine by me. All you have to do is say the word."

Her face softens, and her lips part on a contented sigh. "Thank you, Silas. Underneath all that hard-as-steel-CIA-badass outer shell, you really are a sweetheart."

I smile in return…then finish my thought. "As I was saying, whatever you want to do is fine by me, as long as you're wearing a bikini the entire time."

She laughs out loud, and I can literally see the tension dissipating in the warm air surrounding her. "Well, okay. There go my plans for skinny-dipping in your brother's pool, though. But you're absolutely right. Rules are rules, after all."

She shrugs her shoulders as she hops out of the car without waiting for my reply—and I eventually would've thought of something to say—once I reeled my tongue back into my mouth and the blood flow to my brain resumed. I swear I hear her evil little giggle as she rushes out of the garage to examine the exterior of the house and yard.

When I catch up with her, she's rounding the corner of the house and heading to the backyard. I know exactly what she'll find back there—heaven on earth. A heated pool for year-round use, complete with a waterfall flowing into the attached hot tub, and an outdoor kitchen that would make any professional chef envious. She stops and lets out an excited squeal.

"Are you sure he doesn't mind us staying here? I'm afraid to touch anything—I don't want to be the one to break it."

Her modesty is like a rare gem, one I wonder if I'll ever find again. "I'm positive—he doesn't mind at all. As far as breaking anything, don't even think twice about that. If his three rambunctious kids haven't broken it by now, it's completely indestructible."

"Are they here with us?"

"Not for a few days. They'll be back later in the week, along with their rug rats."

"You don't like being an uncle?"

"Are you kidding? I love it. They're awesome kids. We play football in the house. We play cops and robbers, hiding behind furniture and shooting each other with Nerf guns. I get to spoil them, give them all the sugar their little bodies can take, then walk out the door and leave them with their dad. It's the perfect arrangement. Bull and I have our own competitions—to decide who their favorite uncle is."

"Oh yeah? Who usually wins that game?" Kira's shocked expression tells me she never saw me as a family man.

Up until just a few years ago, she would've been correct. But since I've been back in my brother's and sister's lives, my priorities have shifted.

"Who usually wins?" I hesitate to answer for a second. "Shadow does. Which isn't fair, because he's not even related to them. I'm their uncle by blood, and Bull is their uncle by marriage. But Shadow—who's a great guy, but he's technically a friend of the family—always cheats his way in."

She lifts one eyebrow, amused beyond measure over my sulking and irrational jealousy. "This, I must know. How does Shadow cheat to win the title of favorite uncle?"

"He comes up with the best pranks for the kids to play on the family. They get us every fucking time. It's humiliating, really."

"Give me an example." She's trying very hard not to laugh in my face. She's not succeeding, but at least she's trying.

"During the last game, he had them decorate two round pieces of foam with real cake icing, flowers, sprinkles, the whole works. Then they put it on a cake display stand in the kitchen and hid while we each tried to cut a piece without getting caught by Brianna. They even changed the fake cake out so neither of us would figure it out. He videoed us then played the videos for the whole family after dinner. On the big screen."

When she bends over, gasping for breath and wiping tears from her eyes after laughing so hard, I point out the obvious. "You're not even trying to take my side right now. Just so we're clear."

"I'm sorry. I'm just picturing you, trying to sneak a piece of cake from your sister-in-law's kitchen, only to find out it's not really cake. Then, as if that's not bad enough, your entire family watches you hard at work, trying to cut a piece of foam." Then she breaks out into a laughing fit once again.

"Yeah, yeah. It was so fucking funny. Shadow and all my nieces and nephews thought so, too. Now, get your ass inside and get your bikini on. We're late for our appointment at the beach." I unlock the door with the extra key Noah gave me in case I ever wanted to crash at his place and shoo her inside. "Feel free to look around while I grab our bags."

When I join her inside, she's finally managed to control herself.

"This house is amazing. There's absolutely nothing I would change about it. They must love it here."

"It is a great place. Come on upstairs and pick a bedroom. With a record-high temperature, the weather is perfect for a swim in the ocean today."

"How about a swim in the pool and a soak in the hot tub tonight?"

"If you twist my arm really hard, you might be able to talk me into that too." I waggle my eyebrows at her and show her to the available guest bedrooms upstairs. "I'll be back in thirty seconds. You'd better be changed and ready to go by then."

"Yes, sir. So bossy." Her insults are meant in jest from the smile on her face and the twinkle in her eye. "It won't take me long to change—there's very little fabric to worry about."

There she goes again, giving me the best mental images but leaving me speechless in the process.

As promised, she's changed and ready in no time. The only hitch is she's wearing a cover-up over her bathing suit, so I can't confirm she's wearing the required apparel underneath. But since we're burning daylight, I opt to take her at her word and wait for the big reveal when we get to where we're going.

Once we pull into the parking lot at Lummus Park, I'm surprised to find it mostly deserted, but then, it is late January, so it's not exactly high season. We haul our gear out of the car and walk to the beach and set up our spot, and then she grabs the hem of her cover-up and pulls it over her head. If I thought I was speechless before, I was wrong, beyond a shadow of a doubt. The minuscule triangles of fabric on the top and bottom barely cover her luscious body. Her taut, firm stomach muscles perfectly accentuate her perfectly round, perky breasts. Then she turns around, and I nearly groan out loud.

The bottom is a thong, and somehow, the tiny strings of fabric only make the sexy globes of her ass even more appealing.

"I'll race you to water. Loser buys lunch. Go!"

She takes off running toward the water, leaving me standing rooted to the same spot, still panting after her like a man lost in the desert with no water in sight.

Then she rushes into the water, dives into the waves, and comes up on the other side with a huge smile on her face…and now she's wet. Every inch of her luscious body is dripping wet.

Fuck me.

This is going to be a long day.

"Silas, get your ass in here right now," she yells and motions for me to join her.

I jerk my shirt off and drop it onto my outstretched towel, then jog the few feet to the water's edge. It's cooler than I thought it would be, but obviously not too cold for Kira to enjoy it to the fullest. She's swimming and playing in the waves as if she's the sexiest mermaid in the Atlantic, and I have no doubt she'd win that competition.

When I reach her, she surprises me by jumping into my arms and wrapping hers around my neck. I'm acutely aware of her barely covered breasts pushing against my bare chest, the water serving as a lubricant and a stimulant simultaneously.

"Thank you so much for bringing me here with you and for making this day happen. It's so beautiful here—the turquoise water, the beautiful beach, and the bright blue sky. Every single part of this is magical and wonderful and more than I ever expected. I also want you to know, I can't imagine experiencing this for the first time with anyone else."

With little effort, she wraps her legs around my waist and

locks them behind my back. I automatically move my hands under her bare ass, holding her in place as the waves slightly jostle us in the waist-deep water. Our eyes lock, and the desire blazing in hers is brighter than the sun above us. Beads of water run down her gorgeous face, some disappearing when she runs her tongue over her lips.

Her gaze drops to my mouth just before she closes the gap and presses her lips to mine. Soft and tentative turns to hungry and demanding in a millisecond. I knead the firm flesh of her behind with my fingers when her tongue glides across mine. She lifts her torso, pulling closer to me, and grazes across my already hard cock. When she releases a needy moan in my mouth, any restraint I had a second ago evaporates into thin air. My fingers dig into her skin, holding her tightly against my body. Her hips undulate, gliding against me—over these fucking swim shorts.

Though I never expected to hear her say those words to me, they affect me more than I want to admit. Relationships have never been my specialty. I've never wanted one for longer than a night or two, and I'm still not looking for one at this moment. Something tells me she isn't either, though, so hopefully, we're on the same page. Because with the sun, water, and a beautiful woman in my arms, there's no fucking way I can resist what she's offering.

Especially when she skims one hand down my chest and stops at the band of my shorts. She drags her nails across the sensitive skin of my lower stomach, teasing and tempting me more than I can resist. Her courage surges again. She slips her hand inside, wraps her fingers around me, and caresses me with soft strokes. I was already hard enough to smash boulders before her soft hand found its mark. Now it's becoming painful in the best way.

While holding her up with one hand, I slide the fingers on my other one along the thin G-string fabric until I reach her core. Her fingers dig into my shoulders, and she presses into my hand, wordlessly urging me on.

But I have to be sure. There's no way to undo what we're about to do.

After I break our kiss, she peers up at me hesitantly. "Are you sure this is what you want, Kira? For the record, I don't expect sex from you. You don't owe me anything."

"I know that—and I completely agree. If knowing what I want makes me a terrible person, then I guess I'm the worst person who ever lived. Because the truth is, I want you more than I can bear, and I can't wait one more minute. But if you tell me you don't want this, that you don't want me, I'll stop right now, and we'll go build a sand castle instead."

"Does what's in your hand feel like I don't want you?"

She crashes her lips into mine again, our tongues clashing like the waves on the shore. She pushes the front of my shorts down at the same time I move the small triangle of fabric to the side and plunge my finger deep inside her, stroking her inner walls and increasing her yearning. She digs her fingernails on one hand into my skin as the other aligns our bodies.

"Now, Silas."

With both hands gripping her ass and the strength of my arms holding her up, I push inside her to the hilt while my hands pull her down on me. Then she takes control, rolling her hips front to back then side to side. The more she grinds her hips, the harder it is for me to hold back. She feels like a tight-fitting velvet glove, made exclusively to mold to and match me. The waves help to hide our movements, but anyone with eyes knows better. Somehow, that makes her desire for me even sexier.

Her inner muscles clutch around me, holding tighter and tighter every time she reaches climax, but she's greedy for more. I'm more than willing to accommodate her, until she screams into my neck the final time, urging me to join her. When her loud cries diminish to breathy whimpers, I pull out of her for my own release. Every muscle in her entire body relaxes at once, turning into a quivering, beautiful mess in my arms.

What the fuck do we do now?

Welcome back to reality, Silas.

CHAPTER 13

Kira

Now that the exhilarating high has subsided, the mortification of what I just did starts to set in. It's time to untangle our limbs and climb down from the large tree of a man I just scaled out of the blue. What I'm feeling isn't regret over actually showing my real desire for Silas, but rather the timing. We only just arrived in Miami, and I'd feel less awkward if I'd allowed a little more time to pass before jumping headfirst into a physical relationship.

Relationship? Is that even the correct word for what this is between us?

Association?

Connection?

Frenemies with benefits?

Silas helps steady me when the waves crash into my back as I find my footing. He wraps his hands around my biceps, keeping me upright in the water...but he's also holding me just far enough away from him to avoid our bodies coming into contact again. The flash of pain through my chest is foreign and unexpected. I was never under the delusion of instant love and marriage proposals from him. I'm not that naïve. But then, I didn't expect him to make me feel like a contagious leper immediately afterward either.

"How about that drink I promised you?" His voice is low and intimate, making me question if I'm overreacting to everything and nothing.

Now I realize I've brought feelings into a situation that was only meant to be for fun—a short fling while we're already crossing the blurred line between us. Today wasn't supposed to mean anything. He wasn't supposed to mean anything. My plan was so simple, but I had to complicate it with feelings and insecurities and doubts.

"Right now, a drink sounds perfect."

He releases me so we can work our way through the waves and onto the beach. After I throw on my cover-up, we make our way to the oceanfront bar and slide up onto the stools. He orders our drinks and a couple of appetizers before looking at me for the first time since I forced myself on him.

"Well, it's official. This is now my favorite beach of all time."

When I glance up at him, he's smiling, and the same warm, friendly, yet mischievous glint is there. In his own way, he's letting me know he won't let our frolic in the water make working together feel weird. We're back to business as usual—teasing, laughing, and enjoying each other's company.

Maybe I'll let him make the next move…if there is one.

Usually, sex wouldn't be a big deal—sometimes it's just part and parcel of getting the job done. But my targets were never anyone I wanted to know or spend time with afterward. The bottom line was I'd get the information I needed, then I'd leave. But getting to know Silas so well first has thrown me off-kilter, and now my head and heart are still reeling from just the thought of our every heated touch and passionate kiss.

"It's my favorite, too. But then, it's also the only one I've been to."

"That sly smile doesn't fool me, young lady. You know exactly what I'm talking about, so don't even try to pretend you don't."

The waiter delivers our appetizers at the same time the bartender sets our drinks in front of us. At least now my hands and mouth will be busy for the next few minutes, giving me an excuse to be quiet and bring my thoughts and feelings under control again. We devour the food and drinks in front of us, then Silas orders seconds, prompting me to raise my eyebrows in silent question.

He shrugs his shoulders. "I'm a growing boy. I need food."

Our drink refills arrive first, and I sip on my piña colada while watching the waves lapping against the shoreline. The roar of the water and the soft breeze are instantly relaxing, making me question why I've waited so long to make time for a trip to the beach. My gaze drifts back to Silas, who is watching me with a curious expression, and the full force of how short life is hits me. All the things I've wanted to do and all the places I've wanted to see have been on the back burner my whole life. Like so many others, I lied to myself and promised I'd check them all off my list one day.

One day doesn't exist, though.

"Do you ever feel like life is just one big blur? Like you're just surviving from day to day instead of really living?" I set down my glass but continue playing with the straw, stirring the frozen drink though it doesn't need it.

"I'd say most everyone feels that exact way at some point in life. It seems to come in stages, as you look back at where you've been and look forward to where you're going. It's all a matter of perspective, though, and depends on your frame of mind at the time. We all only have one life. We all have to work to live. We all have trials and troubles and good days and happy memories.

But how we approach every day we have is what makes all the difference. Whether you're happy with what you have, or you think you've been cheated out of having something wonderful, you're right."

"Good points. So, live each day to the fullest, be content with what you have, and keep a good outlook on life. Did I get all that right?"

"You did. I should trademark that and slap it on a bumper sticker before someone else steals it."

"Well, obviously. It's pure gold."

We fall into a comfortable banter over the rest of the meal. Silas finishes off the rest of the food after I've stuffed myself until I'm miserable. I jokingly complain that he'll have to roll me across the sand like a giant beach ball by the end of the week if I go out to eat with him the rest of the time. Resuming our intentional double entendre innuendo and harmless flirting makes the tension from earlier completely fade away.

Which I'm sure is his intention anyway. But the effort he puts into making me feel at ease means the world to me.

"Shouldn't we stake out the spa? See what's happening there today?" I finish off the last drop of my drink just as the waiter leaves the check.

"Not today. I told you—today is all about you having fun. We're going back out on the beach for a while. We can play beach volleyball or swim or rent Jet Skis. If you insist, we can go shopping. Maybe even get you into a luxury spa for a massage— no human trafficking allowed. The world of Miami is all yours, for one day only. So, what will it be?"

"How about…you and I stow away on one of those huge cruise ships I saw on the flight in? Let's go find our own private island to hide away for a few years."

"You honestly have no idea how appealing that offer is. Can't say it hasn't already crossed my mind at least once or twice today."

His flagrant admission takes me by surprise. He's considered running away with me? Maybe there's a romantic bone hidden in that massive, muscled body after all.

"Then my second choice is Jet Skis. Let's go have some fun on the water."

"Perfect choice. A woman after my own heart." He drops cash on the table to cover the bill and a nice tip. "Let's go ride some waves."

At first, I hop on the back of the watercraft while Silas operates it. The spray of water whips by us as we skim across the top of the water. I love it—the speed, the exhilaration, the beautiful water, the sun. I can't stop the laughter from bubbling up inside me and bursting out every time we jump a wave. He takes us out past where the waves break and stops the engine. We float on the water, enjoying the gentle roll of the waves and the scenery surrounding us.

"You ready to drive now?" He glances over his shoulder at me, and I realize my arms are still wrapped around his waist even though we've been still for several minutes.

"Really? You trust me to operate this water motorcycle?"

"Sure. Climb on up here."

We switch places, and he gives me a quick overview of the controls, then we're off again. After a half hour of proving my mettle, he has another idea.

"There's no doubt you're made for this. Let's head back toward shore. I'll rent another one and extend the time on this one, then we'll cruise up and down the shore and sight-see for a while. Sound good?"

"Sounds perfect. I'm having so much fun." I can't help but gush. Taking time for myself has never been my priority. Now I wonder what else I've missed out on after years of work being my sole focus.

We spend the rest of the afternoon acting as if we don't have a care in the world. Jumping waves on the Jet Skis, snorkeling along the jetties, and soaking up as much vitamin D as our bodies can take while sipping margaritas on the beach. This day excursion is exactly what I've needed, only I never realized it before. When the sun sinks lower in the sky, we pack up our things and head back to the car.

"Looks like you've had enough sun for the day." He nods toward the bikini line already showing on my skin. He leaves the top of the convertible up and rolls down the windows instead. The ride back to Noah's house doesn't take long, but it gives me time to collect my thoughts and consider our next steps.

Today's adventures allowed me to recharge my batteries and refocus my intentions. Now I'm ready to put all my energy into getting to the bottom of what the senator is doing and put an end to it once and for all. No more young girls will fall prey to his hands. At least then, there will be one less disgusting man loose in the world.

"Silas, are we going to stake out the spa tomorrow?"

"In a manner of speaking, yes. A couple of friends are actually watching the building today. When you and I go tomorrow, we're going as patrons. We'll get a good look around inside and figure out how they're bringing them in, where they'll hold them, and how we'll get them out."

"You didn't tell me you had people working today. Now I feel bad for taking the day off and having fun all this time."

"That's exactly why I didn't tell you ahead of time. And you can continue to feel bad for having fun instead of working tonight, because I'm taking you out for dinner and dancing in Miami. There's nowhere else like this city at night—you'll love it."

"You're spoiling me. What if I become accustomed to all this doting? Then I could hold you responsible for maintaining the lifestyle to which I've grown accustomed."

He cuts his eyes over to me, so full of playfulness, and grins.

"That would be a shame, wouldn't it?"

Inside his brother's house, he first takes me to the large walk-in closet in the master bedroom.

"Pick out an outfit—whatever you want to wear is fine. Brianna is cool. She won't mind."

Before he leaves me to rifle through her clothes, he shows me where the linens and soaps are located so I can shower and get dressed for a night out on the town. While I try to tell myself that this isn't actually a date, that we're just two friends going out to release some pent-up frustrations before settling into the roles that require our attention twenty-four hours a day, seven days a week until it's over, even I don't fall for that line. This definitely feels like a date. We're getting dressed up.

I mean… I'm wearing heels and a little black dress with long sleeves tonight.

That's definitely only reserved for a date.

When I descend the curved staircase leading to the foyer, Silas stands at the bottom and watches my every step. Hunger burns in his eyes as I approach, heating me from the inside out. The spark between us is still there, and I feel it equally as strongly. He's dressed in a gray suit with a light purple button-down, all exquisitely fitted to his frame. I'm secretly glad I'm not the only one treating this outing as a date.

"You look absolutely stunning. I won't be able to leave your side for a second without every man in the house trying to take my place." He extends his elbow for me to take his arm.

"You don't look so bad yourself, handsome. Don't think all those women won't try to find a way to lock me in the bath-room stall so they can take my place." I wrap my fingers around his arm and step closer to him.

"Guess we'll be stuck to each other like glue tonight, then."

Though part of me knows he means that for the time we're dancing and drinking in the club, another part of me envisions a very different and more satisfying scenario.

CHAPTER 14

Silas

*W*hen she stepped into view, I fought to keep my tongue in my mouth. Otherwise, it would've been on the floor. Not that I haven't found her utterly gorgeous in every other situation I've seen her in, but watching her walk toward me in that tight black dress and those spiky black heels was a full-on fantasy moment.

My plan to take her out dancing until she couldn't walk anymore flew right out the window.

Fuck giving dancing that pleasure.

If there's any reason why she can barely walk later tonight, it'll be because of me and only me. Judging by the way the pulse in her neck jumps from every brush of my fingers and how her breaths become ragged when I lean in to murmur in her ear, I'd say she agrees with me.

We're having dinner at Café Roval, one of the most romantic restaurants in Miami. The Mediterranean food is exquisite, but so is the outdoor seating in the gardens. With the lush green foliage of trees and plants and soft white lanterns lining the path winding around the sparkling pool, we couldn't ask for a more tropical paradise setting. The tables are placed far enough apart to give seclusion and provide us ample privacy. Our chairs are close together, our thighs brush against each other, and our eyes linger on each other's lips for a heartbeat too long to be a coincidence. The fact that we look and act like an enamored couple hasn't escaped me.

Nor has the sickening thought of her being forcibly removed from US soil when this is said and done.

"Silas, this place is amazing. Thank you again for bringing me here." She takes a sip of her wine and releases a little moan of indulgence. She has no idea how much that innocuous noise affects me.

"It's my pleasure, Kira. I hope you have your dancing shoes on. You'll need them." I waggle my eyebrows at her, prompting her to giggle in reply.

"I'm ready to dance whenever you are, big guy. Where are we going?"

"The Copa Room. Heard of it?"

"No, can't say I have."

"I think you'll enjoy it." The wink that follows is entirely automatic, a learned reflex I'm not even conscious of doing most of the time. But in this setting, she may have misunderstood it for something more lascivious.

Not that I mind this small misunderstanding.

"And what exactly is it you think I'll enjoy, Silas?" She folds her hands under her chin and challenges me with her gaze.

"There are cabaret shows and a large dance floor. Loud music and a lot of people. No one sees what you're doing because they're too busy with what they're doing. I'll leave my jacket in the car and roll up my sleeves, then I'll take you out on the floor and spend every minute exploring your body through salsa dancing."

"Holy shit. I don't know which sounds better—salsa lessons

back at the house where we'll be alone, or in the middle of a writhing, grinding crowd with loud music and lots of drinks." The flush starts at the base of her neck and crawls upward, coloring her cheeks the perfect shade of pink.

"Why not both? I can always give you all the private lessons you need later tonight."

"Get the check. It's time to go. I'm ready to dance now."

With a chuckle, I signal for the waiter and quickly settle the bill. Then we make a beeline for the club. The bouncer on duty is luckily an old acquaintance, so we walk directly to the front of the line and into the multicolored light show inside. The music is blaring, the bass is thumping, and all the bodies are grinding on the floor. Without waiting one more second, I grab her hand and lead her onto the middle of the dance floor.

Our bodies align perfectly as if we were made for this. With one hand on her back and the other holding her hand, I pull her much closer to me than needed for typical salsa dancing. The kind I have in mind is a little more intimate, with my invading her personal space so much we look like one body moving in a fluid motion. Pelvis to pelvis, we begin our dance and use it as a preview to foreplay. Her breasts push into my chest, her mouth is a mere breath's distance from mine, and the way her hips rub against my crotch is making an already impossible situation hard.

Very hard.

Obviously hard.

I glide my hand down her side, relishing her curves as I go, and lift her leg until she wraps it around my thigh, ensuring we're effectively dry-humping on the dance floor. So much about her makes me feel like a crazed man. She's sexy and demure, soft and hard, cunning and trusting—all at the same time. She makes me feel so much—too much sometimes. I shouldn't want her as much as I do. I shouldn't cause a scene in the middle of a crowded danced floor, drawing attention to us rather than blending into the background.

Before we're both escorted away in handcuffs for indecent exposure, the song ends and then the main lights dim. The spotlights draw circles on the curtain, drawing everyone's attention toward the stage. A voice comes through the speakers, telling us to put our hands together and welcome the cabaret performers. When the curtain opens, five beautiful ladies take front and center on the stage, singing and dancing their sultry song. The crowd goes wild before settling down to unite as impromptu backup singers. Kira and I join in, ad-libbing and making up our own dance routine while taking advantage of the darkened dance floor.

Though I would love nothing more than to take her home and rock her world until the sun comes up tomorrow, I know tonight is a rare treat for her. Dates, dinner, dancing, drinks—this atmosphere isn't something she's experienced much outside of working her asset for more information. Simply having fun wasn't in her training manual. For now, we are breaking all the rules and crossing all the lines—even that blurred line that still threatens to keep us apart. The line on the map that prompts my country to say she doesn't belong in it anymore.

I'm not ready to accept that decision, so I'm soaking up the time while we have it.

Since we have no intention of leaving anytime soon, I open a tab and keep the beer coming. We don't leave the dance floor all night, exploring each other through our movements with every song coming from the speakers. When the bar finally shuts down, we stumble out the doors with permanent smiles affixed to our faces and not a wisp of air between us. Taking my state of inebriation into account, I consider calling a taxi to take us back to the house. While doing undercover work, I've had to drive while intoxicated plenty of times. Getting a ride after knocking back a few too many doesn't exactly scream "badass criminal."

Though I don't condone it for the average civilian, I have had extensive training in driving under the influence.

Lucky me, I realize I don't have to make that decision the moment we step onto the sidewalk outside the club.

"It's about damn time. You've literally danced your ass off tonight. You have absolutely no ass left now, Silas." Even drunk as I am, there's no way I can mistake his smirk or his smartass remarks.

"Shadow. What the hell are you doing here?"

"What do you think I'm doing here? You have enough people looking for you now to form a regiment. You're not exactly making it hard for them to find you. At least wear a disguise if you're going out and getting caught on every traffic camera from here to Jacksonville." He shakes his head and opens the back door of his truck. With a sideways jerk of his head, he motions for us to get inside. Kira slides in first. "Reaper has your rental vehicle—complete with new tags. And when we get home, you're explaining to my wife why I've been out all night. I'm not taking the fall for this one."

"This is Shadow?" Kira looks between the muscular mountain of a man and me. "The one you told me about?"

"That's him." I nod and shake his hand before sliding into the back seat beside Kira.

"You didn't tell me he's CIA, too." She can't hide the concern in her tone.

"What makes you think I'm CIA?" He closes the driver-side door and starts the vehicle.

"It's not as if you're trying to hide it. If you were with any other government agency, you would've brought a SWAT team and shut down the club to get us. Instead, you're helping us get away. Not many people have the steel balls to pull off something like that."

Shadow throws his head back in laughter. "No wonder you're hiding this one. I like her already. Yes, I'm CIA, but you're safe. Silas, Nick, and Roman are three of the best men I know. The other three men I trust also are waiting to help."

"I don't know what to say. 'Thank you' isn't hardly enough for putting your lives on the line for someone you don't even know." She fights the emotion building in her voice. That small action reveals more than she knows. It tells me she doesn't know what it's like to have a family who supports her regardless of the circumstances.

"We have Silas's back no matter what, darlin'. If he believes in you enough to stick his neck out like this, the rest of us damn sure won't let him do it alone." Shadow glances at us in the rearview mirror as he speaks.

"You know, that's almost enough to make me forgive you for the last time you cheated me out of the 'favorite uncle' title."

"I won that title again fair and square, and you know that's the truth. It wasn't my fault you fell for that old trick."

"What old trick was that?" Kira looks at me, barely able to contain her amusement.

When I'm silent for two seconds too long, Shadow is more than willing to tell the story. "Whoever plays the funniest prank wins. It's as simple as that. He probably told you about the cakes, right?"

"Yes, he did, and I couldn't help but laugh. Just the picture of that scene in my mind was hilarious."

"It really was great. But this one was even better. When we all crash at Noah and Brianna's house, the kids like to help make breakfast for everyone. So we made a special breakfast for Uncle Silas. We poured the cereal in his favorite bowl and covered it with milk...then we put it in the freezer overnight. The next morning, we put just a splash of milk on top to hide the frozen mixture below, then laughed our asses off when he grabbed a spoon and tried to dig in."

"Yeah, that was really hilarious." I rub the corner of my eye, purposely using my middle finger while staring directly into his eyes.

"The kids voted—they said I'm the fun uncle." Shadow shrugs, not giving a shit that he isn't actually related to them.

"Those are awesome pranks. How do you come up with this stuff?" Kira looks at me and laughs. Again.

"I have a few tricks up my sleeve. I'm saving my best jokes for when they're older and won't tell their mother what I've taught them."

"You're more afraid of Brianna than Silas?"

"Absolutely!" Shadow and I answer at the same time.

"I hope I get to meet her one day." Kira's smile beams until she realizes time may not be on our side. The somber thought hits us at the same time, changing the mood in the vehicle in a split second.

In a feeble attempt to regain the lighthearted banter, I wrap my arm around her and pull her against me. "Be careful what you wish for, Kira. You just may get it."

"Starting tomorrow, we have a plan to execute. I've done a little recon of my own while you two danced the night away. Something big is going down in the next few weeks. I don't have all the important details yet, but I've squeezed a few of my old contacts to get as much preliminary information as I could."

"What'd they tell you?"

"Only that they've been put on alert to move precious cargo at a moment's notice once it arrives. They're not keeping these new people around to service local customers this time. Sounds like they're getting the buyers lined up and moving the girls out of the area as soon as they sell. My gut tells me they've been spooked by something—maybe even by your noticeable disappearance. But we'll be here waiting for them, regardless."

"How hot is the heat on us right now?" Although I don't want the honest answer, I need to know. "Will we put their capture at risk by being there?"

"The longer you hide, the hotter it'll get, my friend. You know that. I had a chat with the deputy director earlier today and convinced him he's worrying over nothing. We all go dark when we're eyeball-deep in a case. With everything at stake in this one, you needed some time off the grid. He agreed to cool his jets, but we both know that'll only last for so long. If we can keep you both from looking anything like yourselves, maybe we can pull off this mad caper without a hitch."

Maybe. Exactly.

Kira

When we pull into the driveway, the number of cars parked there is a dead giveaway that the entire team is here. That does give me some peace, though, knowing we have plenty of backup to help us get through this nightmare. The massive show of support by mobilizing at the first sign of a friend in distress from a group of people is largely unheard of these days. It makes me wonder if Silas has any idea how fortunate he is to have all of them by his side. Even knowing the potential consequences, Shadow still stuck his neck out for us in more than one way.

The front door swings open when the truck comes to a full stop, and one of the most beautiful women in the world walks toward us with a determined stride. When I recognize her, even through the beer goggles I'm still wearing, my jaw drops open.

"Is that...Elle Sinclair?" I can't believe my eyes. The famous actress-slash-model is marching straight toward us.

"Elle Kane now, but yes, that's her," Shadow replies before releasing a heavy sigh. "Silas, this is all your fault."

Elle jerks the driver's door open then folds her arms over her body. "Devon, where have you been all night? In what world is it okay for you not to call and tell me you're safe?"

"There is no such world, I know, babe. Trust me. This is actually all on Silas. Since he's gone rogue, I couldn't use my phone and give away our location. I had to wait outside the Copa Room all night while he drank, danced, watched cabaret shows, and had a great time. He closed down the bar. You know I'd much rather have been here with you." Shadow pulls her into his arms and places sweet kisses all over her face until she finally relents and smiles.

"Silas, is that true?" She cocks one eyebrow at him and waits.

"Yes, that's all true. Shadow is covering my ass in so many ways right now that I'll never be able to repay him for all the favors I owe him."

"Then I can't feel sorry for you over what's about to happen." The smile that covers her face is pure evil, and I can't help but laugh out loud in spite of it.

"What's about to happen?" The confused expression on his face instantly changes when another voice calls out his name.

"Well, well, well, as I live and breathe. If it isn't Silas Steele, in the flesh...and in the country. You told me you were in a remote village in Africa, guarding a king against an uprising, so you couldn't make it to my birthday party. Silas, you look me in the eye right now. Did you lie to me about that? Did you skip my birthday party by lying to me?"

Silas drops his chin to his chest and shakes his head from side to side. "Shadow," he mutters under his breath. "I'm so going to kick your ass for this."

Shadow tries to contain his laughter, but it gets the better of him anyway. He tries to cover it up with a fake cough. "You know what happens if you lie to Liz."

"Liz, you know I would've been at your party if I had any other choice. But I was extremely busy with work and couldn't get away. This is Kira, and I've been protecting her from all kinds of threats. I couldn't tell you about her, and I couldn't leave her with no defense either."

Her eyes narrow, crinkling at the corners, and her hands are curled into fists on her hips. She's not completely buying his story. "You should've called me. I'm a super-spy now, you know. All those tricks and tips you withheld from me have been unlocked and are part of my arsenal at last. I can keep her safe much better than you can. No one would dare mess with me."

"There's no doubt about that, Liz. It's just that I'm trying to save you from that pesky little law regarding impersonating a federal officer. They really don't play around with that one."

Another beautiful woman with long blond hair and the sweetest smile joins us. "All right, everyone, you know I love a family reunion more than anyone, but we need to wrap this up. It's either really late or really early, depending on how you look at it. Either way, we only have a few hours to grab some sleep before all the fun starts. Last one up after the kids wake will be sorry."

"You're lucky Brianna saved your ass, Silas. Don't think for one second this is over, though."

"Wouldn't dream of it, Liz." The group chuckles at Silas's expense, but it's all done in love and playfulness. Silas envelops the sweet blond lady in a bear hug and kisses the side of her head. "Thank you for saving me. You're my favorite sister-in-law."

"I'm your only sister-in-law, but you're welcome. It's good to have you home again."

Silas turns to me, keeping one arm loosely slung around her shoulders. "Brianna, this is Kira Petrova. Kira, this is Brianna Steele, my brother's wife and the best damn sister-in-law in the world."

I extend my hand to shake hers, but she bats it away. "Sweetie, we hug in this family. You'll just have to get used to it."

Then she wraps her arms around me and squeezes me with a gentle rocking motion before releasing me.

"It's so nice to meet you. I've heard so much about you—all good, I promise. In fact, I just told Shadow and Silas on the way here that I hoped to meet you one day."

"It's great to meet you. Come on in and get some rest while you can. This house will be crazy tomorrow." She hooks her arm through mine and escorts me inside as if we're long-lost sisters. "You look awesome in that dress. It fits you much better than it does me."

Inside is mostly dark and quiet, probably because the children are asleep, and the parents want them to stay that way for a few more hours at least. We tiptoe up the stairs, and she leaves me alone in the guest bedroom I'd chosen earlier. I close the door behind me to get ready for bed, for what little time I have left to sleep. Once I'm changed and comfortably resting in the bed, I feel a large, warm body slide into the bed behind me before an arm snakes over my waist.

"I didn't even hear you come in," I whisper into the darkness.

"I thought you may already be asleep and didn't want to wake you. But I also didn't want to sleep without you tonight. Hope you don't mind."

"I don't mind at all."

"Good, because I'm comfortable now and I'm not getting up."

We chuckle in the darkness, feeling more relaxed with each other than we did even just earlier today. Sleep quickly takes over, wrapping around me like a warm blanket and pulling me under its irresistible spell. The next time I stir, it's morning and we're still in the exact position we passed out in. Silas's body is so warm. It's as if he has a furnace burning on high inside him. That also makes it impossible to get out of bed—I've never had a more restful night of sleep before.

"I smell bacon," I whisper.

"I smell coffee." His morning voice is a deep and raspy murmur near my ear and sends goose bumps fanning out down my arm. "But it doesn't tempt me enough to get out of bed yet. Go back to sleep."

"Won't they be mad we missed breakfast?"

"Nope. My sister is here, and she's cooking. She got plenty of sleep last night. We didn't. Back to sleep now." He curls his arm tighter around me, not really giving me a choice but to relax against him and indulge in extra sleep.

Just as my thoughts settle and I begin to drift back to sleep, the sound of several little feet rushing toward us jars me awake again. Before I have time to lift my head, small bodies pounce on us from every direction, followed by uncontainable and infectious giggling. I roll over onto my back and watch the three little kids, two girls and one boy, climb all over Silas while he pretends to be asleep.

"Uncle Silas, Daddy said it's time for you to get up." The smallest girl draws out his name, only she says it more like "uncky" in her innocent voice. She crawls up to his face and uses her little fingers to pry one of his eyes open, then leans her eye down close to his. "Are you awake yet?"

He remains completely still until the other two join her at his head, totally surrounding him now. When they're still for more than two seconds, his eyes fly open and he roars loudly as he lifts his head off the pillow. Their shrill shrieks fill the bedroom before they flop onto the bed in laughter. Silas raises up, using his arm as a prop, and tickles them with his free hand.

"Who do you think you are, ambushing me in my sleep like that? When I'm weak and defenseless, even." He grabs one of the girls and blows raspberries on her belly, making her laugh and scream at the same time.

The other two lift their shirts, each taunting him. "You can't do that to me."

"Me either! You can't catch me!"

Of course, he does catch them both with no effort at all and buries his face in their bellies to tickle them. With all three given equal attention, he sits up and pulls them into his lap. Their little faces beam with happiness, making my heart pinch in my chest.

"Amelia, Emery, and Gray, this is Kira. Kira, these are my nieces and nephew. Amelia is the oldest, and as you can see, Emery and Gray are twins. Say hello to Kira, guys."

"Hi, Kira," they say in unison, though the sound of the R is more of a W. They're too adorable for words.

"Hi, Amelia, Emery, and Gray. It's very nice to meet all of you. Seems to me you guys love your uncle Silas a lot, huh?"

"Yeah, we do." Gray nods his head. "But Shadow says not to tell him he's our favorite."

"What? Shadow told you not to tell me that?" Silas asks, clarifying what he heard.

"Yep. Uncle Shadow gives us a dollar every time." Gray's eyes open wide at the mention of the bribe payment.

"Shadows pays you a dollar so you'll say he's your favorite uncle? All three of you?"

"Yeah. We're gonna be rich." Gray smiles and nods.

"Is Silas really your favorite uncle?" I lift my eyes to meet Silas's, waiting for the kids to confirm what I can already see.

"Yes," they all three reply and lean against his chest. He wraps his arms around them, pretending to squeeze them extra hard while their giggles fill the room with so much love, it's impossible to ignore.

"I've lost all three of my kids. Has anyone up here seen them?" Brianna calls from the hallway, her tone betraying her question, though. "They're supposed to be eating breakfast, but they all disappeared at the same time."

"Hurry! Hide!" Silas whispers a little too loudly to be serious. But the kids comply, pulling the comforter over their heads. While they still sit upright in his lap.

Brianna stops in the doorway, smirking at Silas. "Oh my, whatever will I do? I can't find my children anywhere. I guess they're lost forever."

The comforter giggles.

Silas smiles and shrugs. "I'm afraid we can't help you, Bri. As you can see, there are no children in here."

She arches one eyebrow at him, though she can't hide her smile. "I wouldn't go that far, Silas. I think there's at least one big kid in here."

"Don't talk about Kira like that, Brianna. You just met her."

Brianna throws her head back in laughter. "Yeah, you keep telling yourself that, Silas. If you happen to see my kids, tell them I said to get their little butts downstairs and eat, or all four of you will be in big trouble."

"I'll make sure they get the message if I see them."

When we hear Brianna's footsteps on the stairs, Silas pulls the comforter off the top of their heads. "She's gone now. The coast is clear."

Emery, the younger girl, turns around and puts her tiny hands on his cheeks. "I love you, Uncle Silas."

And here I thought my heart already had melted. I was so wrong—that is the sweetest thing I've ever seen.

"I love you too, sweet girl. Now give me a big hug and kiss then go eat before we all get in trouble."

I am pleasantly surprised when all three share their hugs and kisses with me once they've finished with Silas. They're gone just as quickly as they appeared, all rushing out the door and down the stairs. When I glance over at Silas, he's still staring at the doorway with a smile on his face.

"They really do love you. Anyone can see that."

"They're the best. My sister Chaise's kids are too. I can't imagine not being in their lives. There was a long time when I didn't see my brother or my sister. My brother was stationed overseas in hostile territory, and I was undercover God knows where, plus I didn't get along with my dad. But now, you couldn't pay me enough to make me stay away from any of them."

A sobering thought hits me like a two-ton sledgehammer right in the chest. The risks he's taking by simply being associated with me right now will take him away from his family. After years of being apart, not seeing his siblings grow up or his parents grow older, he finally has them back again. The pure delight on his face when they crawled over him as if he was their human jungle gym was nothing compared to confirming he is their favorite. When little Emery told him she loved him, I saw the first sign of vulnerability in him. He's always kept himself well guarded around me.

Those kids have him wrapped around their little fingers, right where he wants to be.

I can't let him put his entire life at risk for me, especially now that I've seen firsthand that his work isn't his whole life the way mine has been.

He won't like what I have to say, because even though he blurs the lines as a CIA officer, honor and duty still guide his every step. But there's no way around it...no way around what I have to do now.

I pause, knowing what I'm about to say won't be received well. It's just not in his nature—and I can't be the cause of his downfall. "Silas, I need to say something."

"Shoot."

"You have to get out of this investigation. You, your family, and your friends all need to leave. There are way too many people involved, and that means too many people have their necks on the chopping block for me. No matter what anyone does to me, I'll never reveal any names or anything about who has helped me. But I have to get far away from you—to protect you. I need to do this. I'll see it through to the end from here."

One side of his mouth lifts in a sexy smirk before he pulls

me into his arms. "No, baby, there's no way you're doing this alone. I've already stepped across that line in the sand, leaving a blurry mark in its place. We're past the two weeks my deputy director gave me to finish this. My family and friends, unfortunately, are accustomed to handling themselves in dangerous situations. They can hold their own in this one, too.

"We're made of Steele, baby. And we know we're stronger with each other, without a doubt. If one person involved didn't want to take the risk, they wouldn't. The fact that they are means they believe you're worth it. You've been inducted into the family, Kira. They'd never turn their backs on you, even if you tried to run away."

CHAPTER 16

Silas

"M ight as well get up now. We won't get any more sleep after all."

After we get dressed, Kira and I head down to the kitchen for a quick bite to eat before our brainstorming session with Noah and his team. Chaise stands at the counter, sipping on a piping hot cup of coffee when we enter the room. She sets down the mug and rushes into my arms.

"Hey, big brother. It's been too long since I've seen you. I've missed you."

"I've missed you too, baby girl. You know you're welcome to visit me in DC anytime you want to come." With a kiss on her cheek, I release her and head for the coffee carafe myself.

"Be careful, I just may take you up on that and leave Colton with the kids."

As soon as the words leave her mouth, her husband enters the room and walks straight to her. "What was that about leaving me behind?"

She dismisses him with a wave of her hand before raising up

385

on her toes to plant a kiss on his lips. "You know I'd never leave you, babe."

One thing I can give Bull full credit for is how much he loves my little sister. His protectiveness of her is second only to his deep adoration. I couldn't have handpicked a better man to care for Chaise.

Bull turns to me and extends his hand. "Good to see you, Silas."

"You too, man." I turn and draw Kira to my side and introduce her to my sister and brother-in-law.

"Now, do you prefer I call you Colton or Bull?" The confused expression on Kira's face is endearing. She's trying to keep up with all the names and faces being thrown at her all at once.

"You can call me Bull. The only person besides my parents who calls me Colton is Chaise."

"That's only because I refuse to admit how stubborn and bullheaded he is." Chaise laughs as she wraps her arm around his waist. "But he knows how much I love him."

Their son rushes me and wraps himself around my leg, holding on as tightly as his hands can grip. When I reach down to ruffle his hair, he grabs my hand with both of his in our standing tug-of-war fight. "And this is their son, Cason. He's six, so only a little younger than Amelia. I'm also his favorite uncle."

Kira smiles and says hello to Cason. He studies her for a second before looking up at me. "Wow, Uncle Silas. She's too pretty for you. She should be my girlfriend. And I'm six *and a half.*"

"Hey—watch it now. We have a guy code around here. No stealing of women. Check the rule book."

"You are such a handsome little man." She runs her fingers through his thick hair. His cheeks lift with a big smile.

"Uncle Silas always says lines are for crossing and rules are for breaking." Cason looks back at me and shrugs. "Your loss, dude."

The room erupts with laughter while Cason and I pretend to have a serious staring contest.

"This little beauty is Chaise's daughter, Lex. She's recently turned a year old. I'm also her favorite." I lift her out of the playpen to cover her little face in kisses. She laughs and puts her little hands on my face. Then she turns her attention to Kira, extending her arms and leaning toward her.

Kira is hesitant to take her at first, but the two seem to form an instant bond. Kira can't wipe the smile off her face as she coos at and talks to Lex. Then Kira's eyes roam around the room, lingering on every face sitting around the table a little too long to be considered casual glances.

Interesting.

"There's one more part of the extended family I want you to meet. This is Rebel and his wife, Heather. Those adorable twins beside them are Kinsley and Elias. They're the same age as Cason. I'm also their favorite uncle."

"Now, Silas. We all know I'm the favorite uncle here." Shadow and Elle walk into the kitchen together, but he has the nerve to smile right to my face after all his games and trickery. At first, I'm tempted to call him on his bullshit, but I decide revenge is better served cold. So he'll choke on it.

"Whatever you say, Shadow. You keep believing that lie."

With introductions out of the way, Kira and I join them at the table and eat until we're stuffed. Kira refuses Chaise's offer to take Kinsley so she can eat in peace. She takes one bite and gives her the next one. One seems to be equally as taken with the other.

"It looks like Shadow and I will both lose our 'favorite' status to Kira any minute now."

"You've both already lost it. You just don't realize it yet." She cuts her eyes up at me and flashes a mischievous grin.

"There's finally someone who can keep Silas in line. I love it," Shadow quips.

As appealing as the initial notion may be, I'm not looking for anyone to keep me in line or keep me anywhere, for that matter. I like my life as it is—uncomplicated with a lot of freedom to do as I please. Roaming from shore to shore or anywhere around the globe at a moment's notice doesn't exactly lend to a happy home. In fact, a serious relationship isn't even anything I've ever seriously considered before.

"I'm glad you're having such a good time at my expense. You'll pay for this later in a very painful way."

He just laughs it off like he does most everything else, then follows up with a shit-eating grin. The bad thing about Shadow is he's a damn good CIA officer himself, with an uncanny ability to see through others, even those who are deep undercover. Knowing he's actively trying to probe my mind through watching my body language is a little unsettling. I don't like being on this side of the equation...and the bastard knows it.

By the time we finish breakfast and head toward Noah's office, we have additional visitors and even more backup for the major trap we're laying for our friendly senator and his partners. Nick, Roman, and Brad arrive with Savannah, Mira, and more kids in tow. We stop in the foyer to greet everyone and chat before disappearing into our version of a war room.

"If all else fails, at least we can build our own army with all these kids around here. They may be more effective than we are anyway. When are you and Elle having kids, Shadow? We may need to start recruiting them sooner rather than later." I turn my attention to my friendly adversary.

A look passes between the couple after my question—Elle is aggravated, and Shadow is uncomfortable. There is no way in hell I'm letting him off the hook with this one. She's ready for kids, and he's not quite there yet. Time to stoke the fire under his ass and use it to my advantage in every way possible.

"Uh, we're in active, hostile negotiations about that very sensitive topic right now. Let's not muddy the waters by bringing that into our more immediate plans." I've literally never seen Shadow nervous in this way before. I really like it.

"All right, let's get this locked down as soon as possible." Noah nips that conversation in the bud before it can gain traction. "Brad, let's get the blueprints up in my office and go over every inch of the building layout."

"On it, Reap." Brad leads the way, and the rest of us follow.

"Savannah and Mira—bring the babies into the den with the rest of us. The guys have plenty to keep them busy for a while in Noah's office. We girls can all get to know each other in a more relaxing setting." Brianna, ever the gracious host, leads the way for her company. That little lady has never met a stranger in her life.

Kira hesitates for a moment until I take her hand in mine and pull her along with me. "You come with me, love. You're part of this op too. You have more at stake than any of us."

"I wasn't sure how much I'd be trusted in a room full of federal agents and military commandos. Especially when they're all here for recon on a covert and illegal operation."

"Are you kidding? You'll fit right in."

We walk into the office together, and Shadow's eyes immediately drop to our joined hands. He hits me with a satisfied smirk, and I know this is only the beginning of our incessant bantering. So I purposely continue holding her hand so that Shadow doesn't think his taunting is getting to me. I mean, it is —a little—but he doesn't need to know.

"Shadow did some initial recon for us, gathering insider information on the senator and what he does in his free time while he's in Miami. Other than the beach, golf course, and a weekly visit to the spa, he doesn't do much else on the regular. The extended stay of three or four weeks is out of the ordinary, though." Noah boots up his computer and turns on the large TV screen so Brad can display the blueprints for the day spa facility.

"Silas and Kira, we have the original blueprints and an expansion filed later for a building permit, but there's always the strong possibility the new plans don't include everything. You two have an appointment for a couple's massage later today. Get inside, get lost, and figure out what's missing from our information."

"Can I request that we get lost inside the building after our massage? I could really use one and don't want to be kicked out before our appointment." I'm only partially kidding. Now that Noah's mentioned it, I actually am looking forward to it.

"That would probably make more sense anyway. When you get dressed again, just turn the wrong way out of the room and have a look around."

Kira examines every detail of the screen, her eyes slowly moving from room to room. "Okay, that layout is burned into my brain now. We shouldn't have any trouble finding a new door or extra room once we're inside."

"Photographic memory?" I ask. "Nice."

"Yes, pretty much, for as long as I can remember. It has its pros and cons. I'd rather be able to forget some of the things I've seen before."

"Not knowing where or how this is going down means we'll have to take shifts on stakeout so that someone is always close by to make a move if needed. We've already set up a schedule with teams of two. Brad, I need you to stay here and help coordinate the tech piece. If Silas and Kira find undocumented rooms, they can put mole cameras in place if they can get a clear signal. Once you have us linked up, we can rotate watching the inside cameras too." Noah's always been the man with the plan. That shows how brothers' personalities can be in stark contrast —he plans every last detail, while I prefer to wing it and see what happens.

Noah gives us the days and times of our shifts for the week, along with our marching orders. He and Rebel are taking the first night. Our working theory is it's too dangerous to bring the people they intend to sell rather than enslave inside the business during the day. They'll most likely attempt to make all their shady deals at night, with each buyer walking their new merchandise out just as quickly as they walk in.

But experience and common sense tell us this will never happen the way we expect, so we have to stay alert at all times. We review the area around the building once again, identifying the best spots to park and observe who comes and goes, walk and peruse the block, and watch different angles of the building for any signs of trouble. When they make their move, I hope I'm the one on watch so I can tear those assholes apart with my bare hands.

"You two should get going. Don't want you to be late for your massage." Noah opens the door and steps out into the hall. "The rest of us will be around here somewhere. If you don't hear from us in a few hours, send help because that means all the kids have hog-tied and stuffed us into the closets."

"Now that I might even pay to see." I grab Kira's hand again and head toward the front door. "We'll check on everyone later —after our relaxing massage and a long stroll inside the building. That should give the kids plenty of time to stage their coup."

Kira and I walk out the front door with a mixture of laughter and obscenities coming from the group of men behind us. She looks over at me and bursts out laughing. Seeing her carefree side tugs at my heartstrings because I know she hasn't had many opportunities just to relax and be herself. Even though we're still technically working, my goal is to make the next few weeks as fun and special as I can under the circumstances.

When we're in Noah's truck on the way to our appointment,

I glance over at her with an intentionally flirty and naughty expression. "You know what?"

"What?" Her bright smile covers her face when she realizes I'm still in playful mode.

"We're getting a couple's massage."

"Yeah, I know. And?" Her eyebrows draw down, and she tilts her head to the side.

"That means we'll be in the same room, so I get to see you completely and totally butt naked. Like, your boobies and everything." I waggle my eyebrows and nod, keeping a huge grin on my face.

When she leans her head back to laugh at my stupidity, her long black hair cascades over her shoulders and down her back. The sheer magnificence of her beauty takes my breath away.

The first thought that fires in my brain is, *How can I ever let her leave?*

Fuck.

I may be in trouble after all.

CHAPTER 17

Kira

Whatever I expected a shady spa that acts as a front for a human trafficking scheme to look like, this isn't it.

This is a five-star luxury health resort with every possible amenity I could imagine, and some I didn't even realize existed. After we sign in and complete the required paperwork, the receptionist brings us each a glass of chilled water flavored with cucumber. Softly in the background, sounds of nature come from the speakers strategically placed around the room. The extra-padded Adirondack chairs instantly put me at ease. The mixture of ambiance and comfort is perfect to create a feeling of serenity.

"Silas and Kira?" A soft voice calls out, and I look up to see an attractive young blonde.

Her hair is pulled back from her face in a ponytail, and she has a welcoming smile. She leads us to the back and shows us to the separate dressing rooms. After explaining how to use the lockers and where to find the robes and slippers, she points out the adjoining waiting room where we'll wait for our massage therapists to come get us.

Nothing about this establishment has raised the first red flag yet, prompting a slight panic attack to flare up in my chest. What if this is the wrong place? What if we've completely misread all the signs? What if this is a wild goose chase, and the very people we're trying to take down have gotten away with everything after all?

After I secure my things in the locker and meet Silas in the posh waiting room, I walk straight up to him, ready to abandon the entire mission. I feel like I've wasted everyone's time and energy on top of putting them all at risk of being arrested just because they wanted to help me.

"Don't say it." His voice is low, and he leans in, his lips close to mine. He rubs his knuckles over my cheek, igniting every nerve ending in my body at once with his simple touch. "We're not wrong. This is a legitimate business, but that doesn't mean they aren't dirty. You have to trust me on this."

"Silas, I do trust you. You have to know that by now." The rest of what I want to say—what I need to say—is on the tip of my tongue. The expression on his face says he knows there's an unspoken "but" at the end of my statement. This is entirely the wrong time to bring it up, though.

His ability to read me like an open book is equally comforting and unsettling. No secrets and no surprises, but that leaves me very few options to protect him...even from himself.

He acknowledges I'm not ready to voice my reluctance with a simple nod. "We'll finish that conversation later. For now, let's suffer through one of the highest-rated massages in South Florida, then we can get lost in the maze of hallways and doorways."

Then he closes the gap between us, and his lips cover mine. The smoldering spark that's always burning just below the surface immediately ignites into an inferno. He slides his hands around my waist, the warmth seeping through the terry cloth robe as if I'm not even wearing it. The tip of his tongue glides across the part in my lips, seeking entry—only he doesn't need to ask for permission. I'm already there, willing and waiting for him when his velvety soft tongue strokes across mine.

I move my hands up his chest, committing every dip and curve of his muscles to memory until I reach the back of his neck. His hair is probably the only soft part of his entire body, and I feel a slight shudder travel through him when I run my fingers through it. My nails lightly scratch his scalp just before I close my fist, gripping his hair with a small tug. His lips leave mine, trailing across my cheek and down the side of my neck. The licks, nips, and bites he scatters across my skin between kisses kick my libido into overdrive. I'm more than tempted to initiate a repeat of our ocean excursion right here in this room —the one anyone could walk into at any moment.

"This is going to be a long fucking day," he murmurs against my skin. "Only one taste of you is cruel and unusual punishment."

"Tonight." My breathy one-word reply is all I can manage at the moment.

"Fucking right, tonight. The first second we're alone, you'll be mine in every possible way."

Is it too soon to say I already am?

Maybe.

But I know, without a doubt, there's no one else who has ever made me feel this way. I never believed in fate before meeting him. Now, I can't imagine our meeting simply being left to chance.

We each take a half step backward from each other when we hear the door open, as if we're a couple teenagers about to be caught making out. Two women in spa uniforms enter, holding clipboards with our paperwork attached. With friendly smiles, they greet us by name and ask what we'd most like to get out of this visit. Two things immediately pop into my mind, but replying my only goal is to finish what I just started with Silas then stop the dirty senator seems inappropriate.

"I carry a lot of tension in my neck and shoulders, so that's my main area of concern." I somehow manage to come up with an intelligent response.

"Same for me." When I look up at Silas, it takes all my willpower not to laugh out loud at his smug expression. He had the same initial thoughts I had.

"We can take care of that for you both. Follow us."

We walk down a long hallway, and I check off the location of each door as we pass, comparing it to the image still clear in my mind. When we reach the couples room, I'm surprised to see a small hot tub in the floor between the two massage beds. Rose petals float on the surface of the water, adding a natural floral fragrance to the room.

"I'm setting this timer for twenty minutes so you two can soak in the tub and loosen up your muscles before we start your massage. When the alarm goes off, dry off and lie face up on the tables. We'll knock before coming in, so don't feel rushed." The therapist puts the timer on the table beside the massage oils before leaving us alone.

"I was only half joking before, but I can't say I'm disappointed at all. Do you need any help removing your robe?" The predatory gleam in his eyes makes my blood boil in the best way.

"Actually, I do need help. This bow I tied in the belt is nearly impossible to untie."

"First of all, let me show you what 'very hard' actually is. Secondly, I'll tear it off you with my teeth if I have to." He grips my hips in his big hands and pulls me toward him, and I go more than willingly. I love his playful alpha side.

Before I even realize the belt is untied, I feel the warmth of his hands on my skin, pushing the robe off my shoulders until it falls to the floor behind me. Not to be left out, I move my hands under his robe and help him out of it. The heat of his body drives away any chill from the air in the room.

"It was only a few minutes ago when we agreed to wait until tonight. Now I don't know that I can wait. But the ticking of that alarm reminds me why I have to—because there's no way I can do everything I've planned for you in less than twenty minutes. Our first time happened way too fast. I didn't get to hear you scream, so I'm making up for that later by taking my time to touch you, taste you, and feel you. I'll make sure you're so fucking ready for me that you're begging for it. Then I'm burying my face between your legs until I feel your thighs quiver uncontrollably. After I have you all worked up into a frenzy, we'll wake the entire house with you screaming my name."

The words simply tumble out of my mouth without a single forethought. "Fuck me, that's so hot."

He skims his hand along my jaw then he gently grips my chin with his thumb and forefinger. The heat radiates from his eyes as he stares into mine. "That's exactly what I plan to do. All fucking night."

"How long is this massage again? I'm thinking we should go check in to a hotel somewhere instead of staying with your family."

"I like how you think. Now, it's time to get you hot and wet."

"I already am."

He quirks one eyebrow and gives me a sexy smirk. "Oh yeah? Maybe I should check?"

My nod may be a little too enthusiastic. He steps into the hot tub and pulls me toward him, his gaze feasting on me as I join him in the water. We sink down into it, our hands instinctively seeking the other. When he skates his fingers up my inner thigh at a painstakingly slow pace, I know he's giving me every opportunity to stop him. There's no way in hell that's happening, though. His hand stills when mine covers it—but the eagerness returns full force when I quickly pull him to his original destination.

He buries one finger deep inside me while rubbing my clit with his thumb. His tongue leaves a hot trail along my collarbone before he dips his mouth to my nipple. When he adds a second finger, he also increases the pressure and speed of his sensual assault. It's all I can do to keep from crying out his name when my climax rips through me. I cling to him, my fingers digging into his shoulders as I ride the wave until it subsides.

I slide my hand down his body and grasp his rock-hard cock, ready and willing to give him the same pleasure, however he wants it. He wraps his hand around mine then halts my movement.

"Hold that thought, babe. If you keep going, we'll end up fucking right here on the floor. Only, I won't stop when they walk back in. When we leave here, we're getting a room for fucking certain."

"Holy shit. Is it wrong that part of me wants to test you to see if you really wouldn't stop?"

A dangerous, feral expression overtakes his features, and it's such a fucking turn-on. Silas is one heartbeat from losing his calm and cool composure. I've wondered if there was a part of him that he kept hidden away, behind the strict lines he never crosses. Now I know for sure—Silas has a very dark and dangerous side.

"I'll fucking show you right now. We'll get kicked out of here and won't complete our assignment, but it'll be fucking worth it."

The alarm goes off, effectively bringing us out of our carnal haze and putting our priorities back into perspective. He steps out of the hot tub and grabs the towels, holding one out for me to walk into. When he wraps the towel around me, he keeps his arms around me too. Then he kisses me softly, showing a stark contrast to the savage man who just made an appearance. With his own Mr. Hyde safely tucked back in his cage, Silas Steele is back in character and back in his element.

Then he helps me onto the massage table and covers me with the sheet before sliding his towel across his skin and lying on his table.

"Make sure she relaxes all your muscles, Kira. You'll need all the flexibility you can get in a couple of hours." His tone is casual, and his face is passive with his eyes closed and a small smile playing on his lips.

What the fuck? How am I supposed to relax now?

Silas

After the best massage I've ever had, Kira and I assure the staff we know how to get back to the changing rooms. Once we're dressed again, we meet in the hall and start our search. We move quickly through the corridors, relying on our collective memories of the blueprints to identify anything out of the ordinary.

"Hold on." Kira stops and looks behind us before pointing to the door to our left. "This one wasn't on the newest design."

"By all means, let's see what's behind door number three." Using my undercover skills, I pick the lock. As softly as I can, I open the door and peek inside. "It's a long, dark hallway. I can't tell what's at the end of it from here."

"There was absolutely not a hallway shown on the plans in this spot. Silas, if they're conducting their side business in a secret room, they could do it at any time of the day or night. How are they moving people in and out?"

"Stay here. If anyone comes back here, just say you got turned around. I have to see what's in here and where it leads."

I creep down the dark hallway, being careful not to make a sound when I move. By the time I reach the door at the end, my eyes have fully adjusted to the dim light. With an easy turn of the knob, I open the door without a creak. The outer door was locked, but they obviously feel comfortable leaving the inner one open.

As I scan the room, the sick feeling in the pit of my stomach grows worse. There's a reason why never underestimating your opponent is drilled into our heads during training. My maxim has always been, "Assume the worst of people and be pleasantly surprised when they don't let you down."

This is what ignoring my training and my gut gets me.

Without caring if I'm heard or seen, I rush back down the hall and find Kira still waiting for me. "Come on. There's someone I need to talk to—I just hope he's still there."

"Who? Where? What's going on? What'd you see?"

"Give me a minute, baby. If I'm right, I'll be able to explain everything very soon."

We reach the door to the men's changing room, and I calm my pounding heart before rushing in and demanding answers. I'm relieved to find just the man I was looking for still inside, cleaning up after the day's patrons.

"Hey, buddy. I'm glad you're still in here. My teenage nephew needs a job in the worst way. This place is so nice, I thought I'd send him down here to put in an application. Can you tell me a little about working here? Does it pay well? How many days off do you get? Stuff like that."

The alarm on his face tells me everything I need to know. He shakes his head quickly from side to side.

"No, no. Uh, no opening." His broken English nearly breaks me. I've been so blind today, focused on Kira instead of my job, I missed all the signs.

The tiredness in his eyes.

His grim expression.

The way his hands shake when he reaches for items.

How his feet shuffle when he walks because he doesn't have the energy to lift them.

"That's too bad. Do you enjoy working here?" I purposely keep my tone easy and my body language friendly and open. I don't want to spook him more than he already is.

One of the manipulation tactics human traffickers use is to convince their prey that everyone is out to get them. That the police will lock them away forever. Even that ICE is always on standby to deport them to a forgotten prison somewhere offshore. If he thinks I'm anywhere in the neighborhood of being a cop, he'll cover and lie for his captors to save his own hide.

When he looks up at me, I can see the desire to spill all the illegal and immoral secrets he's witnessed behind these walls. He glances around nervously, as if he's waiting for someone to rush in and drag him away.

"I haven't even introduced myself. My name is Silas." I extend my hand to shake his.

He takes my hand, and I sense he's warming up to me more with each passing minute. "Cristano."

"Good to meet you, Cristano. Listen, I know you don't know me at all, but I have a feeling you're in trouble. I can help you if you let me before it gets worse."

Panic starts to set in, and I know he's about to bolt.

"If they said you'd be arrested and sent to prison if you were found out, they lied to you, my friend. That's not how our system works. If your employer isn't paying you and not allowing you any days off, they're not good people, Cristano. They're the criminals, not you. In fact, they're the ones commit-ting illegal acts, but you're not. If they took your passport or your identification, they're definitely using you and not keeping up their end of whatever deal they made with you. Let me help."

He's listening—intently—and I can almost see the gears in

his brain turning, putting all the pieces together. But he still doesn't respond.

"Cristano, if you've seen other people come here to work, then all of a sudden, they're gone, that's another bad sign. There are a lot of people who want to help people like you and others who are caught in this unfortunate situation. In fact, a friend of mine has put her life on the line just to stop the bad things that are happening here.

"She found out about it by accident, and her government will likely execute her if she returns home. But it's so important to her, she's willing to risk her life for it. She also found out they're about to bring in more new people. My concern is they'll sell you or someone else who works here to make room for the new people they're taking advantage of.

"If you've seen any of this happening here, I need you to tell me so I can help you. I promise you're not in trouble, and you won't ever be in trouble for trying to make a better life for yourself or your family. We can help you—just tell us what's really happening here."

The aged Filipino man breaks down in front of me, sobs racking his body. Despite the tears and guilt that riddle him, a spark of gratitude still shines in his eyes. Like a dam breaking from too much pressure pushing on a cracked wall, Cristano tells me everything he knows. Everything that's happened. Everything he's seen and experienced in the time he's worked here.

"I will get you out of this, Cristano. You have to trust me. They're bringing in more people to use and abuse soon, and we need to save them, too. Here's my phone number—memorize it or keep it hidden on you at all times. If you're in imminent danger, call me and I'll come rushing in. But if we can save everyone at once, you'll be a hero. Are you with me?"

"I'm with you, Silas." He hugs me, squeezing me as hard as his thin arms will allow.

When I leave, it's with my solemn vow that I'll be back for him. If it's the last thing I ever do, I'll keep that vow to him.

When Kira and I head back to the front desk to pay for our services, I can't contain my disgust for the people who work here, knowing they're helping to exploit destitute people who only want to make their lives better.

"How was your massage, Mr. Steele?" the receptionist asks tentatively. She must sense the fury boiling just beneath the surface.

"The massage was great. Thank you."

When we get in the truck, I relay the entire conversation to Kira. Tears of frustration and disgust well up in her eyes. "Silas, this has to stop. I saw a lady in the women's changing room when I first walked in. She was gone by the time I came out of the curtained area, but now I'm certain she's also being treated like a slave."

"It's going to stop, baby. And the people behind it are going to pay for the shit they've done. We'll make sure of it. Unfortunately, I have to break my promise to you. As much as I want to hide away in a hotel room with you for the next week, this has to take precedent. If we lose Cristano now, I'll never forgive myself."

"Of course. I completely agree. Whatever it takes, let's do it. What did you find when you went into that dark hallway? What's back there?"

"It's one big room that's lined with beds—one after the other, only separated by half-length curtains to create a tiny room. Many of those beds appear to be new—no sheets, no clothes, nothing to show anyone occupies them. They must be making room to hold their 'precious cargo' until the sale is final. They've been keeping the people there to work for them for free…and who knows what else. I saw a few toys down there too, but I didn't see any kids."

"Did you see how they're bringing them in and out of the building?"

"They don't need a secret entrance to bring workers in and out. They can make them wear uniforms and march them in the front or back door without anyone questioning it. For the kids, they could simply hold their hand and walk in with them. It wouldn't seem so out of place that anyone would notify the authorities.

"I have to get back and share all this information with the team. We need to reevaluate our plan and timeline. My main concern is it'll all happening sooner rather than later. I could be wrong, though—that's happened once or twice before."

We get back to Noah's, and I retrace our every step and conversation for the team, with the exception of our time alone in the hot tub. That memory is only for Kira and me to relive… alone…as soon as humanly possible.

"Okay, then. We work just as well together without a plan as we do with a plan. We'll watch it day and night. Everyone be ready to move at a moment's notice." Noah calmly removes Gray from the kitchen countertop he climbed up on.

"Daddy!" Gray's little face contorts to show his displeasure.

"What?"

"You ruined everything!"

"Yes, I'm sure I did, by getting you off the counter where you know you're not allowed to climb. But you still have to get down, little man."

"Seems like you have this dad gig down pat."

"Yeah, you should try it. Chaise and I need more nieces and nephews."

"I'm waiting for Shadow to take the plunge first. Then I'll go." I cut my eyes over at him, not bothering to hide the massive grin on my face.

His response is to flip me off, which only makes me laugh out loud.

"Looks like I'll be taking matters into my own hands soon. If I haven't already, that is," Elle says nonchalantly.

Shadow's eyes bulge out of his head, and his mouth drops open. I quickly turn around and snicker to myself. Otherwise, I absolutely will encourage her.

After a week of round-the-clock stakeouts at the spa and violating the senator's privacy like we're a bunch of peeping toms, we're still no closer to shutting him down than when we started. The man has barely left his house, and those few times have only been to go out to dinner with his wife. I've raised concerns more than once that we're watching the wrong man, but the eyes-only documents he has keep tripping me up.

He wouldn't have those if he were clean.

Unless.

"Shadow, I need you to do me a favor." I find him sitting alone on the deck, staring at nothing while deep in thought.

"It's bothering you too. Isn't it?"

"What, exactly?"

"The idea that we may be focusing all our efforts on the wrong man. But everything we've seen points to him and him alone."

"Yeah, it is. It's a little too convenient, isn't it?" I sit down on the lounge chair beside him.

He nods. "And if my experience has taught me anything, it's not to trust anything that's packaged up all nice and neat. That's a sure sign of misdirection."

"Precisely. Which is why I want you to look into someone else for me. Since I'm technically a fugitive from justice right now, I can't very well call up my friends at Langley and ask for a favor." I hand him a piece of paper. "Find out everything you can on that man for me."

"You got it. Of course, you know this is the first place they'd look if they really wanted to find you, right? Your friends aren't trying too hard to hunt you down."

"You're right. No one is actively looking for me right now. Since I know the CIA has already found me. They're just biding their time right now, in case I'm right about everything."

Shadow nods slowly, weighing my words against his intrinsic understanding of how the agency works. But he doesn't verbally confirm anything.

The door to the deck opens, and Kira calls us both inside. "Brad said he's got something new for us." Shadow and I jump up and follow her into Noah's office.

"The senator is on the move," Brad says from behind his computer screen. "I've got eyes on him, so we're good."

"Just don't lose him. Let's see where he goes and what he's up to, preferably before it's too late." I sit down beside Brad and watch the red dot move on the map.

"They're headed to the private marina," Brad points out.

"I remember reading in his dossier that he has a boat there. Could that be how they're transporting the people into the country?" Kira moves to stand beside me and puts her hand on my shoulder when she leans over to stare at the red dot.

"That's a very good possibility. I'm sure a man of his stature has a large yacht with plenty of holding space." I sit back and fold my arms over my chest. "If he goes out into international waters, that's a sure sign he's up to no good."

"Anyone have an overwhelming urge to rush out and shop for a boat down at the marina right now?" Shadow asks.

"As a matter of fact, I do." I stand and follow him out to his truck. "I've always wanted a boat."

"You're not leaving me behind while you go boat shopping. I'm coming with you." Kira is hot on my heels, refusing to stay here.

The three of us head down to the marina to be there when

Senator Hunt's boat docks again. If he unloads his side business of human trafficking tonight, we'll be there to witness it and put a stop to his activities. The haunted expression on Cristano's face still bothers me. Plus, I have no idea what they're doing with the other people they've reserved beds for in that basement. They're not all working inside the spa, that's for sure.

We reach the docks and prepare to spend a long night waiting for the yacht's return. Depending on how far out they have to run to meet their suppliers and the sea conditions surrounding their return, we could be here until sunrise. We stroll around the boats for sale, looking at everything from a small fishing boat to a luxury yacht that's bigger than my house ever thought about being. Kira ventures off into another ship, daydreaming about what it would be like to own one, and Shadow and I hang outside, keeping an eye on the horizon.

"So, what's your hang-up about having kids with Elle? Why don't you want them?" My casual tone belies the loaded question. Shadow visibly tenses before he answers.

"It's not that I don't want them. I'd love to have kids with her —one day. But we haven't been married that long yet. I'd like to be able to travel more and spend time together as a couple longer before we take that step. Babies will change everything. I've seen Noah and Brianna try to pack up to move across the country for an extended stay at their place in California. There's absolutely no spontaneity—everything has to be planned down to the last snack and nap time."

"Or, you miss being in the middle of danger, chasing bad guys across the stormy seas at a moment's notice. Or jetting off to the Middle East wearing a flak jacket, hunkered down behind a .50 caliber machine gun while cruising across the desert terrain. And you're afraid that having kids will change you."

"Shut the fuck up, Silas."

There's that nerve I've been looking for. Target acquired.

"Convince me I'm wrong." I stop walking and turn to face him.

His deadpan stare is his only response.

"Ah, I see what's really going on here."

"Silas. Let it go."

"Elle doesn't know you never actually left the CIA, does she? You never told her they convinced you to stay on in a specialized capacity when you moved to California. That's why you're avoiding having kids. You're afraid of blowing your cover. You sneaky dog."

"So help me, Silas…"

"Save your threats, Shadow. Your secret is safe with me."

Shadow's phone rings, saving us from an all-out brawl. "That was Brad. He said the boat stopped a short way down the shore. He hacked into the senator's phone camera and verified the senator and his wife are just enjoying some time out on the water. The senator opened a bottle of wine, and the two of them talked about their plans now that the last of their kids is married and off living her own life. He'll check in on them periodically, but there doesn't appear to be anything illicit to their excursion."

CHAPTER 19

Kira

Two and a half weeks.

That's how long we've been watching the spa, the senator, the marina, and combing through every little detail of the senator's life now. Every day, Silas grows more irritated and aggravated. We're somewhat hiding from the government—even though we should've left the country a long time ago if we had any real hope of escaping punishment. But it's his promise to Cristano that weighs the most on his conscience, more and more with every passing minute. Freeing the janitor from his five-star prison is vital to Silas. After spending every minute of the last month and a half with him, I'd like to think I know him reasonably well.

He bends and breaks the rules that don't help with meeting his objective, but there are a few lines he'd never cross. He has a strong sense of protecting the innocent, and failing at that particular mission simply cannot happen. Knowing he's left someone in that precarious position eats him alive inside. Not making any headway on this case makes him a little crazy. But someone beating him at a game where he's usually the victor downright pisses him off.

The only thing that seems to relieve his stress is our time alone, and he uses every precious second of that to work through his frustrations. Night after night, he makes love to my entire body, even my mind. With his whispers and his vows. With his lips and his hands. He elicits feelings and desires that I never knew existed from deep inside me. The licks, nips, and kisses he feathers across my skin in the middle of the night are never enough. He gives until I can't take anymore, but my hunger for him is never fully satiated because I eagerly take him each and every time he reaches for me. When he leaves marks in places that only he and I have seen, it seals a bond between us.

Even if I'm the only one who feels it.

Even if I'm the only one who wants it.

For a long time, I never believed in love. It was only a fairy tale people believed in a hollow attempt to fool themselves into thinking they were happy. I felt sorry for those poor souls, walking around in a self-induced haze until they just woke up one day and realized they weren't "in love" with their partner anymore. Then they left and found the next person they were "in love" with, hoping to fill the hole deep inside them.

Now I have a slightly different outlook.

After watching Noah and Brianna together, hearing their story and seeing firsthand how they never gave up on each other, I'm a believer.

Imagining going back to a life without Silas in it feels empty and pointless.

My instructors back at the Academy never would believe I've turned into a dreamer, trusting in the power of love.

Yet, here I am.

A Russian spy.

Hopelessly in love with a CIA officer.

How can this story ever have a happy ending?

The realization that I only have one ending, and that it's already written in stone, is enough pressure to bear. But every minute that passes with this loving family in harm's way—because of me—nearly destroys me. Watching everyone with their children, so happy, so full of life, and so caring, makes me so envious. I've never wanted that life before. Being trained to never expect happiness beyond what serving my country could bring me set my expectations very low early on in life.

Outside of Mira, I don't remember much about having a family around. I still miss my parents, but my childhood memories were all but pushed out of my mind by the endless drills the Academy put us through. We would whisper our memories to each other at night, trying to hold on to a wisp of our formative years. But we were soon discovered, and they separated us at night, putting us in solitary confinement as punishment until we learned our lesson.

Now I see Mira with Brad, even when they don't think anyone is watching. He's head over heels in love with her, doting on her every need and showering her with affection. She's just as smitten with him, sidling up beside him to steal quick kisses while he works. The way he looks at her when she walks away melts even my cold, black heart. He wants to spend his life with her—that much is crystal clear to me.

I'm afraid to admit, even to myself, that I wish Silas looked at me the same way.

All I really need is a life filled with love and happiness, surrounded by family and friends, with a good man to keep me warm at night. That's my dream life.

Add one more item to that list. I've always wanted a dog, but I was never allowed to have one. A furry, four-legged best friend would complete the perfect picture.

I'm sitting outside by the pool alone, finishing an early morning cup of coffee with only my musings to keep me company, when a voice from the chair beside me nearly makes me jump out of my skin.

"When you went to Russian spy school, did they teach you the art of disguises?" I snap my head to the side, and I find Liz staring me down intently, waiting for an answer.

"Um, yes, ma'am. We were taught how to change our looks and blend in without any distinguishing marks."

"Good, good. And did they teach you other tricks of the trade? Insider secrets that the general public would have no way of knowing?"

"Sure, I guess so. I mean, if everyone knew what to do, it wouldn't be considered a spy trade, would it?"

"Smart girl. Now, here's what you and I are going to do. You'll teach me everything you know, then I'll teach you everything I know, and we'll save the day together." She gives me a long wink along with a sharp nod.

"No. No, no, no, Liz. I've told you a million times. We can't reveal insider practices to you. Stop asking and putting Kira on the spot like that." Silas sits down beside me with two cups of hot coffee and slides one over in front of me. "Keep it up, and I'll slip some sodium pentothal into your drink and make you spill your guts."

Liz stands, leans over the table, and levels her gaze on Silas. "Let me remind you of something, Mr. Steele. You should never make threats to me that you know you can't carry out. They never end well for you. But now that you've thrown down the challenge, I'm thrilled to accept it. The game is on, big boy. I sure hope you're up for it."

She stalks away with a swagger in her step and a scary aura surrounding her.

"She's a formidable foe, isn't she?"

"You have no idea, Kira. No idea. She'd be the world's deadliest weapon if she knew half of what we know." Silas shakes his head, but he can't hide the smile on his face. He loves her, even if she drives him crazy.

"So, what's the plan for today? Since we're not training Liz in the ways of espionage, what else should we do with all our free time?"

"I can think of three or four things that would be a much better use of our time. And a lot more fun for us." He waggles his eyebrows at me. "For one, the pool is heated. We could take a skinny-dip right now."

"Well, if that wouldn't invite the wrath of Liz on us, I don't know what would." I laugh, knowing he's kidding, but the thought is still appealing.

"You have a point there. Although, I'm more afraid of her joining us than anything else." That makes us both laugh out loud. We've grown more relaxed around each other outside of the bedroom, as much as we have inside it. "I suppose we'll have to stick to our standing date of sitting in a car, staring at a building, and waiting for something exciting to happen."

"When it finally does happen, I think we'll have all the excitement we can stand."

"I'm glad you said that. You just jinxed us, so we should have our hands full today."

"It's about fucking time. We should probably get over there in case we just jinxed Nick and Roman."

"Hold up before you two go anywhere." Shadow walks up behind us wearing a grim expression that instantly puts me on alert.

"What happened? Did someone get hurt?" My stomach drops, and I wait for him to relay the worst news possible.

"No, nothing like that. I need to talk to you both about something Silas asked me to look into for him."

"Oh, okay. What was it, and what'd you find? Will it help us put an end to this once and for all?" Looking on the bright side has never been my strong suit, but I'm trying to find a silver lining to balance the solemn expression on his face.

His long, hard sigh isn't a good sign. "I'm legitimately concerned that will be the outcome, but not in the way you meant."

"Just spill it, Shadow. What'd you find?" Silas doesn't even sound like himself. His tone is cold and distant all of a sudden.

"Do you recognize this man, Kira?" Shadow opens the manila folder and holds up a picture.

"Of course. That's David Groves. He's the senator's aide I picked up in the DC bar to get into the secure office."

"His name isn't David Groves. It's Viktor Sokolov."

"As in, Ivan's younger brother?" I take the picture from his hand and stare at it, trying to find some resemblance to how I remember Ivan.

"The same."

"Oh my god. I can't believe it. Are you sure?"

"I'm positive."

"I don't understand how that can be Viktor. How was I able to fool him and gain access to the senator's computer? That makes no sense. He would've suspected something and been on his guard the entire time."

Shadow stares a hole through me for several long heartbeats. Deep inside, I know what he's about to say, but I still hope I'm wrong.

"Those were my thoughts exactly, Kira. So, I did a little more digging. According to Russian intelligence, you and Sokolov have a long history of working together. You've perfected the divide-and-conquer technique. You knew Silas was tailing you, so you concocted this whole charade of drugging 'David,' breaking into the office, and stealing documents to send us on a wild goose chase. You knew Silas would catch you, taking the focus off your friend 'David,' allowing him to finish his mission undetected."

"No, that's not true!"

"You gave just enough information and just enough evidence to lend credence to an otherwise impossible story. It's no secret the GRU has moles everywhere—from personal assistants to congressional staffers. The GRU also knows way too much about Silas—so 'David' just had to find a document from one of Silas's former cases to rein us in. And you just happened to download that file from the senator's files...from the office 'David' helped you get into. That all seems a little too convenient, doesn't it?"

"I have never met Viktor Sokolov before in my life, so I've certainly never worked with him. I met David that night in the bar, on purpose, because I'd researched my target. The only reason I wanted those documents was to show the senator was selling secrets to the Russian government. I didn't even put all the pieces of the puzzle together until Silas and I talked about the human trafficking racket. Even though I know I'll be sent back to Moscow to face the firing squad, I still only want to stop them from abusing more innocent people."

I turn my attention to Silas, who is uncharacteristically quiet.

"Silas, you know I'm telling the truth. You were there. Tell him this isn't true."

"Your involvement with Viktor would explain a lot of things. Like why we haven't found one shred of evidence against the senator when you're the one who implicated him from the beginning." Silas's response cuts me to the core. "And playing on our emotions over sending you back to your death would be an effective ploy."

"Are you serious? You're doubting me now? Yes, I thought Senator Hunt was behind it. But if Shadow is right and that's really Viktor, it makes just as much sense that he's behind it since he has an all-access pass to the senator and all his files, whether Hunt knows it or not. That means Viktor is running the entire operation his brother used to run, only under someone else's name. He's stepped into his brother's shoes and has been doing it right underneath the government's nose."

Silas and Shadow exchange a wordless glance, but the message comes across loud and clear.

I'm once again the enemy.

A seed of doubt has been planted, and they no longer trust me, even though I've done nothing but share what I know and help every step of the way.

"And your documented involvement with Viktor? How do you explain that?"

"Oh, I don't know, Shadow. Maybe if your government found out one of their main operatives went rogue and joined forces with the enemy, they'd conjure up some fake mission reports to discredit her and cause the rest of the team to doubt her motives. Sounds a lot like what we do for a living, doesn't it?"

"Unfortunately, so does that answer, Kira. You could be playing all of us right now. Telling us what we want to hear so your partner can carry out whatever plans he has. With him working in the senator's office in DC, I can't imagine his main objective is to sell slaves in a Miami day spa. He has something much more nefarious going on, and we're a thousand miles away. That takes a lot of heat off him to do whatever he needs to do in Washington, doesn't it?"

"I suppose it would. That is, if you're sure he's still in Washington. Do you know for sure he didn't come down here with the senator? Do you have someone with eyes on him in Washington right now?"

Shadow draws in a deep breath, straightening his back so that he towers over me even more.

"I'll take your silence as a 'no.' I've been nothing but honest about my involvement in this since day one. I've told Silas everything remotely related to this. I've answered every question he's asked of me with honesty, even to my own detriment. I've never lied to him.

"So, to address who can be trusted here and who can't, let me ask you this one question. Does your wife know you're working undercover with the CIA right now? Does she know that while you're helping your friend with your right hand, you're reporting his activities back to the Agency with your left? What happens to Silas when this is over—and how much blood will be on both of your hands that day?"

Silas

The silence inside the truck we borrow from Noah is deafening, and the tension is stifling. The rapport we've developed over the last several weeks seems to have dissipated, along with all the trust we'd built between us. One seed of doubt planted in my mind by Shadow, and it's almost as if the past several weeks with Kira never happened.

Well, not exactly Shadow, but being the bearer of bad news makes him guilty by association. Even though I know he was only sharing information he'd uncovered in the investigation I asked for, that doesn't make it easier to swallow. The Russian government could've altered the mission information to cover their tracks after their agent went rogue, or she could be guilty of everything it said. She could've been playing me the entire time, keeping me from identifying their real endgame. One scenario is as likely to be the truth as the other.

"You know, you can't keep shutting me out like this. When we get back to Noah's house tonight, are you planning to sleep in the other room away from me?"

For once in my career, I honestly haven't thought that far ahead. I'm just trying to get through the current minute before planning what I'll do in the next one. My thoughts are still circling the drain, trying to maintain some semblance of professionalism through my internal battle. Do I follow my head or... that other organ that shouldn't be involved at all?

"Great. That's just fucking great, Silas. I'll tell you what. Since you're so unsure about me and can't make a decision for yourself, I'll make it for you. I won't be in that bed tonight, so it's all yours. Don't bother looking for me either. If you show up anywhere near me, I'll get up and move to another part of the house where you're not. After all this time, you doubt me now. What happened to your fucking lie detector test? Do you think I can beat a system I don't even know about?"

"Are you saying you'd be willing to take that test to prove you're not lying?" The moment the words leave my mouth, I know they're a mistake. I didn't mean it the way it came across, but there's no way I'll convince her of that now.

She surprises me by not answering at all. I expected a smack upside my head. When I glance over at her, the crushed expression on her face and the tears glistening in her eyes do the talking for her. My regret is instantaneous. The sharp pain that shoots through my chest, clawing at my heart like a steel trap, is my own doing.

She swallows hard, regrouping and getting her emotions under control before speaking. Her voice is aloof and distant, not the warm and affectionate Kira I've grown to...know...over time. "No, I'm not willing to do that at all. Go ahead and turn me in. I have nothing left to prove to you."

"Kira—"

"Don't. Just don't. Keep whatever lie you were about to tell me to yourself. It's amazing you're even wasting your time on this stakeout since I'm a complete liar and only diverting your attention to a nonexistent threat. But don't worry. I'll be gone after tonight, and you can drop this case completely. Of course, when it turns out I was telling the truth, you'll look like an even bigger incompetent moron, but that won't be my problem. You can be the one to explain it to Cristano."

Thankfully, we aren't far from the day spa building, and we'll have time for a more rational conversation when I'm not driving and distracted by the road. I know she only lashed out at me because she's hurt, but I don't think she realizes I need time to process everything that's transpired in such a short time. Admittedly, I could've avoided this entire confrontation if I'd just spilled my guts to her, but sharing my feelings never been my style. I've already spent more time with her than all my previous dates combined. Complicated feelings were never part of the equation before now.

But what I don't want to admit is even I know that excuse is utter bullshit. I'm a grown man who can use big words and everything. I'm stopping shy of calling myself a pussy...but the voices in my head are screaming it loud enough anyway.

When I find a parking spot that gives us a line of sight to the back of the building, I put the truck into Park and turn off the engine. Just as I turn in the seat to face Kira and hash out this bullshit once and for all, she jumps out of the passenger door. There's a stronger than usual breeze stirring today with a storm brewing just off the coast. Her long black hair whips around with a mind of its own when powerful gusts come up out of the blue. She takes a seat on a retaining wall in front of our parking spot, pulls a hair band out of her pocket, and pulls her hair into a low ponytail. With her sunglasses in place, she looks like a normal Floridian, enjoying the bright sun and mild late-February temperatures.

Only, I know who she really is.

Or do I?

"Fuck it." I reach for the handle to climb out of the truck, but I stop when I see her perk up.

But she's not paying attention to me. She lifts the pocket-size binoculars toward the spa building across the street. Her back remains straight as a rod, and her muscles are tensed and ready to pounce. I follow her line of sight and recognize a familiar form slinking around the back door. I move swiftly and silently to her side, keeping my gaze trained on the target.

"Isn't that Viktor?"

"Yes, it is. Give me a gun, Silas."

"No fucking way, Kira. You know I can't do that. You're not even supposed to be here."

She lowers the binoculars momentarily to look at me. "But I am here. And so is Viktor. But your rules and laws won't stop him. Obviously. There are laws against human trafficking in this country, right? But he's a criminal, so he doesn't care about your laws because what he's doing makes him money. He's willing to take the risk regardless of what your rule book says." Flames flash in her eyes when she yanks her sunglasses off her face and glares at me.

Seems she's genuinely upset with me, and this isn't just a passing spat.

"I'm trained, licensed, and a US federal agent. I'll subdue him while you help the victims get out of there safely."

"You're impossible. So, just in case you've read me wrong and this is a setup to take you out, you want me to walk into that devil's den unarmed. Is that it?"

"I can't take that chance, Kira." Plain and simple, that's what it boils down to.

"Even if you don't believe I actually have feelings for you and also want to stop this monster, do you honestly believe I could betray my sister like that? She'd be the one who'd be left behind to take the fall for me."

This is but one more reason why I shouldn't have allowed any feelings to become involved in this affair. That thought never crossed my mind. I've been so focused on Kira betraying me, I didn't stop to consider she'd never do that to Mira. I realized how strong their bond was after seeing them together the first time, and that has only amplified over the past several weeks of constant contact. Her sister is the only real family she has left. She'd die before she let Mira pay for her sins.

She turns her face away from me and lifts the binoculars again, hiding her own hurt and anger. But I can see she's at the tipping point—even more so than before.

"It's happening now. They're on the move. Oh my god…that man just shook hands with Viktor, and now he's dragging a little girl away. We have to stop him!"

Kira flings the binoculars to the side and takes off like a bullet, sprinting across the way without alerting the other team or waiting for backup. I race to catch up with her, calling Roman and Nick on my way to get them in place. Viktor rushes back inside the building. We can't risk him escaping through any other door, so I order them to search the building while I follow Kira to the back. Roman cautions me to hang back since this could be the perfect setup to lure me into an ambush once and for all. Pretending a child is in danger definitely would be an effective trap, and the cost of not taking the risk is too high.

When I finally catch up with her, Kira grabs the little girl from the man's grasp. "Hi, sweetheart. Do you know this man?"

The sheer terror on the little girl's face when she looks up at the man in question is enough of an answer for me. Huge tears well up in her eyes as she nervously glances between him and Kira. She wants to answer, but she's obviously been coached and coerced into staying silent. She can't be more than five years old, and that alone is enough for me to empty the magazine into these fuckers.

"It's okay, sweetie. You can tell me. If he's not your daddy, I won't let him take you anywhere. I'll protect you. Have you ever seen him before today?"

The little girl finally shakes her head, indicating no.

"Has he hurt you, sweetie?" Kira's voice is controlled and reassuring as she tries to soothe the little girl.

The heart I deny having shatters in my chest when she nods.

"You sick motherfucker. I should blow your fucking head off your shoulders right now so I can stuff it and mount it on my wall for target practice." The sights at the end of my barrel are set directly between his eyes. With just a twitch of my finger, the leftover pieces wouldn't even resemble a head.

"Who the hell are you?" He somehow thinks he can bluff and bluster his way out of this.

"CIA."

"Then I know you're full of shit. You can't shoot me—I'm unarmed. You are required to arrest me and take me in. I'm entitled to a lawyer." He puffs out his chest, thinking he's won this round.

I laugh in his face, but it's a humorless chuckle. "You obviously have no clue how we work. Get that little girl out of here. She doesn't need to see this."

Kira lifts the girl into her arms, holding the child tightly against her body, and walks briskly toward the truck. I keep my sights steady on him until they're out of sight.

"I have rights. I'm an American citizen. You can't just shoot an unarmed man and get away with it. I'm entitled to a lawyer and due process." His bravado is waning, as it should be.

"Not today, you're not. You're a member of an undercover Russian terrorist cell, putting the lives of millions of Americans at stake. You're a traitor, committing treason against the United States of America of the highest measure."

"That's not true. None of that is true."

"Funny, that's how my report will read. And that's exactly what will be in your obituary." The round leaves the chamber and strikes him before the meaning and weight of my words have time to fully register in his brain.

His is the most satisfying death of my career.

One less piece of shit running loose in the world, preying on innocent children while pretending to be a human being.

Roman and Nick rush through the door with their weapons drawn then quickly put them away when they realize the threat has been neutralized.

"All clear inside, Silas. Viktor got away somehow. There must've been another exit we didn't know about because Roman and I checked every room, every closet, and under every massage table. He gave us the slip."

"What?" I can't believe my ears. We combed over the blueprints and checked the interior ourselves.

"I'm sorry, man. We're thoroughly pissed too. Let's go track him down. He couldn't have gotten far. We'll ground every plane and shut down every mode of transportation out of the county." Roman begins to walk away, ready to be in hot pursuit.

But my feet are rooted to the concrete beneath me. I can't breathe. It feels as if my lungs are filled with water, preventing me from inhaling the oxygen I need to survive. I've never experienced a full-blown panic attack before—nothing even remotely close to it. But I know, beyond a shadow of a doubt, the exact transportation Viktor will use to leave the area.

Because I drove here in it. And I sent Kira and that little girl to wait for me in it.

"He's already gone, Roman. And he took Kira and a victim she rescued with him as bargaining collateral—or human shields—whichever comes first."

We rush back to the parking area, and my worst fears are confirmed.

The truck is gone, along with the two people I should've been protecting.

Approaching sirens grow louder until many different organizations surround us, including my brother and his team. When Shadow and I explain our involvement to the FBI Special Agent in Charge, we're immediately released with his promise to ground all commercial and private flights out of the area. Even though this only took mere minutes from start to finish, I know we're too late. Grounding other flights will only be a nuisance and inconvenience to innocent travelers.

That fucker is a trained GRU agent. His emergency credentials will list him as a visiting dignitary with diplomatic immunity, resourcefully putting him out of our reach. Along with Kira. He'll take her back to Russia to be executed for helping us. God only knows what he's done with that little lost girl.

"Who has my security camera videos? Traffic cameras, ATMs, local businesses. I want them all on my computer in the next thirty seconds!" the special agent in charge bellows to his team, looking for immediate answers.

"I need to see those too." I'm not asking.

The first available footage shows Viktor emerging from a small window at ground level. He must've had his exit planned ahead of time and climbed out before Nick or Roman found him. When we're finally able to see him from a different angle, I have the perfect view of him running toward the truck, climbing inside with Kira, and holding a gun to the little girl's head to make Kira cooperate.

If any lingering doubt remained, it is completely squashed now. Kira was right about one more fact as well. I absolutely am an incompetent moron, and I've left no room for doubt or debate.

CHAPTER 21

Kira

"Viktor, take me but let the little girl go. I can stop and let her out at a hospital or something. She's been through enough. Besides, she'll only slow you down." I don't bother keeping up the "David" charade. We both know who he really is.

"You know, this whole situation is pretty amusing when you think about it."

"I don't think any of this is funny."

"Oh, but it is. I've lived in the DC area for years. Decades. I've worked my way into the office of one of the most powerful senators ever elected. I have access to everything the Intelligence Committee sees. Do you know how important my role is to our government? But everything I accomplished wasn't enough to quiet the storm inside me.

"No one in DC seems to question whatever Senator Hunt wants—he's just trusted implicitly. So, I had one of the senator's CIA contacts locate Silas Steele and share all the information that could be found on him. It's amazing to have that kind of power, so I used it to my advantage to find the one man whose name is still on my list. Do you know what it's like to have the person you're closest to suddenly ripped out of your life?"

"I know exactly what that's like, and you know very well I do."

"Yeah, I guess that was a stupid question to ask you. Anyway, even though we were thirteen years apart in age, my brother and I were very close. When he was murdered, it changed me in ways I never realized until I matured more. I tried to push past the need for vengeance, I really did. But I've accepted that's just not in my DNA. At first, I planned to kill his siblings and be done with it. That would've made us even.

"But while I was watching him one day, I realized he was watching you. Then you started working me, and I realized you had no idea about my true identity. I've never believed in the whole 'it was fate' bullshit. Until that night. There was no other explanation for it. Silas's attention was so laser-focused on you that he never even noticed me. I could've picked him off with a single shot to the head, and he never would've seen it coming.

"That's when I realized just watching him die wouldn't be enough. He would've been a hero, a martyr, and I would've had to hear about it for years to come. No, he has to know he's been beaten, but more importantly, who beat him. The great Silas Steele will be blamed, shamed, and convicted while I have a front row seat to watch all his hard work unravel around him. It's the perfect scenario."

"I don't understand. What do you mean exactly?"

He turns his head and meets my gaze with a sadistic smile. "This may sound odd coming from me, considering I'm not only going to ruin the man but annihilate him completely. I respect you for trying to protect him regardless of what you're facing yourself. But you can stop recording me with your phone now. Where you're going, you'll never be given an opportunity to get it to him. To address your earlier request about the little girl, the answer is no. She'll prove useful to my overall goal. She comes with us."

"Where are you taking us?" He's too forthcoming with information. That's never a good sign. We're trained to be uncrackable vaults, but he's singing like a canary.

"Home, Kira. You're going home. How long has it been since you've visited Moscow?"

"The last time I was there was during my training. I haven't been back for a visit at all."

"Wow…so, about twenty years, then? So much has changed over there since then. It's not the same place you remember. You won't believe the differences."

Somehow, I doubt that. A new coat of paint only hides the repulsiveness underneath for so long. It's bound to rear its ugly head soon after our plane touches down. I turn my head to look out the side window for a moment, hiding my true thoughts and feelings from him.

"And your plans for her?" I motion to the terrified child sitting beside me, so close that she's almost in my lap while I'm driving.

"I have a question for you."

"Okay." My response is drawn out much longer than usual.

"Are you aware that Silas is in love with you?"

I can barely find my voice to reply. "He's not in love with me. Our relationship is just…convenient."

"You really don't know, do you? I'm sorry I have to be the one to tell you this instead of him, but you're wrong about that. I've seen how he looks at you. I've watched you two together when neither of you knew I was there, following your every move. That day at the beach was hot as fuck, by the way. You're in love with each other, but you're both too proud or stubborn or both to say it."

"You're wrong, Viktor. We haven't even known each other long enough to fall in love."

He laughs at that. "Kira, tell me something. Who is this wise and all-knowing person who set a time limit on how long it takes for two people to fall in love? Did they share the rules of love with the rest of the world and get a stamp of approval before making up these ridiculous laws? No, my dear. The people who subscribe to that are sheep—blindly led off a cliff without asking a question. I've seen it happen myself with people I've respected. I was shocked, no doubt, but it was just as real as if they'd spent ten years dating first."

"Why are you telling me all this? You're suddenly a romantic?"

"Hell no, of course not. Don't be ludicrous. I'm telling you this because your death will be much more poignant and impactful to Silas than anyone else in his life. Sure, he'd miss his brother and sister, but he'd move on. But I don't think the man has ever been in love before. And after he loses you, he will never fall in love again." His maniacal laugh sends shivers down my spine.

Part of the reason why he's telling me all this is for psychological torture. If he can break me mentally, he'll revel in that accomplishment more than my physical death. There's a reason why the Academy strongly discourages getting attached to others in our line of work. They can and will be used as pawns against us, putting them in harm's way and compromising us as both agents and informants.

Time to change the subject. I don't want his focus on Silas.

"Everything you did pointed to the senator as the culprit. The leaked confidential documents, the human trafficking through a spa close to his home in Miami, even getting my handler to send me on that mission. That was you, wasn't it?"

"It was, indeed."

"You knew I needed a way in, and you volunteered. Didn't they question why?"

"Of course. I told them I had my doubts about you and your

dedication to the cause. One grain of doubt was all it took for the GRU to test you. But I'm the one who let you pass. When I went to the bar for your refill and you spiked my drink, I took the antidote the Academy made for our special compound. When I 'passed out' in the office, I wasn't actually asleep. After that, Silas was attached to you like a tattoo, which made my job easier."

"You resumed your brother's business since you knew where Silas was at all times and that his attention was on me. You used me as a diversion."

"I played you like a bass drum, girl. You fell in line perfectly. When you disappeared, that only affirmed my suspicions to the GRU. I know you're in love with him the same as he is with you. When I turn you in, the general will take care of you, but Silas's fate will be much worse. You'll probably get a swift and painless execution. Silas will be put through the wringer by his government and publicly disgraced. Once the shitstorm dies down, the CIA will eliminate him and put him out of his misery, and the public will think he's rotting in some federal prison."

"Sounds like you've got it all planned out."

"I've thought about my revenge for a very long time. You're just the first woman Silas has ever shown any attachment to, outside of his family members."

He tells me to pull into a parking garage, and we ditch Noah's truck, forcing the little girl and me into another car nearby. I'm sure Noah has a state-of-the-art tracking system on all his vehicles, but we'll be long gone by the time he gets here. With the barrel held flush against her back, I can't fight back and risk him killing her. I know his training, and I've seen his kind too many times to count. He'll do it in a heartbeat and never look back. Inside the car, we head in the opposite direction, almost doubling back to the area we just left.

He turns down a dead-end street then slows when we reach the water. We pull into the driveway for a private marina, and he opens the gate with a remote he retrieves from his pocket. Boats of all shapes and sizes fill the covered slips along the multiple docks. He forces us out and through the gate toward the ships.

"They'll be watching the airports the most. Private boats leave the docks all the time without any paperwork or tracking at all. Pretty smart, huh?" He's genuinely proud of himself.

"Brilliant." My deadpan response is lost on him. He takes it as a compliment. His only answer is a huge smile, showing he's very proud of himself. I have to physically restrain myself from rolling my eyes. The art of a sharp, sarcastic jab is lost on so many. "You never told me what you're doing with her, though."

He looks down at the little girl for a moment before replying. "I'll give her to the program. The Academy will train her well. You were really too old when they took you—they've figured that out in the last twenty years. Younger is better. If she never knows a different life from the one that we teach her, she'll never betray us like you did. Her mother died tragically, and her father was some low-life thug who traded drugs for sex with her mother. She'll have a better life with the Academy than she would in the foster care system here."

Over my dead body.

I don't voice the words, because that outcome is inevitable, but I'll find a way to get her out before they get their claws into her. She's had enough pain and heartache already in her short life. That needs to end now. Viktor is obviously a sociopath who thinks he's genuinely doing her a huge favor and saving her life with this option.

"Get in." He waves the gun, motioning for us to climb onto the speed boat and into the cabin. He takes my phone from me and throws it overboard, smiling as he watches it sink in the salt water.

He locks the door, leaving us inside, and I immediately look for any communication devices. Marine radio, ham radio, satellite phone, flares, walkie-talkies, anything. But he's thought of that ahead of time because the cabin has been stripped of all radios—even for music. The refrigerator is stocked with food and drinks, and there are clothes in the small closet that will fit me but not the child. Guess he didn't account for every possibility after all.

When I look down at the little girl, her big blue eyes are wide, staring at all the food. That squeeze in my chest is my heart cracking in two for her.

"What's your name, sweetheart?" I kneel down in front of her and brush her long blond hair from her face.

"Amber."

"Hi, Amber. My name is Kira. Are you hungry? Do you want me to make you something to eat?"

She nods enthusiastically, so I start pulling out items out of the cupboard and refrigerator. With all the provisions he stocked in this cruiser, I wonder if we're sailing all the way to Moscow. I know better, but this is somewhat overkill considering what's about to happen. Makes me wonder if this is his boat or if we're just stealing someone else's. Neither would surprise me at this point.

While Amber eats, I check every inch of the cabin, looking for anything to help us escape. Life vests, rope, a net bag, knives —I start making a small stockpile of anything useful I can find. I'll only have one shot at this, so I have to make it the best I can. The windows have already been boarded up from the outside, so I can't even get Amber out one of the small portholes. There's only one way out—the locked door where Viktor is waiting on the other side.

It's either pick the lock...or eat all the chocolate on the way to wherever he's taking us. I hear the engines fire and feel the boat start to move out of the slip just as I being to work on the door.

"You're very resourceful, Kira. But you're not going

anywhere. You don't think I've already taken every precaution, knowing your abilities? I suggest you enjoy the time you have getting to know little Amber. We have a long night ahead of us. The bed in there is for you—I have my own out here."

He's watching me. Of course, there's a camera in here. Secured door. Provisions. Bedroom. Bathroom. No way out.

We're stuck inside here until we reach our destination.

CHAPTER 22

Silas—One Week Later

"Are you shitting me right now?" I'm about to crush this fucking phone in my hand. "You know I'm still working this case. You know what has happened here—you've been updated every fucking day. And I know you have because Shadow has been staying here with me, and he never stays here when he's in town. He has his own place."

I'm pacing back and forth, about to wear a hole in the marble floor of the foyer, arguing with my deputy director about his unreasonable demand.

"No, I'm not flying back to DC when he took her from here in Miami, and he could still have her here somewhere. If you want to see me in person, you can come down here. If I haven't found her by the time you get here, I'll gladly talk to you. But just so we're clear, you are not my priority right now." I end the call before I throw the phone against the wall in a fit of sheer rage.

"He wants you to fly to DC now, knowing what's going on?

What the hell, man?" Shadow stands beside me, regret etched in his face.

"Don't even go there, Shadow. You were only doing your job by reporting the information back to them. I have nothing to hide. I blatantly kept her in the country past the two weeks he gave me. Then I brought her down here to catch the bastard. My eyes are wide open—I did all of that knowing the consequences I'd face because of my actions. And if you hadn't done your job, you'd be in trouble now because of me."

"Let me talk to the deputy director and tell him I have it under control. See if I can convince him to stay out of it for now and let me handle it."

"He won't, but I appreciate the offer. He'll say we let Kira get away with Viktor and that it was her plan the entire time. Then he'll say you and I look like dirty CIA officers now, so the whole agency looks bad."

"You're probably right." Shadow runs his fingers through his hair, aggravated and irritated with the circumstances. "He should know us better than that by now, but he'd use that just to tear us a new asshole."

"He'll say *what?*"

Shadow and I whip around at the same time to face the angry voice demanding answers.

Oh shit.

"Elle." The color drains from Shadow's face, while Elle's quickly fills with red-hot rage.

"The deputy director of the CIA will say you're a dirty officer, Devon' Shadow' Kane? Is that what I just heard?"

Oh shit. She used his full name.

Shadow doesn't answer right away, but his guilt-ridden expression says enough. "Let me explain, darlin'."

"Don't you dare 'darlin'' me right now. How long have you been back with the agency?" She folds her arms over her body and burns a hole through him with her eyes. "What the fuck, Devon? You never left, did you?"

"Elle, wait just a second before you fly off the handle and say something you'll regret later." He holds up his hands in mock surrender, trying to calm her down before it escalates out of control.

My opinion? Her temper is already out of control.

"Too late, Shadow. You've lied to me this whole time. I've always supported you and your career. I even waited months on end for you when you were undercover. But we're married now. We're building a home together, and I'd hoped one day soon we'd start our own family. But after everything we've endured, you decided you didn't trust me enough to let me into your life fully. This secret isn't like you spent too much money on your hobby, or, surprise, you came home with a brand-new motorcycle. You intentionally chose to leave me out of one of the biggest parts of your life, as if I'm not affected at all."

"It's not that I wanted to leave you out of anything. No officer can share what they do with their families. You'd have to be part of the operation or have a need to know—with security clearance—for me to tell you anything."

"Don't try to pull that agency bullshit with me. I've never expected you to tell me anything top-secret. But you could've told me you were working for them. As your wife, I have a right to know that. What if you were out on a mission and didn't come home? Did you ever consider what that would do to me—not having a clue you were still in that line of work?"

Elle walks away and leaves Shadow with his head hanging low in shame. "She's right. I tried to protect her from my life but only ended up shutting her out of it instead."

"You should've known she'd support your decision to stay on the same as you'd support her if she decided she wanted back in front of the camera."

"Is the world's most eligible bachelor giving me relationship advice?"

A knock on the front door interrupts our conversation. Our eyes meet, and I know we have the same questions. Who's here, and how did they get past Noah's security gate?

When I open the door, I'm hardly surprised to find the deputy director standing on the doorstep.

"Graves. Come on in." I step back and let him enter. "Brought your own equipment, I see."

"Sure did. Don't trust yours one bit. Where do you want to do this?"

I show him to Noah's office and make room for the high-tech machine and brain scanner that will tell him if I'm lying.

"Have a seat, Steele. We're going to settle this right now."

"Fine by me. The quicker, the better."

"Kane, you can leave now." Graves arches his eyebrow at Shadow. Being the true friend he is, Shadow looks at me for confirmation before leaving us alone.

"It's fine. Go take care of your business. Graves knows I can take him out with a snap of my fingers. He won't try anything underhanded with me."

Graves doesn't crack a smile. Typical.

After he straps me in, measuring all my vitals along with my brain wave pattern, he pulls a large brown envelope from his briefcase. "I received some interesting documents in the mail today. It's a full dossier on you, actually. I'm going to ask you questions about yourself, the work you've done with the Russians, and the black-market business you've set up here in Miami. I also have a few questions about your girlfriend."

"The black-market business I've set up? What business would that be?"

"We'll get to that."

Over the next two hours, he grills me about every single encounter I've had with anyone of Russian nationality—

whether they were an asset, a spy, or a dignitary. When he brought up Dmitri, the explanations were more complicated than a simple yes or no answer. I gave him more ammunition about our interactions, so we spent a good thirty minutes on my relationship with Dmitri and his wife.

"Are you in any way involved in a human trafficking business operated anywhere in the world?" Just the mere accusation makes my blood boil, but I cool my jets before my temper sets off a false positive.

"No."

"Did you assist in any way with setting up a human trafficking business here in Miami?"

"No."

"Have you visited the spa where a suspected human trafficking ring conducted business?"

"Yes."

I explain the nature of my visits and what occurred each time, including all the days and nights on stakeout time while we waited for someone to make a move. I even tell him about the little girl we rescued from that sick fucker and the bullet I put between his eyes on her behalf.

"Since you passed all the questions for that part, I'm going to tell you what the official documents I received from the Russian embassy contain. You're not going to like it, Silas."

"Go ahead. I need to know."

"Through his work with the CIA and the network he has established in the numerous countries he has worked over his career, Silas Steele has created a virtually undetectable human trafficking ring. One of his main hubs is an unassuming day spa in Miami, Florida. We have a five-year-old girl currently in our custody who was a victim of Mr. Steele's activities. Our agent, Kira Petrova, rescued her and fled the country, as she feared for their lives.

"Silas Steele, in conjunction with Senator Hunt, is passing

top-secret information to North Korea regarding every government with which he has ties. The data to substantiate these claims can be found on Senator Hunt's private server in his Miami home. Attached you will find copies of some of these documents, along with the IP address from where it originated and where it was ultimately transmitted."

Graves hands the documents to me for review, but my dark chuckle holds anything but humor. "You know what's really fucking funny about this? A week ago, Shadow received intel alleging Kira and Viktor Sokolov were in league together, and that she concocted this whole scheme about Senator Hunt selling secrets so her partner could finish his Miami human slave sale without me catching on.

"Now, this intel alleges that I'm the mastermind behind the business, working with Senator Hunt, while Kira and Viktor narrowly escaped the country with their lives. How convenient that the intelligence coming out of this case points the finger all around, and we automatically run after it, like we're a fucking cat chasing a laser light."

"Touché. The next part, I actually believe part of it to be true." He pauses and watches me for a moment before continuing to read from the report. "Kira Petrova has returned to Moscow. Due to the sensitive nature of her position and the grave threat Silas Steele poses, no further communication with her will be possible. If you have specific questions to validate this information, please contact me directly." He finishes reading the ambassador's name and lays the document on the desk.

"So, she's back in Moscow. I knew it, but I didn't want to admit it. I tried to get a flight scheduled under one of my old aliases, but it bounced back. They must have it flagged."

"I'm sure they do."

"Do you think they've executed her yet?"

"My contact says no. She's still being held in an interrogation facility for now. Her father has used every bit of his influence to keep her alive, but his persuasion is waning."

"I have to get to Moscow and break her out."

"You're going to fly to Moscow, break into a secure facility, find an enemy of the state, break her out, and fly back here with her? Do you have some kind of magical powers I'm not aware of?"

"Yes, as a matter of fact, I do. I'm a master of disguises. I'm fluent in Russian. And I'm a man in love."

"You love her?"

"Yes."

"Did you tell her?"

"No."

"Because you're too chickenshit to say the words? Remember, you're still obligated to tell me the truth. Don't start lying to the lie detector now."

"Yes." I grit my teeth and spit out my answer at him. Fucker laughs at me.

"Do you think it's too soon to fall in love?"

"Yes."

"Amateur. I asked my wife to marry me on our first date, and I'd only met her the day before. Finally convinced her to say yes three weeks later. We've been married twenty-seven years now. I haven't regretted it one day of my life. When you know, you know."

He unhooks all the wires and turns off the machine. Then he pulls a smaller envelope out of his bag. "Here are your new passports. Two for you, one for her. Your Russian military uniform and access card are in my car. Get in, get out, and get home. Don't start World War III in the process."

"Yes, sir."

Graves walks out, taking all his equipment with him, and his driver hands me the disguise to get me into the facility. The uniform is freshly dry-cleaned, still covered by the plastic to keep it in pristine condition, and the shoes are buffed to a glossy shine. This will be hard enough to pull off with the full outfit and the keycard to get in. Getting out with her in prison clothes and apparent signs of interrogation without being seen will be impossible.

But damn if I won't give it my best shot. If I die, at least I'll know I died trying.

I close the door as they drive away and turn to find Shadow bounding down the stairs. His eyes are wide, his face is pale, and he's mumbling to himself.

"Shadow, what's wrong?"

"Elle packed her things and left while I was working. She didn't say a word. Didn't say where she was going. Won't answer her phone. Disabled her location services. She just left me."

"I'm sorry to hear that, man. I hate that you got pulled into this because of me."

"It's not your fault, Silas. I've worked on other cases before yours. This is all on me." His eyes finally focus, seeing the uniform draped over my shoulder. "Oh shit. You're breaking in the Kremlin interrogation dungeons, aren't you? Did they leave a uniform for me?"

"No, Shadow. You're not going with me on this one. It's likely to be a one-way ticket, but I've got to try. You should go find Elle, talk to her, and fix your marriage right now. Don't let any grass grow under your feet. You'll regret it if you do."

"It's a pity I have to use my CIA skills on my wife and take relationship advice from my unattached friend." A small smile plays on his face before he gives me a quick, manly hug. "Be careful over there. You don't let any grass grow under your feet while you're rescuing Kira either. We need you back here as soon as possible, to keep us all in line and to save us from Liz."

"Maybe I should take her with me. Those boys in the Kremlin wouldn't stand a chance."

We share a good belly laugh over that vision, but our parting glance holds more sentiment than words can express. Our friends are our family, the people we choose to keep in our lives and share so much of ourselves with. We're all brothers and sisters. The loss of one would be devastating to all.

"Elle and I will see you when you get back, Silas. If you need me while you're there, send a message through Brad's secret system, and I'll be on the next plane out."

"The four of us will go out for dinner and dancing when Kira and I get back. Keep a Saturday night open on your calendar for us."

Kira

"What did you tell the CIA about our operations?" Igor grips my hair near the scalp and yanks my head backward with a forceful tug. "You'll eventually break—one way or another. You can stop all this pain now with a simple answer."

He's lying. Anything I say will be viewed as weakness and used against me in much harsher methods. There's no way for me to win this game he's playing. It was designed to be a lose-lose outcome for anyone sitting in this chair.

"Have it your way, then." He nods to Vlad with a sadistic grin. Igor loves his job.

I'm strapped to a chair in a grungy, dank room in a basement somewhere in Moscow. Viktor knocked me out before we landed. When I first came to, I asked anyone and everyone about Amber, but no one would answer me. I'm a traitor, so they can't be seen speaking to me.

A sharp pain suddenly cuts through my back. I barely had time to hear the crack of the whip before I feel the lash tear into my skin. With strike after strike, I scream and wiggle, trying to shrink away from the agonizing stings. The chair I'm in topples over from my excessive movements, and I try to crawl away, moving like an inchworm across the floor with the chair scraping the concrete since it's still strapped to me.

Igor stands and stomps on my hand, stopping my movement with his wicked smile in place. "She thinks she can get away, comrade. Maybe you should show her what happens to bitches who try to run."

"With pleasure."

Vlad approaches me with slow, measured steps. He swings a pair of pliers in his hand, taunting me with what I know is coming. Igor holds my hand in place with his boot while Vlad clamps the pliers onto the end of my fingernail. His hesitation is a textbook torture tactic—build up the anticipation of the moment, make the victim cry and beg before carrying out the ploy regardless, let him get his rocks off with all the power he holds.

I refuse to give him the satisfaction. With my eyes squeezed shut and the fingers of my opposite hand gripping the arm of the chair as hard as I can, I prepare for the horrible pain that I already know is coming. But I can't stop the scream that nearly splits my throat in two when he rips my fingernail entirely off. Blood pours, my entire hand throbs, and the intense pain almost takes my breath away.

"That's enough!" The stern voice echoes in the concrete block room. "You disobeyed direct orders. Wait for me in the hall."

Vlad's smug smirk disappears as he drops the pliers on the table and scurries away with his tail tucked between his legs. My only consolation is knowing the same will be done to him for not following his commander's orders. He knows what's coming, too. Only he'll have to wait longer for his than I did mine.

"Sasha, get her cleaned up and bandage her hand. Igor, you come with me. Right now." I glance over to see who entered the room and recognize General Krupin. He's one of the few men my father trusts.

I also recognize Sasha from my early days at the Academy. She's an older woman who never quite made it as an undercover operative, but she was always very supportive of everyone who came through the program. She helped Mira and me when we were forced into the program against our will as children. She comforted us every night when we thought we'd drown in our tears. She's the one who helped convince the headmistress to put us back in a room together. She pointed out how much of an asset twins would be when working a complicated case. We could literally be in two places at once, but we had to stay in sync with each other. Over the years I lived in that hellhole, she made it as bearable as possible.

After Krupin and Igor leave the room, Sasha unties me and helps me up before she begins gathering the supplies to wash and bandage my injuries. When she returns to me, the concern in her eyes for my physical state is palpable. She pulls up a chair in front of me and begins wiping my face with a warm, wet washcloth. Her touch is gentle when she cleans my wounds. I think it hurts her worse than it does me. This is why she washed out of the program. She had too much compassion for others, and her every emotion was prominently displayed on her face, giving away her thoughts and intentions every time.

"Sasha." My voice barely reaches a whisper to keep any microphones from picking it up. "Where's the little girl?"

She continues dabbing at the abrasion on my cheekbone, acting as if she didn't hear me. "Dorm."

The dorm—the bedrooms used by the Academy. So, Viktor was telling the truth about putting her in the program and using her as an operative one day.

"Take her to my father."

She stills, pretending to examine my cut closer for anyone watching, but her eyes are solidly on mine. "This one is almost impossible to fix."

I understand her hidden message.

"Saving even just one from the infection is worth all the pain."

She understands my cryptic reply. Save the child from the diseased life we've been forced to live. Give her a chance to be a kid—to run, play, laugh, love—to live. The conflict in Sasha's eyes gives me hope that she's at least considering my request. If she's caught, it'll mean certain death for her. But giving Amber the opportunity we never had would make everything I've endured worth every ounce of pain.

"Don't let them do to her what they've done to us, Sasha. Tell my father she's his daughter now." In a rare moment of showing my own emotions, I feel tears form in my eyes as I wait for her reply. Whether she reports me or consents to my request, I know I've tried to help that baby girl live the best life I can give her under the circumstances.

"Try not to worry. I'll do my best to keep the infection at bay."

I've never wanted to break down and sob in my life as much as I do right now. If anyone can help Amber escape the dorms, it's Sasha.

"Thank you. You have no idea how much I appreciate your help."

She gives me a single nod in response, her throat muscles working hard to swallow the ball of emotion that's threatening to choke her while she continues putting medication and bandages on me. When she works her way down to my hand, her disgust with the process and their tactics is released in a string of curses and obscenities hurled at the two men in partic-ular. After cleaning the area around where my fingernail was, she slathers it with Vaseline before wrapping it with nonstick bandages and gauze. She takes so much time to give me her full attention and care, but I can't help but wonder why. So that I look more presentable when my father identifies my body?

"Tell my parents I love them and that I don't blame them for anything."

She nods and wipes away a stray tear from her eye.

"It's okay, Sasha. I know what's coming. Thank you for everything you've ever done for me. I haven't ever appreciated the people in my life nearly enough. Before it's too late, I want you to know you were always special to me."

"Thank you for saying that, Kira. I've often wondered if my job mattered. It's nice to hear that it does." She stands abruptly, moves to the small wardrobe, and returns with a clean prisoner uniform. It's a very dull and lifeless tan outfit—far from fashionable while remaining utterly functional at the same time. "Let's get you out of those dirty clothes and into some clean ones."

She gasps when I pull my shirt over my head. The bruises and burns I've endured are still relatively fresh, but the recent lashes left the worst marks. Before helping me into the clean shirt, she takes the time to apply ointment and bandages to the raw areas. When I'm finally dressed, she pulls me into her arms and holds me for several long seconds. After the last—I don't even know how long I've been here—however many days it's been, this little bit of warmth is enough.

General Krupin opens the door and starts to say my name but stops when he sees us in an embrace. After a few moments, his patience is worn thin. "Kira, come with me."

We walk down the long, dark corridor and turn left when we reach the end. A few doors down on the right, light filters into the hall from under the door. He opens it and extends his arm into the room, indicating for me to enter. Inside, I find a twin bed, a small desk and chair, and an en suite bathroom.

"As a favor to your father, I've arranged to let you stay in here for the next few nights. No more questioning. Absolutely no more techniques to encourage you to talk. Make yourself comfortable—this is your room now. Your dinner will be here in about an hour."

"Thank you, General. I appreciate your kindness."

Sleep is the last thing on my mind, but as my thoughts drift to Silas and the last interaction we had, my body decides to shut down after all the recent trauma. The darkness pulls me under, my muscles relax, and my mind finally calms. When the need for rest surpasses my desire to stay awake until my execution, I give in and let my dreams take me to the places I've left behind.

The beach with Silas.

Noah's house in Miami.

Our nightly routine of falling asleep in each other's arms after hours of exhausting escapades.

These are the images my dreams are made of.

The next couple of days are much of the same. Rest, recuperate, and refuel with the large meals they bring three times a day. But that all changes the third day in my new room. The guard's personality is entirely different when he delivers breakfast. He refuses to make eye contact with me and acts slightly nervous.

At lunch, the tray is left on the floor outside the door, and he only alerts me with a knock. When I open the door, he's already gone.

He's completely avoiding me.

That means today is the day.

Execution day.

After I finish eating lunch, I stroll into the bathroom and take a long, hot shower. Then I dry and style my hair after rebandaging my hand. There's no reason why Mom and Dad need to see that exposed. There's no makeup in here, so the au naturel look will have to do. Just as well—it's the way I came into the world, and it's the way I'll go out.

Morose. Morbid. Depressing. But true.

A light rap on the door draws my attention just before the doorknob slowly turns. When the door swings open, General Krupin waits with a sad expression on his face.

"I'm sorry, Kira. I argued for a stay of execution, but I was overruled. There's nothing more I can do, my dear. It's time."

The long walk to the execution room simultaneously feels like it takes forever and is over in the blink of an eye. Thick plastic covers the floor, making the cleanup effort an easy job. General Krupin moves to stand behind the desk on the back wall as the lone judge, jury, and witness to the execution. My executioner stands behind me, his hands firmly gripping my biceps to hold me in place.

He knows the drill all too well. He knows what's about to happen.

My knees buckle underneath me from the fear and anxiety coursing through my veins at over 200 miles per hour, and my captor prevents me from crumbling into a heap on the floor before my time. My heart is no longer beating, only fluttering in my chest as it tries to keep up with the adrenaline that's been dumped into my bloodstream. My face is wet from the tears streaming down my cheeks like a raging river during the spring thaw. Strange, since I didn't even realize I was crying until just now.

"I'll leave you to it, then. Goodbye, Kira." In the back of my mind, I hear General Krupin's voice, but his words don't register. All my focus is on the plastic on the floor underneath me.

"I've got you. It's okay now." Strong arms wrap around my waist from behind me and pull me against a hard chest. With virtually no effort, he twists me around, slides his arm under my knees, and cradles me against him. "We're getting the fuck out of here right now."

He jumps to his feet with me secure in his arms, and the whiff of air that envelops me pulls me out of my haze. I know that scent. I recognize that voice. When I peer up at him through my teardrop-covered lashes, the face I see doesn't match who I know the voice belongs to.

"Silas?"

"Yeah, baby, it's me." I've never loved being called that term of endearment more than I do at this moment.

Two men enter from the other end of the room, carrying a limp body to the spot where Silas just stood. She's dressed in the same prison uniform I am. Her hair and build match mine. They lay her down on the plastic and roll her tightly inside.

"Who is she?"

"Her name is Kira Petrova. This lady was an enemy of the state for the murder of the Minister of Health. She injected him with poison after he raped her. Her execution was scheduled to take place today, but she decided to take matters into her own hands and not give anyone else control over her fate." He places soft kisses all over my face, hugs me tightly to him for several long seconds, then helps me to stand on my own again.

The confused expression on my face quickly morphs into understanding. According to all official records, Kira Petrova died in this prison today. That's all that matters to them—that I'm dead and gone. I nod slowly, feeling guilty for being grateful to a woman who took her own life. "Who am I?"

"You're Nadia Utkin, attaché for the Canadian Ambassador. You're here on a diplomatic goodwill assignment to help orphaned children."

The two guards carry Kira Petrova out of the room, and Sasha walks in with a garment bag. "Here you are, Miss Utkin. Your change of clothes just arrived." Tears glisten in her eyes as she passes the packet to me. "I hope you have a safe trip home. I'm sorry you were in a car wreck during your first trip to Russia." She lightly strokes the still visible wounds on my face.

"Thank you." I can barely choke out the words.

She leaves us alone, and Silas turns to face me now that we're alone. "I'm so sorry, baby. I'm sorry I had even one doubt about you and your intentions. This is all my fault—everything you've been through over the last week. If I'd had my head screwed on right, this never would've happened."

I step toward him and put my finger over his lips, shaking my head. "Viktor played us both from the beginning, Silas. He made sure our paths crossed then took advantage of our connection. Since he held all the cards, there wasn't much we could've done to change the outcome. If it wasn't here, it would've happened somewhere else. And I forgive you for questioning me. The story he told was a good one, and you're trained to be suspicious of everyone. It's part of who you are now."

He bends over and places a soft kiss on my lips. "I'll make it up to you, I promise."

"Don't think you'll ever get away with that shit again, though. You used your one free chance. If there's a next time, you'll pay dearly for it." I narrow my eyes at him, but I can't contain the smile that immediately follows. I'm just so happy and relieved and elated and grateful to see him again at all.

"Never again, baby. Let's get you out of that prison uniform and into your regular clothes. We have to move quickly now." He sheds his uniform and puts on a tailored suit in record time.

He doesn't have to tell me twice. In seconds, I'm out of the lifeless tan garb and dressed in a beautiful blue shell dress and matching jacket. Silas clips the required Kremlin identification badge on the lapel of my coat before pulling more tricks out of his pocket.

"So I get a facial prosthesis too?"

"Yes, we can't look like ourselves when we walk out of here. Too many people in this building can recognize both of us on sight." After a couple minutes, he completely changes my facial features, making me unrecognizable as Kira. "Can I escort you out, Miss Utkin?"

I glance at his badge and smile up at him. "Yes, Mr. Fedorov. You do know what that name means, don't you?"

"Absolutely. It's Greek for 'gift of God.' I think it fits me perfectly, don't you?" The teasing, playful glint in his eyes is back.

"Of course. Most days anyway."

"Most days? How about today?"

"Most definitely today, without a doubt." My knight in shining armor. The crazy American who broke in a Kremlin-run prison to free the woman he…what? What am I to him?

"Yes, I love you, baby. With all my heart, I do, and I've never said those words before to a woman outside of my family in my life. I'm afraid you're stuck with me for the rest of yours."

"If you insist. Let's hope that's a long life, with too many years ahead of us to count…and not only the next few minutes while we're escaping from this building."

When we step off the elevator on the main floor, the buzz of workers hurrying from one place to another is a stark contrast to the dungeon we just left. No one even bothers to pass a glance our way. Our indistinct features and visitor passes don't draw the kind of interest and respect the high-ranking officials here do. We head straight for the door that leads outside and to freedom. Every half second that passes only increases the panic rising in my chest. We're so close but so far away.

Stepping out into the sun has never felt as wonderful as it does now. After the last week of torture, waiting to die, and trying to live, my emotions are all over the board. Silas puts his hand on the small of my back and leads me to the waiting car and driver. He's arranged the entire setup and ensured every detail is authentic to our cover. When we slide into the back seat, he tells the driver to get us to the airport immediately. Then he hands me a passport with my new name and picture on it.

"How'd you get a current picture of me?" I'm wearing the prosthesis in the passport photo.

"I'm hurt that you doubt my skills like that, Nadia."

Hurt, my ass. That smile is one of pure pride.

When we get out of the car at the airport, I use all my willpower not to run straight out onto the tarmac and hop on the first plane out of the country. Silas gives no outward indication of being rushed or worried whatsoever, but his eyes scan the area for possible threats more than usual. He's ready to fight our way out if necessary.

He reaches for the door leading into the airport terminal to open it for me but pauses for just a second. "I have a surprise for you before we leave."

"Silas, I appreciate the gesture, really I do, but can't it wait until we get home? I've had enough excitement for one day."

He offers me a small smile, but there's a hint of sadness in his eyes. Then he pulls on the door, and I start to walk through. My feet suddenly stop moving, and my lungs stop working. My eyes bug out of my head, momentarily unable to comprehend the sight directly in front of me. I cover my mouth with my hand to prevent the squeal that's building inside me from erupting.

"Mama? Daddy?" I rush to them. Arms wrap around me from everywhere, squeezing me with all the love my parents have in them.

"I couldn't let you leave without saying goodbye this time. The good news is they'll be able to visit us now that Kira is gone." Silas stands beside us, watching our family reunion after too many years apart.

Daddy holds me with one hand and grabs Silas with the other, pulling him into our tight circle. Through his tears, he somehow manages to speak. "Thank you for this, Silas. I thought I'd never get my little girls back."

Mama cries and repeatedly kisses both Silas and me. We're causing a scene in the middle of the airport, but I'm not even worried now. These few minutes are worth the risk. Then a different kind of panic grips me.

"Mama, Daddy, what about Amber? Did Sasha get her out?" I search their faces, praying Sasha was able to pull off one last miracle for me.

"See for yourself." Silas points toward the security line.

A beautiful little girl waits with her small suitcase, sitting in a chair beside the security checkpoint agent. Her eyes land on mine and a bright smile covers her face.

"Sasha brought her to our house a couple of nights ago. We explained she'd be reunited with you soon, but that you'd look different because you had to hide from some bad men, too. She understood that and promised she wouldn't tell anyone who you are," Mama explains. "She's not your daughter, though?"

"She is now," Silas replies while watching Amber. Then he looks down at me. "She's our daughter."

I jerk my eyes up to meet his. On the one hand, I'm shocked at his declaration, then I realize I shouldn't be. The man only has one weakness, and that's his love for children. I've seen it in the way he loves his nieces and nephews. In how he competes with Shadow and Bull for the honor of being the favorite uncle. In the way he spoils them and dotes on them with complete ease.

"Ours?" Tears again… I thought I'd have run out of them by now.

"Ours."

Silas

We've been back in the US for two weeks, staying at my brother's house for a little rest and relaxation now that we've closed the case against the congressman. Senator Hunt was more than willing to work with us on tracking Viktor's digital fingerprint through his files. But Viktor himself is like a ghost in the wind—he's out there, but he's hiding.

Most of Kira's wounds have healed, all except her hand. That'll take several more months before her fingernail is back to normal. Every time I even glance at it, I'm reminded of how narrowly I made it there in time to stop her execution. A few men who were still loyal to her father agreed to help get her out of the country.

If they hadn't agreed, I would've shot them all on the spot so they couldn't stop me and still gotten her out. Of course, her father didn't take much convincing at all. I sensed he was ready to storm the dungeons himself.

Kira has asked several times about the woman who took her

place. Survivor's guilt still bothers her at times, but I've assured her what I told her about the woman was true. She retaliated against a cruel man for the hell he'd put her through, and the officials sentenced her to die for her actions. She didn't regret what she'd done, though, and chose her own path out of this life. She has my respect for sticking to her guns the way she did. And she has my eternal gratitude for giving me a last-minute Hail Mary to save Kira.

"Here's a question I haven't asked you yet." Kira has peppered me every day with one question after the other about how I got there, how I found her, and how I was dressed in a Russian military uniform.

"There are no questions left in this world you haven't asked me. I'd bet my life on it. This is worse than a hostile inter-rogation."

"Don't bet your life on it—you'd lose. I don't want to lose you again."

"Fine. I'd bet my truck on it, then."

"Does that mean I get your truck when you're wrong?"

"No."

She laughs, shakes her head, and rolls her eyes at me. "The last thing I remember is being locked in the cabin of a boat. Amber and I lay down on the bed to get some sleep, but I was on a plane bound for Moscow when I woke up. How did that happen?"

"The best we can piece together from our contact in Havana is Viktor introduced an aerosol sleeping agent into the boat's cabin to make sure you didn't fight. Then he had Amber and you transferred to the plane."

"Told you I hadn't asked that question before."

"I'm pretty sure you have. Maybe even twice."

"Liar." She swats my arm playfully. "Our vacation is almost over. The real world waits for us to rejoin it. I have to figure out what I'll do for a living now. My Russian spy career is over, you know, since I'm dead and all."

"Do you have any idea how hard it was for me to convince Graves of that? That man is way more distrustful than I am. But he does have a job offer for you if you're interested. You wouldn't have access to any of our files, just to be clear. But he's willing to give you a chance."

"That's amazing, Silas. What's the job? Not that beggars can be choosers, but I'm obviously curious."

"Linguistics. Translating documents and verbal conversations for us. Detecting any hidden messages or ciphers."

"Sounds like that's right up my alley. I can't wait to find out more about it."

My family walks out the back door, joining us on the deck. Noah walks straight to the grill and fires it up, while Brianna and Chaise try to corral the younger kids. Amelia and Amber dash out of the house, running as fast as their little legs will carry them, and dive right on top of me. I pretend to be hurt, as if those little girls could do any damage to me, and I wait until they check on me to reveal my hand.

When they squat down level with my face, patting my head, I suddenly fly up with a roar and grab them in my arms. They squeal and laugh, only pretending they want to get away from me while I act like a monster. Then they settle into my lap, each in the crook of my arms, and lean back against my chest.

"My double A batteries." I kiss each of them on the head.

"We're not batteries, Uncle Silas," Amelia says then cackles.

"You could've fooled me. You have way too much energy. You're always running. You never slow down. You two sound just like batteries to me, little girl."

"Big brother, you look good with two kids on your lap. I bet you'd look even better with two more." Chaise sits down beside us with her daughter asleep in her arms. "You're behind the rest of us. You're the oldest—you're supposed to be setting the example for us youngsters."

"You're so funny, Chaise." My deadpan expression only makes her laugh harder at me. "Hey, where's Shadow? I've only seen him once since we've been back."

"Oh, he's still in the doghouse with Elle. He hasn't been around as much lately." Noah tries to suppress his grin, but it's still there, bright as the sun anyway.

"Did he ever find her?" I look over at Noah to gauge his reaction. He coughs to try to hide his laughter.

"Um, no, he hasn't. The infamous CIA officer who has ways of finding someone in the WITSEC program halfway around the world can't find his own wife here in Miami."

"He knows she's still in the area?"

"Yeah, he's isolated and analyzed every single background noise he hears—when she'll take his calls, that is. He'll think he has it figured out, but she's never there when he arrives." Noah shrugs but doesn't seem overly concerned about her whereabouts.

"You know where she is."

"I have an idea. But she doesn't want to be found, or she'd tell Shadow where she is. I'm giving them time to work out their problems without interfering."

"You're watching him squirm. You should feel bad—he has helped you out of all kinds of problems." Then I think about what I just said and realize it doesn't sound like my brother at all. "Oh, I get it. She asked you not to say anything, didn't she?"

"She made me swear. It's killing me that I can't even give him a clue or a hint."

"You better not, Noah, or you'll find yourself in the same situation. You know I love Shadow like a brother, but he's put Elle through enough. This time, he gets to see what it feels like to be left out." I love my sister-in-law. She keeps my brother in line better than his commanding officers ever could.

"Yes, ma'am. You know I'm not going anywhere, and neither are you. The food's ready. Come and get it before it's all gone."

We gather around the grill and table, piling food on our plates as if we'll never eat again. When we're all settled in and enjoying our meal, Kira's phone pings with a text message. She picks it up mid-bite and glances at the screen before dropping her fork and choking on her food.

"It's Viktor. He sent a picture of the dead woman from Moscow, Silas. He knows." Her hands shake, and she's breathing so fast, she'll hyperventilate soon.

"Kira, calm down, baby. Listen to my voice right now. He won't get to you again—I won't let that happen. You're not going anywhere either."

Her phone vibrates in her hand with another text, and all color drains from her face. She drops her phone on the table, and her hands fly to her mouth. From her reaction, that's the only way she's containing a scream. I grab the phone and look at the picture on the screen.

This picture is of Sasha. She's been brutally murdered.

Working on autopilot, I grab my phone from my pocket and call Dmitri. "Get Nat and get out of your house right now. Take her to the place no one knows about. You remember the place we used to talk about, right?"

"Yes, I remember. We're leaving now." He disconnects, not wasting time asking questions. He knows I would only mention that in a dire emergency. This situation positively qualifies.

"Kira, your parents are okay. They're going into hiding now until we can get them out of the country. If they make it to our secret place, we can extract them without Viktor or anyone from the GRU ever knowing." I hold her hands in mine, waiting for my words to sink in and make sense to her.

"Okay," she stutters, her teeth chattering. "Sasha. Oh my god, he mutilated her."

"I know, and I'm so sorry, baby. We tried to get her to come with us, but she refused. She said that she was home. She was born there, and she would die there. She knew the risks she faced, but she wanted to give you the best life she could because she loved you."

"Mira? Is Mira okay? Find my sister."

"I'm here, Kira. What's wrong?" Mira joins us, walking hand in hand with Brad. She rushes to her sister's side and wraps her arms around her. We give Mira the abbreviated version of what's happening.

"We have to kill him, Kira. He won't ever stop coming after us if we don't. You, me, Mom, and Dad—and anyone else we love—will always be targets." Mira hugs Kira and tries to quiet her tears.

"You're absolutely right. I'll do it—I'll find him and kill him the same way he killed Sasha." Kira's fighting to regain control of her emotions and think somewhat rationally.

"You're not doing anything of the sort. If you get involved in anything to do with this again, we'll both be exiled to Siberia. You'll have to trust me to handle it once and for all. Now that he's contacted you, I'll find him. Don't you worry, baby."

She nods and leans against me. I wrap my arm around her and hold her against me. We quickly change the subject so that the kids don't get overwhelmed with our stress. Kira picks at her food, not really eating much but also not wanting to appear rude. Plus, Amber encourages her every couple of minutes to eat because the food her uncle Noah made is so good.

Kira can't resist that little girl.

When Brianna brings out the dessert, Shadow lumbers in, looking like a shell of his former self. He's in pain, suffering every day without his better half. I know a little about how he feels. The week that Kira was missing and I didn't know if she was still alive was pure hell, and we hadn't even been together for long at that point. Shadow and Elle have a long history together, one he likely relives every night without her.

"There's my brother. How are you today?" Brianna turns and hugs Shadow.

"I'm a miserable fucking fool. That's how I am today."

"Watch your language around the kids."

"Fuck. I'm sorry, Bri."

"Call her, Shadow. Tell her how you feel instead of trying to play the CIA officer investigating your target. She told you what she wanted—for you to open up to her and let her in your life. Listen to her and do what she's asking you to do. You're suffering for no reason."

Shadow considers her advice for a minute before finally surrendering. "Okay, Bri. I know you're right."

He sits down at the table and dials her number on his cell. We all hold our breath while it rings, pretending we're not all eavesdropping on his private conversation.

"Elle? Don't hang up, darlin'. Just hear me out. I've said I'm sorry a million times, but I want to tell you what I'm sorry for this time. You've been my life for as long as I can remember now. But I realize that by trying to protect you from what I do, I've excluded you from being in my life. I know I hurt you by leaving you out, by not telling you the truth about everything, and even by lying about some of the things I did.

"From now on, I want you to be involved in everything in my life. If that means I have to share top-secret information with you so that you'll believe I mean what I say, then so be it. If I need to quit my job and learn to love another line of work, then that's what I'll do. I only want you to come back home to me, be my wife, my best friend, my lover. What would make you happy and make you love me again?"

"I've never stopped loving you, Devon. I had a crush on you as a kid when you were my brother's best friend. I fell in love with you years ago. And I love you more today than I did yesterday." Elle steps out of the kitchen onto the back deck, shocking the hell out of Shadow.

He drops his phone and rushes to her, wrapping his arms around her and squeezing her so tightly, she can hardly breathe. "I've missed you so much, darlin'. I'm so glad to see you and hold you again. Where have you been?"

"That's not important. What matters is that you understand how it feels to be completely excluded from my life. Not knowing where I am, what I'm doing, who I'm with, or if I'm okay. We either make a life together, or we'll be apart for good. Make up your mind right now and stick to it, Devon. Because if you ever do this to me again, I'll make that choice for you, and I won't change my mind again."

"You always have been and always will be my entire life. I understand exactly how I made you feel, and I'll never hurt you like that again. I love you, darlin'. More than you'll ever know. In fact, I'm so in love with you, I'm ready to give you a baby right now. I want a little girl who looks exactly like you."

Tears well up in Elle's eyes as she draws in a ragged breath. She places his hand on her stomach and keeps her eyes locked on his. "I can't promise you it'll be a girl, but we're definitely having a baby in about seven months."

Shadow changes from a downtrodden, beaten soul to an elated and exhilarated man right before my eyes. He lifts her off her feet and twirls her around with the biggest smile plastered on his fugly mug.

"I can't believe I'm going to be a daddy." Shadow's voice is full of excitement. He's so loud, I wouldn't be surprised if the neighbors heard him.

I feel a hand slide into mine and squeeze, so I look away from the happily reunited couple to find Kira watching me with an odd expression. This is one of the rare times I'm unable to read her mind.

"I love you, Silas. I just realized I've never said it, although I should've already told you a million times over. I love you like I've never loved anyone in my life."

I press my lips against hers, relishing the softness there while also wishing I could satisfy the yearning I feel in them. She rubs her fingers along my jaw then into my hair as I deepen the kiss. It's still amazing to me that I can't get enough of this woman, no matter how hard I try.

The urgent tapping of a little hand on my arm ends the tender moment I'm sharing with Kira, and I look down at Amber with her big blue eyes staring up at me. "I love you too. Are you my daddy now?"

Stick a fork in me. I'm done.

Silas

When we returned from Russia, the first thing we did was contact the authorities and the Department of Children and Families about Amber. We were fortunate to have contacts—thank you, Senator Hunt, for your influence—to get an emergency custody order to keep Amber with us while the formal paperwork to foster her is finalized. Fostering is just the first step, though. We've agreed to co-adopt her and raise her as our own. She's already stolen our hearts, and we've proven we're willing to go to the ends of the earth for her, so her assigned social worker was more than happy to keep her out of the normal process.

I fully realize we're blessed beyond measure. Most people who want to adopt don't experience the same speedy service. But just looking at that precious little girl, I know I couldn't have given her up even if they'd said no.

Now that I feel responsible for two beautiful ladies, taking out Viktor is more important to me than ever. After we located him when he took them to Havana, I never actually lost tabs on him. I've just been biding my time. His handler has been protecting him inside the Russian embassy in DC, but a man like him could only take being locked behind the walls of that building for so long.

He's accustomed to moving around freely and playing his games at will. Inside the embassy, he'd be held to their strict rules and code of conduct. Without autonomy, a spy can only drive a desk and do what his superiors tell him to do. The very concept of thinking on his feet flies out the window, and he's left with the memories of the "good old days" when he could make his own decisions.

I know all too well how that scenario would work out for me… It wouldn't. Same line of business, same circumstances, I know it won't work for him. And I know he'll never be content with sending those lame texts like the pussy he is. He'll crave a more hands-on approach to his taunting and mocking, but he'll never have the chance. I'll make sure of that.

Which also concerns me that the job Kira's been offered won't work for her when we get back to DC. Will she be happy working in an office, behind a desk, and shuffling papers? Or will she be bored to tears and looking for something else to fulfill the thrill of the chase?

One major hurdle at a time, Silas. There's one thing we need to focus on at the moment.

When I slip into bed with Kira, I slide my arm over her waist and pull her back against my front. "This is our last night here. Back to DC in the morning. Are you going to miss Miami Beach?"

"Absolutely. I'm not sure I'm mentally prepared to face another DC winter after spending so much time in South Florida."

"Do you think you'd ever want to move here permanently? My parents live nearby. Noah and his crew are here frequently. Chaise and Bull and their kids follow when Noah comes back.

Actually, so do Rebel, Heather, Shadow, and Elle. And Brad, of course. They all work together and count on one another to get shit done."

She turns and looks at me, the moonlight caressing her face through the blinds. "If we did, Amber would get to grow up with a huge family. Aunts, uncles, cousins, and grandparents to make all the bad memories disappear and replace them with only good. That would be perfect."

"Yes, Amber would have that...and so would you. This extended family loves you too, you know?"

"The first time you told me you loved me, I wasn't sure if I'd imagined it or if you'd really said it. That day was the worst. But I realized you made me feel the words long before you spoke them. The way you've protected me, helped me, trusted me, and saved me.

"You risked your own life to save mine. I mean, you came into the Kremlin dressed as a Russian officer in uniform. If you'd been caught...well, I don't even want to think about what they would've done to you. I still can't believe you did all that for me."

"I'd do it all again—and more, Kira. I realize my timing couldn't have been worse, but I knew there was a chance neither of us would make it out of there alive. I couldn't let that happen without telling you how much you mean to me first. Now that I've accepted the fact that I can never go back to being the bachelor who's content with being alone, I'll tell you how much you mean to me every day. It's amazing how much real love can make someone want the things they never wanted before."

"I know exactly what you mean because I feel the same way."

"I don't think it'll be a problem to convince Roman to move back here. He's originally from Florida, so I think he feels the same about the cold and snow as you do. I'm not sure about Nick and Savannah, though. If nothing else, we'd just rely on video conferences for our meetings and cases. We don't have to be in the DC area all the time to do our jobs."

"Just think, if we can convince the entire Scooby gang to live in the same area, we can start our own cult. Noah's house can be our compound." Then she bursts out in uncontrollable laughter, and I join her.

Hearing her laugh, seeing her relaxed and playful, and knowing she's safe and sound in my arms gives me more happiness than I ever imagined possible. Guess it just took meeting the right person, at the right time, and under the right circumstances to change my mind about marriage, love, and a happily-ever-after ending.

Thoughts of a happy ending give me more immediate ideas. With my lips pressed to hers, I roll her onto her back and cover her body with mine. The feel of her body against mine is like pouring jet fuel on the open flame of my libido. After I peel off her clothes, I take my time and give every inch of her body all the attention she can take. With my lips, with my tongue, and with my fingers, I give her my full devotion. When I slide into her, she fits around me as if she is made only for me. The sensation of my every powerful thrust and the sound of her every sexy moan only make me want her more. When we reach the peak of our desire, we tumble over the edge together, our bodies slick with sweat, her nails digging into my back, and our eyes locked in the final throes.

"Just so you know, I'm never letting you go. You're stuck with me now, baby."

"You're the one who's stuck with me. If you ever try to leave me, I'll just follow you."

WE SAY GOODBYE FOR NOW TO MY EXTENDED FAMILY AND HEAD to the private airstrip for our return trip to DC. Nick, Savannah, and their small kids board the plane while we help stow all their luggage. Then Roman, Brad, Mira, Kira, Amber, and I all take our seats. Now is as good a time as any to broach the subject of relocating. As I predicted to Kira last night, the only holdout is Nick, with his meticulous planning and need for order. He won't make that decision without having time to discuss it thoroughly with Savannah, but I can see the wheels turning in his mind. He's thinking about all the same points I had—so many members of our family and friends would be close by, making life easier for all of us.

"What do you think about the prospect of moving, Savannah?" Mira asks.

Mira is Savannah and Nick's live-in nanny as of today, but I have a feeling that'll change soon anyway. Her relationship with Brad seems to be taking on a life of its own. He's as crazy about Mira as I am about her sister. Since the two ladies have been separated for more than a year now, they'll definitely want to live close to each other.

"I'm very intrigued by just the thought. Staying with Brianna for the last few weeks in Miami have completely spoiled me." Savannah looks over at Nick and grins, essentially giving away her final answer.

"Honestly, I think if I said yes right now, she'd have all of our belongings packed the minute we get home." Nick smiles at the thought. "We don't have any family in the DC area. Savannah's best friend and her husband would be welcome to stay with us whenever they wanted. Since she works from home, moving wouldn't affect that either."

"That's a good point, Nick. What about you, Kira? That job proposal was only in the office. You wouldn't be able to do that from Miami. Are you sure you want to give up that offer?" I turn to Kira to gauge her reaction.

"That doesn't bother me. Sitting in an office from eight to five isn't my idea of fun, but I was willing to do it for the opportunity. There are plenty of other jobs I can find, so I'm honestly not worried about it. Besides, according to the government, I'm Nadia Utkin now, and she doesn't have a sordid past. As long as we're all together, I'll be fine." She leans over and kisses my cheek.

We land in DC, and I stop Nick and Kira before we reach my truck. "Nick, I need a favor."

"Of course. What's up?"

"Can Kira and Amber stay with you and Savannah for a while? I have some business to take care of, and I won't leave them alone yet."

Kira looks at me as if I've lost my mind. I offer an apologetic shrug, but that's the most she'll get from me on this. She almost died once—I won't knowingly take her back into a situation where that could happen.

"You got it. Kira, Mira, and Amber are welcome to hang out with Savannah and me for as long as they need. Brad, do you have plans for dinner tonight?"

"Nope, none."

"Good. Join us for dinner. Savannah will love having a house full of adults to talk to for a while longer, and the three of you can finish convincing her to move to Miami."

We get a good laugh out of that. "Chickenshit."

"Hey, I just know who takes care of me. Let's go—the Tucker train is leaving the station."

Kira wraps her arms around my waist and looks up at me with worry in her eyes. "Why do I have a feeling you're about to do something I wouldn't like?"

"I don't know, baby. Maybe you know me a little too well." I smile down at her and place a soft, lingering kiss on her lips. "Don't worry. I'll be by Nick's to pick you up late tonight."

"Please be careful. If you don't show up, I'll hunt you down and make you regret it."

"Yes, ma'am."

Small arms wrap around my leg and squeeze as hard as a five-year-old is capable of. I lean over and lift Amber in the air until she's sitting comfortably on my forearm. She leans her head over on my shoulder and wraps her thin arms around my neck. She doesn't have to say anything because I know exactly what she's thinking. She knows we're going in separate directions, and she wants to hold on to our little family.

"Don't worry, sweet girl. I'll be there to pick you up, too. You believe me, don't you?"

She nods her head, but she still clings to me. When I finally hand her over to Kira, a big piece of my heart goes with her. The sadness on her face at our being separated almost changes my mind.

Almost. But I'm doing this to protect her too.

They all pile into Nick's SUV, and Kira and Amber wave at me as they drive away. Roman is still standing beside me, acting casual but knowing something big is about to go down.

"What's the plan, Silas?"

"I know where he is. I'm going to kill him."

"What do you want me to do?"

"Cover the exits so he doesn't slither away again like the snake he is."

"You got it."

We climb into my truck and head to my place to coordinate our movements. When night falls and it's pitch black outside, we make our way to the rendezvous point. As I suspected, Viktor has been sneaking out of the embassy to frequent his favorite watering holes and go home with whatever willing woman he can find. Tonight, I'm helping him out with a sure thing.

I wait silently in the darkened room for them to get inside the house. She comes in first with her keys still in her hand. He's hot on her heels, holding on to her hips and kissing the side of her neck. She promised him a night he'll never forget, and she didn't lie.

"Oh shit. I left my purse in the car. I need to grab it before someone steals it out of the backseat. We've had a string of car break-ins lately. I'll be right back—make yourself comfortable on the couch." She nods her head toward the sofa, and he takes her up on her offer.

Fucker should've offered to get it for her at the very least.

She closes the door behind her with a smug smile on her face. When she turned the lock on the way in, she activated an automatic mechanism that locks the door from the inside. He won't be able to run out that door when he realizes something is awry. And that realization will hit him in three...two...

"What the fuck?" He jumps up when he hears the car engine start. He's still staring out the window when the car headlights flash across him as she drives away.

He darts to the door to open it, only thinking about getting his rocks off tonight, but the door won't open. The knob only spins freely in his hand. "What the fuck is wrong with this door?"

"Nothing's wrong with it."

He jumps about a foot high and twirls around toward the sound of my voice. His back is pushed against the door, and his eyes are wide with fear.

"That doorknob is working exactly as designed. It's locked and can't be opened from the inside without the right tool. It's keeping you in here with me, where you need to be. No more hiding out in the Russian embassy. No more using the consulate as your errand boy. No more sneaking out of the building at night to grab some pussy. That doorknob's sole job is to make my job of executing you easier." I step out of the shadows and directly into the stream of light coming in through the windows.

I want him to know I'm the one who ends his life.

I want him to die knowing that he lost and Kira won.

I want him to know he's as much of a piece of shit as his older brother was.

"Silas Steele. I have diplomatic immunity. You can't touch me." He juts out his chin, daring me.

Challenge accepted.

With a quick jab, I bust his nose and deflate his puffed-out chest. "Funny, I just touched you. Guess your diplomatic immunity superpowers don't work in here."

"You know what I mean, fucker!"

"I know exactly what you mean. But you don't have that immunity anymore, Viktor Egorov."

"My name is Viktor Sokolov—not Egorov."

"Not according to this passport, it isn't. You're here illegally, and you attacked an NSA agent."

"You work for the CIA."

"Some days, I do. Some days, I work for the NSA. Today, I'm an NSA agent. Guess you're shit out of luck, Egorov. Be sure to tell your pedophile brother I said I hope he's rotting in hell beside you."

Before Viktor can respond or even attempt to run for his life, I draw my handgun and leave a trench in his head wide enough to drive a car through.

"Roman, do me a favor? Call for a clean-up crew."

"You got it, Silas. I'll take it from here. Go pick up your woman and your new daughter. They've waited long enough for a happy home."

"Thanks, man. I'll talk to you later."

Kira—One Year Later

"Mr. Steele?" I call out from the veranda.

"Yes, Mrs. Steele?" Silas replies with an unmistakable smile in his tone. I'm aware a sound can't smile, but somehow, Silas pulls it off, regardless. What can I say? The man is multi-talented.

"I seem to be out of lemonade. Do you mind fixing that little problem for me?"

"Not at all. I'm on my way." My hunk of a man slides up beside me, shirtless, wearing his swimming shorts and flip-flops, and refills my glass.

"Service with a smile. I love it, Mr. Steele."

"I'll service you with a smile any time you want, Mrs. Steele." He waggles his eyebrows at me, making me blush.

"For the love of God, please stop with the Mr. and Mrs. Steele bullshit. You two have been saying that every day for the last month since you got married." Noah shakes his head as he passes by us, but I see the huge smile on his face despite his words.

"The new hasn't worn off yet. We'll stop saying it when it gets old," Silas retorts.

"So, you mean, never. You're never going to stop."

"Exactly." Silas smiles broadly, showing how proud he is of his witty reply.

The past year has held so many changes for us, it's hard to keep up with everything sometimes. We moved from DC to Miami. We left the cold and snow in favor of sand and surf. Our friends and family were all too excited to move with us, even Nick and Savannah. Spending time with them without the constant threat of danger surrounding us made it a much more relaxed atmosphere.

Now I completely understand why everyone loves Savannah so much. She's so giving and caring, but she's also strong and resilient. She had a rough time with a former flame, and she gives Nick all the credit for saving her. He disagrees—he insists he only provided the muscle and she did the rest.

Mira and Brad married soon after we returned to DC. I'd never seen her so excited before. She ran into Nick's house while we were visiting, crying and laughing at the same time, to show off her engagement ring. Brad followed behind her with a red face and a huge smile. He promised me he would love and care for her for the rest of her life. I promised no one would ever find his body if he broke that promise.

I'm positive he believed me.

The adoption of Amber was finalized, so she's officially a Steele now. She had her name changed before I did. She was thrilled to write her new last name on all her school papers. I'm officially Mama, and Silas is officially Daddy. My parents are officially thrilled for all of us and visit as often as they're able, doting on their granddaughter and spending time with Mira and me. In the months between visits, we have weekly video chats so we can all share our lives. They hid in a remote cabin until Viktor was neutralized. Silas wouldn't take any chances of

Viktor's associates getting to my parents. When the smoke cleared from that fiasco, Dad returned to work and announced his retirement. They moved to Zurich immediately after and haven't looked back since.

Amber had nightmares when we first brought her back home. We spent a lot of very late nights calming and soothing her and a lot of days talking to child psychologists about how best to treat her anxiety. She has more good days than bad now, so we're making substantial progress. Oddly enough, it's her daddy she wants when she wakes in the middle of the night. The therapist warned us his imposing male figure may frighten her more after what she experienced, but it seems to be just the opposite. She's comforted by how he protects her because she knows she can trust him. He'd never hurt her or abandon her.

She's definitely a daddy's girl.

"Where'd you go?" Silas sits down beside me and lightly strokes his knuckles across my cheek.

"Just thinking about how different everything is from just a short year ago. We were only here for two weeks last time, detoxing after my stint in a Russian prison and your elaborate prison break scheme, and now we're all closer than ever. Everything we've endured has brought us here, and I wouldn't change our life now for anything in the world. It's perfect. You're perfect. I love our little corner of the world."

"It only gets better from here, baby. I promise you that."

When the sun begins to set, Silas takes my hand and helps me up from the lounge chair. We help clean up the area after our impromptu pool party with the kids and head inside as the night air cools.

"Thanks again for letting us stay here with you while the painters are working on our house. I don't want Kira or Amber sniffing paint fumes all night." Silas puts a stack of dishes and cups in the sink and rolls up his sleeves before loading them in the dishwasher.

"It's no problem at all. You're always welcome here, even if they're not painting. You know we love having you." Brianna pats him on the back on her way to the refrigerator with the leftover food.

"I'm going upstairs to take a shower, babe. Can you keep an eye on Amber? She's a little daredevil, and I'm afraid she'll jump in the pool when we're not watching." I wrap my arms around him from behind and squeeze him tightly.

"Shh—don't give her any ideas." He chuckles. "I've got her, baby. Go enjoy your long, hot shower."

I do exactly that—my shower is long, hot, and thoroughly relaxing. After I towel off and put on my nightgown, I dry my hair and finish getting ready for bed. After thirty or so minutes, I finally emerge from the bathroom and stroll into the bedroom, expecting to find Silas already sawing logs.

What I find instead is unbelievable. And almost inde-scribable.

Silas is lying in the middle of the bed, on top of the covers, sound asleep. He's wearing a French maid uniform, his swim shorts barely peeking out from under the frilly skirt. The fishnet hose that covers his legs from his thighs down to his toes are clipped to the hem of his shorts. Heavy makeup coats his face, complete with bright-blue eye shadow I thought had stopped being made back in the 80s. His lips are painted with very bright red lipstick. Topping it all off is a tiny cap decorated with lace and netting, held on his head with bobby pins.

"Oh, there you are. I couldn't find you earlier, so I had to get my friend Victoria to help me out with this. Be a dear and stay out of the frame for a minute, will you?" Liz saunters by me in a full tuxedo, complete with tails, a top hat, and white gloves, as if it's the most ordinary scene to walk in on.

She climbs up on the bed next to Silas and extends a riding crop toward him until it touches his leg. Victoria snaps picture after picture from every angle while Liz changes her position to show she's the dominant in each frame. When Victoria's tears of laughter flow so hard she can't see to take more pictures, Liz decides they have enough photographs. Then they're simply done—they start to walk out of the room together with no explanation.

"Um, hold on. What the hell is going on here? What did you do to Silas?"

Liz pats my cheek. "Oh, my sweet girl. I'm sorry if you had any plans to get frisky with him tonight. I'm afraid he'll sleep soundly until morning. He's perfectly fine—there are no dangerous side effects, other than he'll be hard to rouse until he's had time to sleep it off. He's probably forgotten the way he threatened to use sodium pentothal on me last year, but I never forget a thing. He has to pay for his crimes."

The two ladies saunter off together, scrolling through the pictures on Liz's phone and discussing which picture they will send to whom.

Noah passes them in the hall on the way to the master bedroom. He stops at our guest bedroom and glances inside. He doesn't appear fazed at all. Then he meets my questioning gaze and shrugs. "Guess he disrespected Liz again, huh?"

"This has happened before?"

"Not this exact payback, but close enough. Whatever he did to her, he absolutely knew better than to do it in the first place. He'll find no sympathy around here. Good night, Kira."

Just like that, Noah's gone too.

Silas told me stories about Liz, but I thought he exaggerated for the sake of storytelling. Now, I think there's no way in hell he told me everything. He left out a lot of crazy details he obviously never thought I'd believe. Before I saw this entire scene firsthand, he would've been one-hundred-percent correct—I wouldn't have grasped the full magnitude.

But now...I can't let this moment pass without snapping a

few pictures of my own. This is the perfect inspiration for ending possible future marriage spats.

I grab a blanket out of the closet to drape over him before sliding under the covers next to him. As soon as my head hits the pillow, I'm out like a light and sleep straight through until morning. When I wake, it's to my husband yelling obscenities and screaming Liz's name…in between trying to unzip the dress he's wearing.

I have to remember to ask Liz where she found his size…

"Kira?"

"Yes, dear?"

"Do you think you can stop laughing long enough to help me out of this getup?"

"I can't promise I'll stop laughing, but I will help you out of it."

"Ha-ha. Very funny."

After I unzip it and help him out of the dress and fishnets, he stomps into the bathroom across the hall, and the cursing resumes full force. He just realized he's wearing full stage makeup.

"Holy hell. This shit doesn't come off with soap and water. What kind of makeup did she put on me? Get the turpentine!"

Liz appears in the hallway with a devious grin on her face. "We're fresh out of turpentine, Silas."

He steps out of the bathroom to face Liz head on. "Then go to the store and buy more."

"The store is sold out of it too." Her tone is casual, unaffected by his mounting annoyance. She huffs on her fingernails then rubs them on her shirt, buffing them to a glistening shine.

"All of them?"

"Tragically, yes. There's a shortage of it in all of South Florida." She folds her arms across her chest. "Every single store is sold out of turpentine."

I feel like I'm watching an old Western movie with a showdown at twenty paces between two gunmen. It's not even high noon yet, so anything could happen before this feud is over. I still can't look away, though. It's all too fascinating to leave before it's over.

"All right, Liz. What did I do?"

"Do you remember threatening me with truth serum to learn all my secrets? You threw down the challenge, and I simply answered it. Of course, I won, as I knew I would."

"I don't recall that specific moment. All I can think is I must've been especially stressed at the time and didn't realize what I was saying." His reply is clearly made under duress, considering the way he's clenching his jaw and gritting his teeth as he speaks.

"Apology accepted. Do you promise never to dis me again?"

"Dis you?" He raises his eyebrows, and it's all I can do to keep from laughing out loud at the bright-blue eye shadow. "Yes, I promise never to do that again."

She hands him a small bottle of makeup remover from her pocket, explicitly designed for the product she applied. He disappears back into the bathroom to shower and scrub all the skin off his face to remove any traces of her artwork. When we finally join the others downstairs for breakfast, everyone's phone pings with text messages simultaneously. When we all look…except for Liz…I know what's inside.

Victoria has pieced the still pictures together to make a movie of Liz's dominatrix cosplay. Silas drops his fork on the plate and covers his bright red face in embarrassment while everyone else laughs, points, and makes crude jokes. I keep my eyes glued to my plate, but I can't stop my shoulders from shaking or the tears from pouring out of my eyes from my stifled laughter. When the replies from Bull, Rebel, and Shadow start pouring in, I completely lose it.

"Nice legs…you should get a job as the poster boy for Nair."

"That dress is fucking sexy. Does it come in men's sizes?"

"I'll never look at a French maid costume in the same light again. Or in any light, for that matter. Ever. Again."

"Liz. You coerced a surrender without telling me about the pictures?" It's not really a question, obviously. I think he simply needs a second to digest everything.

"You didn't ask about any pictures. Our agreement wasn't contingent on anything."

The stare-down occurring across the table tells me this competition isn't over by a long shot.

Looking around the table at this crazy bunch of people, I realize this is the family I never knew I wanted but always needed. They give love so freely, accepting and embracing one another's differences and similarities. When one is down, the others rally around until the situation passes. When one is in trouble, everyone takes it personally and doesn't walk away until the job is done, regardless of the personal costs. Their lighthearted banter is the perfect complement to the stress of everyday life.

I couldn't have picked a better man, husband, or best friend to spend my life with. Our love continues to grow stronger every day, with every passing hurdle we clear, and with every failure we overcome together. Our daughter is healthy and happy and keeps urging us to give her a little brother or sister. We're not quite ready for that yet, but we know it's in the cards for our future.

We somehow finish breakfast without further incidents then make plans to spend time with my in-laws for the rest of the day. The whole family will be there—that includes friends we've claimed as family.

Just over a year ago, this would've been more than I'd ever dared to dream about, to hope for, or to expect.

Today, I'm living my dream life to the fullest.

Roman—Three Years Ago

"I can't do this anymore." Tawnee places her hands on her hips and burns a hole through me with the anger in her eyes.

"You can't do what anymore?" I know she isn't saying what I think she's saying.

"Us, Roman. I can't do us anymore. This isn't working for me. I've put up with too much, and I can't do it one more day. I'm sorry, but this is over between us." She snatches her bag off the bed and starts toward the door.

"You're breaking up with me? Are you fucking kidding me right now?"

"No, I'm absolutely not kidding you at all. I'm done. I'm so done."

"What do you expect from me, Tawnee? I mean, I gave you a drawer and everything."

Ah, shit. That was the wrong thing to say apparently. She's seriously considering drawing her gun and shooting me right now. She's weighing the pros and cons at this very second. I can see it in her expression and the way her muscles are tensed. I don't know what I've done this time to piss her off so badly. All I know is whatever we fight about always ends up being my fucking fault.

"You gave me a drawer? Yeah, let's talk about that drawer, Roman. Let's examine that gesture for a minute. One, it's the smallest fucking drawer in the whole house. Two, why the hell would I put a few items of clothes in that drawer when I still have to go back home for all the rest of my shit anyway? And, most of all, three." She walks over to the drawer I gave her and yanks it open. "You haven't even noticed I've never used the fucking thing!"

She releases it with a jerk, and it crashes to the floor as she walks away, leaving it where it landed.

We'd been dating on and off for a while before that eventful fight. I don't even remember what started the fight now. It was probably something stupid, like I said green is a better color than blue. Who the fuck knows or cares? The point is, she left me and said she was never coming back. I gave her two days to change her mind and her attitude. When I didn't hear a single peep from her within that time, I decided it was time to move on.

And that's exactly what I did. I went out the next night, I met someone new, and I enjoyed the pleasure of her company. Repeatedly.

I haven't seen the same girl twice since the day Tawnee walked out, and I haven't regretted one minute of living my life to the fullest.

Present Day

"Roman, I swear to God, if you tell me that fucking story

one more time…I'm going to take this plastic knife I just used to smear cream cheese on my bagel, and I'm going to slit my wrists with it." Blake holds the knife at his wrist and pretends to saw his skin.

"I've told you that story before?"

"Only once or twice…a week…for three fucking years, man. Listen, I'm going to tell you this one last time as your friend. If you're my friend, you need to listen to what I have to say because I'm as fucking tired of repeating myself as I am of hearing you repeat yourself.

"One. It's time for you to face the truth.

"Two. You are not over being dumped.

"Three. You're not over her moving halfway around the world and never calling you to say goodbye when she left the country.

"Four. You are nowhere near being over Tawnee.

"Five. You're in love with the woman. Still. To this very day. If she walked into this bakery right now and said she wanted you back, you'd jump for fucking joy. And so would I, because at least you'd have a new fucking story to tell." Blake bites into his bagel, tearing it with excessive force, and glares at me over his coffee cup.

"That's ridiculous. How do you get that from what I just told you?"

"Because I'm not a fucking moron, Roman. Unlike you. That's how."

"You're so full of shit. I don't give second chances, Blake. One and done—that's how I manage my relationship issues. Plain and simple. No fuss, no muss. No complications. No baggage. No unresolved issues."

"Yeah, I got it, man. You're still full of shit, for the record. I stick by my original statement and assessment of you."

We walk out of the restaurant and stroll down the street, keeping our target in sight without giving away our position.

My phone vibrates with an incoming text, so I fish it out of my pocket and quickly glance at the screen. My attention is on my mark, but when I glance down at the screen, I forget all about my mission.

I forget about my job.

I forget about my mark.

I forget why I'm following him.

After three long years, Tawnee has sent me a message. But it's not just any message. To anyone else, it appears to be a string of letters and numbers with no discernible pattern. But I know better. I recognize the secret code on sight. With a quick copy and paste into our own software program and our specific key, I decode the message and nearly let my phone slip through my fingers when I read what it says.

Send help immediately. Assassination plot. Extraction needed.

Her life is in imminent danger, and she's reaching out to me for help…from Dubai.

How can I not answer this call?

"What's wrong? Did you just see a ghost or what?" Blake looks over his shoulder at where I've stopped walking in the middle of the sidewalk.

"Something like that. Tawnee just texted me using Brad's secret message system. I haven't heard from her in three years, Blake."

"Yeah. Funny how I got that from the conversation we just had not three seconds ago. What did her message say?"

I hand Blake my phone and take his out of his hand. In seconds, I have my CIA partners, Silas Steele and Nick Tucker, on the phone and I'm relaying the message from Tawnee.

"What do you want to do, Roman?" Silas asks.

He knows damn well what I want to do, but he's testing me in more ways than one. It's not just my commitment to carrying out my duties as a CIA officer he's questioning. It's my commitment to her—someone who once worked alongside me at Steele

Security. Someone who slept beside me, almost lived with me, and loved me. And someone I should've treated better than I did.

"I want to drop everything and leave a blazing trail on our way out of Dubai with her safely in my arms." That's probably the most honest statement I've made regarding her in the last three years.

"Have you done any research into what's going on and why she's involved in an imminent assassination attempt?" Nick asks, ever the level-headed hero.

"No, Nick. I just got the text and immediately called you two." I grit my teeth to keep my impatience under wraps.

"So, we could be walking straight into an ambush. It could all be a ruse to get you there for some reason. Or Silas. Or me. Or all three of us, for that matter. You have nothing but a simple text that could be from anyone pretending to be Tawnee."

"It came through Brad's encrypted system. Only Tawnee would know what secret key to use so I could decode the message. She sent it to me—not you and not Silas. Me. She needs me, and I'm going with or without you two."

"That's what I wanted to hear. Get your shit together, Roman, and screw your head on straight. If she's in a volatile situation, what do you think is waiting for us? We have no idea what we're walking into, so you need to check your emotions at the door and think logically. What is she working on? Who is she working with? Who are their friends and enemies?" Nick has been in so many dangerous situations in his career, this line of questioning has become second nature to him.

He's right, though. I saw her plea for help, and I was ready to run headlong into the fire, no questions asked.

Maybe Blake is right after all.

"Tell Blake to pack his gear. He's going along for the ride, too. I'll contact Langley and get all the intel we have on the situation. There's a flight leaving Miami today at 5:35. Let's meet at the airport and prepare for the long-ass flight to Dubai. Leave your guns at home. You'll never make it through customs with a weapon." Silas is the most seasoned CIA officer of us all.

Even though we're assigned to a joint task force with the NSA and CIA, we mostly perform under CIA rules. Meaning, there are none. This should be an interesting trip.

~

Tawnee

"Rafael, it's time to go. We've cleared the hallway." I approach my handsome Latin employer and try to urge him out of the luxury hotel suite for the third time this morning.

"Tawnee, you have to relax. You're far too pretty to be so stressed all the time." He finally stands from the overstuffed sofa and slides his sunglasses over his eyes.

"Unfortunately, my looks have no bearing on my stress levels. Ensuring your security does. You not taking your own security seriously also does. Why hire me and make me travel around the world with you if you don't listen to me?" I turn and walk back to the entrance to check the hallway before letting him pass through the door.

"There's nothing I have to worry about. I know you've already worried about it a thousand times over before I've even considered it."

"I don't doubt that's true. Not even for a second. Which makes me even more stressed since, again, you don't take your own safety seriously. We're caught in a vicious cycle, you and I. So I need you to help me out here and don't make me old before my time. Stay close to your security team, be vigilant about watching your surroundings, and do exactly as you're told to do."

"I love it when you're bossy like that. It's so sexy."

"I'm serious, Raf."

"So am I. And your ass looks awesome in those pants. You should wear those every day."

I stop and turn to look him dead in the eyes. "Rafael, I do wear the same style of pants every single day that I'm with you. They're basically my work uniform. And you can't possibly watch your surroundings if you're watching my ass."

His dark chuckle makes me smile. He knows he drives me crazy—that's why he does it on purpose. He's a shameless flirt, but he's also harmless. If he thought for one second his comments offended me or made me uncomfortable, he'd apologize profusely and buy me a mega yacht to make up for it. But then, he can afford to be so lavish since he's one of the richest men in the world. As the owner of a very profitable holding company, he controls the majority of shares in a lot of very high-powered, high-profile companies. Those businesses have made him an extraordinary amount of money, but he's still the same down-to-earth man he was before the cash starting rolling in.

All the money he has made is why I have a job today, albeit one that makes me crazy more than anything else in my life at the moment. Buying the controlling shares in companies whose owners aren't ready to give up control hasn't made him the most popular man on the Forbes Top 100 list. Corporate enemies can be ruthless. Kidnapping is a real threat for someone who is worth so much. Then there's the matter of his life insurance policy—it requires him to have private security in most circumstances...like when he leaves his house for any length of time, goes out on dates with unvetted partners, or when he's traveling to Dubai for both business and pleasure.

We're in the UAE for both reasons on this trip.

He's taking a tour of a recently built high-rise condo building as he considers expanding his interests. Not that he needs more income, but he's bored with managing his life against where the stock market closes or how a company performs. Expanding into real estate in one of the most popular destinations in the world makes good business sense to him.

Buying the entire building in this destination mecca isn't something many people would be able to afford.

But Rafael Cruz isn't just anyone.

We finally make it to the waiting car and get him inside without incident. On the way to tour the high-rise, Raf makes another business call while I watch our surroundings.

"Tony, change lanes abruptly." Our driver, Tony, is used to my obsessive behavior by now, so he does as I ask without question.

All the hairs on the back of my neck stand at attention. I speak into the comms, alerting the rest of the team in the other cars. "We have a possible tail. White Nissan Altima. Two males. Two cars behind and speeding up fast to catch up with us. Tony, make an unexpected turn, but not down a dead-end street. Make sure there's an easy out."

Tony's more alert now. His eyes are glued to the rearview mirror when he identifies the turn he'll make. Rafael, on the other hand, continues his conversation for a few more seconds before disconnecting the call as if nothing out of the ordinary is happening around him. The other car is traveling too fast in an attempt to catch up with us, so they're unable to make the same turn. They slam on their brakes, and the tires screech against the asphalt. Then they turn, and the front wheel jumps the curb before they speed up again, racing toward us.

"Tony, get us out of here. Now."

We race through the crowded city, drawing way too much attention in a culture that doesn't appreciate such outrageous behavior. But these guys aren't stopping. If anything, they're becoming more aggressive.

"Raf, you need to get down out of sight."

"Don't you have your gun? Shoot their tires out." He slides

down in the seat, snatches his shades off his face, and looks at me with fear in his eyes for the first time since this chase started.

"Do I have a gun in Dubai? No, Raf, we're not residents here. We can't carry firearms without a special invitation from the sheik himself. Even you don't have that kind of clout here."

"Then how exactly do you plan to protect me?"

"By losing them and getting you to a safe place until we can work with the police to identify the owner of the car and the men inside."

Suddenly, another car appears out of nowhere and rams us from a side street. While we were watching the car behind us for the last several miles, they coordinated a sneak attack. Our car spins around in the middle of the street and slams into the side of a building. The initial shock of the crash takes me a few precious seconds to clear my mind, then I check on Rafael to make sure he isn't hurt.

He assures me he's fine, so I immediately survey our surroundings to get my bearings. Tony and the second car of security guys surround our car, ready to fight off our attackers. Raf's door is pinned against the building, so I turn and shield him with my body since there's no way out and nowhere to run. The ruckus outside the car is fierce, with aggressive yelling in Arabic and English. The men start to scuffle, leaving me exposed inside the car. Arms reach in, grabbing at me, trying to pull me out. But I plant my feet against the side of the vehicle and push with all my might, staying between them and Rafael.

Tony dispatches the man who had distracted him then rushes back to help me. Two other members of our detail soon join him, effectively beating back the attack with fists and brawn. The entire scene lasts mere seconds, but it feels like it takes forever. The next thing I see, the attackers run back to their cars. One turns to look at me again before he slides into the passenger seat. He angrily yells something in Arabic...but I distinctly hear my name right in the middle of his rant.

Now I'm not so sure Rafael was the intended target after all.

~

Haven't read Nick Tucker's story yet? Get it now in *Fine Line*. Read Roman's story in *Hard Line*.

Want more of Nick Tucker? Read ***Her Dom*** and ***Her Dom's Lesson***!

Want more of Nick, Silas, Roman, Reaper, Bull, Rebel, and Shadow? Find them and more the ***Steele Security series***: ***Wicked Games***, ***Wicked Ties***, ***Wicked Nights***, ***Wicked Intentions***, and ***Wicked Shadows!***

~

ACKNOWLEDGMENTS

Writing a book is much harder than one would think. The finished product only takes a few hours to read, but months to agonize over every single word, plot point, and character action. Only speaking for myself, I can honestly say I put my heart and soul into the story, taking time away from family and friends (and cleaning house….oh, the messy house!) to write just one more chapter.

When I finally reach those two little magical words, a weight is lifted from my shoulders and I'm able to breathe again. Until I start the next book. Which is usually while my editor works on the recently completed one.

My writing journey includes chatting with several people I trust and admire to give feedback and suggestions. There are also people who encourage and support me along the way, taking a chance on a new type of book or a storyline outside the norm. Those who aren't afraid to step outside the box and give "different" a chance. These are my people—my tribe—whether they realize it or not.

Acknowledgments are hard to write because I never want to leave anyone out or make anyone feel their place in my life isn't important. If you've ever read my books, you hold a special place in my heart. There are a few special people I want to recognize for helping make this book special to me.

First and foremost, I thank my Lord and Savior, Jesus Christ, for his unending love, mercy, and forgiveness of a sinner like me. Without Him, I am nothing. Yes, when I say I fall short, I realize I fall way short, but thankfully, there's no such thing as being too far from Him. He knows my heart. Someone recently called me a hypocrite for adding this to my acknowledgments. Since I openly admit I'm a sinner, I don't see it the same way she does. To me, a hypocrite implies someone denies any wrong-doing WHILE actually doing wrong. Adding this is my way of sharing my belief and thanking Him for the many blessings in my life, even though I'm well aware I don't deserve them.

Michelle Dare, you've been with me since the beginning of this crazy journey. All these years later, it's very clear that you're stuck with me. FOR.EV.A. Sorry for your bad luck. ;)

Victoria Renteria, you are an AWESOME alpha reader! Thank you for your time, feedback, and belief that I could actually finish this book. Silas was quite the PITA, but you made it feel much easier with you wittiness and awesomeness!

Lisa A. Hollett with Silently Correcting Your Grammar, my editor and my friend, thank you once again for working through this book with me and polishing it until it's as perfect as possible.

Wander Aguiar, the photographer for the covers in this series, is always wonderful to work with—although he does make choosing one photo very difficult. Fortunately, I was able to find three that perfectly fit this series.

Sommer Stein with Perfect Pear Creative Covers, thank you for creating these awesome covers. I'm always in awe of your amazing talent.

To the readers, whether you love, like, or hate this book, thank you for taking your time to read it. Thank you for your reviews, even if all you say is you liked it or not. Thank you for your support—you have no idea how much every little bit means to me. You are the best!

All my love to you,
Angel

Lines are for crossing.
Rules are for breaking.
HARDLINE
A CROSSING LINES NOVEL
USA Today Bestselling Author
A.D. JUSTICE

HARD LINE.

A CROSSING LINES NOVEL.

Copyright © 2019 A.D. Justice.

Cover photo by Wander Aguiar.

Cover model is Forest H.

Cover design by Sommer Stein, Perfect Pear Creative Covers

My rule: Never let an old flame burn you twice.

Other people gave second chances—I didn't. My modus operandi was to move on to the next girl in line and forget the previous one.

So when Tawnee Milano said she needed her space, I let her go. Then I left our mutual employer for a new job with the CIA and didn't look back.

But a coded distress message from her sends me right back to where I was when we first split up. The possibility of losing her forever forces me to relax my rigid stance. With her life in danger, I'm finally facing my true feelings for her.

Mottos are all fine and good in theory. Not so much in practice.

Now my hard line policy is to get her back—and keep her this time.

PROLOGUE

Roman—Three Years Ago

"I can't do this anymore." Tawnee places her hands on her hips and burns a hole through me with the anger in her eyes.

"You can't do what anymore?" I know she isn't saying what I think she's saying.

"Us, Roman. I can't do us anymore. This isn't working for me. I've put up with too much, and I can't do it one more day. I'm sorry, but this is over between us." She snatches her bag off the bed and starts toward the door.

"You're breaking up with me? Are you fucking kidding me right now?"

"No, I'm absolutely not kidding you at all. I'm done. I'm so done."

"What do you expect from me, Tawnee? I mean, I gave you a drawer and everything."

Ah, shit. That was the wrong thing to say apparently. She's seriously considering drawing her gun and shooting me right

501

now. She's weighing the pros and cons at this very second. I can see it in her expression and the way her muscles are tensed. I don't know what I've done this time to piss her off so badly. All I know is whatever we fight about always ends up being my fucking fault.

"You gave me a drawer? Yeah, let's talk about that drawer, Roman. Let's examine that gesture for a minute. One, it's the smallest fucking drawer in the whole house. Two, why the hell would I put a few items of clothes in that drawer when I still have to go back home for all the rest of my shit anyway? And, most of all, three." She walks over to the drawer I gave her and yanks it open. "You haven't even noticed I've never used the fucking thing!"

She releases it with a jerk, and it crashes to the floor as she walks away, leaving it where it landed.

We'd been dating on and off for a while before that eventful fight. I don't even remember what started the fight now. It was probably something stupid, like I said green is a better color than blue. Who the fuck knows or cares? The point is, she left me and said she was never coming back. I gave her two days to change her mind and her attitude. When I didn't hear a single peep from her within that time, I decided it was time to move on.

And that's exactly what I did. I went out the next night, I met someone new, and I enjoyed the pleasure of her company. Repeatedly.

I haven't seen the same girl twice since the day Tawnee walked out, and I haven't regretted one minute of living my life to the fullest.

Present Day

"Roman, I swear to God, if you tell me that fucking story one more time…I'm going to take this plastic knife I just used to smear cream cheese on my bagel, and I'm going to slit my wrists with it." Blake holds the knife at his wrist and pretends to saw his skin.

"I've told you that story before?"

"Only once or twice…a week…for three fucking years, man. Listen, I'm going to tell you this one last time as your friend. If you're my friend, you need to listen to what I have to say because I'm as fucking tired of repeating myself as I am of hearing you repeat yourself.

"One. It's time for you to face the truth.

"Two. You are not over being dumped.

"Three. You're not over her moving halfway around the world and never calling you to say goodbye when she left the country.

"Four. You are nowhere near being over Tawnee.

"Five. You're in love with the woman. Still. To this very day. If she walked into this bakery right now and said she wanted you back, you'd jump for fucking joy. And so would I, because at least you'd have a new fucking story to tell." Blake bites into his bagel, tearing it with excessive force, and glares at me over his coffee cup.

"That's ridiculous. How do you get that from what I just told you?"

"Because I'm not a fucking moron, Roman. Unlike you. That's how."

"You're so full of shit. I don't give second chances, Blake. One and done—that's how I manage my relationship issues. Plain and simple. No fuss, no muss. No complications. No baggage. No unresolved issues."

"Yeah, I got it, man. You're still full of shit, for the record. I stick by my original statement and assessment of you."

We walk out of the restaurant and stroll down the street, keeping our target in sight without giving away our position.

My phone vibrates with an incoming text, so I fish it out of my pocket and quickly glance at the screen. My attention is on my mark, but when I glance down at the screen, I forget all about my mission.

I forget about my job.

I forget about my mark.

I forget why I'm following him.

After three long years, Tawnee has sent me a message. But it's not just any message. To anyone else, it appears to be a string of letters and numbers with no discernible pattern. But I know better. I recognize the secret code on sight. With a quick copy and paste into our own software program and our specific key, I decode the message and nearly let my phone slip through my fingers when I read what it says.

Send help immediately. Assassination plot. Extraction needed.

Her life is in imminent danger, and she's reaching out to me for help...from Dubai.

How can I not answer this call?

"What's wrong? Did you just see a ghost or what?" Blake looks over his shoulder at where I've stopped walking in the middle of the sidewalk.

"Something like that. Tawnee just texted me using Brad's secret message system. I haven't heard from her in three years, Blake."

"Yeah. Funny how I got that from the conversation we just had not three seconds ago. What did her message say?"

I hand Blake my phone and take his out of his hand. In seconds, I have my CIA partners, Silas Steele and Nick Tucker, on the phone and I'm relaying the message from Tawnee.

"What do you want to do, Roman?" Silas asks.

He knows damn well what I want to do, but he's testing me in more ways than one. It's not just my commitment to carrying out my duties as a CIA officer he's questioning. It's my commitment to her—someone who once worked alongside me at Steele Security. Someone who slept beside me, almost lived with me, and loved me. And someone I should have treated better than I did.

"I want to drop everything and leave a blazing trail on our way out of Dubai with her safely in my arms." That's probably the most honest statement I've made regarding her in the last three years.

"Have you done any research into what's going on and why she's involved in an imminent assassination attempt?" Nick asks, ever the level-headed hero.

"No, Nick. I just got the text and immediately called you two." I grit my teeth to keep my impatience under wraps.

"So, we could be walking straight into an ambush. It could all be a ruse to get you there for some reason. Or Silas. Or me. Or all three of us, for that matter. You have nothing but a simple text that could be from anyone pretending to be Tawnee."

"It came through Brad's encrypted system. Only Tawnee would know what secret key to use so I could decode the message. She sent it to me—not you and not Silas. Me. She needs me, and I'm going with or without you two."

"That's what I wanted to hear. Get your shit together, Roman, and screw your head on straight. If she's in a volatile situation, what do you think is waiting for us? We have no intel on what we're walking into, so you need to check your emotions at the door and think logically. What is she working on? Who is she working with? Who are their friends and enemies?" Nick has been in so many dangerous situations in his career, this line of questioning has become second nature to him.

He's right, though. I saw her plea for help, and I was ready to run headlong into the fire, no questions asked.

Maybe Blake is right after all.

"Tell Blake to pack his gear. He's going along for the ride too. I'll contact Langley and get all the intel we have on the situation. There's a flight leaving Miami today at 5:35. Let's meet at the airport and prepare for the long-ass flight to Dubai. Leave your guns at home. You'll never make it through customs with a weapon." Silas is the most seasoned CIA officer of us all.

Even though we're assigned to a joint task force with the NSA and CIA, we mostly perform under CIA rules. Meaning, there are none. This should be an interesting trip.

~

Tawnee

"Rafael, it's time to go. We've cleared the hallway." I approach my handsome Latin employer and try to urge him out of the luxury hotel suite for the third time this morning.

"Tawnee, you have to relax. You're far too pretty to be so stressed all the time." He finally stands from the overstuffed sofa and slides his sunglasses over his eyes.

"Unfortunately, my looks have no bearing on my stress levels. Ensuring your security does. You not taking your own security seriously also does. Why hire me and make me travel around the world with you if you don't listen to me?" I turn and walk back to the entrance to check the hallway before letting him pass through the door.

"There's nothing I have to worry about. I know you've already worried about it a thousand times over before I've even considered it."

"I don't doubt that's true. Not even for a second. Which makes me even more stressed since, again, you don't take your own safety seriously. We're caught in a vicious cycle, you and I. So I need you to help me out here and don't make me old before my time. Stay close to your security team, be vigilant about watching your surroundings, and do exactly as you're told to do."

"I love it when you're bossy like that. It's so sexy."

"I'm serious, Raf."

"So am I. And your ass looks awesome in those pants. You should wear those every day."

I stop and turn to look him dead in the eyes. "Rafael, I do wear the same style of pants every single day that I'm with you. They're basically my work uniform. And you can't possibly watch your surroundings if you're watching my ass."

His dark chuckle makes me smile. He knows he drives me crazy—that's why he does it on purpose. He's a shameless flirt, but he's also harmless. If he thought for one second his comments offended me or made me uncomfortable, he'd apologize profusely and buy me a mega yacht to make up for it. But then, he can afford to be so lavish since he's one of the richest men in the world. As the owner of a very profitable holding company, he controls the majority of shares in a lot of very high-powered, high-profile companies. Those businesses have made him an extraordinary amount of money, but he's still the same down-to-earth man he was before the cash starting rolling in.

All the money he has made is why I have a job today, albeit one that makes me crazy more than anything else in my life at the moment. Buying the controlling shares in companies whose owners aren't ready to give up control hasn't made him the most popular man on the Forbes Top 100 list. Corporate enemies can be ruthless. Kidnapping is a real threat for someone who is worth so much. Then there's the matter of his life insurance policy—it requires him to have private security in most circumstances...like when he leaves his house for any length of time, goes out on dates with unvetted partners, or when he's traveling to Dubai for both business and pleasure.

We're in the UAE for both reasons on this trip.

He's taking a tour of a recently built high-rise condo building as he considers expanding his interests. Not that he needs more income, but he's bored with managing his life against where the stock market closes or how a company performs. Expanding into real estate in one of the most popular destinations in the world makes good business sense to him.

Buying the entire building in this destination mecca isn't something many people could afford.

But Rafael Cruz isn't just anyone.

We finally make it to the waiting car and get him inside without incident. On the way to tour the high-rise, Raf makes another business call while I watch our surroundings.

"Tony, change lanes abruptly." Our driver, Tony, is used to my obsessive behavior by now, so he does as I ask without question.

All the hairs on the back of my neck stand at attention. I speak into the comms, alerting the rest of the team in the other cars. "We have a possible tail. White Nissan Altima. Two males. Two cars behind and speeding up fast to catch up with us. Tony, make an unexpected turn, but not down a dead-end street. Make sure there's an easy out."

Tony's more alert now. His eyes are glued to the rearview mirror when he identifies the turn he'll make. Rafael, on the other hand, continues his conversation for a few more seconds before disconnecting the call as if nothing out of the ordinary is happening around him. The other car is traveling too fast in an attempt to catch up with us, so they're unable to make the same turn. They slam on their brakes, and the tires screech against the asphalt. Then they turn, and the front wheel jumps the curb before they speed up again, racing toward us.

"Tony, get us out of here. Now."

We race through the crowded city, drawing way too much attention in a culture that doesn't appreciate such outrageous behavior. But these guys aren't stopping. If anything, they're becoming more aggressive.

"Raf, you need to get down out of sight."

"Don't you have your gun? Shoot their tires out." He slides down in the seat, snatches his shades off his face, and looks at me with fear in his eyes for the first time since this chase started.

"Do I have a gun in Dubai? No, Raf, we're not residents here. We can't carry firearms without a special invitation from the sheik himself. Even you don't have that kind of clout here."

"Then how exactly do you plan to protect me?"

"By losing them and getting you to a safe place until we can work with the police to identify the owner of the car and the men inside."

Suddenly, another car appears out of nowhere and rams us from a side street. While we were watching the car behind us for the last several miles, they coordinated a sneak attack. Our car spins around in the middle of the street and slams into the side of a building. The initial shock of the crash takes me a few precious seconds to clear my mind, then I check on Rafael to make sure he isn't hurt.

He assures me he's fine, so I immediately survey our surroundings to get my bearings. Tony and the second car of security guys surround our car, ready to fight off our attackers. Raf's door is pinned against the building, so I turn and shield him with my body since there's no way out and nowhere to run. The ruckus outside the car is fierce, with aggressive yelling in Arabic and English. The men start to scuffle, leaving me exposed inside the car. Arms reach in, grabbing at me, trying to pull me out. But I plant my feet against the side of the vehicle and push with all my might, staying between them and Rafael.

Tony dispatches the man who had distracted him then rushes back to help me. Two other members of our detail soon join him, effectively beating back the attack with fists and brawn. The entire scene lasts mere seconds, but it feels like it takes forever. The next thing I see, the attackers run back to their cars. One turns to look at me again before he slides into the passenger seat. He angrily yells something in Arabic...but I distinctly hear him say my name right in the middle of his rant.

Now I'm not so sure Rafael was the intended target after all.

Roman

Blake and I rush into the Miami airport as if we'll miss our international flight that doesn't even leave for three more hours. I'm so keyed up, it's not even fucking funny. Three years of no word from Tawnee evaporated into the Miami heat when I opened her message. Anything could happen in the eighteen-plus hours it'll take to reach the Middle East, including the layover time in Paris. Then there's the issue of actually finding her once we land. But one way or another, that's precisely what I plan to do. Then I'll carry her home, kicking and screaming over my shoulder if needed.

Both Silas and Nick are already here, waiting with the flight reservations for Blake and me in hand when we approach them.

"Courtesy of Uncle Sam," Silas says with a smile when he hands us our itineraries. "Seems there may a need for us to be there in an official capacity after all. We have established contacts in the area who can get us what we need once we land, but there's a catch. We're not allowed to carry firearms in the UAE because we're not Emirati citizens and the sheik won't give us permission. Our big brass has already tried to convince him. The details are sketchy because Rafael Cruz is a private citizen who travels to foreign countries more than he stays in his own, but word has it he's involved in a lot more than what we see in his public persona."

"Such as—what?" Silas is fucking crazy if he thinks he can leave me hanging with a statement like that and get away with it.

"Go check in, then we'll talk more in the private lounge inside the international terminal."

I know waiting until we're in more secure quarters makes sense, but the rational part of my brain has taken a back seat to the impetuous man inside me. The man who wants to rush in with guns blazing and no backup plan. Even though I don't have a gun on me at the moment and won't have one for the foreseeable future.

The check-in line is too fucking long.

The agent is too fucking slow.

The people surrounding me are too fucking annoying.

"Look, I know you're worried about her, but she said she needs evacuation from the country. Not that she's taking heavy fire and about to be bombarded by cruise missiles. If you don't chill the fuck out, Silas will leave your ass here, and you know it. If you can't take the heat of this mission, you need to bow out on your own. Don't put all our lives plus hers on the line because you can't control your emotions." Blake keeps his voice low and controlled, but his aggravation simmers just below the surface.

He's right, and I know he's only looking out for me. I never would've dared to approach another case with this train of thought. Rash decisions and tunnel vision put my team in even more risk of danger... or worse. They have enough at stake as it is. I take a deep breath and slowly release it, letting the stress leave my mind at the same time. With my thoughts clearer and my attention better focused on the tasks we have to accomplish, I turn to Blake, the man who's been my best friend for more years than I can remember.

"Thanks, man. I appreciate your kicking my ass and making me deal with the problem at hand."

"That's what friends are for, Roman. I know this is more personal than any other mission you've ever had, but that's exactly why you always have to keep a clear head. Regardless of how unnatural that is for you."

Spoken like a true smartass. But his infusion of humor works, making us both burst out in laughter.

We get through security and find the lounge without a hitch then settle into a private corner with drinks in hand.

"Rafael Cruz made his billions from buying stock in companies until he had enough shares to influence the overall direction. Sometimes, he springs hostile takeovers on companies. His portfolio is vast—the more he makes, the more he invests into both upcoming and existing companies. He's involved in such varied industries, it's hard to find a common theme." Silas stops to sip his vodka.

"But you found one, didn't you?" I know Silas well enough to know he wouldn't bring up a specific topic without a good reason.

"I think so. They built Dubai to be a tourist destination because the sheik who owns it realized oil production can last only for so long. It'll eventually run out, and he didn't want his country dependent on a single source of income to sustain them. Mr. Cruz has recently started investing in multiple oil conglomerates that all directly compete with that very sheik. In fact, some of his investments even compete with one another.

"The working theory is Cruz's company is trying to gain the maximum number of shares for each company under the radar. If he succeeds, he'll ultimately combine them into one company that makes him the biggest oil tycoon in the world. Imagine if the majority of the world had to get their supply from either Cruz or Russia. The boys at Langley are working on pulling the documentation to put the puzzle pieces together."

"Russia because it's a state-owned oil company, right?"

"Exactly. And Saudi Arabia's main production company recently went public. They're the most profitable company in the world. A Westerner taking over that business would provoke a lot of people in that part of the world."

"It definitely would. If news of that reached the general public, there would be riots in the street and lynch mobs out for his head. I'll call my dad when we land and ask if he's heard anything about someone making a quiet takeover bid for the world's oil. The time difference between Dubai and South Africa is only two hours." All I can see is Tawnee in the middle of that chaos, with angry men not caring if she is to blame or not. She'll be guilty by association, and they'll kill her because of him.

"What does your dad do?" Nick asks.

"He's the head chemist for the largest oil production company in South Africa. He moved there a couple of years ago to take over as the leader of his division. Since he's in senior management, he may be privy to information about potential mergers or acquisitions, but I doubt it. That information is usually reserved for the CEO and the board of directors to avoid massive stock dumps and insider information violations.

"But what we do know is time is of the essence. Silas, did you find out anything about the assassination attempt she mentioned in her message?"

"The oil shares piece is a working assumption. We don't have concrete evidence of that yet. As far as the message, my sources on the ground relayed information about a car chase that ended in a wreck. By the time the authorities arrived on the scene, the other vehicles involved had fled. They originally listed it as a hit-and-run, but they noted suspicious events surrounding it.

Since then, the traffic camera feeds have been scrubbed, and any evidence has disappeared." Silas raises one eyebrow, conveying his distrust without a word.

"Scrubbed from inside Dubai?" They're not known for their dishonesty in state affairs, so that information shocks me.

"No, they were hacked from outside their network. Their computer forensics department is working on tracing the hack, but the sophisticated method is taking time to sort out. They're willing to work with us—to an extent. Remember, we're foreigners, but we're still expected to abide by their rules and their laws. They're lenient with tourists, but only to a certain point. But we're not entering their country simply as tourists, so don't expect to be treated as well as their guests would be."

"So, they know we're coming in an official capacity and will watch us closer?" Nick asks.

"Exactly."

Once we've mulled over all the details we currently have until we can recite them in our sleep, I stroll over to the bar and have a seat alone. After I've been lost in my own thoughts for about an hour, Silas slides onto the bar stool next to me and orders a double shot of vodka. He doesn't say anything for a couple of minutes, which I appreciate, but I know it's coming. Words of wisdom from the great Silas Steele.

"How are you holding up, Roman?"

"On the one hand, I'm okay. On the other, waiting is killing me. I'm not a patient man. You know that."

"I do. And I know all too well how being impatient can get you hurt or killed. Or worse, get someone else hurt or killed. You don't want that on your conscience. Trust me."

All I can do is nod, showing I understand what he's telling me. He's worked countless missions, putting his spies in harm's way every day. I have no doubt Silas felt terrible when his previous asset's cover was blown, but Tawnee is more than a resource to me.

"Have you stopped to consider why she contacted you after all this time? Why not someone else in Cruz's organization? He has more than one team. Tawnee doesn't work nonstop around the clock. So why bring you into the equation, halfway around the world, when she knows you can't get there immediately?"

"No. I haven't stepped back and looked at the entire situation as an outsider, honestly. I saw the message, my world blew up, and I started picking up the pieces without asking all the right questions. Do you think they coerced her into it? Are we walking into a trap? And, if so, what could they possibly want from us?" The wheels in my mind are turning at breakneck speed now. I'm not asking all the right questions or considering the various possibilities.

"Stop beating yourself up. If I got the same message from Kira, I'd find a way to teleport across the galaxy to reach her. These are just some of the questions I'm asking after sitting back and examining the entire situation. Something isn't adding up for me, and I think that variable is one that's still unknown. I'm not blaming you for not seeing it because I don't think it's been revealed to any of us yet."

"What fun would it be to have all the answers upfront and know exactly what to do when we arrive?" I finish off my whiskey with one large gulp and stand. "Our flight is about to board. I can't wait to spend eighteen hours in the air with you. We'll have some great bonding time."

"Don't sit close to me." He throws back his shot and walks over to the others to get his carry-on luggage.

I'm close on his heels, laughing at his dry sense of humor and his way with words. It's good to have friends to keep me grounded regardless of the chaos around me. I have a strong feeling I'll need exactly that kind of friend once the wheels touch down on the tarmac in Dubai. When the shit hits the fan and we're scorching up the roads to find Tawnee—wherever she is.

We board the flight and take our seats in the first-class section. The enclosed window suite gives me plenty of privacy to sleep on the long haul, but I also have way too much time to think. Too many images of what could possibly happen to Tawnee before I reach her. Too many visions of her caught in the crossfire between some underhanded, unscrupulous businessman and his enemies. She'll do her job and defend him with her life—and he'll, no doubt, allow it. I've never met the man, but I already don't like him.

My thoughts drift to the last time I saw Tawnee and what our fight was truly about. The topic that kicked off that exact conflict isn't significant, but the underlying resentment that kept our relationship on edge is all on me. That's one part of the story I've never admitted to Blake, though he knows the truth anyway. It's not hard to figure out, considering how well he knows me. My reluctance to commit fully to her—to be a couple—created a sore spot between us that never healed.

Her words during that confrontation have haunted me since the day she left.

"Roman, do you want to be with me or not?" She met my gaze without hesitation, but then, that was just Tawnee in a nutshell. She stood her ground and never backed down from a fight.

"If I didn't want to be with you, I wouldn't be."

"Do you really think that answer is sufficient?" She put her hands on her hips and glared at me, her eyes narrowed and her normally full lips pulled into a tight line.

"It's the truth. What more do you need? Our relationship is self-explanatory. We're together, so that means we each want to be with the other."

Her hands flew to her forehead then her fingers started kneading her temples. She worked to remain calm, but the anger and frustration were building inside her like a volcano about to explode. "You have about thirty seconds to make this right, Roman. I'm not exaggerating, and I'm not being overly emotional."

"I don't know how you expect me to make it right. I don't even know what's wrong. We have a great relationship, sweets. What more do you want from me?"

"Roman, we've been together long enough now that we either move forward together or we should go our separate ways. I'm not some young kid fresh out of college. I know what I want. If you're still on the fence after all this time, tell me now so I'll know what I should do next."

"You know, pushing me into marriage before I'm ready won't work out well for either of us."

"Marriage? You think I'm pushing you into marriage? Why the hell would I want to marry you when you won't even commit to an exclusive relationship with me?"

"What are you talking about? I'm not seeing anyone else."

"Well, isn't that a relief." Her words dripped with sarcasm. "You're still waiting to see if someone better comes along. You've never said you love me. You've never talked about our future—how you see it, what you want, nothing. Apart from when we're literally having sex, we live completely separate lives. Is that all you want from us?"

"Look, I'm sorry, but I don't know what to tell you other than I'm content with our current arrangement. I think it works out well for both of us. We both have independent personalities, and we like our separate space. Why ruin a good thing by changing it now? You know the old saying, 'Don't fix what's not broken.' Well, I'm not broken, so stop trying to fix me."

"I'm not trying to 'fix you' or change you or make you do anything you don't want to do. All I want is for you to man up and finally tell me what it is you want for us—as a couple. For our future. For our relationship. For you and me together. Do you think you can manage that?"

"I don't think of it in those terms, Tawnee. I don't say, 'Roman, in exactly sixteen-and-a-half months, you're going to ask Tawnee to move in with you. Then, exactly five-years-and-nine-months later, you'll ask her to marry you. Then ten-years-eleven-months-and-

twenty-nine-days after that, you'll start thinking about getting married. Then double that time, and you'll start thinking about having kids.' I'm more of a take-it-day-by-day kind of man."

The change in her expression and demeanor was instantaneous. Her face fell and her shoulders drooped. I saw something on her face I'd never seen before—defeat. She'd accepted it and waved the white flag of surrender in that very moment. While I never meant to hurt her, I realized that's exactly what my snide remark did. I confirmed all her suspicions and concerns about me and killed her love for me in the span of a few seconds with careless words. I wanted to take it all back right then—I wanted to drop to my knees and beg her forgiveness.

But I didn't.

I stayed rooted to my spot, hanging on to my pride instead of showing my true feelings.

It's not that I didn't love her; I just assumed she knew.

"Tawnee, look, let's not do this right now. Let's both just calm down, and we can talk about this rationally later."

"There's nothing left to talk about, Roman. You've made your feelings and intentions crystal clear to me now. If nothing else, I do appreciate that, but I can't stay here with you one minute longer. I am calm, and I am rational—so don't expect my decision to change anytime soon."

"What are you talking about—what decision? You're not acting like yourself. Are you on your period or something? Oh fuck. You're not pregnant, are you? I definitely can't handle that shit right now."

Famous last words of a fool.

CHAPTER 2

Tawnee

"Tony, it's been two days since the incident. The report from the local police should be available now. Call them to ask if we can get a copy and see what else you can find out about their investigation. I'm sure there's information they're withholding from the general public, but we need eyes on everything we can get.

"Tabitha, Mr. Cruz's meeting is scheduled for next week, but he can't be late again when it's time to go. You know how he is about punctuality, and it's considered incredibly rude in this culture. They were very gracious about our mishap this week. Map out a new route and note any possible deviations so we're not caught unaware when we're on the move again.

"Carter and Jason, you two comb through the local news, online forums, and the dark web. Investigate anyone who posts or comments about the details. No one has claimed credit for it yet, which leads me to believe there'll be a follow-up attempt.

"John, talk to the head of security about getting the hallway camera feed sent to our secure laptops for extra monitoring."

After giving out the team's marching orders, I walk back into Rafael's royal suite and climb the elegant staircase in the entryway to complete a thorough search of the expansive accommodation for the third time since we got up this morning. We changed hotels and opted for this ultra-lux and uber-secure resort after the failed attempt to grab us, erring on the side of caution, though the manager of the original hotel tried his best to dissuade us from leaving. Having someone of Rafael's stature at a hotel only increases their bragging rights along with the number of people—mostly women—who frequent the bars and restaurants, hoping to run into him accidentally and have him fall madly in love with them at first sight.

If they only knew how many other women have attempted those same tactics and failed miserably.

He may be the world's most eligible bachelor, but he's also extremely discerning in choosing his dates. If there's no chemistry after they serve the main course, he politely thanks her for a lovely evening, excuses himself, and arranges her transportation home. That very scenario has happened more times than I can count. Not that I blame them for trying. He is one fine specimen of a man. At six-foot-four, he's an intimidating figure both inside the boardroom and out. His jet-black hair and dark brown eyes perfectly match his bronzed Latin skin. He turns heads everywhere he goes.

"How do you feel, Raf?" His usually handsome face is scrunched, and he's carefully kneading the back of his neck. "You're still in pain, aren't you?"

His sheepish grin is the only answer I need.

"Some days, I feel more like your assistant than the head of your security. Tabitha already rescheduled your building tour for later next week. The hotel concierge can arrange for a private physician to visit your suite. It's technically been thirty-six hours since the collision. You can't put off an exam any longer. If the doctor thinks you need X-rays or scans, we're going to the hospital, even if I have to taser you to get you there."

"Whatever you say, boss lady." He winks at me, knowing that term riles me up but also knowing I can't stay mad at him for long. "We've been together so long now that I think you know me better than I know myself."

"That's because I do. After the last three years of working for and traveling the world with you, I don't see how you could possibly have any secrets left I don't already know."

"You're my personal stalker. I kind of like that, Tawnee. Makes you even more mysterious and sexy, if that were at all possible."

"Did you hit your head in the wreck? Maybe I should take you for that CT scan after all."

He playfully bats away my hand when I reach to check his forehead for a fever. "Don't act like you don't know. I tell you all the time—you could wear a burlap sack and still be the most beautiful woman I've ever seen."

"And just like every other time you've said that, I call bull-shit. You've dated Victoria's Secret models. I'm nowhere near their league."

"You have that backward. They're nowhere near yours."

I shake my head at his antics. "You are a shameless flirt, Raf. Do you need a bag of ice for your neck until the doctor arrives?"

"No, I don't think so. I'll just kick back here and relax until then. Thank you, though. I appreciate how well you take care of me."

Though it takes several phone calls and a lot of waiting, the doctor shows up and conducts a thorough exam. With no pressing business meetings this week, Rafael has plenty of time to rest and recuperate. Tony talked to the local police depart-ment, but their report isn't available yet—at least, not for us anyway. Without the additional information it contains, there's not much we can do at this time of day, other than finally relax and have a team dinner on the expansive balcony of Raf's royal suite.

The worried expressions on everyone's faces match my somber mood. What happened this week was much too close for comfort, and we're in a part of the world where I have no contacts available to help me out of a jam. Whoever is behind this and whatever their plans are, this team will have to handle it on our own.

"Penny for your thoughts, Tawnee." Rafael catches me staring into my wineglass.

"My thoughts are worth much more than that." My smile is as normal as possible under the circumstances. I don't want to add to the apprehension I already feel from the group.

"You know I'm good for it—however much you charge." He's like a dog with a bone.

"I'm thinking we should have your suite's assigned butlers clear the table now so you can get some rest after a very long and trying day. We'll all feel more refreshed in the morning."

"If you say so. That's not what you were thinking, but you're not wrong."

The entire security team stays in his suite while the staff cleans off the table and resets everything to perfection, watching every movement like a hawk stalking some unsuspecting prey. I'm not willing to trust anyone outside our circle at this point in the game. There are way too many variables still unknown. When the last of the waitstaff leaves the room, the rest of us follow close behind.

"I'll see you in the morning, Raf. But if anything happens tonight, call me immediately, and I'll come right back up here." I'm the last one out the door, hesitant to leave him alone just yet.

"Plan on joining me in my suite for breakfast first thing in the morning. I'll put the order in tonight so it's here on time."

"Okay. Goodnight."

"Goodnight, Tawnee."

~

His request for me to have breakfast with him isn't anything unusual. He hates to eat alone, even when he's in his room away from all the prying eyes.

His request to me *after* breakfast throws me for a loop, though.

"Tawnee, let's go down to the beach and relax. Just you and me—we'll leave the rest of the team here. We both need a break and some time to destress. We have all day to ourselves."

I stop walking, making yet another round after breakfast, and stare at Raf in disbelief. My jaw is slack, and my eyes fly wide open. "You've got to be kidding me right now."

"Not at all. No one will recognize us in bathing suits and T-shirts. They'll expect me to be in an Armani suit, silk shirt, and leather Louboutin dress shoes. I'll wear flip-flops and an ugly Hawaiian shirt with cheap sunglasses."

"As much as I'd love to see you in that get-up—and take pictures of it to blackmail you with later—I wouldn't be very good at my job if I agreed to your crazy request so soon after there was an attempt made on your life." I move closer to where he's sitting on the sofa, staring out the floor-to-ceiling windows at the inviting waters of the Persian Gulf. The people on the beach and in the water below look like ants from this height. But one fact is clear—Rafael is jealous of those ants and their carefree lives. "Talk to me, Raf. What's really going on? You've never mentioned wanting to swim in the ocean or wear Hawaiian shirts and flip-flops before now."

"I've made a lot of mistakes in my life, Tawnee. Some I'd give up every dollar I've made to go back and change, but we both know that can't happen. I've worked more than I've played. I haven't spent enough time with the people who mean the most to me. I've been on plenty of dates, but I've never felt that instant spark or connection with anyone." He turns and looks at me with deep sadness and regret in his eyes. "Except you."

I've never had an occasion to use the word flabbergasted to describe my own feelings and reaction, but now is as good a time as any. I've also never had a problem with using my vocabulary or conveying my thoughts—until now. An invisible tether holds our gazes in place. I'm staring into his gorgeous dark brown eyes, waiting for the punch line to pull us out of this awkward staring contest.

"This must come as a surprise to you, judging by your reaction. Or lack of reaction, I should say. Our flirting started out innocent enough—I used it as an icebreaker to get to know you better as a person, not just as my security officer. But the more time I've spent with you, the more my feelings have changed. Since the day we first met, I've compared every woman I've dated to you. Not one of them measured up to the high standards you set, though, and that's why I haven't kept anyone around."

Nope, this awkward moment will not pass by unnoticed. At all.

"Rafael—"

"Don't say anything yet, Tawnee. I haven't reached this level of success without being able to read people. You've always been the consummate professional, keeping any personal feelings separate from the job I hired you to do. Our relationship has always been one of employer and employee, and you haven't allowed yourself to consider any deviation from that course even though I flirt with you relentlessly. I understand why, and I respect you for it.

"What I'm asking of you is this—search for your true feelings for me, and I think you'll realize they run as deep as my feelings do for you. We've spent a lot of time together and grown to know each other very well. I've fallen in love with you, Tawnee.

I believe you secretly love me too. Don't look at me as your employer. Simply see me as a man."

With our eyes still locked, I sit down on the couch beside him. I'm glad I was standing so close because my knees were about to buckle at any moment. "To be completely honest, I'm not sure I know how to separate my professional and personal life anymore. That has nothing to do with you and all to do with me. I've poured every bit of myself into my business for so long. I don't know if there's anything left of me outside of work."

His eyes soften as he watches me, understanding immediately lighting in them. "He broke your heart, didn't he?"

"Who?" I draw my eyebrows down in confusion for a moment. I'm certain I didn't mention any names. Or, more precisely, a single name.

"The man you loved once. The guy who wasn't man enough to love you in return, not the way you deserved to be loved, anyway."

I'd feel less exposed in a two-piece thong bikini while standing in the center of the Dubai mall than I do fully clothed right now. He wasn't exaggerating when he said he could read people. He sees right through me as if I'm a transparent pane of glass.

"You deserve so much better than that. This week's events opened my eyes to how blasé I've been toward my own safety, even though you've warned me a million times. You know as well as I do, I've always considered the security measures to be overkill. I thought it was more that the insurance company was trying to save the money on my life insurance policy. Now I understand there's much more than money at stake. You may think my change of heart is only because I saw my life flash before my eyes, but what's really happening is I refuse to waste one more minute of hiding what I genuinely feel for you.

"That said, I'm willing to take whatever risks come our way to spend the day with you on the private beach at this ultra-secure resort. Do you have an indemnity waiver I need to sign first?" A sexy smirk covers his face, and his handsomeness strikes me with full force for the first time in the last few years I've known him.

His skin is naturally tanned, blessing him with a natural sun-kissed complexion. Those dark brown eyes and full lips are accentuated by his perfect cheekbones and strong chin. But it's that one dimple on his left cheek that's the finishing touch.

"Sorry. I must have missed something. What indemnity waiver are you talking about?"

"The one that absolves you of any liability when we put on our bathing suits and join the party crowd on the beach. My swimming shorts are calling my name. Did you bring a bathing suit with you?"

"Yes, I always bring a couple since I swim laps at night to get in my exercise."

"It's too bad I never knew that before now." He waggles his eyebrows and smiles seductively at me.

"Even though I have bathing suits with me, we're not going to the beach. I'm sorry, Raf. I appreciate your epiphany about taking your security seriously, but you've got to realize you're not doing that *right now*. Putting yourself out in the open on a very crowded beach is the opposite of being aware of your safety."

"You're right—see, I don't even consider these things because I know you will. We'll take my entire protection detail with us. They can take turns standing guard and playing in the water, so they'll blend in without being miserable in the sun. Just to be clear, I'm going either way, so..."

"Fine, only because I know you will. Then I'd either be forced to drag your ass back inside and cause a huge scene, or I'd have to quit and fly back home."

"You can never leave me, Tawnee, though the whole concept of you dragging my ass back to my bedroom has merit. Now, about that dip in the ocean. I'm going to go change into my bathing suit now, so I suggest you do the same. You'll sweat your ass off in those clothes outside."

With that, he walks off to his bedroom and leaves me on the couch, still searching for the best witty reply—though I come up short even with the extra time to think. Apparently, my only recourse is to give in to his whim and join him since he'll go with or without me. After I inform the rest of the team to join us at Raf's last-minute beach party, I head to my room on the next floor down to put on my bikini and slide a cute cover-up over my head. Dubai is more liberal than the other Arab nations, especially for foreign visitors, but strolling through the hotel wearing a few shreds of fabric held together by dental floss is still frowned upon.

The beach, however, is fair game.

When I walk out of my suite, the others are waiting for me in the hallway near the elevators. I hear Raf talking to them as I approach.

"To be perfectly clear, I'm the one pursuing Tawnee, not the other way around. In fact, the only thing she has agreed to so far is going down to the beach, and that's because I twisted her arm. She would never let me go alone, regardless of the professional cost to her. So, I wanted to be upfront with everyone in the event she agrees to go out with me on a personal level. I wouldn't want anyone to think she behaves in any way other than professional. I'm the one who confessed I'm in love with her. She hasn't admitted to any feelings for me yet, but I hope to rectify that very soon." Rafael's words stop me in my tracks.

It's one thing to have a private discussion with me about this, but quite another to share everything with my team without clearing it with me first. As he said, I haven't agreed to anything, but now everyone who works for me knows much more about my personal life, or potential personal life, or lack of personal life, than I wanted to share.

Yes, technically, he pays them, but they report to me. I'm the one who picked all his detail teams.

"Well, boss, this may surprise you, but we actually have a pool going on when you'd finally break down and ask her out. It's been clear to us for quite a while you've had a thing for Tawnee."

Thanks, Tony. That's exactly what I wanted to hear.

"Is that right?" Raf sounds proud. "In this pool, did anyone have any thoughts on how long it would take Tawnee to agree?"

Now, this, I have to hear. Only, the hallway is now completely quiet except for the nervous shuffling of feet. Then Tony finally opens his big mouth again.

"We pretty much agreed that would happen when hell froze over. Nothing against you, boss. But she's pretty hard-core when it comes to her job, and we didn't think she'd jeopardize it for a potential relationship. That's not really her style."

"Interesting. Well, maybe I should fire her first then ask her out."

The group breaks out in laughter until I turn the corner to join them, then everyone has a sudden coughing fit.

"Very convincing, guys. Not obvious at all." I make it a point to glare at every single one of my team before turning my attention to Raf. "And you. May I have a minute in private?"

I turn and walk back to my room, open the door, and hold it open until he walks inside first.

"How you're still single is such a mystery to me when you're so romantic. 'Fire her then ask her out'? Really?" I roll my eyes and shake my head.

Raf laughs, clearly amused at the circumstances. "Don't blame them, Tawnee. That was my impromptu meeting. Just in case you come to your senses and realize you're as madly in love with me as I am with you, I wanted to avoid the uncomfortable conversation we'd have to have at that time."

"Well, why didn't I think of that? Yes, that makes perfect

sense. So, instead of giving me more than fifteen minutes to absorb everything you said, you thought it was a good idea to have an uncomfortable conversation with the entire team today. Because, why not? We were just in a high-speed car chase then a wreck less than forty-eight hours ago, and now we're all going to the beach together after you announce your feelings toward me to my entire team. Just your average, ordinary vacation troubles."

"Exactly." He has the audacity to be proud of himself.

"Rafael, I really don't appreciate the position you've put me in at all. My personal life is none of their business. Your personal life is their business—to a degree—but you and I are not there yet. I haven't committed to anything more than our current relationship, which is employer and employee, border-line friends. If we progress into anything else, I'll be the one to have the talk with my team. Are we clear?"

"Crystal. But you have to admit one thing."

"And what's that?"

"At least you'd know life with me would never be boring." Rafael's smile crawls across his face, and his eyes twinkle with laughter. He turned what I intended to be somewhat of an insult into a positive.

"Always looking for the silver lining, huh?" I can't help but smile back at him.

"Absolutely, and I usually find it too. Now, let's go—the team is waiting, and they may get the wrong impression of us being in your room alone for so long." He extends his elbow toward me and nods his head toward it. "We have to look like normal tourists, remember?"

"I do remember. I also remember any public display of affection here, even simply holding hands, can result in the police being called on us. I think we've drawn enough attention to ourselves today, don't you?"

"You win this round, Miss Milano. But the next one will be

mine. I guarantee it." His predatory gleam sends shivers down my spine, but I mask my reaction

"I can hardly wait. Can we go now? We're burning daylight in here." I take the designer beach bag Rafael is holding and stuff my towel and sunblock inside before hoisting it onto my shoulder. We rejoin the others in the hall, and I press the down button for the elevator, ready for a couple of hours of relaxing with the ocean waves as my white noise.

Now that the tension is dispelled after Rafael's announcement, we can enjoy the rest of the day in the sun, sand, and surf. Stepping out into the extreme heat takes my breath away at first, but the breeze from the ocean helps me acclimate quickly. Each suite has a private cabana reserved on the beach with a lounging platform that resembles a queen-size bed. The four corners of the frame have gathered curtains, and the top has an optional cover for a shield from the intense Middle Eastern sun.

I set the bag down on the lounger and begin pulling out the contents, specifically the sunblock for my shoulders, when Raf tosses his shirt in my face. Playfully, of course. When I look up at him, I have every intention of hurling an insult his way, but my eyes drop to his perfectly chiseled torso, and whatever thought I had leaves me.

Speechless.

Breathless.

And busted. So very busted.

"You aren't the only one who exercises." I can't see his eyes behind the mirrored frames and the bright sun, but I can feel the blatant satisfaction in them.

My senses finally return, and I grasp the hem of my cover-up and pull it off, leaving it in a heap on the outdoor bed. Now it's my turn to gloat and leave him speechless while he watches me rub the lotion into my skin before heading to the water.

It's been a long time since I've enjoyed flirting with a handsome man.

CHAPTER 3

Roman

"If you come over here one more time, I'll throw you out of this plane, Roman."

"You're not very nice when you first wake up, Blake. Has anyone ever told you that?"

"No, because you're the only one who has ever been brave enough to wake me up several times in one night. We've been traveling for too many hours to count, and we have several more hours to go yet. When they tell us we're coming in for a landing, that's when we'll be there. Not a minute before. So go back to your own suite and leave me alone until we get there."

"Here's what's bothering me." I ignore his loud groan—and when he turns his back to me—and keep talking. "I only received the one message. Nothing from her since then. If she hasn't been captured or killed, why wouldn't she have sent a follow-up message?"

"I understand what you're asking, but we can speculate for the next six hours until we get there and still be wrong. Write down all your questions, see if you find any common threads in them, and we'll be sure to cover all the angles as soon as we can. You're worried about her, I get it, but we can't do anything from here."

"You're right. These questions are just nagging at me. If she was okay, she would have sent a follow-up message. But she hasn't, so that leads me to believe—"

"That she's in a position where she can't send another message. Not that she's dead. Don't even go there, man. But *do* go back to *your own suite* and get some rest so I can too. We'll both need it in a few hours when Silas has us running nonstop."

I move back to my seat and spend the rest of the flight trying to rest, but the questions swirling in my mind make it next to impossible. Now that we've finally landed in Dubai, I realize I'm more keyed up than I was before we took off in Miami. Needless to say, after all the traveling and time difference, it's too late in the evening to canvass the area for information. Just my luck.

We walk into the FIVE Palm Jumeirah hotel, and I'm instantly floored by the opulence and attention to every minute detail. I've heard of Dubai and its growing popularity as the place for tourists, but I never realized the full extent of exactly how much until now. Our rooms are in one of the upper floors with fantastic views of the Persian Gulf, and we're all practically speechless over the lavishness surrounding us when we start to make our way to our rooms.

"And I thought Noah had a nice place," I mumble while we walk down the corridor.

"He does. This place is a completely different world altogether, though. Maybe we should send for the gang so we can all live here instead of Miami." Silas chuckles. He's kidding, but he still appreciates the beauty surrounding us.

"Just wait until tomorrow morning when you're not dying of jet lag and too many hours of flying. You probably won't want to leave the hotel grounds after all. Call Tawnee and tell her to come to us—we'll protect her from here." Blake unlocks his door, steps into the doorway of his room, and drops his suit-case. "Holy hell. Yeah, she needs to come on over and stay here with us."

When I open my door, I understand exactly what he means. Low lighting along the walls creates a soothing atmosphere, instantly sweeping stress away. The sliding glass door beside the bed gives an unobstructed view of the water surrounding the hotel. Silas stops me before I'm able to take in the entire room.

"Roman, I assume she still hasn't answered any of your texts or encrypted messages since we landed?"

"No, and I've been checking every thirty seconds or so. I've sent enough unanswered texts to be considered a stalker at this point."

"I get it, man. Order room service for tonight. Get some rest. We'll meet out here at seven in the morning, grab breakfast, then pay a visit to the local police and see what we can find out. Don't go out on your own and get arrested—the laws are much different here than they are at home."

"That's over the line, Silas. You know I can't promise that at home, much less here." I flash a smile and shrug one shoulder.

"Don't make me have to lock you in your room for the night."

After looking over every square inch of my new home for however long it takes to find Tawnee, I unpack my suitcase and crawl into bed after ordering room service for the evening. I leave the curtains open so the rising sun will wake me, giving me the perfect morning view to set my mood for the day. I can only hope these small, positive touches help settle the sinking feeling in my gut. Tawnee has never ignored texts—even if she only responds to tell me to fuck off. The only way she wouldn't answer me is if…

Like Blake said, I can't let my thoughts go there again. One step at a time.

After enjoying a full four-course meal from the room service menu, I lie back on the bed and start listing all the things we should be doing right now that don't include resting, eating, or sleeping.

The next thing I know, the room is filled with bright sunshine. When I open my eyes, I fling my arm over them as a shield until they adjust. Then I catch a glimpse of the shimmering water outside. The bright blue sky above. The breathtaking view is exactly what I need to encourage me to rush through my morning routine and get dressed to accomplish my goals. First, find Tawnee. Second, take her home with me and keep her there forever. Third, make her fall in love with me again.

When I step out of my room, I'm surprised to find I'm the first one. After I glance at my phone, I realize I'm way ahead of schedule. Sunrise comes much earlier here than at home, one more thing to get used to, but I feel more rested than when we walked off the plane last night. I take a calculated risk and guess Silas is already up and rummaging around in his room while he waits for the rendezvous time, so I knock on his door.

As I expected, he's fully dressed and ready to go when he opens the door.

"A little eager, are we?" He smirks at me but holds the door open wide so I can pass through.

Then I turn to him, ready to get down to business. "You know I am. I was ready to go out and conduct a grid search last night when we got here. I was just thinking, maybe you should try texting her. You know, in case she's ignoring me for some reason but will answer you."

"I've already thought of that and tried. Although I didn't reach the stalker level you did, I did send her a few messages. She hasn't replied to me either, so it's not that she's avoiding you. She's off the grid."

"Is it strange that makes me feel better and worse at the same time?"

"That's a normal reaction—not strange at all. I've been looking into the guy she works for more in-depth this morning. I've already started a file on Mr. Rafael Cruz with some interesting information."

"You didn't sleep at all last night, did you?"

"Not much. I slept too long on the plane to make the flight go by faster, so I couldn't sleep once we got here. Did you know he's one of the richest men on the planet?"

"No, I didn't. I mean, I knew he was some bigwig in the corporate world, but I had no clue he was that wealthy. No offense to her skills, but does it make sense that Tawnee is his head of security?"

"First of all, never say that around her if you want to keep your balls attached to your body. She'll snatch them off and have them stuffed and mounted as fuzzy dice to hang from her rearview mirror. Yes, it makes sense. She's good at what she does, and she has the experience to back up her decisions. That black belt in Brazilian Jiu-Jitsu doesn't hurt either—she knows how to use it to subdue much larger opponents. Plus, she has an efficient and logical approach to coordinating coverage. You underestimate her way too much, and you always have."

I've never really considered it in that light before, so I don't have much of a comeback to deny his assessment of me. I suppose he's correct, though. She obviously impressed one of the richest men in the world enough to nab that high-level job right off the bat. Makes me wonder what Cruz sees in her I didn't. Maybe I've just been wearing blinders where she's concerned without even realizing it.

"You're right. When we worked together for Noah, she was nothing but competent and reliable in every situation. In all honesty, I don't know what's wrong with me, Silas."

"Really? You don't know?" He looks amused, but I'm very serious.

"No, I don't. You think you do?"

"Oh, I know I do. I don't even have to think about it."

"Let's hear it, then. This should be good." I fold my arms over my chest and wait for some enormous revelation about myself.

"You're selfish, self-centered, and take others for granted."

"Selfish and self-centered are the same thing."

"No, they're not. At all. You're selfish because you have no consideration for others. You're self-centered because you only focus on what *you* want or what *you* need, never putting anyone else's needs before your own. On top of that, you expect everyone in your life to keep giving their all for you, while you keep taking but never giving in return. Then you're shocked when they throw up their hands and walk away from you. That combination takes a lot of nerve—or stupidity. Which one is it?"

Fucking hell. The reflection I see in the mirror Silas just thrust in front of my face is not attractive.

Is that really how everyone else sees me?

Is that an accurate description of me?

Deep down, I already know the answer to both of those rhetorical questions. I also know that's exactly what Tawnee thinks of me—because I haven't given her any reason to believe otherwise. Now that I can't hide from the defects in my character, I'm one hundred percent committed to changing them, especially where she's concerned.

"Has anyone ever told you you're a shitty profiler?" I know he's not, but I have to throw some kind of barb back at him.

"Nope. Never. I'm an excellent profiler, and everyone at the agency knows it. In fact, you should ask around and find out for yourself. It'll do you good." He quirks one eyebrow and nods toward my tightly crossed arms. "Even your body language says you're closed off. I knew you wouldn't accept what I had to say before I even said it. You don't fool me for one second, Roman."

"For argument's sake, let's say you're right about me. How would I go about fixing those character flaws?"

"Well, you could always say, 'What would Roman normally

do in this situation?', then do the exact opposite. Or you could just stop and consider Tawnee's feelings for once in your fucking life. You're a grown man—start acting like it, for fuck's sake. I shouldn't have to tell you how to keep your girlfriend happy."

"Ouch."

"Tough love. You need more of it, along with a good, swift kick in the ass. Let's get the others and go to eat breakfast. I've made reservations for a late lunch at the Burj Al Arab Jumeirah."

"What's that? I thought we were going to the police?"

"We were, until I found out that Rafael Cruz is checked in at the only hotel in Dubai nicer than this one. He's staying in one of the royal suites at that exclusive resort. There are also a few regular rooms are reserved under his company name, so we'll go over there and see what we can find out first. Without reserving a room, we can't even get on the grounds. The only way around that is to have reservations at one of their restaurants."

Silas's evaluation of me sticks in my mind, clawing at my sanity and making me second-guess my every move. But I can't deny what he said is true. Several times over breakfast, I wanted to rush the other men through their meals so we could get on the road. But I refrained from saying anything and simply listened to them while I drank another cup of coffee.

"Silas, you've been married for a couple years now. Can we expect to hear the pitter-patter of little Silas or Kira feet anytime soon?" Nick asks. He's been on Silas for the last year to give Amber, Silas's adopted daughter, a little brother or sister.

"You know, you're the sole reason why Amber asks us about that every single day now. Kira and I talked before I left to come here, and we've decided it's time. When I get back, we'll start practicing more." We all laugh, knowing exactly what he means. "When are you going to settle down, Blake?"

"Never."

"You're not allowed to hang around with Roman anymore. He's a bad influence on you."

"I don't know, Silas. I've been seeing this girl, but I'm hesitant to make our relationship a big deal. We're still taking it slow right now, nothing exclusive." Blake suddenly finds his fork very interesting.

"Do you love her?"

"I'm not sure."

"If you found out she'd been seeing some other guy while you've been away, how would that make you feel?" Silas already knows the answer. I can see it in his eyes.

Blake shrugs but doesn't look up.

"What if she told you she was in love with him and didn't want to see you anymore? What if she was letting him do everything to her body that you do?" Silas keeps pressing those buttons.

"I'd hunt him down and kill him." Blake pins Silas with an intense, murderous gaze.

Silas laughs in his face. "That's what I thought. You need to reevaluate those feelings you claim not to have before it's too late, my friend."

Too bad Silas didn't give me that exact advice three years ago. But I'm not sure I would have listened to him anyway.

CHAPTER 4

Tawnee

"Tawnee, are you awake?" If the pounding on my door wasn't loud enough to wake me, the yelling of my name from the hallway would have been. Fortunately, I've been up for quite a while already, trying to recall every detail about the incident without the police report as a reference.

We didn't stay on the beach for very long earlier this morning because I couldn't shake the feeling of being watched. When we adjourned to our rooms, I took a few hours of much-needed time off—and had an extremely productive nap.

I jerk the door open and face Rafael. He's dressed in his casual yet expensive attire, but he's carrying the same designer bag we used at the beach earlier. "Why are you out of your room without an escort?" I cross my arms and tap my foot while waiting for what I already know is an unacceptable answer.

"We're in the most secure hotel in the entire Middle East. This place is sitting on its own private island with a closed bridge manned by private security guards. They have a fleet of

Rolls-Royces that pick guests up at the gate and drop them off at the front door. Who do you think can get me in here?"

"Anyone with the means to hire hitmen, Raf. You're not the only man in the world with money and who stays in fancy hotels when he travels. Whoever was behind that chase could have reserved rooms here too. You're making my job impossible. I mean, how am I supposed to get another security job if you get killed in 'the world's only seven-star hotel' on my watch?"

"Fooled you. Tony escorted me down, checked out the hallway, found no assassins, so I sent him back upstairs. But I promise I'll call you from my room next time I decide to venture out of my room… into the hallway… only one floor down from my suite."

"Since you're already here, come on in." I open the door wider to let him pass through. "What's on your mind?"

"First, I actually did try to call your cell a couple of times, but you didn't answer. You always answer, so that alone concerned me enough to rush down the flight of stairs to check on you." He takes a seat on the couch, his eyes never straying from mine. "Were you avoiding me?"

"You know better than that. With all the excitement, I didn't realize it until last night, but my phone is missing. Then with the impromptu beach excursion, I forgot to tell you. It must be in the rental car—maybe it fell under the seat when we crashed. I've looked everywhere else for it, and I know for a fact that I didn't take it to the beach with me. I was just about to call the wrecker service and ask them to look inside the car."

"Let me talk to them. Even though this area is more tolerant of women than others in this region, there are still plenty of prejudices. I don't think a wrecker driver would appreciate you asking him to search the car for your lost cell phone. In fact, that may ensure you never get it back. We won't be here long enough to have another one shipped. I guess you'll just have to stay close to me at all times. You can even move to my suite—it has three bedrooms."

"Yes, I guess I could do that. Or, here's a novel idea, you could just use the phone in your room to call me when I'm in my room."

He smiles, his dark eyes sparkling with dangerous flirtation. Dangerous to me, that is. "I like my idea much better. You can protect my body with yours much easier if we're in the same suite."

"If you don't open your door to strangers or go wandering around the hotel alone, we won't have to worry about that, will we?"

"You never know, Tawnee. Anything is possible. We certainly didn't think we'd be chased and nearly nabbed this week, did we?"

"Actually, I always consider that it is a very real possibility. That's exactly why I was watching our surroundings so closely. Now, did you come down here just to try to convince me to move into your suite with you?"

"No, that wasn't why I came down here at all. I just now had that brilliant idea. The reason I've been trying to call you is to take you to the restaurant in the lobby for a nice lunch, then we can spend the rest of the day on the beach together. This morning was perfect. I haven't felt that relaxed in a long time, even though you saw ghosts everywhere. Since Tabitha rescheduled my meeting for later next week, we're free to do whatever we want to until then. What do you say?"

"Well, you are my boss, Raf, and it's my responsibility to make sure you're protected at all times. If you're on the beach, I'll be on the beach with you, along with several members of the team to keep an eye on the perimeter. But grabbing lunch then spending the rest of the afternoon in and around that crisp blue water sounds like heaven on earth. Give me a minute to change clothes and alert the guys then we can head down to the restaurant."

"I'll call Tony so he can alert the rest of the team to meet us downstairs. You just put your bathing suit on under that dress so we can start doing as little as possible as soon as possible."

~

"I'M NOT EATING AGAIN TODAY. MY GOD, I'M SO STUFFED NOW I can barely move. You are a terrible influence on me." I plop down on the lounger in our cabana, ready to take another nap after the feast we just enjoyed.

"Au contraire, my love. I'm not a bad enough influence on you—yet. I'm working on it, though."

"Just lie down in the hot Dubai sun and shrivel up like a prune in silence, please."

He chuckles beside me. "Are you going to relax this time so we can enjoy it?"

"Yes, if you'll behave and not try to swim up and down the coast alone."

"Done. I'm staying right here beside you. I'm not quite up for the Iron Man today."

"How does your neck feel now?" I glance over at Raf as he stretches out beside me in the beach cabana, his bronzed skin already darkening in the sun.

"A little sore. Maybe you should massage it for me and make it feel better." A smile plays on his lips, though he tries to hide it.

"Or maybe I should make you an appointment with the spa and let the professionals handle that for you."

"I'm positive I would feel much better if you rubbed it instead of someone I don't know."

My thoughts immediately stray directly where they shouldn't—ever—especially not about my boss. Nevertheless, I don't believe for one second that we're still talking about rubbing his *neck* at the moment.

"I'll call the doctor again and have him give you a hand sooner than expected. If you're still in pain, he should make sure nothing else is going on—even if that means a trip to the hospital."

"Nothing else is going on, *that's* the whole problem." Now he does smile, and his white teeth glimmer against his tanned skin. "I'm trying to fix that little oversight, if you'd just let me."

"Excuse me, sir. I'm so sorry to disturb you." The hotel concierge appears next to the cabana, waiting for Rafael to acknowledge him before continuing.

Raf opens his eyes and sits up when he sees the man is wearing a hotel uniform and name tag. "No trouble at all, Ahmed. What can I do for you?"

"There are four gentlemen at the beach entry gate who claim they urgently need to speak with you. They claim to be acquaintances of Miss Milano." His eyes momentarily skim over to mine.

"What are their names, Ahmed? Do you know?" Four men are here to see me? That's not ominous at all.

"Yes, ma'am. Their names are Silas Steele, Nick Tucker, Blake Mills, and Roman Scott." Ahmed reads the list from a piece of paper in his hand, then waits for instructions from us.

Since they aren't guests of this hotel, they're not allowed on the grounds without specific reservations for the restaurants or spa. But, I'm beyond shocked and concerned. What the hell are those guys doing here?

"Rafael, I know them. I used to work with all of them in Miami. If you don't mind, I'd appreciate your giving permission for them to join us. Something must be terribly wrong for them to be here, asking to see you."

"By all means. As long as you know them, they are welcome to join us. Ahmed, please show them to our cabana when they arrive. Thank you." When Ahmed walks away, Raf turns his attention to me. "What do you think all this is about?"

"I have no idea why they would be here. Miami is a long way from here, and there's an eight-hour time difference on top of that. Combined with what happened a couple of days ago, their arrival in Dubai is more than a mere coincidence."

"How would they have found us? It's not as if this hotel would give out customer information."

"They have the skills and means to get that information without calling the hotel. How they found us doesn't concern me as much as why they want to find us. Something big must be happening. We may need to cut this trip short and get you out of here on zero notice."

"I'm sorry, love, but that's not happening. If I don't see this through now, it'll never happen. The sellers weren't offended with the first change of plans because they're well aware most of the people here drive like a bat out of hell. But if I bail on them and leave the country, they'll never speak to me again."

"It really isn't my place to say this, but because I genuinely care about your safety, I feel like I should. Raf, you have more than enough money. Is closing this real estate deal really worth risking your life over?"

He pulls my hand to his mouth and kisses the back of it. "Thank you for worrying about me. I know you take your work very seriously, but I also know I'm more than only a job to you. But there's something you should know by now, Tawnee. There's no such thing as having enough money. Besides, I also trust that you'll keep me safe."

"You are an impossible man."

"Impossible to resist? Impossible to forget? Impossible not to love? There are so many possibilities to finish that thought. Which did you mean?"

"Rafael, I've worked for you for nearly three years now. If

there's one thing you know about me, it's that I say exactly what I mean."

He laughs and nods. "This, I do know. Absolutely." He pauses for a moment, looking at me with a thoughtful expression, and part of me wishes I could read his mind. Then he lifts his knuckles and skims them over my cheek. "You're so beautiful. Your black hair shimmers in the sun. Your deep hazel eyes both captivate me and see straight through me. For the longest time now, I've been dying to kiss your luscious lips just to know how you taste. And, for the record, the more you blush like that, the more I'll tell you exactly what I'm thinking. That fact that you have no idea how fucking sexy you are makes you even more special."

Ahmed clears his throat from behind us, saving me from trying to come up with a reply. Rafael casually turns to greet his guests while I slide off the end of the lounger to say hello to my friends. Then I stop dead in my tracks when I see Roman's face, even though I knew he was on his way in. The red creeping up his neck to his face isn't because of the sun. His hands are curled into tight fists at his sides. His eyes narrow, crinkling at the edges as they draw tighter and tighter. His teeth are clenched so hard, I can see the muscles jumping in his jaw.

After three years apart—because of his bullshit—he has the nerve to show up here and glare at me like that?

I don't fucking think so.

When I see Silas, Nick, and Blake, I ignore Roman and rush to hug the other men. I haven't seen them in three long years either, and I'm genuinely happy they're here.

"Silas, what are you doing here? It's hardly a coincidence that we're in the Middle East at the exact same time."

"It's not a coincidence at all, Tawnee." Silas looks over at Roman, who still hasn't spoken to me, before cutting his eyes back to me. The other men exchange curious glances—confusion, shock, relief, lots of questions—but no one says anything.

"Roman received a coded message from you on our secure system. It said you needed immediate extraction from the country because of an assassination attempt."

"What? Are you joking? I haven't used that system in three years. That message wasn't from me."

All eyes shift to Roman as we wait for him to further explain this mystery message.

"What? Why are you looking at me? I showed you the message—I sure as hell didn't send it to myself."

"Oh shit." I close my eyes and mentally berate myself for my stupidity. "We had an incident a couple of days ago that resulted in a wreck. There was also an altercation and a lot of commotion. My phone has been missing since then, but I just assumed I dropped it in the car while I was fighting off those men. What if one of them took it and cracked the code?"

"Cracked Brad's code? Come on." Roman automatically dismisses my theory. Seems nothing has changed in the last three years.

"Roman, think it through. That's the simplest explanation, no matter how improbable you think it is. We already know someone hacked into Dubai's traffic cameras and deleted all the footage of the wreck. Why couldn't that same someone hack Brad's system?" Silas turns his attention back to me. "Can we finish this conversation somewhere a little more private and a little less exposed to potential sniper fire?"

"Thought you'd never ask."

CHAPTER 5

Roman

Tawnee pulls on a summer dress over her bathing suit then heaves a massive bag onto her shoulder. Not that she's incapable of handling it on her own, but my mom raised me better than to stand by and not offer my help. The rest of the team is busy gathering their personal items and making introductions, so I take the opportunity to get a few minutes alone with Tawnee. When she walks between Silas and me on the way toward the hotel entrance, I grab the straps and slide it off her arm.

"Why do you have such a huge purse, Tawnee?" I chuckle as I turn and walk beside her.

"That's not my purse, Roman. It's Rafael's very expensive designer bag." She shakes her head at me, but I see how she looks down at the ground, trying to hide her smile.

"Rafael carries a purse?" I know exactly what she meant, but I couldn't miss the chance to get a little jab in.

Her laugh bursts free before she can stop it. She turns to look at me and pushes her sunglasses up on top of her head.

Fuck, I've missed those dark hazel eyes—warm golden-brown mixed with olive-green that sparkle and shine with her personality. "No, he doesn't carry a purse. You know better than that. Don't play dumb with me. You forget that I know you too well for you to get away with it."

"No kidding. I can't get away with anything around you. You're worse than Silas." I glance over at her and smile, trying to keep our banter light. My first thought took me back to when she left me, and how stupid I was ever to let her go.

"I'm going to take that as a compliment."

"You should—that's exactly how I meant it. Seems your team falls in line with your lead, following your orders to a T."

She doesn't respond right away, which naturally catches my attention. After a loud sigh, she meets my questioning gaze with a shrug. "You know how some of these macho former commandos are. To them, taking orders from a woman is the equivalent of… carrying a purse."

"So, you've caught shit for having the elite skills and the intense grit needed to be the head of security for one of the wealthiest men in the world? Sounds like they're more threatened by you than anything else."

"It's not everyone—just one or two who have been more challenging than the others. Let's just say I've had to prove that I mean what I say more than once, but they always see it my way sooner or later."

My first instinct is to come to her rescue by taking names and kicking asses of anyone who has disrespected her. But I push those feelings aside because it won't help our situation, and it won't earn me any points with her. If anything, my outburst would make her lose the hard-won respect she's earned so far. However, I am absolutely willing to put those assholes under a microscope and find out every one of their deep, dark secrets.

Jealousy makes men do stupid things, but when their

masculinity is threatened, they can be deadly. That may be just the catalyst one of these guys needs to stage an attempt on their employer, making it appear as if Tawnee was caught in between. Since Tawnee wasn't the one who called me to her rescue, this could be a case of premeditated friendly fire. Maybe we should use this time to kill two birds with one stone—flush out any potential traitors and cement her place of authority.

"Which ones have given you the most grief?" I keep my tone nonchalant and conversational to avoid spooking her.

"Until recently, Tony seemed to be the ringleader. He was Raf's driver long before I came along and thought he could spot a seasoned tail with one glance. We've had a couple of instances occur where that wasn't the case at all, and we narrowly escaped. He resented my input on more defensive driving maneuvers. The last time he disobeyed a direct order, he and I had a 'come to Jesus' meeting, and I ended up telling him it was my way or the highway. He's still with us, so he chose my way, and I haven't had to give him an order twice since then."

Note to self: *Kick Tony's ass.*

"And what about Raf?" I can't keep the sarcasm out of my voice when I say his name. *Raf.* He makes me want to ralph.

Her head jerks in my direction, and I know without a doubt she picked up on the subtle change in my voice. "What about him?"

"What does he say about his security team disobeying your orders?"

She narrows her eyes at me but ultimately decides to leave it alone. For now, anyway. "Rafael offered to fire Tony and let me choose a suitable driver as his replacement. He fully supports me and my abilities to handle his safety—no matter what it takes."

"That must've chapped Tony's ass to hear that."

"I think it made him realize how seriously Rafael took my role in his organization and made Tony appreciate my input more." The words are there, but her tone lacks conviction. She may have believed that at one time, but now she's not so sure. "Wait a minute, do you think one of my own staff is behind this? Like they're staging a coup against me or something?"

"I'm not prepared to accuse anyone on your team of attempted kidnapping, but I also can't vouch for them. Until I've vetted them, I have to view everyone as a suspect."

"And who asked you to vet anyone? You know I appreciate you how you dropped everything at a moment's notice and came running because you thought I was in trouble. But as you can see, I'm not in trouble. I'm fine, and I'm not asking for your help or your interference with my job." She stops walking and confronts me face-to-face.

I'd expect nothing less of her.

"I'm not trying to take over your job, Tawnee. I have a job. The four of us are here for *you*—no one and nothing else. We didn't just come running at a moment's notice. We hopped on the next flight out of Miami and flew halfway around the world. For you. After someone has already chased you and erased the traffic camera footage, do you really think they'll just slink back into the shadows and disappear? Someone hacked into Brad's system and sent an encrypted message to me—and only me—and made it appear to come from you. Only someone who knows you would know to contact me through that app."

A shocked expression passes over her features for half a second before she hides behind her mask again. Her chest rises as she takes a deep breath then she puts her hands on her hips. "You're right. None of this is a coincidence, and I'm clearly not thinking straight. I'm sorry for overreacting—I know you're just trying to help. Thank you, Roman. Your showing up here means more to me than you know."

We begin walking again, though the rest of the clan has nearly caught up with us now. "How have you been? You know, before this week went to hell in a handbasket."

"Fine." She glances in my direction but doesn't make eye contact with me. "I've been very busy, obviously. Rafael travels constantly, and his security team is always with him. We rotate days off, but we're almost always in a different country. We're scheduled to be here for a month before we get to head home and stay there until the end of September. I can't tell you how much I'm looking forward to that long of a break in his schedule."

"You two seem close." Yeah, I had to go there. It's eating me alive. Since the moment I saw her lounging in the ocean-side cabana with him in her barely there bikini, oiled skin, and care-free smile. He doesn't deserve that smile from her.

"We are."

That's it? No elaboration? No explanation? Only a confirmation of what I've already witnessed for myself. They're close.

We reach the entrance to the hotel, and I open the door to let her go in first. "After you." Then I follow her inside the elegantly decorated space.

"Thank you. And I should have said this before—thanks for carrying the man-purse for me. It was a little heavy." She doesn't even try to hide the smug grin this time.

"I have no shame in carrying the man-purse for you. I'd even drive to the store and buy the biggest box of tampons they have if you asked me."

"As always, you're too kind." She pushes the button for the elevator then quickly turns to me. "Oh, I forgot I need the room keycard inside the elevator."

She unzips the bag and starts rifling through the interior pockets while it is still on my shoulder. She's so close to me—her face is so close to mine. All I want to do is press my lips against hers right now. To feel the softness. To taste her one more time. To take back every fucking thing I did and said that ever hurt her.

Instead, I only watch her, unable to tear my eyes away from her face.

Just like my assessment of Rafael being undeserving of her smile, I don't deserve her kiss.

I haven't earned her affection.

Yet.

The others surround us as we wait for the doors to open, carrying on their conversation as usual. Silas asks Rafael about any enemies who feel strongly enough to act on their anger, before urging him to return to the US—apparently not for the first time since Rafael's response is a little terse. "I can't do that, as I explained. My business comes first. That's why I have a security team in place."

Nick is chatting with someone about the details of the wreck and the altercation afterward, asking a million and one questions. Blake has yet another side conversation with the only other woman of the group. The additional security members chime in here and there, adding tidbits of information that may or may not come in useful later. But in the several seconds we all wait for the elevator car to arrive, I feel the unmistakable sensation of angry eyes burning a hole through me.

When I abruptly turn to confront the glare like a man, Tony quickly averts his gaze and suddenly finds the adjacent wall riveting. Undeterred, I continue to stare and wait for him to grow a pair. The elevator doors open, and even though he knows he's being watched, he refuses to make eye contact with me again. We move into the elevator, Tawnee uses her card to access the resident floors, and the doors slide closed.

The silence inside the confined area is conspicuous and uncomfortable—for some. But I use it to my advantage while observing the other members of the security team. Beads of sweat gather on one guy's forehead. Another man shifts awkwardly, unable to stand still from nervous energy. A single glance at Silas, Nick, and Blake confirms my assessment. Their postures are relaxed and calm, and they remain completely still. No fidgeting whatsoever.

When we reach his floor and file out into the hall, Rafael's security team jumps into high gear, sweeping his gigantic royal suite before allowing him to enter.

"Wow, this place has multiple levels. I've never been in a hotel room quite like this one before." I look around the entryway, astounded at the ornate marble stairway leading up to the next story.

"I need ample space to stretch out." Rafael doesn't bother with the common courtesy of looking at me when he speaks to me.

Personally, I think he's compensating for something with this oversized suite for only one man. He must have a micropenis the size of a Tic Tac.

"Rafael, do you have any business deals in the works with the potential of putting you in harm's way?" Nick asks, getting straight to business as usual.

"My business ventures don't exactly invite new best friends, but I can't think of anyone who would want to hurt me—especially someone with Arab connections. Tony and I have had long discussions about this over the last couple of nights, going through all my recent acquisitions. But nothing has stood out to either of us so far."

"We need to review that information as well. There may be names on that list of business associates we recognize." I appreciate how Nick doesn't really ask for what he wants. He just says how it'll be, and that's the end of the story.

"Absolutely, we can arrange that right away. Any help you can give is very much appreciated. Where are you staying?"

Nick gives the name of our hotel then goes into full agent mode, talking with Rafael about hotel security, his security team, and a barrage of other questions. Silas and Blake join in when the rest of the security team rejoins us, and we're finally able to enter the main sitting area. While they're busy talking, I take advantage of the opportunity to steal some time with Tawnee.

"Which way is your bedroom?" I pat the side of the beach bag I'm still carrying.

"My suite is on the next floor down. I'm not staying in the same room as Rafael."

"Do you want to head downstairs to your room and change? I'll escort you." I gesture toward the door with my head, hiding my satisfaction at knowing she has her own room.

"Why would you assume I need an escort to my room?" She pierces me with her angry eyes as they narrow at the corners.

I cock my head to the side and draw my eyebrows down, trying to find the words to answer her. "Tawnee, I didn't mean it like that. I saw your face when Nick started questioning Rafael, and I know there's something you haven't told anyone yet. I thought maybe you wanted to talk about it in private."

She folds her arms over her chest, shakes her head, and rolls her eyes at me. "You know me too damn well, Roman Scott."

"Apparently not well enough to know why you're withholding vital information when you know how dangerous that is."

"Lower your voice, Roman."

"You're right—you know how pissed Silas will be when he finds out you haven't said anything about it yet. But I'm the one he'll take it out on. I suggest you come clean to me first, so I can help mitigate the damage."

"Fine, but only because I want to get out of this bathing suit and into real clothes. Come with me." She steps forward into the room and gets everyone's attention. "Roman and I will be back in a few minutes."

Rafael doesn't appear pleased at all with her announcement, but Tony looks downright pissed off.

CHAPTER 6

Tawnee

My thoughts and feelings are all over the place when Roman and I step outside of Rafael's suite. Seeing Roman again immediately erased the three years we've spent apart, and I feel as if I'm right back at the moment when we split up. I mentally force my thoughts back to the present several times, trying to leave old memories and unresolved feelings in the past where they belong. We're in the middle of the most dangerous situation of my entire life, not to mention my career, and I'm distracted by a former flame like a foolish schoolgirl.

If anyone on my team knew how their head of security reacted when faced with a hostile opponent from her past, they'd band together and have me committed for losing my mind.

I wouldn't be able to blame them either.

This behavior isn't like me at all.

"Man, this hotel is so far out of my league, I'm afraid to even ask how much they charge per night."

"Well, Rafael's room is obviously more upscale than the rest of ours. His is around twenty-grand per night. Mine is much more economical at almost ten thousand a night."

Roman stops walking and gawks at me for a few seconds. "You're shitting me."

"Not at all." I can't help but laugh at that typical Roman response.

"You're talking US dollars, right? Not pesos or some fucking obscure denomination that equates to a hundred dollars a night." Roman pushes the elevator button, and we wait for the car to arrive.

"US dollars, yes."

"And you're here for how long?"

"A month." We step inside the elevator and move to opposite sides.

"Fuck me. I've never known anyone that rich before. Seriously, how do you amass that much wealth without being involved in some seriously shady shit?" While I'm almost positive Roman didn't mean that as a direct insult to Raf, I still feel the need to defend my employer and friend.

"I'm sure that's true for a lot of people, but Rafael made his money by learning the stock market inside and out, watching the signs, and getting in on the ground floor of stocks that paid huge dividends when the company took off. The more he made, the more he invested in his vision. It took years of hard work, losing large sums of money, and facing almost certain bankruptcy before he turned it all around. But that wasn't by doing anything illegal. He took a long, hard look at himself and his missteps, then he never made those mistakes again."

Roman simply watches me, his blue-gray eyes assessing my body language while he processes all the information I just dumped in his lap. But it's the intimate sensation his eyes evoke that rattles me to the core. The doors slide open and I step out of the elevator first, but I can feel Roman hot on my heels. The arcs of electricity are still there when we're near each other—regardless of how inconvenient or unwanted they are. One thing our relationship never lacked was sexual chemistry. Even now, my senses have kicked into overdrive from his closeness, and all my nerve endings are firing relentlessly.

It's as if my body craves him on a purely carnal level, and there's not a damn thing I can do to stop it.

My hand shakes when I lift the room key to open the door. As I should have expected, it doesn't work when I first attempt to open the door. It also refuses on the second try. After the third time, now I'm pissed off at the door, at Roman, and at the world. All for no reason other than I've allowed this man to affect me to the point I can't even open a fucking door.

Roman's hand slowly moves toward mine. I feel his chest barely brush my back, but the contact is enough to send chills down my spine.

"Let me try. Probably just needs an easy touch."

His mouth is too close when he speaks. The deep timbre of his voice combined with the feel of his lips brushing against the shell of my ear nearly makes my knees buckle underneath me. His fingers slide across my hand until they reach the room key.

All while I remain as still as a statue because I can't fucking move. Not that I'd ever admit this to him, but I'm equally afraid of brushing against him more... and not being close enough to him. My entire body is on fire in the best way—and this is a sensation I haven't felt since I was last with him. It's been three years since I've felt this alive.

He takes the card from me and tries it.

Naturally, it opens the first time for him.

"Oh, look, it opened for you. I warmed it up for you." I've got to dispel the mounting tension inside me with a little humor before I whirl around and mount *him* right here in the hallway.

"You certainly did." His voice is too low... too close... too intimate. "From the first second I saw you in that itty-bitty hot black bikini on the beach." He steps around me and holds the door open. The desire I see in his eyes not only matches mine, but reaches out and grabs me by the throat, making it impossible for me to say anything witty in return.

When I finally step across the threshold, he closes the door behind me but motions for me to stay put. Much like the security team did for Raf's safety, Roman silently moves through my suite, checking every possible hiding place for potential intruders.

"All clear, sweets. I thought I'd read this hotel had complimentary butler service to cater to your every need—even unlocking your doors for you."

The half-second hesitation in answering is only because I haven't been called "sweets" in so long, it hit me like a blast from the past. That was always his pet name for me. "Yes, they normally do. But for obvious security reasons, we declined the service. We like to know exactly who has access to our rooms at all times."

"I concur—I'd like to know who has access to your room at all times too. Let's make a list right now." He smiles from ear to ear, so proud of his little funny.

"You know my rule on that, Roman. It doesn't matter which hotel we stay in; I only allow them to make one key for my room, and I know where it is at all times. That way, if it's ever missing, I know not to return to the room alone, and I'll change rooms for added measure."

"Yes, I do know you—better than anyone else does. Want to tell me what you're hiding now? I have a sinking feeling I'll beat Silas to the punch and go ballistic before he even has the chance."

"I'm going to shower and get dressed before we have this conversation. But I will say one thing about it and leave you to ruminate on it."

"What's that?"

"You have good intuition. You should go with it."

"Fuck, Tawnee. I fucking knew it." He drops his chin to his chest and stares at the floor, keeping his hotheaded temper under wraps. He's trying to, at least.

I've got to give him credit for that—the old Roman would fly off the handle and pop off with something smartass. Then we'd end up in a huge argument because I'm every bit as stubborn as he is.

"You have a few minutes to digest it and come to terms with the terrible unknown, then we can speak calmly about it."

He nods, not making eye contact, but also not destroying the room in a fit of rage.

Baby steps.

"Is there any beer in the fridge? I'll probably need twelve or thirteen to get through this."

That makes me smile. "Yes, as a matter of fact, there's a twelve-pack in there. Don't tell anyone, though—I don't normally share my beer."

He finally looks up at me again, and what I see in his eyes makes my heart skip a beat. Here I thought it was anger simmering just below his skin, waiting for the right moment to unleash hell on earth, when it was essentially deep-rooted fear he was fighting to control. Fear for me.

"You'd better call down and have another twelve-pack delivered before you're finished with your shower if you plan to drink any." The slight upturn of his lips betrays his halfhearted sarcastic jab.

"I'm not worried about it. I mean, technically, it's almost considered contraband here. But I have my sources if we need more."

"It's the butler you dismissed, isn't it? He's your beer source."

"Damn, you really do know me too well." I point toward the kitchen area. "Help yourself. There are snacks in there too."

I leave him to rummage through the suite and find whatever

he wants while I head toward the master bedroom. When I'm standing under the hot water in the massive shower, my thoughts once again return to the problems in our relationship instead of focusing on the more pressing issue at hand. Since those thoughts won't leave me, I let them run rampant to get it out of my system so I can do my job.

His last words to me the day we broke up were to ask if I was either on my period or pregnant since the only reason for my outburst must have been hormone-related. I've never wanted to shoot someone before or after that event—but the fleeting thought was there. In my military and security careers, I've been required to shoot, but those instances were all about self-preservation and nothing related to revenge. In the heat of the moment with Roman, I finally understood the meaning of "crime of passion." Questioning my sanity and what I was possibly capable of doing haunted me for months after that encounter.

But it forced me to do a lot of soul-searching and being entirely honest with myself. The reason I reacted so strongly— and borderline violently—was because his flippant response to my legitimate heartbreak confirmed the facts I'd chosen to ignore for far too long. I loved him much more than he loved me, and that made me feel much too vulnerable and nowhere near good enough for him. His player days weren't far enough in his past to satisfy me, and his commitment phobia only rein-forced the thoughts that constantly plagued me in those days. I couldn't shake the notion he was always waiting for someone better to come along... that I was only his "Miss Right Now" instead of his "Miss Right Forever."

Over the last three years, I've tried persistently to avoid comparing Roman and Rafael in any way. But there's no way around it. The stark differences are there in my face every day. One of the reasons I've been so loyal to Raf, even when he makes outrageous demands—such as going to the beach so soon after a deadly threat—is because of how well he treats me. Before he shocked me by professing his feelings for me, I knew the deep-rooted respect between us was mutual. I felt it, saw it, and we both appreciated it, never taking it for granted.

I've never felt as if my heart were in danger of being shattered into a million pieces with Rafael. With Roman, I waited for the other shoe to drop every day. Every time Roman started a conversation with the dreaded phrase, "We need to talk," I just knew it was to tell me he'd fallen in love with someone else. When Rafael says we need to talk, I feel no qualms about the unknown topic. The understanding that whatever we're facing, we'll face it together, is simply ingrained in our working relationship.

Until today, our relationship has been strictly platonic with only harmless flirting and innocent teasing. The line we crossed today put us in an all-new territory, and I'm not sure how to handle it. Roman showing up right at that moment only complicates the situation further, though my rational mind knows that's silly. It has been three years, for crying out loud. He shouldn't still affect me like this.

With my eyes closed and my head leaned back, I drop my hands to my sides and let the pouring water from the rain-like shower head rinse the conditioner out of my hair. My heart is racing, and I can barely catch my breath. When I saw Roman on the beach, looking at me with his dangerous and feral expression, the flush I felt had nothing to do with the temperature outside and everything to do with the desire that immediately engulfed me. He looked delicious enough to eat in his dress slacks, button-down shirt, and blazer.

The man I used to know thought dressing up meant wearing jeans with no visible holes in them. Back then, if I'd asked him to wear what the rest of the world considered dress clothes on the beach, I'd be in a psychiatric facility on a seventy-two-hour hold for a full mental health evaluation. Clothes do not make the man; that idiom, I firmly believe. But can a change in the man's choice of clothing signal a difference in the man himself?

Or am I putting too much stock in subtle variations and setting myself up for disappointment yet again?

"Fucking stop obsessing over this already, Tawnee. You'll end up driving yourself to the psych ward if you don't get a grip, girl." Talking to myself with a firm tone and a no-nonsense, practical approach usually does the trick.

I've been around Roman all of thirty minutes—max—and my thoughts are already running away from me. My cart and my horse aren't even in the same time zone at this point. With a shake of my head, I attempt to clear the fog from between my ears. Then I pick up my razor to shave all my lady parts. I set one foot on the tiled seat in the corner of the shower and slide the blade across my skin.

"Don't take this the wrong way, okay, sweets? I couldn't help but notice when I first saw you down on the beach that you look like you've lost quite a bit of weight. Not that you don't look fucking hot as hell, but I never thought you had any extra weight you could lose in the first place. You were always muscular for a woman, and it looked damn good on you. I've searched your entire kitchen and what you call snacks is more like raw rabbit food. I'm worried you're not eating and maybe even starving yourself or something.

"Fuck, this is coming out all wrong. I'm sorry—I know I sound like a complete dick, but I don't mean it that way. What I really want to know is if you're okay. That's all that matters to me, Tawnee—if you're happy and healthy and taking good care of yourself."

At first, the deep timbre of his voice emanating from inside my bathroom makes me jump. The sudden jerk of the razor against my leg nicks my skin, causing a tiny rivulet of blood to form instantly. The sheer audacity of him just waltzing into my bathroom while I'm obviously still in the shower and very naked strikes a chord in me. He's crossed a hard line—one he will immediately regret when my scrawny, too-skinny ass kicks his arrogant, self-absorbed ass to kingdom come. While he's mid-sentence, I grab the handle and swing the glass door open, ready to crack his skull.

Then three things hit me, one after the other, and they knock the wind out of my sails.

First, I didn't close the bathroom door all the way.

Second, he's standing in the opening with his back to me and his eyes closed.

Third, his apology is sincere and heartfelt—and so is his concern for my well-being.

Before he realizes I'm standing behind him completely naked and dripping wet, I step back inside the shower and softly close the door.

"I'm not sure how to answer the part about the weight loss. I guess I've lost some since you last saw me. But, yes, I'm taking good care of myself. We travel a lot, and you know how hotel gyms are compared to real ones. Their weights aren't as helpful, so I've been swimming laps and building up my cardio lately. And clean, healthy eating is not rabbit food. It's good for you— you should try it."

"Sweets, I'm not eating a plain stalk of celery. That's not a snack. A party-size bag of Cool Ranch Doritos is a snack. A giant Halloween-size bag of frozen Reese's—the best snack of all. Carrots, celery, and broccoli are meant to be combined with other ingredients to make a full dish—not to graze on like rabbits eating grass."

I laugh out loud as I turn off the water and grab my over-sized plush towel. After a few quick swipes to dry off, I wrap it around me and step out of the shower. "Must be nice to eat all that tasty-good junk food and not have it go straight to your hips and thighs. Not all of us are as fortunate as you are, Roman."

"Is it safe to open my eyes and turn around now?" I can't help but think how sweet it is of him to ask that. Not that I should expect less from any man, but being respectful of anyone's privacy has never been in his nature.

"Yes, it's safe now. Thank you for being considerate of my privacy."

"No thanks needed, sweets." He looks over his shoulder, and his steely gray eyes darken with desire. He moves to face me fully while leisurely perusing the length of my body from my towel down to my toes. On the way back up, he notices the blood on my shin. "Your leg is bleeding. I saw some bandages in the kitchen cabinet. Have a seat and I'll grab them."

"Don't bother. It's only a small nick from shaving." I follow him out of the shower room and into the outer sitting area, but my protests fall on deaf ears. Within seconds, he's back with the small first aid kit I always take on trips.

"Let's have a look." He motions toward the chair in front of the vanity mirror as he opens the container.

"Really, I'm okay—"

"Sit."

"Fine." I plop down on the seat and scowl at him. Then he hits me with that sexy smirk of his, and I forget why I'm irritated with him.

He kneels in front of me and picks up my leg to examine the minuscule cut. The rush of electricity that zings through my body makes me grip the sides of the chair, my fingers curling into the wood and holding on for dear life. I'm intentionally holding my breath to avoid saying something I'll regret later and praying he doesn't say anything that requires an intelligent reply. He slides his hand up the back of my leg to the bend of my knee. A whimper nearly escapes my throat from the warmth of his hand and the memory of his touch.

With a cotton swab soaked with peroxide, he cleans the area then leans closer and lightly blows on it to dry it. He's solely focused on my nonexistent wound, not at all affected by what is essentially foreplay for me.

I think I may die now… It's been way too long since I've been with a man.

He removes the smallest bandage from the kit, covers the cut, and sets my foot on his thigh before looking up at me. He doesn't move from his position at my feet. His hand is still on my leg, and his thumb lightly brushes back and forth across my skin…lovingly, reverently, longingly.

A sea of emotions washes across his features while we remain locked in a silent battle of desire versus reality. Part of me wishes I could read his mind, but a greater part is afraid of what I'd find there. Despite the number of times I've denied the truth since we parted, I can't fool myself any longer.

I've never really moved on from Roman Scott.

But I won't allow this old flame to be rekindled.

He not only shattered my heart beyond repair—he crushed my spirit and my belief in an eternal love in one fatal move.

"All better now. Thank you for taking care of me. I'll join you back in the living room once I'm dressed, and we can have that talk you're so looking forward to." My friendly smile is securely in place on the outside, but inside, I'm mentally hardening my heart.

Disappointment flashes across his face before he masks his features and gains control of his emotions. There's no doubt in my mind that he understands my underlying message. "As I said, there's no need to thank me. Taking care of you is my pleasure. Take your time, Tawnee. I don't mind waiting for you, regardless of how long it takes."

His hidden message isn't quite as ambiguous as mine… I hear what he's trying to say loud and clear.

The problem is, I took a hard-line stance against too-little-too-late men three years ago.

CHAPTER 7

Roman

Walking out of that room when I was so close to reminding Tawnee of what we once had was sheer torture. I was one step closer to convincing her to give me another chance. Then she completely slammed on the brakes and stopped the forward momentum I'd gained. Not that I can blame her, but I admit I was hoping our first meeting would've gone better.

So, I'll back off for now and give her a little space to deal with the changes and shocking turn of events that have been thrown at her in the last few days. My surprise arrival must make her feel awkward, to say the very least, but I know it sure as hell can't be as hard as seeing her cozy with another man. When I walked up and saw her with Rafael, I wanted to tear him apart. Silas's questions to Blake about how he'd react to seeing his girlfriend with another man echoed loudly in my ears.

Now I know exactly what it feels like—it fucking sucks, that's what.

She walks into the living room wearing tight-fitting black

pants, a champagne-colored shirt, and a short white dress jacket. The way her thick black hair falls over her shoulders only accentuates her sex appeal, making me salivate like one of Pavlov's dogs on sight. Before she even glances in my direction, she sets her bag down and continues straight to the kitchen. When she returns, she has a beer in each hand, offers one to me, then sits in the chair across from me instead of on the couch beside me.

Aha, so this is how we're playing it. All right. If this makes her feel safer to keep her distance from me, I'll just use methods other than innocent touches or rendering first aid to win her over. That includes anything and everything under the sun. When I raise the longneck bottle to my lips, I keep her in my sights as the nectar of the gods slides down my throat. She stares at the bottle in her hand before taking a swig, then she starts peeling the label.

That act alone gives me more satisfaction than it should. Since receiving that encoded message, verifying her safety is the only thing that has made me feel better than seeing her make that little sign. At least she isn't getting any satisfaction from Ralphy-boy.

"You've been keeping a secret long enough, sweets. What is it you're hiding from us?" I prop my ankle on my knee and lean back against the overly plush cushions.

"You're not allowed to yell."

"Oh fuck. That's never a good sign." My deadpan expression really says it all.

"Promise me, Roman."

"You have my word. I don't fly off the handle and yell at people like a lunatic anymore."

"Good to know. Hold on to that thought for the next few minutes." She tilts the bottle up, and I'm mesmerized by the way the muscles in her throat work when she swallows.

When she turns her attention back to me, I purposely keep

my expression neutral and my body language open. The last thing I want is to seem closed off to her. "Talk to me, Tawnee. Let me help if I can."

"I'll probably regret leading with this, but I don't think you'll appreciate the suspenseful buildup to it if I start at the beginning." I simply nod in understanding to avoid interrupting her. "I'm not entirely convinced Rafael was the intended target. When the Arab men heard the sirens approaching, they ran back to their cars. One of them was still yelling in Arabic, but I distinctly heard him say my name.

"Before you get your panties in a wad over this, I've gone over the scene in my mind repeatedly, dissecting every moment. During the altercation, I used my body to shield Rafael. His side of the car was pinned against the building, so there was only one way in and out—straight through me. Since I don't speak Arabic, I can only guess what he was yelling about. But it makes sense that if they'd researched Rafael, they would know I'm the head of security. So, he could have been cursing me because he lost that fight to a woman. Maybe he was mad because I dared to fight him off instead of bowing to his wishes. Or maybe he was pissed because I kicked him in the head. There are so many possibilities, it didn't make sense only to focus on a single reason at the time."

"At the time? But now you've changed your mind about that?" I know where she's going with this, but I'm trying hard not to be the overbearing asshole I usually am and simply blurt it out. But it's fucking killing me inside. My every instinct screams at me to throw her over my shoulder, march her fine ass out of this hotel, and put her on the next flight home.

"Yes. I can't stick my head in the sand and pretend I don't see what's happening. The team takes risks to keep Rafael safe—but we do what needs to be done to mitigate those risks as much as possible. Circumstances are different now, though, with the scrubbed camera feed, the hack into Brad's system, and the encoded message sent directly to you. All signs point to one fact. Their mark wasn't Rafael—it was me. And my staying here creates more danger for both Rafael and the team. I can't expect anyone to work double security details to cover both of our asses."

"Now that I know the finer details of what happened, I have to say I agree with your assessment. I know coming to this conclusion was especially difficult for you. You'd never voluntarily give up your responsibilities unless there was no other way. Those guys absolutely wanted you—but that doesn't automatically mean they weren't trying to nab Rafael too. Sending me the distress signal was a brilliant move. They get extra-credit points for that one."

As soon as the words leave my mouth, my spy senses start tingling all over.

Fuck me.

"Wait a minute… Let's talk this through, because something is way off base here. Sending me that message wouldn't help them get to you—they knew that. The only purpose that message served was to get *me* to come here to find you. What could they possibly have to gain from that?" Her lips part in surprise as my words sink in. The wheels in both of our brains are spinning out of control now.

"Do you have any Arab enemies? Anyone in this part of the world who would have used me as leverage against you?"

"No, I've never worked in this region before now. I don't know what this could be about or how I got on their radar."

"Roman, I have to tell you I'm freaking out a little now—and you know I don't do that. Ever." She jumps to her feet and starts pacing back and forth in front of me, unable to contain the nervous energy coursing through her veins. "But none of the scenarios in my mind included you as a target. Now that you've pointed out that someone wants both of us here—in Dubai, at the same time—that's all I can focus on. We should leave. All of us. Right now. Let's go explain it to the others and leave before they finish what they've started."

On her next pass toward me, I stand and block her path. With my hands wrapped around her biceps, I bend my knees to put us eye to eye. "Tawnee, slow down, sweets. Take a deep breath. I agree we need to talk to the others about this—but not *all* the others just yet. I'd rather start with Silas, Nick, and Blake, then go from there. Okay?"

She nods. "Okay, you're right. That makes perfect sense. They have the most experience with life-and-death situations in hostile enemy territories. Surely the five of us can put our heads together and come up with something resembling a good plan."

"You bet your *sweet ass*, we can." I waggle my eyebrows at her.

"Roman." She's using her stern voice. That's a good sign that she's getting her anxiety under control. "Did you have to remind me of the real reason why you call me 'sweets' right at this moment?"

"Yep, I sure did. It worked, didn't it?"

She's fighting against the smile that's trying to break free.

"In case you were wondering, I still think you have the sweetest ass in the world. Now that I've flown halfway around the actual world and have seen a lot of asses on my way here, I'm confident in officially claiming my title as the *numero uno* ass-expert now."

The smile wins.

"Well, you've certainly had enough experience in being an ass to make you an expert on the subject."

"Ha-ha. You're still so funny. Do you want to call up to Rafael's room and have the guys come down here to talk so we'll have more privacy?"

"I think it's best that we head back up there. Raf's suite is enormous—we can use one of the spare rooms to strategize then share the plan with the others when we're ready. Plus,

Raf would probably be very suspicious of our motives otherwise."

By all means, let's not make Raf suspicious.

She cuts her eyes over to me, and I immediately wonder if I said that out loud instead of just thinking it. "Wait a second. You don't still think one of my security team is in on this, do you?"

"At this point, I don't trust anyone except for you and my team. Like I said earlier, I don't know anything about your employees, sweets, so I can't vouch for them. But I sure as fuck don't like the thought of your life in their hands."

"Don't hold back, Roman. Tell me what you really think."

"All right, I will. I absolutely think someone on your team is behind this whole thing, or at least involved. What's worse is you think so too, but you won't admit it yet. You hold on to this notion that everyone you trust is implicitly good and has your best interests at heart. But they don't, sweets. Not everyone."

"When did you become so insightful about other people?"

"Ever since I started working with Silas a few years ago. It's the only way to survive around that man. He's worse than a lie detector—he can read your thoughts."

"Good to know. I'll watch out for his telepathic abilities. Maybe I'll wear an aluminum hat or something."

"It won't help. I've tried it."

She rolls her eyes and shakes her head at me. "Let's go. We have work to do."

When we rejoin the others in the expansive suite, the eye daggers being thrown at me from both Rafael and Tony nearly make me laugh. Instead, I make it a little more interesting by pouring gasoline on the fire.

"Sorry to keep everyone waiting. Tawnee and I needed a little longer than we first thought." Nothing like leaving my comments vague enough to at least conjure the very images they're trying to avoid thinking about. "Silas, Nick, and Blake— can we talk to you privately?"

"Sure. Please excuse us for a few minutes." Silas stands and walks out of the living room without waiting for a reply from anyone.

We adjourn in a spare bedroom, Silas ensures his signal jamming device is on, and Tawnee and I bring everyone up to speed on the details she shared with me. When all their questions have been answered, the heavy blanket of silence covers the room as they digest the information.

"What do you think, Silas? Do we stay or do we go?" He rubs his hand along his jawline, weighing our options against the risks we face. But I already know what he'll say—his hesitation gave it away.

"We're staying until this is done. She's one of us—she helped you protect my parents when that lunatic was running around unchecked several years ago. I won't leave her to face this alone. Rafael is adamant he won't leave until he completes his real estate deal. If that's what he wants to do, that's fine with me. But I've got to tell you, it thoroughly pisses me off that he's so indifferent to his team's safety. Tawnee could head home and let someone else take over running the detail, but she can't live her life looking over her shoulder, waiting for some random man to grab her."

"Your director told you to stay on the job, didn't he?" Tawnee tilts her head to the side and raises her eyebrows.

"He may have suggested we need to identify who's luring Roman to the Middle East and neutralize the threat while we're here."

"Ah, you're shitting me. He figured it out before I did?"

"That goes without saying, and it's why he's the director. He's been doing this a lot longer than you have, Roman."

"Yeah, you have a point there. So, Tawnee… do you want to hang out in Dubai, put your life on the line with a group of Arab men who want to kidnap you, and cheat death out of the pleasure of using his sickle on you?"

"Well, Roman, when you put it that way...how can I possibly resist?"

Before this is over, she'll be saying I'm the one she can't resist. That is now my personal mission. It just so happens she and I will have plenty of time together in the very near future. I glance over at Silas and notice he's doing his Jedi mind trick shit again, reading Tawnee like a book. I've also learned to interpret the subtleties in his expressions better, and it's clear he respects her even more now.

"Nick, tomorrow morning, take Blake and go talk to the police. See what information they'll release about the scene or any angle they're working. I'll have a closer look at the security team members. Roman, you're on bodyguard duty for the time being. Don't let Tawnee out of your sight."

Thank you, Silas. I'll even babysit your daughter when we get home in return for giving me this assignment.

I will guard Tawnee's body with mine any time of the day or night. Vigorously.

Tawnee folds her arms over her chest and pins me with her glare. Maybe Silas isn't the only mind reader of the group. "Wipe that grin off your face and get *that* thought out of your mind right now, Roman."

Her direct order only makes me smile more.

CHAPTER 8

Tawnee

*W*hen we emerge from the spare bedroom, Rafael and the rest of the team stop talking, and all heads turn to us. Raf is the type of man that enjoys being the one in charge of everything, regardless of the circumstances or who else is involved. In this case, he doesn't have the expertise to be the one who calls the shots. And that really bothers him.

"Did the five of you solve the problems of the world in your impromptu bedroom meeting?" Raf asks with only a hint of sarcasm bleeding through his typically controlled tone.

"As a matter of fact, we did. Did you expect any less of us?" Roman throws his own sarcastic jab back.

Maybe all of us staying in Dubai isn't the best course of action after all. I can already see the frustration building in Rafael, and Roman isn't likely to back down to any man.

I'll be caught in the middle of their virtual pissing contest. That's just fucking great.

"Tawnee alone has my confidence. I don't know the rest of

you from Adam. You could be the most incompetent of all the agents for all I know."

"Officers."

"Pardon?"

"We're CIA officers, not agents."

"So?"

"So, your assumption is wrong right off the bat. We're not the most incompetent agents at all." Roman's goading is intentional. He remains completely calm while Rafael uncharacteristically shows signs of his increasing aggravation. "But we're damn good officers."

"Rafael, Roman, that's enough from both of you. This isn't helping our situation at all." I shoot dirty looks at both men for putting me in this predicament in the first place. "Rafael, I can personally vouch for these men. They are the best at what they do, and they've already identified key factors I completely missed in all the chaos. You need to give them a chance."

"For you, I will do my best." His attention remains on me, not bothering to give the men helping us even a fleeting glance. I know exactly what this means. Rafael won't take orders from them out of spite. Instead, he'll wait until the word comes directly from me.

"Everyone—take a seat so we can talk as a team. Silas, I'm passing the speaking baton to you since you're the senior officer here. We're working together, but he's in charge of the plan." I glance around the room at every member of my team, wordlessly driving home my point.

"To be blunt, there are too many variables in this equation for anyone to assume anything. That's why I've already given each person on my team very specific marching orders. The message Roman received wasn't a fluke—someone wants him here for a reason. They may have been trying to kidnap Tawnee as a means to draw him in. When that didn't work, they grabbed her phone and used a system our IT guy created from scratch.

It's not available to the public, so they have their own tech guru working behind the scenes too. Until we know exactly what they want with Tawnee and Roman, I've instructed them to stay by the other's side.

"As I understand it, Mr. Cruz, they rescheduled your real estate meeting for next week and that's your only business here in the Middle East. Is that correct?"

"Yes, it is." The skeptical expression is still firmly intact.

"In that case, it's best that you stay on the hotel grounds with your security team around you at all times. We don't have enough intel yet to confirm if you are a target or not. It's best not to roam around out in the open like a walking bull's-eye. To be clear, I'll help keep you safe as much as I can. But I've been given orders from my superiors, and they don't include being your bodyguard. So, if you decide to venture off the grounds, know that you're doing so at your own risk and without my team or Tawnee."

I understand Silas's directness. As an officer in perilous situations, he can't risk being misunderstood. His edicts must be followed to the letter—dotting all the I's and crossing all the T's. However, Rafael isn't quite as understanding as I am.

Rafael deserves plenty of credit, though. He commands the room when he walks into a meeting. There's an innate air of authority about him that makes people flock to him everywhere we go. The way he carries himself, the way he dresses, and the way he speaks show a refinement most people don't possess. His charisma draws others in, but his shrewd business side leaves no doubt in their mind that he can be ruthless when he must be.

But he has a definite problem with authority. I think that's the underlying reason he started buying the controlling shares in various companies several years ago. He felt limited by the decisions and practices of the nameless and faceless company insiders. Since he had no power or influence to change their rules, he worked until he took over the company itself and changed what best suited him.

"So, if they're after Roman and were planning to use Tawnee as leverage to get to him, why would you put the two of them together? Doesn't that just make it easier for the bad guys to nab them both at the same time?"

"I can understand why you would think that, since you're not an expert in security measures. But, no, it doesn't make it easier at all. Think about it. If Tawnee is overseeing your security team, it divides her attention. She's responsible for making sure you're safe, that her team is following orders, and adjusting coverage on the fly when you decide to change plans at the last minute. She doesn't have the luxury of focusing on her own protection in that scenario. Whereas, by putting two highly trained and skilled operatives together, they can focus on their own safety and help each other. They'll assess their surroundings through a different lens automatically because that's what they're trained to do."

"If you say so. Tawnee and Roman can stay here in my suite. I have two extra bedrooms they're welcome to use." Rafael is speaking to Silas while looking at me.

Maybe I should feel flattered Rafael doesn't want me to be alone with my ex-boyfriend because he recently confessed his feelings for me, but his response isn't exactly a compliment. In the years since I met Raf, he's always had a domineering demeanor, but this reaction is different. His demand is more like a manipulation and control tactic, and I don't appreciate it at all.

"Rafael, that's not necessary. I'm already settled into my room downstairs, and there's plenty of room in it for Roman too. We'll be fine—no need for you to worry about us."

"We've had a long day. Let's all go upstairs to the rooftop restaurant and have dinner together. The sunset views are stunning."

Avoiding the subject won't make it go away and won't change my mind, Raf. But then you already know that about me.

"Good idea. Full bellies and empty bottles of wine are exactly what we need right now."

"My thoughts exactly. I'm glad to see we're on the same page."

My witty sarcasm is wholly lost on Raf.

Inside the elegant French restaurant on the highest floor in the hotel, the pissing contest continues when we take our seats. Roman slides into the seat beside mine before Rafael can claim it. The two men act out their juvenile charades with glares, passive-aggressive verbal jabs, and accidental hits with elbows. I choose to ignore them both and stare out the floor-to-ceiling windows at the Persian Gulf in awe.

The setting sun shimmers on the water like a million brilliant diamonds in full display. The lights of the city begin to blink on in the dusk of the day. Brief moments like this make me wish for a less hectic life. One that would allow me the chance to slow down and enjoy these exotic locales instead of only having a passport stamp to prove I've visited. A few cheesy tourist photos would be terrific—when I'm feeling nostalgic or want to show my kids what an exciting life I've lived. One day. Hopefully.

While everyone else is engaged in lively conversations around the table and enjoying the exquisite meals, I use the time to observe each person silently. After Roman and I split, I quit working for Steele Security and moved away from Miami. Noah Steele, Silas's younger brother, freely gave me advice and recommendations, viewing me as an ally rather than competition. Tabitha was one of the first people I hired for Rafael's detail. She's been with us almost from day one of venturing out on my own. Seated next to her is Carter, another long-term employee. While I haven't confirmed anything, I have my suspicions those two are more than friends after work hours. But all

I care about is that they've both had my back in every situation we've encountered.

Next to Carter is Tony, a longtime employee of Rafael's. When Raf hired me to oversee all his security details, vetting everyone who had direct access to him—that included Tony. A few questionable charges came up on his background check that made me want to dig deeper, but Rafael explained them away as cases of either self-defense or defending his employer. He assured me Tony had earned his place in the ranks several times over. He wouldn't allow the acts of greedy people who only wanted Raf to pay them off to make the charges go away tarnish Tony's years of loyal service.

The stories seemed plausible at the time, and I was willing to give Tony the benefit of the doubt—until the first time he disobeyed my direct order. Then I called in a favor to a law enforcement friend who provided more detailed information about those charges. Raf's explanations were generous, but it seems Tony was defending Raf against someone in every instance. Whether Tony committed the crime in question, or he simply took the fall for something Raf had done, was never firmly established.

Either way, Tony had gone above and beyond to prove his loyalty to Rafael, so I dropped the crusade against his arrests. Even though he and I still butted heads repeatedly afterward because he resented taking orders from a woman. If I had to guess, I'd say it bruised his ego when Raf didn't choose him for my role, especially after taking hits to his credibility because he covered for Rafael. *Allegedly* covered, that is.

Jason and John both joined Raf's protection detail after they completed their stints in the military. They haven't been with us for as long as Tabitha and Carter have, but they've both proven their mettle on multiple occasions. Anyone would be hard-pressed to walk away with the high commendations those two men have.

Roman suspects someone on my team is behind this attack, but there isn't one person I can point an accusing finger at and still sleep at night. The security breach isn't on my team—I would bet my life on it. That only leaves one person who has the access, motive, and means to take me out of the equation. Only one man who would benefit the most from my permanent absence.

But the puzzle piece that doesn't fit is probably the most important one of all.

Tony doesn't even know Roman, so why send the fake distress call to get him here?

In fact, Roman and his coworkers' presence only makes the situation more difficult for Tony. So, what's his angle?

"There are tricks to flushing out a double agent. They all trip up eventually. It gets harder to keep all the lies straight. The reasons why they're sticking their necks out don't make as much sense anymore." Silas is answering someone else's question, but he's looking at me. "The signs are usually there if you know what to look for."

"What signs are those?" Tony asks. His tone is more of a challenge than curiosity... or maybe I'm biased against him.

"In my line of work, it's almost always a large windfall of money that arrives out of the blue. I'm always suspicious of anyone who says their rich uncle died and left them a hefty inheritance."

Silas is right... the signs will present if I just keep my eyes open and watch for them.

"Tawnee, do you think we could go down to the lounge on the ground floor? I've read the terrace is beautiful in the evening, and that bar is the best place for evening cocktails." Tabitha's hopeful expression makes it nearly impossible to tell her no. She only wants some free time with Carter that doesn't involve a locked hotel room. "There are a lot of outdoor tables with triangle-shaped lamps to light up the veranda."

Hopeless romantic to the end.

"What do you say, guys? Think we'll be safe around the pool, in the waning light of day, with all of us together?" I glance around the table, waiting for a rousing round of "no" from the alpha-male league.

"I think that's a great idea. Let's go. We'll have a few drinks, listen to some music, observe the male peacock in his natural habitat." Silas lifts his glass to his mouth to hide his smirk.

Funny, but I'm not sure which strutting peacock he's referring to at the moment—Rafael or Roman.

"If there's music, then there's dancing." Roman turns to me and waggles his eyebrows.

"Do you have no sense of culture or propriety at all?" Rafael's patience is hitting a breaking point. "You are in Dubai, Roman. You don't dance in public unless you want to be arrested for indecency. By all means, have at it. Dance until your heart is content—but do it alone so no one else has to pay for your stupidity."

Roman's face burns bright red—even his eyes have a fiery flare in them. He starts to rise out of his seat, his hands curled into tight fists, but I put my hand on his arm to distract him.

"Sit down. You are not fighting in here." Roman does as I say, so I turn my attention to my employer. "Rafael, that was uncalled-for and impolite. Roman isn't here on vacation. He rushed here to help me. You'll have to forgive him for not researching the rules and customs ahead of time and be a little more gracious for the additional help."

"You're absolutely right, Tawnee. I offer my apologies to you, Roman. That was rude and condescending—two traits I abhor in other people. And, as she pointed out, I'm in your debt for helping keep us safe. I think a little time out on the terrace in the warm ocean breeze would do us all some good."

Roman keeps his gaze locked on Rafael, but he finally nods,

signaling his agreement. I suppose that's the best response I can hope for from him.

"Thank you, Rafael. I appreciate the effort you're showing. I'm ready for some fresh air myself."

We take the elevator down to the mezzanine level and then ride the two-story-high escalator down to the lower lobby level. Tabitha and I chat and laugh, finally letting go of the stress I've been carrying. Until something catches my attention in my peripheral vision. When my eyes lock on to the source, my lungs seize in my chest, and I reach for the nearest source of comfort I can find. My fingers dig into Roman's arm, squeezing and clawing out of equal terror and disbelief.

"What's wrong? What is it?" His hand covers mine as the urgency in his tone increases. "Tawnee, talk to me."

"That's him, Roman. The one who tried to grab me in the back of the car." I point to the man strolling across the lower lobby floor as if he owns the place. He's not in a hurry. He's not concerned with being seen. He's staying in the same hotel as us.

"Which one? The man in the white dress with the red-checkered do-rag on his head?"

"He's wearing a thobe, the traditional Arab garment. And that's not a do-rag, it's his headdress. But yes, that's the one." At least Rafael doesn't sound as patronizing while he explains customary Arab clothing.

"I don't care what he's wearing. His ass is mine." Roman winds around the people in front of us before sprinting down the escalator and across the lobby. Blake and Nick are close on his heels, chasing the unknown assailant. All three men disappear through the automatic doors leading to the expansive gulf front terrace.

"I'm taking Tawnee back up to my suite right now." Rafael wraps his hand around my upper arm and starts to push me forward.

"No, wait a minute, Raf. I'm a security professional too—I'm *your* head of security. I should help Roman chase him down and make him tell me why he was after us. We need to know who's behind this and why."

"Tawnee, I agree with Rafael on this one. Let's all go back up to his suite. One of your guys can stay down here and bring my guys back upstairs—with or without an extra visitor." Silas is a little too calm, making me question if he knows something he isn't telling. I narrow my eyes at him, looking for any of those clues he promised would surface. "Trust me, Tawnee."

"All right. Jason, you wait down here for Roman, Nick, and Blake. They can't get back upstairs without scanning a guest keycard in the elevator."

"Yes, ma'am. I hope they catch the bastard. If they do, we'll make him talk. Don't worry."

Fucking right, we'll make him talk.

CHAPTER 9

"He got away?" Tawnee stares at me in disbelief when I show up back in Rafael's suite empty-handed. "How? They built this hotel on a man-made island."

"Yes, he did." I want to fucking punch a hole in something. I pace back and forth, more aggravation building inside me with my every step. "We almost had him outside, but he pulled a fast one on us. The fucker in the white dress jumped on a speedboat that was already waiting right there."

"Which way did he go?" Silas asks.

"Straight out to sea, man, until we couldn't see the boat anymore. If I didn't know better, I'd say the whole thing was very carefully staged." Nick scans the room with his accusing glare, never one to hold back what he's thinking.

"Staged how?" Rafael sets down his drink and stands to face Nick. I almost laugh—as if Rafael could ever intimidate a veteran DEA agent who spent two years undercover with one of the most notorious motorcycle gangs in the world.

"Staged so that Tawnee would see the very man who caused

a wreck, forcibly tried to drag her out of the back of the car, and said her name as he climbed into his car. Turn around and look out of the window right behind you. Do you see a dock out there anywhere? That boat was in that exact spot for a reason. This hotel wouldn't have allowed that to happen for just anyone." Nick takes a step toward Rafael, daring the man to challenge him a second time. "I think someone expected Tawnee to go after him. If I were a betting man, I'd say we would've encountered a shitload of resistance outside had she taken the bait. They would've disappeared into the horizon with her in the boat, and we would've had no way to stop them."

"Are you implying someone in this room is responsible for this? That one of us is a traitor?" Tony steps up beside Rafael.

I stand shoulder to shoulder with Nick and face down both men. "If Nick isn't saying that, then I am. I don't believe in coincidences."

"Neither do I. You know, at first, your accusation really pissed me off. But now, I absolutely agree with you. Someone in this room is responsible for all the bullshit that's happened this week, and I know exactly who it is." Tony glares at me with murderous intent in his eyes.

Bring it on, fucker. I've faced much worse.

"What are you saying, Tony?" Rafael asks, his eyes wide and his jaw slack as he stares at his right-hand man. "Do you know something about the attack we don't?"

"I've been retracing our steps, trying to isolate the one thing that would've given us away. We never give out our itinerary with enough advance notice for anyone to plan a well-coordinated attack like this. There's only one possible solution I've come up with... Roman is behind all of it so he can rush in, save the day, and be Tawnee's hero again. He's the one who staged the kidnapping attempt."

"Have you lost your fucking mind?" I'm about to go nuclear on his stupid ass.

"You're the only one who received this mysterious message from her. On a private, secure app no one outside of a select few people that you know can access. In a country where we have no means to verify anything you say is true. That's exactly why you weren't in any danger when you took off after that man—because you know he's not really after you. You look pretty damn guilty from where I'm standing."

"You son of a bitch!" I lunge at him and slam my fist into his face. When he goes to the floor, I pounce on top of him and keep pummeling until I shut his fucking mouth for good.

Strong arms wrap around my shoulders and drag me off Tony. Everyone in the room stands between us as we continue to hurl insults at one another. I fight against the stronghold my team has on me, wanting to tear Tony apart for even suggesting this is all on me. Tawnee's life is in real danger, yet his main concern is that I want to play a hero game. He's a fucking moron.

"Everyone, stop!" Tawnee moves to the center of the ruckus and yells at the top of her lungs.

I mean, it works. Everyone shuts up and waits for her to continue, including me.

"Tony, you're way off base with accusing Roman. He is not behind this. He had no way of knowing where we were either. He and I haven't spoken in three years until he showed up here *to help us.*" She runs her hands over her face out of utter annoyance. "And you, Roman, have no right to accuse my team of doing anything underhanded. You've known them all of a few hours now. You may not trust them, but that doesn't give you the right to doubt them.

"I consider everyone here as a friend. Roman, Silas, Nick, and Blake are not private security contractors. They work for the US government, and they're here on official business. My team is private security, but we're all damn good at what we do. We've wasted enough time being suspicious of one another. Get your shit together or get the fuck out—it's that simple."

She's so fucking sexy when she takes charge. I don't know why some men have a problem with a woman giving them orders. I personally find it's a massive boost to my libido. Maybe that's because I also picture her—Tawnee—wearing a skintight leather suit, spiky heels, and brandishing a whip she isn't afraid to use. Shit, I have to get that image out of my head before a tepee forms in my pants.

She walks across the room toward me, and I watch the men move out of her path. While she doesn't appear to be especially pleased with me, I don't see that look she gets in her eyes when she wants to hurt me either. That's undeniably a good sign. When she reaches me, she picks up my hands and inspects my knuckles.

"Are you okay?" Her voice is low, only loud enough for me to hear her now that the crowd has dispersed.

"I'm fine, sweets. His hide isn't as thick as he likes to pretend it is." I wink when she finally meets my gaze.

"Do you need to ice your hands?"

"Are you trying to get rid of me? We're stuck together now, remember? Mano a woman-o." I waggle my eyebrows at her suggestively, and she finally rewards me with a smile. She can't resist my juvenile wit and charm.

"Mano does not mean man, so your little catchphrase doesn't even make sense. However, I remember you chasing that man and leaving me on the escalator when you're supposed to be my personal security officer."

"I never would have left you had Silas not been right there to protect you. When you grabbed my arm like that, I knew you needed me to be the strong one even before you said the first word. Then when you told me he was the man who'd tried to grab you, I saw red. If I'd gotten my hands on him, I would've killed him right there in front of everyone. You may get a call from the front desk any minute now, telling you to get me out of here because I scared the other guests. They were tripping over their feet to get out of my way."

"Why, Roman? Why after all this time do you care so much about what happens to me? We haven't been together for a long time now." She looks down, afraid to look directly into my eyes and find something she's not ready to face.

But she doesn't have to worry about that.

Tawnee, time and distance have no influence on my feelings for you. I've loved and missed you more every day we've been apart. I should have told you forever ago, but I let my stupidity and pride stand in the way.

But I don't say any of that, because they're only hollow words. My recent good deeds are nowhere near enough to make up for my prior cruel actions. And professing my undying love right now will only drive her further away. I didn't make sure she knew how much she meant to me when I had her. Why should she believe it now?

"Ah, sweets, if there's one thing you should know about me better than anyone, it's that I'll always come running when you need me."

She peers up at me through her lashes, and the spark of hope shining there is unmistakable.

"Roman—"

"Tawnee—"

Fucking *Ralph*.

The invisible fetter holding her to me is broken by the sound of his voice interrupting our very private conversation. The moment is gone, and I'll probably never know whatever she was about to say to me, thanks to him.

"Yes, Raf?" She turns her back to me and faces him, which I'm sure was his intention.

He strolls across the room to her, not speaking but keeping his eyes trained on her. Yeah, we get it, dude. You just used your strutting peacock swagger to hold her attention. Whoop-de-freaking-doo. We're all so fucking impressed. I don't even bother trying to hide my disgusted expression.

He wraps his arms around her shoulders and pulls her closer to him. "It's been such a long and trying day for you. Why don't you lie down in the spare bedroom and sleep here tonight? I'd feel so much better knowing you're close to me and safe tonight."

I really want to tear his arms off his body and shove them up his ass right now.

"It's probably best that Roman and I head down to my suite. Silas, Nick, and Blake can use your extra bedrooms for tonight. It doesn't really make sense for all of us to play musical chairs with our belongings, especially this late in the evening."

"That sounds like a perfect plan to me." I beam with pride at Raf.

Roman—one. Raf—zero.

"Don't you need to go back to your hotel and pick up a few of your things?" He's trying hard to get rid of me for some reason.

"Give me your room key, Roman. I'll grab what you'll need for tonight and tomorrow, then we can assess our next steps." Blake steps up beside me and extends his open palm.

Have I mentioned how great my best friend is?

"Perfect. Thank you, Blake." I retrieve the keycard from my wallet and hand it to him. "We'll be in Tawnee's suite when you get back, so stop by her room on the way up."

"I'll go with you, Blake. I can grab Silas's and mine too." Nick takes Silas's room key from him.

"Raf, do you mind giving them your extra room key? They'll need it in the elevator to get back up here. I have a master key, but I'd rather hang onto it, if that's okay." I'm glad Tawnee remembers the minor but vitally important details. I'll be tucked away in her room and not even thinking about where my coworkers are in just a few minutes.

"I don't mind at all." He's lying—he minds a lot. When he fishes his wallet out of his pocket, he removes the cards and hands one to Blake before putting the other two back in their place.

"You keep multiple room keys on your person at all times?" My brows draw downward, and the corners of my eyes tighten. I know Tawnee would have strongly suggested otherwise.

"Why wouldn't I? I never know when I'll need to ask one of my staff to fetch something from my suite."

Fetch? Does he think they're his dogs now?

I may be overly biased against him. Or maybe he's just a douche.

"Nick and Blake—be sure to bring back one of our business suits. There's somewhere else we need to be tomorrow that calls for us to look nice." All heads turn to Silas, who has been unusually quiet during this entire exchange. "Tawnee, you'll need to join us too. I wouldn't ask if it weren't important."

"Sure thing, Silas. I trust your judgment."

"Let's meet in the lobby at nine in the morning and go from there. Rafael, you should be safe with the rest of your security team here. But I still wouldn't recommend leaving the hotel grounds just yet."

"Even though that's exactly what you're doing with Tawnee and Roman tomorrow?" Tony counters. "After you've said they're both in danger?"

"Yes." Silas backs Tony down with his don't-fuck-with-me expression.

Most people don't understand Silas when they first meet him. He has two modes: all-business and all-family. When he's in all-business mode, he gets shit done. He rarely smiles, he's lethal when needed, and every move he makes is thoroughly calculated. When others say, "it's just business," they're justifying a decision that hurt someone else, rationalizing to relieve their own guilt. But Silas doesn't feel guilt over anything business-related. That's why he's earned the right to command respect at the agency.

When he's in all-family mode, no one from Langley would even recognize him because of the differences in his personality. He laughs, he plays practical jokes on family and friends, and he lets his daughter put makeup on him for their afternoon tea parties—it's almost as if he's an entirely different person.

The hard line no one wants to cross with Silas is questioning his commitment to his job, his country, his decisions, and especially his family—friends included. That seems to be a family trait because his brother is the same. Both men are my unsung heroes. The people I secretly wish I could be more like. But with all my character flaws, I don't see that happening anytime soon.

"Well, now that that's settled, maybe we should say good-night and let these fine people get some rest." I take Tawnee's hand in mine and pull her out of Raf's embrace. I've watched him paw at her long enough.

My actions are as transparent as glass, which is why I refuse to acknowledge the dumbfounded expression on her beautiful face. In my defense, I don't mean to be a self-absorbed asshole who wants what he wants and pursues it with a vengeance. But that's also who I am, so I'm going with it for the time being. If Tawnee were to tell me she needed me to be something more, that would be different. I'd do everything in my power to be what she wanted because losing her the first time made me face my faults. Not that I'd dare claim to be perfect... but we are matched perfectly.

Raf cuts his eyes to look directly at me for the first time since the moment we met, but there are no warm and fuzzy feelings in those cold, dark eyes. He's severely pissed off—probably because he's not getting his way, but mainly because he's not getting Tawnee. He steps toward her, puts his hands on her face, and gently kisses her forehead.

Right fucking in front of me.

Blake grabs my arm, stopping me before I even realize my body is in motion. I guess one round of fisticuffs isn't enough for me tonight.

Shit. Now I'm thinking about fists and cuffs in an entirely different light.

"Sleep tight, beautiful. I'll dream of you tonight." Raf's intimate whisper to Tawnee makes me want to punch him even more.

"Goodnight, Raf." Tawnee tries to act casual, but I can detect the subtle changes in her tone. His display of affection is out of the ordinary.

So… his majesty is threatened by the old Ro-Man.

Good.

"Come on, Tawnee. I'll tuck you in and get you some warm milk to help you fall asleep."

Blake covers up his snicker with an unconvincing cough, and I'm especially surprised to see Silas fighting a smile while he stares at the floor, suddenly refusing to make eye contact with anyone. As for me, I'm all smiles while saying goodnight to everyone on the way out of the multilevel, royal suite.

Dude must have more dollars than sense to pay that much for a hotel room.

We reach the elevator bank, and I press the down button, whistling a happy tune while we wait. Tawnee pulls her hand loose from mine, folds her arms over her chest, and cocks one hip out to the side—then glares at me.

"What?" Innocent. Oblivious. Charming. All at once. That takes real talent.

"I feel like a fire hydrant."

"Okay, I'll play along. How does a fire hydrant feel? Hard as steel? Holding back a lot of pent-up energy? Ready to squirt and shower someone with all that wetness inside?"

"Like every damn alpha dog in the surrounding vicinity has hiked his leg, pissed on me, and marked his territory without even the common courtesy of first asking if I enjoy golden showers."

My eyes bug out of my head, and my jaw drops open. "Are you into them?"

"No!"

The elevator bell dings, the doors slide open, and she stomps inside with her arms tightly closed over her body. She moves to the far back corner on the opposite side from the buttons and glowers at me from under her heavy brows. I push the button for her floor and face her as the car begins to move.

"Tawnee, come on, sweets. I'm sorry—forgive me. I didn't mean any harm—just trying to make you laugh. I swear I was kidding about that. Couldn't you tell?"

She draws in a deep breath, blows it out on a long sigh, and releases her arms to her sides. "Yes, Roman, I know you were only kidding. But sometimes I need you to be serious. When I say something bothers me, you should know that it *really* bothers me. I need to know that you hear and understand me."

"You're absolutely right. Again, I'm sorry. So, if I've interpreted this correctly, you're saying you don't want me to compete with Rafael for your attention or affection. Does that sum it up?"

"Yes. No. I don't know. What? You're competing for my affection?" She clamps her mouth shut and steels her spine. "I'm not a piece of property for anyone to fight over. I have my own mind, and I'm perfectly capable of deciding who 'wins' my affections without being put in the middle of some juvenile turf war."

That's not at all what I wanted to hear her say, but I'll respect her wishes.

"Point taken. I won't get in his way anymore."

When the elevator stops, I hold the doors open with one arm and motion for her to exit first with the other. She walks past me, hesitates for just a moment as if she wants to say something, then thinks better of it. Once we're inside her room, she tells me to help myself to her secret stash of beer while she goes through her nightly bedtime routine.

But I don't.

While Tawnee is in the master bath, Blake drops off my clothes and toiletries, which I stow in the second bathroom and change into my lounging pants. After locking the door, checking all the windows, and adding additional security to the balcony's sliding door, I grab the extra blanket from the hall closet and settle on the overstuffed couch to get some sleep.

A few minutes later, she emerges from the bedroom and stops when she reaches the darkened living room. I'm sure she expected to find me wide awake, beer in hand, and waiting to throw sexual innuendos her way. Maybe about the way her nightgown barely covers her sweet ass. Or how her toned legs look ultra-sexy peeking out from under the thin, silky material. Or even how her nipples appear to prefer the cold, air-conditioned air in here since they're standing at attention in perfect form.

But I don't say any of those things out loud.

Her eyes haven't fully adjusted to the dark room yet, so she stands over me, trying to determine if my eyes are open or closed. She chews on her thumbnail, unsure if she should say anything and chance waking me. Then she tiptoes back to her room and climbs into the bed… but she leaves the door open.

I close my eyes and let sleep overtake me.

Tawnee

After a night of tossing, turning, punching pillows, and sleeping in short stints, I finally decide it's time to face the day. The enticing aroma of fresh-brewed coffee is so strong, I can almost taste it. In the living room, I find Roman is not only already awake, but he's fully dressed in his suit and has had breakfast delivered to the room.

"Good morning. Sleep well?" He's a little too chipper first thing today.

"Fine. You?"

"Like a rock. That couch is surprisingly comfortable. I think I like it better than my bed at the other hotel." He hands me a cup of piping hot java. "Still take yours the same as usual—a little bit of coffee with your sugar and vanilla flavoring?"

I take a sip, close my eyes, and smile. "It's perfect. Thank you." He remembers exactly how to mix all the ingredients to suit my taste. How can that be? And why?

"Have a seat. Breakfast is ready too." He lifts the silver dome off my plate, and I lick my lips in anticipation. "You ordered pancakes? I haven't had them in forever. They smell so good."

When I finally come up for air after a few minutes of gorging myself, the subtle shift in my reality instantly slaps me in the face. My throat clogs with emotion, making it hard to swallow my food. The scene right in front of me could have been my idyllic life. The dream feels so real and so close that I could simply reach out and grab it.

A handsome man sits across the table from me, enjoying the breakfast he so thoughtfully made for us. The comfortable silence we enjoy means we don't have to fill every moment with words for our time together to be meaningful. The butterflies fluttering in my chest when I look at him are evidence my love for him will only increase every day. Our individual strengths and weaknesses only make us stronger as a couple.

But that's only a pipe dream with Roman. The man who barely gave me a drawer to keep extra clothes in. The man with an aversion to commitment and a fear of missing a better opportunity waiting around the corner. The man who prefers to remain a lifelong bachelor, never opting for marriage or kids to fulfill him. Like a bad case of déjà vu, I've been in this exact scenario before, and I recall how badly it ended.

I won't put myself in that position again. I won't give my love to a man who can't return it.

"Is anything wrong with your food? Do you want something else?" He lowers his fork to his plate and moves toward the phone to order whatever I want. Too bad it's not on the menu.

"No, this meal is delicious. No need to change anything."

"All right. Want to tell me what's on your mind, then?" He retakes his seat and directs all his attention to me.

"No, I really don't. Let's just focus on getting through today and whatever it is Silas has planned for us."

"All right, sweets. If you change your mind, I'm ready when you are."

"Ready for what, Roman?"

"Anything you want, Tawnee."

He seems so sincere, making it far too easy for me to be pulled under his spell and get lost in his eyes. That tug on my heartstrings? That's the direct line this man still has attached to me to this day. It's also the warning signal confirming how badly I want to believe him. And emphasizing why I always need to stay on guard. I never thought I'd fall back into the same old routine so quickly and easily.

If I were forced to examine why I don't simply ask him what I want to know or tell him exactly what I'm feeling, the conclusion would be something along the lines of... ignorance is bliss. I can't handle his rejection a second time around, so it's better that I don't go there in the first place.

We resume breakfast with idle chitchat, avoiding any topic that remotely relates to the two of us. When I manage to stop just short of licking the last few crumbs off my plate, I thank him for his thoughtfulness and disappear into my bedroom. All I know about today is Silas has plans for us that require dress clothes and leaving the hotel grounds. Since he hasn't shared intel on what's waiting for us out there, that helps me decide what to wear—black dress pants, a flowing shirt, and flats.

Once I'm dressed and ready to go, Roman and I meet Silas in the lobby.

"Where are we going?" Not knowing what's on the agenda makes me a little nervous.

"There's a conference nearby at the Dubai World Trade Centre that we need to check out." The smile Silas tries to hide makes me nervous. He rarely smiles while he's working. We all know and love this about him. Usually.

"Oh, a conference? That sounds... fun." That's a lie. Complete and utter bullshit. Conferences bore me to tears. I've attended enough as Raf's security to know I'd never voluntarily sign up for one.

"Doesn't it? I thought so too." Silas strolls through the main entrance, and the attendant opens the back doors of the Rolls-Royce limousine.

The two rows of plush leather seats face each other, leaving plenty of space in between to stretch out with the electric footrests. "I think I could get used to living in the lap of luxury like this. Have you ever seen anything like this before?"

Roman turns and looks out the side window, but Silas grins and nods his head at me. "This is very nice. It's way out of my price range, but I'm not above letting someone else pamper me for a while."

"I'm surprised your boss doesn't cart you around in one of these every day." There's no malice in Roman's voice, but there's an unmistakable deeper meaning to his words.

"Rafael certainly has the money for it, but he's not pretentious like a lot of men in his position are. Yes, he has nice things and travels the world, but he doesn't call unnecessary attention to himself by announcing to everyone around how much money he has. He has a security team in place to *avoid* trouble, so he doesn't want to do anything that will encourage it."

"Smart man."

"He is a brilliant man. There's no denying that." I'm stating facts, not boasting about my employer. But when I catch a glimpse of Roman's reflection in the glass, my heart drops to my stomach. The faraway stare. His down turned features. The clipped replies.

He's giving me exactly what I asked for—what I said I wanted. He's not competing with Rafael anymore. He's not trying to win me over or convince me he's the better man. When I said I'll be the one to decide who I'm with, I wasn't implying I'd chosen Rafael. But then, I suppose I haven't *not* chosen Raf either.

This is what happens when I'm around Roman. He makes me feel like a crazy woman. I'm never indecisive. I can't be hesitant—other's lives are literally in my hands in my line of work. But give me twenty-four hours with this man, and I'm the most wishy-washy person I know. If any of my employees were in the same state of confusion, I'd sideline them until they got their shit together.

When I turn my attention toward Silas, his knowing smirk makes my face burn red hot. Without conscious effort, my eyes jerk to the empty seat beside him. His light chuckle at my discomfort only makes it worse. My skin is melting off my bones by now, I'm sure of it. I take a deep breath, trying to calm my racing heart and erratic pulse, but it does very little good.

The driver stops to let us out at the exhibition center, and Roman extends his hand to help me out of the car. We follow Silas through the main entry doors, and I stop in my tracks when I find hundreds of people milling around, looking at the exhibits, and asking questions of the oil and energy professionals on hand. Why did Silas bring us to an oil conference? I feel so lost and completely out of my element.

Silas pulls three badges out of his jacket pocket and hands one to each of us. With a quick glance at it before clipping it to my shirt, I realize Silas has been hard at work. The badge already has my name imprinted on it. He didn't make this in his hotel room last night. Before I pepper him with questions, I peek at Roman to gauge his reaction. The only response he gives is a slight nod of his head before donning his badge.

No questions. No hesitation. No doubts.

Roman begins walking again, checking out several booths and talking with the men and women staffing them as if he's an energy expert. Since our badges show we all work for the same company, I follow his lead and try to sound somewhat knowledgeable about the topics at hand. I mean, I'm not, but I'm doing my best to bluff my way through the crowd. Silas loosely follows behind us, stopping at opposite stands and waiting for us to move ahead first.

When we finish one long row that spans the entire length of the center, we stop at the refreshment center to get a couple of drinks. I've talked more over the last couple of hours than I have the past year combined. After a long gulp of ice-cold water, I twist the cap back on and look up at Roman.

The intensity in his blue-gray eyes steals my breath. Every time I look directly into his eyes, I have a physical reaction to him. My heart beats faster. I have a hard time controlling my breathing. Butterflies take flight inside my chest, swirling like a miniature tornado inside me. The man is dangerous to my sanity in so many ways.

"What are we doing here, Roman? What are we looking for?"

"I'm not sure, but I have a strong feeling we'll know when we find it." He lifts his water bottle to his lips, and I'm instantly mesmerized by the simple act of swallowing. Is it the way his tongue darts out of his mouth, barely grazing the opening of the bottle? Is it the way his full lips purse, kissing the rim? Is it because I want to lick the droplet of water left on his mouth?

The answer is most likely yes, to all three questions. And to anything else he asks me right now because I'm clearly out of my mind.

He cocks his head to the side and arches one eyebrow. One cheek rises with the most seductive half-smile. "Are you thirsty, Tawnee?"

I know that look—I've seen it all too often. He sure as hell isn't asking if I want more water. But I have no words to answer him. I stutter and stammer before I give up and nurse my water bottle instead of trying to speak until it's empty.

"Let's keep going. We're bound to find something interesting." Roman tosses his empty bottle into the recycling bin, and we start down the second aisle.

From my vantage point a couple of steps behind him, I have an excellent view. His broad shoulders taper down to his slim waist. Even when he's wearing a business suit, his muscular ass looks fantastic. Other women stop chattering and check him out when he passes by them. Not that I blame them, obviously, since I'm doing the same.

"Tawnee?" A familiar voice in the crowd pulls me out of my reverie over Roman's ass. "Oh my God. Is that really you?"

When I locate the face behind the voice, I know without a doubt we've found exactly what we're looking for... or, I should say, *who*. "Gerald?" He wraps his arms around me, pulling me into a full embrace.

It's funny... and sad... realizing how much I've missed him after seeing him again.

"Dad? What the hell?" At least Roman looks and sounds as bewildered as I feel. "I've tried to call you several times, but you haven't answered. What are you doing here?"

"I'm working—this is an oil conference. It's sort of what I do for a living, son. It's so late every night when I get back to my room, I haven't had a chance to call you. The real question is, what are you two doing here? And at this oil conference, no less? Why didn't you leave a message and tell me you were in Dubai too?" Gerald grabs his son in the same kind of bear hug he gave me, not the least bit concerned with the odd looks others send our way.

"First of all, I had no way of knowing you were even here. Second, I didn't leave a message because it's a sensitive topic. I couldn't leave it on your voice mail and chance someone else hearing it first. And last, I'm here helping Tawnee out—not for an oil conference."

"All right. Well, I can't leave the booth for a while since it's my turn to stand here and look pretty. How about we meet around one for lunch? Most of the crowd will be in breakout sessions by then. The session with my big reveal doesn't start until three."

"Sounds good, Dad. You're giving one of the session speeches here?" Roman's spy senses are tingling.

He stands up straight, drawing up to his full height, and begins carefully scanning the room. He shifts his gaze slowly and methodically, assessing everyone in his field of vision. When his eyes linger on one spot for more than a second, I follow his lead and find Silas standing off to the side with a satisfied smirk on his face.

"Yes, I am, and my topic is one of the more controversial ones, too. I can't wait to share my work with all the bigwigs in this industry." Gerald looks so proud. He makes me want to stay and listen.

"Do you speak fluent Arabic?" I don't mean to sound as shocked as I do.

He laughs. "No, sweetheart, I wish I could. They graciously hold this conference in English since it draws oil executives from all over the world."

"Ah, I see. So, what's your session about, Gerald?" I know he's a chemist for a major oil company in South Africa, but that's the extent of how much I understand about his job.

"I've created a synthetic product that can replace crude oil—and it lasts a lot longer. It'll revolutionize the entire oil industry. Instead of drilling and fracking and wrecking the environment, we can redirect our resources to manufacturing this synthetic compound instead. I'm so excited about it. Our initial trials are extremely promising."

I'm happy for Gerald—honestly, I am. But even with my limited knowledge of the oil industry, I understand he just painted an enormous target on his back. Roman stares at Gerald, his eyes wide and bottom jaw slack, shaking his head from side to side. He doesn't want to believe it either.

"Ah, shit." Roman drops his chin to his chest and stares at his feet. He's visibly uneasy in a way I've never seen him before. "There's no way it's a coincidence we're all three here at the exact same time."

Panic rises in my chest and stops at the back of my throat,

nearly choking me as I work hard to restrain the scream that desperately wants to break free. He's right. There's no fucking way. Statistically speaking, that can't ever happen.

Yet here we are.

An Arab man who knows my name and tried to kidnap me.

Someone sent Roman an SOS message from an encrypted app on my personal phone to get him here.

Soon Gerald will reveal a creation that will effectively stop the need for oil production around the world at an oil convention with worldwide business leaders.

Ah, shit is exactly right.

"We've been set up, haven't we, Roman? We're here as the bait, aren't we?"

CHAPTER 11

Roman

"Tawnee, I didn't expect to find you here." Rafael sidles up next to us, resting his hand on her lower back in a passive-aggressive intimate display.

Is this fucker serious?

I'm just about to rearrange his face when I remember my discussion with Tawnee yesterday. She doesn't appreciate my ogre ways, so I throttle down my reaction before she sees my face. She's too busy staring up at Raf's face, anyway.

"What are you doing here?" She keeps her voice low and her anger controlled, but there's no mistaking the way she enunciates each word with purpose. "You weren't supposed to leave the hotel grounds."

"Yes, I know that was the original plan. But while I was working from the hotel room, I received an email about the topics for today. It's rather fortuitous that we couldn't reschedule the property tour for this week. This conference is one of a kind, and now I'm available to attend all the discussions." His smile reminds me of a used car salesman I used to know… slimy and underhanded.

"Don't worry, Tawnee. We have him on a short leash." Tony pats her shoulder while smiling. He knows his boss is a douche. "We'd better go find the meeting room if you still want to catch the session on industry trends."

"You're right, Tony. I can't miss that one. Let's have dinner together tonight, Tawnee. We haven't finished the discussion we started on the beach. I'm deeply interested in hearing your thoughts on the matter."

"Sure. Call my room when you get back to the hotel, and we'll complete our plans." She doesn't smile like I expected her to do. She's probably still mad that he disobeyed orders.

Like clockwork, I scan the area again for any potential threats and my eyes land on Silas in his hiding place. When Rafael walks off, Silas makes a walking motion with his two fingers, signaling for us to follow. Now I know Silas expected Raf to make his appearance here, but I can't wait to hear his explanation for not clueing me in on my dad being here.

My cell pings with a text, so I fish it out of my pocket.

Silas: *Don't worry. I'm covering your dad.*

Me: *Would've been nice to know he was here…*

Silas: *I had to verify it in person. Stick with RC. He's here for a reason.*

Me: *Copy that.*

"What was that about?" Tawnee looks up at me, knowing I'm only on my cell phone while working if it's an emergency.

"Silas said we need to stick with Raf. Let's go listen in on the thrilling topic of what's new and exciting in the oil and energy industry." I didn't lie… I just didn't tell her the entire truth of why we're following Raf around.

"Does Silas know of a credible threat against Raf?" Naturally, she's more concerned about his safety than her own.

"No, that's not what he said at all. But if he says we need to go with Raf, then we go with Raf without arguing over it. So, let's go."

The only seats left in the entire room are in the very back. Funny, those are usually the seats I scrap over to get to first. This subject must be more exciting than I thought. If we'd waited much longer, we'd have to stand. The tables along the front of the stage where Rafael and Tony sit are packed. When they announce the speaker, I understand why everyone is crowding the platform.

This is a fucking terrible idea. My brain screams at me to yank Tawnee out of her chair and bolt from the room before it's too late. My gut says to stay for as long as it's safe, gather the intel, and be thankful our seats are beside the exit door. Aside from Raf and Tony, every other guest at the other end of the room is wearing a thobe and head covering...much like the man who attacked Tawnee.

Only, from the back, they all look alike. There's no way to tell if that specific man is in this crowd or not. But the hairs standing straight up on my arms assure me he's here.

"Please welcome Saudi Arabia's Minister of Energy, Industry, and Natural Resources, Nizar Al Aiban. In his previous role, he was the CEO of the world's largest oil and natural gas production company, SAOR, Inc." The announcer steps aside and shakes hands with a sleek businessman before exiting stage left.

Nizar steps up to the podium and shares his insights on where we are today, where we should be, and how we will get there. He discusses environmental protection policies, company projected earnings, and the sustainability odds of current oil production. Though I have no interest in these benign topics at all, I know the other shoe will drop at any moment. I split my focus between what the speaker says and how the crowd reacts.

An hour later, he finally reaches the end of his prepared comments and opens the floor microphones for questions from the attendees. Numerous men clamor to one of the four stands located around the room. The announcer steps back up to the podium to quiet the low roar of voices. Though I don't speak Arabic, they sound angry to me.

"As a reminder for our international guests, please phrase your question in English. If you need a translator to ask for you, we have many in the room who will gladly help." He takes his seat off to the side again, giving Nazir the floor once again.

Nazir motions toward the man waiting at the first stand. "Please go ahead with your question."

"Thank you, Minister Al Aiban. As I'm sure you've already expected, many of us have the same question about the recent unpleasant developments. More specifically, the rampant rumors that have surfaced since SAOR, Inc. became a publicly traded company last year rather than remaining state-owned. Men whom I respect said a *Jewish woman* from the United States is behind the company that has overtaken SAOR. Is this sacrilege true?"

Before Nazir says one word in response, the room erupts in a cacophony of angry shouts, low growls, and chairs scraping against the floor as more people jump to their feet. Although I don't understand what they're saying, I can take a few calculated guesses and feel confident I'm dangerously close to the mark. From citizens of a country that reviles Jews, Christians, Israelis, Americans, and basically all women around the world, their reactions are not hard to deduce.

Death to the Jewish-American woman.

Kill the foreign woman—take our oil back.

Allah forbids this blasphemy.

Tawnee leans over to whisper in my ear. "Um, wow. So much hatred in this confined space is stifling, isn't it? I've never seen a group of men have so much animosity toward women despite having four wives each."

"Their wives know their places—and that place is never equal to or above their man. A woman taking over the world's largest oil company, which happened to be Saudi-owned for the last three decades, is a direct slap in their faces. The fact that she's Jewish on top of that makes it even worse. I hope they never find out who she is because they will drag her body through the streets behind their vehicles without a shred of regret."

"How would they know she's Jewish? It's not as if they stamp our religious beliefs on our passports."

"Maybe she has a traditionally Jewish last name."

"Maybe that's her married name. It's just odd."

"Could be. Women don't take their husband's last name in Saudi Arabia. They're required by their religion to keep their father's name, so it's entirely possible they haven't considered that angle. But I will not be the one to enlighten them today."

When the room settles down enough for Nazir to answer, I notice more than a few heated glares cast in our direction. Seems they're willing to throw their anger in the direction of any woman unfortunate enough to be in the room.

"I can assure you these are all lies, carried out with the greatest of intentions. But their sole purpose is to undermine our operations and discredit our great country. We are working tirelessly to identify where these rumors have originated and stop them at the source."

He's lying. All the signs are clearly visible on his face, in his body language, and in the pitch of his voice. He's hiding the truth to save his own ass but also to keep this information out of the news. If the affluent Saudi investors find out a woman is taking over at the helm, they'll dump their stock so fast, the company will fold next week.

But then, maybe that's the whole point.

If I wanted to take over the most profitable company in the world at an unheard-of low stock price, that would certainly do it.

Rafael and Tony stand, say their goodbyes to their table-mates, and turn to leave. Raf's eyes land directly on mine. A visible jolt runs through his body when he realizes I've been watching him this entire time, studying his every reaction. Though he's unsettled, he plasters that same pretentious smile on his face to remind me I'm still beneath him.

That's all right, buddy. I've got your number.

Tawnee and I stay put as Raf makes his way toward us on his way to the exit. He stops beside Tawnee, addressing her rather than facing me. "I see you couldn't help yourself. Here you are, watching my back when you should be taking care of yourself."

"Roman and I have each other's back just fine right here. Don't worry about us."

That shitty grin Raf gave me just a minute ago? Yeah, I'm giving it right back to him now in spades. He focused solely on her, and she responded for the two of us. I really like how that minor action feels.

"Why don't you join us for lunch? Tony and I are eating with a few businessmen we just met. You're welcome to eat with us." He takes her hand in his, preparing to help her stand. Presumptuous much?

Not that he included me, but I feel obligated to decline his invitation, nonetheless. "What a shame. Tawnee and I already have plans for lunch. Maybe some other time, though."

"Some other time, then." He leans over and kisses her on the cheek. "I'll see you at dinner tonight."

When Raf and Tony are out of earshot, Tawnee turns to me. "All right, spill. Gerald, Raf, you, and I are all here. This is not a coincidence. What is going on?"

"You know as much as I do, sweets. I'm sure whatever is

coming will make itself known very soon. What fun would it be if our luck changed now?"

"Only you could make me see this situation as a game." She shakes her head at me, but her smile is there just the same.

"Sometimes it's better to think of these situations as a game. That way, you don't freeze up with fear or indecision. Everything we do is about moves and countermoves... beating our opponent's next play before it's even made. That approach helps me anyway."

"You know, that actually makes sense. I'll try that."

"Looks like we can make our way out of here now. The crowd around the door is thinning out. Let's go see who Rafael and Tony are having lunch with before we check on Dad again. I'm a little curious."

"Curious? That's not the word I'd use. More like suspicious." We stand and make our way into the crowd and through the doors.

"That word fits too." With my hand on her lower back, I steer her clear of the masses and start walking toward the exhibit booths.

"Roman, I've worked for him for three years. That's a long time to be that close to someone and not know them inside and out. Do you not trust my judgment?"

"You know I do. But people change, Tawnee. Sometimes when you're looking right at them. The people closest to you know how to hide their lies because they know what you'd notice. You wouldn't see the most subtle changes, though. Psychopaths have this shit down to an art."

"Are you saying Rafael is a psychopath?" She arches one eyebrow.

"No. But I'm not saying he's *not* one either."

"You're impossible."

"Impossible to stay away from? Impossible not to fall head over heels in love with? I know. It's both a blessing and a curse, but I'll take one for the team and bear this heavy burden, anyway." I expect an eye-roll, maybe even a sarcastic huff, but I'm more than a little pleased to see an amused smile instead.

We take the long route along the deserted hallway and swing by the rear doors of the ballroom where the expansive buffet is underway. This affair isn't quite up to par with Rafael's usual dining preference, but no one would know that from the huge smile on his face. Even Tony is laughing and joking with several of the Arab men sitting around them. Then Tony sees us standing in the doorway and lifts his hand in a small wave. The man sitting on Tony's right looks to see who he's waving at, and his cheerful expression instantly changes.

He points toward us, his finger exaggeratedly jabbing at the air.

Then everything turns black.

Someone slips a hood over my head.

Muscular arms wrap around my neck from behind, pulling me backward at a fast pace.

Tawnee screams my name from beside me, her cries for me muffled. But my captor has me effectively incapacitated and unable to help her.

I hear the heavy metal door of the conference center open, then we're thrown inside a darkened space, with Tawnee landing on top of me. More arms grab us, holding us down to prevent us from putting up too much of a fight. But they obviously don't know who they're dealing with, because Tawnee and I both let our legs and arms fly, contacting whatever flesh we can find.

During the fight, I realize we're in the back of a panel van from the unmistakable sound of a door sliding shut—just as the engine whines and the tires squeal in the rapid getaway. We're jostled around on the floor when the van jumps the curb and swerves right into the already heavy traffic, and several heavy bodies pounce on top of us. Horns blow from all directions and angry shouts soon follow, but our getaway driver never misses a beat.

"Keep your heads down and stay quiet if you want to live," the angry, gravelly voice commands as someone else binds our hands and feet with zip ties.

Tawnee

"Irecognize your voice, even though you're trying to disguise it. Take these cheap-ass cuffs off me, or you'll get a thorough ass-kicking when I get free." Roman controls his tone, but I sense the hostility behind his words. I'm still pinned on top of him despite the terrible driver behind the wheel throwing us around the interior like rag dolls.

"Wait a minute—I know that voice too." At first, I was too freaked out to realize who grabbed us. Now I know exactly who it is. "Take this bag off my head and untie me right now. Or so help me God, I will taser you right on your balls, film it with my phone, and upload it to every social media site known to man."

Laughter fills the vehicle, then the man lying on my back slides off. Fingers wrap around my shoulders and upper arms to help me up since my hands are bound behind my back, then someone removes the thick black bag covering my face.

"Hello, Tawnee. So good to see you again." He has the nerve to smile at me.

"Rebel. Take these ties off my hands and feet right now."

"Do you promise not to punch and kick me again? You have a mean swing. That last one nearly broke my jaw." He raises his eyebrows, waiting for me to assure him I'll play nice.

"I promise if you don't release me right now, the damage will be much worse than a broken jaw when I'm through with you."

"Can someone take this fucking bag off my head? Now!"

All our eyes drop to Roman, who's still lying on the floor of the van, as if we forgot he was there. When I look back up at Rebel, Bull, and Shadow, we all burst out laughing, immediately dispelling the tension from just a moment ago.

"Yes. This is all real fucking funny. Just so you know, I'm kicking everyone's ass when I get out of here. Everyone involved. I don't care who you are." Roman's hands also are bound behind him, so even though he manages to sit upright, he still can't remove the covering.

"Leave Roman's on. That's a much better look for him," Reaper calls from the front.

"I should have known you were driving, Steele. You never could drive for shit," the talking bag retorts. After Bull releases my hands and feet, I help him free Roman. He glares at each man individually for a minute, contemplating a brawl in the back of the van. I can see it in his eyes. "Was all that shit really necessary?"

"We had to make it look convincing." Shadow shrugs one shoulder, as if we already should have known that.

"I meant being hog-tied once we were already in the back of the vehicle." Roman's eyebrows draw downward.

"Oh, that. Well, we weren't going to originally, but we came prepared just in case it came to that. You both fought like two feral cats in a burlap sack. You two gave us no other choice, so that was really your fault." Bull leans back against the side of the van and grins.

"You boys are enjoying this a little too much. Let me guess. Silas called you the minute they landed, and you decided to get in on the action too." I fold my arms over my chest then watch as each man cuts his eyes to the next one.

"Close, but not quite, Tawnee. We were here before you arrived. Shadow is here on official assignment, and he asked us to join him as private contractors. Silas called me when he got to his hotel room, but he didn't know we were already here until then." Reaper pulls into a driveway in a residential area and jumps out of the driver's door.

He slides the side door open, and we all file out, following him into an elaborately beautiful Italian-themed beachfront home. Strike that—this is a mansion. Should have known these guys wouldn't have anything less.

"Here's your new home sweet home for the next few days. The kitchen is fully stocked, but let me know if there's anything else you want. This neighborhood is safe for you to move around in, but don't venture out into the tourist areas. We want everyone to think you're being held for ransom." Shadow takes us on a quick tour to show us the layout and where to find everything we'll need.

"I'm starting to think I don't charge anywhere near enough for my services." I stroll through the interior behind him, amazed at the expensive marble on the floor and the walls. Every room is professionally decorated and offers every amenity anyone could possibly want. "This place is way out of my price range."

When we reach the back of the house, I realize exactly what love at first sight means. The entire wall is floor-to-ceiling windows, overlooking a lush, green yard, an outdoor kitchen with spacious seating, a gorgeous pool, and a private beach on the turquoise water of the gulf. I'm claiming this area for myself.

"There are some perks that come with the job. When you conduct business in an area known to attract the world's wealthy, you can't stay in a run-down shack. This house leaves no doubt about my status in society." Shadow is enjoying this part of his job a little too much.

"Yes, your image as a wealthy kidnapper is critical. Got it."

"Well, yeah. Even us kidnappers have to look good while doing it. Where have you been, Tawnee?"

"With my head under a black burlap sack, evidently."

"Good one. I knew I liked you for some reason." He smiles and winks, then moves to the refrigerator to grab a few drinks. He passes around the cans of beer, and we all take a seat outside.

"We knew something was up when we saw Silas hiding in the shadows at the convention center, but we didn't know what. How did you know we'd be in that hallway?" Roman takes a sip and waits for someone to fill us in.

"Silas called and told us which route you'd taken. It was the perfect timing. There were enough people around to authenticate the story, but none close enough to interfere. And, Rafael was right there in our line of sight—so it was perfect." Shadow quickly lifts and lowers his eyebrows before his smile covers his face.

"I don't get it. What am I missing?" I search their faces, waiting for the punch line—something—to explain what they obviously already know.

"You know, Tawnee... we had to ask ourselves if you knew what was going on. Ultimately, we decided there was no way you knew. But I've got to tell you, the evidence against you looks very damning." Reaper moves to sit down across from me and levels his assessing gaze on me.

"Evidence against me? What the fuck are you talking about? And how could you ever suspect me, Reap? You're the one who hired me after a thorough background check." I'm still so lost. I've worked on dangerous cases with these men. I've trusted them with my life, and they've trusted me with theirs. Reaper trusted me to protect his parents. But now they are looking at me as if I'm the criminal under investigation. "Someone needs to explain right now."

"Wait here." Bull walks into the house and returns with a file in his hand. "You need to read this. Just don't kill the messenger."

With an unsteady hand, I take the folder from him and flip it open. The first page is mundane business information, but I take note of the key details and move on to page two. As the pieces of the scattered puzzle start to fall into place, I flip the pages faster and faster. When I reach the end of their research and have the full picture clear in my mind, I slam the file shut and stare at it for a long, heated minute.

"Now you see why we needed a moment to gather our wits?" Reaper asks.

The sympathetic tone of his voice nearly shatters my outward façade. I need to hold on to this anger… this hatred… because the last thing I want to do is cry in front of these men. I haven't fought the stereotype of women in the security game all these years just to let it crumble in front of me now over this bullshit.

"Yeah, I see it all very clearly now… and I know what I have to do. I have a bullet with someone's name on it." My fingers curl around the manila folder, gripping until my knuckles are white. It strikes me as funny since I just watched my unconscious reaction happen right before my eyes.

But I'm not laughing right now.

The betrayal is far too fresh. The wound is way too deep. My revenge will be all too swift.

"You can't kill anyone, Tawnee. Not yet, anyway. You and I know who the villain is, but all of that is circumstantial. You'll take the blame for everything if we don't handle this exactly right. We're on your side, and you know we won't let you down." Shadow loosens my grip one finger at a time then takes the folder from me.

"Someone want to clue me in?" Roman stands and faces Shadow, waiting for his chance to read the file.

"No. We talked it over with Silas, and he wants you to remain in the dark about what's happening with this case. Tawnee needs to know what she's facing, but it's best that you don't know yet. Your reactions to everything that happens from this point forward must be genuine. No acting allowed on your part." Shadow walks back into the house, slides the folder into his laptop bag, and rejoins us on the lanai.

"You're fucking serious? I thought you were just pulling my leg with that whole keeping me in the dark fuckery. This isn't funny, man. What is Tawnee being blamed for? Who's setting her up? How am I supposed to have her back when I don't know what to watch for?"

"This is no different from any other job you've done before, Roman. It's no different from it was ten minutes ago when you knew even less. You'll never know all the variables, but you still have to find a way to account for every possible scenario. Stop putting your personal feelings in the mix and look at this from the same standpoint as you would for any other mission." Reaper stares Roman down until he submits.

"You're right, man. I know you are. Okay, if it's that important to Tawnee's safety, I'll be the odd man out and act all surprised over whatever's coming our way. Doesn't mean I have to like this shit, though." His sarcasm is spot-on. I only recognized it because I know him so well.

Plus, I know Roman better than to believe he'll just let this go with no further explanation. The first second he catches me alone, he'll grill me with every question under the sun. When I don't cave in, we'll end up in a huge fight and be right back where we started.

It's kind of our thing.

Or, it used to be our thing, anyway.

"Next steps are easy," Shadow continues, ignoring Roman's

sarcastic digs if he even realized them. "Hang out here until we 'release' you. Try not to kill each other. If you do, hide the body so it doesn't smell. Don't do anything to get the police called on you."

"Where's the best place to hide a body around here?" I ask. Completely serious.

"Probably dump it in the gulf and let the sharks eat it. Tiger sharks are mean, you know." Shadow gets me.

"Are you guys not staying here in your posh kidnapper pad?" I ask when they all stand and walk toward the garage door.

"No, this place is way too shabby for us. We'll check back in on you soon, though." Shadow smiles and walks out first. They climb into a Range Rover parked in the second carport and wave goodbye.

Roman and I stand at the door to the garage and watch our captors leave. As soon as the garage door closes, Roman turns to me, folds his arms over his chest, and quirks one eyebrow.

"Let's have it, Milano. Don't leave out one single word of what you read in that file. I don't care what they say. I can't cover your ass as well if I don't know who and what we're up against."

"Sorry, Roman, no can do. I really do agree with the guys on this one. It's best that you don't know what was in there ahead of time."

"Fuck that, Tawnee. If I have to hold you down and torture you all night, you will give up the intel I need. One..." He takes a predatory move toward me with a sinister gleam in his eye.

I turn on my heel and dash through the house, trying not to scream and laugh too loud as I outrun him. When I reach the bedroom, I grab the lock on the doorknob, ready to turn it the second the door shuts, but a size thirteen shoe slips inside the opening at the last second. Then he squeezes his face between the door and the frame, his eyes wild and crazy, and a grin so big it shows all his teeth.

"Let me in, Tawnee. Open the door and let me in on your own. If I have to open it, you'll be very sorry."

I can't stop laughing. "No, Roman, I'm not letting you in here. You're not holding me down and torturing me. Now move your foot and your face before I cut them off with the door."

"Nuh-uh, sweets. My fingers are itching to get to you. Every second that passes only makes it worse...for you. When I get ahold of you..."

"Roman, no. I mean it. No, no, no, no, no!"

When another fit of laughter hits me from the crazy expression on his face, he pushes the door open and rushes toward me. I stumble backward, trying to stay out of his reach, but the back of my legs hit the edge of the bed. It's too late to get away. He pushes me down on my back and pounces on top of me, placing his knees at my sides to cage me in. He holds my hands above my head with one hand and wiggles his fingers on the other while hovering over my ribs.

"Tell me... or the torture session commences."

"I can't tell you anything."

His fingers move closer, and I squirm involuntarily at the mere thought.

"Tawnee. You know I won't stop."

"Roman, this is not very nice of you at all."

"It's not nice to keep secrets from me. Last chance, Milano. Tell me what was in that file."

I shake my head. "You know I can't. This is Shadow's job. What he showed me in that file is classified."

"I don't care. I'm a CIA officer, too. I have top-secret clearance the same as he does. Two..."

"Don't do it, Roman!"

"Three!"

He is relentless. His brand of torture is to tickle the information out of me. The bad thing is, it usually works because I can't stand it for long. He uses my weakness against me, and he enjoys it immensely. He releases my hands so he can use both of his to torment me more. I try to push his hands away, but he's much stronger than I am, so it does little good.

"Ready to talk yet?"

"Yes! Now let me up. I need something to drink after all that screaming."

His face is barely an inch above mine. His lips hover just over my mouth—so close, but so far away. The heady scent of his cologne envelops me, lingering in the air until all I want is to breathe him into me. "Hmm. I think you're trying to trick me. You know what'll happen if that's what you're up to, Tawnee."

Busted. I planned to run into the other bedroom and lock the door. To save myself from doing something even stupider than telling him what I read in that file. "Fine. You win. Just stop tickling me now."

"Good. Let's go raid the fridge and talk over a nice, long meal. I'll even cook for you. All you have to do is whisper in my ear and tell me all your secrets, sweets."

It's times like this that make me miss Roman more than usual. But that's one secret I won't spill tonight.

Roman

Shadow wasn't kidding when he said they stocked the kitchen with everything we could possibly want to eat or drink. I'm keeping my promise to Tawnee and cooking a meal to make up for the lunch we missed earlier.

"You know, I wish they had let us stay long enough to hear Dad's speech. I'm not worried about him because I know Silas is watching him, but I would have liked to hear about his work." I start taking out all the ingredients I need to make our date night meal. Or, afternoon date. Whatever.

"I would have enjoyed hearing him speak, too. It's been so long since the last time I saw him. Too long. I've always loved your dad. Don't suppose he got remarried in the last three years, did he?"

"No, there's no way he'll ever do that. Losing my mom so suddenly and at such a young age scarred him for life. He won't put his heart out there and risk having it sliced into a million pieces again." I drop the ground beef into the frying pan and chop it until all the small pieces crumble.

"Guess you still don't get to see him very often, huh?" Tawnee moves to the refrigerator to retrieve a bottle of wine.

"Can you hand me the lettuce, tomatoes, cheese, and sour cream while you're in there, sweets?" She pulls one ingredient out at a time and passes it to me. "No, I don't get to see him in person nearly enough. We video chat at least once a week, but it's always so bittersweet. I know his work is important to him, but I wish he'd move back to the States. He could have retired years ago and spent his remaining time with me."

"He loves you more than anything in the world, Roman. But he obviously never healed from his broken heart. Everything back home reminds him of your mom." The memory of the phone call telling us Mom had died of a sudden heart attack grips me, stealing my breath all over again. Tawnee continues speaking, thankfully pulling me back into this moment. "I'll never forget what he said to me one day. It struck a chord so deep inside me, I haven't been able to shake it to this day. He said, 'Tawnee, you only get one love of a lifetime. When you lose that, you lose the will to love again.' What scares me the most is thinking he's right."

I force air into my lungs again and quickly turn toward her. "I never knew—" Not realizing she was standing so close since I was in my own little world, I crash into her outstretched hand holding my glass of wine. The cold liquid splashes all over my shirt, soaking me until the fabric sticks to my chest. "Shit, that's cold!"

"Oh no—I'm sorry, Roman. I hope I didn't just ruin your shirt."

I chuckle to myself as she rushes to the sink to wet a dish towel. "Don't worry about it, Tawnee." Reaching behind me, I grab the back and snatch it over my head. "I'll throw it in the washer, and it'll be as good as new. No big deal. It's not like it's one of those thousand-dollar silk shirts your boss wears."

"Still, I feel bad for pouring wine all over you. You'll be all sticky now."

"I've been worse than sticky before. I'll survive." I wink at her and toss the shirt in the general direction of the laundry room. "How about getting me a refill while I start on our side dishes?"

"Sure. I'll try not to give you a bath in it this time." She tops off my glass and hands it to me.

After a few sips in between removing the skins and pits from the avocadoes, I kick off my shoes and make myself comfortable. I'm focused on making homemade guacamole, adding all the ingredients, and ensuring it tastes perfect, when I remember what we were talking about.

"Hang on. You said you were afraid my dad was right about only having one love of a lifetime. I never knew he told you about his 'love theory.' He started saying that shortly after Mom died."

"Yeah, we were talking one day when he came home to visit. I think you were working. He was struggling with all the memories of Barbara hitting him at once, and I tried to console him. The hollow expression in his eyes broke my heart. He truly believed what he was saying. He doesn't think he can ever love or be loved again. It's sad because he can still have a full life, with love and laughter and family. From what you've both told me about your mom, I don't think she'd want him to be unhappy for one second. She certainly wouldn't want to be the cause of him not finding love again."

Tawnee's insight hits me like a bolt of lightning—all one billion volts strike me square in the chest. I have trouble catching my breath again while small black dots dance in the air in front of my face. My grip around the handle of the frying pan tightens, but I can't move the rest of my body.

"Here, let me help you with that. You're about to burn our dinner. It takes a special talent to ruin tacos." Under normal circumstances, I'd have a quick retort to her joke about my culinary skills.

But I can't think of a single comeback now.

When I realize I'm no longer holding the pan or the spatula, I take a step back from the stove and lean against the island before I fall to the floor from the smallest puff of air. She adds the finishing touches to our meal and turns to me with her beautiful smile in place.

Then it instantly fades.

"Roman, are you okay? What's wrong? Should I call an ambulance?" The sheer panic in her voice clears the fog from between my ears.

"What? No. Why would you think I need an ambulance?"

"Because you're gripping your chest. Your face is all contorted as if you're in pain, and you're suddenly as white as a ghost."

"Oh." I look down and realize my fingers are curled into my skin, over my heart.

"I thought you were having a heart attack or something. You scared me. What's going on, Roman? And don't tell me it's nothing because it's clearly something."

"All right. Let me finish making the guacamole and salsa for the chips, then I'll tell you. I promised you a full meal after all."

The skeptical look she shoots me isn't exactly subtle, but she arranges the fixings for the tacos along the bar while I finish the sides. When we sit down together, she watches me expectantly, and I know without a doubt she won't let me off the hook with this one. Not that she should... I deserved that slap in the face of perspective and self-awareness.

"Tawnee, first I want to apologize for how we split up. You were right about a lot of my deficits, but I never corrected you about one assumption you made. I was selfish, immature, stupid, bullheaded, and all the other idiotic things. But I never —*never*—thought there was someone better waiting around the corner. I've always known there's no one better than you. There's no one I'd ever want more than I want you. There's no one who would ever compare to you."

Her throat muscles work to swallow the emotion bubbling up. Unshed tears glisten in her eyes. Her chest heaves, rising and falling rapidly with her ragged breaths. She gently shakes her head from side to side as if she doubts her own ears. This confession has been a long time coming, and there's a very real probability I'm too late.

But it's now or never, and I can't let this moment pass without trying.

"Mom and Dad's love was like a fire that could never be extinguished. It kept them warm, protected… alive. One thrived off the other, and everyone around them could feel how pure their love was. Even when they fought, it was always with the understanding that nothing could take their love away.

"But then she died. Without warning. Without a chance to say goodbye. There was no way to prepare for the devastation she left behind. My father's very essence withered up and died without my mother there to give him a reason to go on. Obviously, he loved me and provided for me. He was a great father. But he couldn't teach me the right way to love a woman, because he simply didn't have it in him anymore."

We both need a second to digest all that I'm throwing at her, so I empty my wineglass. She's still fighting the emotions raging inside, unable to verbalize what's she's thinking or feeling. So, I continue.

"It was devastating, losing someone I loved with all my heart. Somehow, I forgot how good it felt to love. My father's vow never to allow anyone into his heart became mine, although not intentionally. What you said to me just now nearly drove me to my knees, Tawnee. Mom would be furious with Dad and me if she knew how we'd shut ourselves off from sharing our love with someone special. She'd say we were cowards for being afraid of getting hurt again. She'd also blame herself for causing us so much unnecessary pain. She'd be so disappointed in us—in me. She'd be disappointed in *me*... for not making a life with the woman I still want more than anything. All this time, I never realized the truth until you said it."

Tawnee stares at me, the silence stretching between us. She searches my eyes, part of her wanting to believe me, wanting to accept this is real. But then her shields fly back up. Her expression hardens when her self-preservation kicks in. She shakes her head harder this time, and her lips form a thin line.

"Nope. No way. I'm not falling into this trap again, Roman Scott. Do you have any idea how many times I gave you 'one more chance' over the years we were together? Too many, that's how many. I wasted so much time trying to give you love that you never wanted, and you made that painfully clear to me—repeatedly. Your little speech just now was very convincing, I'll give you that. For a few seconds there, I *actually* considered giving this dog and pony show of ours one more try. How stupid am I?

"You have this wonderful moment of clarity about how shitty you treated me and how disappointed your mommy would be in you, so you want to make it up to her. I mean, what the fuck, Roman? You're a grown man. Whether she's here, you know what love is... and you know what it isn't. You're trying to make amends to someone who isn't here anymore, not to me. I promise you this—I won't put my heart out there for you to trample all over it again. Any chance you had of reconciling with me has long passed."

She pushes back from the table, takes the wine bottle and her glass, and walks toward the back door.

"Tawnee, put all the other bullshit aside and answer one question for me with the full, unadulterated truth."

She stops in her tracks, only turning her head to look at me over her shoulder. "What do you want to know?"

"Do you love me?" I hold my breath and wait for her honest answer.

"Roman, if I thought any good would come out of it, I'd answer that question. But since I don't see anything changing between us, we should leave this subject alone."

"I deserve that after driving you away like I did. I've wanted to tell you how sorry I am every day since then. But I was too proud… too stupid… too scared to do anything about it. That coded message kicked my ass into gear—because I realized I didn't want to live anymore if I'd lost you for good.

"Then seeing you again nearly made me lose my mind. I've almost bitten my tongue off a million times since that moment to keep from shouting out how much you mean to me. But I knew if I just threw my feelings at you all at once, you'd run away again because you wouldn't believe me. I'm telling you now because it's the truth. If I die tomorrow, I want you to know no other woman has ever held my heart. Telling you has nothing to do with seeking my mom's forgiveness. I only want yours."

She lowers her face, staring down at the floor. I watch help-lessly as big fat tears fall straight down from her eyes. I slip out of my chair and take a couple of steps in her direction. I don't want to crowd her, but I don't want to give her an easy out to turn away from me either.

"I'm right here, sweets, waiting for you with my heart wide open. All you have to do is step into my arms, and I'll shower you with all the love you can stand. For the rest of your life. For the rest of *our* lives together, Tawnee."

"I can't." Her whisper is so full of both pain and longing. She wants to, but she won't allow herself to chance playing the fool again.

My next play is a gamble… and I'm betting the house on it. I'm sending up silent prayers it works.

"Bullshit. You can, and you know it. You're just scared. You think you need this brick wall up all the time. Never let anyone see your weaknesses. Never admit to having any. Keep your emotions out of everything—including relationships—so you'll be taken seriously.

"You should know better than anyone that's not how any of this works. Teams are built based on the strengths and weaknesses of the individuals in them so there's a balance. Emotion plays its part the same as logic does. Brute strength is just as important as intellectual power. Persuasion can be more effective than force.

"Do you know what's both your weakness and your strength?"

"What?"

"Love, sweets. Love is. You are my weakness, Tawnee. I'd lay down my life for you this very second. But you're also my strength. There's nothing I wouldn't do for you. If you can honestly tell me you don't love me, I'll let you go right now, even though I know I'll never be happy again. But if it means you will be, that's all that matters to me."

Actions speak louder than words.

Sometimes the words need to be said, though.

Now that I've completely opened my heart and mind to her, the decision is all up to her. What will she choose?

Walk into my arms—or walk out the door?

CHAPTER 14

Tawnee

Roman takes another step closer to me. I want to believe him, and that's why I'm hesitant. Am I considering giving in and walking straight into his outstretched arms because I think he has changed? Or is being with him what I've wanted for so long, I can't see myself with anyone else now?

With my eyes closed, I drop my head back, inhale a deep breath, and slowly release it and try to blow the stress out on my exhale. When I envision my future, who do I see at my side? Who's there to comfort me, love me, and share even the most mundane details of my day with? I relax the tight control I've kept on my feelings and let the scene flow freely in my mind. I can see every detail as clearly as if I'm watching a movie on the silver screen.

When I open my eyes, I turn to face Roman. Those hypnotic blue-gray eyes are laser-focused on my every move. His inner turmoil swirls in them—fear, unease, and love. Now I know I'm not wishing it into existence. He's showing me in the only ways he knows how.

Hot tears spill over onto my cheeks, but I don't bother to wipe them away. They'll only be replaced by more waiting for their turn. My heart knows exactly what it wants, regardless of whether my brain agrees. My feet move of their own accord, rushing toward his waiting embrace. Somehow, in the few feet that separated us, I manage to put the wine bottle on the counter just before launching myself at him.

He catches me in midair, and his strong arms engulf me. I wrap my legs around his waist as I encircle his neck with my arms. He crushes his mouth to mine, and everything around us disappears. Our lips and tongues explore urgently, needing more and more, until we're consumed with unfulfilled need. The inherent electricity between us arcs, igniting our bodies with so much heat, our shirts seemingly melt off us and fall into a puddle on the floor.

My back hits the wall, jarring me out of a Roman-induced haze, and I break our locked lips for one more confirmation that I'm not in this alone. His arm, leg, and the wall hold me up while he searches my face, his love for me still shining brightly in his eyes. His gaze lingers on the wetness still on my cheeks. He wipes away the remnants of my tears with the pad of his thumb then leaves soft kisses in their place.

"I've missed you so fucking much, sweets." He leans his forehead against mine and closes his eyes. "Now that I have you back in my arms, don't expect me to let you go ever again."

There's so much regret in his voice and so much tenderness in his touch. Is it too much to hope the childish man I knew before has matured since we've been apart? Honestly, I don't want him to change everything about himself. He's still the man I fell in love with long ago. Our problems weren't all his fault. Now that he owned up to his shortcomings, I owe it to him to do the same.

"Roman, I…" His lips are back on mine before I can say another word.

"Unless you're about to talk dirty to me, and I mean *filthy, nasty*, dirty talk, whatever else you want to tell me can wait. But my balls are bluer than the water out there in the gulf. They can't wait one minute longer."

Leave it to Roman to make me laugh and put our current situation into perspective with only a few well-chosen words. "Yep, it can wait. Absolutely."

"Can't tell you how glad I am to hear you say that. I was about to strip those pants off you, bend you backward over the couch, and feast on you instead of the tacos still on the table."

"Oh, okay. Put me down, and I'll be glad to help you out with that."

His sexy smirk of reply is enough to dissolve my panties right off my body. He lowers my feet to the floor, skims his fingers down my chest, and relieves me of the rest of my clothes. With his arms wrapped around my waist and his hands resting on my ass, he walks me backward until we find the couch.

"Lie back, sweets. A growing boy needs to be fed. And I'm fucking starving."

Before I can respond, his mouth is on me. His tongue licks, flicks, and teases. Stars burst behind my eyelids when he sucks my clit into his mouth. His teeth barely graze over the sensitive bud, and my hands automatically fly to his head. I curl my fingers into his hair, gripping it tighter as each wave of pleasure crashes through me.

This man makes me crazy in so many ways. Every touch reminds me of when we were a couple years before. The memories of our good times have gotten me through so many dark patches when we were apart. The way he makes love to my body always left me more than satisfied and thoroughly spent. He takes his time, finding the exact spots that drive me wild, and uses it to our mutual advantage. Every touch, every kiss, and every bite only make me crave him more.

His hands slide under my ass, lifting me off the couch to give him better access. Then he begins his thorough feast yet again, until my screams fill the room and my body quivers from the overstimulation. He sheds the rest of his clothes and helps me upright again. The tender kisses he gives convey his feelings without words. The way his hands cover my cheeks, reverently holding me while our tongues perform their own mating ritual.

"I'm the luckiest fucking man in the world," he whispers in my ear, then leaves a trail of kisses and nips down the sensitive cord in my neck. "It's been too fucking long, Tawnee. Too long since I've tasted you, since I've felt you wrapped around me, since I've heard you scream my name loud enough for the neighbors to complain. I will rectify all of that several times tonight."

"They warned us not to have the police called on us." My breathy reply is hardly an objection. Merely an observation.

"I never agreed to that stipulation." He pulls my hair to one side and follows it around the back of my neck. "Now, be a good girl and bend over for me."

Goosebumps spread out across my skin, and a shiver runs down my spine when I do as he commands. I know what's coming next, so I grab the edge of the couch in a death grip. I feel him behind me, skimming the head of his impressive cock along my slit. Teasing. Tempting. Torturing. The anticipation builds inside me, making all my muscles tense into tight coils while I wait for his next move. Every second that passes only adds to the thrill.

Then all of a sudden, he ends my anguish when he thrusts inside me. He fills and stretches me to accommodate him, and my body loves every second of it. The soreness I'll feel later is more than worth the intense pleasure he's giving me right now. His fingers dig into my hips as he holds tightly. His hips thrust harder and harder, punishing me mercilessly while stopping just short of inflicting pain. He is the only man who has ever had the power to make my body obey his every command.

After we christen every surface in the room and my body has been bent in more ways than a contortionist could manage, he finds his release. At last. My legs are about as useful as overcooked spaghetti noodles. My arms shake from overuse. Every inch of my body is covered in sweat—his and mine combined. I'm basically a pathetic bag of skin and bones lying in a heap on the floor, unable to move, barely able to speak, and incapable of removing the permanent smile that's now etched on my face.

"That was an incredible first round. Let's eat the tacos, chips, and dip then I'll be ready for round two." He springs up from lying on the floor to standing straight up as if he's an acrobat. Not a single sign of fatigue or lethargy in his demeanor.

"Make my plate and bring it over here. I'll eat mine from right here on the floor," I mumble into the throw rug. The one that gave me carpet burns in places no one should ever have carpet burns.

He chuckles from above me. "No can do, sweets. As much as I love looking at your sweet ass up in the air like it is…and all the ideas your current position gives me… we're still having dinner together. Come on."

His strong arms wrap around my waist, and he hoists me up to stand with no effort at all. With his hands on my cheeks again, he places sweet kisses on my lips.

"Thank you for getting me up off the floor." My weak smile is only because I obviously don't have his stamina. But he knows, so there's no explanation needed.

"My pleasure. Let me grab you a shirt to wear, and we'll finish the gourmet taco meal I cooked." He winks and jogs—*jogs*—to the bedroom to find whatever clothes the guys left here for us.

While he's rustling through the closet and drawers, I reheat the taco meat and shells. Taking a moment to examine the spread he made for us, I realize how much work went into it. He made the dips from scratch with all fresh ingredients. The toppings for our tacos are all neatly cut up in small bowls. The entire presentation was important to him... and it was all for me.

Tacos and guacamole shouldn't make me feel all emotional. This isn't the reaction of a normal, sane person.

The small gestures do matter the most. His attention to the details that others overlook shows how much he cares. The dedication to making every facet as perfect as possible confirms he values my opinion. Was his impromptu speech truly spontaneous and unrehearsed, or has he been holding in all those thoughts and feelings much longer than I realize?

"I found a T-shirt you can lounge around in."

When I turn from the stove to take the shirt, I realize he's been watching me, assessing my reactions while I didn't know I was being observed. "Thank you." I pull the shirt over my head and turn back to finish reheating our food.

"Want to share what you were just thinking about with me? You were latched on to something intense." He takes the reheated food from me and moves back to the table.

"I've been angry with you for a long time, and I just realized how I never gave you the credit you deserved. There were so many little things you did for me every day that I never even acknowledged. You took care of a lot of things without my asking you to or even knowing you did. If I hadn't reacted the way I did at the end, I wonder where we'd be today."

"You're not the one to blame for our problems, Tawnee. The little things I did never made up for everything you did for me. Not that I've changed *that* much, but I was immature and unappreciative. Your leaving me was the slap in the face I needed to wake the fuck up. At first, I thought you'd be back in a day or two. But then you struck out on your own, got this sweet gig with one of the world's wealthiest men, and you were gone.

"That made me grow the fuck up. I couldn't depend on you to take care of all my bullshit anymore. When I had to take responsibility for all the little things I'd counted on you to handle for me, I couldn't deny how shitty I'd treated you. As far as commitment goes, you had every right to expect that and more from me. For the record, I was always committed to you. I never even looked at another woman, much less thought about holding out for someone better.

"Where would we be if you hadn't left me? We'll never know. As much as I hate to admit this, I don't think we'd be right here, right now, in this new relationship we've found. For that, I can't regret losing you three years ago, because now I can promise I'll never do anything to make you want to leave me in the future."

His words still echo in my mind long after he spoke them. He urged me to fix my plate before the hot food got cold again and the cold food got warmer. Every bite was better than the last, because I knew it was made by his hands with love—for me. He hasn't said those three little words yet, but his deeds have proven it to me time and again.

Over dinner, we talk nonstop, catching up on every insignificant detail of the last three years we can possibly think of. We intentionally avoid discussing any kind of romantic relationships that may have occurred while we were split up. As Ross so eloquently said, "We were on a break!" The truth is, it doesn't matter if either of us sought comfort from someone else—we're human, we're alive, and we both had to keep moving forward. Our love and our relationship are just that—ours. If we focus our attention on anything else, we'll be no better off than we were before.

Neither of us wants that.

For the first time, Roman and I are on the same page, and it feels better than I ever imagined it could.

"You know, I saw some bathing suits in there while I was rummaging through the clothes to find that shirt. What do you say to a long, leisurely dip in the ocean from our private beach? I think we've earned that perk after the day we've had. I mean, we were kidnapped today. That's very traumatic."

"I agree. We deserve a little fun in the surf. I'm sure I've read somewhere that it helps prevent PTSD after a traumatic event."

"You read that in one of those tabloid newspapers you love so much, didn't you?"

"Let it go, Roman. I told you they have the best crossword puzzles."

This feels so right—the joking, the sarcasm only he and I seem to get, the way we know each other inside and out.

"Let's go change into our suits. I would love to skinny-dip, but I'm positive that would end in our arrest."

"You're absolutely correct. So will any public displays of affection out there, so don't even think about ocean sex. They barely tolerate it when tourists hold hands in public, so we're not testing them on anything else."

He huffs loudly, disgusted by my ocean sex refusal. I knew that was what he had planned. "Fine. But only because I know you'd be in a lot more trouble than I would."

"Whoever said chivalry is dead? We have living proof of it right here, ladies and gents."

"Tawnee?"

"Yeah?"

"You should be running right now."

I squeal and take off toward the bedroom. It's only when I cross the threshold that I realize this is exactly where he wanted me to go. Too late—he's already right on my heels and blocking the exit.

"I suppose I'll just have to settle for pre-ocean sex to hold me over." He waggles his eyebrows at me before stalking toward me with that damn sexy swagger and irresistible smirk.

Putty. I'm putty in the man's hands.

CHAPTER 15

Roman

"What types of sharks are in the Persian Gulf again?"

"The only shark you have to worry about is me, Tawnee. Now get your ass in this water with me right now."

She wades in, coming toward me with a sly smile on her face. "The water feels good."

"Yes, it does. I know how to make it feel better."

"No, Roman. I mean it. The answer is no, no, no."

"Spoilsport. Taking away all my fun." She rolls her eyes at me, but the smile on her face is genuine. I've missed seeing it and missed being the reason behind it even more. "Let's grab the masks and fins so we can snorkel over by the rocks."

After we put on our gear, we swim the short distance to a retaining wall that has large rocks piled against it, creating a man-made reef. We spend hours swimming back and forth, watching the small, colorful fish dart in and out of the rocks. When she reaches for my hand to get my attention, I don't let go. We move in tandem with our fingers laced together. I couldn't care less what anyone thinks about it—I'll hold my girl's hand whenever I want.

"I think we've worked off all the food we ate earlier. I'm starving." Tawnee looks up at me from her seat in the sand. She's removing her fins, beads of water drip down her face, and her smile is brighter than the desert's setting sun. "It's time to go inside, finish off the leftovers, and make something sweet for dessert."

"Yes, ma'am. Your wish is my command. Thrice-heated tacos and one homemade buttermilk pie coming up. Though I suppose it would be called laban pie here. Doesn't have quite the same ring to it, does it?"

"Those don't really sound like they go together." She scrunches up her nose and grimaces at the same time.

"Trust me. You'll change your mind after your first bite of pie." I extend my arm and offer her my hand to help her up.

"If you say so. I guess I should trust you—everything else you made was delicious." She cups my cheek with her soft hand. "Thank you for doing that."

"My pleasure, sweets. Now it's time for you to eat and build up your energy again."

Her jaw drops open, and my only response is to wink at her. The nervous expression on her face is adorable. She turns to walk in front of me, but I hear her mumble under her breath, "I'm going to buy a chastity belt and hide the key for at least a week."

"That's fine by me, sweets. I know how to pick locks."

The house phone rings when we enter through the back door. I hesitate for a moment then decide to answer just in case.

"Roman, it's Shadow. We won't be back by the house for two or three more days. We can't leave our posts for the time being. Do either of you need anything urgently before then?"

"No, man, we're good. Thanks for checking, though. We'll be here when you're ready. Don't hurry on our account." Literally

—I don't want them to hurry at all. We're good. We're so good here.

We disconnect, and I relay the message to Tawnee. "Looks like you're all mine for at least two more days. There's no way for you to escape from me. Isn't that great news?"

"On the one hand, yes. On the other, it makes me wonder what they're up to and what's coming next. Did he tell you and you're just withholding information from me?"

"Nope. I wouldn't do that, sweets. You know as much as I know."

"Then I suppose we'll just have to find ways to entertain ourselves while we're held hostage in this house." She shrugs her shoulders and lifts her hands with her palms up. But I do love that grin on her face. "I'm going to shower and wash all the salt and sand out of my hair. I'll help you make that pie when I get out if you want an extra pair of hands."

"Don't worry about it. I've got it. Enjoy your hot shower in that enormous master bathroom. I'll take my shower while it's baking, then we can relax for the rest of the night."

She walks over to me, raises up onto her toes, and softly kisses my lips. "Thank you. You're spoiling me, and I'm loving every minute of it."

"It's about time I returned the favor. You spoiled me for a long time, only I was too thickheaded to realize what I had until you were gone. I don't want to lose you again, Tawnee. I've been miserable without you—just ask Blake. He caught the brunt of it."

She giggles, picturing the two of us going at it like brothers. "Remind me to send him a gift basket as a thank you for putting up with you in my absence. You know, after we're rescued."

"Hell, he'll be so happy to get rid of me, he'll send you a gift basket for taking me off his hands."

After we finish dinner and scarf down half the dessert, we settle on the spacious couch with a fresh bottle of wine. I sit at the end with my legs stretched out on the ottoman, and she snuggles against me in the crook of my shoulder. The familiar scent of her shampoo lingers in the air around me, and I inhale a deep breath, trying to remember the last time we took a moment just to chill and enjoy each other.

Not a single time comes to mind.

Did we never do this as a couple?

What the fuck was wrong with me?

We find an English-speaking channel and let the movie playing transport us to other worlds. We chat about the plot and laugh off the inconsistencies, unconcerned with reality versus fantasy in our choice of entertainment. We have so much in common in some ways, but we're polar opposites in others. But we can use all of that to our advantage if we simply focus on what's most important this time around.

Before long, I know she's fallen asleep by her rhythmic breathing and lax limbs. Watching her rest comfortably in my arms makes me feel ten feet tall. She feels safe and protected with me. She knows she can trust me and that I'm a man of my word. I'd die before I'd hurt her again… and anyone else who hurts her will be the proud owner of a shallow, unmarked grave in the middle of the desert.

The credits end on the movie we were watching, and another one begins, before Tawnee stirs. She lifts her head from my chest and glances around the room, momentarily confused, until her eyes land on mine.

"Hello, sleepyhead."

Cue the sheepish grin. "Hush. You're so warm and comfortable, I couldn't help but fall asleep. What time is it?"

"Not too late yet. We've just had a very long day. You can go back to sleep if you want, I don't mind. I'll stay right here and hold you."

"If we turn off all the lights in here, it's dark enough outside that no one could see us…" She lets her voice trail off, raises her eyebrows, and bites her bottom lip.

"No one could see us, huh? And what would we be doing that no one needs to see?" I like this adventurous side of her.

"Skinny-dipping in the pool."

Correction. I love this adventurous Tawnee.

"I will go turn off every light and night-light in the house right now. Are you wearing anything under that little silky robe?"

"Nope."

"Perfect. I'll grab a couple towels and meet you in the back-yard in two seconds."

"Okay. Don't make any noise when you come out. I'll be the naked one in the pool waiting for you."

"You're killing me, sweets."

She slips out the door while I rush to grab the towels. If that thin, silky robe she's wearing gets wet, she may as well be completely naked. We're trying to avoid any jail time, if possi-ble. I can't guarantee the neighbors won't hear her moans and cries after I catch a glimpse of the moonlight shimmering off her wet, naked body.

When I step outside, I drop the towels on the lounge chair beside the pool, kick off my shorts, and ease down the steps where Tawnee sits. I step in front of her, push her knees apart, and settle between her thighs. The warm water acts as a natural lubricant, and her body is a natural aphrodisiac.

She pulls my face toward hers and lightly brushes her tongue against the part of my lips before taking full control of our kiss.

Then she wraps her legs around my waist, pushing the warmth of her pussy against my cock, and all bets are off. With a slight adjustment, I'm poised and ready at her entrance. I drive inside her with full force, and her back curves from the intense pleasure. Her sexy moans only make me thrust harder. The water sloshes around us as her bare chest arches out of the water, and I slide my hand from her stomach to her throat.

"You feel so fucking good. I can't get enough of you."

We twist and change places, with me sitting on the step and Tawnee straddling me. The grinding of her hips combined with her inner muscles tightly gripping me nearly pushes me over the edge first. With the first peep of her uncontrollable scream, I cover her mouth with mine and meet her stroke for stroke. In perfect sync, we reach the peak together and tumble over the other side in unison.

She collapses against me, and I lean back against the top step, holding her close with one hand and drawing lazy circles on her wet skin with the other.

"I didn't mean to attack you like that as soon as you got in the pool with me. I thought we'd have a few minutes to swim first." She giggles against my chest.

"You already know you can pounce on me anytime you want without permission or explanation. I truly do not mind one bit." I feel her smile against my skin. "We can swim now if you want. Wear you out a little more so you'll sleep like a rock tonight."

"I'm a little too comfortable lying on top of you to move just yet."

I pick her up and glide through the shallow end, semi-swimming but mostly letting the water flow over us. "How's this?"

"Perfect. Everything here is perfect. Feels like we're on an exotic vacation and makes me never want to go back to the real world."

A nagging doubt starts at the back of my mind. Like one tiny seed, just a fleeting thought, but it's taking root in my mind and growing faster than the speed of light. I've mentioned our future several times… over the last twenty-four hours… but she hasn't. Does she see this as a vacation fling? Having fun while we're here, but leaving it all behind when the fairy-tale escape ends?

But that's not Tawnee's nature. It never has been. She wouldn't use me like that. She wouldn't listen to my professions of love only to rip my heart out with pure spite. I push those thoughts out of my mind and refocus my energies on the beauty who's stuck on my body like a tattoo.

"Roman?"

"Yeah, sweets?"

"I think it's time to take me to bed, snuggle with me all night, and make sure I have sweet dreams."

"My pleasure." We exit the pool, and I wrap her towel around her. She peeks up at me from under her eyelashes, then places a soft kiss on my lips.

"If I'm already dreaming, don't wake me."

"You're not dreaming. This is all real, and it only gets better from here."

We head back inside and straight to the master bedroom. So much has happened over such a short time, all the other days start to blur into one. But not today. From now on, my hard-line stance is firmly in place—I'm not leaving here without her by my side. I won't lose her again.

We crawl into the middle of the king-size bed, our arms and legs wrapped around each other, and wait for sleep to overtake us. Tawnee is out like a light first, and I watch her sleeping soundly for a few minutes... captured by her beauty, captivated by her heart, and addicted to her love.

The next three days follow much of the same pattern as the first one. Shadow said they'd be back in a couple of days, but at this point, I don't care if he takes a couple of weeks. Or months. Years would be acceptable too. I've spent hours upon hours of making love to her, cooking meals together, swimming in the ocean and the pool, and enjoying a few days of having no responsibilities at all. We couldn't have planned a better vacation, or a more deserved break from reality.

Every day, I've considered pressuring her for information.

What was in that file? Who was she threatening to kill? Why can't I know about it? But I haven't been able to bring myself to broach the subject. The mere mention of work or anything about our real lives may burst the bubble we're living in. Something tells me I'll need every possible minute to convince her we are real, what's happening between us is meant to be, and we can overcome anything together. I never gave her a reason to believe in me before, so I have to give her every reason to take a leap of faith now.

On the fourth morning of our captivity, Tawnee and I are at the table having breakfast together, joking about not knowing what we'll do today. Then we hear the garage door open, and a truck pulls into the empty space.

They turn the engine off, and we rest our forks on our plates.

Our eyes meet as the large door slides shut.

The knob jiggles just before the interior door swings open.

Shadow, Reaper, and Silas all file into the kitchen with their solemn, grim expressions in place.

Our small slice of heaven is about to turn into a pit of pure hell.

"Well, if it isn't the three horsemen of the apocalypse. To what do we owe the pleasure?" I lean back in my chair, preparing for the worst.

The three men glance at one another nervously, uncertain of who should be the one to share the bad news they're harboring. That truly makes me feel worse, because I've never seen any of these men hesitate to say what's on his mind. Silas steps forward, maintaining eye contact with me the entire time to keep my attention focused on him.

"Roman, there's something I need to tell you. It's about your dad."

CHAPTER 16

Tawnee

My hands fly to my face, covering my gaping mouth, and my heart drops to my feet. If someone killed Gerald because I didn't tell Roman what I know, I'll never forgive myself.

Neither will Roman.

Roman flies up from his seat, and Silas puts his hands up in front of him, signaling for Roman to sit back down.

"He's okay now. He—"

"Now? What do you mean *now*? So that means he wasn't okay at some point in the last few days?"

"Roman. This behavior is exactly why we've kept you out of the loop. You fly off the handle without having all the details. I know for a fact that you've been trained better than that." Silas straightens his spine, pulling up to his full height, and looks down at Roman with the stern expression of a displeased superior.

It works. Roman's demeanor changes immediately, and he

nods in agreement. "You're right. When it comes to the people I love, my reactions may be a tad bit heated."

One side of Silas's mouth lifts briefly. It only lasts a split second, but it's enough to make me relieved to have seen it. "That's better. No more talking until I've finished briefing you. I promise to answer any remaining questions afterward. Deal?"

"Deal."

"As I said, he's okay *now*. He was attacked just after his speech at the oil and energy conference. There were quite a few people who didn't share his enthusiasm over his project. We were there, but a crowd surrounded him when he left the stage. Most of the people were peaceful and professional. They only wanted to ask more questions about his research after the panel said they had to move on to the next speaker.

"As the crowd dispersed, two men used that opening to move closer to him. One stabbed him and the other grabbed him, trying to drag him outside, very similar to the way we had you and Tawnee taken. Only they were stupid, because they didn't make sure he was alone before they made their move. Shadow and I immediately took him to the hospital, while Reaper and Bull cornered the two assailants. We have them in custody now and have been putting them through the wringer to squeeze every last bit of intel out of them.

"His injuries were not life threatening, but that doesn't mean he enjoyed it. They kept him overnight for IV antibiotics in case of infection. We arranged a privately chartered flight to get him out of the country and to Noah's house in Miami. Brianna is taking care of him now, and he's perfectly safe. She even took him in for a second opinion, against his will, but she managed it anyway. I received a message this morning from him. He sends his love to you both and said to tell you—and I quote—'Work your shit out so I can have grandkids before I die.' It seems he's fallen in love with all the kids coming and going at the house of Steele and wants his son to start contributing."

"Oh great, a new crusade for my dad to take an interest in. This one only involves my reproductive status. Do parents not realize they're encouraging their kids to have sex when they say shit like that? It just has the opposite effect. That's not uncomfortable at all." Roman's reaction makes me smile and stifle a laugh, but now that's exactly what I'll think about the next time I'm around Gerald.

"Our two idiot guests have confirmed our original suspicions that the three of you were not here by coincidence, but their boss only told them their part of the plan. We're confident they're not withholding information from us about that. The reason your dad was here is obvious. His name has been listed as a speaker on the agenda for months. But why the group behind this needed Tawnee and you here with him isn't clear to me yet.

"Now it's your turn to talk. What did I leave out?"

"Give me a second to process everything, man." Roman props his elbows on the table and rests his forehead on his hands.

Though I can't see his face, I can feel the full range of emotions flowing through him. I want to reach across the table and hold his hand, to show he has all my support, but I don't want to interrupt the moment he needs to collect his thoughts.

"Silas, I can't help but think this wouldn't have happened if we'd moved faster on investigating who was behind the documents you showed me. Is this my fault for not telling Roman about them before now?" I lean forward in my chair, my chest filling with dread at the mere thought.

Roman's head jerks up, and his eyes search mine. I know the underlying heartbreak he's dealing with right now—he's remembering when he lost his mother and thinking about how close he came to losing his dad too.

If I contributed to that by my inaction, by not telling him everything when I had a chance...

"You know, Tawnee, I've been over and over that in my mind. I've let the other guys go through every page and tell me if I missed the mark too. None of us has found anything that even remotely connects the information in that folder to what Gerald is working on. Not one single piece of it." Silas scrubs his hand over his face. I've never seen him look as weary as he does this morning. Makes me wonder if he personally escorted Gerald to Miami then flew straight back here.

"Here's a novel idea. Why don't we just tell Roman what's in the fucking folder so he can help decide if his dad is in any way connected to what everyone else fucking knows but Roman? Why don't we just do that?"

Shadow, Reaper, Silas, and I all stare wide-eyed and slack-jawed at Roman for several heartbeats. When he refers to himself in the third person like that, he's pretty much at the end of his rope. Then Silas folds his arms over his chest and levels Roman with his piercing gaze.

"You're doing it again, rookie. We didn't show you the file to begin with because you'll go ballistic when you read it. I know you all too well. There's still another part of this operation we'll execute next. You won't like it at all, but you'll suck it up and take it like a man, regardless. If you can't do your job, I'll get your walking papers drawn up right now, and we'll finish without you. You feeling me, Roman?"

"Yeah, man. I hear you. I refuse to say I'm feeling you."

I don't know why I bother trying to hide my outburst of laughter behind a cough. Shadow and Reaper respond with full belly laughs. Silas smiles—a genuine ear-to-ear smile—and nods.

"All right, then. Do whatever you have to do to find your Zen-zone. You will need it." He walks out to the garage and returns with his laptop case. When he hands the folder to Roman, I instinctively hold my breath.

Here we go.

He flips the front cover open and is mainly unimpressed with the list of Rafael's businesses. Then he turns the page and starts reading Exhibit B.

State of Florida.

Application to Marry.

Name of Spouse: Rafael Tomas Cruz

Name of Spouse: Tawnee Lia Milano

Both "spouse" signatures are in place, along with the first two state seal stamps to certify its authenticity. All that's needed now are the signatures and the seal under the "Certificate of Marriage" section that confirms the ceremony took place.

He holds that page in his hands a little longer than the average CIA officer would. His jaw muscles tick and flex with the gritting and grinding of his teeth. I remain silent because there are still several more documents to go through. He finally flips the page and begins reading the next one—the prenuptial agreement. After seeing Raf's and my names, he's not interested in the details, so he flips to the last page and sees the signature lines are complete, as is the witness' signature.

He blows out a hard breath, but the red creeping up his neck toward his jawline is a dead giveaway.

The next document is a copy of significant life insurance policies that were taken out on Rafael and me, listing each other as the beneficiary in the event of the other's death. Roman's empty hand curls into a tight fist, and his perfectly plump and kissable lips disappear into a hard line. Following the lump-sum payout are several property deeds showing my name has been recorded as the new owner recently. Though Roman didn't take the time to read it, the properties I now own are the ones that were negotiated in the prenuptial agreement, regardless if the marriage survives. The deeds to the homes, businesses, and land combined put my new tax bracket somewhere in the stratosphere.

He runs his fingers roughly through his hair in frustration, making his already tousled strands even sexier without trying, then he drags his hand along his short beard. He's working hard to keep from blowing up. The old Roman would have already smashed the glass table and stormed out of the room. The man sitting in front of me is earnestly trying to see past the betrayal he's feeling right now.

All eyes are on him, patiently—or impatiently, in my case—waiting for him to turn the page. I can't save him from self-destructing this time. His genuine reaction is important to me... and to us, but he doesn't realize that yet. He suddenly jumps to his feet, sending his chair flying backward from the force. But he doesn't leave. He plants his hand on the table beside the folder, takes a deep breath, and flips the document over at last.

Since I already know what he sees, my eyes are glued to his face. Just a second ago, his gorgeous features were distorted by rage and distress. Now they're slowly morphing into shock, then confusion, and ultimately understanding. He quickly goes through the remaining images, recognizing what he's seeing without realizing the significance yet.

"All right. I've memorized everything in this file. I can assure you that every single page is burned into my brain for all time now. Can someone explain to me why this is evidence against Tawnee? And why the fuck did I need to see this?" He's not looking at anyone when he speaks. In fact, he hasn't looked away from the last image at all.

"The answer to both of your questions is the same: because none of those documents are real, except the pictures of Tawnee and you at the very back. Those were printed from her phone... the same phone that was stolen after the car chase here in Dubai. And all of the documents are hidden in a single folder on Tony's laptop." Silas speaks slowly and calmly so Roman can follow the bread crumbs.

Roman looks up at Shadow. "So, when you said you had to make sure Tawnee wasn't involved, you meant in forging the documents so everything would go to her if Rafael meets an untimely death."

"Exactly. She'd be too smart to keep that kind of proof on her own laptop, especially if none of it appeared on Rafael's. But it would make sense if Tony was the keeper of one set of the documents. As Rafael's right-hand man, he'd be privy to their personal life together," Shadow explains.

"Wouldn't he need to update his will with all this for it to be binding?"

"Not in this case. The prenuptial agreement is evergreen, so there's no expiration date. It meets all the parameters of being fair and just to both parties—it even spells out the distribution of any properties, businesses, or financial gains after the agreement is signed. I'm waiting for a full copy of his will to verify who his beneficiary is, but prenups trump state property laws in most states, if they meet certain criteria. This one meets all the criteria."

"So how does a fake marriage and prenuptial agreement between Rafael and Tawnee connect to my dad and me?" Roman paces back and forth, the wheels in his mind spinning as he attempts to complete the puzzle. "Did the men who stabbed my father say anything when they got close to him? Anything at all?"

"Unfortunately, I wasn't close enough to understand their words. They just sounded like angry Arabs to me." Reaper shrugs his big shoulders, aggravated that he doesn't have more to go on. "I don't know what the fuck to think anymore. I've racked my brain trying to make a connection between all these bits and pieces."

Roman stops dead in his tracks, and he swivels his head toward Reaper. "Wait. What did you just say?"

"I can't make a connection." Reaper's eyebrows draw downward, and he cocks his head to the side in confusion.

"No. Before that. You said the men after my father were just angry Arabs."

"Yeah. So? Is that supposed to mean something?"

"Shadow, when you pulled this list of Rafael's companies, did you have the analyst look at Rafael's name only?"

"Yes. He's never been married. No kids. No family to speak of—not immediate anyway. What are you thinking, Roman?"

"I think you should have them run the trace again, but search under Tawnee's name this time."

"Let me help you out there," I interject. "The only business I have is my security business that you men have pulled me out of this week. Why would you think... *That motherfucker!*" I drop my head in my hands and bite back a scream. How could I be so stupid and blind?

"My sentiments exactly, sweets. *That motherfucker.* Now, can I kill him?"

"Only if you beat me to him, Roman."

Okay, now I get it, and I can't blame Roman for feeling this way ever again. The urge to throw shit, break glass, and pitch the biggest fit the world has ever seen almost overpowers me. I think I would feel much better if I could demolish everything in my path and get all this rage out of my system.

"Does someone want to include us in this big revelation? We may be able to offer some assistance if we know what's going on." Reaper waits for a reply from either Roman or me.

"Reap, if the information on the search comes back with what I think we'll find, I'll fill in all the holes. Since we can't dismiss the possibility that Tony's the beneficiary and the one behind all this, I don't want to get too ahead of myself. For once." Roman turns his attention to the other Steele in the room. "Silas, what's the next step in your plan? The one you said I wouldn't like. Might as well lay it all out on the table now."

Silas glances between Roman and me before a devilish smirk appears. "Rafael is paying the ransom for you two. The money drop is tonight. After we confirm the payment, we'll send him instructions on where he can find you. Once Tawnee is back on his team, her job will be to stay as close to him as possible, so he doesn't suspect we're investigating him. Our focus is still on both Raf and Tony, but one doesn't go anywhere without the other. Since Raf has professed his feelings for Tawnee, she'll confess she realized her mutual feelings for him after the harrowing ordeal with her kidnappers."

There's a pronounced moment of silence while the two men have a silent face-off in the breakfast nook. Not exactly an area conducive for the whole duel at twenty paces analogy, yet that's exactly where my thoughts go, anyway.

"Are you fucking insane, man?" Roman bellows and throws his arms up in the air, conceding to Silas. "You want to send her right back into the arms of the two men we suspect most of all?"

"Exactly. You can't say I didn't warn you first." Silas beams at Roman. He may enjoy this part of his plan a little too much.

Roman

After that announcement, I need fresh air to clear my head and accept this ridiculous plan Silas is pitching. I turn and walk out the back door and straight into the ocean, where the waves lap at my bare feet and the soft breeze provides some respite from the scorching sun overhead. I close my eyes and drop my head back, soaking up the rays and using the salt and sand to calm this storm raging inside.

When I hear the door open behind me, I assume Tawnee is coming out to check on me. That was an intense few minutes in there, going through all the documents that suggested she was set to marry another man. My thoughts and emotions were all over the board as I moved from one piece of evidence to the next. What grounded me were the memories we'd made over the past few days. The woman they have held me captive with isn't someone who could spend several days in my arms then run off to marry someone else.

Keeping that in the forefront of my mind wasn't easy, though. Flashes of her lounging in the cabana with Rafael fought for their place in the equation too. I'd be stupid and careless and reckless if I didn't at least consider there was more than an employer-employee relationship between those two. I couldn't bring myself to look at her while looking through that folder—I had to work through my own issues with it first.

"How are you holding up, Roman?" Silas asks.

When I open my eyes, he's standing beside me, shoulder to shoulder. "Great. I'm about to send the love of my life right into the viper's nest. Other than that, really good."

"Unfortunately, I know exactly how you feel."

"I know you do, man. Would you do it again if you had to?"

"That's not a fair question, Roman. Kira's out of the game."

"Yeah, she is. But she'd jump right back in if she had no other choice. How would you deal with that?"

"You know what I'd do. I'd break shit, punch holes in walls, and bite everyone's head off who dared to speak to me." His dark chuckle matches mine.

"That's what I thought. You couldn't patch into his comm lines and eavesdrop on his conversations since we've been abducted?"

"Do you honestly think I'd violate Rafael's civil rights like that? He's a private citizen, Roman. That hurts."

"Cut the bullshit, Silas. What'd you hear? And why are you keeping it from Tawnee?"

"My allegiance is to you, Roman. I'm trained to suspect everyone until they give me a reason not to—it's simply the way I'm wired now. Shadow and I talked about it beforehand. I allowed her to review that file, and I had him keep it from you for a reason, and it wasn't because of your temper. Though you do need to control yourself better.

"She's been with him for the last three years, practically around the clock. She excuses his behavior when she shouldn't. She gives him the benefit of the doubt when she should question his motives. That's all normal for someone who has an established relationship. We want to see the best in the people we're closest to, so it's not a big deal on its own. But I thought her reaction to the forged documents and life insurance policies would be stronger. And I thought she'd tell you everything over the past few days when you were alone. But your reaction to seeing the file for the first time was genuine. She didn't tell you about any of it—and what he did is just cause for a serious ass-kicking. Don't you find that odd?"

"Are you saying the documents are real and she planned to marry him? Or are you saying you think she's involved in something shady and trying to hide it from us?"

"After hearing Rafael's phone calls on what he thought was a secure phone, I don't believe she's involved in anything shady at all. But it's my job to question if the documents are forged or if they're legitimate. We need to know exactly where her allegiances lie, because when she goes back to him, she may realize how much she's missed him. That was a great call to search for companies in her name, by the way. Good catch."

"Silas, I don't know if anyone has ever told you this or not, but I think you need to hear it from someone who knows you very well."

"This should be good. Let's hear it."

"You should never, ever go undercover as a therapist. Especially not a relationship counselor. You can't say shit like that to people then follow up with an attaboy comment. That's not even in the same hemisphere of how that's supposed to be done."

"I felt it was important to end my little speech on a positive note. That didn't do it for you?" He has the nerve to look offended.

"No, it didn't work for me at all. Your people skills need a lot of work, man."

"I'll get right on that. I'll take sensitivity training or whatever bullshit it is all you pansies do." He gestures toward me when he refers to "pansies." Nice.

"That's Step One, right there, Silas. Self-awareness."

"Oh good, maybe I don't need that class after all."

"Just tell me what you heard on his secure phone calls."

"He called our Arab friends and very angrily demanded to know why they took the two of you early. Apparently, they were supposed to get all three of you at the same time. We caught wind of that plot a few days ago, which is why we took you and Tawnee when we did—because Rafael was watching it happen.

"He came to the conference to have plenty of alibi witnesses when you two were reported missing. But he was so focused on being innocent, he couldn't improvise and change his behavior when the deed went down. Even his table buddies were trying to alert you to the danger coming up behind you, but Raf didn't move a muscle. When he realized Gerald was still there, he lost his shit and called his buddies on their burner phones."

"What did they have to say about that?"

"They swore up and down they hadn't made a move yet and that they didn't know who had you. When they finally convinced Raf they were telling the truth, that's when he really started panicking. He hung up and made another call to his lawyer, who advised him to get Tawnee back immediately because it takes seven years to have someone declared legally dead. Everything he has in her name would be in limbo without a body and confirmation. There was also a vague reference to multiple attempts in a short period of time being too suspicious and therefore not recommended.

"Just before we had our impromptu meeting in the spare bedroom of his suite, I slipped my own bug into the living room. It's a new design that's not detected by normal sweepers. He seems to spend more time in that room than any other. Perfect timing, too, since we wore out our welcome as soon as you two went missing. We've been listening to the others' conversations from our hotel room, too. So far, Tony is the only potential accomplice out of the people on his staff. He's overly stoic about her disappearance. Normal people would be more concerned than what he's displayed."

"Tony wants her job. Tawnee told me she's had trouble with Tony not following her orders and she's had to jump his shit more than once to get him in line."

"Makes sense. Maybe he thought he was about to be promoted from driver to head of security. But when Rafael agreed to pay the ransom for both of you, he squashed Tony's hopes. If that's the case, Tawnee may not be out of danger just yet."

"I don't think she's out of danger with Rafael either. It may not be smart to arrange another hit on her, but that won't stop him from doing it in this part of the world. Dubai may be relatively safe, but it borders Saudi Arabia, and we both know that country is not safe."

"Tell me why you wanted to check for companies in Tawnee's name. That wasn't just an off-the-wall idea you had. Something prompted it."

"Tawnee and I followed Raf and Tony into a breakout session at the conference. There were a lot of angry Arabs in there. They kept saying a Western Jewish woman was buying up the controlling shares of the primary Saudi oil producer. Think about it—they despise Westerners, they hate Jews, and they're widely known for their mistreatment of women in general. But this puts all three of those demographics together. Give a Western Jewish woman the controlling shares of their oil company, and you have an instant recipe for disaster.

"Rafael's business is buying the controlling shares of companies, right? So maybe he's staying under the radar on this one, using Tawnee's name to take the heat off him. His business model has never involved touring a real estate property before deciding to buy it. He's hanging around here for a reason. Now we have a bunch of marriage documents—fake or not—and he inherits everything when she dies. Milano is historically an Italian-Jewish name. Even though Tawnee's family isn't Jewish. They were raised as Christians. These men could easily find out she's from the US, though. Rafael may be the one who released the rumors to get the old-fashioned Arab men up in arms about it."

"That does up the ante. We need that report back immediately. If she's the shareholder they referred to, they won't believe her when she says she didn't know. They'll charge her with some other high crime and execute her after a one-day mock trial." He retrieves his phone from his pocket and sends an urgent email to his analyst at Langley.

"Are we still sending her back in there knowing all this?" I already know the answer, but I'll make him confirm it.

"We have to. We expect no less of our assets in hostile territories. We push them to get us the information we need to carry out our jobs. Tawnee has a business to run too, and her sole client is paying for her release. Just be glad he didn't negotiate for her release and not yours."

"That doesn't make me feel any better, Silas. Now I have to live with thinking he bought and paid for me... and know that he sees it exactly in that way." That pisses me off even more.

"We'll split the ransom money. That'll make you feel better. You'll get his money for your abduction. Pretty sweet deal, huh?"

"Until he has the real kidnappers come back and finish their job. Did he ever say why Dad and I were part of his plan?"

"The working theory is your dad was a target because of his new compound. The oil investors aren't ready for it, especially not Rafael if he's trying to corner the market with the Saudi oil company. You were most likely on his radar because of the pictures still on Tawnee's phone. The coded message was probably a test to see if you'd answer her plea for help. When you came running, they confirmed you as a threat. If she disappeared, he knew you'd never stop looking for her.

"Taking all three of you out at the same time, in the same place, would have been easily explained. Your dad was here for a conference, you'd reconnected with an old girlfriend, the three of you went off together and got lost in a bad area. Accidents happen to tourists every day."

"We should take this back home to finish it. The odds of this playing out in our favor in this part of the world are slim to none. And who would believe Tawnee would want to stay here and stay on the job, after being kidnapped? No one."

"Roman, listen carefully, because you'll only hear me say this once. You're absolutely right." Silas smiles, and this time, it isn't his usual sarcastic grin. "But the bosses have declared your dad a higher priority for national security than Tawnee, so we don't have a choice. We finish it here, one way or another. Gerald is safe at Noah's, but if we bring two more targets back to Miami —or anywhere in the US—we put him in more danger. They'll revoke our passports to keep us out if we force their hand."

"We are surrounded by motherfuckers."

"Speaking of, we need to review our strategy for picking up the money and releasing the hostages tonight. Nick will be here any minute now. Blake, Bull, and Rebel escorted your father back to the States, and they're taking turns standing guard over him. You know they'll keep him safe."

"But can they protect Dad from Liz? That's the real test."

"No one is safe from Liz. There's a new national security threat level named after her. Maybe we should have brought her with us—she'd have them confessing to crimes they didn't even commit in no time."

We both crack up over that. Laughing again feels so good after such a stressful day.

"I know we have to consider anything is possible, but you

should know I trust Tawnee with my life. Maybe she does want to see the best in everyone and gives too many chances, but I love that about her. She wouldn't have stayed with me for as long as she did if that weren't part of her personality. And she wouldn't be back with me right now if she weren't willing to see the best in me, because we both know I didn't deserve a second chance. If you don't think she's part of anything illegal, you should tell her what you know before she walks back in there. She deserves to know... She deserves that much from us."

"I'll think about it. We have a few hours before this goes down. We'll all be around the table while we build our strategy. I'll be able to get a better read on her before we release you tonight."

"You already know if you don't tell her, then I will. Don't you?"

"Do I look like I was born yesterday? I'm not stupid."

With my temper cooled off and my head screwed on straight, Silas and I head back inside with the others. Tawnee eyes both of us skeptically when we step through the door. She has her own sixth sense, and I know her Tawnee-senses are tingling all over right now. Silas and I had a long conversation, and that is out of the ordinary.

"Did you two finally decide to ask my opinion before running off to solve a problem that revolves around me?" She glares at both of us. Apparently, she thinks we were discussing her role in this plan without her. As if.

"That never crossed our minds, Tawnee." Silas keeps a straight face for as long as he can then bursts out laughing. "Just kidding. I would love to hear your thoughts on sending you in to spy on your employer."

"I'm in. It's the only way we can get to the bottom of this anytime soon. You'll never get anything against Rafael out of Tony. I believe the rest of my team is loyal to me, but they're also not close enough to Raf to have anything useful or incriminating. It has to be me."

"You do realize what I'm asking you to do, right? You'll have to convince him you're interested in pursuing more than a friendship with him. Hopefully, he'll drop his guard easier that way."

Her eyes float up to mine. We don't have to speak the words to know what the other is thinking.

This will be the hardest fucking assignment I'll ever have.

I'm not exactly the sharing type.

CHAPTER 18

Tawnee

fter hours of walking through the plan for the money drop, the hostage release, and what'll be expected of me as an undercover double agent, we take a much-needed break for food and adult libations. Lots of them. I load the machine with ice, alcohol, and drink mix for an extra-large pitcher of frozen margaritas. The guys work on grilling steaks and making baked potatoes and tossing a side salad.

We carry everything outside to the lanai to enjoy our last day in our private paradise. Roman has been exceptionally quiet and withdrawn most of the day. Not that I don't understand—I don't like this setup any more than he does, but I don't know of another way to find out what Rafael's endgame is. Though, to be honest with myself, it doesn't take a genius to figure out what he's doing after creating all those documents with my signature forged on them.

Being near him without stabbing him in the neck with my pen will be hard.

Not recoiling when he touches me will be very difficult.

Pretending to be romantically interested in him knowing everything I do, especially after reconnecting with Roman, will be nearly impossible.

We finish our meal, with Nick, Reaper, Silas, and Shadow carrying the conversation while Roman and I only occasionally engage. The margarita pitcher is empty, so I walk back inside to replenish our supply. One last drink as a team to toast our upcoming success—because failure isn't an option. While the machine shaves and crushes the ice, I'm lost in my own thoughts and memories. Rafael's betrayal stings worse than I've outwardly shown. Not because I'm in love with him or anything remotely like that, but I thought we were truly friends. I believed he'd have my back the same as I've had his all this time.

I've learned firsthand how much it hurts to care more for others than they do for me.

But there's no time to dwell on that when it's painfully obvious he has more nefarious plans for me than I ever believed him capable.

"Are you okay, sweets?"

Roman's voice in my ear makes me jump almost out of my skin. "Holy shit, Roman. I didn't even hear you come in with the ice grinder running. You scared me."

"You were deep in thought. Want to share what you're thinking?" He brushes his knuckles along my cheek, and I instantly melt into his touch.

"I'm dreading this assignment for so many reasons. You know I don't do well with hiding what I'm thinking—I don't have a poker face at all. I really don't want to be thrown into a Dubai prison for murder, but that could very well happen if they find my fork sticking out of Rafael's neck. And…"

"And?"

"I don't want to leave you. These few stolen days have been amazing. I'm afraid to leave and break the magic spell we've been living under."

He pulls me into his arms and holds me, reassuring me as only he can. "Our magic spell can't be broken, sweets. Nothing will come between us again. I've been waiting all day for Silas to tell you the other part of the story, but he hasn't. I'm not letting you walk into this trap without knowing all the facts. I'll pour us a couple of drinks, and we'll talk in here."

When he reaches for the margarita pitcher, I put my hand on his to stop him. "We'll keep the straight tequila. Give them the pitcher."

"Good idea." He presses his lips to mine then takes the pitcher outside.

When he comes back in, I have several shot glasses lined up on the bar, and I'm pouring the tequila in each one. "If Silas is keeping information from me, I have a feeling we'll need these. It'll be harder for me to inflict injury on him if I'm shit-faced."

Roman begins laying out the backstory Silas shared with him earlier. The plot to kidnap all three of us and leave our dead bodies somewhere to be found at a later date. Raf's calls to the Saudi men demanding an explanation for their fuckup. The call to his lawyer and the vague reference to not making another attempt so soon after the first. Raf's inaction when they grabbed us right in front of him.

Silas questioning where my loyalties lie—with Rafael or with Roman.

I've already downed several shots, but I have so much adrenaline and rage coursing through my veins, I don't even have a buzz yet. I'm still fully capable of causing massive damage. So many thoughts swirl through my mind as I pace back and forth along the length of the kitchen and dining area. The longer I walk, the madder I become.

"Tawnee? Did you hear anything I just said?"

With quick strides, I walk toward Roman until we're standing toe to toe. "Look me in the eye, Roman Scott. Where did you say my loyalties lie—before you told me everything?"

"I told Silas I trust you with my life. My trust in you has never wavered."

He's telling me the truth. I can see it in his eyes. "As long as you believe in me, I don't care what Silas thinks. Now, what did you just say? I'm sorry, I didn't hear you."

"I asked if you're still sure you want to do this. Knowing Raf's behind everything and wants you dead, are you sure you want to go back in there with him?"

"More than ever."

He drops his head back and stares at the ceiling, clearly not pleased with my decision.

"Roman, is there something else you're not telling me?"

"Nothing concrete yet. Just the theory on the secret company in your name we're waiting to confirm. I know in my gut we've hit the nail on the head, and that makes this charade even more dangerous. That oil company was state-owned since it began decades ago. The government took a gamble by putting it on the stock market, but the more traditional nationals never approved of that move. So, if Tawnee Milano, an Italian-Jewish Western woman, dares to attempt a hostile takeover, a lot of angry men will be gunning for you."

"You know, when I first saw those documents with my signature forged on them, I actually believed he was just so cocky, he assumed I'd accept his proposal on the spot. That he'd had them prepared ahead of time because he doesn't like to wait for anything. He'd just shared his feelings for me not long before you showed up at the cabana. He'd always been a flirt, but I never took him seriously. When he confessed that he was in love with me, I was too shocked to give an intelligent reply. Then he told my entire staff he was pursuing me and not the other way around, I believed he was legitimately trying to save my reputation. How stupid am I?"

"You're not stupid at all. He had a long time to plan and scheme to get to this point. You couldn't have known what he was up to or how far he'd go to pull it off. But you can't underestimate him now, sweets. He's dangerous, and we don't know how much Tony is involved in this. You've got to assume he's just as bad. Bury your feelings deep inside, knowing you can tell me all about them when it's over. But you can't give anything away until we get the notice to make our move on him."

"Am I trying to get him to admit to conspiring to kidnap and kill us? Or to forging my signature on documents? Or to working with Saudi nationals? Or to creating a fake company and buying shares in my name? What is our endgame, Roman?"

"We can't return home until we neutralize the threat. Dad is a high priority for our national security, so we can't go back and put all three targets close together again. If we can get a line on who Raf is working with inside Saudi Arabia, maybe we can shut it all down at once. That's why Shadow was here first, and why he recruited the others to help him. This is bigger than just three Americans in trouble in the Middle East."

"Well, I have to tell you… none of that makes me feel any better. At all."

We both start laughing, knowing it's the truth but there's not a damn thing we can do about it except ride the wave wherever it takes us.

"We have several hours left before we put our dirty clothes back on and stage our release. Is there anything special you want to do until then?"

"Yes, there is. Tell the guys to leave and give us the rest of the time alone. Let's swim in the ocean, snorkel along the rocks, have more pool sex, eat junk food, finish off the margarita mix, and snuggle on the couch while we watch movies. One more day of our real world before we have to leave here and pretend to be someone we're not."

"Sounds perfect to me, sweets. I'll tell them to hit the road right now."

Roman walks outside, and I hear him ordering his friends to

"get the fuck out of here right now." The guys walk through the house to the garage door, each with a knowing grin on his face. Not a single one even tries to pretend he doesn't understand why we're kicking them all out. But that's fine with me—I don't have to hide my feelings for Roman here. Silas stops at the bar on his way out, watching my reaction for a moment before he speaks.

"You two are good for each other. He loves you, Tawnee. He never stopped loving you. Hold on to that until this is over."

I simply nod, unable to speak, then Silas continues walking to the garage. When the large automatic door shuts, confirming we're alone again, we rush to change and grab our gear. We have a short time left to do all the things we enjoy together, so we'll make the most of it. All this will change as of eleven o'clock tonight.

I just hope and pray it's only a temporary inconvenience rather than a permanent situation.

"THE MONEY DROP HAPPENED WITHOUT A HITCH, JUST AS WE KNEW it would. He wants you back more than he wants the money he paid for your ransom. We've had the hostage exchange site under surveillance for the last several hours with no suspicious activity detected. We'll still cover you from all sides, though. We're not taking any chances. Are you two ready?"

"As ready as we'll ever be." Roman glances over at me. "You got this, sweets. You'll do great."

"Yeah, I got this." I'm not as convinced as I sound, but I can't go home until this is finished. And I'm more than ready to go back to the US now.

Shadow drops us off on the sixth floor of a deserted parking garage. He drives up to the top of the garage, ditches the van, and uses a keycard linked to someone else to enter the office building. Keeping his face covered and turned away from security cameras, he makes his way out the side door and into a waiting car. Though I can't see them, I know the other guys have eyes on us because I have the distinct feeling of being watched.

A few minutes later, the unmistakable squeal of tires and an engine revving echoes through the garage. Roman and I are tied together, back to back, with the thick black hoods covering our faces. Our clothes are dirty, our hair is matted and stuck to our heads, and we have splotches of dirt smeared all over us. I'm also missing a shoe, which I heavily protested because I really like these shoes. Silas promised I'd get it back when this is all said and done.

"Tawnee? Is that really you? Thank God you're safe! Did they hurt you?" Rafael is obviously a better actor than I gave him credit for. He's laying the brokenhearted hero bit on thick while untying our restraints and removing our hoods. He holds my face in his hands and kisses me squarely on the lips. I think I just threw up a little bit in my mouth. "I'm so happy to have you back, love. What did they say? What did they look like? Who are they? I'll pay someone double the ransom to hunt them down and bring them to justice."

"We're okay, Raf. It was terrifying, but they didn't harm us. I guess they wanted the ransom money more than anything. They spoke very little English, and even that was broken, but I didn't get a good look at any of them. Did you, Roman?"

"No, I didn't. But I'd recognize their voices if I heard them again. Thank you for paying the ransom. That couldn't have been easy for you to negotiate with terrorists like that." Roman extends his hand to shake Rafael's. There's a brief hesitation on Raf's part, but he does accept the olive branch.

"Don't mention it. I wouldn't have it any other way." Raf and Roman share an uncomfortable moment of simply looking at each other, so I clear my throat and force a fake cough to break the tension.

"Tawnee, it's so good to see you." Tony pulls me into a full embrace. "I'm so relieved you're okay. Let's get you out of here before they decide to come back."

On the ride back to the hotel, Raf turns to Roman. "Which hotel are you staying at, Roman? We can drop you off."

Subtle.

"I'm staying in the suite with Tawnee. I'm not convinced she's out of danger."

"No offense, but I think she'd be safer staying in my suite with me at this point. You both were taken from a very crowded conference. I will hire additional staff to stand guard outside my door around the clock to ensure no one gets to her again. After my business concludes next week, she'll be on a private jet headed back home."

"It's okay, Roman. I appreciate your offer, but maybe Raf has a point. I'll stay inside the resort and wait this out. We only have a few more days until we can make our trip home." Keeping my tone neutral is much harder than I thought it would be.

"If you say so. I'll be around for a few more days if you need me. What about the police, Rafael? Do we need to go give any statements or anything?"

"No, the kidnappers were very clear about that. If we contacted the police, they would kill you both. I wouldn't take the chance they weren't bluffing about that, so I didn't involve any of the authorities."

Isn't that convenient? The problem is, I remember Silas said he didn't give that stipulation, purely as a test.

You just failed that test, Raf.

CHAPTER 19

Roman

The smug bastard drops me off at my hotel and barely waits for me to get out of the car before telling Tony to drive away. Silas and Nick are already here, waiting for me to join them in Silas's room. I can't stop the sinking feeling in my gut as I watch Tawnee drive away with him. No matter how many bugs we have in his suite or how closely we watch him, we're not there if—*when*—something happens.

After a quick rap on the door, Nick opens it, and we walk straight back to the command console where Silas is. The bug in Rafael's living room is on speaker, so we have a front-row seat to hear all his conversations. I just wish we could listen to what was being said inside the car while they're on the way back to their hotel. We couldn't slip a phone on her since they stole hers in the wreck. Someone would be sure to check her for listening devices after being out of their clutches, so there was no use in even trying.

In her capacity, she wouldn't have allowed a device to stay on her person, anyway. If she'd walked in and gotten caught with one, Raf would know instantly, and she would be in danger just as fast. We have to trust her to get the information we need and get out of there as soon as she does.

"How'd they act in the car?" Silas asks.

"Rafael couldn't wait to get rid of me. I said I was staying in Tawnee's room with her, but he shut that down real fast. He wants her in his suite in no uncertain terms. He said they're leaving here after his meeting next week instead of staying for an entire month. That means whatever he has planned will go down soon. He said he'd hire additional security to stand guard around the clock. He could be lying, or that could be how he betrays her again."

Tawnee's voice comes across the speaker, and I can breathe easy again for now.

"I'm going to take a shower now, Raf. I can't wait to get out of these dirty clothes and into my pajamas."

"Are you hungry? I can order room service and have it here waiting for you when you get out."

"Can I pass on it for tonight? I'd love to have breakfast with you in the morning, though."

"Breakfast is our thing, isn't it? That's a great idea, love. I'll order it tonight, and it'll be delivered first thing in the morning."

"Thank you again for everything, Raf. I wouldn't be here now if it weren't for you."

"It's my pleasure. A feast fit for a queen will be waiting for you in the morning."

Silence on the speaker means Tawnee escaped to the shower. I don't know if I can listen to this guy much longer without stabbing my eardrums until I'm completely deaf. I don't know how she's endured it for the last three years.

"Silas, can I just go over there, strangle him to death, and close this case once and for all? The world would thank me if they could hear him."

"Yeah, Roman, for once, I think your anger is warranted. I'm very tempted to send you over there and put us all out of our misery."

The shrill sound of a cell phone ringing comes across the speaker, making both Silas and me perk up.

"Hello?"

"No, you listen to me. You will do exactly as I say, when I say to do it, and not one second before or after. This must be executed flawlessly. I understand you're not accustomed to perfection, but you will learn quickly."

There's silence, presumably while the other party responds. What I'd give to have that comm line in my ear.

"Yes, Yousef, I'm back in my room now. She just went to bed. Bring Omar, Khalil, and Ahmad with you first thing in the morning. Don't be late."

"Don't be late for what? Do those names mean anything to you?" I turn to Silas and Nick, ready to bolt.

"Other than being four of the most common names in Saudi Arabia, no, they don't. Sit tight. We don't want to show our hand unnecessarily. That could be his additional security team coming on duty." Nick continues to concentrate on the speaker.

"Have you heard him order a team since we've been out of the picture?"

"No. I haven't. But that doesn't mean he didn't do while he was away from the bug where we couldn't hear him."

I know Nick's right, but that doesn't stop me from wanting to tear down the place to get her out of there. Now we wait and see what happens next. I know Tawnee is capable and a badass; that's part of what I love about her. It's because I love her that I don't want her to face this alone.

After Rafael hangs up with Yousef, he calls room service and orders one of everything on the breakfast menu to be delivered to his room by seven o'clock tomorrow morning. That may be a slight exaggeration because I can't stand the guy, but he's definitely overcompensating now. He's desperate to impress her and show her he can give her the world on a silver platter.

Or the illusion of it, anyway.

He doesn't want to stay with her any longer than it takes to pull off his scheme without being the target of a nation of angry men.

"That shower felt so good. These clean pajamas feel even better. Thank you for having my clothes brought up here ahead of time. That was so thoughtful of you. I just wanted to say goodnight."

"Goodnight, Tawnee."

Silas turns to me and shrugs. "I'll leave the speaker on and listen for anything out of the ordinary tonight. You two can go back to your rooms and get some sleep. We'll probably be very busy tomorrow."

"As much as I hate to leave her in there with him all night, I guess you're right."

"She may be in there with him for several nights before we get any real answers. Now it's a waiting game, and I know how impatient you are. If you stay in here and drive me crazy, I'll have to hide your body beside his." Silas cuts his eyes at me and lifts one brow.

"Fine, fine, fine. I can take a hint. I'll be back in the morning. Silas, wake me if anything happens."

"You got it."

AS PROMISED, I'M BACK IN SILAS'S ROOM AT FIRST LIGHT, bearing gifts. When he opens the door, I offer coffee, donuts, and breakfast sandwiches. That seems to brighten his mood some.

"Nothing exciting happened last night?" I know he already would've told me if it had, but I can't resist asking.

"Not a peep all night."

"In a way, I hope today is more exciting because I'm ready to take this motherfucker out and go home."

"You and me both, man. You and me both."

When they finally stir, several voices carry through the speaker at once. I distinctly hear "good morning" and "sleep well," standard early morning greetings.

"You've been through quite an ordeal, and I'm sorry to put such an imposition on you by asking for a favor."

"Are you kidding? You saved my life, Raf. Any favor you need isn't an imposition. What's on your mind?" She's very convincing. I know she hates every second of being fake.

"I'd really appreciate if you could find the energy to finish the conversation that we started a few days ago but never had a chance to complete. I know my timing is terrible, but I almost lost you, and I don't want to let more time slip away."

"I understand what you mean. We can talk over breakfast. Thank you again for ordering in—I'm not ready to face a restaurant full of people just yet."

"I actually prefer it this way because I get you all to myself. I hope you're hungry—I may have ordered an overabundance of food. It'll be here any min—" A chime rings throughout the spacious suite. *"Ah, that's probably the food now. Tony, can you get the door, please?"*

"Sure thing, boss."

"Raf, did you leave anything for the rest of the hotel to eat?" Tawnee laughs. To the untrained ear, it's a normal laugh. To my Tawnee-tuned ears, it's forced.

"Only the very best for you. Would you like to eat at the formal dining table?"

"Actually, no, I'd rather eat in here if that's okay with you. The couch is so comfortable, and I've had enough of hard chairs and floors this week."

Good excuse, sweets.

"That's perfect. I prefer the more intimate setting for our discussion, anyway. Shall I make your plate for you?"

"That's very kind of you to offer, but I think I can handle it."

When they settle down on the couch, their voices come in loud and clear.

"I realize this is very sudden and may seem completely out of the blue, but I assure you I've given the matter a great deal of thought. Even before this week and everything that's happened. This ordeal has only magnified the importance of not wasting another moment. Tawnee, will you do me the honor of marrying me?"

Silas and I turn our heads to look at each other at the exact same time.

"No fucking way. He did not just ask her to marry him."

"He did. He's escalating his timeline." Silas picks up his phone and texts the rest of the team to give them a heads-up.

"Raf, I don't know what to say. This is very sudden." Tawnee doesn't hide the surprise in her voice, but she's careful to keep her tone from sounding harsh.

"We're in one of the most beautiful cities in the world. We can get married on the hotel grounds. The wedding coordinator can arrange for a local Christian minister to officiate the ceremony so the courts will recognize it. It'll be the perfect setting, and you won't have to lift a finger."

"They can't get married here. They're not residents—the UAE courts won't recognize it. Right?" I'm grasping at straws here.

"The Dubai courts will recognize it if a minister of their faith conducts the ceremony—especially since they're of the same faith. Dubai is much more accommodating to visitors than the other Emirates. They know this place is a wedding destination gold mine. Had Tawnee truly been Jewish, they obviously wouldn't allow it."

"I really don't know what to say, Raf."

"Say yes, and make me the luckiest man in the world."

"Say no, and make me the happiest man in the world, Tawnee," I yell at the speaker, willing her to hear me.

"I'm very flattered, Raf, but I have to say no. It's too fast for me. We've been friends and have gotten to know each other after all this time. But if I do get married, it'll be for the rest of my life. We need time to get to know each other as a couple before we even think about marriage."

"I completely agree that marriage should be until 'death do us part.' We are on the same page there. But I think you know if someone is your match or not. When someone is your soul mate, you can feel the connection regardless of the distance or time apart. And when you're close to that person, your very essence tells you. Electrified touches, knowing glances, finishing sentences for the other, and understanding deep feelings without the words to describe them—these are all signs that your soul has found its mate."

Not that I ever thought I'd agree with this tool, but he's one-thousand percent correct about soul mates. All of that is what I feel when Tawnee is near... what I've always felt around her, but I was too stupid to realize it. I used to think love made me weak. Now I recognize love makes me the strongest man alive. I'm nothing without her in my life and by my side. When I get her back—this time—I'll hold on to her for the rest of my life. Now that I know exactly what I've been living without, I see I haven't been living at all.

"That explains so much." I can tell by the inflection in her voice that she's lost in thought. She's thinking about what she feels for me.

"It certainly does."

"Be ready to move at a moment's notice, Roman. Nick is packing his stuff now. She just turned him down, and she just confirmed she's still in love with you. Even though she didn't say your name, he can tell she wasn't referring to him with that last comment. He won't wait much longer to get rid of her now. There's something else I need to check—your question about them getting married raised a red flag for me." Silas opens his secure CIA laptop and starts clicking away.

I try to watch what he's looking for and listen to the speaker for strange noises at the same time. If someone rushes in and nabs her, the only signal I get could be a muffled cry for help. Silas zips through the website, letting our special encryption translate each page while hiding his online presence.

"You're looking at the deeds for the property he's touring next week? Why?"

"I have a hunch from something you said before... Yep, there it is. He already owns that building. He's not here to consider buying it—he already owns it. That means he has an automatic resident visa. Now, let's go to one more site and check one more thing... Son of a bitch. They just processed Tawnee's resident visa as his employee. He must know it's approved for her to stay here long term as his employee. He's not planning to return to the US in a few days. He's staying in Dubai, gaining control of the most profitable oil company in the world, and setting up residence as an expat right here on the Saudi border."

"We know everything has been a setup from day one. The trip to Dubai, the wreck, the attack on my dad—let's just go in and take him out of play altogether. Don't give me the company line that the CIA doesn't assassinate people. I know better than that shit. We are the elite team that goes in when others can't or won't. Get her out of there, remove him from the picture, and let her dump all the shares. She'll make a ton of money, and they'll leave her alone since they'll have their company back."

"Not a bad idea. Maybe we can sell that to the State Department so that they'll let us back into the country—it's still iffy. We have direct orders to identify the conspirators because of the high probability of terrorism. We may have to stop over in another country first to give her time to close out the sales and get her name off all the dark web hit lists. She'll have to change her name for a while too." Silas is thinking out loud.

"She can change her name permanently—to mine. Let's just

go over there and get her the fuck out of that place, man. Before it's too late." I'm already on my feet, moving toward the door.

"All right. Go pack your shit and take your suitcase with you. We'll have to gain entry by sea. The only way in or out of their hotel by land is blocked by guards. Rafael won't let us in again. As soon as we have her, we'll have to flee the country."

When I step out of his room, I hear him calling Shadow and Reaper to let them know we're making a move on Rafael today. I don't even feel the least bit guilty—he's plotting to kill my girl, but he's the one who will get a six-foot-deep surprise.

Before the door closes, I hear voices on the speaker again, so I stop and listen.

"Oh, yes, I almost forgot. I have a surprise for you. Stay right here, and I'll fetch it from the bedroom."

"Raf, you really didn't have to get me anything."

"Nonsense. I enjoy spoiling you. It's quite breathtaking. One moment."

"Okay, if you insist."

Silas's cell pings with a text then his laptop signals an incoming secure email. When he double-clicks on the attachment, he leans back in his chair with his bottom jaw hanging down to his lap.

"What? What the fuck is it, Silas?"

"Hey! What are you doing in here? Get out before I call security! Let go of me! Noooo..."

"Tawnee!" I scream at the speaker, as if she can hear me, as if it'll stop whoever is doing whatever to her. "Silas—fucking say something!"

"Rafael listed Tawnee as the beneficiary for his entire estate —everything he owns is automatically hers upon his death."

"Good. But his death isn't the one I'm concerned about right now. Move your ass—we have to go help her!"

"They have also recorded a will in Tawnee's name, leaving everything she owns to Rafael in the event of her death. It was dated six months ago." He jumps up as he speaks and opens a zippered compartment of his suitcase, retrieving a packet of guitar strings and two short metal poles. "Here. You'll need this."

When I realize he just handed me a garrote wire, I'm impressed with his knowledge and skills all over again. I was ready to go in with fists flying. This will be much more effective. Steal up behind Rafael, wrap the guitar string around his neck, and twist the poles until he's dead. It results in a silent kill, no need for a gun, and no ruckus to alert security.

"Perfect. I hope this cuts his fucking head off."

CHAPTER 20

Tawnee

Four large men in expensive Armani suits stormed into Rafael's room, dragged me off the couch, and down the steps to the first floor of the suite. Raf casually strolls down the stairs with a carefree grin on his face.

"Ah, I see you've met my associates. Good. Formal introductions aren't exactly necessary at this stage. You know, I wasn't sure about going through with this at first. After all this time you've been my head of security, I thought you were loyal to me. I was confident I could convince you to marry me by confessing my love for you.

"But all of a sudden, your entire personality changed. You didn't argue when I had your personal belongings moved from your room to mine. That's not the Tawnee I know. She would've raised hell with me over that. Then you kept favoring a certain seat on the couch, and you wanted to eat on the couch instead of at the table. Those signs were just a little too telling. We didn't find your bug, but I know it's somewhere in that room. Your friends have been listening to our conversations, checking up on me." He turns his attention to the brutes holding me. "Get her ready."

One wraps a roll of thick, black duct tape around my head, covering my mouth and underneath my chin several times. Another man binds my hands behind my back. The third man approaches with a boshiya, a thick black veil that completely covers my head and face. There isn't even a hole for my eyes. Then they cover me with an abaya, a traditional Muslim dress that hides my regular clothes underneath, all the way down to my shoes, and makes me feel as if I'm wearing a heavy tent.

"Perfect. Your friends will be here soon, looking for you. I know that. But when they break in and find my suite empty and all your belongings gone, they'll assume you've been taken elsewhere. Then they'll leave. The best part is you'll still be on the property, attending our wedding. When the wild goose chase ends, and they realize they were never anywhere close to you, it'll be far too late for them to backtrack and find you. No body, no crime."

I can't flip him off, tell him what I think, or even give him a dirty look. He wouldn't be able to see or hear anything from under all this garb, anyway. Now I wish I'd taken him out when I had the chance. Never, in a million years, would I have thought he could be this devious.

Then Tabitha walks down the steps, wearing a gorgeous, modern, A-line wedding dress with spaghetti straps and a plunging neckline. Lace appliques cover the skirt. She styled her hair the same as mine. She applied her makeup to look like mine, right down to the eyeliner that changes the shape of her eyes. Even if I could speak through the layers of duct tape covering my mouth, I wouldn't be able to say a single word.

"Ah, *Tawnee*," Raf greets Tabitha. My eyes dart between the two of them, even though they can't see me under this thick black veil. "Are you ready to marry me today?"

"I'm more than ready to marry you, Raf. I've been in love

with you for so long, and after my kidnapping, I finally faced my true feelings. I'm so excited to become Mrs. Tawnee Milano-Cruz today." Tabitha's smile beams, exactly like a true bride.

She walks straight to me, searching for my face under the black shawl. "You must wonder why, after all this time, I'd betray you like this. It's really very simple—my loyalty was never to you. Rafael is the one who has paid our salaries all these years. Without him, none of us would have had such a prestigious position. And for marrying him today while pretending to be you, he will set me up for life. Carter and I will be able to sail off into the sunset together, debt-free and without a care in the world. You could have had this for yourself, Tawnee. All you had to do was say yes when he asked you to marry him."

They may have tied my hands behind my back, but my legs are still free. For now. *Time to sweep the leg, Johnny.* My Brazilian Jiu-Jitsu training comes in handy right about now. With a standing leg sweep, I knock her to the ground, pounce on top of her, and squeeze with my thighs until I hear ribs crack. She may sail off into the sunset, but it'll be with a long-term reminder of who she stabbed in the back to get there. The men surrounding me are too shocked at first to react quickly, but when they do, arms grab me from every direction and pull me off her. I squeeze my thighs tighter, lifting her off the floor with me until my legs can't hold her weight and I drop her flat on her back with a thud.

"Enough!" Raf bellows. "Tabitha, go fix yourself up again until you look perfect. We'll be waiting for you downstairs for the ceremony. Carter will walk you down the aisle and give you away."

I glance around, looking for the other members of my team. I'd love to know if they're part of this mutiny or if something has happened to them. They weren't here when we came in late last night after the hostage release. Has Raf killed Jason and John or turned them to the dark side with Tabitha and Carter?

She limps away to fix herself up, but not before throwing a nasty scowl my way. If only she could see the eye daggers I'm tossing her way.

Raf holds up his phone, showing me a live feed of Roman and Silas in the car. "Did you really think I wouldn't have them followed after they dropped you off last night? I know they're on their way here to rescue you. Perfect timing. Let's go get married, shall we?"

Two of the men from behind me walk toward the spare bedroom and return with my suitcases. I know they have packed all my personal possessions, leaving no trace of me behind. There are ways to make everything disappear—security footage, passports, people—with the right amount of money. Raf has that in spades.

"Bring her."

The other two men grab my arms and force me to follow Raf out of the suite, to the elevator, and outside. The wedding planner has been hard at work decorating the grassy court-yard with white linen-covered chairs, a shimmering walkway lined with white flowers and glossy green foliage, and a flowing gossamer-wrapped arbor. Set against the blue sea, sky, and bright sun, it's a ceremony any bride would dream of having.

If she's standing next to her groom of choice, that is.

The chairs are already full of guests, all excited to see Rafael Cruz get hitched. My goons force me into a chair in the middle of the row, next to other women in varying degrees of similar dress, where I'm less likely to be noticed. The music starts, quickly followed by *oohs* and *ahs* from the crowd. The only reason I even glance over at Tabitha is to see if she's grimacing from her cracked ribs and shallow breaths.

She's in a lot of pain.

That makes me smile on the inside. I can't physically smile under all this duct tape.

They must have told the minister to zip through the formalities because he takes no time in getting to the vows, the I Do's, and pronouncing Mr. and Mrs. Cruz as man and wife, sealed with a kiss and exchange of rings. When the guests stand to clap and cheer, my bodyguards force me up and quietly slip away from the adoring fans waiting to throw birdseed at the happy couple.

When we reach the fleet of Rolls-Royce limos, one man stops me, harshly jerks me to face him, and lifts my veil. "Your name is Tawnee Lia Milano? Is that correct?"

Anger burns in his eyes and his face is scrunched up in disgust. This instantly feels very different from just a few minutes ago.

I nod my head slowly, afraid to confirm his question. How would he know my full name?

"This is her. This is the one. We're taking her back with us."

"But Rafael said—"

"I don't care what he said. He lied to us about her name. She is the one we've been looking for after all. We're taking her now." He puts the veil back in place, shoves me into the back seat of the car despite my kicks and fighting, and instructs the driver to go.

As we drive away from the hotel, I continue to struggle against them, trying to reach the door to fling myself out of the moving car, then one of the men punches me in the face, knocking me out.

When I come to, everything is upside down. Then I see feet below me, moving swiftly. Shifting to get a better look, I realize I've been flung over one of the brute's shoulders, and he's carrying me toward a small jet. I begin to fight again, knowing certain death awaits me if I allow them to take off with me aboard that plane.

"Be still or I will break your neck and leave your body right here for the animals to eat while you're still alive." His angry growl sends shivers down my spine because he means what he says.

I look around to figure out where we are, but all I see in every direction is flat sand and heat monkeys jumping in the distance. Nothing distinguishable for miles. Without knowing exactly how long I've been out, I make an educated guess that I'm outside of Dubai, in the UAE, on my way to Saudi Arabia.

As a woman, they will strip my rights away from me the moment I cross into their country—no voice of my own, no way to get across the border, and no value as a fellow human being. And that's the best-case scenario I can hope for now. The odds of Roman—or anyone—finding me are statistically impossible. Not improbable. Impossible.

He deposits me in a seat at the rear of the plane where two other women wait. When he rejoins the other men at the front of the aircraft, the two women act quickly to untie my numb hands and remove the tape from my mouth and hair—as much as they can. When the blood rushes back into my hands, the pain is excruciating. With the first noise I make, the women shush me and nervously glance toward the men. One massages my hands while the other woman applies oil to my hair to loosen the adhesive residue. Seems they have more than a little practice at remedying these medieval torture tactics.

After she removes the last of the tape, the lady working on my hair removes a new scarf from her bag and wraps it around my head and neck, covering my hair and every inch of exposed skin. With my arms untied, I'm able to wear the abaya correctly, making it much more comfortable than before. But from the way the man spoke my name, I'm not convinced an abundance of comfort will be found when we land.

"Do you speak English?" I whisper to the ladies.

"Yes," the younger of the two whispers back. "I am Anisa, and this is my sister, Farrah."

"I'm Tawnee. Where are they taking me?"

"To a village on the outskirts of Riyadh." Anisa watches the front of the plane closely. Her discomfort with talking to me is clear.

"Why? What do they want from me?"

The sisters lock eyes, silently deciding whether to answer my question.

"Please tell me. I do not understand why they want me or what they expect from me." That's not a complete lie. I have ideas, but they're unconfirmed suspicions. To know what my next move should be, I need confirmation.

"Because they know you're the woman who's trying to take over our oil business and overthrow our Crown Prince." Farrah sounds as though she completely believes the rumors that are no doubt running rampant about me throughout the kingdom.

Exaggerations and fabrications only add to the hysteria, making me public enemy number one across the country. Next, they'll say I'm after their husbands. Not a chance, sister.

"Farrah, I promise you neither is true. Look at me—do I look like I have the money to buy the controlling shares in SAOR? I don't own shares in any company. Also, I have no interest in being your new Crown Princess, or whatever that title would be. All I want is to go back to my home in my country. How can I do that? How can I get home?"

"This is not possible, Tawnee. The mutawa—the virtue police—have you in custody now. They can hold you indefinitely for such severe offenses." Anisa is clearly the more empathetic of the two.

I know what the religious police are about—they're the plainclothes officers who roam the streets to enforce their public morality laws however they deem fit.

The sisters take their seats when the plane starts to move

and stay silent for the two-hour flight. I know exactly how long we were in the air… because I count every second of it. If I have any hope of escaping back to Dubai, I need a way to calculate the distance and direction. Getting out of this country is my one and only goal.

When we land, the morality police—which is a complete oxymoron to me, because I believe it's immoral to mistreat women—snatch me up out of my seat and haul me off the plane and straight into the back seat of yet another car. When we stop, it's at a dull, tan building, mostly made of clay. The windows are all covered by a thick rattan wood. An eight-foot fence lines the edge around the entire rooftop of the building to prevent the prisoners from escaping or jumping to their death.

I'm thrown into a dimly lit cell, with only a hard cot, a thin blanket, and a toilet. Male guards patrol back and forth along the path in front of the bars, simultaneously sneering at me with disgust and leering at me with lust in their eyes. Pitiful sounds echo throughout the sparsely furnished common room. Women cry from every corner of the prison—some scream, some make strange animal noises, and others sound as though they're talking to themselves.

None of this bodes well for me.

A loud bell rings and all the guards congregate in one corner of the room, unroll their rugs, and bow to begin their mandatory prayer time. While they're all busy, I crouch on the floor at the edge of my cell, closest to the woman beside me, and loudly whisper to get her attention.

"Hey, what's your name? Mine is Tawnee. Do you understand English?"

"Yes. Most of my country does. My name is Lara."

"Why are you in here, Lara?"

"Because I ran away from my brother."

"I'm sorry, I don't understand what you mean."

"He was my guardian, but he was very cruel. He used to beat

me and make me into his slave. When I ran away, the police caught me and put me in here. My brother refuses to get me out, so the police can keep me as long as they want, or they can sell me as a bride to anyone they choose."

My heart breaks in two for her. She's resigned to her fate and doesn't have the strength to fight it any longer. "Lara, I'm so sorry, but maybe we can help each other. Is there a way out of here? Any way out?"

"No, there's no escape from this place. I've been here more than five years now, and my brother still refuses to take me back. Even if I could escape, I have nowhere to go."

"You can go with me. If we get out, I will take you with me."

"We won't be allowed out of the country without my male guardian's approval. Since I no longer have a male guardian, I can't get approval to leave. You can't either. Even as a foreigner, you're required to have a male escort at all times when in public." I'm sure her argument makes sense to her—this is her culture and what they have ingrained in her since birth. I'm not as willing to accept the rule of another over me.

"Lara, if we break out of jail, it'll be without the help of a male guardian. We'll also sneak across the border without the permission of a male guardian, because we'll be badass prison escapees by then. Who needs a guardian when you're a badass?"

"There's a moment when they leave us alone in the infirmary after the electric shock torture. The woman who runs the infirmary is the commander's wife, so none of the male guards can stay in there with her. If we could somehow pull ourselves together inside that room, we could make a run for it."

"Do they take everyone for torture at the same time?"

"No, it's scheduled by which cell we're in. You and I will go together in two days, according to our cell numbers."

So much can happen in this hellhole over the next two days.

Is it wrong that I wish for our torture session to come sooner?

Roman

"Dude, run over them, knock them out of the way, push them off the road. Do something!" I yell at Silas, knowing there's nothing he can do about gridlock traffic on the main road in Dubai that runs parallel to the beach.

"Don't look now, but we're being watched. There's a guy in the car two lanes over, one car back, who's been following us. Assume the worst when we rush in." Silas checks the rearview mirror again, watching our tail while they watch us.

"Are you above being a pirate?"

"Not at all. It's my dream job. What's your plan?"

"Pull in to that marina and let's commandeer one of those boats from the rental place. Since we're making a water entrance to the hotel anyway, we might as well do it in style. We can ditch our stalkers while we're at it."

"Great idea. There's no way they'll get over in this bumper-to-bumper traffic to follow us out there. Now to get past the guys on the docks."

"Leave them to me. You and Nick pick out a fast boat and let's haul ass."

Silas barely wedges between the line of cars and the pedestrians on the sidewalk to get us out of traffic and onto the side road. The instant we moved out of line, the cars behind us surged forward, cutting off anyone who may have thought about getting over. Before our vehicle comes to a stop in the marina parking lot, I'm already out and running toward the docks.

A party of at least seventy people is lined up to board a large yacht. The deckhands are busy checking in each person and assisting them on board. The captain is in the cockpit, running through his last-minute inspection, and the guests are lively and animated in their formal dresses and black-tie tuxedoes.

I stick out like a sore thumb.

There's no way anyone will buy the line I'm late for this party.

All the more reason for me to distract the couple of guys who don't have their hands full already. I trot toward them, frantically looking around, and stop when I get just past them. They turn, and their gazes track my movement.

That's it, fellas. Eyes on me. I'm over here.

"Have you seen a little girl wander by here? She's five, wearing a pink princess dress. She has a little tiara on her head and a purse on her arm. She was beside me one minute and gone when I looked down the next. I'm afraid she got on one of these boats, pretending it was hers. Or, God forbid, she fell in the water. You haven't heard a splash, have you? You don't think she's under one of these boats, do you?" I'm laying it on thick, letting the alarm overtake my voice and my face.

Panic-stricken, they leave the guests to the other workers and rush to help me. If I keep them busy checking the multitude of yachts lining the five rows of docks, Silas and Nick can manage to get one of the smaller, faster fishing boats untied and ready to take off without being seen. The engines on the party yacht are loud enough to mask a vessel the size we need… for a few minutes, anyway. They'll realize it soon enough.

The two men split up and board each boat, checking every nook and cranny inside after they've finished with the outside. I would feel bad for my blatant lie and their dedication to finding the lost child if a life wasn't truly in danger right now. But Tawnee is my first and only priority—so I can't focus on anything except reaching her.

While the men are busy, Silas and Nick slip past me and hurry to the end of the dock where the smaller center console boats are tied. Nick unties one of the lines while Silas starts the engines, then he unties the second line before pushing off. The longer he lets it idle in neutral, the better off we are. When they drift far enough away from everything that Silas can put it in gear to go forward, Nick motions for me to join them. I rush to the end of the dock, Silas swings by close enough for me to jump on, and we haul ass out of the marina and around the bend to the hotel.

I haven't worked out how we'll get up to Rafael's suite yet. The elevator requires a room key to move off the lower floors, making it almost impossible. We arrive at the hotel in no time, thanks to the powerful engines on the back of the fishing boat. They're designed to take the fishermen out far and fast, so they can be the first to the prize. Now if I can just make it to my prize in time. Silas sidles up alongside the concrete retaining wall around the hotel so Nick and I can jump off to secure the boat's fore and aft lines to the palm trees.

We race across the green grass and through the middle of an ongoing wedding reception. I don't think much about it until I catch a glimpse of Tony lurking in the back. After he checks our surroundings, he motions for me to join him around the corner. I'm well aware it could be a setup, but I'm willing to take the chance. His expression before he saw me was genuinely distressed. I'm going on a hunch that he truly wants to share information with me.

When I turn the corner, Tony's leaning against the side of the hotel with his head hung low and his shoulders drooping.

"What's happened, Tony? Where is she?" I can barely catch my breath, but it's not from exertion. My heart is racing a hundred miles an hour.

Then it stops beating when I realize what I just ran through.

"Did he force her to marry him somehow?" I'm about to lift Tony off the ground by the lapels of his dress jacket if he doesn't start talking.

"No, he let something far worse happen to her." He begins talking and doesn't stop until the entire sordid story is out in the open. "He was in league with a handful of Saudi oil investors in a bid to take over the oil company. Most of the Saudi men are very traditional—and very resistant to change. They didn't want their state-owned company on the New York Stock Exchange. They didn't want foreigners to have any piece of it, but they were willing to do business with Raf under the pretense they'd get it all back. Only Raf never told his business partners that he bought the oil shares under Tawnee's name. He did that to protect himself because he knew the Saudis would be enraged if they found out he planned to keep his shares. He's still an outsider, you know. His business partners could have snuffed him out at any moment.

"Raf thought he had more time to convince her to marry him before things got out of control. He could put the company in both their names without her ever knowing. By then, it wouldn't matter if they got to her—he'd be in control of it all without having lost anything. Later, he could dump the shares at more than twice the price, knowing the Saudi people would buy them up to regain control. Or he could decide to keep them long-term."

"Okay. What went wrong? Whose wedding was today? Where is she now?"

"What went wrong? Everything. He overestimated his charm and underestimated Tawnee's love for you." That "you" was a little forced and a little bitter. "Tabitha pretended to be Tawnee today—fake identification included—and married Raf. When his Saudi business associates heard Tabitha say Tawnee's full name, they immediately realized who she was… and that they didn't need Raf anymore. Raf never dreamed they'd double cross him, but then he never seemed to consider all the angles of his cockamamie plans. That's why he's had so many advisers over the years—he didn't build this empire alone like he tells everyone."

"You advised him, didn't you? That's why he kept you so close to him."

"Yes, I did. But he wouldn't listen to me on this one. I told him those men couldn't be trusted. I told him that Tawnee wasn't here for his money or his status, that she wasn't that type of person. He believed everyone wanted him for his wealth and nothing else, though, so he quit caring about others at all. He hid it well, but I knew better. Tawnee and I butted heads more than a few times over the years when Raf was being an ass and putting her in more risk than necessary. I couldn't tell her that, though."

"Why are you telling me this now? And where is she, Tony?"

"His four Saudi business partners took her before the wedding was over. They didn't even wait until Raf and Tabitha made it down the aisle as man and wife. One of them punched Tawnee, knocked her out, and threw her in the back of a car. I tried to stop them, but I was too late. Raf was furious when he found out because he sank a lot of money into those shares and they just cut him out of it altogether. He doesn't care about her, though.

"I'm telling you all this for three reasons. First, I just quit my job because Raf refused to go after them and save her. Second, you've got to save her because she's about to die. They would have taken her outside of Dubai to a private airstrip to board a jet bound for Riyadh. That's where they were every time Raf had a video conference call with them. And third, because I love her. I've been in love with her for a long time, but I know she never felt that way about me. I was willing to step aside and let her marry Raf if that's what she wanted—at least he could provide for her in a way I never could. But now, I'm done with him, I can't help her, and I'm hoping you can."

"What were their names, Tony? Who are his associates? I need names to find out where they'd be and where she'd be held."

"Here are their names." Tony hands me a folded piece of paper from his pocket. "And I can tell you where they'll hold her —where they hold all the women they to torture and get away with whatever they want. Dar Al Reaya, the female torture chambers in Saudi Arabia where they send all the victims to pay for the crimes they didn't commit."

Ice-cold blood runs through my veins at the mention of that name. I've heard of those places. I know what they do to women in them. My Tawnee is a prisoner in one of those godforsaken locations, where the guards get their rocks off by torturing, raping, and mentally abusing women who have no one to care about them. Sometimes they sell the women in an arranged marriage, where they face the same horrors, only in some man's house instead of a typical prison cell.

"So, they'll torture her, break her down, and make her transfer her shares to them... then they'll kill her anyway."

"Exactly. Raf is a coward. He wouldn't even try to save her from their clutches. In his twisted mind, he blames her for making him lose all that money. I mean, her name is the one on the company, after all. Right?" His laugh is humorless and full of disgust.

"Where is Raf now?"

A helicopter takes off from the landing pad that hangs off the top edge of the building. Tony looks up at it and points. "On his way to his 'honeymoon with Tawnee.' He's getting out of town before any Saudis come back for him. They're going to Paris."

Without looking, I know Silas and Nick are behind me. They have been there the whole time, ready to give support when I need it. "One of you tell me you have pull in Saudi Arabia to get us across the border without visas."

"Sorry, man, but I don't. Had it been Russia, maybe I could have helped. The border crossings into Saudi Arabia are heavily guarded, and the airport customs and immigration area is just as strict. They don't want foreigners in their country."

"You know I don't have Saudi contacts. Sorry, Roman," Nick adds.

"I can help." A man steps out from behind the landscaping, seemingly out of nowhere, and I didn't even know he was there. I jerk my head to the side, and my eyes fly wide open.

I openly gape at him for a minute. Something about him is very familiar. "Oh my God. Shadow? Is that you? Where have you been?" I can't believe my eyes.

"We've been working, Roman." He motions to the man who steps up next to him.

"Reaper? What the hell is going on? What have you two been doing?"

"Holy shit. I didn't even recognize my own brother." Silas laughs and steps back to get a good look at both men.

"That's because he's wearing a dress, Silas. I bet you've never seen either of them in a dress before."

"Roman, they're not dresses. They're called thobes, and nearly every Saudi man wears one exactly like it. We had to blend in and appear to be one of them while doing recon."

"You two can speak and read Arabic?" My tone is notably skeptical.

"Yes, we can. We had to learn it for this mission. Imagine being caught while dressed up as a Saudi man and not being able to speak the language. Our paperwork is all set, and we're your sponsors to enter the country. They will hold Reaper and me responsible for your behavior while there, so don't make us look bad."

"I would never. I'm just going to kill anyone and everyone who gets in my way. But I'd never make you look bad while doing it."

"Do you have a way home, Tony?" Nick asks.

"Yes, don't worry about me. Just hurry and get Tawnee out of there before it's too late." He walks off with his shoulders hunched and a shuffle in his steps.

"What's the plan, Shadow?" I'm back to business. Tony is a big boy. He can find his way home.

"Tell me, how do you feel about wearing a dress?" The huge grin on his face not only confirms I'm fucked but also that Shadow will enjoy this particular screwing more than he should.

CHAPTER 22

Roman

"Y ou've got to be fucking with me right now." I look at my reflection in the mirror and still can't believe my eyes. "This will never work."

"It'll work because you'll be sitting in the back seat, keeping your mouth shut like the good little girl that you are." Shadow points his finger in my face as he issues his implied threat.

"Just so we're clear... your ass is the first one I'm kicking when we get back home."

"Is that any way to speak to your male guardian? No wonder I'm throwing my daughter in the detention center. She's disrespectful, disobedient, and just plain ugly." Shadow walks off laughing, leaving me to stare at my reflection again.

I'm in a head-to-toe black triangular tent. There's no other way to describe it. I have an opening for my eyes—one slit in the fabric—that's it. "They will never believe I'm a woman, Shadow. Look at me. I'm too tall and too broad to be a Saudi woman."

"It'll be fine. They won't pay much attention to you, anyway.

Plus, we'll be in a Land Cruiser, not some tiny compact car. We'll put you all the way in the back, in the third-row seat."

"Whatever works, man. I don't care. Just get me to her."

We pile into the SUV, but we're so much farther behind the men who took Tawnee than we already were because every move we make takes planning, discussions, and contingencies. My impetuous nature still has a hard time dealing with all the waiting this job requires. It's not that I don't understand the reasons—it's knowing Tawnee needs me and I'm not there to protect her.

We're driving across the UAE to the border of Saudi Arabia, roughly 600 miles, because they will definitely question my status as a woman in an airport. But with the Saudi license plate and registration, we're simply returning home from a family visit to Dubai. Once we're inside the country, Shadow has a private plane waiting to take us the rest of the way to the capital. All we have to do is make it past the border guards first.

Piece of cake.

When I look like an enormous woman in a country where the average female height is barely over five feet tall.

I can't help where my thoughts stray on the six-hour journey to the border. Only six, thanks to the liberal speed limits throughout the UAE and Shadow's lead foot. We roll up to the covered booths, where groups of soldiers wait for the nod to descend on someone trying to gain illegal entry. My instincts tell me to account for every threat—the location, the type of threat, and estimate the likelihood of an attack. But I'm scrunched down in the back seat to make myself appear smaller. I purposely keep my gaze low to avoid eye contact with anyone outside the vehicle. And my demure little girl act is keeping us all alive.

The guard takes the documents from Shadow, and they have a brief conversation in Arabic. The reason I don't look at them now is that I'm afraid he'll speak to me and I have no way to reply. I'm at a complete disadvantage in this country on every front. But there's no part of me that wants to back out of this. My girl is in an even worse position, and I know she isn't giving up. She doesn't have it in her to surrender.

I release a huge sigh of relief when we're waved through the checkpoint without an extensive search. When we pick up speed again, I finally feel safe enough to speak.

"Can I take this ridiculous outfit off now?"

"Silence, woman. You're not allowed to speak until spoken to first. Learn your place."

"Shadow, you should know that I'm telling Elle every mean word you say to me. She will make you pay for it when we get home."

"That's cold, man."

The entire vehicle breaks out in laughter, releasing some of the stifling tension that's made it hard to breathe all day.

"Seriously, you can't take it off yet. They're known to have random roadblocks just to harass people, make sure they have all their paperwork in order, and that they're following all the religious laws. We can't let them see your face."

"Good point. I'll keep it on. But you should know this thing is really uncomfortable and I'm developing claustrophobia under here."

"I get it. You hate wearing a niqab and an abaya. But a lot of women in this region like them. It's usually by personal prefer-ence, but in this case, your father has deemed you unworthy of staying with the family. So you have to wear it to cover your disloyal face."

"The entire world needs therapy, man. You. Me. Them. Everyone."

After another two hours on the road, we finally reach the private jet that will carry us the rest of the way. When we land outside of Riyadh, I calculate they had a ten-hour head start on us, and we're still not caught up. The men we meet on the hard-packed sand landing strip are obviously also CIA, putting their lives and their covers on the line to help a fellow brother-in-arms.

"Are you sure you want to go through with this?" One man approaches me, wearing the traditional thobe and headdress.

"Without a doubt. Holy shit. You're Jason, aren't you? You worked with Tawnee."

"Yeah, that's me. John and I were on assignment to follow Rafael Cruz." He nods toward the other man helping us. "We had to pull back when everything got crazy with the whole fake wedding bullshit. We have tabs on where he'll be, though, so we're helping get Tawnee back first."

"We appreciate the help. Why didn't you tell us we were on the same team when we first met? You must have known Silas and I were CIA."

"Sure, we did. Silas's reputation precedes him. But then so does Shadow's, and we were under orders not to give anything away. We knew we couldn't trust the others, so we just kept playing along until we couldn't anymore."

"We're glad to have you on our team. What do you have for us?" Nick asks.

"I don't know where you'll stick this to keep them from finding it, but I'll leave it up to you to find a spot." He hands me a small military-grade stun gun.

"Well, if they grab my crotch on the way in, they'll get two handfuls of a big cocky surprise anyway, so I think I'll add this to the package." I lift my dress and stuff the stun gun into my briefs.

The guys chuckle, but they know the seriousness of what we're about to do... and the slim-to-none odds of pulling it off successfully.

"We'll be right here with our finger on the engines, ready to roll when we see you coming. Try not to bring too much company back with you. I really don't want to test my pilot skills against the Royal Saudi Air Force fighter jets." John shakes my hand—equally in a symbol of wishing me good luck and in saying goodbye to me for good.

"Roman and I are going to the detention center now. The rest of you should stay here—nearby. I don't know how long it'll take us to get in and out, but it doesn't make sense to put everyone's lives on the line. If you don't hear from us by morning, get out of the country and get yourselves to safety." Shadow makes it a point to look at each man individually when speaks, driving his point home.

"You're my brother. I'm going in beside you." Noah steps up next to him. "My nickname is Reaper for a reason."

"Noah is my brother—literally—and I'm going in beside him. Roman is my junior officer. I'm going in beside him." Silas steps beside me.

"None of you are going anywhere without me. We're in this together." Nick puts his hands on his hips and stares us down.

Shadow drops his head and stares at the ground. "Noah, your wife will murder me if I go home without you. And Silas, your wife is a trained agent. She'll kill me in my sleep if I go home without you. Nick, your wife and her nanny will have my head and my balls on a pike."

"You don't think Elle would do the same to us if we let you go in there alone?" Silas counters.

"Look, I'm the one going in as a woman. I think you all should stay outside. You can get ready to give us a hand when we get out, and they're hot on our asses. That way, we have the element of surprise on our side inside and outside of the facility."

"I don't like it." Silas shakes his head.

"How many fathers tour the facility when they send their wayward daughters off to a torture center? None. They kick them to the curb and drive off on their merry way. If I have four male guardians escort me inside, they'll know right away something is up. We can't raise all those red flags."

"He's right, Silas. Let the kid have this one. We'll cover the outside and push them back long enough for Roman and Tawnee to make a break for it." Noah claps his brother on the shoulder. "You know this is the right plan."

"Shit. Okay, fine. Let's get this over with. Everyone ready to go?"

"I've been ready all fucking day. Let's go." I slide into the back seat, putting on the shamed demeanor of an unruly adult child.

Shadow drives us through the capital city until we reach the outskirts on the other side and the night grows darker. He drops the guys off about a block from the destination so they can get in place. The lack of consistent streetlights only amplifies the misery and gloom of the women's prison. I've heard horror stories about these places—the women who were arrested for having premarital sex because they were raped, the morality police threw them in prison for not meeting their religious standards, and some women were imprisoned for having a job without their husband's permission. Daily lashes. Torture by electric shocks. Prolonged solitary confinement.

He parks in front of the center to drop me off and talk to the guard. We had already decided he'd tell the guard my vocal cords were damaged, so I don't speak, rendering me worthless to him since he can't marry me off. He'll ask to see where I'll be kept, ensuring I don't have to answer any questions between the door and my cell, but then the rest will be on me.

Escape from my cell.

Find Tawnee.

Get us both out.

Alive. That one is important.

By morning.

No pressure.

Shadow bangs on the door, and a guard opens it almost immediately. They talk while I keep my head bowed, not daring to look at them while they discuss how terrible I am. Shadow grabs my arm, pushes me forward, and I follow in line behind the guard. While they speak in a language that makes no sense to me, I scan the area for exits, the total number of guards, and the proximity of the cells.

As we pass the inhabited cells, I search each one for Tawnee. My anger grows with every woman I see on the stroll toward my cell. Abused, neglected, and forgotten—every one of them. Rocking in the corner, talking to herself, crying or screaming, and every variation in between. Then I stop dead in my tracks when I see a woman passed out on the floor, swollen bruises and scratches across her face and neck, and wearing torn clothes.

After several steps, the guard notices I'm not right on their heels anymore and turns to yell at me. I don't care what he's saying. I don't care how mad he is. Nothing else matters.

Because that woman on the floor who has been beaten unconscious is Tawnee.

And culpable or not, this motherfucker is guilty as sin in my eyes.

He comes closer, getting in my face to scream at me, his spittle spraying on me while his horrible breath could knock me out on its own. Under normal circumstances. But nothing about this is normal. My rage has burned past the point of madness. Now, I'm emotionally numb. The cold and calculating side of me has emerged, and he only wants to witness the carnage.

Shadow searches my eyes and realizes something is horribly wrong. His gaze jumps to the cell beside me, and the ruthless assassin he's rumored to be comes to life.

The guard continues to spew his vitriol, and I've heard enough of it. With a quick jab to his nose, I knock him backward. He stumbles over Shadow's foot and falls to the ground. I move to stand over him, jerk the ridiculous garb I'm wearing off me, and punch him directly in the throat. His hands wrap around his own neck, then he sputters and coughs as he tries to breathe, and he flails on the ground when his oxygen reserves expire. I could easily end his suffering rather than letting him slowly suffocate to death, but I don't want to.

I grab the keys off his belt and unlock Tawnee's cell door. Men's voices carry down the hall, growing closer to where we are. The other guards on duty tonight, no doubt. The man who's barely moving on the floor probably drew the short straw and had to work through his break time.

"Shadow, you should get out of here before the rest get in here. We don't know what kind of weapons they have access to in here." I whisper to him as I kneel beside Tawnee and remove the stun gun from my briefs.

"You're full of shit, Roman. I'm not leaving you alone now. We still have the element of surprise, and we have more backup outside. Let's get her out of this cell. She needs to be close to the front door when the fighting starts."

After we lift her off the floor, we each wrap an arm around her waist and pull her arms around our necks. With her supported between us, we sprint toward the front door to get her to safety. The chattering voices enter the room and turn to angry shouts. Sirens blare throughout the facility, doors fling open and more men run out, and the automatic door locks slide into place.

A dozen men descend on us, but I don't feel panicked at all. There's no fucking way they're taking her back into that cell. They'll have to go through me to reach her, and there's no fucking way that will happen. Shadow releases her into my arms and prepares to fight off the first wave. I gently set her down in the corner behind me, then take my place beside Shadow.

The guards brandish a variety of weapons. Some carry a

flogger, others have a cattle prod, and a few have whips. But we're ready for them. We're trained Special Forces operatives and CIA officers. The more weapons they bring my way, the more I'll have to use against them. The first man moves in too close, and I hit him with the stun gun. He screams loudly from the electric shock, and I wonder if he realizes he's only receiving a small taste of his own medicine. When he goes down, I take the flogger from his hand and give it to Shadow.

Several more rush us at once, and though we don't escape entirely unscathed, they definitely hobble away worse for wear. Shadow now holds out two charged cattle prods, fending off the brave but stupid men who try to advance on us, while I try the different keys on the front door. When I find the correct one, I cradle Tawnee against my chest while I run outside, and Shadow covers my back. Reaper, Nick, and Silas meet us at the curb and jump into the fracas to lend a hand. A crowd gathers in the streets, lights in the surrounding apartments blink on, and angry voices increase in volume and numbers.

"Get in. Get the fuck in, and let's get out of here before the whole neighborhood descends on us." Silas slides behind the wheel and peels away from the building before we've even closed the car doors.

No matter. We disappear into the night, park the car in a crowded parking lot, and quickly jump into another one. When they eventually find the original vehicle, we'll be long gone— flying far away from here.

"Tawnee, sweets, can you hear me?" She hasn't opened her eyes yet. I don't know if she needs a hospital or a good night's sleep. I don't know if they've drugged her or if she has brain damage and internal injuries.

Nervous glances come from everyone in the vehicle, but no one says anything. We can't get her medical help in this country. Our only choice is to see our original plan through until we're in a country where she's safe. We can't stop in Dubai because the religious police have been known to snatch Saudis off the streets there and take them back home to face their punishment.

"Can we get her to Paris tonight? Or Frankfurt?" My voice sounds hollow, but I'm grasping at straws here.

"They're both about the same flight time away. We're looking at a six-hour flight to reach either city." Shadow scrubs his hand over his face. "Let's get back to Jason and John, put her on the plane, and we can do a field assessment on her. Then we'll talk about next steps."

Next steps?

I don't have any next steps without her. I took a hard-line approach when I vowed to get her back, and nothing can make me back down from my promise. Under the passing illumination of the streetlights, I examine her wounds, her skin color, and make sure she's breathing regularly.

"You have to wake up, sweets. There's something I never took the time to tell you, and I need to say it now more than ever. But I'm not saying it until I know you can hear every word." I place a soft kiss on her forehead and say a prayer, asking God to give her back to me.

Jason and John wait inside the plane with the engines fired up, knowing we're coming in hot. When we board with her, John assures us he can take off alone so Jason can tend to her wounds.

"Scoot back just a little, Roman. I was a medic in the Army and a paramedic on the truck when I got out of the service. I promise I'll take good care of her."

I move to the floor and let them stretch her out on the long bench seat. I feel the thrust of the jet engines when we start down the runway. The plane lifts off the ground, but John keeps us low, avoiding radar for as long as possible. Jason continues his assessment of her, checking her pupils, her breathing, and her heart sounds. Her pulse is a bit slow, but that's not unusual for her condition.

"She doesn't have any obvious signs of internal bleeding—either in her torso or her brain. My guess is they gave her a dose of pain medication, or something similar, to knock her out after they tortured her. Her wounds are still very fresh. My advice is to let her sleep for a couple more hours then we'll decide if we should land somewhere for medical attention." Jason sits back on his heels and looks at me, waiting for a final decision.

"Okay, that's our plan, then. Keep monitoring her and reassess after a couple of hours. I'll stay right here beside her and watch for any change in her condition."

After the longest ninety minutes of my life, John announces we have cleared Saudi airspace and are on route to Paris unless we tell him differently.

"Tawnee, sweets, can you hear me? Hey, Tawnee, can you wake up for me now?" I kiss the back of her hand and stroke her hair, being careful not to touch any of the bruised or scratched places.

Feeling helpless, I look at Silas and wait for advice.

Tawnee

I hear Roman's voice, calling my name, but I can't open my eyes to see him. He sounds so far away, and my eyelids feel so heavy, as if they're nailed shut.

Every inch of my body hurts. Snippets of memories flash in my mind, like a movie reel that tries to play but keeps getting stuck. I try to focus on what I remember, but a dense fog has settled on my brain and I can't think straight.

Then it all comes rushing back at me at once.

The men who took me.

The prison guards who tortured me.

The woman in the infirmary who gave me an injection of something, though she wouldn't tell me what it was. She wasn't pleased that they'd been so rough with me on my first day. Apparently, they prefer to dish out the torture in metered doses so they can remind the wayward girls on a daily basis. She mumbled to me, in English, about how I wouldn't be able to take my punishment tomorrow because they'd had too much fun with me today.

Lovely lady, that nurse.

"Tawnee, sweets, you have got to open your eyes now so I know you're okay, or we'll be forced to land wherever we are right now and take you to the hospital. It's now or never—this is your last warning." Roman sounds so distraught.

I fight against my welded-shut eyelids and finally manage to pry one open. The ecstatic expression on his face from my opening one eye makes me wonder if I look as banged up as I feel. He gently wraps his hand around mine, not squeezing but sharing his strength with me just the same.

"Thank you, God." He kisses the back of my hand over and over. "Tawnee, can you speak? Do you want to go to the hospital right now?"

"No." My voice is hoarse and barely audible, but I force it enough for him to hear me. "I'll be okay."

"Do you know if they gave you any medications?" That's Jason's voice. I manage to open the other eyelid and focus on his face.

"Yes. An injection to make me sleep."

"Okay, I'm putting the portable oxygen on you just to be on the safe side. We'll take turns staying up to watch you until we reach Paris. John's flying the plane, and he's an excellent pilot. Between all of us, we've got you covered." Jason smiles, and I realize I'm happy to see him. Those two didn't turn to the dark side after all.

"No need to take turns. I won't be able to sleep until I know she's all right. You guys should rest while you can, though. I'm not leaving her side." Roman leans in and softly kisses me on the lips. Even though it's only been about twenty-four hours since I last saw him, it feels like an eternity that we've been apart.

"Never again," I whisper.

"Never." He shakes his head. "You're stuck with me forever, sweets. There's no getting rid of me now."

My eyes are too heavy to keep open, so I let them close on their own. Sleep overtakes me again, but this time, it feels different. A warm hand holds mine close to his heart, and I feel him at my side throughout the entire flight. He checks on me, he makes sure my oxygen mask is on correctly, and he whispers sweet nothings to me. Wrapped in the warmth of his love, I'm able to relax and let the dreams flow. Dreams of him and me. Dreams of our future. Dreams of our love. The best dreams I've ever had.

But not better than the real thing.

When the medicine starts wearing off and the grogginess fades, I open my eyes and find Roman still sitting guard over me. He's sitting on the floor and must be uncomfortable after all this time. After I slip the oxygen mask off my face, I move against the back of the bench as much as I can then pat the empty space.

"I don't want to hurt you." He looks up and down my body. I don't bother to look at the scratches and gashes and bruises. I can feel them without needing to see them.

"You won't hurt me."

He turns off the oxygen canister then gingerly moves to join me, facing me as he lies down. "I thought I'd lost you for a while there. You wouldn't wake up, even when I carried you in my arms."

"That was only because of the medicine she gave me. I'll be all right after a little R&R."

"I'm sorry I didn't reach you in time to stop them. I'll never forgive myself for that." He closes his eyes then squeezes them, fighting back the emotions inside.

"None of this was your fault. Not one single thing that happened. Don't you dare try to take the blame for it. This is all on Rafael, and he's the one who will pay for it. Not you." I run my fingers through his hair then along the scruff of his beard.

"Tawnee, there's something I have to tell you, and I should have told you a long time ago. I shouldn't have kept this from you."

"What is it?"

"I love you. I've always loved you, and only you. I will only ever love you. You are my soul mate…the other half of my soul."

"I love you, too, Roman. You're the only man I've ever loved, and I still love you after all this time."

His kiss holds more urgency this time. It's not as soft. He's not as afraid of hurting me. It's perfect.

"You're right about one thing. Rafael will absolutely pay for this. He won't get away with it."

"Neither will Tabitha or Carter. They were both in on it too. I will hunt them to the ends of the earth if I have to."

He lifts his hand to my face and skims his fingers from my forehead, along my cheek, and down to my chin. His eyes search mine before lingering on every wound, no matter how large or small. There's a question in his expression, but he's afraid to ask it.

"What do you want to know, Roman? You can ask me. I won't break, I promise I'm not that fragile." I smile as widely as I can without wincing to convince him.

"Your clothes were torn when I found you…"

"No, they didn't rape me. Not that they were above it, but they didn't. One of the guards grabbed at me. I stepped backward, trying to get out of range, but he snagged my clothes instead. The fabric ripped from the force."

"What did they do to you?"

"Electric shocks, slaps, punches, kicks—they stopped short of lashes. The woman who gave me the injection suggested that would come soon, though. They wanted the SAOR shares. Seems Raf did set me up, huh?"

"He certainly did. But they wouldn't believe that you couldn't give them what you don't have, right?"

"They didn't believe me at first, but I think they began to after the abuse went on so long and my story didn't change."

"Interesting. Were the men who took you also guards at that place?"

"No, I don't think so. The guards treated those four men with much more respect than anyone else in there. I wish I had their names to give you."

"I have their names." That shocks me speechless. I raise my eyebrows, waiting for him to continue. "We arrived at the hotel right after the fake marriage ceremony. Tony stopped me and filled me in on everything. He gave me the names of all four Arab men and said he quit his job because of what Rafael did to you."

"Tony quit his job because of me?" I must not be hearing him correctly.

"Yeah. Seems Tony has been in love with you for quite a while, but he knew you didn't feel the same. He still tried to look out for you, though, and sway Raf's decisions when he could."

"Knock me over with a feather… I never would have thought any of that."

Roman shrugs one shoulder. "This may come as a total shock to you, but sometimes men have no clue how to express their true feelings. So, they resort to doing stupid shit instead."

I start to giggle at him. Then he chuckles along with me, and before I know it, we're both trapped in a fit of laughter. "Stop making me laugh—it hurts." I hold my side, but to be honest, I don't want to stop. This carefree moment feels too good, despite my sore body, to let it go just yet.

"You can't blame this on me. All I did was tell the truth. Is it my fault that sometimes we men can be functional idiots? If I had any kind of power, I wouldn't get into half the trouble I do. So, if anything, this is mostly your fault."

"Your deductive reasoning prowess blows my mind. Care to explain how this is my fault?"

"If you weren't so smart, you wouldn't recognize my stupidity. Then it wouldn't be such an inconvenience to you. Have you tried being less intelligent? I think it could really help you just be happy all the time."

"Yes, you're exactly right, Roman. I mean, everyone says ignorance is bliss for a reason, right? I could live in complete bliss if only I were just a smidge stupider, right? That's your story, and you're sticking to it?"

He looks down and pulls his lips between his teeth to keep from smiling. When he regains his composure and lifts his eyes to mine, the love shining in them makes my heart skip a beat. "You know I wouldn't change one single thing about you, sweets. I fell in love with a strong, independent, intelligent woman, and I'm more in love with her today than I've ever been."

Tears of pure happiness spill over onto my cheeks. "You can't say things like that to me in my current state, Roman. All that strength, independence, and intelligence melts away, and all that's left is a blubbering, emotional woman."

His smile is warm and understanding. "I love that woman just as much. We'll balance each other, Tawnee. You don't have to be 'on' all the time. If you'll trust me to be your rock, I promise I'll never let you down again."

"I trust you with my life, Roman."

Shadow walks over and kneels on the floor beside us. "Hey, Tawnee. How are you feeling now? Should we divert to Rome, or do you want to wait until we get to Paris? It's no trouble—we can protect you either way."

"I'm okay, Shadow. I'll just rest until we get to Paris. I can't thank you enough for coming to get me out of there."

"My pleasure, darlin'. I'm just sorry it took us so long to reach you."

"There was a woman in the cell next to mine. Her name was Lara. Did either of you see her when you passed by?"

"No, sweets, there was no one in there when we walked by. I was counting cells and bodies until I found you," Roman replies.

"I think they killed her for talking to me, and it's my fault. I initiated the conversation, and I encouraged her to go along with me. We were planning to escape together as soon as possible."

"That isn't your fault, Tawnee. She obviously wanted out if she was so willing to put her life in the hands of an American stranger. The risks were worth it to her, because either way, she's free now. If all those women weren't being held prisoner in there, I'd call in a drone strike and raze that place to rubble." Shadow's hand curls into a tight fist, anger roiling through him over the inability to stop their cruel practices. "I'm glad you're already feeling better, though. We were worried about you. I'll leave you two alone to rest now."

Snuggled against Roman's warm body, I close my eyes and fall back asleep. When we start our approach for landing at our destination a few hours later, my entire body still feels like one big sore muscle. But the medication has largely worn off, so I'm much more alert and ready to face the next part of this journey. Though no one has shared any information with me, I know we're stopping over in Paris for much more than refueling the private jet for the next leg of our trip.

"Does anyone have my passport?" I ask tentatively.

"Now that you mention it, this one in my bag may be yours." Noah winks and hands over my passport.

"How did you get this?"

"We had a gut feeling Rafael would betray you. If that happened, I wanted to make sure we protected your identification, so I took it for safekeeping before you left the beachfront house."

"I'm surprised I didn't even notice. I was so focused on what I had to do that I didn't even check for it."

"That happens to all of us at some point in our careers. Don't sweat it. That's why we have each other's backs."

"Who wants to tell me what we're really doing in Paris, then? This is where Raf and Tabitha are on their fake honeymoon, isn't it?"

"I'll tell you exactly what I'm going to do here, sweets. I will find out where Raf is staying and get word to his Saudi partners. When they show up, I will kill every single one of them in a very unpleasant way. Then we can finish our trip home."

Roman isn't joking in the least. Though his expression is passive and his tone is neutral, he's deadly serious.

"And the other two?"

"If they're with him, they will die with him."

"No qualms? No second thoughts?"

"None. They conspired to kill you, Tawnee. They were active participants in sending you to the executioners—or worse, life imprisonment in a place where women wish for death long before it finds them. They had no qualms, no second thoughts, and no remorse. When I get ahold of them, I won't have any either. Maybe God will have mercy on them because I sure as hell won't."

"You're exactly right, Roman. I'll help you... in Lara's memory."

When the plane touches down, the guys exit first to give me some privacy to change clothes. Roman stays to help me, though I tried to convince him otherwise. I know what his reaction to seeing the still-fresh wounds will be, and I want his head clear when we go after Rafael. But I should have known he wouldn't leave me to struggle alone.

When every stitch of clothing is removed, he circles me and takes note of every abrasion I have. Every location. Every imprint of a hand, fist, or boot. He commits all my wounds to his memory. Then he turns, picks up the pile of clothes one by one, and takes his time to help me into them.

"I promise, he will feel everything you felt and more." He finishes with an extended kiss to my forehead.

Roman

"I can tell you where Raf is staying. He always stays at the same hotel in Paris. He wouldn't give up his favorite place just to avoid me." Tawnee and I descend the steps of the jet and walk across the tarmac at the private airstrip.

"Good. Will it be hard to get to him at this hotel?"

"No, not like at the last hotel. It's still a high-end resort, but much more accessible to the public. We can even get a room there, and he'll never know. He'll be in the penthouse suite on the seventh floor, where he'll have meals on his private terrace overlooking the Eiffel Tower. He'll think he's safe and secure in his upper-class suite."

"That's okay, sweets. Let him be smug right up until the end. I have special plans for him."

Inside the terminal, we move through immigration without a hitch. The private airport is small but busy. Most of the visitors passing through here are CEOs of major corporations, royalty, or other officials in high places, so the immigration personnel are proficient at their jobs. Tawnee receives more than a few raised eyebrows because of her injuries, but she assures everyone that she's just grateful she walked away from the car wreck with the terrible drivers in Dubai. Their empathetic nods end any further questioning.

"Two rental cars are waiting for us. Where are we headed?" Jason asks.

"The most luxurious hotel in Paris," Tawnee replies.

"I'm making our reservations there now. There will be several unhappy guests when they arrive and learn their rooms have been given away, but our cause is more important than theirs." Shadow clicks away on his special CIA phone, hacking through firewalls and employee log-ins to gain access to their reservation system. "Done. Roman and Tawnee, I put you two in the royal suite just below his. Let me know if you need any help getting into his make-believe fortress."

"Thanks, Shadow, but we've got it. He's not going anywhere except to the morgue. I promise you that."

"You already have a plan in mind?" Shadow asks.

"Yes, I do. An especially cruel one that I'm looking forward to carrying out."

"How can we help?" One side of Shadow's mouth lifts in amusement. He wants in on the action.

"Have you ever been a waiter?"

"Are you kidding? There's not much I haven't been while undercover."

"Perfect. I'll be waiting inside his suite when you bring up his special delivery. You're welcome to stay for the show."

"Let's finish this. I love cosplay."

Shadow leads the way to the rental cars. We divide up in the two vehicles and drive toward the hotel. On the way, I turn to Silas for the other part of my plan.

"We need some partially fake news to go viral and draw out our Saudi friends. They need to pay Raf a visit here in Paris so we can end the threat to Tawnee and my dad at the same time."

"Partially?"

"Yes. The pictures we release need to show Raf and the real Tawnee in their wedding photos. Then reveal she's the woman who bought the shares, but Raf is taking over as CEO, effective immediately. His first act in his new position will be to dump the stocks and try to bankrupt the oil company. They won't allow that to happen—it's a matter of national pride. They'd buy the shares back no matter who was selling them, but putting Raf's name and location out there will bring our friends out to play. They won't let him take all the money and run."

"Devious. I love it. It'll spread like wildfire within an hour after I post it, I'll make sure of it." Silas retrieves his computer and begins doctoring the photos and writing a thorough press release, including the exact address where the newlywed couple is honeymooning.

"I figure we have about eight or nine hours before the goon squad lands. Sweets, where can I take you after we check in?"

"Straight to our royal suite." She smiles up at me. The bruises on her face and neck do nothing to detract from her beauty.

"I see your sassiness is making a full recovery already." I quirk up one eyebrow at her, but she knows I love that answer more than anything else she could say.

"I'm guessing it has a huge bathtub that would be perfect for at least two people to soak their aching muscles in until their skin shrivels up like prunes. Then there's room service, with chocolate-covered strawberries and champagne as an appetizer. Maybe a nice juicy steak and lobster tail for the main course. Thick, plush robes and fuzzy slippers to laze around in. Then we can get dressed, scale the wall outside the hotel, and kill a few people before bedtime."

"You are the perfect woman and traveling companion. Has anyone ever told you that?"

Chuckles fill the car, and I'm struck by how fortunate I am to be surrounded by the best friends a man could ask for. I only wish Blake were here to lend a hand, but I'm thankful he's standing guard over my dad right now. He's not exactly in the clear yet. Even eliminating the four we know of doesn't guarantee others won't come for him later, but he'll never be without the protection of the best people in the world.

"There are probably a few places I need to go first. The Saudi men took all my clothes with them, so I have nothing else to change into. I don't even know whose clothes I'm wearing right now." Tawnee's gaze drifts to the window, not exactly focusing on anything as the memory plays in her mind.

"The last people to use the plane left them behind. Sorry if the fit is a little big on you," Jason says from the front.

"They're fine—I'm glad they're not tight. That would be uncomfortable with all these bruises. Thank you for finding them for me, Jason."

"My pleasure, Tawnee. You know, John and I both wanted to tell you a long time ago that we're CIA, but we had orders. I hope there're no hard feelings about that. If it makes you feel any better, we've always had your back, though."

Tawnee's jaw drops open, and she looks up at me. "Did you know that?"

"Only recently—as in the last few hours. Everything is running together. I may have forgotten to tell you that part with the whole thinking you were about to die in my arms thing."

"All right. I forgive you."

"Thank you."

"You're welcome. Just don't let it happen again."

"Yes, ma'am."

"I have to tell you both—I really like this version of Roman. Pliable. Easy-going. Takes orders well. Blake will never believe our boy has changed so much." Silas turns in the front seat to look at me as he speaks. I reply by pretending to scratch my eye with my middle finger. "I can see you, Roman. Don't make me tell Tawnee on you."

I wrap my arm around her shoulders and pull her close to me, planting a kiss on her temple. "Tell her whatever you want about me. Just be sure to include telling her how much I love her."

"We're in the most romantic city in the world, and the only one who has his woman with him is Roman, of all people. How the fuck did this happen?" Silas asks and shakes his head.

"Silas, do you have all the details of my secret company?" Tawnee's question intrigues me.

"Yes, ma'am. Our analysts found every last detail about it after Roman suggested we search by your name."

"It's in my name alone? No one else's?"

"Just yours." Silas turns around again. His eyes narrow, and a wily grin begins to form.

"And the shares? They're all mine?"

"That's right. Let me guess... you want to dump them for real?"

"Yes, that's exactly what I want to do. Can I?"

Silas checks his watch and mentally calculates the time difference. "Wow. We're working through a lot of time zones. We left Riyadh around midnight their time. Flew six hours to Paris. Now we're an hour behind Riyadh and six hours behind New York. So, when the stock exchange opens in nine hours, you will absolutely be able to sell them."

"Do you have the log-in and password for the account they're in?"

"I can't believe you'd even ask me a question like that, Tawnee. That hurts me. What kind of officer do you take me for?"

"That means yes, he has it and has been closely monitoring it. In fact, he's probably already transferred them to a new account that Raf doesn't know about." If I know anything about Silas, it's that he's always two steps ahead of the enemy.

"Finally. Some respect for the senior officer." Silas smiles and turns to face the front. "When you're ready for them, Tawnee, they're all yours. Since you got them legally, there's nothing we, the government, can do about your investments. Enjoy the fruits of your labor." He jots down the account information and hands it to her.

"I never dreamed I'd have a sugar momma. This is so exciting." The moment the words leave my mouth, Tawnee playfully jabs me in the ribs.

"I'd be a dead sugar momma without you. Our prenup will say I get to kill you if you ever leave me."

"Show me the dotted line. I'll agree to those terms and sign it right now. I've already experienced how dark my life is without you, and that's not a place I want to return to ever again."

She nestles closer to me, lying her head in the crook of my shoulder and wrapping her arm around my waist. "I wish you could feel how happy you make me, Roman. Silas, when my shares are sold and they settle the accounts, what do you think about bringing the whole family here for an extended vacation?"

"I think that's the best idea ever. You won't hear any objections from anyone."

"Good. We could use some fun, family time after all this is over."

It'll all be behind you in a few hours, sweets. One by one, I'll cross the names of those who betrayed you off my list. Then we'll focus only on everything good in our lives and celebrate our reunion in the best way possible.

"THAT'S IT? ALL I HAVE TO DO IS SET THE PRICE I'M SELLING THEM at and wait for someone to accept it?" Tawnee checks the information on the screen for the fifth time before executing her trade.

"That's it. Just make sure the price per share is the minimum you want because that's all you'll get." Silas has been so patient with her. She still thinks of this as stealing no matter how many times he's explained she's the legal owner of all the shares. She can't steal from herself.

When she submits the order, she sits back and stares at the screen. "Now, we wait?"

"Yeah, but I promise we won't have to wait very long." Silas chuckles to himself, knowing the news he submitted online earlier has already created such a buzz in Saudi Arabia, we can hear the hum all the way from Paris.

We checked in to our procured, not stolen, room and went on a shopping excursion the minute the stores opened. She was so excited to buy new clothes and shoes in Paris. She rolled her eyes at me so many times in the hours she dragged me from one store to the next that I warned her they'd get stuck in that position. She thinks I'm hopeless because I don't get what the big deal is about the clothes here. We can buy clothes anywhere.

It's obviously a chick thing.

She retorted it's a chic thing.

Then she laughed when I asked what the difference was.

Whatever. She's happy. I'm happy. She has new clothes that I can take off her later. We all win.

"When will I know if they sold?" She refreshes the screen. Again.

"As soon as people start snatching them up. At the end of the day, all the day's trades will be called, and most of the money will be transferred to your account right away, but they have three days to pay up. You'll have access to the full amount after the end of those three business days." Silas has explained that a few times already.

"Okay, it's done. I'll check back later and see how much has moved. Why don't we order some room service? I'm hungry, and we need to finish making our plans for Rafael."

Silas glances up at me, and I nod.

"Tawnee, we have orders to neutralize this threat for national security reasons. But I can't approve for you to go with us. Please trust me. Jason and John will stay here to protect you while Roman, Nick, Noah, Shadow, and I handle the rest. If you get involved, I won't be able to protect you from French or US laws." Silas carefully explains the precarious situation we're in, and I can only hope she understands.

She glances up at me, the anguish and distress immediately clear in her expression. "He did this to *me*, Silas. Not to you or anyone else. But you're telling me I don't have the right to defend myself?"

"What we're doing isn't self-defense, sweets. You know that. It's the preservation of our way of life, which happens to coincide with fulfilling a deep need for vengeance in me. Please let me take care of this for you. Trust me to do that."

She taps her nails on the tabletop for a solid minute, considering her options against our request. "All right. I'll stay here. But if anyone comes into my room, they're fair game to me, and you two will stay out of it."

"Deal," Silas and I reply at the same time.

"Will you at least include me in the planning session so I'll know what's happening?"

"Yes, we will. You need to be prepared in case anything goes off plan. I don't want you getting caught unaware."

We order enough food and drinks for an army then call the rest of the guys up to our suite. While we eat, talk, and laugh, the time ticks away. Silas's phone pings with incoming information at the same time as Shadow's. The two team leaders have just been alerted to an incoming threat.

"The four camel-men of the Saudi apocalypse just landed in Paris, didn't they?" My question is rhetorical. I already know that's what their alert is about.

"Yeah, they're here, and they're searching hotel databases for

Rafael's name to verify this is where he is. This hotel is full, so they'll be looking for their own room next. My guess is they'll only stay one night—long enough to do the job and get back home the staff finds his body." Silas pushes back from the dining table and stands. "It's time to put our plan into action. Roman, I'm going to change clothes and will meet you in the stairwell. Shadow, you have your uniform, right?"

"I do. I hope he's a big tipper. I hate serving ungrateful people." He walks out with a spring in his step, headed back to his room to change with the other guys on his heels.

I turn to Jason and John. "Don't let her out of your sight or out of this room until we come back. I don't care if every fire alarm in the building is going off—if I'm not at that door, do not open it."

"Got it. We'll keep her safe." John assures me as he steps up beside her. "Don't worry about us. Just focus on getting the job done upstairs."

After I change into my nondescript black clothes, I meet Silas, Shadow, Nick, and Reaper in the stairwell. Shadow carries a silver platter covered with a white linen napkin. The covered plate is compliments of the chef. Having heard Raf was in the building, the chef wants to welcome him personally.

"I'm going in. The terrace doors are wide open, just as Tawnee said they would be. After a quick climb up one floor, I'll be inside his room in no time. Give me ten minutes, Shadow, then deliver his gift."

"Ten minutes—mark. Get to climbing, Roman."

I rush back into my suite and straight to the balcony directly below his expansive terrace. I scale up the ornate concrete decoration and over the wrought-iron fence. From my vantage point, I see Rafael lounging on his couch while watching TV. I expected him to have it on the news or a business channel, but I realize he's so confident in his underhanded dealings, he's not the least bit worried anything will go wrong.

Kneeling behind the small round table with two chairs, I watch for any other movement inside the suite. If Tabitha and Carter are in there with him, I'll deal with them first. My guess is they're in a separate room. His insistence on having the three-bedroom royal suite to himself in Dubai tells me he doesn't share well with others. After eight minutes, I feel confident he's alone, and I move into place inside the suite. Right on time, Shadow knocks on the door and announces he's with room service with a perfect French accent.

When Raf opens the door, he barely acknowledges Shadow. "I didn't order anything, so you can take that off my bill immediately."

"This is compliments of the chef, sir. He heard you were staying with us this week and wanted to send your favorite rare delicacy to you, free of charge."

"Really? What is it?"

"Pufferfish, sir."

"Chef Olivier does know how to tempt me. Bring it in—I can never resist pufferfish."

Shadow walks in with the tray and waits for Rafael to give him instructions. "Where shall I put it, sir? Would you care to dine at the formal table?"

"No, just put it there by the couch. I'm watching this show, so I'll just enjoy my fish with the wine I've already opened."

"Very good, sir. With compliments from the chef, we hope you enjoy this small treat."

"I'm sure I will. Thank you." Raf pulls out a €100 bill, hands it to Shadow for his tip, then closes the door in his face before he can respond.

Raf sits on the couch and removes the silver dome cover, humming to himself when he sees the thinly sliced pieces of fish. He leans back on the couch, taking the plate with him, and mindlessly pops slice after slice into his mouth while watching TV. When he has scarfed down almost the entire fish, he sets the nearly empty plate on the coffee table and starts punching his lips and tongue with his fingertip.

I grab him around the neck from behind and force him down onto his back. When he opens his mouth to protest, I release several drops of the pufferfish's deadly toxin down the back of his throat.

"You've already eaten enough tetrodotoxin to kill thirty people, but those extra drops I gave you will ensure the job is done faster. The tingling you felt on your lips and tongue was the neurotoxin already going to work on your nervous system. With as much as you've consumed, you'll be paralyzed in the next few seconds. You'll lie here, fully aware of what's happening to your body, but unable to do a fucking thing about it.

"Before you die, I want you to know what else is happening right now. Tawnee is here—she's alive and well. We rescued her from that women's detention center you let your piece of shit friends throw her in. All those shares you were waiting to cash in are still in her name, and she just opened the order to sell them all. By the close of business today, she'll have more money than you ever dreamed of having. But there's more—she doesn't know this part yet. I'm waiting to give her the rest of the documents as a wedding gift.

"Look at this picture, Raf. It's one of the real Tawnee and you getting married. We also have a copy of your marriage license and a copy of your will. The will you changed eight months ago to leave everything you own to her. So, you can lie here, you fucking coward, and die in your own piss and shit as you lose control of your bodily functions. You think about how you had it all when you had her, and how you lost it all when you betrayed her and left her for dead in a Saudi prison."

When I release him, he remains rigid and still on the couch. But his eyes confirm his brain still functions at full capacity. He'll be dead within twenty minutes, but I'm not going anywhere until I see it with my own eyes. No fucking ghosts will come back to haunt my love.

His breaths become ragged and shallow as his diaphragm short-circuits from the poison coursing through his body, shutting down his organs. The light in his eyes is extinguished, and there's no way anyone can bring him back now.

One down.

When I step out into the hallway, Silas, Shadow, Nick, and Reaper have all four of Tawnee's kidnappers on the floor. "Bring them in here with Raf."

We lift their limp bodies and haul them into the suite and arrange them in the other chairs. After a few drops of toxin into each man's mouth, and the leftover contaminated fish on the plate, the cause of death for all five will be easily explained. Since pufferfish isn't on the hotel menu, it will clear the chef of any wrongdoing, and they'll assume he brought the delicacy in from somewhere else. It won't be traced back to anyone in this city; we've already made sure of that.

The five of us walk back down to my suite with a weight lifted off our shoulders and smiles on our faces. We can go home soon—or we can bring the family to us for a while first—because the menaces to society have been dealt with expediently. When I reach the door to our suite, my heart jumps up in my throat when I see it's not latched shut.

I gently push it open the rest of the way and peek inside. Tawnee has Tabitha subdued on the floor, while John holds Carter with his hands cuffed behind his back.

"What the hell happened here?" I know I specifically told them not to open the door unless it was me.

"These two idiots got the room numbers mixed up and tried to get into this suite. When Tawnee heard their voices, she bolted for the door before we could catch her. But we got them, anyway. INTERPOL is on the way to get them and help process the paperwork for the other mess—our director called theirs and explained the situation. Carter and Tabitha are going to spend a long time in prison," Jason explains.

"Is that what you want, Tawnee? For them to live their lives behind bars?" I want to make sure because we still have time to make them disappear.

"Yes, I decided death was too quick and easy for them after what I've been through. They'll spend the rest of their lives thinking about what they did to me, though. In separate prisons. In separate cells. Alone."

She made the right choice. But then, so did I. Rafael never would've gotten what he deserved, and those four kidnappers would've been national heroes when they returned home. Now, they'll all go home in pine boxes.

For all intents and purposes, this is over. For Tawnee and me, we're finished with their deception, betrayal, and greed. My focus is solely on her from now on—whatever it takes to make her happy.

That's my new hard line perspective... my only rigid stance going forward.

Roman

"You want to tell me what really happened in here?" I turn to Tawnee when the last of our squad leaves the room.

The slightly guilty expression on her face gives her away. *You're totally busted, sweets.*

"Whatever do you mean?"

"I gave those men strict instructions before I left. That door should have been barred from the inside. They should have tied you to a comfortable chair with silk ropes and sat in your lap to keep you from opening it. So, do you feel the need to confess anything?" I put my hands on my hips and straighten my back, and using my intimidating glare, I wait for the truth.

"I confess… I regret nothing." She lifts on her tiptoes to kiss me. Her lips are so soft, and I'm so grateful to feel them again.

"You're trying to distract me. I know your tactics." I manage to state my accusation between luscious kisses. "Not that I'm complaining… much. I'd just like to know the truth."

She pulls back and looks up at me from under her lashes. I know the very second when she accepts the inevitable.

"All right. Here's the full truth. You took off on your own to exact your revenge against Rafael when I'm the one who was wronged. I appreciate your doing it on my behalf, but it's not the same, Roman. There are some things I need to do and standing up for myself is one of them. But I agreed to your plan, even though you still haven't told me what you did to him, for the record—so I had to improvise.

"Jason and John follow the rules pretty well, so they had set up surveillance in the lobby to keep tabs on who was coming in and out. When John saw Tabitha and Carter coming back in, laughing and enjoying themselves, I may have snapped. Just a little. Not like a Roman-level snap, but enough. As Raf's head of security, I still have access to his messaging network, so I used Jason's phone to access it. Raf was never tech-savvy enough to handle it on his own. So, I messaged them as Raf and told them the hotel had to change their room, but their keycards would still work."

"They didn't know that's impossible? The front desk would have to re-key them to work with this lock."

She shrugs. "Tabitha and Carter never questioned Raf like the rest of us did. I guess they just thought he magically made it happen. Anyway, when they showed up at the door, Jason, John, and I were ready and waiting for them. Tabitha was easy to overpower since I cracked her ribs when she confessed to stabbing me in the back. John and Jason had no problem restraining Carter. And you know the rest."

"But you decided to let them live." I'm questioning if I'm worthy of her love. She shows mercy and forgiveness while I charge full steam ahead and let a man die a cruel death.

"I gave it a lot of thought, and I even wavered when I had her in my grasp. But something she said to me stayed with me. She planned to ride off into the sunset with Carter and the money

Rafael promised them. Spending her life with him was her ultimate goal, regardless of who she hurt along the way. Then I realized how devastated I would be if you and I were separated for the rest of our lives. I realized how devastated I've been since the day we split up. Doing that to Tabitha and Carter would be worse than ending their lives, putting them out of their misery. Their hell is only starting… and they'll be in it for a long time to come. They don't deserve death."

"And Rafael? What do you think he deserved for his offenses?"

"He deserved to die. He planned this scheme for a long time. All the paperwork he had drawn up and forged. The trip to Dubai under false pretenses. The wreck that put us all in danger. He had someone attack your dad. He arranged my kidnapping, and he knew where they'd take me. Then that led to Lara's death. Even though I don't have proof that she's dead, I heard her screams after they caught us talking. If she's still alive, she's wishing for death. This is all on him.

"He hurt so many people simply to make more money that he didn't even need. He already had more than he could ever ask for—money, possessions, respect, admiration, and loyalty—but none of that mattered to him in the end. It's as if everything he did was a game to him to see how much he could get away with before someone stopped him."

"I'm glad you feel that way because his death wasn't an easy one. He suffered. He felt every second of it right up until the end. And I wouldn't change a single thing about it. I'm sorry you feel I took away your right to exact your own revenge. Maybe I did. But when I carried you out of that shithole, I thought you'd die before we could get out of the country. Maybe it was selfish of me to leave you out, but I couldn't take the chance of something going wrong and losing you for good. I can handle anything any man throws at me, but I'm not strong enough to lose you. So, when Silas pointed out we couldn't cover for you if things went sideways, I jumped at the loophole to keep you safe."

"Tell me how he died."

We sit on the couch, and I proceed to tell her every step I took, every word I said, and every reaction Rafael had to the toxin up until the moment he took his last breath. She listens intently but silently, taking everything in. I can't help but wonder what she thinks about me now. Will this change her feelings for me? Will she feel unsafe around me and walk away?

"What are you thinking, Tawnee?"

She purses her lips and slowly nods her head, considering how to frame her response. "I'm impressed. That was a great idea—very imaginative. I especially like how it can't be traced back to anyone so there's no fall guy in this scenario. Thank you for taking care of everything and seeing it through until the end. And thank you for taking care of me. I understand your reasons. All I ask is you include me in the discussions in the future instead of deciding for me. And I promise not to be so independent that I don't listen to your concerns. Deal?"

"Deal. Let's shake on it." I extend my hand, and she tentatively accepts it after a moment's hesitation.

Then I drop one knee on the floor in front of her.

"Tawnee, will you marry me? Will you promise to stand beside me regardless of how stupid I act? Will you be the woman who snaps me back in line and keeps me from self-destructing? Will you sleep beside me every night, donating your body to the Roman Scientific Study Foundation from this day until death parts us? Will you be my everything for the rest of time?"

She uses her free hand to whisk away the tears that escape from her eyes. Then she nods enthusiastically. "Yes. Yes, I will, Roman."

I reach under the sofa cushion and retrieve the small velvet box I bought during our Paris shopping excursion. While I hold it, she opens the hinged lid and gasps.

"I can't believe you bought my ring and proposed in Paris. When did you become such a romantic?" She smiles through the tears that fall freely from her eyes now.

"Like I said, we can buy clothes anywhere. But an engagement ring from Paris is something to brag about." I take it out of the box and slide it onto her ring finger. "Perfect fit. Just like you and me, sweets."

She slides off the couch onto my leg, and I gently pull her into my arms. "I'm yours, Roman. Always."

"And I'm yours, sweets. Always have been. Always will be."

She brushes her lips across mine, and fire immediately engulfs us. Within seconds, I'm stripping off our clothes and burying myself deep inside her right there on the floor. Her body shudders and shakes beneath mine. Every soft moan urges me on. Every fingernail scratch down my back only makes me go harder. When beads of sweat cover our bodies and drip from my brow, we find the edge of ecstasy and leap off the cliff together.

As I stand, I gather her in my arms and carry her to the bathroom. After a long, hot shower, I wrap her in the thick, warmed towel and use a second to dry her off. "I didn't make your wounds worse, did I?"

"No, baby. You made me feel better all over." The peaceful smile on her face makes me proud, because I know I put it there.

"You called me 'baby.' You've never used a pet name with me before."

"Then I'd say it's way overdue, wouldn't you?"

"Absolutely."

After she finishes drying her hair, we retreat to the bedroom to sleep after a long and trying day. The minute our heads hit the pillows, the laptop chimes with an alert. She groans in frustration but checks it all the same. Not knowing what it was about would drive her crazy all night.

"Is this a joke? Holy shit, Roman! I keep forgetting about the time difference between here and New York. Look at this!"

She shows me the final settled amount from selling her shares. All I can say is, I'm glad I'm already lying down, because I'd be face-first on the floor otherwise. "That is unbelievable. But I'm thrilled for you, sweets. I mean, what else do you say to *that?*"

"You're thrilled for *us*, Roman. Not just me. We're really getting married, aren't we?" Her tone is uncertain, but I'll squash that doubt immediately.

"As soon as possible—just try to stop me. I only assumed you'd want a prenuptial agreement after the recent developments. Oh, there's one more thing I legitimately forgot to tell you about with all the excitement. Rafael had a fake will made six months ago, showing you left everything to him in the event of your death. But, about eight months ago, he changed his actual will to leave his entire estate to you. So, on top of the shares you just sold, you're also set to inherit everything else he owns."

"Are you kidding me, Roman?"

"No, sweets, you really get it all. Houses, properties, bank accounts, his holding company—"

"Not about that! About wanting a prenuptial agreement. After all this time and everything we've been through—including today—you nonchalantly throw that comment out there. Have you lost your mind?"

"I honestly just thought—"

"Well, stop thinking. You're not allowed to think for either of us anymore. I'll handle all of that going forward."

"Yes, ma'am. You'll get no more thinking from me." I can't help but smirk. "I'm not trying to be an ass. I'm willing to do whatever it takes to protect you, Tawnee."

"I know you will. That's why I don't feel the need for anything else. Some say that's naïve, but I can live with that. You put yourself in danger to rescue me. You've taken care of me, whisked me out of the country, and gotten rid of all my problems. As far as I'm concerned, half of this is already yours as payment for your services. You know, as soon as I have access to the funds."

I shake my head. "I'm not interested in an IOU. But I will take an 'I do' as payment."

"Consider my debt paid in full, then. Because I'll 'I do' you so many times, you'll have a permanent smile on your face."

"I don't know about you, but I'm wide awake now. What do you want to do?"

"Let's go wake up all the guys. They need to call everyone back home and start making plans to join us in Gay Paree. Do you have any idea how many more clothing shops there are here? It could take weeks before we work our way through them."

Not exactly what I had in mind, but also not a bad idea.

"There's only one clothing shop I want you to go to. The rest of the time, you won't need any clothes."

"Oh yeah, and where's that?"

"A bridal shop for your dream wedding dress."

"What kind of ceremony do you think we should have?"

"I don't think. That's your job, remember?" She swats me with the pillow, and I laugh. "Sweets, listen. Most guys don't care about that. I'll show up where and when you tell me to, and I'll be happy to wear whatever you pick out. Except one of those Arab dresses. I have to draw the line there after the past few days."

"I promise—no thobes, headdresses, or anything related. I can't wait to see you in a custom-tailored Armani tuxedo. I bet you'll look so hot."

"I can't wait to see you in absolutely nothing all day, every day, on our honeymoon, because I already know for a fact you look hot in your birthday suit." I waggle my eyebrows at her, and she rolls her eyes at me. "Time for a confession, Tawnee. I know you're not a materialistic person—you never have been. But I questioned how you would ever choose me over Raf. I knew I'd never be able to give you the finer things like he could or take you on trips around the world on a whim."

"You give me what he never could, Roman. I can feel you when you're near. Electricity runs through me when I simply touch your hand. You've offered all of you, holding nothing back from me. My soul recognizes you as its mate. You're the other half of me."

"You're the best part of me, Tawnee."

Now that we're unable to sleep, we get dressed and share all the wonderful news with our friends who have had our backs every step of this journey. After we pop the cork on some champagne and toast our announcements, the guys contact our friends and family at home to fill them in. They're all excited to start making travel arrangements to join us on a European tour. When we finally head back to our room, we stand in the window, staring at the Eiffel Tower lights as they twinkle against the night sky.

"Roman?" she whispers to me, though her back is flush against my chest.

"Yeah, sweets?"

"If I ask you to give up something for me, would you resent me for it later?"

"I highly doubt that, Tawnee. How could I ever resent you? Tell me what you want." My curiosity is piqued.

"I want you to quit your job. We'll have more than enough money—neither of us will ever have to work again." She turns to face me, searching my eyes for an answer.

"What do you want to do with all our time if neither of us works?"

"I want to be the voice and an advocate for those women in the Saudi prisons. How can I escape and never think about the ones who are still stuck in there? They're probably facing worse punishment because I got away. I'll have the resources to build a platform for awareness of their plight and to help stop the inhumane treatment. That's what I really want to do, and I'd love to have your help with it."

"You've got me, sweets. I'll be right beside you every step of the way. I have one condition, though."

"And that is?"

"You're never going anywhere in the Middle East again. Ever. Travel to that area of the world is strictly off-limits unless we have the entire US military as an escort."

"Agreed. You don't have to ask me twice."

We both know she'd never be safe there, and I'm not willing to risk her life for anything, no matter how noble the cause. I'm just glad to hear we're on the same page. Otherwise, I'd have to look into investing in building a house with secret rooms, hidden passages, and interesting dungeon furnishings to keep her in until she came to her senses.

EPILOGUE

Tawnee

About an hour outside of Paris, we found the most gorgeous castle, complete with a moat, and beautifully manicured adjacent grounds.

"This is perfect for a wedding, Roman." I can't help but gush over the towers, balconies, and turrets lining the 52-bedroom, genuine 1500s French chateau-turned-hotel.

"Sweets, you know we can't officially get married here unless we've been a resident for thirty days. Refusing to leave France after an extended vacation does not meet the residency requirements."

"I know, spoilsport, but it's still fun to pretend."

"Gerald and I are into the pretending, too. He pretends to be the big, bad wolf, and I pretend I don't want to be eaten." Liz walks by and blurts out way more personal information than I ever need to hear.

"Liz, come on. Keep that shit to yourself." Silas shakes his head and sticks his fingers in his ears. "I think my ears are bleeding."

"Let me tell you something, Silas Steele. You and Shadow are both just jealous because you lost the chance to experience your reverse harem fantasy with me. Gerald is my main man now, and we're not into sharing. We're devoted to each other, and there's nothing you two can do about it."

Shadow mumbles under his breath beside me. "I don't know whether to congratulate Gerald or have him committed for a psychiatric evaluation."

Silas steps up to my other side and mutters, "Never use the words pretend, role-play, prophylactic, or flogging around Liz. It never ends well."

"So, Liz, you never told me how you ended up dating Gerald." I'm not letting these guys off the hook that easily. I love how she makes them squirm, even if I think she's crazy, too.

"Well, sweet pea, it was like this. Blake, Rebel, and Bull brought him home to the Casa de la Steele. That's fancy language for the Steeles' house. Anyway, you know someone stabbed him in that third world country over there."

"Liz, Dubai is far from a third world country." Noah stops her. "They're very wealthy."

"Anyway, before I was so rudely interrupted, I was saying someone stabbed Gerald, so they brought him to Miami so I could patch him up. You know, these boys can't exactly do their job without me. While he was on the mend, Gerald and I had a lot of time to talk. He couldn't give me a good explanation for why he'd been single for so long.

"He finally said it was because his wife had died, and he was afraid of getting hurt again. So, I took my flogger and whacked him across the back of the legs with it. He screamed out, 'That hurt!' and I told him it was supposed to hurt."

"Naturally." *Where the hell is this going?*

"That's when I explained to him that regardless of whether he loves again, he'll still get hurt. He'll still feel pain. There will never be a time in his life, while he's alive, that he can escape all pain. Then he finally understood me."

A time in his life... while he's alive? Is there a time in his life when he's dead? I can't ask these questions because I'm genuinely afraid of the answer.

"After that, I put the flogger away until he was ready for it. But when he asked for it on his own, that was a beautiful thing. I knew then he was ready to love freely and not worry about getting hurt. That just freed us up for so many other possibilities. Ball gags, whips, chains—I don't even know what some of those toys are called. Doesn't make them any less fun, though."

When I glance around, all the men have their hands over their ears and are running—*running*—away from us. The women are all wiping away tears of laughter. And Gerald, sweet Gerald, is standing next to Liz with the biggest smile I've ever seen anyone wear.

There's a man in love if I've ever seen one.

We continue our stroll around the castle before piling back into the stretch limousine. I've felt a little guilty for enjoying all the spoils of our victory so extravagantly. But if I've learned anything, it's that we only have one life, and the best we can do is live it to the fullest.

"Please, sweets, for the love of all that is holy in this world, can we go back to Miami now? I've loved every minute of the last three weeks I've spent with you in France, but I'd love some time alone with you. Completely alone. Locked in our own home. Tell you what—I'll even have a moat built around it the second we get back, complete with a drawbridge that only I have the access code to open." Roman pleads with me, keeping his voice low enough so the rest of the crowd can't hear.

"Okay, I suppose we have been away for a long time now. If the others are ready to go back, we can alert the pilot and head home tomorrow."

"Thank you, thank you, thank you. Have I told you how wonderful and sweet and beautiful and precious you are today?"

"Yeah, I think that's what I heard you say right about the time you ran away and left me alone with Liz."

"There's a standing rule with this group. I'm not proud of it, but I have to live by it."

"And that is?"

"It's every man for himself when it comes to Liz. If you fall, it's up to you to get yourself out of there on your own. That's the only time we'd purposely leave a man down behind." He smiles and winks, but I know every one of these men would take a bullet for her.

Though they won't take a flogging from her.

"Hmm, I'll have to remember that. It may come in handy one day very soon."

The smug smile disappears from his face, and it's quickly replaced by a concerned, haunted stare. Now it's my turn to smile.

"As fun as this vacation has been, is everyone ready to go back home?" Roman asks the group.

"Ready when you are. This has been an amazing vacation, and we appreciate your generosity so much. I think we all needed this time to relax and unwind." Brianna, Noah's wife, grabs his hand and squeezes. "Noah works way too much. I've tried to get him to slow down and not take so many cases."

"I was actually hoping this group would take on a different type of case—one everyone can take part in. But I don't want anyone to feel pressured. This isn't a tit-for-tat. Only join if you're sincerely interested."

"Tell us. The suspense is killing me!" Chaise, Bull's wife, bounces in her seat.

"Roman and I have plans to start our own nonprofit organization to work to help end human rights violations in Saudi

Arabia. It won't be easy, but I feel very strongly that we have to try. Even if all we can do to start out is put public pressure on our government to stop doing business with them, or levy economic sanctions against them until they stop their travesties against women and the other minority groups they target. After seeing it firsthand, I can't turn a blind eye now."

"I'm in, Tawnee. You know I was an investigative reporter. I can dust off my writing skills and start publishing scathing articles about their mistreatments." Brianna reaches over and grabs my hand, showing her support.

"That's a great idea. Bri. I've worked in human resources for years. I can help you with setting up your nonprofit and writing the bylaws. When we're ready, I'll be right beside you on Capitol Hill to make our case." Chaise adds her hand on top of Bri's.

"While we're at it, I'll chime in. I'm a nurse, and I'll use my medical expertise to help in all sorts of ways. I can detail what happens when they deny women healthcare. I can help examine those who have escaped and document their injuries." Heather, Rebel's wife, puts her hand on top of ours.

"I'm still a Hollywood movie director and an actress. I will use my public voice to affect change. Count me in." Elle, Shadow's wife, plants her hand with ours.

"My sister and I have a variety of special skills. We can get all the information you need, and no one will ever be the wiser." Kira, Silas's wife, adds her hand.

"I'm an author—I'll be glad to write a book about it, get on the interview circuit, and get more people involved." Savannah, Nick's wife, joins her hand with ours.

"I'm Liz. I'm a superspy and a force to be reckoned with. I'll put those men in their places—under my feet." Liz places her hand on top.

"I'm feeling all the girl power in this vehicle. Tell you what, I'll just kick whoever's ass tries to get close to you ladies.

Consider me your full-time bodyguard." Roman kisses me on the temple and squeezes me to him.

"The rest of us are with Roman. We'll carry your purses and kick asses, too. Just point us in the right direction, and we'll do what you need us to do." Noah grins, content to pitch in wherever he's needed.

"Thank you, all of you. I don't know how far we'll get, but every little bit has to help. Right?"

When we get home, I immediately start planning our wedding. It's been a long time coming, and we're both finally ready to make that leap. Since Roman and I first met in Miami, and so many of our pivotal moments occurred at the beach, that's where I've chosen to have our wedding. It seems fitting to make our new beginning match our original one.

I'm wearing a sexy backless mermaid dress with thin spaghetti straps. The scalloped top meshes perfectly with the beach theme, and the white lace chiffon sets the tone for an elegant evening wedding. The length is perfect to wear my jewel-embellished barefoot sandals, with the strap extending down the middle of my foot and looping over my toe. Roman is wearing a white linen suit that fits him perfectly.

As I walk down the aisle to meet the man I love, the one who drives me crazy, makes me laugh, rocks my world, and would move heaven and earth for me, I realize I'm the luckiest woman alive. When we say I do, exchange rings, and kiss for the first time as husband and wife, I genuinely feel as if my life is finally starting.

And what a beautiful life it'll be.

∼

Two Years Later

THE OFFICE BUILDING BUZZES WITH EXCITEMENT AS THEY RELEASE the news from the Middle East. The newly named Crown Prince has allowed women to drive in Saudi Arabia. The fight is nowhere near over since the detention centers are still dotted throughout the land, and male guardianship rules are also still firmly in place.

But we'll take this win for the team and press on until we reach the next milestone.

Brianna is working on another exposé story, having met with two sisters who managed to flee their home for the country of Georgia, pleaded for asylum from any country that would help them, and they were finally given safe passage to Canada. Their stories of male domination, abuse at the hands of family members, and no rights to choose whom they wanted to marry make my skin crawl. If this venture helps just one of those women, all the hours we put into the cause are worth it.

Chaise walks by, stops, and backs up. She can't pass by me without rubbing my belly, as if the protrusion is there for good luck.

"I can't wait to be an aunt again. Hello, baby, it's Auntie Chaise. Again." She bends and speaks loudly to my stomach. "He can hear me, you know. He'll know my voice as soon as he's born."

I shake my head when she hurries on her way, late for another conference call with a senator's office. Her brother, Silas, used some of his DC clout to arrange the direct meetings to give us a chance to push for more concessions.

Roman steals up behind me and wraps his arms around my now extended waist. His hands slide down across our baby bump as he kisses my cheek. "Hello, sweets. How are you and my baby holding up today?"

"We're tired. He's heavy, Roman. I can't comfortably sit down, lie down, or stand. I think he'll make his grand entrance into the world any day now."

"I have to admit, I'm ready for that day. Then you'll be forced to take time off and spend it with the baby and me. We'll allow close family and friends to come over, but we will lock the rest of the world out. No senators. No CEOs. No foreign dignitaries."

"Oh shit."

"What? What's wrong?"

"You just wished it into being. Quick, wish for a fast delivery. Say it!"

"What are you talking about, Tawnee?"

"My water just broke, Roman. It's running down my leg right now, like I just peed all over myself. This baby is coming today."

"Oh shit. Let's go—your suitcase is already in the car." He takes my hand in his, then stands up on the chair in the middle of the expansive room.

"Can I have your attention, please?" he yells at the top of his lungs. Everyone stops and stares at him, waiting for him to continue. "Tawnee and I are leaving the building... because we're having a baby today! We love you all—but we're out of here as of right now since she's in labor."

Cheers and clapping fill the room, and with my pregnancy hormones, my emotions get the best of me. With tears in my eyes, I thank all our employees for their tireless work, their well-wishes, and their support.

On the way to the hospital, Roman keeps my hand in his to share his strength. It's scary, knowing a tiny human is about to be ejected out of my body through an opening that frankly doesn't seem big enough. But he reassures me the entire way, letting me know he's right beside me with all his love. Those sentiments continue all the way to the birthing room, where the nurses prepare me for the inevitable conclusion to this condition.

Once I'm settled and comfortable, our family begins

streaming in. Silas and Kira, with their children, Amber, Laci, and Ryan. Those two have been busy the last couple of years. Then Nick and Savannah, with their twins, Gavin and Kinsley. Blake and his girlfriend, Julia. I still have hope for them.

Our extended family also comes to show their love and support. Noah, Brianna, Bull, Chaise, Rebel, Heather, Shadow, and Elle—all our brothers and sisters in love if not in blood.

I can't leave out Liz and Gerald. They married soon after Roman and I tied the knot, and they've lived in wedded bliss since that day. Gerald has said many times the reason he waited so long to fall in love again was that his soul knew he had to wait for Liz. They're precious together, even if Liz is still crazy and makes me laugh every day. At least I can honestly say I love my mother-in-law and my father-in-law as if they're my own parents. After losing both my parents in a tragic car wreck when I was in my early twenties, I'll take this family over being alone any day.

When the nurse comes in to recheck me, she announces it is time and shoos them all out of the room. With Roman by my side cheering me on and giving me encouragement, we welcome our son into the world. After the staff finishes their work and leaves us alone, we enjoy some much-needed quiet time—just the three of us.

"Hello, Ethan Matthew Scott, my little love." I nuzzle his cheek and gently kiss his little button nose. "He already looks like you, Roman."

I look up at my big, strong man and see tears glistening in his eyes for the first time in all the years I've known him. "I can't even remember all those years I lived without giving all my love away now. I wouldn't know how to go back to that life, and I'll never want to. I'm the luckiest man alive, with the most beautiful wife anyone has ever seen and the most perfect baby boy ever born. I promised you this on our wedding day, and I'll say it again now. Our little family is my entire world. You have all my love, all the time, no matter what."

"I love you too, Roman."

With Ethan asleep on my chest and Roman asleep at my side, all three of us wedged into this twin hospital bed, I drift off to sleep happier than I've ever been, loved deeper than I could hope for, and giving more love than I even knew was inside me.

This is the perfect life.

$\sim$

Want more of Nick Tucker?
Read *Her Dom* and *Her Dom's Lesson*!

$\sim$

Want more of Nick, Silas, Roman, Reaper, Bull, Rebel, and Shadow, and Liz?

Find them and more the *Steele Security series*:
Wicked Games (Book 1)
Wicked Ties (Book 2)
Wicked Nights (Book 3)
Wicked Intentions (Book 4)
& Wicked Shadows (Book 5)

Have you met Damon Marchetti, the sexy anti-hero mafia capo? Danger, intrigue, murder, betrayal, and oh-so-steamy times are waiting in *Warning, Part One*, *Warning, Part Two*, and *Warning, Part Three*!

Find all my books at www.authoradjustice.com

Are you on Facebook? Join my reader group! No requirements or expectations — just readers having fun! :)

ABOUT THE AUTHOR

A.D. Justice is the award-winning USA Today bestselling author of the Steele Security Series (Wicked Games, Wicked Ties, Wicked Nights, Wicked Intentions, Wicked Shadows), the Crazy Series (Crazy Maybe, Crazy Baby), the Dominic Powers series (Her Dom, Her Dom's Lesson), the Immortal Obsessions series (Immortal Envy), and a few stand-alone romance novels, such as Saving Grace, Completely Captivated, Just One Summer, Intent, and Mistletoe Not Required.

When she's not writing, she's spending time with her own alpha male character in their North Georgia mountain home. She is also an avid reader of romance novels, a master at procrastination, a chocolate sommelier, a twister of words, and speaks fluent sarcasm. An avid animal lover, A.D. Justice has two horses, three cats, and two very spoiled dogs.

While the primary focus of her books has been romantic suspense, she has expanded into different sub-genres of romance. Stay tuned to read what she has in store for you!

Connect with her online!
Newsletter
Facebook Reader Group
Website

Immortal Envy (Book 1)

Stand-alone Romance Novels

Saving Grace

Completely Captivated

Intent

Just One Summer (Novella)

Mistletoe Not Required (Novella)

ACKNOWLEDGMENTS

Writing a book is much harder than one would think. The finished product only takes a few hours to read, but months to agonize over every single word, plot point, and character action. Only speaking for myself, I can honestly say I put my heart and soul into the story, taking time away from family and friends (and cleaning house. Oh, so messy!) to write just one more chapter.

When I finally reach those two little magical words, a weight lifts from my shoulders, and I'm able to breathe again. That is until I start the next book, which is usually while my editor works on the recently completed one.

My writing journey includes chatting with other authors I trust and admire to give feedback and suggestions. Others encourage and support me along the way, taking a chance on a new plot twist or storyline that's not mainstream, and who aren't afraid to step outside the box and give "different" a chance. These are my people—my tribe—whether they realize it or not.

Acknowledgments are hard to write because I never want to

leave anyone out or make anyone feel their place in my life isn't important. **If you've ever read my books, you hold a special place in my heart.**

There are a few select people I want to recognize for helping make this book special to me.

First and foremost, I thank my Lord and Savior, Jesus Christ, for His eternal love, mercy, and forgiveness of a sinner like me. Without Him, I am nothing. Yes, when I say I fall short, I realize I fall way short, but thankfully, there's no such thing as being too far from Him. He knows my heart.

Someone recently called me a hypocrite for adding this to my acknowledgments. Since I openly admit I'm a sinner, I don't see it the same way she does. To me, a hypocrite implies someone denies any wrongdoing WHILE actually doing wrong. Adding this is my way of sharing my belief and thanking Him for the many blessings in my life, even though I'm well aware I don't deserve them.

Michelle Dare, you've been the bestest BFF ever. You listen to me whine and cry and puff up, only to tell me to suck it up and get over it already. I LOVE YOU! You're still stuck with me.

Victoria Renteria, you are an AWESOME alpha reader—even though you ditched me at the end of this book and went on a family vacation (the audacity!!!)—then you laughed about it. THAT is real friendship. Thank you for your time, feedback, and for making me add *just a little more*. MUAH!!!

T.K. Leigh, I don't know what I'd do without your bad influence and spot-on advice virtually every day. I'm so fortunate to have you in my tiny circle and count you as one of my very best friends in the world. I love you to death!!!

Lisa A. Hollett with Silently Correcting Your Grammar, my editor and my friend, thank you once again for working through another book with a penciled in due date then helping make it as perfect as possible at moment's notice. I hope your other clients aren't like me! :)

Wander Aguiar, the photographer for the covers in this series, is always wonderful to work with—although he does make choosing one photo very difficult. Fortunately, I was able to find three that perfectly fit this series.

Sommer Stein with Perfect Pear Creative Covers, thank you for creating the awesome covers for this series. I'm constantly in awe of your amazing talent.

Candi Kane with Candi Kane PR, you are a godsend! Thank you for all your help and support. I think I'll just keep you.

To all the bloggers, thank you for the cover reveal posts and the release day shares. You don't get nearly enough credit for all you do. We need you more than you know!

To the readers, whether you love, like, or hate this book, thank you for taking the time to read it. Thank you for your reviews, even if all you say is you liked it or not. Thank you for your support—you have no idea how much every little bit means to me. You are the best

All my love to you,
Angel